FUTURE WORLD HISTORY TRILOGY

RUSSELL FINE

Other Novels by Russell Fine

Science Fiction
Janus

Frank Carver Series
Frank Carver Mysteries I
Frank Carver Mysteries II
The China Strategy
The Eternity Gene
Dreamscape
McBain's Redemption
New Terra

Political Fiction
The California Experiment
Quest For Power

DEDICATION

This book is dedicated to the people who helped make this book a reality and I would like to take this opportunity to thank them all for their assistance.

First, my wife Sherry helped me by reading every word many times, correcting my frequent keying errors, and offering helpful advice with the plot and content.

My son, Randy, for his assistance editing and proofreading the story.

And finally a special thanks my editors who are also my friends and neighbors, Suzanne Horsfall and Cheryl Adamowski. As always, they did an excellent job. Without these people this book would never have seen the light of day, nor would I have a final edition worthy of you, the reader.

PREFACE

I decided to write this series of books because it was apparent to me that our schools no longer teach history. While it is true that almost nothing of historical significance has occurred for at least a thousand years, during the five hundred years between about 2000 and 2500 there were massive changes in the world. It's impossible to provide the information about all of the changes that occurred during that time in a single book. So, I've written three books and combined them into a single novel. The first book will provide the reader with information about some of those people and the events that occurred which still affect our lives on a daily basis. The first book covers the period from 2035 to 2120. The second book covers a much shorter period of time, 2120 to 2136. The third book talks about the events between 2136 and 2500.

I expected this series of books to take about a year to write. However, when I began my research, I discovered the information I wanted was difficult to find. I wanted to be as accurate as possible, so I searched for months through old video records and newspaper articles. (For those of you who don't know what a newspaper is, I suggest you do a little research yourself.) Many of the conversations in this volume are extracted directly from those sources. In the end, it took more than four years to complete the novel.

As everybody knows, we currently have a World Government, we all speak the same language, and we all use the same currency. However, the world was a very different place back then. At that time, the world was divided into political and economic areas that were referred to as "countries," and there were over two hundred of them. In most cases, each country had its own independent government, and in many cases, its own currency and language. Additionally, differences in religions and skin color had caused conflicts for hundreds of years. These differences were the cause of many major wars and terrorist uprisings.

The two most successful countries in the world at that time were the United States of America and Russia. They were adversaries, but there was no actual fighting between the countries. The United States was economically the more powerful of the two, and because of its robust economy, most of the scientific research was conducted there. That's where this book starts.

Much of the first book covers how our sources of energy changed from the use of fossil fuels like oil, natural gas, and coal to the way we produce our energy today. In 2035 there were thousands of large electrical generating facilities all over the world using either fossil fuels or nuclear fission to generate electricity. That electricity was distributed by wires to homes and businesses. Transportation was also dependent on fossil fuels.

Little did the people of Earth have any idea how drastically their world was about to change.

Russell Fine

03/16/3504

FUTURE WORLD HISTORY BOOK 1

2035 - 2120

PART ONE – THE INVENTION
AUGUST 14, 2034

The tropical depression had been growing in strength since forming just west of Africa over a week ago. When it became a tropical storm, it was named Felicity. Felicity was heading west and three days later it was upgraded to a hurricane. All of the predictions were that Felicity would make landfall on Montserrat on August 24th as a category 2 storm.

Charles and Catherine Simpson retired in January and had planned the vacation they were currently enjoying on Cat Island more than a year earlier. Charles had worked at NASA for more than thirty years as an engineer, and for the last five years was in charge of propulsion systems development. Catherine worked as a high school science teacher. They both loved the beach, and really enjoyed snorkeling and scuba diving. They were in the second week of their three-week vacation when they heard about Felicity. But Montserrat was hundreds of miles south of Cat Island and they weren't concerned.

On August 22nd Felicity made a surprising sharp turn to the northwest and was heading straight for Cat Island. The storm was upgraded to a category 3 level. It had sustained winds of one hundred fifteen miles per hour with gusts that exceeded one hundred fifty. The storm was enormous, with hurricane force winds extending more than ninety miles from the eye.

By the time Charles and Catherine were aware of the danger it was too late to get off the island. They were staying in a stone cabin that looked like it could withstand anything Mother Nature could throw at them. Early in the morning on August 25th they were sheltered inside their cabin and the hurricane shutters were tightly closed waiting for Felicity to strike.

Charles decided to call their son, Albert, and let him know about the situation while they waited for the storm. They talked for a few minutes and Charles assured Albert that they were in a safe place and would be okay. He promised to call again after the storm had passed.

As the storm approached, the sound of thunder was constant and almost deafening. It was impossible to speak so they just sat silently on the chairs in their room. Although it seemed impossible, the thunder got even louder right before the power to the cabin died.

Now they could hear the wind too, and it was almost as loud as the thunder. Suddenly they heard a loud cracking sound. They both looked up and saw the slate roof of their cabin beginning to crumble. Before either of them could react, the entire cabin collapsed, burying them under several tons of stone. Their bodies remained buried for days in the debris before they were found.

FEBRUARY 16, 2035

It was Saturday and Albert Simpson was alone in the lab at Simpson Metallurgical Laboratories. An impressive name for a company with only three employees. Albert was thirty-four years old, about six feet tall, and thin. He had brown eyes and matching dark brown hair that he kept perfectly groomed. Albert was very intelligent, and many of his acquaintances thought him handsome. But, despite his intelligence and good looks, he often felt uncomfortable around other people. As a result, he had few friends and hadn't been on a date in years.

The work he was doing was boring and his mind wandered back over the events of the previous six months. His life made an abrupt change when his parents were killed while on vacation. Before his parents' death, he had been a professional student. He graduated high school at the top of his class at sixteen. He received his first bachelor's degree in electrical engineering at nineteen. In the fifteen years that followed, he earned master's degrees in electrical engineering, mechanical engineering, chemical engineering, computer science, and metallurgy. He was working toward his first doctorate when the disaster struck. His parents had supported him both financially and in his quest to continue his education. Now he was on his own.

Albert inherited the house and their savings. It was obvious he was going to have to drop out of school and find a job. During the time his father worked at NASA, Albert had met several of his colleagues. He reached out to them in hopes of finding a job, but the openings available all required work experience. He certainly had the required education, but never having held a job disqualified him. Albert sent out dozens of resumes, but it was a wasted effort. He received only a few polite responses indicating they would retain his resume in case a position opened in the future that met his qualifications. Albert was growing depressed.

He had enough money to last a while and moved into his parents' home, so his living expenses were minimalized.

3

He needed something to do and had thought about taking a job that he was over qualified for just to keep busy until something better came along. Before he took that plunge, one of his father's business associates contacted him. Albert had met Jeff Leonard several times and was both surprised and pleased to hear from him. Jeff said that NASA was in the process of developing a new propulsion system and suddenly realized they required an extremely strong magnetic field to make the system feasible. They wanted to subcontract the analysis of potential materials to a third party. Jeff, who was aware of Albert's situation, explained that if Albert set up a company that could do the work, he would help Albert get the contract.

Albert gratefully accepted the offer and immediately began the process of starting up the company. Realizing he knew nothing about starting a business, he turned to one of his few friends, Susan Woods, who had recently received an MBA. She agreed to help him and also expressed an interest in joining the company. Susan was not interested in working for a large corporation where it would take many years to even be noticed. Additionally, she liked Albert and found him interesting. The excitement in her voice was a clear indication that she thought it would be fun to work with him.

Albert also reached out to Tim Martin, another friend and professional student, in hopes that he could convince him to join the company and help with the technical aspects of the operation. Like Susan, Tim expressed interest in working for a smaller company. He had already earned several degrees and he wanted to do something besides go to school, so he thought this would be a great opportunity.

Albert, Susan, and Tim were well matched. Each of them was very intelligent and somewhat introverted. Tim was a few inches shorter than Albert, but was built like a football player. He was very strong and agile. He had green eyes and black hair that showed definite signs of receding. Susan, at thirty-one, was the youngest of the group. She had an obvious Nordic heritage, with blue eyes and long blond hair. Susan was thin and very attractive. She exercised for at least an hour every day to make sure she stayed that way.

4

In exchange for their efforts in helping Albert get the business running and because he was unsure at this point how much he would be able to pay them, it was decided they would form a partnership. Albert would have 70% of the business and Susan and Tim would each have 15%. Since Albert was putting up all the money, they agreed this was a fair arrangement.

Albert had about five hundred thousand dollars in the bank. Most of that was the result of the life insurance policies his parents had. The rest was money that had been left to him by his parents. Susan thought that would be more than sufficient to get the business going. They had forty-five days to get the business operational and submit the bid to NASA. Because of Jeff's involvement with the project and the short time frame, he was given the authority to award the contract. So, if they won the bid, and Jeff assured Albert they would, they would have to be ready to start work within thirty days after the contract was awarded.

Susan got busy with the legal requirements while Albert and Tim looked for a suitable place for the operation. It took only a few days to find the perfect location: a three thousand square foot building previously used as a meat storage facility. The refrigeration equipment had been removed but the "cold storage area" was perfect for the lab. It also had an area set up for offices that would easily house three desks, the computers, printers, and other necessary office equipment. An additional reason for selecting the building was that it had the needed electrical service and natural gas service available for the alloy manufacturing and testing equipment. (Please note that at that time, natural gas was the fuel of choice for many heating applications. It was often used for cooking and heating homes.)

By the time Albert and Tim found the location for the business, Susan had completed the paperwork and Simpson Metallurgical Laboratories was created. The building lease was signed and Albert and Tim began the process of ordering the equipment that was needed for the operation. The three of them spent the next several weeks setting up the business, so by the beginning of November 2034 they were ready. All they needed were some customers. Albert kept Jeff aware of their progress throughout the process of setting up the company, so when the business was ready, they could immediately submit their bid.

True to his promise, Jeff helped Albert with the bid, and three weeks after it was submitted, Albert was notified by NASA that his company had won the contract. They would have to begin the work on January 2, 2035.

The contract with NASA required Albert's company to create metal alloys and evaluate the magnetic properties of them. The alloys were created by melting all of the component metals and combining them. The goal was to find the alloy that would create a magnetic field strong enough to contain the plasma that was the heart of the new propulsion system while using a minimal amount of power.

The metal alloys were created in rods an inch in diameter and three inches long. The testing was simple. The alloy rod to be tested was placed in a hollow plastic cylinder tightly wound with very thin, enamel-coated wire. When an electric current was applied to the coil, the testing device would evaluate the magnetic field strength at several distances from the alloy rod. The testing apparatus was automatic. It applied twenty-four different voltages to the testing coil starting at .5 volts and increasing in .5 volt increments until twelve volts was applied. The test results were automatically transferred to a file on their computer system and displayed on a monitor so the operator would see the results.

The first group of alloys to be tested was made from iron, silver, and nickel. The differences between each alloy sample were very small. The amount of one of the component metals was increased or decreased by .5 gram. Each sample took about an hour to make, and only a few minutes to test. The work was easy and boring, but it paid well and Albert, Tim, and Susan enjoyed working together.

The testing apparatus beeped to indicate the test for the sample labeled 178 was over. The sound brought Albert's mind back to the testing. His face had a look of astonishment when he looked at the results of the test. Realizing the magnetic field created by the sample was about ten times stronger than any previously tested sample his heart began to race. The results were absolutely astonishing. With a new-found excitement and a smile you could not wipe off his face, he moved on to the next sample.

All the samples were sequentially numbered. So, Albert picked up sample 179 and placed it into the testing apparatus. He decided to test this sample manually. He started at .5 volts and he could not believe the results. This sample registered almost twenty times the field strength of the previous sample. He slowly began increasing the voltage, carefully watching the results. As the voltage reached one volt, the magnetic field created by the sample exceeded the capacity of the system to measure it.

At first, Albert thought the testing system was giving false readings, but when he increased the power to two volts, the resulting magnetic field was so strong that a pair of needle nose pliers on a workbench four feet away flew toward the sample, narrowly missing him on the way. The pliers banged into the sample with a loud clang. Albert shut down the test as his mind began to race. He simply could not believe the results of the test. He picked up his phone and called Tim.

Tim answered after a few rings and Albert exclaimed, "Tim, you need to come to the office as soon as you can. I have something to show you that you may not believe! In fact, I'm not sure I believe it. I want you to run this test yourself."

"Okay, I can be there in fifteen minutes. Is this something good or something bad?" Tim asked curiously.

"If the testing results are correct, we may have made the scientific discovery of the century. Please hurry!" Albert replied. Tim said he would leave immediately. Albert returned to the testing apparatus and recorded his results while he waited for Tim to arrive.

The implications of the test results were astounding and Albert was certain this alloy would meet NASA's requirements, but he was thinking far beyond that. He was already imagining new, more practical applications. By the time Tim arrived at the office, Albert was fairly sure what that application would be.

Albert was deep in thought and didn't even notice when Tim walked into the lab. He was startled when Tim said, "Hi."

"Please test alloy 179. Do it manually, not automatically, and increase the voltage in .25-volt increments. If your results are the same as mine, and I'm certain they will be, I think you'll agree we've found something pretty spectacular. The sample is already in the coil."

"Okay, do I need protective gear or a Kevlar suit?" Tim joked. He sat down in front of the testing console, reset the system, and started the test. At .25 volts, the alloy created the strongest magnetic field they had ever measured. He raised the voltage to .5 volts and the field had increased in strength by almost ten times. At .75 volts the field exceeded the system's capacity.

"Oh my God! Is this for real? Are these the same results you got?" Tim inquired.

"Yeah." Albert picked up the pliers placed them back on the work bench, about five feet away and said, "Raise the voltage to two volts and watch the pliers."

Tim did as Albert suggested, and just as it happened before, the pliers flew off the work bench and banged into the end of the alloy sample with a loud clang.

"Pretty amazing stuff, wouldn't you agree? When I tested sample 178 it exceeded every previous sample by a factor of ten. Please continue the testing to verify the results. While you are doing that, I'm going to work on increasing the capacity of the testing apparatus. After you verify the test results, please make additional samples. The difference between 178 and 179 was the nickel content. So, increase the nickel by .1 grams in each sample. Sound good?" Albert asked excitedly.

"Sure. Let's get going," Tim replied.

For the next two days Tim worked on creating the samples and Albert modified the testing equipment to increase its measurement capacity. Albert's first modification increased the measurement capability by a factor of ten, but when he attempted to measure the magnetic field from sample 179 at one volt, he realized his design was inadequate. The system still could not measure the field strength, because it still exceeded the system capacity. Each test came with a newfound realization that they were on the cusp of something very special.

For the next modification, Albert decided to increase the measurement capability by one hundred, so now they could test the fields one thousand times stronger than his original design. Using his new design, he tested the field produced by sample 179 at one volt. At two volts, the field reached 70% of the system's capacity. He had to shake off the initial shock, and it took him a few seconds to realize what he had discovered. When the shock wore off, he yelled, "Tim, you have got to see this."

Tim ran over and looked at the computer screen. Like Albert, he could hardly believe what they had found. "Oh, my," he whispered.

By late Monday night the samples were ready. Albert and Tim decided to begin evaluating the new samples on Tuesday morning. They went to a nearby restaurant for dinner. Up to this point they had not really discussed what the potential application for their discovery would be. Now that they had some free time, this would be the ideal opportunity to talk about it.

They found a booth at the back of the restaurant and sat down. A waitress brought menus, took their orders, and left. Then Tim said, "I'm sure you've been thinking about how we could use this discovery. Did you figure out how this is going to make us rich?"

"Not only rich, but famous, too," Albert said with a big smile on his face. "What we have is basically an electromagnetic amplifier. We can take a small electric charge and from that create a very powerful magnetic field. We could then use that magnetic field to create a much larger electric charge. In fact, I think if we do this right, we could even make it self-sustaining."

With an astonished look on his face Tim asked, "You think we can make the first perpetual motion machine?"

"Except there's no movement. I'm thinking in terms of the first perpetual battery," Albert responded excitedly. "All we need is an oscillator to drive the electromagnet and a transformer to pick up the resulting field. We would need some simple circuitry to clean up the output to make true sine waves and we could siphon off some of the resulting power to keep the oscillator running. If it all works, and I don't see any reason why it wouldn't, we would have a self-sustaining power source!"

"It sounds crazy. It would appear to violate several known laws of physics. But perhaps we're discovering new laws. In any case, if it works, we're going to change the world!" Tim said.

Albert couldn't sleep that night, so he got up at 4:30, showered, dressed, and left for the office by 5:15. When he arrived, he found Tim was already there. He had apparently been there for some time, because he was putting the finishing touches on a big box made from what looked like steel plates.

"What is that?" Albert asked.

"I was concerned about the strength of the magnetic fields. This building has a steel support structure and a strong magnetic field. It could possibly damage the structural integrity of the building. I thought we should have something to contain the magnetic field, so I built this protective box." Tim replied.

"I thought about that too, but I think all we need to do is test the samples manually. You saw what happened at two volts, so I think if we start the testing at .5 volts and increase by .25 volt increments, we'll minimize the risk and still get the results we need. However, since you went to the trouble of building the box, I see no reason not to use it."

It took an hour to mount the testing apparatus inside the box. Albert started the test with sample 178 and there was no change from the previous test. The rest of the 178 samples also showed no change until Albert tested 178.9. The results really changed. At two volts sample 178.9 registered 13%.

Obviously, a significant increase, but not even close to test results from the original 179 sample.

Albert was nervous as he inserted the new sample 179 into the testing coil. If the results were not the same as the original 179, they would have to spend days or weeks trying to figure out what had happened. As he started the test, his concern vanished. The results were identical to the first sample.

Next on the list was sample 179.1. Albert began the test at .5 volts, and the results were almost identical to sample 178.9. He continued the testing for the rest of the samples, and with each sample the resulting magnetic field dropped by about 10%.

"Do you realize how lucky we were to stumble onto this alloy? We could have easily missed it," Albert said.

"Do you think we should try it again with slight variations in the silver and iron content?" Tim asked.

"Yes, I think we have to do that, but I have a feeling the field strength will probably be less than with 179. Please make samples using the formula for 179 as a base and vary the iron and silver content by one-tenth of a gram in both directions. While you're doing that, I'm going to start working on our power source. Sound like a plan?" All were in agreement and they proceeded accordingly.

For the next few days, Tim concentrated on making the new alloy samples and Albert worked on what he called the "Simpson Power Module." He started by designing the electronic circuits that would supply the power to the coil wrapped around the alloy rod. He designed it so the voltage being supplied to the coil could vary from one volt up to six volts. For the output, he used an iron rod six inches long and a half inch in diameter. He wound insulated copper wire around the rod one hundred times and mounted it a half inch from the alloy rod. He attached measuring devices to the input and output of the device to check the results.

Albert turned on the device and verified the input was one volt. Then he checked the output: it was fifty-six volts. He needed the output to be one hundred twenty volts so he made modifications to the device until it matched the output he wanted. It took over an hour, but Albert was very pleased with the initial test results.

Then he modified the modified the design so it could use a battery to start the device. Albert also designed the circuit that would convert the device's output to match normal household power. That way it could supply electrical power to any household device. It took two days to design and build the required components. He assembled the prototype device and called Tim over to watch the test. The output of the device was now going to a standard electrical outlet and a probe was plugged in to verify the output. On the input side was a spot for a standard 1.5 volt, D-size battery. Albert inserted a battery, turned on the device, and the output was a perfect sine wave that measured normal household power, one hundred twenty volts.

Next, he plugged in a one-half horsepower motor and turned it on. The startup current for the motor was ten amps and he expected to see a drop in the output voltage when the motor was turned on, but that didn't happen. The voltage stayed constant, and the motor ran perfectly. He had calculated the current drain on the battery powering the system and he expected it to run for an hour. It actually ran for almost an hour and a half before the system shut down.

Albert and Tim watched the test for the entire time, barely speaking, both of them were waiting for something to go wrong. When the test was over, Albert and Tim looked at each other with extreme surprise and approval obvious on their faces. They did not need words to acknowledge that it was possible to make the system self-sustaining.

The next step was for Albert to design a power supply for the device so it would no longer need a battery after the device was started. While he was working on that, Tim began testing the new alloy samples.

Just as Albert had predicted, the new samples with varying amounts of silver and iron did not exhibit magnetic fields that exceeded alloy 178. It was now apparent the only alloy formula that would work was 179.

By the following Monday, Albert had completed the necessary design modifications. Tim and Susan both came into the lab to watch the test. The prototype didn't look very pretty, but when it was turned on it worked perfectly. Albert removed the battery and the system kept running. He plugged in the motor and turned it on. It ran as expected and the system output was still constant at one hundred twenty volts.

Albert and Tim had created the first "perpetual" power supply, and Tim was right. The world would never be the same.

"I'm not sure how to market this, but for now we need to build some additional systems. I also have to contact NASA and let them know we found the material they need to contain the plasma for their new engine," Albert said to Tim, then turning to Susan, "Please have an attorney look over the contract we signed with NASA to make sure we own the rights to this. Tim, please make another twenty rods with the 179 formula. I think we should make the next prototypes look more professional, and then set up a test and invite the press. Do you guys agree?"

"Yeah, but don't you think NASA is going to figure out what we did? Even if the contract doesn't indicate that NASA owns the formula, they're part of the federal government and could tie this thing up in court for years," Tim said with obvious concern.

"Let's find out what the lawyer thinks before we do anything. I think we should go ahead and build the prototypes, but we should wait to call a press conference until we get some legal advice. I'll contact a lawyer immediately," Susan responded.

"Good, while you're doing that, Tim and I will work on the prototypes."

During the next few days each of them worked on their tasks. Tim created the silver alloy rods while Albert refined his power supply design and found some plastic boxes that could be used to hold the prototypes. On Tuesday, Susan met with the attorney, who promised to review the contract and get back to her in a day or two.

13

On Thursday morning Albert was assembling the first prototype when Susan came into the lab. Albert was so engrossed in his task that he didn't notice her until she tapped him on the shoulder. He looked up at Susan and saw a big smile on her face.

"I just heard from the attorney. He said that according to the contract, your only responsibility is to notify NASA of the test results every month. NASA has no rights to anything we develop in the course of our testing. He even said that according to the contract, any side-discoveries are ours and can be used as we see fit. Of course, he paraphrased that for me as it was far more complex." Susan said happily and then continued, "So, I guess we're all going to be very rich, right?"

"If these prototypes work, and I'm sure they will, I'm certain that's true. Aren't you glad you dropped out of school to join the company?"

"Yeah," Susan replied smiling. "Just don't screw things up. I'm already dreaming about what it would be like to be wealthy and not have to worry about my monthly bills."

"I promise I won't screw this up. We have another job for our favorite lawyer. Please find out what we need to apply for a patent and ask him if he can handle that for us. If he can't, ask him to recommend a good patent attorney. One more thing, please go tell Tim what he already said. I'm sure he'll be very happy to hear the news."

Susan left to talk to Tim as Albert continued working on the first prototype.

An hour later Susan came back into the lab and said, "I heard from our lawyer's assistant. She told me he doesn't handle patents, but he did recommend someone. I called her and she's sending over a package of forms and documentation regarding the patent process. She said we should call her after we review the material and she'll come here to get the process started."

Albert nodded, "That sounds perfect."

By Friday morning the first prototype was ready. The unit now utilized a 1.4 volt watch battery that would last for many years. He added a green LED "Power On" light to

14

indicate the system was functioning normally and a red LED "Problem" light if the system was malfunctioning, or if an excessive amount of power was being drawn from the unit. It also had four standard outlets built in.

For a test this time, Albert plugged in a refrigerator, a toaster, and a coffee maker. He flipped on the switch and immediately the green light turned on. Then he made a pot of coffee and some toast, and sat down to the best breakfast he'd had in a very long time. It seemed as though everything was working perfectly.

After twelve hours everything still appeared to be working, so Albert, Tim, and Susan all went home. They were all anxious to see if everything was still okay when they came in Saturday morning.

Albert arrived first at 6:00 AM. When he entered the lab, before turning on the lights, he could see the green light on the prototype. He turned on the lights and walked over to the refrigerator. It was obviously working correctly. Then he made a pot of coffee and waited for Tim and Susan to arrive.

At 7:30 Tim arrived, and Susan showed up a few minutes later. Albert poured them each a cup of coffee. It was obvious that everything was working perfectly.

"I have to file a report with NASA in a few days, so I'll be working on that," he said. "I would like both of you to concentrate on building the prototypes. I also want to build a unit that can power my house. I think that would be a great test, but I need to make some changes to the power supply. I would like to connect it to my circuit breaker box, and in order to do that we need to match the line from the power company."

"When do you want to schedule the press conference?" Susan asked.

"I would like to have my house running off a power unit for a few weeks before we do that. I also want to give each of the reporters a prototype to take home and use. We really need to think about who we should invite, so give it some thought. If we tell them in advance that we have a self-sustaining power supply, they'll think we're nuts. So, we need to give some thought to what we can say that will entice them to come. Albert smiled at both of them and continued. "We deserve some time off away from this place. So, no work tomorrow."

Albert spent the day completing the report for NASA and decided he would call Jeff Leonard to make him aware of the properties of alloy 179. He thought that since he had found what NASA was looking for, they would consider the contract terms fulfilled and terminate the contract, but that was okay. He had more important things to work on now.

Tim and Susan looked at Albert's circuit design and realized they didn't have the parts in stock to build more than two power supplies and oscillators, so Tim ordered the parts they needed. Tim and Susan spent the rest of the day building two power supplies and two oscillators.

On Monday morning Albert e-mailed NASA the report and called Jeff Leonard to let him know what he had found. Jeff seemed to be skeptical, to say the least, but Albert told him he would send an alloy rod to him overnight so he would have it in the morning. That way they could test it for themselves. He also told Jeff that he would send the plans for the testing apparatus he was using if they wanted to duplicate exactly what he did.

He put together everything he needed to send and included a note cautioning them to apply the test voltages in .5 volt increments. He set up the parcel pickup online, and according to what the attorney's office said, this would complete his obligation to NASA.

At 10:00 AM a messenger arrived with the package from the patent attorney. Albert looked it over. The process appeared to be pretty simple, but he was concerned about whether it was possible to patent the alloy composition. It was a question for the attorney when she came for the meeting. They were going to need photographs, drawings, and schematics for the power module. But since the product was still in the prototype stage, he wasn't ready to do that yet. He asked Susan to set up a meeting with the attorney later in the week. Then he began working on the device that would power his house.

Carol Lawton, the patent attorney, arrived a few minutes early for her appointment Thursday morning, but Albert, Tim, and Susan were already waiting for her. They all met in Albert's office.

Once introductions were over, the patent attorney got down to business. "The purpose of our meeting this morning is to begin the patent process by establishing some evidence for the granting of a patent. Ms. Woods has given me some basic information about the device. Based on that information, I see no reason for a patent to be denied. Personally, I'm very excited about this device. I'm going to record this meeting so I don't have to take any notes. Is that okay?"

"I have no problem with that," Albert said.

"Good," Carol said. She opened her briefcase, removed her cell phone, set it up to record an audio file, and placed it between them on Albert's desk. At that point, she asked Albert to provide some history regarding the device. Albert spoke for several minutes about how the company was formed, their contract with NASA, the discovery of the magnetic properties of the alloy, and the subsequent creation of the power module.

"That's exactly what I needed to know. I'll need the dates of the events you told me about. I also need some pictures of the prototypes, and I really want to see one these things."

They walked into the lab where Albert showed her the first unit they built which was powering the appliances.

Carol took pictures of the original unit and some of the current prototypes. "I think that's all I need for now. My only concern is the ability to patent the contents of the alloy used in the devices. That can be a little tricky. I really don't think there'll be a problem because the application is certainly unique. In any case, I'll get back with you in a week or less."

After Carol left, Albert continued the work on his "home" power module. Just as he was making the finishing touches, he received a call from Jeff Leonard. Jeff told him what he already knew: the alloy created the most powerful magnetic field they had ever measured and they were very excited because they were sure it would enable them to build the new plasma engine. Albert asked if he should continue testing new alloys. Jeff told him to hold off testing new alloys until they had more time to evaluate the current sample. That was exactly what Albert wanted to hear. Now he could concentrate full time on the power modules.

Albert took the power module home and decided to wait until the following morning to connect it. Tim and Susan wanted to be there when he did. Arriving at his house at 8:00 AM, Tim took the cover off the breaker box and disconnected the wires from the power company and attached the power module. Then he turned on the power module and walked over to an outlet and verified the power was correct. Next, Albert went into his kitchen and checked the oven and stove. Both worked normally so he proceeded to turn on the TV and that worked too. There were zero problems.

"This is too easy, we must be missing something," Albert mused.

"Maybe, but I have no idea what. In any case we'll soon know if there's a problem. Let's give it a few days. If nothing explodes and your house doesn't burn down, we did it right," Tim replied with a grin.

"Okay, I agree. Now, any ideas who we should invite to the press conference?" Albert asked.

"I think we should invite somebody from the university newspaper," Susan stated.

"I agree, but we need to get national press coverage. We should probably ask ABC, CBS, Fox, and NBC to send somebody," Tim said.

"Yeah, that sounds good, but I would also like to invite somebody from some magazines like Popular Science, Physics Today, and maybe Consumer Reports as well. I was also thinking that we should have an additional demonstration. Susan, please see if you can find a used all electric car to buy, not a hybrid, it has to be all electric. We can remove the battery and replace it with a power module. You can spend up to $30,000," Albert said.

"That's a great idea. I'll get on it this morning," Susan replied happily. "I've never been able to buy a car and not finance it myself or otherwise have to pay for it."

It took Susan two days, but she found a 2030 Paxton Electro. It was perfect for the demonstration. Tim and Susan went to buy the car and Albert began researching what would be required to modify it. A majority of the car's electronics were centered on the battery status and remaining miles before the battery would have to be recharged. He was not going to attempt to modify any of that, but he thought it would be interesting to see how the system would cope with a power source that never required recharging.

For the next week Albert and Tim worked on the modifications to the car. Aside from some minor problems related to the display, which they decided to ignore, the car ran perfectly. To test it out they decided to take an evening off and drive about a hundred miles to a very expensive restaurant to celebrate. Susan expressed some concern regarding the reliability of the modified vehicle, but both Albert and Tim were sure there wouldn't be any problems. It turned out to be a perfect evening. The food was excellent and the car ran perfectly.

The following day Carol called Susan and told he the patent was pending and she was sure it would be approved in a few days. She also said that their rights to the power module were fully protected. Since Albert's house had been running off the power module for three weeks they decided it was time to announce their product to the world. Susan started making calls. The university newspaper immediately agreed to have someone there. Others were more difficult. They insisted on knowing exactly what was going to be presented. Susan told them they were going to demonstrate a unique new power source. Additionally, she promised to reimburse them for any expenses if they ultimately felt it wasn't newsworthy. In the end they all agreed to send someone to the demonstration.

Everything was in place for the demonstration. The modified Paxton Electro was parked in front of the building. There were eight prototype power modules ready to be distributed, with the original unit still providing power to a refrigerator, toaster, and a coffee maker in the lab. Two worktables had been cleaned off and set up with chairs, and coffee cups were placed by each seat. By 10:00 AM everybody had arrived. Albert greeted them as they walked in. He stood at the front, facing them, and began.

"Hi. I'm glad you all could make it here today. My name is Albert Simpson and next to me are my two partners, Susan Woods and Tim Martin. Before we get to the demonstration, I want to give you some background information. Until last fall we were still students, but a personal problem occurred that required I start earning a living. Using some contacts that my father made while he was working for NASA, I managed to secure a contract to test materials that would be used in a project for NASA. Our company was formed specifically to service that contract and we started doing that right after the first of the year.

"In the process of doing the evaluations we came across a metal alloy that exhibited properties that were, to say the least, quite remarkable. That metal alloy is the key piece of the products we are going to show you today."

He went on to explain the workings of the metal alloy as a kind of magnetic amplifier, finishing with, "What we created and will demonstrate for you this morning is a self-contained power source that will run indefinitely.

"If you look to your right, you'll see our first device. It has been providing power to the three appliances plugged into it for about two months. We also designed a unit that provides two-phase, 240-volt, 200-amp service for home use. I disconnected my home from the electric company lines about a month ago and the power module has been providing power flawlessly since. Additionally, we purchased a Paxton Electro

21

a few weeks ago, removed the battery, and replaced it with a power module. I have driven it a thousand miles since we completed the modifications without a single problem.

"I understand you may be skeptical, but when you leave today each of you will be given a prototype to take home. I urge you to use it and test it in any way you see fit. Each of these prototypes produces normal household power. It's limited to 15 amps. If you try to exceed that, the unit will power off. Please feel free to look at our first unit. I'll be happy to answer any questions you have."

There was a uniform look of disbelief on the guests' faces, but each of them got up to look at the power module on display. After studying it for a few minutes, the representative from NBC looked at Albert and said, "You're going to put all the oil companies out of business."

"No, there will still be a need for oil. However, there won't be much of a requirement for gasoline. I don't think we'll see electric planes or ships, at least not in the near future," Albert replied.

"My name is Marcia Poston. I work for Fox. This is all very impressive but I'm not very technical. Can you explain, in simple terms, how this device works?"

"Of course, Ms. Poston. Do you understand how a transformer works?"

She frowned and admitted, "No, not really."

"Okay. I'm sure you're aware there's a relationship between electricity and magnetism. In high school science you probably made an electromagnet with a battery, some wire, and a steel nail. All you did was wind some wire around the nail and connect the wire to the battery. Now imagine you have a large iron donut. You wind wire around half the donut one hundred times and connect that wire to a source of alternating current, like you use in your home. On the other half of the donut, you wind wire around two hundred times. You've just made a transformer. The input side has one hundred turns and the output has two hundred turns. So whatever voltage is applied on the input would be doubled on the output. Do you understand?"

22

"Yeah, I think that's pretty simple."

"Good. What happens is the input creates a magnetic field in the steel donut, and that magnetic field induces a current into the coil of wire on the output. The steel donut simply acts as an electromagnet. In our devices, we use a coil of wire to create the magnetic field in the silver alloy rod. The big difference between a regular transformer and our device is that the silver alloy rod actually amplifies the magnetic field substantially, so with less than a two-volt input we can create a much more powerful output. It's the first device ever designed that has more than 100% efficiency. It produces enough surplus power in the output that some of that power can be used to supply the input voltage. As a result, it's self-sustaining."

Marcia nodded. "I think I understand. The key to the whole device is the silver alloy rod because it can amplify a magnetic field."

"You're correct, Ms. Poston. If there are any of you who still don't understand, just think of it as a battery that will never run down. You just plug your appliances into it and it will continue to supply power forever. Or, attach it to your car and it will run without ever having to buy fuel for it."

"Can we see your electric car?" somebody asked.

This time Tim replied, "Sure, come with me." He walked outside and everybody but Ms. Poston followed him.

"Do you think big oil, the electric companies, and the government are going to let you sell these devices?" she asked. "This has the potential to wreak havoc with the economies of not only the United States, but many of the richest nations in the world."

"I know that, and that's why I invited you very important people here. I expect you to report this and spread the news all over the world before the government can come in and stop us. It's true that many people will be hurt financially by this, but far more will benefit. If the people know about it, there's no way the government will be able to stop it. I'm not sure what these devices will cost, but wouldn't you like to spend $500 and never have to give the electric

23

company another penny? Besides, you'll never experience another power outage."

"Of course I would." She smiled. "I think it would be even better to buy a car that never needs gas or to be recharged. As I said, I'm not a very technical person, but I'd like to have someone who is talk to you. Would that be okay?"

"Sure, but please arrange it as soon as possible. I don't want the release of this information to be even slightly delayed." Then Albert gave her his card and said, "Have them call me on my cell."

"I'll call right now. I just hope they believe me."

A few minutes later, Tim and the reporter from the university came back into the lab.

"Where is everybody?" Albert asked.

"The guy from Consumer Reports said he recently spent a week driving a new Paxton Electro, so he could write an article for the magazine and he asked if he could drive the car. So, I gave him the keys. He went for a ride with the reporters from the networks. I think they think this is some kind of hoax. My guess is they're looking all over the car to find another source of power or something. Anyway, I'm sure they'll be back shortly," Tim said.

"You look familiar. I think you were a teaching assistant in one of my electronics design classes," the university paper reporter said to Albert.

"Yes, you're correct. I remember you because you asked me some questions about some high-speed switching circuits. I wanted you here today because I would bet you have a lot of Facebook and Twitter followers. Is that right?" asked Albert.

"Well, I don't have that many, but the paper has seven or eight thousand on each. I assume you want me to put the information about these devices out on the web."

"Yes, and as quickly as possible."

"Okay, I'll be happy to do that."

At that moment Albert's phone rang. He excused himself from the reporter and Tim, then he walked away. He looked briefly at the display and noted that the call came from

24

New York City. He touched the screen to accept the call and said, "Hi, this is Albert Simpson. How can I help you?"

"My name is Matt Brewer. I'm a technical reporter for Fox News. I was asked to contact you regarding the power module you claim to have invented. I'll tell you right now that I am very skeptical, but I am willing to look at what you have because it would be impossible to believe without seeing it firsthand."

"Okay, you have every right to be skeptical. If you come here, I'll prove it to you and I can even give you a prototype unit to take back with you."

"I'll be there at 9:00 tomorrow morning. I'm expecting to be amazed."

"I promise you won't be disappointed. I look forward to meeting with you. See you tomorrow morning," Albert said as he ended the call. Walking back to the shop he saw Tim.

"Tim, we're going to have another demo in the morning. A reporter from Fox News named Matt Brewer. I've seen this guy on TV and he appears to be very smart. I would bet he's going to want to see a more informative demonstration. Before you leave tonight, please hook up some oscilloscopes so he'll be able to see exactly what's happening."

"That's easy. I'll take care of it," Tim replied happily.

A few minutes later the reporters who had taken the Electro for a joy ride came back.

"The car drives perfectly. It appears to accelerate a little faster than the 2035 models, and that's a plus. You said you were going to give us units we can take with us. Are they ours to keep, or do you want them back after our evaluations are finished?" the reporter from Consumer Reports asked.

"I would like you to contact me when your evaluation is completed and I'll let you know at that time. I expect some of you will open them up to see what's inside. That's okay, but I caution you, please don't mess with anything inside. If the magnetic coil becomes misaligned, the unit won't function correctly. If that happens it will be worthless unless you want to use it as a door stop," Albert responded. He thought for a

25

moment, then added, "Tomorrow morning a technical reporter from Fox News will be here. We're going to give him a more comprehensive demonstration. If any of you are interested, please be here at 9:00. Tim will give each of you a prototype now. He can also answer any questions you have. I have some concerns regarding how the government and some large corporations are going to react when the news of this discovery becomes public knowledge. So, I want the news about these power modules to be spread as quickly as possible. Once the public knows about this, nobody will be able to stop it."

After all of the reporters left, Susan came into Albert's office. "Carol Lawton called earlier and said there won't be any problems with the patent. She has already filed some of the paperwork and said we're fully protected."

"Perfect, that's a big relief," Albert said with a big smile on his face.

The following morning Albert arrived at the office at 7:30 to find Susan and Tim already there. Tim was in the lab preparing for the demonstration. Susan sat at her desk drinking a cup of coffee when the phone rang. Albert was sitting at his desk in the lab and heard Susan's half of the conversation.

"Good morning, Simpson Metallurgical Laboratories, how can I help you?" After a pause she added, "Yes, he's here. I'll get him for you right away." She walked into the lab. "Albert, Samantha Pratt is on the phone for you," she said.

"The vice president? That Samantha Pratt?" he asked.

"Yeah, and she didn't sound very happy."

Albert picked up the phone and said in a cheerful voice, "Good morning Madam Vice President. How can I help you?"

The voice on the phone was anything but happy. "You can tell everybody this invention of yours is a hoax."

"I'm sorry Ms. Pratt. I can't do that because the power module is not a hoax. What's your problem with it?"

"No problem, other than the possibility it will put a few million people out of work, reduce tax revenues by more than 10%, and maybe as much as 20%. It will decimate the oil, gas, and utility companies. I'm sure there are many more industries that would be adversely affected. Did you think about any of these things before you made your announcement yesterday?"

"Of course I did, but I believe the benefits easily outweigh the problems. I seem to remember a speech you gave a few months ago where you said climate change was one of the biggest problems our world faces. I don't believe that, but we all want cleaner air and water. These devices would allow us to reduce carbon emissions by over 90%. We'll still need oil, just much less of it. I agree the need for electric and gas utilities will disappear eventually, but the water, sewage, and garbage utilities will be fine. The automobile companies will make a fortune, since everybody will be buying new electric cars. They'll probably need to hire a lot of new workers, and let's not forget that somebody will have to manufacture the

27

power modules, and they'll need workers too. I'm sure you are aware that our petroleum resources are limited, and this invention completely eliminates the problems associated with that. Additionally, it will take years before the full effect of the availability of these devices occurs."

She sighed deeply and said, "I suppose you do have some valid points, but I still foresee a lot of problems."

Albert continued, "Have you considered how the availability of cheap, unlimited electrical power will benefit the poorer countries of the world? With these devices, even the most remote places on Earth could have electrical power. They would be able to provide light, heat, and perhaps even water anywhere. Also, consider the fact that most of our adversaries are economically dependent on oil. What do you think will happen to them when the need for oil drops by 90%? Without money to fund terrorism, we might actually find ourselves with world peace."

"I think you're dreaming, but that's a nice thought." She paused for a moment and asked, "Have you thought about how you're going to manufacture these things?"

"Actually, I have. I don't want to be directly involved in the manufacturing process. In the next few days I'll probably get a lot of offers from large companies who want to manufacture these devices. You may rest assured I'll pick an American company. If you like, I'll keep you informed as things progress."

"Okay, that would be great. You've given me some things to think about, but I'm still concerned this could devastate our economy. I'm going keep a close watch on you. If you do anything that even has a tinge of illegality you might find yourself in federal prison. I'll have my assistant contact you later this morning and let you know how to get in touch with me. I expect to receive regular reports," she said, and she hung up the phone.

Susan was staring at him during the whole conversation. "That went better that I thought it would," he said to her.

At a few minutes before 9:00 Matt Brewer came into the office. A minute or two later the reporter from the school newspaper came in too. Albert greeted them and turned them over to Tim for the demonstration.

Albert went back to his office thinking about his conversation with Vice-President Pratt. He wondered if there really would be companies eager to make the power modules. He had neither the money, nor the knowledge, that was needed to set up a manufacturing operation. After thinking about it for a while he decided that, for now, all he could do was wait and see what happens.

Tim walked into Albert's office and said, "The demo went perfectly and Matt is no longer skeptical. I'm going to show him the car and take him for a ride. We should be back shortly."

"Do we have another prototype to give to Matt?"

"Yeah, I set that up as soon as I got in this morning. Matt said he was going to try to get a story ready for the news this evening."

"Perfect, I want to make sure everybody knows about this as soon as possible."

"I'm sure you realize that as the information about the power modules spreads, people are going to want to know when they can get them."

"I've been thinking about that since my conversation with the vice-president this morning. I told her I expected some large companies to contact me about making them. I hope I'm right about that."

"I suspect we'll be inundated with offers within the next few days. Don't worry about it. I'm going now. Matt's waiting by the car," Tim said as he left Albert's office.

An hour later Tim and Matt walked into Albert's office.

"You were right. I'm impressed. I really thought it was some kind of hoax. I'll be on the 6:00 PM news today with the story. At this point I don't think it would be wise to tell the public about you or your company. Do you agree?" Matt asked.

29

"You're probably right. I should've thought about that yesterday, but by now the news is probably all over the Internet. I even got a call from the vice-president about it early this morning, so it's too late. I think we'd better hire some security guards before the crowds show up at the door. Tim, please backup all of our files and then take the backups to the bank. Put them in the safe deposit box."

"I see you're busy, so I'm going to leave. I'll send you the piece for the news before it airs so you can review it. Thanks for everything. Good luck," Matt said as he shook hands with everyone there.

After Matt left, Albert walked over to Susan's desk and asked her to contact a security company and arrange to get twenty-four hour security at both the office and his home as soon as possible. Then he went back to his office. He was worried about two things: security and manufacturing.

Albert ultimately decided, despite the security, he didn't want to go home. He was concerned there would be crowds at his home and he didn't want to have to deal with that. So, he went shopping for the clothes he would need for the next few days and checked into a hotel.

APRIL 12, 2035

Albert arrived at the office at 7:15. He was surprised to see there were at least a hundred people outside the office being held back by the security team. As he walked into the office the crowd screamed questions at him, but he ignored them until he got to the office door. Then he turned around and facing the crowd said, "There's no schedule for manufacturing the power modules yet, and the prototypes are not for sale. I promise that when we know when and where you can buy one, the information will be made public."

When he went inside the office the phone was ringing. He decided not to answer it because he was sure it was somebody wanting the same thing the people outside wanted. He was wondering how he was going to get anything done in the office when his cell phone rang.

It was Tim. "I drove by your house this morning to see if there was a crowd there. I think there were fifty people and the police were there as well. Apparently, somebody tried to break into your house to steal the power module you have. The security guards you hired stopped him and called the police. I think we're going to have a problem. Perhaps you can arrange to be interviewed on the news tonight so we can dispel the crowds."

"I think that's a good idea. I'll call Matt and ask him to arrange it."

Albert called Matt, but Matt didn't answer so he left a message telling him what he wanted. He also told Matt to call back on his cell phone because he wasn't going to answer the office phone today. After he hung up he looked out the window, but the crowd hadn't dispersed.

At 7:45 Susan came in. The people outside screamed questions at her and, like Albert, she ignored them. "I think they got mad because I wouldn't answer their questions. I don't have any answers for them anyway," she said.

"I told them we would make an announcement about the availability as soon as we know anything, but that didn't seem to help. I took the phone off the hook because it was ringing constantly and I don't want to answer it. Also, Tim called to tell me somebody tried to break into my house last night to steal the power module, but the security guards caught him and called the police."

Susan went to make coffee and saw Albert had already attended to it, she turned and watched him walk to his office. He was still thinking about how to manufacture the power modules when his cell phone rang. He answered it without looking to see who was calling and was surprised to find it was Vice President Pratt again.

"Good morning, Mr. Simpson. I saw the news last night, and apparently so did a lot of big shots at Vextor Motors, Kingman, and Chapman. Since they all made substantial contributions to us for the last election, they all called to ask me to use my influence in order to secure the manufacturing rights to your invention. I told them to contact you and gave them your cell phone number. I also received calls from Toyota and Honda, but I told them this product was going to be manufactured by an American company. They weren't happy. I hope you realize you have the opportunity to make or break some of the biggest companies in the country," she said.

"I've thought about that. It won't be an easy decision. It's probably better they called you instead of me because they would never get through on our office phone. I'll be happy to listen to their offers. I expected offers from car companies, but I also thought some of the appliance companies like GE or Westinghouse might be interested as well. Would you like me to keep you informed?"

"Yes, I would. I know which company I'd like you to pick, but because of our political differences I won't discuss it with you. It may negatively affect your choice."

"My choice will be based solely on the company's ability to manufacture and distribute the power modules. There won't be any politics involved in my decision."

"Okay, that sounds good. I hope you'll make your decision in the next few days. I'll be waiting for your call."

By noon Albert had received calls from all three of the car companies. He set up meetings with Vextor Motors for the following Monday morning and with Chapman for late that afternoon. He was going to meet with Kingman on Tuesday at 10:00 AM. All of the meetings were going to be at his hotel. He called the hotel and reserved a small conference room.

Albert walked over to the lab, where Tim was playing computer games. Albert said, "Tim, I need three more prototypes. Do we have them?"

"No, we only have two left. I still have a few more alloy rods. Do you want me to make another one?"

"Yeah, I won't need it until the day after tomorrow. I'm going to leave now. Please bring all three over to the hotel when they're ready. Also, see if you can find a safe place to store the Electro for a while."

"No problem. I'll take care of it. See you later."

Albert went back to the hotel and was relaxing in his room. At 5:00 PM there was a knock at the door. Albert looked through the peep hole and saw it was Tim. He was carrying two power modules. Albert opened the door and Tim came in. He put the two power modules down on the desk. "The third unit is in my car. I thought we could go to dinner and you can get it when I bring you back to the hotel," Tim said.

"That sounds good. Let's go."

After they were seated at the restaurant Tim asked, "Are you ready for your meetings tomorrow?"

"I hope so. I'm going to ask for a royalty to be paid to us for each unit they sell. I think 5% of the retail price would be about right. You and Susan would each get 25% and I'll get 50%. But I want to hear what they offer before I make any suggestions. I suspect they would be able to manufacture in excess of one hundred million units in the first year of production," Albert replied.

Neither of them said anything for a few minutes. Then Tim said, "You were right when you said we were going to be rich. I just can't imagine having that much money. Dinner's on me!"

"OK, but don't spend it yet. I suspect it will take some time for the attorneys to work out the details."

They ate mostly in silence, both of them thinking about the future. After dinner Tim drove Albert back to the hotel. Albert picked up the power module and said, "Thanks for dinner. I'll call you after my meeting with Vextor Motors. Goodnight."

"You don't mind if I call Susan and tell her what we discussed, do you?" Tim asked.

"No, of course not."

APRIL 15, 2035

At 9:45 the next morning Albert's phone rang. It was the front desk telling him a Mr. Walters from Vextor Motors was here to see him. Albert told the clerk to send Mr. Walters to Conference Room C and he would be there in a few minutes.

When Albert arrived at the room, he found Mr. Walters seated at a small conference table. Mr. Walters stood up and said, "Good morning Mr. Simpson. My name is Aaron Walters. I'm in charge of the New Product Development at Vextor Motors. We're very interested in the power modules you have developed."

"Good morning. Please call me Albert. Is it okay if I call you Aaron?" Albert replied.

"Certainly."

"Would you like me to order some coffee or anything?" Albert asked.

"No, I just had breakfast. I would like to ask you some questions about the power module."

"Go ahead, ask me anything you like."

"I saw the story about the power module on the news and it just seems too good to be true. What is the longest any of these devices have been running?"

"Well, my home has been running off of a power module for months, the original unit in our lab has been running even longer, and the unit we installed in a Paxton Electro has been powering the car for almost that long. I have a prototype in my room that I'll give you later. You're free to test it, examine it, and even take it apart if you like."

"Have you patented it yet?"

"The process has been started. Our attorney has assured us we're fully protected."

"Can you give me some history regarding the development of the power modules?"

Albert spoke for the next several minutes outlining the highlights of the development of the devices and then asked, "Is that what you wanted to know?"

"Yes, that was great. If our testing proves the validity of the product, we are prepared to offer you twenty-five million dollars for the rights to the product. That would make you and your partners very rich," Aaron said.

"Aaron, I appreciate the offer, but I suspect whoever has the manufacturing rights to the power modules is going to make billions of dollars. I would estimate the cost to manufacture a power module would be about forty dollars. The most expensive part of the device is the alloy rod, which is primarily silver, and at current market prices the materials for the rod would cost twenty-eight dollars. I'm sure that during the first year you'll be able to sell every power module you make, and that number could be close to one hundred million. If you sell the modules for two hundred fifty dollars each, your profit would be two hundred billion dollars. Additionally, since you would have the only cars that don't require any fuel, your car sales would be unbelievably high. Based on that, I would think you could offer us a lot more."

"Okay Albert, I see your point. What did you have in mind?"

"I was thinking more in terms of a smaller cash payment, perhaps five million dollars, and a royalty of 5% of the retail price on each power module that is sold. Would Vextor Motors agree to that?"

"I don't know. That decision would have to be made by the board of directors."

"Okay, I'm going to go back to my room and get your power module prototype. I'll be right back."

Albert left the conference room and went back to his room to get the prototype. When he got back to the conference room Aaron was on the phone. He could not hear what Aaron was saying, but the call ended a few seconds later.

"I believe the board of directors will agree to your terms," Aaron said.

"Great! Please put that in writing. I have a meeting this afternoon with Chapman and a meeting tomorrow morning with Kingman. After all the meetings, I'll make my decision. Additionally, I want to know your plans for distribution of the product for home use so your response should include some marketing plans. I don't want the modules to be made strictly for automobile applications."

"Okay, I understand. It will probably take a few days to put all that together. If there's any delay, I'll let you know. Is that my power module?"

"Yes, please take it with you. I'm looking forward to receiving your response. Goodbye for now, Aaron." Albert said as he shook hands with him.

As Aaron picked up the power module and his briefcase, he said, "Goodbye, it's been a pleasure meeting you, Albert."

Albert went back to his room and waited for his next appointment, which was not scheduled for several hours. He called Tim on his cell phone and found out the crowds were still outside the office and his home, but there were fewer people. He gave Tim the details of the meeting with Aaron and asked him to inform Susan. Tim was very happy with the results.

"Have you considered what's going to happen to the price and availability of silver when the power modules go into full production?" Albert asked but not waiting for a response he continued, "I checked and found the worldwide annual production of silver is about seven hundred million ounces, and the power modules will use a big chunk of that. That could make the power modules very expensive, perhaps too expensive for some people to buy. I don't want to price anybody out of the market, but I have no idea how to prevent it. Anyway, give it some thought. Perhaps we can find a solution before it becomes a problem."

"Okay, I'll do that, but unless we find another material to use instead of silver, I can't imagine any way around it," Tim replied with a hesitation as though he was already trying to think of a solution.

"I'll call you after the meeting with Chapman," Albert said as he hung up the phone.

Albert was relaxing in his room when the phone rang at 1:50. It was the front desk informing him Dr. Emma Foster from Flexton Chapman was here to see him. Albert told him to direct her to the conference room and let her know he would be there in a few minutes.

Albert walked into the conference room carrying a power module. He introduced himself and asked Dr. Foster if she wanted something to drink.

"Good afternoon Mr. Simpson. Some coffee would be great if it isn't too much trouble."

"It's no problem at all." Albert picked up the phone, called room service, and ordered coffee for two. Then he turned to Dr. Foster and said, "I'm sure you have some questions, so please feel free to ask anything you like."

"Okay. You've been using these power modules for over two months. Have you had any problems?"

"No, we haven't had any problems whatsoever. Every device we have has functioned perfectly since they were turned on."

"That's amazing, but the devices do look rather simple in design. The key is the alloy rod you're using to create the magnetic field. How did you discover it?"

Albert proceeded to give Dr. Foster the history of the product. Just as he was finishing, a waiter came in with the coffee. Albert poured two cups and passed one to Dr. Foster and asked her if she would like cream or sugar with it.

"Thank you, black is fine." She said as she smiled at him. "I'm sure you're aware that Flexton Chapman is very interested in obtaining the manufacturing rights to the power modules. Unfortunately, we're not in a position to offer you what the product is worth in cash, but we have an offer for you to consider. I don't know if you're aware that we've been buying back shares of stock for about a year. We currently own 53% of the outstanding shares. We're prepared to offer you a 10% ownership in Chapman and a seat on the board as compensation. That would make you the largest personal stockholder in the company."

Albert tugged at his left earlobe for a few seconds while he thought about what Dr. Foster said. "That's an interesting offer. Do you have the manufacturing capacity to build the power modules for both automotive and home use? I want to be sure the power modules will be available for both applications."

"Chapman has facilities in North America, South America, Europe, Africa, and Asia. In less than three months we could have manufacturing in production in every major market. We don't have a retail marketing system in place, but I'm certain that could be done very quickly. I can't imagine any large retailer that would not be interested in selling the products."

"You're probably correct, but you can't sell them at discount stores because the 'whole house' units have to be professionally installed. In any case, those are problems that should be fairly easy to resolve. I have a question for you: Since Flexton Chapman stock doesn't pay a dividend, would you also be willing to pay $5,000,000 up front?"

Dr. Foster paused for a few seconds and then she said, "Yes, I think that could be arranged, but if we acquire the manufacturing rights to the power modules, the stock would increase in value substantially."

"Yes, I realize that. That's the reason why your offer is financially sound. I would like you to make your offer in writing and include a marketing plan. Please try to have that back to me within ten days so we can review it and make our decision within the next thirty days."

"That won't be a problem. I'll call you as soon as we're ready."

"Perfect. Also, I have a prototype for you to take with you. I'm sure you'll want to evaluate it."

"Yes, thank you. I'll call you in a few days. Goodbye Mr. Simpson," Dr. Foster said as she stood up to leave.

After Dr. Foster left, Albert went back up to his room and called Tim to ask him if he was at the office.

"Yes, and the crowds are still here. How did things go with Chapman?"

"They made an interesting offer. Please get Susan and put your phone on speaker and I'll tell both of you about it."

"Okay, give me a minute." There was a pause, and then he said, "Okay Albert, Susan and I are both here."

"Flexton Chapman offered us a 10% stake in the corporation, a seat on the board of directors, and five million dollars up front. That seems to be a very attractive offer because, if they have the rights to the power modules, the stock will very likely double or triple in value. Susan, since you have some contacts in the financial industry, please try to find somebody who knows more about this than we do. Perhaps they could give us some idea of how much the value of the stock would change. I realize it would only be a guess, but it would be an informed guess."

"I agree, that sounds very attractive. I do know somebody who might be able to help us with an estimate. I'll call him this afternoon," Susan replied.

"Does the stock pay a dividend?" Tim asked.

"No, it doesn't, but that could change. I also don't know how many shares are involved. Anyway, they're putting everything in writing. Why don't we meet here at the hotel at 5:30 and we can have dinner together? We can continue our conversation then."

"That sounds good. Tim's nodding so I guess it's okay with him too. See you soon," Susan said and ended the call.

They met right on time and went out to the best steak house in town for dinner. It was lavish and expensive, but they knew that soon each of them would be wealthier than they ever dreamed was possible, so the cost was not an issue.

The dinner conversation was primarily about what they were going to do with the money. They all agreed some of their new-found wealth would go to setting up a charity that would provide educational benefits to children who, for financial reasons, were unable to attend either college or a trade school. Albert surprised them by saying he wanted to get into politics, and that he was going to run for congress. Because of the money needed to run a political campaign, virtually every candidate for public office would owe favors to somebody. However, he would be able to fund his own campaign and would be free to do what he thought was right. Both Susan and Tim thought it was a good idea.

APRIL 16, 2035

After breakfast Albert went back to his room. He checked his e-mail and was surprised to find a message from Kingman containing a complete marketing plan and a contract. Albert read the document and was very impressed. The message said David Becker, the Vice President of Technology, would be there this morning. It also appeared Kingman had put together an excellent marketing plan that not only covered the use of the power modules in cars, but also the home and business applications. However, the thing that impressed him the most was that Kingman was going to license the automotive version of the power modules to other car companies one year after the first Kingman car powered by a power module was released.

The contract indicated they would receive an upfront payment of ten million dollars when the contract was signed and an unspecified royalty for each module that was manufactured by either Kingman or any other company Kingman licensed to build the power modules. The royalty amount would be negotiated after Albert and his attorney had an opportunity to thoroughly review all of the material.

Albert decided to go to the conference room prior to the meeting, so at 9:30 he asked the clerk at the front desk to send David Becker from Kingman to the conference room when he arrived, where Albert would be waiting for him. He also asked the clerk to send over coffee for two.

A minute or two after 10:00 there was a knock at the door. Albert got up, opened the door, and said, "Good morning. Mr. Becker, I presume?"

"Yes, I am. It's a pleasure to meet you, Mr. Simpson."

The two men shook hands and Albert offered coffee.

Once they sat down, Mr. Becker asked Albert if he had seen the e-mail from his company.

"Yes, I did. I was very impressed by your marketing plan. I really liked your idea to market the 'whole house' units through the major hardware store chains. I was also pleased with the idea to allow other car companies access to the technology."

"While it would be nice from a financial standpoint to have an electric car monopoly, it isn't practical. Kingman would not be able to meet the demand for electric cars, and we want people to like us, so they keep buying our products. Besides that, we feel we could find ourselves in trouble over some antitrust statute. The federal government wasn't happy with Kingman anyway because, unlike VM and Chapman, we were able to get through the last recession without government assistance."

"I agree completely. Do you have any questions regarding the power modules? I have a prototype here for you to take with you."

"I guess I cheated a little bit. Matt Brewer is a friend of mine and he and I partially disassembled the power module you gave him. I was actually surprised how simple the design is and I'm sure that simplicity will result in excellent reliability. From a manufacturing standpoint, the only potential problem is the positioning of the alloy rod and the transformer. We'll need a design that will withstand the rigors inherent with placement in a car. We have to be sure sudden movements or low speed accidents won't affect the power module. But that won't be very difficult. In fact, I already have an engineer working on it. It must have been a real 'Eureka' moment when you saw the results of your test."

Albert allowed himself a chuckle. "I must admit I was very surprised. Perhaps even more surprising was the fact we could have easily missed finding that alloy because a change in the composition of the alloy by one tenth of a gram of one of the component materials completely changes its magnetic properties."

"That will increase the manufacturing cost a little. What do you think would be a reasonable price for a 'whole house' unit?"

"With installation, I would think the cost should be in the five hundred to seven-hundred-and-fifty-dollar range. One consideration should be the cost for the alloy materials. The principal material in the alloy rod is silver, and each rod contains 1.5 troy ounces. When these devices go into full production, the cost could rise from twenty dollars per troy ounce to two hundred, or perhaps more. That should be factored into the retail price for the device."

"I don't believe we considered a potential increase in the cost of silver to be a factor, primarily because I wasn't aware of the amount of silver in each rod. I think we should have a retail price based on silver at two hundred fifty dollars per troy ounce. We would make some extra profit at the beginning, but that will change very quickly."

"How many units will Kingman be able to manufacture per month?"

"We're planning to make them in six locations: two in the United States, one in Germany, one in South Korea, one in Australia, and one in South Africa. Once we're in full production, I believe each facility would be able to produce between two and three million units per month, so a total of about fifteen million units."

"So, at one hundred eighty million units per year, or in terms of silver, two hundred seventy million troy ounces, that's about 40% of the annual worldwide silver production. I don't know much about precious metal trading, but Kingman might want to consider investing in some silver mines," Albert said.

"I see your point, but we don't know the size of the worldwide market. Eventually the market will become saturated and demand will decrease substantially. Of course, that could take twenty or thirty years, and there's a potential for a silver shortage before the saturation occurs. That would really drive up the price. I'll have to discuss this with our procurement group."

"That's a good idea. I don't think the people who want these devices, and that includes almost everybody, will be happy about material shortages pushing up the price. They'll probably think Kingman is doing it on purpose just to increase profits."

"Are there any other potential problems you're aware of?"

Albert thought for a moment and said "Not that I can think of currently. I want you to know Kingman was the only company that presented me with a full marketing plan and an agreement for the rights to the power modules." Then Albert smiled and continued, "So far, I'm very impressed with your presentation and I'm leaning in your direction. I'll give the contract to my attorney so he can review it."

They talked for another half hour or so and made plans to talk again in a day or two. After David left, Albert stayed in the conference room going over the conversation in his mind. He was almost certain he was going to give Kingman the manufacturing rights, but he would discuss it with Tim and Susan before making a final decision. He gathered up his papers and went back to his room.

Albert called Tim and Susan and told them he would be in the office in the morning so they could discuss all the offers. Before going to bed he set his alarm for 5:30 and tried to sleep, but he had so much on his mind he found sleep almost impossible. He finally got out of bed at 4:30 and left to go to the office by 5:15. When he got there, he found twenty people milling around in the parking lot. As he got out of his car several of them began shouting questions at him. He decided he should say something, so just before going into the office he spoke to them.

"A decision will be made in the next ten days regarding which company will receive the manufacturing rights to the power modules. All the contenders are United States automobile companies. Each of them has promised they will make power modules for both car and home use. Additionally, they should be able to make the products available to the public in about ninety days after receiving the manufacturing rights. There will be more details regarding the availability of the products in the next two weeks. There's no point in staying here because we have no products for sale. I urge you to go home. I realize there's a great need for these products, and we're doing everything we can to make them available as soon as possible."

Albert went into the office. The first thing he did was scan the documents he had received from Kingman and e-mailed them to his attorney for review. Then he made a pot of coffee and sat down in his office to relax. He looked outside. It appeared that a few of the people had gone home. He wanted to go home too because he was tired of living in a hotel. He wanted to make the decision quickly so his life could get back to a semblance of being normal.

Susan arrived at the office by 7:00. She stopped briefly at Albert's office to say good morning, got a cup of coffee, went back to Albert's office, and sat down. "So, what happened with Kingman?" she asked.

"They were prepared, unlike VM. They had a preliminary marketing plan, a contract, and a manufacturing plan as well. They realized they would be unable to meet the demand for the product, so they planned on granting manufacturing rights to other companies after a year. I think that's a good idea. Overall, I was impressed."

"Did they specify how they were going to pay us?"

"That also surprised me. The contract calls for a ten-million-dollar payment up front and royalty payments for each device that's manufactured, by either Kingman or any other manufacturer they license, but the amount of the payments was left blank on the contract. That's something we need to discuss this morning when Tim gets here."

Tim arrived a few minutes later, and after getting his coffee, joined Albert and Susan.

"Now that we're all here, I would like to discuss the offers we've received. Financially, any of the offers will make us very wealthy. Kingman made us the best offer. They'll give us ten-million up front and royalty payments that we must specify. But I think there are other considerations besides the financial ones. Needless to say, these companies are not altruistic. They're primarily interested in making money, and I can't blame them for that. However, I think the company we choose has to look beyond the obvious automotive

47

applications. There's probably not as much profit potential in manufacturing power modules for home and business use, but I think that's very important. I want to bring electricity to the remotest parts of the world and improve the lives of the people who live there. We have the ability to do that now and the company we select has to agree," Albert said.

"I agree with you," Susan said.

"Yeah, I think that's important too," Tim agreed. "But there's no way we could force the company we select to do that."

"The offer from Flexton Chapman includes a position on the board of directors, and that would give us some ability to push them in the direction we want them to go. But my concern is that they're not as financially sound as either Kingman or VM. Of course, if we gave them the rights to the power modules, their financial position would change dramatically. At this point I'm inclined to eliminate VM for several reasons. First, they tried to take advantage of us by making a ridiculous offer, and second, they were totally unprepared for our meeting. Flexton Chapman and Kingman made reasonable offers and they were better prepared."

"Is there any reason we couldn't give the rights to both Flexton Chapman and Kingman?" Tim asked.

"That's an interesting option. Legally, I'm sure there's no problem, but I'm fairly certain both companies would alter their offers if they didn't have exclusive rights. However, I'll call them this morning and discuss it with them. On a different subject: Tim, did you come up with any ideas on how to minimize the silver usage?"

Tim nodded. "I thought perhaps we might be able to reduce the size of the alloy rods by 50% by reducing the amounts of each component by the same amount. So, I made a few smaller rods and tried them. You'd think the size of the rod wouldn't matter, but it does. The smaller rods didn't exhibit the same magnetic properties as the larger rods. I made these rods with a smaller diameter, so now I'm going to try making them shorter. I should have the results by tomorrow morning."

"Thanks, that was a good idea. I believe the availability of silver is going to become a problem very soon. Please keep me informed. Susan, did you get any answers on our Flexton Chapman stock questions?"

"Not yet, it was late Monday when I asked about it. The people I asked have only had one day to work on it. We probably won't get an answer until next week," she replied.

"OK, I guess we can wait a few more days. I sent our attorney a copy of the materials I received from Kingman this morning. I suspect we'll have documents from VM and Flexton Chapman before the end of the week."

The meeting broke up. Tim went to the lab to work on the shorter alloy rods and Susan went back to her office. It was too early to call his contacts at Kingman and Flexton Chapman, so Albert sat in his office and thought about how his conversations would go.

About thirty minutes later his cell phone rang. He was surprised to see that the call was from Emma Foster. "Good morning, Dr. Foster. I was about to call you. I have a question for you."

Before he could ask his question, Dr. Foster interrupted him. "I want to advise you that Flexton Chapman has withdrawn their offer. We've decided we're not in a position that would enable us to take full advantage of the rights to the power modules. Unlike VM and Kingman, we don't have a lot of experience with electric vehicles. It would probably be at least eighteen months before we could release a car that utilized a power module, and we know the public won't wait that long. What we would like from you is an agreement to supply us with prototype units we could use for our product development, and when the product is ready, we would like to be able to either buy or manufacture the power modules for use in our vehicles. Is that possible?"

"Well, I'm surprised by your request, but I do understand your position. What I was going to say was that we're considering offering the rights to the power module to both you and Kingman. But if you have no immediate interest, that's okay. In my discussions with Kingman, they felt they would probably find themselves under pressure from the government to allow other companies access to the technology, so their plan was to license the technology to other companies one year after their first power module vehicle was released to the public. I'm certain we can include the requirement that Kingman supply you with power modules you can use for development purposes in our contract. We'll do that for Vextor Motors too. Does that meet your needs?"

"Yes, I believe it does. We'll probably need at least one hundred units, but possibly more. I'll ask our R&D group how many they think they'll need. I want you to know I appreciate your consideration and I'm pleased you understand our position. Once the public knows the power modules are being made, there will be panic and we really don't want to be the object of public wrath. As I said before, Kingman and VM are in a much better position to utilize the power modules than we are. Will you keep me informed regarding the agreement with Kingman?"

"Of course I will. I'm certain I'll be discussing this with Kingman today and I'm also positive they won't have any problems with the requirement to supply you with the power modules you need."

"Thank you, Mr. Simpson. I'll be waiting for your call," and the conversation ended.

Albert was stunned. He couldn't believe Flexton Chapman wasn't interested in the manufacturing rights, but based on the people who were still outside his office, he did understand their position. Now, for the first time he began to think about the impact on the automobile industry. The public knew at some time in the near future they would be able to buy cars that didn't require any type of fuel. That meant car sales would drop like a rock and all the car companies would be hurt financially. He suspected most of the car dealers would be put out of business. But that was the price of progress: gasoline-powered cars would go the way of the horse-drawn carriage.

An hour later he called David Becker, his contact at Kingman. After exchanging pleasantries, David asked Albert if he had any questions.

"I do have some questions, though they aren't specific to the proposal. I sent my attorney a copy of the documents this morning. I'm sure I'll hear from him by the end of the day. I wanted to know if Kingman has a timetable for the availability of vehicles that will utilize the power modules."

"Yes, we do. We're already working on the changes for the STZ electric car. We expect that to be available for sale about three months after we have a signed contract. Also, a year ago we started working on a high torque electric motor that was going to be used for an T3000 hybrid truck. Obviously, that vehicle won't be a hybrid now, but we expect that to be available about three months after the STZ. We'll probably look at using the T3000 engine in an A-Trek and possibly a Flex too. I have no idea what the time frame will be for those vehicles at this time. Why do you want to know?"

"I want to be sure that whoever gets the rights to the power module will be able to release a vehicle fairly quickly because the public is going to get impatient. I think three months is reasonable. I'm sure you'll be inundated with orders. Have you given any consideration to how you're going to handle them?"

"We have. To keep things simple there will only be one model of the STZ. There will be no options, except color. There will also be a fixed price, which will probably be around forty-five thousand dollars. We'll be able to make about two hundred thousand cars per month and we expect to sell out the first years' production in a week or two. There are going to be a lot of disappointed consumers, so we decided the fair way to do this is by some kind of lottery. If you want one you go to your local Kingman dealer, fill out a form, leave a deposit, and you'll receive a ticket that has a number from one through one hundred. When the first cars are ready for delivery, we'll randomly select a number and those people with that number will get their cars during the first week of availability. That process will continue for a year. If, at the end of the year, we still can't meet the demand, the same process will continue. We'll also be checking so nobody will be able to buy more

51

than one car. We don't want somebody to buy a bunch and re-sell them."

"It sounds like you've really thought this out. I suppose you'll do the same thing for the electric T3000 truck?"

"Yeah, we'll probably begin taking orders for the T3000 at about the same time the STZ is released. I know it has only been a day since we met, but we're somewhat anxious to know where we stand. Can you tell me?"

"I think we're leaning in your direction. Flexton Chapman withdrew their offer this morning because they felt it would be eighteen months before they would have a vehicle ready for release, and they were sure the public wouldn't wait that long. VM came to our meeting unprepared so, as I said, we're inclined to go with Kingman."

"That's terrific! Please contact me immediately if you have any questions."

"Actually, I do have a request. Flexton Chapman asked if the company that received the rights to the power module would provide them with units they can use for development purposes. I think that's a good idea. In fact, I think Kingman should agree to make units available to any car manufacturing company that wants them, within reason, of course. Flexton Chapman asked for one hundred units. Do you think that will be a problem?"

"No, I'm fairly certain we can do that. I'll have to ask the directors for approval. However, we don't want to be making thousands of units for them, but one hundred shouldn't be a problem. Anything else?"

"No, I think that's it for now. I'll probably have an answer for you regarding the contract tomorrow after I hear from my attorney. I'll call you."

"Thanks Albert, all of us at Flexton are very excited about this. I'll be waiting for your call."

"Your welcome, David. Goodbye."

Later in the day Tim came into Albert's office and said, "I'm really confused. I mentioned to you that I was going to make some alloy rods that were the same diameter as the original ones, but half the length. They didn't work. So far, the only rods that work are the ones that are identical to sample 179. That means any deviation from the original sample in even the slightest way probably won't work. I don't understand why. Why would the diameter or the length of the rod change its magnetic properties?"

Albert was silent for a few moments while he thought about what Tim just said. Perplexed, he replied, "I have no idea. But this is going to become a serious problem. Did the smaller samples exhibit any enhanced magnetic properties?"

"Yeah, but the fields weren't strong enough to create a sustained reaction. They were only about 10% of the normal field strength."

"So, we not only stumbled onto the only correct metal alloy, but also the correct size. That's really quite incredible. The odds of winning the lottery are probably better. If we can't use smaller rods, then we can't reduce the silver requirement. Kingman is going to have to deal with that. I'll let them know."

"It will be a problem, but not for many years. Perhaps somebody will find an alternative material before the situation becomes serious. In any case, it's not our concern. Our biggest problem now is what to do with the money we're going to get," Tim said with a smile.

"That's a problem that will be fun to deal with. But before you spend your money, we have to conclude this deal with Kingman. I think that will happen quickly. Why don't you take a few days off? I don't think there's anything for you to do right now. I'll keep you informed about how things go with Kingman, and if something comes up, I'll let you know."

"You know I've wanted a new fishing boat for a long time. I think I'll go boat shopping this afternoon." He grinned.

Albert grinned back. "Okay, have a good time."

After Tim left, Albert thought about going home. He called the security company only to learn there were still a lot of people hanging around outside his house, so he decided to go back to the hotel again. He stopped by Susan's desk on his way out and asked her if she wanted to go to dinner with him.

"Are you asking me out on a date?" she asked with a smile.

"Yes, that's exactly what I'm doing. Are you interested?"

"Yeah, I'm interested. Are you going back to the hotel?"

"I am. Why don't you join me at 5:30? Tim left to go boat shopping and you should probably go home too. Nothing is going to happen for the rest of the day."

Her smile widening, Susan agreed.

On the way to the hotel, Albert received a call from his attorney who told him he didn't see any problems with the contracts other than the blanks for the royalty amounts. Albert thanked him for his efforts and continued his drive to the hotel.

He was waiting in the lobby when Susan arrived at 5:30. "Where would you like to go to dinner?" he asked her.

"Have you ever been to Venice?"

"You mean the city in Italy with all the canals? No, I've never been there. Besides, even though we have a lot of money coming, don't you think going to Europe for dinner is a little extravagant?"

"I didn't mean the city in Italy. I meant the restaurant downtown."

"Oh, I haven't been there either. Let's go."

They went to Susan's car and listened to some classical music during the drive. Susan found a parking space and they went inside the restaurant. There was soft background music playing and beautiful pictures of Italy and Venice adorning the walls. Albert asked the hostess for a private booth. She showed them to a small room with a table for four. They sat down and the hostess handed them menus. They looked at the menus for a few minutes, discussing some of the choices, and then the waiter appeared. They ordered a bottle of red wine. After the waiter left, Albert said, "We'll probably have the initial ten-million-dollar payment from Kingman next week. Do you have any idea what you're going to do with the money?"

"I'd like to get a new car, but I'm going to wait and get one that's powered by our power modules. I've never had a lot of money before and I really don't know what to do with it."

"I'm sure if I ask, Kingman will give you a car. However, since we can afford to pay for them, I'll ask them to sell us three cars as soon as they're available. I would guess Tim would like one too. Do you want to travel or buy a house?"

"I'd like to travel. I haven't seen much of the world outside of the United States, but I don't want to do it alone."

"I can understand that. I went to Europe a few times with friends, but all we did was go to bars and restaurants looking for girls. I never got an opportunity to really see the countries we were in. One place I visited several times when I was young was an area around the Smokey Mountains. My parents loved nature. We rented a cabin on a lake and every day we went fishing, swimming, or both. We went hiking through the forest as well and we saw deer, raccoons, and lots of rabbits. It was a wonderful place, but I don't remember exactly where it was. I'm fairly sure it was in eastern Tennessee or western North Carolina. Anyway, I want to buy a house in an area like that."

"That sounds wonderful," she said with a new light in her eyes, "I spent most of my life in Chicago and my only real exposure to nature was the city parks. They were nice, but nothing like what you described. I have an idea! How about after this deal with Kingman is completed, we go together to look for your new house?"

"That's a great idea. You know, I've often thought about asking you out. But I didn't have much money and I simply couldn't afford to take you someplace nice for an evening."

Susan reached across the table and grasped Albert's hand. "Had you asked, I would've been happy going to Burger King with you. I really wouldn't have cared where you took me or what we did."

Albert smiled and said, "Okay, I guess I was being stupid. But that's in the past. Here we are, on our first date, and we're in Venice."

At the moment Albert finished speaking, the waiter came back with the wine, hot bread, and two small plates with spiced olive oil. Albert and Susan ordered dinner and the waiter left them alone again.

They talked for a while about the discovery they had made. Then Albert turned their conversation toward the future. "Susan, do you think I would make a good politician?"

"If there's such a thing as a good politician, then it would be you. But I don't understand why you want to do that. What do you hope to accomplish?"

"I know our invention is going to change the world. There will be unintended consequences and I'd like to have some say in how our government handles those things. That means I have to plunge right in at the federal level. I think when we look for a house it should be in an area where the people are somewhat conservative or I'll never have a chance of winning an election."

"You could just make a huge contribution and ask for an appointment to some cabinet position."

"I suppose that's also a possibility. I'll have to think about that."

Albert ordered veal parmesan and Susan asked for the fettuccini alfredo. Their food came and it looked absolutely delicious. They ate mostly in silence, both thinking about the future.

After dinner they both ordered coffee. As they slowly drank their coffee, they soon found themselves holding hands across the table. Their affection for each other obviously growing.

When dinner was over Susan drove Albert back to his hotel. They both got out of the car and near the hotel entrance they embraced for the first time. Then their lips touched as they kissed. After several seconds they broke the embrace and said goodnight to each other. Albert went to his room, smiling broadly. Susan drove home smiling too. Both of them were thinking about the future, and wondering if they would spend it together.

APRIL 18, 2035

The next morning Albert arrived at the office at 8:00 and was surprised to see Tim's car there. There were only about fifteen people milling around outside the office. He thought about speaking to them but changed his mind. If things went according to plan, he would make an announcement to the media this afternoon.

He went inside to find Tim waiting for him in his office. "I thought you were going to take some time off to go boat shopping. What are you doing here?" Albert asked.

"I went boat shopping and I found something I really like. It's a little pricey, so I wanted to find out how things are going with Kingman before I make a decision."

"I hope to conclude everything today. How much is this boat you want?"

"It's more like a yacht than a boat, It's thirty-five feet long, and it'll sleep four, or perhaps six if they're very friendly. It costs around four hundred and fifty thousand dollars."

"Where are you going to use it? There are no big lakes around here."

"My parents live on the shore of Lake Michigan near Muskegon. They have a dock where I can keep the boat during the summer, and there are places there that will store the boat during the winter. I love that area and I'm going to look for a house there."

"I'm also going to look for a house," Albert said, "but I'm not sure exactly where yet. I think it will be in eastern Tennessee or western North Carolina. Susan is going to go house hunting with me."

Almost on cue, Susan walked into Albert's office, walked over to Albert, kissed him on the cheek, and said, "Good morning."

"That's new," Tim said with an amazed look on his face.

"We went on our first date last night," Albert said with a smile.

"Well, it's about time!" Tim exclaimed.

"Better late than never, right? I guess it's good we're all here. I'm going to call Kingman at 9:00 and I hope to conclude our negotiations today," Albert responded.

For the next forty-five minutes they talked about the boat Tim wanted to buy, about the house Albert wanted to buy, and about Albert and Susan traveling around Europe together. They all kept nervously looking at the clock on the wall, which seemed to be moving in slow motion.

At 9:00 Albert picked up the phone and called Kingman. He asked for David Becker, and a few seconds later David answered the phone.

Albert said, "Good morning David. How are you this morning?"

"Good morning Albert, I'm very well so far. I hope you aren't planning on ruining my morning."

"No, I think you'll be happy with what I'm going to say. My attorney had no problem with the contract other than the blanks for the royalty payments. As far as the royalty payments are concerned, I think 5% of the retail price per unit is fair. Do you agree?"

"Yes, I was actually expecting you to ask for more."

"I see no reason to ask for more. With the number of units I expect will be sold, we'll have more money than we'll know what to do with. When we spoke yesterday, we were discussing the plans for the automotive units. I would like to know your plans for the home and business units," Albert requested.

"Nothing is set in stone yet regarding the distribution, but as I said, we're discussing this with all the major hardware retailers. The manufacturing will begin within forty-five days after receiving the signed contract, and we should be able to begin shipping shortly after that. That's assuming we don't run into any major manufacturing problems. Our expectations are we'll be able to make nine hundred thousand units per month for homes and businesses."

"Is that worldwide or only United States production?"

"That's worldwide. About seven hundred thousand will be available in the United States. As you noted yesterday, there may be a problem with the availability of silver. We're going to begin researching other materials immediately."

Albert thought about telling him about Tim's efforts to reduce the silver requirement, but decided he didn't want to do anything that would mess up the negotiations. So, he replied, "That sounds like a good plan. I want to call a press conference for this afternoon and announce that Kingman will be manufacturing the power modules. Is that okay with you?"

"Yeah, I think that'll be fine. But you're going to get questions you can't, or shouldn't, answer. Tell them we'll call a press conference tomorrow. I'll get a new contract e-mailed to you within fifteen minutes with the royalties inserted. Please sign it and have it witnessed. Then e-mail a copy to me and overnight the original. I'll get the original signed tomorrow and e-mail overnight the fully executed contract to you. Also, send your banking information to me and I'll have the initial payment wired to your bank tomorrow. Please review the contract completely before you sign it."

"Okay, I'll do that. I'll also get my attorney over here to review the changes and witness the signatures. I'll call you as soon as it's signed and on its way to you. I'll be waiting for your e-mail."

"You'll have it shortly. Thank you."

Albert called his attorney, who agreed to be there at 1:30. A few minutes later he checked his e-mail and found the message from David. He printed a copy of the contract and read it. He didn't find any problems and gave it to Susan to read. She read it and didn't find problems either so she gave it to Tim. He simply put it back on Albert's desk and said, "I don't like reading legal stuff. If you guys read it and didn't find any problems, I'm sure it's okay."

At 1:15 the attorney arrived. He read through the changes and his only comment was, "The contract looks fine. You people realize that you are all going to be very wealthy? That means you should all think about creating a last will and testament so your money will be distributed the way you want in the unlikely event of your death. Everybody puts it off, but I urge you not to do that."

Albert hadn't thought about that at all, but he realized the attorney was right. "We'll do that within the next month or so. I'll call you and set it up. I need you to witness our signatures on the contract."

Albert, Tim, and Susan each signed the contract. Then the attorney signed as a witness. Albert asked Susan to make each of them a copy of the contract, scan it, e-mail it to David at Kingman, and send the original to Kingman by overnight courier. While Susan was doing that, Albert called David and told him the signed contract was on its way.

Then Albert called Aaron Walter at Vextor Motors. "Mr. Walter, this is Albert Simpson. I'm calling to inform you that we've made the decision to give Kingman the manufacturing rights to the power modules. The Kingman offer was more than I expected and they were the most prepared."

For a second, there was only silence on the other end of the line. Then Aaron replied, "I'm sorry to hear that. I would have sent out our contract to you tomorrow. It included everything we talked about. We could have continued the negotiations, but if you have made your decision, we have no choice but to accept it."

"Kingman has agreed to make the power module technology available to other companies in about fifteen months. They've also agreed to make power modules for other automotive companies for development purposes. That way Vextor Motors will be able to develop the products they want to build during that fifteen-month period," Albert said.

"That will certainly make things better," Aaron said with a brief sigh. He continued after a pause, "Will you get me a contact at Kingman?"

"Yes, I'd be happy to do that. There will be a press conference this afternoon where I'll make the announcement, but I wanted you to know before that. Please feel free to call me if I can be of assistance to you."

"Thank you, Mr. Simpson," Aaron said and he hung up the phone.

60

Albert said, "I don't think he was very happy with our choice."

Susan came back with the copies and gave each of them one. Then she said, "I put the original in an overnight envelope and called for a pickup. I also e-mailed a copy to David at Kingman."

"Thank you. Please call our media contacts and set up a press conference for this afternoon. And try to call Vice-President Pratt as well. I promised I would call her when I made a decision."

"Okay, I'll call her now. Then I'll call our media contacts. Do you think 3:30 would be okay?"

"That would be perfect. That way the story will be ready for the 6:00 news."

About fifteen minutes later Susan walked into Albert's office. "The news conference is set for 3:30. The vice president was traveling, so I spoke to her aide and told her we've decided to give the contract to Kingman. She said the vice-president wanted the contract to go to Vextor Motors and she probably was not going to be happy with our decision. I basically said Vice-President Pratt could call you about it, but I was sure you wouldn't change your mind."

Albert said, with a note of anger in his voice, "you're correct. I really don't like politicians, once they have a little power, they think they're Gods. Anyway, the contracts are signed and I couldn't change my mind even if I wanted to." Then Albert smiled at Susan and said, "Thank you for taking care of it."

"If you don't like politicians, why do you want to become one?"

"I intend to be humble," Albert responded.

"Then you're going to have to change your personality," Susan said.

"Yeah, I guess I will."

They decided to hold the press conference outside the office. It was sunny and the temperature was a perfect seventy-four degrees. The people from the local TV stations began to arrive at 3:00. There was also a reporter from the local newspaper.

By 3:30 everything was ready, so Albert walked outside and stood on a small landing at the top of the stairs leading to the office. In addition to the reporters, there were perhaps twenty other people waiting for him to speak.

"I'm pleased to announce we have concluded an agreement with Kingman to manufacture the power modules we developed. I know you're all anxious to know when these devices will be available, so I'll tell you what I know.

"Kingman has already started working on modifications to one of their vehicles to work with the power modules. I believe it will be based on the current all electric version of the STZ. We anticipate it will be available for purchase in about three months. However, because of the limited supply, and a substantial number of potential purchasers, Kingman is going to conduct a lottery of some type to determine who will be able to purchase one. I don't have the details of how the lottery will work. I assume that Kingman will make that information available shortly. I can tell you there are no options on the car. The only choice will be color."

At that point, somebody yelled a question. "Do you know what they will cost?"

"No, I don't know what the retail cost will be. That's a question for Kingman. We also anticipate people and businesses will be anxious to get the power modules that will enable them to disconnect from the power grid. Kingman is going to make those devices available through the major hardware retailers like Home Warehouse, Lance, Markman Hardware, and others in about sixty days. They'll only be sold with installation. You won't be able to go to the store and just pick one up. I also anticipate there will be limited availability for a long time and I have no information on how the retail sales of the power modules will be handled. Before you ask, I don't know what the devices will cost."

"Do you know how many of the home type devices Kingman is going to make?" somebody asked.

"No, I really don't. I can tell you that Kingman is planning to have a press conference tomorrow. I'm sure they'll be prepared to answer your questions at that time."

"How long did it take to develop the power modules?" another person asked.

"We had a contract with NASA to research the magnetic properties of materials that were to be used in a new project. During that evaluation, we found a material that had very unique properties. We realized the material could be used to make a self-sustaining electric power source. It only took a couple of weeks to design the first prototype. That unit is still running in our lab."

"Have you given any thought to the effect these devices are going to have on the world economy? They could put millions of people out of work," another reporter chimed in almost accusingly.

"Actually, I had that conversation with the vice president. I'm sure there will be changes in the economy all over the world. For some, like countries that are largely dependent on oil for their economy, there will be major issues. For countries with more diverse economies, the problem will be minimal. Yes, it's true many people will lose their jobs and some businesses will fail. But the auto industry will see phenomenal growth and will likely increase employment substantially. I'm sure there will be new jobs to cover the ones that are lost. I want to thank you all for coming," Albert said. He really didn't want to answer any more questions so he went back into the office.

Albert decided to call David and let him know what had happened at the news conference. He warned him to be prepared to talk about product availability and pricing.

"We're prepared," David assured him. "Just so you know, the price for the home unit is going to be just under one-thousand dollars, not including installation. We decided on that price because that way we'll be able to absorb the price increase in silver for the first year or two and keep the retail price constant. When people realize the product is dependent on silver and the public sees the price of silver increasing, they'll understand we'll be forced to increase the price of the devices. Also, we're currently in the process of making long term agreements with several silver refiners so we'll have an uninterrupted supply of silver at stable prices."

"That sounds reasonable. I wanted to ask if you'll allow my partners and me to each purchase a STZ when they become available."

"Sure. The first STZ will go to our museum, but you guys will get numbers two, three, and four at no charge. Do you care about color?"

"I don't, but I'll ask Tim and Susan if they have a preference. Also, before the news conference I called my contact at Vextor Motors and made them aware of our agreement with you. I also told them Kingman would make power modules available for development purposes and he asked for a contact at Kingman. Can you give me a name and phone number?" Albert asked quizzically.

"Just have them call me. I'm sure we'll be setting up an industrial sales group, but until that happens, I'll take care of it."

"Okay, I'll give your name and number to both Vextor Motors and Flexton Chapman. I'm sure they'll be contacting you shortly. Good luck with your news conference tomorrow."

"Thanks Albert. Please feel free to call me anytime."

"Okay, I'll do that," Albert said as he hung up with David.

APRIL 19, 2035

Many historians look on this date as the first day of a new era. Although Albert had told the world about the power modules weeks before, and held a press conference the previous day, it was the announcement by Kingman that made the world take notice. For the previous one hundred and fifty years the people who had oil were rich. It started with John Rockefeller, who had become one of the richest people in the world by selling oil for lamps that brought efficient light to homes and businesses for the first time. Then it was the people who controlled the governments in the oil exporting countries who were rich. They all knew it would end someday, but that day always seemed to be many years away. Yet today they finally realized the end was in sight.

Kingman scheduled the news conference for 4:30. Minutes after Kingman announced they would be selling cars that didn't require any external fuel within three months, there was panic. Not only were the oil exporting countries worried, so were all of the other automobile manufacturing companies. In several countries, automobile manufacturing was their biggest industry.

The following Monday the price for oil futures dropped from one hundred and ten dollars per barrel to sixty dollars per barrel. It would never recover. Within three days, oil futures were down to twenty-two dollars per barrel. Every car company, other than Kingman, saw their stock prices tumble. Kingman stock increased by 30%, and it kept going up for weeks. The big oil companies were hit even harder. Some oil companies saw their stock prices drop by 75%.

Albert was forgotten by the public, at least for a while, and that was all right with him. He and Susan went house hunting together, and while looking for a home they found each other.

Tim bought his boat and went to live with his parents again. He bought some land nearby and had a house and boat house built. He decided to use most of his very substantial income for charity, setting up a foundation that provided full

65

scholarships for children whose families could not afford to send their children to college. He also gave large sums of money to charities that carried out medical research.

SUMMER 2035 THROUGH SUMMER 2039

In late June 2035 Kingman announced they would begin taking orders for the new "No Fuel STZ" on July 8, 2035. They decided to set the price at forty-seven thousand five hundred dollars, and that included a ten-year warranty on the power module. The cars were available in white, black, blue, and silver gray. That was the only option. When an order was placed the customer was required to give a $5,000 deposit. They explained the lottery system that would be used, and nobody would be able to purchase more than one vehicle. They expected the first deliveries in the United States to be made the week of August 26, 2035. Deliveries in other countries would begin two weeks later.

They also announced they would begin shipping home power modules to retail stores in the United States on July 15, 2035. Each retail store would determine how the devices would be sold. They expected to ship two hundred thousand units that week, and one hundred and fifty thousand units per week after that. The units would be available for Europe and Australia a week later.

Despite the fact Kingman made it clear that placing your order first did not increase your chances of getting one of the first vehicles, people began lining up outside Kingman dealerships as early as July 5th. As expected, the entire first year of production was sold by July 12th. Less than 5% of the orders had a color specified, and not one order stated the purchaser would not accept a different color if the color they specified was not available.

In the United States, Home Warehouse and Lance Home Stores began accepting online orders for the home devices. They were charging $695 for the unit, and estimated the installation for a typical home would be an additional $400. A credit card number had to be supplied with the order, but the card would not be charged until the device was available for installation. Many of the local municipal governments quickly passed laws that forbid these units to be installed in homes without a permit, and in some cases, where the municipalities owned the local electric companies, they were charging $2000 for them. That did slow down sales in some areas, but consumers filed lawsuits claiming the permit fees were too high, and ultimately, the consumers won.

Kingman was forced to delay delivery of the STZ vehicles by a week because they realized they had to make the vehicle, and the power module, theft proof. Every STZ was equipped with a keyless entry system, but after you got into the car you had three tries within thirty seconds to enter a five-digit code on a screen on the dashboard. If you failed to enter the code within thirty seconds, all four wheels were locked. To unlock the wheels, you had to exit the vehicle, lock the doors, unlock the doors, and start over again. Kingman also placed the power module inside a steel box that could not be opened. It could be removed with a special tool, but only if the vehicle was raised on a lift.

In August 2035 Kingman ceased production of all gasoline-powered passenger cars worldwide so they could begin conversion to manufacturing electric vehicles. They also ceased production of gasoline engines for those cars at the same time. The engine manufacturing facilities were converted so they could make electric motors and power modules. This move allowed the power modules to be more easily distributed all over the world.

On September 3, 2035, Kingman began accepting orders for the T3000E electric pickup. Like the STZ, the first year's production was sold in a week.

Kingman did supply power modules for development purposes to every car manufacturer that requested them. By early fall of 2036, they began making the production devices for Vextor Motors, Flexton Chapman, and the other automotive manufacturers that had the ability to stay in business after a 90% drop in sales.

By the summer of 2038 there was an enormous selection of electric vehicles available, not just family sedans and pickup trucks, but sports cars, sport utility vehicles, motorcycles, and even a few small motor homes. The automotive industry was booming, and all of the surviving companies were making more money than they had ever thought possible. Kingman was doing better than the others because they had a fifteen-month head start and the largest selection of vehicles. As a result of both car sales and power modules sales, Kingman had become the largest corporation in the world.

In early 2039 Kingman decided to set up a Marine Division. Their first task was to design an electric replacement for outboard motors. In February 2039 they announced a line of electric outboards. The smallest was a 20-horsepower motor and there were also 50, 75, 100, and 150 horsepower versions. The price for these motors was half of the equivalent gas-powered motors. Additionally, these new motors required no maintenance and they weighed nearly 75% less. In under two months Kingman had captured over 85% of the outboard motor business.

There were still a few applications for electric vehicles that remained to be resolved. There were no electric motors for the big eighteen-wheel trucks available yet, but Kingman was working on those too. Additionally, motors for ships, airplanes, and construction equipment were not even being worked on at that time.

At the end of the summer of 2039, 65% of all the vehicles on the road were electric, and 35% of homes and businesses got their electric power from power modules.

OIL COMPANIES

After the initial drop to $22 per barrel for crude oil the price continued to drop, but much more slowly. By the summer of 2038, crude oil sold for just under $12 per barrel. Gasoline in the United States was selling for seventy-five cents per gallon and almost all of that was tax. Almost nobody used heating oil anymore and even the use of natural gas had dropped by over 60%.

The only bright spots for the oil companies were big trucks, airplanes, and ships. But that was not enough to keep most of them in business. By the summer of 2039 there were only three oil companies left: Western American, Universal, and Craver. The other oil companies were bought by one of these three for pennies on the dollar.

Gas stations were disappearing as well. Drivers who still used gas-powered cars discovered they couldn't let their gas tanks drop below half full because they ran a substantial risk of running out of gas. It was especially bad in rural areas, where there hadn't been many gas stations to begin with.

The reason these three companies survived was because they had diversified and made other things like plastics, cleaning products, and pharmaceuticals.

In the summer of 2035, oil companies employed over two million people. By the summer of 2038 that number had dropped to less than two hundred thousand and was still headed lower.

RUSSELL FINE

POLITICAL CHANGES

The political changes as a result of the decreased demand for oil were extensive. As stated previously, many countries were either completely dependent or very dependent on the sale of oil to keep their economies running smoothly.

The part of the world hit the hardest was what was referred to as the Middle East. Saudi Arabia, Iran, Dubai, Qatar, the United Arab Emirates, and Bahrain were all facing bankruptcy by the summer of 2038. The citizens of these countries were, for the most part, given everything they needed or wanted from the government. That changed quickly, and the people were growing frustrated with government interventions. There were riots and threats of revolution in most of these countries.

There was one positive change for the world, which mostly involved Iran. The government was a theocracy, based on Islam. Additionally, they felt their religion should be practiced by the entire population of the Earth. To meet that goal, they financed acts of terrorism all over the world. However, when the money disappeared, they could no longer afford to do that, and the Islamic terrorists disappeared as well.

Other major oil exporters like Russia, Mexico, and Venezuela were facing bankruptcy as well. The wealth their countries had was never really seen by the ordinary citizens. It was kept by the politicians running the government. When the ruling politicians saw their lifestyle changing, they tried squeezing more money from the people by raising taxes, resulting in democratic revolutions in Venezuela and Russia. In both cases truly free elections were held for the first time and the corrupt people in power were thrown out of office, if not exiled or imprisoned.

Mexico was different because of close financial and geographical ties to the United States. It became part of the United States in April 2038. Many historians believe this was the first step in the process of forming the government we have today.

Silver became the most valuable precious metal by the end of 2037. At that time gold was selling for $2400 per troy ounce and silver was selling for $2490 per troy ounce. The price of silver continued to rise, and by the summer of 2038, silver was selling for $2910.

Although Kingman tried to keep the price for the power modules constant, they were forced to raise prices several times, and by the summer of 2038 the cost for a home power module was $4895.

The increase in the price of silver was good news for the corporations that owned silver mines. Many mines that produced low grade silver ore or mines that appeared to be almost devoid of silver were reopened and being actively mined. This increased the supply of silver by 15%. It didn't increase the supply of silver to the point where it had a negative effect on the price, but it was definitely good for consumers.

However, like all minerals, there was a limit to the supply. Some scientists estimated the supply of silver would be exhausted in as little as ten years, while others estimated it would last over one hundred years. But they all agreed at some point in the not too distant future, there would not be enough silver to meet the demand.

ALBERT AND SUSAN

After several weeks of searching, Albert purchased three acres of wooded land in Marshville, Tennessee. Albert and Susan met with an architect to design a house. Following several discussions with her, the architect had a fairly good idea of what they were looking for, and about a week later she showed them some preliminary plans. After a few minor modifications were made, they were ready to start construction. Albert made arrangements with the architect to act as the general contractor for the home and he set up an account for her to handle the construction expenses. The architect estimated the construction would take a year and the cost would be about four million dollars. Obviously, that wasn't a problem.

With the house situation resolved, Albert and Susan decided to go traveling. Susan wanted to spend some time in Paris. She had been there before but never had enough time to really explore the city. Also, Susan spoke some French and she wanted to use it. They drove to Atlanta, turned in their rental car, and purchased first class one-way tickets to Paris. During the flight, Albert made reservations for a hotel and car rental so they would be prepared when they landed.

After they checked into their hotel and got comfortable in the room Albert said, "Susan, please sit down. I want to discuss something with you."

With a look of concern on her face she said, "You sound very serious. Is there a problem I'm not aware of?"

"No, in fact almost everything is perfect. To make everything perfect I would like you to answer a simple question. Okay?"

"Sure, ask anything you like."

Albert said, "Susan, in the past few weeks we've spent a lot of time together." Then he hesitated for a moment to build up his courage. Then he said softly, "During that time, I've been very happy and have grown to love you more with each of the days we have spent together." Then Albert knelt down before her and opened up a small blue box containing a ring.

75

Then he said, "I hope you feel the same way about me. I want to spend the remainder of days, weeks, years," he takes a deep breath, "my life with you. So, my question is, will you marry me?"

"Oh my God, Albert! I've loved this time we've spent together, and I love you too. So, my answer is yes. Yes, I'd very much love to marry you. But as you probably know I'm very wealthy now. Are you sure you're not marrying me for my money?" she asked with a big smile on her face.

They hugged each other tightly, and kissed passionately for several moments. Then, breaking the embrace, Albert looked into Susan's eyes, wiped the tears of joy from her cheeks, and said gently, "I promise I'm not marrying you for your money. I don't want to wait. I think we should get married while we're in Paris. Who should we invite besides Tim?"

Susan thought for a few moments and replied, "I would like to have my parents here. They're kind of old-fashioned and they were upset we went traveling together. When they find out we're going to get married, it'll make them very happy."

"Anybody else? I have no relatives to invite. You and Tim have been my only family for the past few years."

"I'll ask my parents if there's anybody they want to invite. I suspect my mother will want to invite my aunt. I'll call her and ask later today. Do you know what's involved in getting married in France?"

"I have no idea, but I suspect the hotel concierge will be able to handle everything. Let's go talk to them."

They went to the concierge desk and explained what they wanted to do. The desk clerk said the law was recently changed and a license was no longer required, so he could arrange everything. Then he asked if they wanted to have a religious ceremony or a civil one. Since neither Susan nor Albert were religious, they asked for a civil ceremony. Then they asked if the clerk could schedule it for the following week, so they could plan for the guests to arrive. The clerk asked how many guests they were expecting, and Albert told him there would probably be less than ten, but they would let him know for sure by the end of the next day.

When they got back to the room, Albert called Tim and invited him to the wedding. Once Tim recovered from the surprise, he said, "Congratulations! Of course, I'll be there. Is it okay if I bring my parents? They've never been to Paris. This would be the perfect opportunity for me to give them the vacation of a lifetime."

"Sure, I'd love to meet your mom and dad. If you want to invite anyone else, just let me know so I can arrange hotel reservations for them. Do you guys have current passports?"

"Yeah, I got mine renewed two years ago when I went to Japan for a conference. I'm sure my parents have current passports because they go to Canada frequently. Have you set the date for the wedding yet?"

"No, not yet. I'll call you tomorrow."

"Okay, I'll be waiting for your call. I'm very happy for both of you."

Albert didn't realize that while he was talking to Tim on the phone Susan went into the bedroom. When she came back from the bedroom she had a big smile on her face.

"I just spoke to my mother. She was very pleased with our decision to get married. She and my father want to get here as soon as possible to become better acquainted with you. They barely know you. I think there's a travel agent in the hotel. Can we go talk to them now?" Susan blustered out in nearly one breath. Her excitement level was off the charts.

"Sure. I just spoke to Tim. He's also coming with his parents. I told him I would call him when we have the date set. Did your mother want to bring your aunt as well?"

"She was going to call her and then call me back. I want to arrange first class tickets for everyone," she said while zipping around the room, getting her things together for an outing.

"Of course. We could even charter a plane to pick them up and bring them to Paris if you like," Albert said, putting on his leather shoes.

"I don't think that's necessary. In fact, it might frighten my mother since she's a little afraid of flying anyway. I'm sure she'd be more comfortable in a big plane."

Albert and Susan decided the wedding would be on Tuesday, June 11, 2035. That gave them the time they needed to make the travel arrangements. Albert called the concierge desk and told them the date they had picked and asked them if he would be so kind as to arrange the hotel rooms for his guests. He also asked about flight reservations. The desk clerk told him he could take care of that as well. Albert said he would stop at the desk later and give them the information they would need for the travel reservations.

Albert and Susan had thought the world had forgotten about them, but they were wrong. On the Friday before the wedding there was an article about it in the newspaper. They started receiving calls asking for interviews, but Albert turned them all down. They wondered how the newspapers had found out, but at this point it made no difference. Albert called the front desk and asked them to screen his calls and not allow any calls from news agencies. That seemed to work, but about two hours later the phone rang.

When Albert answered it a woman said, "Hi, you must be Albert. My name is Lisa Thomas. I was a roommate of Susan's for our freshman year at college. I live in Paris now and I read about the wedding in the paper this morning. I wanted to call Susan and congratulate her."

"Okay, I'll get her for you." He turned toward Susan and said, "Somebody named Lisa Thomas is on the phone for you."

Susan smiled and walked over to get the phone. "Hi Lisa, it's great to hear from you! How are you?"

"I'm fine. I live in Paris now and when I read about the wedding I had to call. Actually, I'd like to come over and meet your future husband. Would that be okay?"

"Sure, when do you want to come?"

"I'm a doctor now and have appointments until 4:00. Could I come over at 5:00?"

"That would be perfect. Albert and I would love to take you to dinner. We're in room 1640."

"Sounds great, I'll see you at 5:00."

Susan told Albert they were going to dinner with Lisa and that Lisa was a doctor now. Albert said that was fine with him. Then they put together a list of the guests who were coming for the wedding and included their addresses and phone numbers. When the list was completed, they went down to the concierge desk and gave the clerk the list. He asked the clerk to contact each guest and book roundtrip first class flights for the days and times they requested. Albert also told him to charge his credit card for everything.

After making the travel arrangements, they decided to take a walk. They strolled around the area near the hotel, stopped at a few stores but didn't buy anything, got back to the hotel at 4:30, and went up to their room.

A few minutes after five there was a knock at the door. Susan looked through the peephole and told Albert it was Lisa.

Susan opened the door and said, "Hi Lisa. Oh my gosh, it's been what? Seven or eight years since we last saw each other and you look great! I guess being a doctor agrees with you."

"Thanks, you look pretty good yourself. I assume this is Albert," she said. She walked over to Albert and kissed him lightly on each cheek. "It's a pleasure to meet you."

"It's nice to meet you too. Susan told me you live in Paris now. How did that happen?"

"Well, after I graduated from medical school, I did my residency at a hospital in Orlando. While I was there I met some people from a charity that provides free medical services to people in poorer countries," she stated, continuing, "After my residency was completed I went to work for them and they sent me here for additional training on STD's and to become fluent in French. In six months or so I'll be assigned to work somewhere in Africa where French is the primary language."

"That sounds very rewarding," Albert said.

"I agree," said Susan. "This is something you talked about doing when we were roommates."

"I know, and I'm very happy. When I saw you were here, I wanted to see you, but I also have an ulterior motive. We're trying to set up some medical facilities in the more remote parts of Africa and we really need Albert's invention to make it possible. We've been using gasoline generators, but it's often difficult to get the gas we need. We can afford to buy them, but there's strict rationing because of demand and they're simply not available. I was hoping you could help us."

Albert replied, "I would be happy to help in any way I can. How many do you need?"

"Ten would be okay, but twenty would be better."

"I don't think that will be a problem. I'll call my contact at Kingman and ask him to ship them to the hotel. Do you want 110-volt or 220-volt units?"

"We'd prefer 220-volt units, but we'll take what we can get. How do we pay for them?"

"You don't pay for them. We will, and we'll give you an additional two million dollars as well."

Lisa's eyes welled up with tears. "Wow! That's very generous. I don't know how I can ever thank you." She wrapped her arms around Susan and they hugged tightly. She looked over at Albert and he accepted a hug from her as well.

Susan said, "We appreciate what you're doing and Albert and I are happy to help. Let's go to dinner now because I'm hungry."

"Give me a minute to call David and ask him for the power modules," Albert said as he walked into the bedroom to make his call.

When he called, he was surprised to discover David was also aware of his impending marriage. He didn't think the news had made the United States papers, but he was wrong. David said he would have twenty units shipped to Albert's hotel and they should be there within a week. Albert thanked him and ended the call.

When he got back into the living room he said, "Lisa, it's all taken care of. The power modules will be here within a week. If you give me the account number and routing number for the bank your charity uses, I'll have the funds transferred tomorrow."

"I'll be happy to do that. Thank you so much. This is incredible," Lisa said to Albert, looking at Susan, "You have got yourself a good one. I am so happy for you." And Susan just smiled back. She knew.

They went to dinner and Albert spent most of the time listening to Lisa and Susan talk about the times they had lived together. Susan invited Lisa to the wedding and Lisa happily accepted the invitation.

When Albert and Susan got back to their room there was a message from the concierge that said all the travel arrangements had been made and the guests would all be there by Saturday evening.

All of the guests arrived, although Tim and his family arrived early Saturday afternoon. Albert thought about going to meet him at the airport but decided against it. De Gaulle Airport was too big to try to meet somebody without prior planning. Tim told him they would get a car and drive in themselves and not to worry about him, that they could see some sights on the drive. So, he and Susan spent the afternoon in their room talking about what they should do for their honeymoon.

Tim arrived at 4:00. He and Albert shook hands and Susan walked over and kissed Tim on the cheek. Then Tim reached into his pocket and removed an envelope which he handed to Albert.

"What's this?" Albert asked.

"It's your honeymoon plan. Open it," Tim said smiling. "It's the least I can do. After all, without you I would not be where I am today.

Inside the envelope were boarding passes for a cruise from San Francisco to Hawaii and French Polynesia, returning to San Francisco. It was a twenty-eight-day cruise and Tim had arranged for them to have a suite. The cruise was scheduled to depart the Friday after the wedding. Albert and Susan both smiled and Albert said, "We were just talking about our honeymoon plans. Thank you, Tim." Then Albert put his arm around Tim and said, "We didn't know what to do, other than staying in Paris for a while. This is really terrific."

"That deserves another kiss," Susan said, and she kissed Tim a second time.

"There should have been a note in your room telling you about the plans for Monday. Was it there?" Albert asked.

"Yes, I think that's a great idea. None of us have been to Paris before and I think a city tour would be perfect."

"It includes a six-hour tour of the Louvre and dinner at the Eiffel Tower. We're looking forward to it too."

They talked for about an hour and made plans to meet for breakfast at 9:30 Sunday morning. Then Tim went back to his room.

The next few days went by quickly and before they knew it, the day of the wedding had arrived. That morning at breakfast they decided to give each other rings during the ceremony, so as soon as they were finished, they went to a jeweler a few blocks from the hotel and purchased two simple gold bands. The jeweler promised to have them sized and delivered to the hotel by one o'clock.

The hotel had arranged to have a minister from a nearby church perform the ceremony. The minister called Albert at two o'clock and asked if he could meet with him and Susan an hour prior to the wedding. The wedding was scheduled for 7:00, and at 6:00 the minister arrived at their room. After the introductions the minister asked what kind of ceremony they wanted, and they spent a few minutes talking about it. Albert and Susan wanted something simple and informal. The minister agreed and suggested that they arrive at the room at ten minutes after 7:00 so that everyone would be seated and waiting for the ceremony to begin.

Both Albert and Susan were dressed casually, and they asked their guests to do the same. They arrived at the room where the wedding was to be held a few minutes early. The door was closed so they waited until 7:10 to enter the room. There were surprised to see a photographer waiting for them as they walked in. They posed for a few pictures and then walked up to the minister who was standing at the front of the room. The guests were seated around one large table and they all stood up and applauded as Albert and Susan walked past them. The service was short, only about ten minutes. When it was completed Albert and Susan kissed for the first time as husband and wife. Then they sat down at the table with the other guests and had a meal created by the best of gourmet chefs in the area.

On Wednesday morning Albert and Susan flew to San Francisco and stayed at a hotel near the cruise terminal. Friday afternoon they went to the terminal to board their ship. Neither of them had ever taken a cruise before and they were looking forward to it.

Because they were booked into a suite, Albert and Susan bypassed the long check in lines and were personally escorted to their cabin. It was much larger than they had expected. There was a large bedroom, a spacious living room, and a full bath. There was also a large balcony overlooking the sea and it could be accessed from either the living room or the bedroom. After Albert looked around and said, "Wow! I really wasn't expecting this. I'm not going to have a problem spending the next month here!"

Susan replied, "I agree, this is much bigger than my first apartment."

The first five days of the cruise were spent at sea, crossing the Pacific Ocean on the way to Honolulu. Susan and Albert spent most of the time in their room enjoying each other's company. And, like most people on cruises, they spent a lot of time eating. Because they were somewhat famous, they also were invited to have dinner at the captain's table on several occasions.

After stopping at Honolulu and Lahaina, the ship was at sea again on the way to Fiji. Albert suggested they purchase a yacht, but Susan said she was perfectly content to let someone else manage the ship while she enjoyed being waited on. The cruise was wonderful, and they enjoyed all the ports they stopped at. During the return to San Francisco Albert and Susan decided that they would take cruises regularly.

83

After the cruise they went back to Marshville to see how the construction was going on their house. They had been receiving messages about the progress regularly from the architect so they had some idea of what to expect, but they were surprised to see the progress that had been made. The house was ahead of schedule and it looked like everything would be finished within sixty days.

Albert and Susan spent the time waiting for the house to be completed buying furniture and other things for the house. They both thought it was fun to buy things without having to worry about the cost. The other thing they did during that time was to give some serious thought about the best way to use their enormous wealth. They both wanted to do something that would help others, but they were not sure exactly what they wanted to do. They decided that, for now, they would make substantial donations to existing charities. However, they both wanted to create a foundation that would help others in some unique way.

They lived a quiet life together. Mostly forgotten by the media. They loved their house and enjoyed the time they spent there. They went hiking almost every day. It provided a way to exercise and watch the wildlife that surrounded their home. They took a few more cruises too.

In the spring of 2040 Albert started his political career. He ran for a congressional seat that was currently held by a republican who had decided to retire after spending almost twenty years in congress. There were several contenders for the seat, but Albert managed to win the primary, so he would face off against a democrat in the November election. Just prior to the election, the man holding the congressional seat for which Albert was running was accused of accepting money in exchange for political favors. Apparently, it had been going on for several years, and the proof was so overwhelming he didn't even try to deny his guilt. As a result, Albert lost the election.

In January 2042 Albert and Susan had their first child: a girl they named Emily. Shortly after Emily was born Albert had decided to start his political career again, and was running for the congressional seat he previously lost. The man who won the election decided not to run again. Albert won the Republican primary election again, and won seat with 73% of the vote.

2041 THROUGH 2051

In 2041 Kingman released large high torque electric engines that could be used in large trucks and buses. It would take until 2045 before the majority of the "over the road" trucks and buses were electric powered. This became a necessity because there were almost no gas stations left.

In 2042 most of the companies that manufactured home and farm tractors began offering electric versions of their products and they were an instant success. They were less expensive and more reliable than the gas-powered equivalents. They were so successful that by the summer of 2043 it was impossible to find any new gas-powered tractors or lawn mowers.

Because the cost for the power modules continued to rise, cars, riding lawn mowers, tractors, and other farm equipment were designed so the power module could be removed and moved from one device to another. This was one factor that kept the cost of the new equipment down. In fact, when people traded in their cars for newer models, they usually kept the power module to use in their new vehicle.

By the end of 2048 there were no gas-powered vehicles in regular use anywhere. Only planes and ships used fossil fuels.

In 2049 a group of college students in London discovered the correct formula for the silver alloy rod that was the essential part of the power module. However, by that time it really made no difference. Kingman had over one hundred manufacturing facilities dedicated to making power modules, and they never really made excessive profits on the sales, so it would have been impossible to sell them for substantially less than Kingman. They didn't even try to make power modules, but they did publish the formula so it was available to everybody.

By the end of 2050 over thirty billion power modules had been sold.

Also, by the end of 2051, all of the coal fired and nuclear power plants had been decommissioned. The only power plants left were the ones that used water, wind, geothermal, or solar power to generate electricity and they didn't have very many customers.

However, despite the fact that air pollution and carbon emissions had been reduced by over 90%, it was still impossible to satisfy the radical environmentalists. They still claimed Earth was doomed due to the excessive release of methane gas concentrated over dairy farms and cattle ranches. In other words, cow farts.

POLITICAL CHANGES

In 2043 Canada and most of the Central American countries joined with the United States to form the North American Union. All of the countries agreed to use the United States dollar as their currency, which most of them were already doing, and English as a common language. Later that year the United States dollar became the Universal Dollar.

In South America all of the countries joined together in 2045 to form the South American Union. They also selected the Universal Dollar for currency, but they decided to use Spanish for their language.

In Europe most of the countries were already members of the European Union. They had a common currency, the Euro, but many different languages. In 2044 they decided to adopt English as their common language, and in 2046 gave up the Euro in favor of the dollar.

Perhaps the greatest change was in what was referred to as the Middle East. All of the countries in that part of the world, including Israel, formed an alliance called the Middle East Partnership, or MEP, in 2047. The practical benefits from forming the partnership easily outweighed the members' religious differences, and since the Arab countries no longer had vast amounts of wealth needed to provide goods and services to their citizens, many of the people became farmers and ranchers. The homes and palaces that were used by the royal families or political leaders had mostly been converted into expensive resorts. The member countries had not yet decided on a common language, but they did decide to use the dollar as their currency.

Finally, in 2048 Australia, New Zealand, and many of the smaller countries in that part of the South Pacific began talks aimed at forming a union.

SILVER

In 2035 when the power module was invented, the world was producing seven hundred million ounces of silver per year. That increased to over one billion ounces per year in 2043. It was impossible to find that much silver by 2048. That year the world was only able to produce four hundred fifty million ounces, and that was not enough to meet the demand, as many had predicted ten years prior. Because of the demand for silver, the price increased to more than $6000 per ounce.

As the cost of silver continued to increase, so did the cost of the power modules. At the end of 2038 the cost for a new power module was eight thousand dollars. That made them a prime target for thieves. The previous theft deterrents, which seemed to be adequate in 2038, were no longer sufficient to prevent power modules from being stolen. In order to prevent theft, new power modules were made with a circuit which prevented the module from being used unless an electronic key was within a few feet of it. That did seem to reduce theft, but in many cases the owners were robbed of their keys when the module was stolen. To prevent this, in 2041 Kingman offered keys that were inserted under the owner's skin. It was a painless procedure and it almost completely resolved the theft problem, but it did create some problems too. For example, you could not use a parking attendant to park your car or lend your car to anybody.

ALBERT AND SUSAN

In 2042 Albert ran for a seat in House of Representatives again. This time he won easily, After two terms in the house, Albert decided to run for a seat in the Senate and was elected to the North American Union Senate in 2046. He almost immediately joined with other members of the government who wanted to have one government for the entire world.

By the end of 2038 Albert and Susan decided that, although they already were donating large amounts of money to their favorite charities, it was not enough, so they created the Susan and Albert Simpson Foundation. The goal of the foundation was to provide financial assistance to people who needed money for either educational or medical purposes. Susan ran the foundation, along with a staff of twenty other people. They gave away more than ten billion dollars per year and improved the lives of thousands of people all over the world.

Albert and Susan had their second child, a boy they named Terry, in January 2043. He was named after Susan's father, Terrance, who had passed away in December 2040.

2056

The year 2056 is often thought of by historians as the year peace broke out all over the world. In the preceding few years more countries joined with their neighbors to form trade partnerships. One of the largest included India, Japan, Malaysia, South Korea, North Korea, Taiwan, and all of the countries in South East Asia. It was called the Asian Common Union, or ACU. Also, in 2056 the African countries formed the African Union. Both groups chose English as their language of choice and the dollar for their currency.

The only large countries that had not joined with their neighbors were Russia and China. However, Russia joined the European Union in 2057.

China insisted on using the yuan as currency, and since the rest of the world used dollars, they lost most of their trading partners. That, combined with decades of predatory trading practices, meant they were now almost completely isolated. Without trading partners, China had no way of bringing much needed capital into the country so they were on the verge of bankruptcy. But they were stubborn. It would take another thirty years before they finally agreed to join the ACU.

As a direct result of all of these unions and trading partnerships, the threat of war had completely vanished. Although many countries maintained their armies, albeit at substantially reduced levels, the armies were now mostly used to handle natural disasters and to do scientific research. The savings that resulted ushered in a new era of prosperity for almost everybody.

Since many of the larger countries had budget surpluses, they were spending the money on scientific and medical research.

By 2056 heart disease had been almost completely eradicated. New drugs were found that were able to cure many of the more common heart conditions. If there was no drug to help patients, there were also artificial hearts that could allow you to live a normal life. At that time there were already more than one hundred thousand people living with artificial hearts.

Most forms of cancer had been eradicated as well. Breast and prostate cancer had been eliminated by 2046, and in 2056 colon, liver, and pancreatic cancers were no longer a threat.

One other major problem eliminated was Alzheimer's disease. It could not be cured, but a medication was found in 2053 that would prevent people from contracting the disease.

Most of these medical advancements were the result of creating genetic based drugs. Once the public realized genetic research actually improved their lives, they began to accept genetically modified food. This meant increased crop yields for farmers and the elimination of hunger as a worldwide problem.

Much of the scientific research was centered in the North American Union. NASA was given the funding to build new ships that would allow people to travel to other places in our solar system in reasonable comfort and at much greater speeds. Much of the credit for the new NASA ships was due to the silver alloy Albert had discovered. It allowed NASA to build plasma-based engines that were more efficient and developed more power than the chemical based engines used previously. In 2051, people returned to the moon and two years later, a permanent base was established there and was used for the next fifty years.

In 2056 the first of many manned flights to Mars occurred and NASA had plans to build a permanent base on Mars as well.

2080

It had been almost fifty years since the power module was invented and the world had gone through some major changes as a result. Some of the changes were easy to predict. Nobody used fossil fuels for energy production anymore. Every home had its own power source. Every mode of transportation now used electricity. The last to convert were ships and airplanes, but by 2060 even those were using electric power. The world continued to improve economically as well. Since nobody paid for energy anymore, everybody had more money to spend.

Some of the changes were less obvious. Now that electric power was available everywhere, governments and charities were able to set up medical facilities in the most remote areas. They could now provide light, clean water, heating, and cooling, and even sanitation facilities wherever they were needed. As a result of the improved living conditions, infant death rates were cut in some areas by over 90%, and average life spans increased in these remote areas as well.

Of course, these advances were not limited to the remote areas of the world. With the advances that had been made in medicine, many of the most common causes of death had either been eliminated or significantly reduced. The result was a substantial increase in the population. These people needed homes, transportation, and energy.

People all over the world were now dependent on the power modules, and as the population increased so did the demand for them. Kingman was no longer the only company that manufactured the power modules. There were at least twenty other companies making them. The problem was not a lack of manufacturing facilities, but a lack of silver. Worldwide silver production had dropped to two hundred fifty million ounces per year and resulted in nearly a 50% drop in power module production.

From 2046 to 2076 every new home or apartment included a power module. Now, depending on where you lived, you might have to wait for six months to get one. As a result, new home construction had dropped by more than 60%. That created a housing shortage, and most parents found themselves living with their adult children since they couldn't find homes of their own.

Cars had also included power modules for many years, but as the cost for the power modules increased, that feature was eliminated. By 2080, if someone needed a power module for a car, the wait was at least four months. This meant if anyone purchased a new car, they had to have a power module for it, and car dealers no longer accepted "trade-ins" because they couldn't be sold. The result was thousands of abandoned cars, many only a few years old, littered streets and empty lots in the large cities. If a car was in an accident and the power module was damaged the owner could find themselves in real trouble.

By the summer of 2080 there were mass protests and more than a few riots caused by the situation. For the most part, people understood the problem, but they were frustrated and felt something should be done. There was some talk about bringing back power stations and even gas-powered cars, but the infrastructure was gone and there was no way to bring it back. The world had moved on, but something had to be done.

PART TWO – THE SOLUTION
SEPTEMBER 2080

Robert Townsend was President of the North American Union and was currently serving a two-year term as the Leader of the World Council. He was about six feet tall and kept himself fit by walking five miles a day and watching his diet. As a result, he looked much younger than his actual age of seventy-one. He had been a politician for almost his entire adult life, but he had never faced a problem as serious as the lack of silver the world was currently experiencing.

Robert Townsend stood up in front of the group and said, "I want to thank you all for coming. We have a serious problem and I think we should decide, as a group, on the best course of action. As you all know, we've been looking for an alternative to silver to use in the manufacture of the power modules for years, but nothing else works. Our ability to find additional sources of silver haven't met with great success either. In fact, the estimates for this year's production is two hundred and fifty million ounces, and next year will probably only be around two hundred million ounces. That's less than half of what we need to keep up with demand. These are facts all of you are aware of, but the reason I called this meeting is that we've made a discovery recently that could resolve our problem."

He now had the attention of everybody in the room. In attendance were the heads of all of the major trading groups. In the room were the presidents of the South American Union, the European Union, the Asian Common Union, and the Australian Union. They controlled the world economy and had to make a very important and very expensive decision, but with the exception of Robert Townsend, they didn't know that yet.

"One of the space probes we launched in 2079 landed on Jupiter's largest moon, Ganymede. I was given a report last week indicating Ganymede has substantial silver deposits, perhaps exceeding the deposits on Earth. Each of you has a copy of that report in the folder in front of you. I propose we finance an expedition to Ganymede to determine if the report is correct. The cost for this expedition is just over one trillion dollars."

He waited for a moment for them to absorb what he had just said and then he continued, "NASA believes they can have the equipment and crew ready in eighteen months. The trip to Ganymede will take eight months, the crew will need at least three months on Ganymede to complete their analysis, and then they'll have an eight-month trip back. These figures are based on current engine design which will allow the ship to travel at speeds up to eighty thousand miles per hour."

When he finished speaking, Aki Hoshiko from the ACU asked, "Even if they find Ganymede is 90% silver, how can we get it back to Earth without going bankrupt?"

"That's phase two of the plan. NASA believes they can develop an engine that would enable ships to travel at speeds up to 60% of light speed, or one hundred twelve thousand miles per second. That would reduce travel time to Ganymede to ten days. The actual travel time would be less than two hours, but it takes time for the ship to accelerate to maximum speed and then slow down again as it approaches Earth. The ships would be unmanned, because it would be impossible for a human to endure the gravitational forces during acceleration. Also, the ships would be quite large, perhaps fifteen hundred cubic meters, so each ship could carry millions of ounces of silver ore."

"A ship that large can't land, can it?" asked Maurice Le Carré from the EU.

"No, you're right, it can't land on Earth. We have to unload the cargo and put it into ships like the ones we currently use to bring supplies to the International Space Station. The ships could land on Ganymede, however, because the gravity is only 15% of the gravity on Earth. The low gravity will also make it easy to mine the silver ore and easy to load the cargo ship."

"This sounds a lot like science fiction, but even if it's possible, what's it going to cost?" asked Gordon King from the Australian Union.

"That's an excellent question, Gordon, and one I knew would be asked. It won't be cheap. NASA estimates the cost will be between one and two trillion dollars. Once we have the technology, we would be able to explore all of the planets and moons in the solar system. Think about what we might find," Robert said with excited nervousness, "You should also be aware that this is a long-term commitment. It will take three or four years of development to complete and test the engine design. Some work has already begun, and once that's finished, we'll have to build a ship to test the engine. That will probably be another year at least. The testing will take perhaps six months. If no additional design changes in the engine are required, which is unlikely, work can begin on the cargo ships. I would assume some engine changes will be required and then tested, so I would add another year to the schedule. Since the cargo ships won't be carrying any people, the design is much simpler, and the design of the cargo ships will probably start while the engine is being tested. Of course, the cargo ships have to be built in space, so the process will be slower, but I think it will take a year to build each ship. With luck, we might be able to launch the first cargo ship in as little as eight years. The first ship will be sent to Ganymede with the materials required to build a habitat for the workers. Again, if everything works according to plan, the first cargo ship with silver ore should be back to Earth ten years after the program starts."

At that point Robert paused for a few moments and Gordon King asked, "Is there a plan to build a ship with a new engine that will be able to carry people? I don't think unmanned ships can really carry out much in the way of scientific research."

"Yes, there's some research going on in that area already. We know the human body can't withstand more than 3 g's for any extended length of time, but we think by placing the crew in some kind of chamber that will mitigate some of the forces, combined with a form of "suspended animation" if you will, we can keep the acceleration at 6 g's. At that rate it will take the ship two weeks to reach twenty thousand miles per second, which should be fast enough to make travel within the solar system reasonable. Obviously, a lot of this is theoretical, but it's based on sound scientific principles. Any questions?"

"Yes," said Eric Estivez from the South American Union. "How many cargo ships do you plan on building?"

"The plan is to build three ships. We don't know how difficult it will be to mine the silver ore, but it should be easier than it is on Earth because of the lower gravity. We think with three ships there'll always be one in orbit by the space station to be unloaded."

"How many people will be on Ganymede?" Maurice Le Carré asked.

"Probably one hundred to start. The habitat will be designed to comfortably hold two hundred. The cargo ships won't go back to Ganymede empty. They'll bring everything necessary to keep the people there comfortable."

There were quiet murmurs in the room amongst the constituents. Robert cleared his throat to signify that he was not done yet. Once everyone's eyes were focused on him again, he took a moment to organize his thoughts.

After a few more seconds, Robert continued, "I realize this is a lot to think about. I'm going to put together a written plan over the next week and send a copy to each of you. That plan will include the financial contribution each of you will be required to make. I would like to get together again one month from today and make our decision. If anybody has an alternative proposal, please let us know at that meeting. If there's no alternative plan, please be prepared to vote on this proposal at that time. We can't postpone our decision. I'm sure we've all heard the rumors about bringing back power generating stations and gas-powered cars. None of us want that, so we must be proactive. Thank you all for coming."

When he finished speaking, he sat down and the meeting broke up a few minutes later.

OCTOBER 2080

All of the people who attended the September meeting were at this meeting as well. Robert Townsend spoke to the group. "It's good to see all of you again so soon. I know each of you received a copy of the report I sent out after the last meeting. I've spoken to each of you several times during the last month and I know all of you have read the report. If any of you have any comments or suggestions, now would be the time for us to discuss it."

Aki Hoshiko from the Asian Common Union stood up and said, "I believe you have done an excellent job. The report contains all the information I needed to make my decision. Speaking for the ACU, we fully support the recommendations outlined in the report. I met with my top science advisors and they also agreed this is probably the only reasonable solution to the problem."

"Well, I appreciate the vote of confidence. Has anybody come up with an alternative solution we should consider?"

Eric Estivez from the South American Union asked, "Since we already have a small colony on Mars, have you considered Mars as a possible source for silver?"

"We did consider that, but in the twenty years we've been exploring Mars, we haven't found any deposits of materials that are not abundant on Earth. If we ever run short of iron or nickel, then Mars might offer a solution, but there's no indication there are any large deposits of silver there."

Maurice Le Carré said, "I agree with Mr. Hoshiko. This appears to be the only possible solution to the problem. Do any of you disagree with that?"

Since nobody spoke up, Robert said, "There have been some interesting developments since our last meeting. First, NASA is currently building a ship that was meant to be used for the next Mars mission. It's much larger than the current ships because it was supposed to transport twenty-five people. The current ships have a maximum capacity of twelve. NASA has agreed to repurpose that ship for the trip to Ganymede.

There'll be some changes required for the longer trip, but they believe they can have the ship ready in six to eight months. I think you might also be interested to know the captain for that trip to Mars, who will now be going to Ganymede, is Terry Simpson. He's the son of Albert Simpson who, as you all know, was the inventor of the power module."

Robert continued, "There has also been some good news in the development of what is now being called the sub-light engine. Computer simulations indicate the design will work and the engine should allow the ships to reach approximately 62% of light speed, or about one hundred fifteen thousand miles per second. One of the NASA engineers tried to explain how the engine works, but even though I took several physics courses in college, I wasn't really able to understand it. In any case, a computer simulation isn't the same as a real test, and according to the engineer, the real testing probably won't start for two or three years. I know this is optimistic, but these two developments put us two years ahead of where I thought we were at the last meeting."

"I think that's very good news. Let's put this to a vote," Gordon King said.

"Okay, you all know the financial contribution you're required to make so, unless there's some objection, I would like to ask all who are in favor of proceeding with the Ganymede proposal say 'aye'."

Everybody in the room said "aye" and Robert said, "Thank you all. I believe we made the correct decision. I'll prepare a press release and send it to each you for comments by the end of the week. I would like to announce this to the world sometime next week."

All of the attendees agreed again and Robert said, "I'll keep each of you informed with monthly progress reports, and if something important occurs, each of you will be informed immediately. I would also like to ask each of you to let me know if you have somebody from your area you think would be useful to the project. I'll arrange for them to be made part of the NASA team. Thank you all for coming."

A few days later Robert arranged for a worldwide broadcast to explain what was going to happen. After a brief introduction, he began to speak. "Good evening. As all of you are aware, the world has become dependent on power modules. Currently we are unable to mine the silver needed to meet the demand for them. I want you all to know those of us in government are aware of the problem and now we believe a solution has been found.

"Over a year ago a probe was sent to Ganymede, the largest moon of Jupiter. Actually, it's the largest moon in our solar system. Although the intent of the probe was not specifically to search for silver, it did discover what we believe are massive silver deposits. And although it may seem like science fiction, we have found a way to mine the silver on Ganymede and bring it back to Earth. I wish I could tell you we'll have all the silver we need shortly, but I can't do that. It'll probably be several years before that silver begins to arrive on Earth. We know this time table isn't much help for those people who are currently waiting for a power module.

"Last week NASA began modifications of a new ship that was originally going to be sent to our colony on Mars. It's now going to be used for a trip to Ganymede. This ship should launch within six months and its mission is to verify the silver deposits on Ganymede and determine the best methods to extract the silver. While this mission is going on, we're designing a fleet of new ships that will be used as cargo vessels. These ships will be powered by a new engine that will allow the ships to travel at speeds of up to 60% of light speed. These ships will be unmanned and will be able to make the trip between Ganymede and Earth in ten days. Each ship will have a capacity of fifteen hundred cubic meters of cargo space and will be able to transport twenty million ounces of silver ore. These ships are, needless to say, very complex and they'll require a lot of time to develop. We expect to begin development of these ships shortly and expect them to be fully operational by the time we begin the mining operations on Ganymede.

"Additionally, we want you to know we're doing exhaustive searches for new sources of silver here on Earth as well, and those explorations will continue. We have found some areas that appear to be promising, and we will keep you informed regarding our progress. Also, we'll set up an online site within the next forty-eight hours that will contain the latest status for all of our endeavors. The public can also submit questions at these sites that will be answered promptly. We want to keep you informed. Thank you all for your time this evening."

The reaction to the speech was predictable. Nobody was really happy with the plan because even if everything went according to the schedule, which few believed would happen, the problems would continue for many years to come. It didn't stop the demonstrations, and some of those demonstrations turned somewhat violent. Nobody was hurt, but there was some significant property damage and most of that was directed at Kingman. Many of the demonstrators felt Kingman was responsible for the current problem and the world was better off before the power module was invented.

However, a week after Robert's televised speech, the discovery of a huge, previously unknown silver deposit, was going to play an important interim roll. Initial indications revealed it could produce two hundred million troy ounces of silver per year when it was in full production. It would be a few months before that happened, but that was a lot less than the eight years before the silver ore from Ganymede would be available.

Once Robert had been made aware of the silver deposits in Argentina and confirmed the information with the mining engineers who were on site, he arranged for another worldwide broadcast.

Smiling broadly, he began, "Good evening. Four weeks ago, I spoke to you about our plans to bring substantial amounts of silver back from Ganymede, but I also told you that we were searching on Earth for additional silver resources as well. I'm very happy to tell you the search has found what may prove to be the largest silver deposit on Earth. It was

106

found in western Argentina, twenty-five miles west of the city of Mendoza. The initial estimates indicate that when this mine is put into full production, which will happen in the next sixty days, we'll have enough silver to meet 90% of the demand. That means there will probably still be a wait for a power module, but it will be a matter of days rather than months. We expect within five months all the current pending orders will be filled, and we're going to try our best to reduce that time as well.

"Please understand, this silver deposit won't eliminate the need for bringing silver back from Ganymede. However, there's every indication it will largely eliminate the problem until that happens.

"I'm also happy to announce the launch for the initial trip to Ganymede has been moved up and we expect that launch to occur in sixty days. One additional positive thing has happened regarding the engine design for the cargo ships that will carry the silver ore from Ganymede back to Earth. Computer models indicate the design will work and next week we'll begin construction on the first prototype engine.

"In my last announcement I stated we'll keep you informed and that's exactly what we did tonight. You may rest assured as progress is made, we'll make that information available to you as soon as possible. Thank you for your time this evening. Goodnight."

This time the public reaction was much more positive. For the most part the demonstrations stopped, but there were still some minor outbreaks of violence. Those outbreaks were eventually tied to professional rabble rousers hired by people who simply hated all forms of government and sought to cause chaos for whatever reason they could find.

The mine in Argentina began to produce massive amounts of silver thirty-five days after Robert's speech. In less than two weeks the additional silver began to make a difference in the backorder status for many people. It was anticipated that by the time the ship to Ganymede launched in December, the backorders would be gone.

DECEMBER 2080

The Captain of the ship, Terry Simpson, looked a lot like his father. He was tall, thin, had brown hair and matching eyes. He also had his father's intelligence. He graduated at the top of his class in high school, at seventeen. He attended MIT where he received a master's degree in Aeronautical Engineering. Immediately after graduation he went to work for NASA where he was trained as a pilot. After he completed his pilot training he was assigned to work on the missions to Mars. He started out as a copilot, but after two years he was given a ship of his own. He had completed 13 Mars missions as captain when he was given the job of Captain of the ship going to Ganymede.

The ship for the mission to Ganymede was ready by December 1, but it would be twenty-two days before the Earth would be in the best position to launch the ship. All of the crew members had spent time in the habitat on Mars, so they were familiar with the rigors of space travel. The crew included a geologist whose job was to evaluate the silver deposits on Ganymede. There was also a medical doctor, Ross Daniels, whose job, aside from taking care of the crew, was to work with Sheila Nelson, an exobiologist, to check for any living organisms on Ganymede. They were not expected to find any, but they would have sixty days to look. The other seven members of the crew were there to make sure the ship functioned normally, and to make sure they arrived at the intended spot on time and left for Earth on schedule.

NASA received constant messages from the probe on Ganymede, although there was little new information. It was expected the probe would continue transmitting for decades since it used a power module as a power source.

On December 20 the crew went to the space station to prepare for the launch. All members of the crew were given extensive physical exams and the ship's operation was checked by the crew. On December 23 everything was ready and the ship, now named Ganymede I, was launched at 3:00 PM eastern time.

Several hours later, they passed the orbit of the moon. By the end of the second day, Earth was just a large bright dot in space. The flight was uneventful until the morning of December 31. They received a message from NASA telling them the Ganymede probe had stopped transmitting a few hours earlier. There was no indication of any malfunction, although all of the data had not been analyzed yet. The crew was given the additional task of trying to determine the cause for the failure of the probe.

GANYMEDE

The trip to Ganymede was, for the most part, unremarkable. All of the crew members were used to living in cramped spaces and had long ago lost any need they had for privacy. There were a few minor disagreements between the crew members, but these problems were quickly resolved.

In order to pass the time, they all read books and played games. Additionally, the ship had an advanced communication system which enabled them to receive copies of the latest movies and television programs. They also sent and received messages to and from friends and family. The delay between the time a message was sent from the ship and the time it was received on Earth was thirty-five minutes, so real time communication was impossible, but they were used to that.

On August 23rd, the ship's computer put the ship into a low orbit around Ganymede that would take them over the area of the probe. Terry Simpson, the ship's captain, spoke to the navigator, "Lieutenant Parker, we know the coordinates of the probe, so let's find it and then we can look for a nice smooth place to land nearby."

"Yes sir, we should be over the probe's location in forty minutes," Lieutenant Parker replied.

After fifty minutes had passed Terry asked, "Shouldn't we have seen the probe by now?"

"Yes sir, I expected to see it ten minutes ago. I just finished double checking the coordinates and they're correct. It would be much easier to find it if the transmitter was still working, but obviously that's not an option. That area will be in visual and computer scan range again in ninety minutes. I'm going to program the computer to look for any metallic object on the surface. That should be ready to begin processing in ten minutes, so there's no reason we shouldn't find the probe on the next pass."

All of the crew members waited patiently for the next pass over the area, but neither the computer nor any of the crew could find the probe. Terry was confused. "Lieutenant Parker, I don't understand. Are we looking in the correct area?"

"Yes sir, we're absolutely looking in the correct area. I don't understand this either. The probe isn't there," Mark replied, with obvious confusion in his voice.

Terry asked Lieutenant Cohen, the geologist onboard, "Is the surface geologically active? Could the probe have been buried in a landslide or something?"

"There's no evidence of any recent seismic activity sir," she replied.

"Okay, Lieutenant Parker, before we pass over that area again, double check the scan program. Also, I want everybody to man a monitor and visually check every square inch of that area for the probe. It has to be there."

"Yes, Captain."

On the third pass over the area where the probe should have been, nothing was found. Terry said, "They'll never believe this back at NASA headquarters. They're going to think we're all nuts, or incompetent, or perhaps both. Lieutenant Parker, on the next pass look for a landing site. We're going to land the ship and then do our own ground search."

Four hours later the ship touched down on Ganymede. An hour later Terry and Lieutenant Cohen left the ship to search for the probe. Before they left, they studied pictures the probe had taken of the area around it. There were some unique rock formations that would help confirm they were looking in the right place. After forty-five minutes of searching, they were certain they had found the location where the probe landed. The surface was slightly indented and it was obvious the probe had been there, but nobody had any idea what had happened to it. They went back to the ship more confused than ever.

"Okay, we aren't crazy. The probe was there and now it's not. Does anybody have any ideas?" Terry asked.

Lieutenant Parker said acidly, "Isn't it obvious? The Ganymedeians took it inside their underground lair."

"Do you want to send that report back to Earth with your name on it?" Terry retorted.

112

"No, I really don't think that would be a good idea. But somebody, or something, had to have taken it. It didn't vanish on its own."

Terry recorded the following message: "Sir, we now know why the Ganymede probe stopped transmitting, and I'm certain you'll think we're all insane, or incompetent, when I tell you what we found. Actually, I have to tell you what we didn't find. The probe's gone. We made three passes over the area where it was supposed to be. The first one was visual, and the probe is large enough that it should've been easy to spot, but we didn't see it. For the second pass we programmed the computer to search for any metallic object on the surface. The computer didn't find anything. We made a third pass with both computer and visual scans. Again, nothing was found. We landed at the probe's last known location and two of us went out to search for it. We found indications it had been there. There are pictures attached to this message. We are, of course, open to any suggestions regarding our next course of action regarding the probe. We'll begin our evaluation of the silver deposits within the next twenty-four hours. By the way, after eight months without gravity, we're all enjoying being on the surface of Ganymede. I'm waiting for your response."

The response from Earth was short: "That is an interesting, and completely unexpected development. We'll get back to you shortly."

The NASA scientists' first thought was that the ship was looking in the wrong location, but the ship's location was pinpointed by the transmission they had sent. The probe was saucer-shaped and about seven feet in diameter. It was five feet high and made of polished aluminum. It would have been very easy to see against the gray, almost flat surface of Ganymede. The obvious conclusion was that there was finally proof we weren't the only intelligent life forms in the universe and these lifeforms had taken the probe.

NASA sent the following message back to Ganymede: "We verified the location of the ship and you're within three hundred yards of the probe's location. We're forced to believe another intelligent lifeform took the probe in order to study us.

113

Since there is a possibility that you are not alone on Ganymede, we're concerned for your safety. Please complete your research as quickly as possible and return to Earth. Additionally, please consider the information regarding disappearance of the probe as secret. It is not to be divulged to anyone. We'll inform President Townsend and let him make the decision on when and how to make the information public."

Terry hadn't given any thought about the safety of the crew until he received the message from Earth. He got the crew together and read the message. There was a unanimous decision among the crew to continue the mission as planned. They all felt that any beings intelligent enough to take the probe were not likely to be violent. Terry decided on a compromise. It took them eight months to get to Ganymede, and he did not want to return to Earth empty handed. He ordered that a member of the bridge crew monitor the scanners for any indication they were not alone, and they would abort the mission and return to Earth immediately if anything was found.

Terry sent a message back to Earth informing them of his decision.

The response was short again: "Acknowledged."

The entire crew of the ship couldn't stop thinking about the possible presence of an alien ship nearby, but little was said about it. They spent the next five days prospecting for silver and they weren't disappointed. There appeared to be massive silver deposits a few feet below the surface. The geologists also found there were veins of water ice less than ten feet below the surface and there was probably liquid water deeper, where it was substantially warmer than on the surface. The search for water would have to wait for the next mission, however, since the equipment on the ship wouldn't allow them to scan more than a few hundred feet below the surface.

The next couple of months passed quickly. During that time, the crew accumulated a substantial amount of silver ore to bring back to Earth for analysis. The geologist also spent time gathering information regarding the size of the silver

114

deposit and it appeared to be larger than any silver deposits found on Earth. They began to wonder if there were other large silver deposits, so two weeks before they were scheduled to begin the return trip to Earth, they put the ship back into orbit and searched for a similar site. During the passes over the moon, they found two sites that looked promising. They selected the larger of the two sites and landed again.

Daryl Cohen, the geologist, and Sheila Nelson, the ship's exobiologist, left the ship to explore the surface. Lieutenant Cohen was pleased to find what appeared to be another substantial silver deposit. They also found a small amount of water ice a few inches below the surface. Lieutenant Nelson took a sample of it back to the ship for analysis.

Upon returning to the ship, the geologist prepared her report for NASA and Sheila began to prepare the ice sample for analysis. The ice sample was placed into an airtight container and allowed to melt. Then Sheila put the sample into an electronic microscope to begin to look at it. The sample looked perfectly clear, but microscopic examination revealed something she had never expected to see. She found what appeared to be something with a cell-like structure. It was definitely something that had been alive at one time. Sheila spent the next several minutes looking at other areas of the sample and everywhere she looked she found more of these cell structures. She couldn't believe what she was seeing. She called Terry, and trying to contain her excitement, asked him to come to the lab. When Terry came in, Sheila said nervously, "Sir, please look at the display."

Terry stared at the display and after several seconds, stammering, he asked, "Is this for real or is it some kind of joke?"

"I can assure you it's not a joke and the image isn't the result of any contamination. There are hundreds of those cells in the water sample."

"Please prepare a report for NASA and I'll send it with the geology report later. I think it would be a good idea to get another sample and verify those cells are really there. I want to be sure before I send this information to Earth."

"Yes sir. I'll go get another sample now."

"Please take Lieutenant Parker with you and have him verify everything you're doing."

"I'll go talk to him now and then I'll create another sample tube using the bio-system."

"Great, please let me know what you find immediately." A few seconds later Terry asked, "Did you ever find anything similar on Mars?"

"No, we never found anything that would definitely prove life ever existed on Mars. We did find what appeared to be the fossil remains of some very small organisms, but it was impossible to prove."

"Okay, I want to see the results from the next sample as soon as possible."

The news about Sheila's discovery spread quickly around the ship and within a few minutes everybody stopped by the lab to look at the sample.

Forty-five minutes later Mark and Sheila left the ship to get another sample. When they returned Sheila prepared the sample for viewing as the entire crew of the ship watched. A few seconds later the image of a cell appeared on the monitor.

"I guess that verifies your discovery. Get your report ready as soon as possible," Terry said.

"I'll have it ready in two hours."

When Terry had the reports from Sheila and Daryl, he sent the following verbal message to Earth: "This is Captain Simpson. As I reported to you, we left our original landing site and from orbit found two promising areas for potential silver deposits. When we landed, Lieutenant Cohen and Lieutenant Nelson left the ship to explore the landing area. I'm pleased to tell you we found another large silver deposit. Lieutenant Nelson found something possibly just as important and definitely more amazing. While examining the silver deposit, they found some water ice a few inches below the surface. Lieutenant Nelson took a sample of it back to the ship for analysis. The sample showed evidence of what were, at one time, living organisms. Their reports are attached to this message."

116

When the reply from Earth was received, Terry read it to the entire crew.

"Congratulations are obviously in order. The Ganymede mission was far more successful than we ever dreamed possible. Not only did you confirm the presence of substantial silver deposits but you proved, beyond question, that life exits elsewhere in the universe. If life could have developed in the harsh environment on Ganymede, it could probably have developed almost anywhere. Additionally, we can be fairly certain that some of that life is intelligent and probably capable of interstellar travel. Our people here are anxiously awaiting your return. They want to analyze the single cell organisms you found as soon as possible. Until we've had a chance to complete our analysis of the cells, we must ask you to keep the information regarding this discovery secret. We're all very proud of the job you and your crew have done."

A few days later the ship left for Earth. The entire crew had been concerned the aliens who took the probe would come back, but once they left the orbit of Ganymede, that concern had mostly vanished.

THE RETURN TO EARTH

The return trip to Earth was uneventful until July 23, 2082. The ship received a private message for Terry from his mother, "Terry, I wish there was an easy way to tell you this, but there really isn't any. Your father passed away last night. He had a stroke and by the time we got him to the hospital it was too late. The doctor said his death was quick. Emily and I both wish you were here and I'm sure you'd like to be here as well. I thought you would like to know that this morning I received a message of condolence from President Townsend, who said he'd be honored to be at your father's funeral. He asked if he could deliver the eulogy, since you can't be here. I'm going to tell him it would be fine, but I wanted your permission first. I think this is something that would've pleased your father."

The news was completely unexpected and it hit Terry hard. He was sitting at the command console when he read the message. He felt tears welling in his eyes. Ross was sitting next to him and saw the change in Terry's face as he read the message and could see he was obviously disturbed by the message. He asked Terry, "What's wrong?"

Terry handed Ross his communicator so he could read the message.

Terry went back to his cabin. It took a few minutes for him to regain his composure. Then he responded, "I do wish I could be there. I'm sorry you and Emily have to go through this by yourselves. I have no problem with President Townsend giving Dad's eulogy and I'm sure he'd be pleased. I'm really looking forward to getting home and spending some time with you and Emily."

A few days later at Albert Simpson's funeral, President Robert Townsend spoke. "Few, if any, people in the world have touched as many lives as Albert Simpson. Every one of us uses his contribution to the world every day. The device he invented powers our homes, offices, factories, and virtually every mode of transportation. Thanks to the power module, the air we breathe is cleaner and the water we drink is purer. His invention made it possible to have medical facilities, schools, water, and sanitation systems in places where only fifty years ago it would have been impossible. He cured us of our dependence on oil and the result has been peace and prosperity all over the world."

President Townsend spent the next few minutes giving a history of Albert's life. He concluded the eulogy by saying, "Albert did more than just invent a device that changed our lives. He served in our government with honor for thirty-six years, first as a congressman and then as a senator in the North American Union. He's probably the person most responsible for the formation of the North American Union. He led the fight in congress to get the approval for the legislation that was needed to make it happen. I think we all owe him a debt of gratitude for having the vision and desire to put in all the hard work that was required to guide us into creating a successful world government and a more prosperous and peaceful world.

"He and his wife, Susan, did not start out wealthy, they became wealthy as a result of hard work and determination. Once acquired, they shared that wealth with the world through their generous donations to charitable organizations everywhere. Additionally, the Susan and Albert Simpson Foundation has provided financial assistance to more than three hundred fifty thousand people since its formation almost fifty years ago, and even though Albert is no longer with us, the foundation will continue to help those in financial need for many years to come."

President Townsend then turned and faced the casket and said, tearfully, "Rest in peace my friend. Thank you for all you have done for the people of the Earth. It's my fondest hope you will be remembered for the contributions you made to improve all of our lives." Then he turned toward Susan and smiled warmly before he stepped down from the podium.

By Christmas of 2082 the members of the ship's crew were getting very anxious to finish their long journey. They all sent and received Christmas messages from friends and family and those messages only made them feel far lonelier in the vastness of space.

The NASA scientists were also very anxious for the ship to return, but for a different reason. They wanted to study the specimens the ship was bringing back. It was their first chance to study an actual alien organism. All of the lab equipment had been ready by early December and now all they could do was wait.

THE GANYMEDE SPECIMENS

On January 19 the ship docked at the space station. The crew spent the next few days going through an extensive debriefing, medical examinations, and relaxing in more normal feeling of gravity for the first time in more than two years. They were also able to hold real conversations with their loved ones, something each of them spent several hours doing.

On January 23 the crew of the ship, the silver ore, and the cell specimens all went back to Earth. Terry's sister, Emily, was waiting for him when he walked inside the NASA building. They hugged and went to a private plane that would take them back to Tennessee so Terry could see his mother again.

Although the primary purpose of the mission had been to determine the extent of the silver deposits on Ganymede, the silver ore was largely ignored by NASA. Almost everybody at NASA wanted to begin the analysis of the Ganymede cells as soon as possible.

Visually, the cells appeared identical to many of the single cell plants and animals found on Earth, but when the DNA analysis was completed the results were surprising in the extreme. A DNA molecule in all living things on Earth looks like a ladder that has been twisted into a spiral shape. The DNA of the Ganymede cells was similar, but with one striking difference: it looked like a ladder with an additional center support, or two ladders attached to each other and then twisted into a spiral shape.

In our DNA, the vertical components are made up of sugar and phosphate. The horizontal components are called base pairs. The Ganymede DNA had an additional vertical component between the base pairs, so there were no base pairs, instead there were base singles.

It was certainly one of the most important scientific discoveries ever made. When this information was given to President Townsend, he immediately called the other world leaders to let them know what was found. It was decided to make the information regarding both the cells and the disappearance of the probe public.

On January 28, 2083, Robert Townsend again spoke to the world. "As you all know, the ship we sent to Ganymede returned to Earth several days ago and I wanted to take this opportunity to make all of you aware of the results of the mission.

"I'm sure you are all aware of the substantial silver deposits that were found on Ganymede. Initial estimates are that there's probably more silver on Ganymede than there is on Earth. That is, of course, very good news. But that's not the reason I'm speaking to you now.

"We believe two other discoveries made during the mission are more important than the silver deposits. The silver deposits on Ganymede were found by a probe that landed on its surface in January 2079. Shortly after the mission to Ganymede was launched, the probe stopped transmitting. We added the task of determining why the probe failed to the mission. The ship was going to land near the probe's location anyway, so the task should have been easy. However, after entering orbit around Ganymede, the crew of the ship made a startling discovery. The probe was no longer there."

He paused for a few seconds to give people a chance to absorb what he had just said. Then he continued, "The obvious conclusion is that someone, or something, took the probe. We now have the answer to one of our greatest existential questions: we're not alone in the universe. Because we were concerned for the safety of the crew, we asked them to return to Earth as soon as possible, but they felt that if there were other lifeforms intelligent enough to go to Ganymede and take our probe, they were unlikely to be hostile. So, under orders to make safety their top priority, they stayed and completed their mission.

"I must tell you now that just before leaving Ganymede the mission crew found something else that is equally startling. Just below the surface of Ganymede there are veins of water ice. Upon examination of that ice, they found evidence of single cell organisms. Those samples were brought back to

Earth and the analysis of those samples found that the DNA in those cells are unlike the DNA of living organisms on Earth. I don't want to go into the technical aspects of the differences between our DNA and the DNA from the Ganymede cells now, but when the analysis is complete the information will be published. Ganymede isn't a very hospitable place, and if living organisms could develop there, then we must conclude that life is far more common than we ever thought possible.

"The mission to Ganymede was expensive, but I think we'll all agree it was one of the best investments ever made. One final thought I would like to pass along: I don't think the fact we now know that life exists elsewhere in the universe should cause us to alter our religious beliefs. It simply means God's responsibilities are bigger than we thought. Goodnight."

The reaction to the speech was, for the most part, positive. Most people had already been fairly certain we were not alone in the universe, but some people were concerned because of the possibility that whoever took the probe may be more advanced scientifically. A few people were convinced life on Earth was now doomed. There were also the religious fanatics who simply could not accept the idea that God would have created life anywhere else in the universe besides planet Earth.

A few days after the speech, the results of the analysis of the silver ore brought back from Ganymede was made public. The ore had a higher silver content than almost all of the silver deposits found on Earth. The information the government released said that once the mining operation was in place, Earth would have enough silver to last for at least a thousand years. It was also announced that the initial design for the sub-light engine was complete and construction of the prototype would begin immediately.

THE GANYMEDE DNA

In Washington, in a conference room at the North American Institute of Health, several of the world's leading genetic experts were gathered to discuss the implications of the alien cell DNA found on Ganymede.

The leader of the Genetics Division at the North America Institute of Health, Dr. Wayne Sommers, went to the podium and spoke to the group.

"I want to thank you all for coming today. All of you have a copy of the report on the DNA structure we found in the Ganymede cells and I'm sure you all have studied the report. To say we were surprised is a gross understatement. I think we all believed the structure of DNA would be the same for all lifeforms anywhere in the universe. This was proved to be untrue with the first sample of alien DNA. What does this do to our perception of life elsewhere in the universe? Please feel free to ask a question or contribute."

Dr. Simon Chambers, from the EU Health Institute, said, "I think it's too early to reach any conclusions. I believe we should try to create a living organism with this DNA and see if it can survive in the environment we have on Earth. We already know they live in water, so it might not be very difficult to do. Then we can really study the organism."

Dr. Susan Pike said, "I think that would be an incredibly bad idea, unless we do it on the Moon or Mars. These cells could prove to be toxic to organisms with our DNA structure."

"Susan is right," Dr. Sommers replied. "We can't take any unnecessary risks. There are some unused labs on the Moon that could be used for this. They're not equipped for genetic experiments, but that's easily resolved. Simon, do you want to take on that task?"

"Yes, I'd love to do that. I can be ready to go in two weeks. I'll arrange for the equipment I need to be shipped immediately."

Dr. Charles Farrow, also from the North American Union, said, "While I think it's probably a good idea to try to

127

create a living organism with that DNA structure, I think we should also consider that the organism found was probably the highest form of life to develop on Ganymede. If you think about its DNA structure, you realize the possibility of a genetic mutation is almost nil. On Earth the weak link in the DNA is between the base pairs and that's where mutations can occur. The bond between the base pairs and backbone is very strong and does not break. These cells have no base pairs, so I suspect any mutation would be impossible. The lifeform we found may be as complex as they can get with that DNA structure."

"You may be correct. I thought about that too, but even if that's true, I would still like to know more about the cells we found, and I think this may be the best way to do it," Dr. Sommers added.

They spent another hour or so talking, but in the end the decision was made that Dr. Chambers would set up a genetics lab on the moon and attempt to create a living organism with the Ganymede DNA.

Instead of two weeks, however, it was almost three months before the genetics lab was ready on the moon. The lab they decided to use was two miles from the main moon base. It had been empty for twenty years, so some time was needed to make it operational again. It had to be set up with an air and water supply. It also needed furniture, a kitchen, sleeping quarters for three people, and a bathroom. Additionally, the equipment had to be set up and tested. To prevent any possibility of contamination, the people who worked at the lab would not be allowed to go to the main base. Before anybody could leave the lab, they would have to spend three days in a decontamination chamber.

In addition to Dr. Chambers, there were two graduate students working at the genetics lab on the moon. They thought the task they had to perform would not be overly difficult. They didn't have a large amount of cell material from Ganymede to work with and it would probably be some time before they could get more, so they used what they had carefully.

The first thing they did was remove some DNA from the cells in order to implant it into an amoeba. Within minutes it died. Then they tried implanting the DNA into other single cell organisms, both plants and animals, but they all died. Then they tried small reptile eggs, but nothing worked. Finally, after almost six months of continuous failures, they gave up.

Dr. Chambers called Dr. Sommers to tell him the genetic experiments were a total failure and that he and his students would be closing the lab and returning to Earth in a few days. Dr. Sommers agreed that was probably the best thing to do for now. However, on the next trip to Ganymede they were going to attempt to find some living cells and transport them back to Earth, and the genetics lab they now had on the moon would be the best place to study them. So, when Dr. Chambers and his students left the lab, all of the equipment and furniture was left in place.

THE GANYMEDE CARGO SHIPS

While people from the North America Institute of Health were doing the genetic experiments with the Ganymede cells, substantial progress was made on the sub-light engine. As they were closing the lab on the moon, it was announced that the prototype engine would be ready for testing in three or four months and construction had started on the ship that would be used for the test.

Computer models indicated the engine would be able to accelerate up to four hundred and fifty miles per hour per second, but the initial test was going to keep the acceleration rate at no more than one hundred and five miles per hour per second. At that rate of acceleration, the ship would be subjected to less than 5 g's of force, which was far more than a human could withstand for more than a few seconds, but the acceleration would not affect the ship. The ship would accelerate at that rate for four days and would reach a maximum velocity of ten thousand miles per second, or a little more than 5% of light speed.

After four days the ship would have traveled one and a half billion miles. Then it would decelerate to zero, which will also take four days, turn around, and return to Earth. The entire test would take sixteen days.

By mid-December everything was ready. The ship, which was not much more than an empty shell with computers and instruments, was ready by early November. The engine was mounted in the ship, and some very low power static tests were run in early December. All of the tests appeared to be successful and the launch was scheduled for December 16.

The ship left Earth's orbit accelerating at 1.5 g's. After an hour the rate of acceleration was increased to 5 g's, and shortly after that it could no longer be seen visually. However, the instruments indicated that everything was normal. That continued until the deceleration phase began and then things started to go wrong. The instruments indicated the ship did not decelerate as it was supposed to. In fact, it didn't decelerate at all, and kept traveling away from Earth at ten thousand miles per second. After two days no more transmissions were received from the ship. There was no way to determine what had happened.

However, the test was not a total failure. The sub-light engine worked as designed. The failure appeared to be in the computer that was controlling the flight. There was some speculation the failure could have been caused by subjecting the computer to 5 g's of acceleration for four days, but there was no way to verify that.

Construction on the next ship was nearly completed when the first ship failed. This time all of the components in the ship were subjected to 10 g's for five days to ensure that they would not fail during the next test. Additionally, multiple redundant systems were set up so if the primary and secondary systems failed, a third backup system would take over control of the ship.

During the high gravity testing, some component failures were found and those components were redesigned so they could withstand the rigors of the test. It took four months before NASA had substantial confidence the ship's controllers would function correctly. A new ship had already been built and the engine installed. By early July 2084 the next test ship was launched.

This time when the deceleration phase began, the ship indicated that it was, in fact, slowing down. As expected, four days later the ship began its return journey to Earth. Four days out from Earth the ship began to slow again, and by the time it reached the orbit of the moon it was only moving at about fifteen thousand miles per hour. At that time the crew on the space station switched the ship to external control and brought it back to within one mile of the station.

Although the sub-light engine had been tested and was considered functional, the design for the unmanned cargo ships was not completed. The ships were several times larger than any ship that had been previously constructed. It was decided that the structural integrity of the ship and the control systems had to be capable of withstanding up to 10 g's of force during both the acceleration and deceleration portions of the flight, even though that would never happen during the trips to Ganymede. The design was completed in October 2084 and in November construction began on the first cargo ship, which was named the Albert Simpson.

The construction of the ship near the space station was a monumental task. It had a cargo capacity of one thousand six hundred cubic meters. There were one hundred full time construction personnel working on the project. It was anticipated that it would take eighteen months to finish the job, but it took longer than expected, and it wasn't completed until February 2085.

The first test was scheduled for March 15. During the test, the ship would move to a high Earth orbit of fifty thousand miles. Once it was in a stable orbit it was scheduled to accelerate at 1.5 g's until it reached a velocity of fifteen hundred miles per second, a process that would take thirty hours. That velocity would be maintained for twenty-four hours while the control systems were checked out. By using the Earth's orbit, if there was a failure, the ship would not be lost like the first sub-light engine test ship had been.

The Albert Simpson performed perfectly for the first part of the test. It easily transitioned into the correct orbit and accelerated to fifteen hundred miles per second as required. It was now the fastest object orbiting the Earth, completing one orbital pass in slightly less than a minute. Testing of the control systems was progressing normally until an unexpected massive solar flare occurred. As the ship was bathed in radiation, some minor failures were noted in the control systems. The test was cut short and the ship brought back. Over the next two months additional radiation shielding was added to the ship. The next test was scheduled for June 1.

The second test went as planned, but there were no solar flares to contend with. However, it was decided that a longer-range test was in order. For the next test, the Albert Simpson would be accelerated to twenty-five hundred miles per second and placed in an orbit around Mars. The plan was for the ship to maintain a Mars orbit for ten days before returning to Earth. The test was set for June 20.

133

On June 20, the ship accelerated slowly away from the space station and then the acceleration was increased to 5 g's. After twenty-two hours the Albert Simpson's velocity was twenty-five hundred miles per second and the ship was almost to the orbit of Jupiter. At that point the ship was three hundred fifty million miles past Mars, so the deceleration process started, and the ship was turned around and put on course for Mars. It arrived at Mars twenty-eight hours later and was placed into an orbit around Mars where it stayed for ten days. It was then moved out of orbit and returned to the space station. The trip back was much slower, but the Albert Simpson still arrived at the space station twenty hours after leaving Mars. The test was a complete success.

RETURNING TO GANYMEDE

Due to the successful test of the Albert Simpson, work began on the ship that would transport the first twenty-five people to Ganymede. That ship would also be their home until the habitat could be completed.

The design of the ship was complete, but the construction would take ten months. Then, if all went well during the testing after the ship was completed, it would launch for Ganymede about two months later. The ship was named the Ganymede Express.

While the Ganymede Express was being built, the Ganymede habitat was designed and the components were built and placed inside the Albert Simpson. It was also loaded with enough food, water, medical supplies, and air to last the crew at least eight months.

With everything that had been learned about space ship construction over the past several years, the task of building new ships was simplified. The Ganymede Express was finished a month ahead of schedule. The testing began immediately, and only a few minor problems were detected. Those problems were quickly resolved and by June 2087 the ship was ready. The entire crew from the first Ganymede mission was going on this mission as well. Fifteen additional crew members were also selected. Most of the new crew members were mining engineers and people with experience building habitats on Mars. Terry Simpson was again chosen as the captain of the mission.

Once the habitat was complete, the Ganymede Express would return to Earth, leaving only those people who were needed for the mining operation and Ross, the ship's doctor. Ross was staying primarily because he hoped he would be able to search for living organisms in the liquid water a few hundred feet below the surface, and of course it was essential to have a doctor onboard in case of illness or injury. It was expected that the habitat would take sixty days to build and the plan was to begin silver shipments thirty days later.

Because of some improvements in engine design, the Ganymede Express would be able to make the trip to Ganymede in only six months. That meant if everything went according to schedule, Terry and his crew would be back on Earth in fourteen months.

The Ganymede Express was launched on July 6. The trip to Ganymede was uneventful. There were no problems encountered during the flight, although some of the crew members were concerned about the possible presence of the aliens who had taken the Ganymede probe. By the time the ship entered orbit around Ganymede the Albert Simpson was ready for launch. The plan was to launch it as soon as the Ganymede Express landed. On the third orbital pass, the ship landed in almost the same location as the first landing spot on the previous trip. Terry sent a message to Earth telling them the ship had landed. Two hours later a message was received telling them the Albert Simpson was on the way. It would be there in a little over eight days and placed into an orbit around Ganymede. It was Terry's responsibility to land the ship nearby. This was something he, and his navigator Mark, had practiced extensively using simulators before the Ganymede Express left Earth. He hoped the simulator was a perfect emulation of the real thing because there was no way to practice with the real thing at that time.

It took the ship's crew a few hours to get accustomed to the gravity on Ganymede, but after that several members of the crew decided to go exploring. The mining engineers had seen pictures of the silver deposits, but it was not the same as seeing it in person. The geologists and the mining engineers went out and spent an hour exploring. They came back excited and anxious to get started. A few hours later the head of the habitat construction crew and his assistant went out to look for the best location to build the habitat. They were gone for two hours. They not only found a good site, but they marked off the position for the base of the habitat. They too were anxious, but they would have to wait for the arrival of the Albert Simpson before they could get started.

136

While they were waiting for the arrival of the cargo ship on Ganymede, the NASA propulsion engineers back on Earth conducted the first test on a miniature version of the sub-light engine. The engine used in the Albert Simpson was huge, almost twenty-three cubic meters. They were hoping the smaller version of the engine, which was only about four cubic meters, would be able to power smaller ships, like the Ganymede Express, at speeds up to fifteen hundred miles per second, using a constant acceleration of not more than 1.25 g's. That would allow them to go to any part of the solar system in days or weeks, rather than months.

The test results were far from perfect, but still promising. They would be making some changes over the next week or two and then do another test. The computer simulations indicated the design was good, but the first test was disappointing. After studying the test results there was agreement on the design changes needed and they began implementing those immediately.

The Albert Simpson was placed into orbit around Ganymede on schedule. Terry and Mark were seated at the command console and initiated the system which gave them control of the Albert Simpson. When the link was established Mark said, "You realize we now have control of the most expensive piece of equipment NASA has ever built, and on top of that it was named after your father. We're about to do something nobody has ever done before. Let's make sure we don't screw this up."

"You're making me nervous, and I'm nervous enough already," Terry replied. "Please shut up."

For the next hour Terry and Mark made small maneuvers with the cargo ship and everything appeared to be working properly. On the next orbital pass, they slowed the ship down and it entered the thin atmosphere around Ganymede. As it approached the landing site, the ship ceased horizontal movement and they began the slow vertical descent. The Albert Simpson landed gently within a few feet of the designated landing site. They shut down the engine, extended

137

the boarding ramp, and opened the hatch. Terry sent a simple message back to Earth:

"The Albert Simpson has landed."

A few hours later the entire crew put on their suits and went outside. The temperature was a relatively balmy -112 degrees Celsius, about as warm as it ever got on Ganymede. Their suits were bulky and made movements difficult, but the low gravity made the task a little easier. First, they unloaded two trucks from the cargo ship. Then they unloaded the base of the habitat, which was made up of two-inch-thick, four-foot-square interlocking plastic panels. On Earth they probably weighed seventy-five pounds, but on Ganymede they only weighed eleven pounds, so they were easy to handle. There were five hundred and six of these panels. All of the panels were loaded into the two trucks and moved to the construction site. The base had to be put on flat ground, so the next thing they unloaded was part of the mining equipment. That was used to prepare the ground for the base panels. After that was complete, they started connecting the panels for the base. Once they had one hundred of the panels placed, they decided to call it a day and went back to the Ganymede Express.

They decided they would work in six-hour shifts, with eight people per shift. The only one excluded from the work detail was Ross. He stayed onboard and was available in case of an accident. After a six-hour break, the first shift went out to continue working on the base. The base was completed the following day and the next things they had to work on were the side and roof panels. After the sides and roof were finished, they could begin working on the inside. The side panels were all identical. They were basically eight-foot squares with a titanium frame and a one-inch-thick opaque plastic insert. There were no windows anywhere and the only exterior door would be an airlock. Like the floor, the sides were designed to interlock, so it made building the exterior walls fairly easy. Each wall was three panels high because the building would have three floors. After the walls were finished, they were connected with titanium bars at the top and at each floor level.

138

Then they added vertical supports at sixteen-foot intervals. When all of the supports were in place, the roof panels were put on to complete the exterior construction, except for the air lock. That was the last and most complicated part because it had electrically controlled doors that had to be opened and closed in a specific sequence. So far, the exterior construction of the habitat had taken fifteen days. Completing the air lock took two more days.

After the air lock was completed, all of the plastic seams in the building had to be sealed. This involved spraying each seam with a thick plastic adhesive that cured when exposed to ultra-violet light. Sealing the building took another three days. Now they were ready to pressurize the building and begin heating it so the work could be done inside without the crew having to wear the bulky suits.

Air tanks were brought in and the building was pressurized to the equivalent of seven thousand feet on Earth. A comprehensive leak test was performed and a few leaks were found that were quickly repaired. One hundred electric space heaters were brought in and forty-eight hours later, the temperature inside the habitat was twenty degrees centigrade.

The interior of the habitat would be completed by the members of the crew who were brought there specifically for that purpose. The other members of the crew began working on their assigned tasks.

Now Ross had the undivided attention of two of the mining engineers. Their task was to drill a hole deep enough into the surface to find liquid water so Ross could continue his search for lifeforms. There was a lot of speculation regarding how deep they would have to drill, but they were equipped to go up to fifteen hundred feet.

Eight hours after they started drilling, they had reached a depth of two hundred and fifty-three feet, but there was no sign of liquid water. However, seven hours later, at a depth of four hundred and sixty-nine feet, they found liquid water. In order to prevent the water from freezing, they lowered a heated canister that could be opened and closed remotely down into the water. After the canister was filled and brought back to the surface, they gave it to Ross for analysis.

Ross went back to his lab in the ship and first looked at the sample under a microscope, expecting to see the same cells he had seen before, but living this time. He was disappointed because there was nothing to see, just plain water. He put a sample into a higher power electronic microscope, and still nothing was visible. Then he performed an extensive analysis of the water to see what was in it. When the analysis was complete, all it showed was water with trace amounts of some common minerals dissolved in it. Although it was not what he had been hoping for, it was still a remarkable find because now they had a source for drinking water.

He sent a report back to NASA, but he also decided they would have to look in the location where he had found the samples on the previous visit, but that was hundreds of miles away and there was no way to get there now. He would discuss it with Terry later. After the habitat was complete, perhaps he could convince Terry to take him and the two mining engineers there so he could get another sample.

When NASA responded to his report, they were very happy with his discovery of drinkable water. They also suggested that he test some of the veins of water ice just below the surface in the area where he was now. He had actually already thought about that and was planning on doing it as soon as he could get one of the mining engineers to help him.

For the next few weeks the construction crew worked on the interior of the habitat. While that was going on, the mining crew began extracting silver ore and putting it into the cargo ship. That process was slow, but at the end of three weeks they had extracted seventeen cubic meters of ore. They wanted to get ten times that amount before the ship returned to Earth, but the Albert Simpson was scheduled to return to Earth in six weeks. That wasn't enough time for them to reach their goal.

While the miners were busy extracting ore, Ross and one of the mining engineers went to find some water ice that

Ross could test. They found some eight feet below the surface and Ross took some samples. He wasn't surprised to discover these samples showed no trace of the organisms he had seen in the samples from the other location. He went to Terry and made his request that he take him and two of the mining engineers to the location of the second silver discovery to look for liquid water samples. Terry said it was okay with him, but he would have to get approval from NASA. He sent a message to NASA and they approved it.

The six weeks were going by quickly. The habitat was finished, and everyone was happy with the results. It was warm and comfortable. The food was still the prepackaged NASA stuff, but at least they could sit in a makeshift dining room with tables and chairs and eat it. When the Albert Simpson returned it would have some real food and all of the people who were staying on Ganymede were looking forward to that.

Two weeks before the Ganymede Express was scheduled to take off, Terry called Ross and Ben, who was one of the mining engineers Ross was working with, into the ship's control room. "I asked you both to come here because I think you two are the most qualified members of the crew to handle a very important job. This ship is returning to Earth in two weeks, but before we leave, we're going to launch the Albert Simpson. When it comes back, somebody has to know how to land it. Since neither Mark nor I will be here, I would like you two to do it. If you agree we'll start your training immediately. It's a delicate task, but not difficult. The computer will help, but it's a manual operation. Are you interested?"

Both men immediately agreed and Mark started their training using a simulator. They learned quickly, and Terry decided to let them handle the departure of the Albert Simpson.

Three days before the Ganymede Express was scheduled to return to Earth, Terry took the ship to the other location where Ross had found the lifeforms before. As soon as the ship landed, Ross and the engineers left the ship with their equipment. They went two hundred yards from the ship and set up the drill. At four hundred and ten feet they found liquid water and Ross got a sample. He hurried back to the ship while the engineers dismantled the drill. When Ross got back to the ship, Terry was in his lab waiting for him. He put the sample into the microscope and found what he was hoping for, the organisms he had seen before. But this time they were alive! As he and Terry watched they saw one of the cells divide. Ross was so happy he could barely control himself. He smiled and said happily, "Do you realize we're the first people from Earth to see a living alien lifeform?"

"Yeah, I guess we've both secured our place in history," Terry agreed.

When the engineers returned, the ship went back to the original landing site. They all got off the ship and went to the habitat which, they discovered, had now been named the Ganymede Hilton. Two days later, Terry and the other people who were leaving said their emotional goodbyes to the people who were staying. When they left, they never expected to return. Terry had planned on resigning when he got back to Earth.

Before the Ganymede Express took off, Terry and Mark watched as Ross and Ben launched the Albert Simpson for its return to Earth. The launch was perfect and Terry congratulated them both on a job well done. Contained in the cargo hold of the Albert Simpson was seventy cubic meters of silver ore, which took up only a small fraction of the space. It was not enough to make even a small dent in the Earth's silver shortage, but it was important for the people to know that the Ganymede mission was a success.

Once the Albert Simpson was gone, the Ganymede Express took off too and began the six-month journey back to Earth.

The trip back to Earth was long, boring, and completely without incident. Terry and Mark discussed their future and Terry told Mark he was planning on retiring after they returned to Earth because he was tired of being gone so often and wanted to find a nice girl, get married, and provide his mother with grandchildren. Mark was about ten years

142

younger than Terry and he liked what he was doing. He planned on continuing the space travel for a long time.

While the Albert Simpson was on its return trip to Earth, the NASA engineers continued tweaking the miniature sub-light engine. They decided it was time for a real test of the engine. They found one of the early Mars mission ships that was scheduled to be scrapped parked near the space station and spent almost two months retrofitting it with the new engine and control systems. After a few successful static tests, it was ready. They decided to test it the same way the Albert Simpson was tested. They moved the ship to a fifty-thousand-mile orbit above the Earth and accelerated the ship at 1.25 g's. After thirty-six hours the ship was traveling at one thousand miles per second, or three million six hundred thousand miles per hour. They left the ship in orbit for five days before slowing it down and then bringing it back to the space station. The engine and control systems were removed and the ship was scrapped.

Two months after the Ganymede Express started its return trip, Terry received a message telling him the Albert Simpson had returned to Ganymede and landed successfully. It was something Terry and Mark had been concerned about and they were happy to get this news.

When the Ganymede Express arrived at the space station, Terry was surprised to find his boss waiting for him. "Hello Barbara, I wasn't expecting you to meet me here. I thought we'd meet after I got back on Earth, but it's nice to see you. Is there a problem?" Terry asked.

"No, there's no problem. But there has been a development and I wanted to discuss it with you and Mark. I didn't want to wait. Please come with me."

Terry and Mark looked at each other with a confused look and followed Barbara to the conference room a few hundred feet down the hall. When they were comfortably seated Barbara said, "I know you guys just got back from a fifteen-month mission, and I'm sure you want some time off. You've certainly earned it, but I'm hoping I could talk you into one more mission. This one will be much shorter, probably not more than two months."

Before Barbara could continue, Terry said, "I was planning on telling you that I want to retire when we had our meeting."

Barbara said, "I actually thought about that, but before you make up your mind, I wanted to tell you about a new engine our engineers have developed. They made some substantial modifications to the sub-light engine and created a much smaller version which can be used to power ships the size of the Ganymede Express. The engine is designed to accelerate at no more than 1.5 g's and reach a maximum speed of one thousand miles per second. The ship could make the trip to Ganymede in two weeks. We're going to retrofit the Ganymede Express and send it back to Ganymede. We want you two to head up the mission."

"Why the big rush?" Terry inquired.

"Because the silver mine in Argentina is almost out of silver and we have to get more people to Ganymede as quickly as possible. The public is not aware of the problem, so we want to make sure the solution's in place before there's a shortage of silver again. You two are the most experienced people we have and this mission has to be perfect. So, can I count on you for one last mission?" Barbara asked pleadingly.

"Yeah, I guess so," Terry responded unenthusiastically. Then he asked, "How long will it take for the retrofit?"

"About two months and it'll start immediately. You can have six weeks off, but I need you here to go over the new control systems before we launch. Okay?"

Mark and Terry both said, "Yes," at the same time.

Terry and Mark took the next shuttle back to Earth. After they landed, they said goodbye and agreed to meet again in six weeks for the flight back to the space station. Terry went home to Tennessee to see his mother and sister for the first time in almost a year and a half.

Emily met Terry at the Knoxville airport and drove him to their mother's house. They hadn't really talked for almost two years. He told her he was going to make one shorter trip to test some new equipment and then he was going to

144

retire. Emily asked about the details of the trip but it was classified so he couldn't discuss it. Terry told her that upon his retirement he wanted to get married and have a family. She told him she knew several eligible young women and when the time came, she would be happy to help him find somebody. He thanked her but he was sure it was something he could do on his own. Then they talked about their mother's health and several other less important things.

After they arrived at their mother's house, they spent some time catching up on the events of the previous two years. The conversation was pleasant and after talking for an hour they went to a local restaurant and had a very good dinner. When they got back to the house, Susan said, "I have something I want to talk to both of you about. Since we're not together very often, this seems to be an ideal opportunity."

Terry and Emily looked at their mother and Emily asked, "Mom, is something wrong?"

"No, everything is fine. I miss your father very much of course, but aside from that I'm okay if that's what you're concerned about. When your father and I started receiving royalty checks from Kingman, we suddenly found ourselves with more money than we knew what to do with. This was before we set up the foundation. Your father was sure the price of silver would increase substantially over the years, and he was right. He started buying one-hundred-ounce silver bars when silver was still under forty dollars per ounce. He stopped buying them after he'd accumulated five hundred bars. Each of those bars is now worth over eight hundred fifty thousand dollars and I'm giving each of you two hundred and fifty of them. I certainly don't need the money, and when my time comes my income will be diverted to the foundation, so this is your inheritance."

Terry was stunned. "Thank you, I appreciate the gesture. But I really don't need the money."

"It's yours to do with as you please, but don't be too hasty in saying you don't need it. You never know what's going to happen in the future."

"Thanks Mom. I might sell it and give the money to the foundation, but I'll think about it for a while," Emily said.

"Okay, as I said you can do anything you want with it. So, Terry, you'll be retired soon, and that makes me very happy. Have you given any thought about where you're going to live?"

"I thought I'd stay here for a while and then decide. I've always liked this area, so I'm sure I'll find my own place nearby. Besides, Emily has promised to help me find a wife. I can't pass up an offer like that!"

Susan smiled at that comment, and Emily gave him a dirty look.

THE QUICK TRIP TO GANYMEDE

By mid-February 2089, the new engine had been installed on the Ganymede Express. It was now the fastest passenger space ship ever built. The static tests were perfect, as was the Earth orbit test. Terry and Mark both returned to the space station to begin their training by the third week of February, and after two weeks they were ready for their first test flight. They were going to duplicate the Earth orbit test. That was scheduled for March 1.

Terry and Mark were a little nervous. Until now, the fastest anybody had ever traveled was one hundred thousand miles per hour. They were going to be moving at three million six hundred thousand miles per hour. At that speed there was no room for error. They left the space station and moved into the same fifty-thousand mile orbit that had been used before. While moving the ship into orbit, they kept the speed at a modest thirty thousand miles per hour. Once the ship was in orbit, Terry increased the acceleration to 1.25 g's. Terry and Mark were pushed back against their seats. It was a little uncomfortable, but after half an hour they had adapted to it. They both thought it was more comfortable than being weightless. This rate of acceleration would continue for another thirty hours. Then the engine would cut out and they would be weightless and uncomfortable again. The ship, Terry, and Mark all performed flawlessly. After five days they began the thirty-hour deceleration process. When the ship slowed to thirty thousand miles per hour, they halted the deceleration, moved out of orbit, and returned to the space station.

While the Ganymede Express was being tested, the passengers who were going to Ganymede were told about the new engine, and that the trip would take less than two weeks. They were thrilled. A few of them had been to Mars, but most were space flight novices. None of them were concerned about the thirty hours at 1.25 g's. During their preflight training at NASA, each of them had been subjected to 4 g's for a few seconds, and 2 g's for ten minutes, so the acceleration wasn't considered a problem. They were all brought up to the space station a week before departure for training and additional medical testing.

The Ganymede Express left for its flight on March 21. For the first half hour the acceleration was kept to .2 g's. Terry announced that everyone should be seated because in five minutes the acceleration would increase to 1.25 g's. After fifteen minutes at full acceleration, Terry announced that people could leave their seats, but they should use some caution when moving around the ship because of the increased gravity. Thirty hours later Terry again asked everybody to be seated because he was shutting off the engines and they would be weightless for three days. At that time the deceleration process would begin.

Right on schedule they began slowing down the ship, and by the time it was two million miles from Ganymede, the ship had slowed to one hundred thousand miles per hour. Terry informed the passengers that they would be landing on Ganymede in twenty hours.

Just as they were about to enter into orbit around Ganymede, there was a control system failure in the engine propulsion module. Terry noticed it immediately and switched to a backup system, but they missed the orbital entry point and flew past Ganymede. It took three hours to maneuver the ship back into the correct position, and on the third orbital pass they slowed the ship down and dropped toward the landing site. Mark asked if he could handle the landing and Terry agreed. Mark landed the ship perfectly, and all of the passengers came into the control room and thanked Terry and Mark for a wonderful trip.

As the passengers got off the ship, they were welcomed by the people stationed on Ganymede who were all very happy to see some new faces after nine months. They all went to the Ganymede Hilton where they were directed to their rooms and given a big dinner.

Terry spent some time with Ross, discussing what he had learned about the lifeforms on Ganymede. What he was told concerned him a bit. It seemed any lifeform based on

Earth's type of DNA would die if exposed to Ganymede cells. There had been a plan to use the water they found on Ganymede for drinking and cooking, but that plan was put on hold until they were absolutely certain there was no danger. In the meantime, every trip made by the Albert Simpson included ten thousand gallons of fresh water. The ship was making monthly trips now, but the people on Ganymede would not survive very long if there was a problem with the ship. NASA had started construction on another ship, but it wouldn't be ready for a year.

Terry and Mark spent five days on Ganymede. This time, when Terry said goodbye to the people he had worked with for nine months, he told them his return to Earth was his last space flight. Mark would be making regular flights to Ganymede, although the schedule was not set yet.

One of the new people on the flight was a doctor who was going to replace Ross. There were also twenty people who would be working as miners extracting the silver ore. The plan was that with the additional people, they would be able to work continuously in eight-hour shifts and would be able to extract six hundred cubic meters of silver ore every week. That meant the hold on the Albert Simpson would be nearly full every time it returned to Earth.

With the exception of Ross, everyone else was staying on Ganymede, so when the ship went back to Earth there were only three people onboard. The return trip went smoothly, and the Ganymede Express arrived at the space station twelve days later. When Terry got off the ship, he sent a brief message to his boss, Barbara: "I'm done. I enjoyed working with you for these past several years. If you need me, I'll be at my mother's house. Thanks for everything. Goodbye."

Mark stayed on the space station to be briefed on his next assignment. Terry and Mark said goodbye and Terry took the next shuttle back to Earth.

Terry returned to Tennessee, and at a Christmas party being given by the foundation, he met Roberta Cook. She was a few years younger than him. Her husband had been killed in an accident two years earlier. Roberta had an eight-year-old son named Brandon. Terry and Roberta dated for a few months and then decided to get married. Terry had grown very fond of Brandon, and Brandon loved the idea of his mother being married to a famous space pilot.

The wedding was held at Susan's house. There were a lot of famous people in attendance, including President Robert Townsend. Terry was happy to see Barbara and Mark at the wedding. He spent an hour or two talking with them about old times before he and Roberta left for their honeymoon. Barbara and Mark would remain his best friends for many years.

Shortly after the marriage Terry adopted Brandon. As he grew up, Brandon and Terry became very close. Perhaps it was because of their relationship that Brandon eventually became the top engineer at NASA.

PART THREE
INTERSTELLAR TRAVEL

When the sub-light engine was put into the Ganymede Express, a new era of exploration followed. The silver shortage was resolved. With that problem gone, it was a matter of pure scientific curiosity to study the other planets and moons in our solar system. By 2092, some additional improvements were made in the sub-light engine that allowed it to reach a velocity of 5% of light speed, or about ninety-three hundred miles per second. It took fourteen days to reach that velocity, but the ships didn't need to travel that fast. Even the distant dwarf planet Pluto could now be reached in less than two weeks.

Missions were sent to every planet, with the exception of those planets that had extremely hostile environments. They were Mercury, Venus, and Jupiter. Also, every moon with a diameter of more than five hundred miles was studied extensively. Samples were taken so that if Earth ever ran short of any raw material they would know where in the solar system to find it.

Many of the people on Earth were certain of the presence of alien beings because they believed aliens had taken the Ganymede probe, while others were unsure. However, most felt that now that we could easily travel anywhere in our solar system, we should begin to examine how we could travel to other solar systems regardless of the possible presence of aliens.

What a lot of people didn't realize was that interstellar travel was impossible with the current technology. The distances were many times greater than the distances required to travel to parts of our solar system. The fastest ships could only travel at 60% of light speed, and people would be unable to withstand the acceleration required to get to that speed in a reasonable length of time. Even if a way was found to allow people to survive the acceleration, it would take fifteen years to reach the nearest star system with planets. Not many people would sign up for that.

In February 2100 a meeting was held that included all of the world's brightest and most respected physicists and engineers to discuss ways of building a ship that could travel to the stars. There were many problems to solve, but they were sure it could be done because they believed the beings who took the Ganymede probe had already done it.

The first problem was that interstellar travel required velocities exceeding the speed of light in order to minimize the travel time, and it was impossible to do that. As an object was accelerated to the speed of light its mass increased and approached infinity, and it would take an infinite amount of energy to accelerate an infinite mass. Obviously, that was not possible. Additionally, if you could travel at the speed of light, there's also a problem of time dilation. That means time moves more slowly for the people who are traveling at the speed of light than for the people back home on Earth. For example, if a person traveled at the speed of light for five years to reach our closest neighbor and then spent five years returning to Earth, that person would have aged ten years, but on Earth eighty years would have passed.

The only possible solution to the problem was to take a different approach. To quote an old science fiction book, *Dune*, they had to learn how to fold space. That would enable somebody to travel without moving. It was thought if a wormhole could be created between two locations, an object placed into the wormhole would be instantly transported to the other end. But that was only a theory, so the esteemed scientists at the meeting decided to try to prove it.

The immediate problem was how to create a wormhole in the first place, and then how to create a termination point at a remote location. It took thirty people working full time for five years before they were able to create a wormhole between two known locations. The wormhole was fifty feet long and it appeared to be stable. It had a diameter of two feet. A ball was thrown into one end of the wormhole and they were expecting it to appear at the other end. Instead, it disappeared completely. When the power was turned off the wormhole collapsed, but the ball was gone.

The engineers looked at the design, came up with a few ideas, and a month later they were ready to try again. They created the wormhole as before, gave it a few minutes to stabilize, and threw a ball into one end. This time the ball came out the other end of the wormhole, but it was shredded into thousands of little pieces. Nevertheless, they had made progress.

It took three more years of experimenting with the device before there was a successful test. They tried other objects and they all went through the wormhole unharmed. Up to this point, no living object had been put through the wormhole, but they decided to try sending a mouse through it. A small white lab mouse was placed in a clear plastic container and pushed into the device. It came out the other side, but it was dead. It didn't appear to be physically harmed, so they would have to examine it to find out what had killed it. The distance was so short it was impossible to tell how much time had elapsed, if any, for the objects put into the wormhole to travel fifty feet.

Now they had two problems: they had to know what killed the mouse, and they had to build a longer wormhole so they could measure the elapsed time. However, determining how the mouse was killed was more important. The tests on the mouse didn't immediately reveal any cause of death. They dissected it and looked at every part of it, but everything appeared to be normal. Then they decided to look at the cell structure to see if there was any cell damage. They discovered there was substantial damage to the brain cells. The engineers remembered how the rubber ball they had put into the device when it was first tested came out shredded. They thought the same type of adjustments could be made, but to a much greater degree, and that might resolve the problem.

It took a few weeks to make the changes and they tried again. The results were the same. The mouse died. They looked at the changes they had made, they tweaked a few things, and then they killed another mouse.

One of the engineers suggested that there might be some sort of radiation exposure inside the wormhole and perhaps if they shielded the mouse from any potential radiation it would resolve the problem. They built a steel box and lined it with lead, put the mouse into the device, and then retrieved it from the other side. They opened the box and fully expected to find another dead mouse, but the mouse was alive and appeared to be okay. The biologists assigned to the project put it into a cage and watched it for five days, but it didn't exhibit any problems. Five days later the mouse was killed and examined for cellular damage, but none was found.

Now the engineers knew there was some kind of intense radiation inside the wormhole, but they didn't have any idea what kind of radiation it was. All attempts to check the radiation levels with sensors failed. They suspected the passage through the wormhole was too fast for the sensors to react. They were going to have to wait until a longer wormhole was ready.

It was decided a mile-long device would give them enough distance to determine the speed of the objects passing through it. Some thought was given to building a mile-long structure to test it but ultimately, because it had to work in any environment, they decided to build it outside. It took four months to build. When it was ready, sensors were placed at both ends of the wormhole. The sensors were connected to a computer that could accurately determine when an object entered the wormhole and when it arrived at the other end. The device was accurate to a ten millionth of a second.

They decided to test it with a rubber ball again. The ball was thrown into the device and it instantly appeared at the other end. The computer indicated zero time had elapsed, which meant less than one ten-millionth of a second had elapsed between the ball's entry into the wormhole and its exit. Then they tested it with another mouse, and it went through the system in its shielded container without any problems.

They also put radiation sensors through the wormhole, but again there was no indication of any radiation found. So, either the sensors were not fast enough to detect the radiation or the radiation was something the sensors were not designed to detect. Either way, the team had no idea how to figure out what the radiation was.

Another milestone in the development of the wormhole system had been reached, but there were still many problems ahead. Being able to move an object a mile is not the same as being able to move it a few trillion miles. Additionally, the most perplexing part of the problem was how to create a termination point for the wormhole from the entry point location. That was the next issue the engineers decided to work on.

The engineers at NASA spent months proposing various ideas for ways to create the wormhole termination point remotely. They tried a few ideas and all of them failed, but that did not deter them. There was a consensus that a solution existed, but nobody had thought of it yet. Finally, a year later, an engineer named Dr. Carlos Ramirez came up with a possible solution. It involved projecting a high energy particle beam that could be used to control the direction of the wormhole, and when the beam was shut off the wormhole would collapse. The design was similar to particle beam weapons that had been invented back in the 2040's, but this one would be much more powerful. They ran computer simulations and it looked like it would work. Construction of the device commenced, and ten months later, it was ready for testing. The way it worked was the particle beam was started first, and then the wormhole was created around it. It was a line of sight system because any dense object would collapse the particle beam.

The first test involved creating a wormhole on a flat area near a mountain with a sheer cliff wall two miles away. The particle beam was turned on and then the wormhole was created. It was difficult to see because it only created a slight distortion in the air. Cameras were set up at the entry and exit points of the wormhole so they would be able to see the results instantly. It was tested with a rubber ball again. Dr. Ramirez threw the ball into the wormhole and it instantly flew out of the wormhole and hit him in the chest. He wasn't hurt, but extremely surprised. Analysis of the video showed the ball striking the wall and bouncing back into the wormhole.

The test was an amazing success, but now they had to figure out how far they could project the particle beam. It was decided that the test should be done either in space or from the surface of the moon because they were sure that projecting the beam through the atmosphere would weaken it, and it was, after all, designed to work in space. Two days later, Dr. Ramirez and two other engineers went to the moon with all of their equipment. The test was set up on the surface of the moon and the particle beam was aimed at a point on the Mojave Desert. When the beam was turned on it was instantly detected by engineers on Earth. That was a distance of more than two hundred and forty thousand miles. The results were better than they had hoped, but now they needed to test something farther away with no atmospheric interference.

For the next test, a ship was launched from the space station and moved to a location five hundred thousand miles from the moon. The particle beam was aimed at the ship, but when it was turned on it was not detected on the ship. It was a little disappointing, but not unexpected. The ship was moved in fifty thousand miles and another test was performed. The results were better. A very weak field was detected, but it may not have been strong enough to prevent the wormhole from collapsing. The ship was moved twenty-five thousand miles closer and the test was successful. The particle beam could be projected 2.28 light seconds into space.

The engineers realized they could create a wormhole 2.28 light seconds long. It was interesting, but useless from the point of traveling to other solar systems. The only practical application was to build a kind of elevator going from Earth to the moon. That would certainly be useful, but it wasn't what they were trying to accomplish. The next part of the task was to figure out how to project the beam far enough to make it useful.

Over the next several months they conducted more tests, but the results were always similar. The beam dissipated at four hundred twenty-five thousand miles. A more powerful beam generator was built and when it was tested the results were only slightly improved. The beam was still useable at four hundred and thirty-four thousand miles, but obviously still not what they were looking for.

The NASA engineers were holding meetings every three days, but for the most part the meetings were just excuses to talk, drink coffee, and eat snacks. But finally, at one of the meetings, Dr. Ramirez again thought he may have come up with a solution. "I think that our approach to resolving this problem has been wrong from the beginning. We've been trying to project the particle beam to the ship's final destination, or at least far enough to make it useful. I believe what we have to do is project the beam from the ship as it's moving through the wormhole. As long as the ship stays within the particle beam it will continuously move through the wormhole. I realize for that to happen the ship can't travel instantly through the wormhole, and I'm certain it doesn't. If it did, the mice that were killed during our early testing would not have had any time to be exposed to the radiation inside it, but obviously they were. So, it must take some time to go through it. I would like to run another time test, but this test should be at four hundred and twenty-five thousand miles. If there's a measurable amount of elapsed time going through the wormhole, I'm sure we can resolve this problem."

Everybody agreed that was a good idea. At least it gave them something to try. The test was arranged for two weeks later. They used the same system that was used to test the one-mile-long wormhole. After the test was completed, the computer indicated the time required for the object to pass through the wormhole was .017 seconds. So, it actually traveled one hundred and thirty-four times faster than light.

The next test was to use a mouse again. The shielded container holding the mouse was placed into the wormhole and retrieved by the crew in the target ship. When they opened the container, the mouse appeared to be in perfect condition. A check of the time for the mouse to pass through the wormhole was unchanged from the previous test. It was still .017 seconds.

When Dr. Ramirez saw the results of the test, he said to the other people at the moon base, "I think now we all know that the physical laws that apply in our universe do not apply inside a wormhole. I should have realized this when we put the first rubber ball into a wormhole. If the physical laws were the same, it would have exited the wormhole at a much greater velocity than its entry speed. We also know objects are moved through the wormhole, not just instantly transported. That should've been apparent when the first mouse died. I think we can correctly assume objects are instantly accelerated to more than one hundred times the speed of light when they enter a wormhole and instantly decelerated to their entry speed when they exit the wormhole. So, if the laws of motion were applicable inside a wormhole, any object placed into it would have been subjected to unbelievable gravitational forces and would have been crushed. We also know some time elapses between the time an object enters a wormhole and the time it exits. I believe the .017 seconds it takes to transit the wormhole will be enough time to extend the wormhole another four hundred twenty-five thousand miles, so our ship should be able to move continuously. I suspect there's no time dilation inside the wormhole, but it needs to be tested. Does anybody disagree?"

None of the other people at the base disagreed with Dr. Ramirez's ideas. They could sense that their task which, at the start seemed to be insurmountable, was coming close to being completed. They had been working on this project for almost nine years and they were ahead of schedule. At the first meeting of the team working on the project in 2100, it had generally been thought it would take at least twenty years to complete.

They had to create a system capable of generating a particle beam directed at a specified position in space and allowing that location to change every .017 seconds. They also had to design a system that would create a wormhole large enough for a ship to travel through and small enough to be placed on the ship. Of the two tasks the first one was far more difficult, and it took almost three years to create the first

158

working model to test. The larger wormhole generator was ready eighteen months earlier. The devices had to be put into a ship to be tested.

The ship had to have a human pilot. It would have been impossible to control remotely because one second after the ship departed it would be twenty-five million miles from Earth and out of control range. This was a dangerous mission. While the ship was being built, several human tests were performed sending the subject on a four hundred and twenty-five-thousand-mile journey. There were no problems found. In fact, the people who were tested said they felt nothing. There was no sensation of movement at all. Of course, being sent four hundred and twenty-five thousand miles may not be the same as being sent a light year away. These tests were too short to determine if there were any time dilation effects, so that was something else that would be evaluated during the test.

This first test was going to be short. The ship would move out beyond the orbit of Pluto, turn around, and come back. The outbound part of the trip would take about fourteen seconds. On the return trip it would stop somewhere between Mars and Earth. Then the ship would use its sub-light engine to return to the space station.

They wanted an experienced space pilot for the test mission, so they asked for volunteers. Of the fifty active space pilots, forty-seven volunteered. After going over all of the volunteers' qualifications, Captain Jeffery Whitestone was selected.

Jeffery was born in England, but emigrated to the North American Union at age eleven when his father accepted a teaching position at Harvard. He graduated high school at seventeen, and not surprisingly, went to Harvard where he obtained a bachelor's degree in mathematics and then a degree in electrical engineering. After obtaining his second degree, he went to work for NASA as a junior engineer. A year later he applied for a position as a pilot and was accepted into the two-year training program. He completed that in 2108 and had been making regular trips to Mars and Ganymede since that time.

159

One of the reasons Jeffery was selected for this mission was his engineering background. The general feeling was that somebody with his background would be better able to understand the systems on the test ship, and if there was a problem, he would be more likely to find a solution.

There was a discussion about having two pilots on the test mission, but since the mission was so short, and potentially dangerous, it was ultimately decided a single pilot would be best.

The test was scheduled for September 16, 2116. Jeffery had been training with the engineers who designed the propulsion system for six months. He felt more than ready when the time for the test had arrived. The plan was to move the ship a thousand miles from the space station, orient the ship so it was pointing to a star several light years away, program the controls system to go in the direction of the star, travel along that path for fourteen seconds, and then collapse the wormhole.

A shuttle pilot took Jeffery to the ship and stayed with him until he was comfortably seated in the pilot's seat. Then the shuttle pilot left. Shortly after the shuttle pilot closed the hatch, Jeffery powered on the engine control systems. He moved the ship to the designated position and contacted the space station to tell them he was ready. They told him to launch the ship. He pressed the button to launch the ship while he was looking at a monitor that showed his designated flight path. He felt nothing, but the view in the monitor became fuzzy. When the ship stopped fourteen seconds later, the view instantly cleared up and what he saw was much different than the view he had before he pushed the launch button. He checked his position with the computer and it confirmed that he was now more than three billion miles from Earth. The ship was equipped with external cameras and he spent several minutes taking video pictures from the ship. Then he turned the ship around and pointed it at the sun. He programmed the system to take him to a position seventy thousand miles from Earth. When the computer was ready, he pushed the launch button again, and several seconds later, when the view in the monitor cleared up, he could see something he had seen many times before from space: Earth. He contacted the space station to tell them the mission was successful and he would be back at the space station in less than two hours.

Fifteen minutes later Jeffery received a message from Max Hiller, his new boss: "Great job, but this is only the first step. We'll discuss this when you get back to the station." Max was in charge of product development for NASA, and that included the development of the ships that would be used for interstellar exploration. Jeffery thought this test flight was a onetime event and afterwards he would go back to flying his regular trips to Mars and Ganymede. Now it didn't appear to be the case. He wondered what Max had planned for him.

The shuttle was waiting for him just outside the docking location. A few minutes after stopping, Jeffery heard the familiar sound of the shuttle docking with his ship. He took the shuttle for the ten-minute trip to the space station. When he got inside, there was a crowd waiting for him and they began to applaud. He really didn't think he had done anything to rate the applause, but he appreciated it anyway. He saw Max standing in the crowd and when their eyes met, Max began to walk over to him. Max shook Jeffery's hand and said, "Congratulations, you have now flown faster and farther than any other human. Now, I want to discuss some future plans with you as soon as possible. When you get back to Earth, you'll probably be swarmed by reporters and I want to be sure you have something to tell them. I'm going to ask for a lot of money to build the next ship and train the crew, so we're going to need some good publicity. Can you meet me in conference room ten in an hour?"

Jeffery excitedly replied, "Of course, I'll see you in an hour." Then Jeffery went back to his small room, took a quick shower, changed clothes, and went to the conference room for his meeting. As he walked in, he was surprised only Max was there. Max looked up at him, smiled, and said, "Please sit down. I ordered some coffee and snacks."

"Thank you, I'm kind of hungry."

161

Then Max, looking very serious said, "Jeffery, I really appreciate what you did today. I know you don't think it was a big deal, but it really was. Your flight will make headlines across the world, and you're now a celebrity. Your flight today was the first step in developing our first interstellar space ship, and NASA wants you to be the captain. Are you interested?"

Jeffery could hardly believe what he had just heard. He was so excited he could barely speak, but finally he blurted, "Yes. Yes, I'm very interested."

Max smiled at Jeffery's response and said, "Perfect, so now I'm going to give you a synopsis of our plan. I've already sent you some preliminary drawings of the ship's design. It's classified, so please don't discuss it with anyone. The ship is twenty-five thousand cubic feet. It has fifty-four cabins, each designed for one person. They're all the same except for yours and the executive officer's cabin, which are slightly larger. There's a fully functional medical facility with the capacity to perform major surgery if required, and research capabilities to analyze any lifeforms you might find. There are kitchens, dining rooms, a large recreation room, and a hydroponic garden area so you can grow some of your own food. It will also carry its own shuttle so you can land a crew on any planet you want to study more closely. The idea is to provide the crew with a comfortable place to spend a year or two."

"That sounds great! What can I do to help?"

"Actually, quite a lot. I want you to study the ship's design and let me know if you see something that should be modified, or something we missed. I also want you to think about the other pilots you've worked with over the years and find somebody you think would make a good executive officer. Additionally, I want you to work with the personnel people to select the qualifications for the other crew members."

Jeffery was both excited about the job and worried he wasn't up to the task. "Wow! That's a lot of responsibility." Then he paused and asked modestly, "What makes you think I'm capable of doing all those things?"

162

Max smiled and said, "When we selected you for this mission it wasn't just because you were a good pilot. We went over your college records, talked to the people you've worked with, studied your psychological reports. I admit we even followed you around for a few months. We had to be sure we were picking the right person, and I'm very confident we did."

Jeffery was wondering if they planted a camera in his bedroom, but decided he didn't want to know. He had actually dreamed about being the first person to visit another solar system, and now it was probable that his dream was about to come true. He replied, with a note of humility, "Okay, if you're sure I'll certainly give it my best."

"I never expected anything less."

There was a knock on the door and a steward brought in the coffee and snacks. After they each poured themselves a cup of coffee Max continued, "We expect it'll take about three years to build and test the ship before we start the first interstellar mission. While the ship is being built, we'll be training the crew, so when the ship is ready, we'll be ready to go. Your first mission is going to be to the closest star system with multiple planets, Gliese 876. That system is fifteen light years from Earth. It will take you forty days to get there. We want you to study the planets for a month or so and then return to Earth."

"That sounds very exciting. Can I assume if the mission is successful, the following missions will be longer?"

"Yes, the next mission will probably last two years."

"Have you given any thought about how we would handle an encounter with another intelligent lifeform?"

"Actually, we're hoping that happens. We know they're out there because somebody took the Ganymede probe. Of course, we have no idea where they're from, but we think it's probably somewhere in Earth's neighborhood, perhaps within a hundred light years."

"That's a pretty big neighborhood. It would probably take several lifetimes to study that much territory."

"I never said this was going to be easy. However, we hope to have several ships within ten years, so you won't be

163

doing this alone. Also, after the mission to Gliese 876, we'll only be going to star systems with Earth-like planets, so that diminishes the task substantially. I'd like to meet with you again in a day or two after you've studied the plans for the ship. Just call my office and they'll set up the meeting. I'd like you to stay here until after our next meeting. Then you can go back to Earth if you want to."

"Okay, I'll start looking at the plans after I get a few hours of sleep. Thank you for this opportunity. I promise I won't let you down."

"You're welcome. Have a good rest."

Jeffery left the meeting and headed back to his room. He was more excited than he had ever been in his whole life. He was tired because he hadn't slept more than an hour or two the night before the test flight, but he was sure he wouldn't be able to sleep. He got back to his room, stripped down to his underwear, and laid down on his bed. As excited as he was, he still fell asleep almost immediately.

After sleeping for a few hours Jeffery got up, still excited about the job he had been given. He went to his computer and brought up the plans for the first star ship. He was amazed at what he saw. It was apparent a great deal of effort had gone into the plans. After studying them for a few hours, he called Max and set up an appointment for later in the day.

He met Max in the same conference room where they had met the day before. When Jeffery walked into the room, Max was already waiting. Jeffery asked, "Am I late for our meeting?"

"No, you're right on time. I just got here a few minutes ago. What did you think about the plans for the ship?"

"I was very impressed. After studying them for several hours I have a few questions, and one suggestion."

"That's fine. I really want your opinion and comments."

"The one suggestion I have is that I believe we need a room with enough capacity to seat the entire crew. I suspect we'll probably have meetings and there's really no place to meet."

"Okay, that seems reasonable. What else?"

"Obviously, we'll be going into areas where we've never gone before and there may be some situations that come up that may require us to defend ourselves. Is the ship going to be armed?"

"We hope you'll never need it, but the ship will be armed with particle beam weapons. The design's not all that different from the particle beam used to create the wormhole path. There will also be handheld weapons, although the design is still being worked on. You and your executive officer will be given weapons training, and there will also be at least four crew members who will be given weapons and security training, so they can provide protection for the ship and crew in addition to their primary function onboard the ship. The ship will be a small, self-contained city. We won't be able to help you with any problems that might develop, so we want to cover as much as possible before the mission starts."

"I noticed there are three kitchens, one on each floor where there are living quarters. Is there going to be any kitchen staff to prepare meals?"

"Not really. There may be someone who wants to work as a cook occasionally, but each person will have the responsibility of preparing their own meals. We haven't decided on the makeup of the crew yet. We'll be discussing that over the next month or two. We know we'll have a doctor onboard. There will be two engineers to manage the equipment and handle repairs. We'd also like to have a zoologist and an exobiologist who will study any plants and animals you find during your explorations."

"That still leaves about forty people." Jeffery said.

"I realize that, and that's why in the next few months we want to figure out what staff will be needed. I know it's early, but if there's anyone you think you'd like to have as your executive officer please let me know as soon as possible. I think the tasks ahead will be easier if you have somebody to discuss it with," Max replied.

"Okay, I'll do that. I can probably give you a few names tomorrow. I'll also think about the staffing requirements. That's a lot of positions to fill, perhaps more than we need."

"If we end up with empty cabins, I'm sure we can find people who'd love to have an opportunity to study other planets."

"Are you still going to be on the station in two days or are you going back to Earth?" Jeffery inquired.

"I plan on being here for at least another week. My wife's coming up on a shuttle later today and we're going to relax for a while. But whenever you want to meet again, just let me know."

"Okay, enjoy a few days off. I'm sure you need it. By the way, I wanted you to know, if it's okay with you, I plan on staying on the station instead of going back to Earth," Jeffery said as he got up to leave.

"If that's what you want to do, it's okay with me. Some reporters may be disappointed, but I'm not concerned about that in the least," Max said. Then he smiled, stood up, and shook Jeffery's hand.

For the next two days Jeffery thought about nothing other than the mission personnel. He finally decided to tell Max he wanted Debbie Murphy for his executive officer. She had been flying the same Mars and Ganymede flights that he was on, and she had been doing it for a year or two longer. More importantly, she had experienced something that only happened once. On a flight back to Earth from Ganymede, her ship experienced engine failure. She managed to repair the engine problem and keep everybody on the ship calm during the thirty-six hours the ship was out of commission. He was sure she would be perfect, and he knew she had applied for the test pilot position, so she would not be concerned for her personal safety. In addition to being qualified, she was also a very close friend.

Next, he thought about the ship's crew. He simply could not think of any reason to have more than twenty crew members. So, he was going to give Max a list of what he thought was needed for the first mission. If there were any missing positions, they could be filled before the second mission.

Two days went by and Jeffrey met with Max in his office. Max was on the phone. After he hung up, he looked at Jeffery and asked, "Did you decide on an executive officer?"

"Yes, I gave it a lot of thought and I decided on Debbie Murphy. I think she'd be perfect for the job."

"I agree. I know she's between flights now so I'll contact her when we're done. Did you think about personnel requirements?"

"I did that too. I can only come up with twenty positions. I'll send a list to you, unless you'd like me to go over it with you now."

"I have some time, so let's talk about it."

"Okay, but I want to point out this list is only for the first mission. If we discover we need additional personnel they can be added before the second mission. This is in addition to the positions we've already discussed. I think we should have a person trained as a combination shuttle pilot and navigator. That way we'll have additional backup in case I become incapacitated. I'd like to have a photographer who will keep video records of everything accomplished during the mission. I think we should have a linguist, in case we have to communicate with an alien race, and although the officers onboard will keep personal logs, that person would also be responsible for maintaining a written log for the mission. Since we have room, it might be a good idea to have two people who will cook and maintain the kitchens. I'd like to have a geologist onboard and somebody to manage the hydroponic gardens. I also think we will need a minimum of four engineers to maintain the equipment and three or four full time security officers."

"I'm sure you realize most of the time these people will be sitting around doing nothing."

"Yeah, I know that. But as you pointed out, we'll be on our own during the mission and I want to make sure we'll be able to handle any problem we run across. Oh, I almost forgot. I would also like to have a nurse and doctor onboard."

"Okay, send all that in writing to me. I don't think any of this is a problem. I agree with what you want."

"Please let me know about Debbie as soon as you can."

"I'm sure I'll have an answer within an hour or two. By the way, the group that designed the ship will be here the day after tomorrow and they want to meet with you."

"Just let me know when and where and I'll be there. Say hello to your wife for me."

"I'll do that. Actually, why don't you join us for dinner? Meet us in the restaurant at 6:00."

"Okay, I'd like that. Thanks." Jeffery left Max's office and headed back to his room.

Jeffery got to the restaurant a few minutes early and ordered iced tea. Max and his wife, Ann, were a few minutes late. Jeffery got up and hugged Ann briefly and said, "It's nice to see you again. It's probably been two years since we last met. You look very nice."

"Thank you. I'll bet you're pretty excited about your new assignment."

"I certainly am," Jeffery replied, then he turned to Max. "Did you speak to Debbie?"

"I did and it took her almost three seconds to agree to her new assignment."

"That's great! When will she be here?" Jeffery asked with a big smile on his face.

"She's scheduled to go to Ganymede next week, but she'll be here in a few days. After the trip, she'll stay here so you two can work together. I hope you only asked for her because of her abilities, not because you're attracted to her."

"We're friends, and have been for eight or nine years. We had dinner together a few times, but our relationship is based on mutual respect. There won't be any romantic entanglements. I promise."

"Good. Now let's order dinner. I'm picking up the check," Max said.

THE STAR ROVER

A few days later, Debbie arrived at the station. She went to Jeffery's room and knocked on the door. Jeffery had ordered breakfast to be delivered fifteen minutes earlier so he didn't think twice about answering the door, even though he was only dressed in a robe and white cotton briefs. When he opened the door Debbie looked at him, smiled, and said, "Were you expecting me? I thought I'd surprise you."

Jeffery replied, "I knew you were coming, but I thought it was going to be in the afternoon. Besides, you've seen me wearing less."

Debbie came into the room and they hugged and kissed each other lightly on the lips. Then Jeffery said, "I told Max we're simply friends, and there wouldn't be any romantic entanglements. I don't want him to think I lied. Besides, you're still the most qualified of all the pilots for this job."

"I know, and I think we can manage to keep our hands off each other for a while. Don't you agree?"

"Yes, this mission is too important to let anything stand in the way. I'm sure we'll be able to find some time to get together in private. Anyway, as long as you're here, I have some things I want you to look at. The plans for the Star Rover are on my computer. So is a list of the crew positions. Please review them and let me know your opinion."

"Okay, but I have a meeting with Max in fifteen minutes. I'll come back after the meeting." They kissed again and Debbie left.

A few minutes later the steward brought Jeffery his breakfast. He was relieved the steward hadn't come while Debbie was there.

When Debbie returned, she said, "Max and I had a long talk and he made it very clear we can't be more than friends at this time. I assured him that wasn't a problem. I really don't know why he's so concerned, but I think it will be best if we don't do anything that can create any kind of problem. I asked him about the mission parameters, but he told me to discuss that with you. So, what are they?"

"There are two missions planned. The first one is short, only four months. We'll be going to Gliese 876. That system has four planets and we'll spend a week or so studying each of them before returning to Earth. Gliese 876 is fifteen light years from Earth, so it will take forty days to get there, a month to study the planets, and forty days to return to Earth."

"That should be very exciting. Is the second mission longer?"

"Yes, that mission will last two years. I don't think a decision has been made as to where we're going, but I think the goal is to find intelligent alien life. Anyway, the computer is set up for you. Please go over the plans for the Star Rover. In a few minutes I'm going to a meeting with the designers to review the plans. I think they'll be here for a few days and I'll make sure you're included in the next meeting."

"Okay, I'll see you here after your meeting."

There were several meetings with the ship designers over the next several days. In the end, they decided to build one large dining room with the capacity to hold up to seventy-five people and a single large kitchen next to the dining room. The kitchens on the other floors were converted into small break rooms. The rest of the design was unchanged. Construction was scheduled to start in January 2117 and was expected to take three years.

After Debbie was permanently assigned to the project, four additional people were selected for engineering positions. Their job was to maintain all of the equipment onboard and be able to rebuild anything from spare parts. After the selection of the engineers, Jeffery, Debbie, and the engineers were scheduled to go through an eighteen-month program to learn everything about the ship's systems.

During that time Jeffery and Debbie were also responsible for managing the construction of the Star Rover. It made for some very long days, but they loved every minute of it. By the time their training class was completed, the ship was half finished. The hull was done and the work on the inside of the ship was started. The first step was to pressurize the inside of the ship and heat it so the construction crew could work without space suits. Once that was accomplished, the pace for the construction increased quickly. In fact, it appeared that the ship would be ready three months ahead of schedule.

Jeffery and Debbie spent a lot of time selecting their crew members. The most difficult position to fill was the ship's doctor. It wasn't a problem for the first mission, but they had to interview fourteen doctors until they found one who met the qualifications and didn't object to being gone for two years. In fact, the doctor they chose, Dr. Frank Weber, was very excited about the idea of possibly having an opportunity to study alien organisms. Dr. Weber knew a nurse who would be interested as well, so the medical positions were filled. There were literally hundreds of people who were interested in the biologist, zoologist, and geologist positions, and even more were interested in the photographer position. It took some time, but both Jeffery and Debbie were very happy with their choices.

NASA found people for the chefs' jobs, the linguist, the hydroponic gardener, and the security positions. As a result, the entire crew had been selected by November 2118. They were scheduled to start their ten-month training program in February. The idea was that every crew member would be able to do almost any job required.

The Star Rover was completed and ready for testing on October 1, 2119. All of the onboard systems were tested extensively over the next three months. However, they had not tested the propulsion systems. The first propulsion system test was scheduled for January 12, 2120. For that test, only Jeffery and Debbie were onboard. The test was for the sub-light engine and was the same test that had been performed before. Jeffery put the ship in a fifty-thousand mile orbit and accelerated at 1.25 g's to fifteen hundred miles per second. Other than a few minor problems with the steering control system detected during acceleration, everything was perfect. They spent two days in orbit before slowing down to twenty-five hundred miles per hour and they returned to the space station.

It took a day to repair the steering control. The test of the wormhole system was scheduled for January 25, 2120. This was going to be a one-week test and the entire crew was going to be onboard. Enough supplies were brought onboard to last three months, so if there was an engine failure, they would be able to get back to Earth by using the sub-light engine without running out of anything critical.

The plan was for the Star Rover to use the wormhole system to travel out past the orbit of Pluto. They would spend six days cruising using the sub-light engine and testing the onboard systems. Then they would use the wormhole system to return to the space station.

The crew was brought onboard the day before they were scheduled to begin the test. It was the first time most of them had actually been on the ship. Everything was functional, except the hydroponic garden, but the woman who was responsible for it was onboard.

The crew had two hours to unpack and explore the ship. Jeffery called a meeting in the dining room. When the crew was assembled Jeffery addressed them. "I'd like to welcome all of you aboard the Star Rover. I hope you found your rooms comfortable. This brief trip is to test as many of the onboard systems as we can. So, play with everything, and if you detect even the slightest problem report it immediately. On the table to your left as you walked into the dining room are small communicators that have your name on them. Please make sure you pick yours up. The system has been designed to use either the communicator number, which is a two-digit number on the back of each device, or simply by speaking either the person's last name, or position. For example, if you wanted to speak to the doctor you could say 'Doctor,' or 'Weber.' By the way, I hope you all like steak and lobster, because that's what the chefs are preparing for dinner. However, don't expect we'll be having that kind of food every night.

"We'll be starting our voyage early tomorrow morning, so be at your assigned post by 7:30. If you have any questions please don't hesitate to ask Debbie or me. Also, since there are only twenty crew members, we're not going to be concerned about rank. It's not necessary to address me as Captain or sir. Jeffery is fine. My executive officer is Debbie, not Lieutenant Commander Murphy. Thank you. Have a wonderful evening."

By 7:00 the following morning every member of the crew was already at their assigned positions. There was a security office and three of the security officers were there. The fourth security officer was assigned to be on the bridge, potentially manning the weapons stations. The bridge was manned twenty-four hours a day. There were always at least two people on the bridge, a security officer and the person in command of the ship. The command position changed every eight hours, it was either Jeffery, Debbie, or the ship's navigator, Lieutenant Mike Parker.

For the initial launch, the bridge was fully manned. Jeffery was at the command console. Sean Richards, the chief security officer, was seated at the weapons control console. Mike was at the navigation console, and Debbie positioned herself by the long-range scanners. At exactly 7:30, Jeffery told Mike to power up the engine and move the ship out of orbit and away from the space station. As the ship started to move, a message was received from Max: "Good luck and Godspeed."

When the ship was two thousand miles from Earth, it was pointed at Polaris and the wormhole system was energized. Jeffery announced that in ten seconds the ship would enter the wormhole and would exit fourteen seconds later. Once again, as the ship entered the wormhole all of the external monitors displayed a solid light gray screen. When the ship exited the wormhole, the display was completely different. Jeffery announced that the Star Rover was now more than three billion miles from Earth.

The sub-light engine was engaged with an acceleration of .75 g's. The low gravity would make everybody onboard more comfortable. The next six days would be spent testing the ship's systems. So far, the only failure was one of the ovens in the kitchen, and one of the maintenance people took care of that very quickly.

During their first full day on the ship there were a few plumbing problems with the showers and toilets, but they were soon sorted out.

On day two the weapons systems were supposed to be tested. They used the shuttle to place several eight-foot diameter targets five miles from the ship. After the shuttle was back onboard, the weapons were powered up. The security officer with the most experience using the system was Lieutenant Bruce Phillips. Bruce was waiting at the weapons console for permission to fire the particle beam weapon. Jeffery told him to proceed, so Bruce took careful aim and fired the weapon. It missed the target by several feet. Bruce adjusted the aiming software and fired again. This time he missed, but by only two feet. He made another adjustment, fired again, and the target was demolished. He aimed at the second target and missed by a foot. He adjusted the aim again and fired. The target disappeared. He fired at the third and fourth targets. Both targets were hit with the first shot. Everybody on the bridge was pleased with the results, but several people expressed their hope to never have a reason to use the powerful weapon.

Things were going very smoothly until late in the afternoon. There was a sudden power fluctuation and an external radiation sensor sounded an alarm. Jeffery was in his cabin, but was immediately called to the bridge. "What happened?" he asked Debbie as soon as he arrived.

"I'm not sure. We went through some kind of intense radiation field. I've never experienced anything like it before. This ship is shielded extremely well and nothing should've been able to penetrate it. Or at least nothing we've ever experienced," Debbie answered.

Jeffery opened his communicator and said, "Chief Engineer." He waited a few seconds for Ron Rice to answer and then asked, "Did the radiation field cause any damage to the ship?"

"There was no detectable damage, at least not so far. One of our sensors indicated the radiation was similar to a very powerful x-ray."

Jeffery looked at Debbie and asked, "Could we have been scanned?" He didn't wait for an answer. "Debbie, use our long-range scanners and see if there's anything out here that might have generated that pulse."

Debbie went to the scanner console, entered a few commands into the computer that controlled the system, and said, "We're scanning now for any object larger than a few feet, but the scanner's range is limited to three thousand miles. A few minutes later the scanner announced, "Unknown object detected." Debbie looked at the image on the monitor and could not believe what she saw. Her mind was trying to absorb it. She yelled, "You'd better look at this!"

Jeffery moved quickly over to the monitor and looked at what Debbie was pointing at. There was no doubt about what he saw. It was another ship! Jeffery asked excitedly, "We are recording this, aren't we?"

Debbie answered, "Yes, everything we scan is recorded."

As everybody on the bridge watched the monitor, the ship suddenly disappeared.

Jeffery said, "Debbie, send that recording to Earth. I know they won't get it for a while, but if something happens to us, they'll know what happened."

He walked over to the command console and sent the following message to Earth: "At 4:43 this afternoon our ship was scanned by another ship. There's no apparent damage. Long range scanners detected an alien ship. While we were watching the alien ship, it disappeared. We sent the video to you."

Jeffery then ordered his crew, "I want the long-range scanners set to scan at maximum range constantly. If anything is detected, call me immediately."

"Yes sir, my staff and I will man the scanner non-stop," Lieutenant Sean Richards, the chief of security replied.

Jeffery announced to the rest of the crew what had happened and he told Debbie, "Get Mike and come to my cabin immediately."

"Okay," Debbie replied and left the bridge. Jeffery was in the process of leaving the bridge, but stopped and said to Sean, "Get another one of your people up here to help you. The ship is yours." He left without waiting for a response.

A few minutes later Jeffery went into his cabin at sat down at a small table. A minute later there was a knock at the door. Debbie and Mike came in and sat down at the table.

Jeffrey said, "The three of us have more experience in space than all the rest of the crew combined. We have to decide what to do about this situation. Debbie, how far was that ship from us?"

"It was twenty-seven hundred miles away, almost at the limit of our sensors."

"The limit of our weapons is five hundred miles, so they were way out of range. But I really don't think they meant to harm us. I think they just wanted to know more about us and our ship," Mike said.

"I agree. Do either of you think we should—" Jeffery stopped speaking because his communicator rang. When he picked it up, he could see it was Ron Rice, his chief engineer. He opened his communicator and said, "Yes Ron, what…," but before he could continue Ron said, "I have to see you right now, it's urgent."

"I'm in my cabin with Debbie and Mike."

"I'll be there in two minutes."

"I think we should delay any decisions until Ron tells us what's so important," Jeffery suggested to the others, who had heard what Ron said.

He opened the door to his cabin and then went back to the table.

A few moments later Ron came in and said, "I was running some ship diagnostics. One of those is a check of the ship's chronometer. It compares our time with the time on Earth by picking up a time signal. The diagnostic takes our distance from Earth into its calculations and then compares the two. Normally any discrepancy is very small, less than a millisecond.

However, when the test was run today, it was off by three hours. I ran the diagnostic a second time and the results are the same. Time stopped on the ship for three hours."

Nobody said anything for a few seconds and then Jeffery said, "I won't ask if you're sure this information is correct, because you wouldn't be here if there was any doubt. Is there any way to find out what happened during that time?"

"I don't see any way to do that. It appears every system and person on the ship was frozen in time for three hours. In fact, I can't even tell when the event started," Ron replied.

Jeffery, clearly concerned for the safety of the crew said, "So, the ship could have been boarded and inspected and we would never know! Obviously, we are dealing with technology far more advanced than our own, but I think they had no intention of harming us. They certainly could've done that and we would've been completely helpless. I want the ship thoroughly searched and let me know if anything, no matter how trivial it may appear, is out of place. Ron, your people know more about this ship than anybody else so you're in charge of this task. I want a report in two hours."

"Yes sir," Ron replied and he left.

Jeffery, Debbie, and Mike went back to the bridge and Jeffery made an announcement. "As you all know by now, it appears our ship was scanned by the alien ship that was detected by our sensors. What you don't know is that the encounter with the ship didn't last just a few minutes. It actually lasted three hours, but for some unexplained reason none of us were aware of it. I've instructed the ships maintenance staff to search the entire ship for any evidence we might have been boarded during that time. If any of you see anything that looks suspicious, please let me know immediately."

Jeffery sent a message to Earth informing them of the missing three hours. Then he looked at the rest of the people on the bridge and asked, "Should we continue the mission, or should we go back to Earth? I don't believe meeting with an alien ship was simply a chance encounter. I believe they knew we were here and I suspect these are the same beings that took the Ganymede probe."

Debbie said, "I agree meeting the alien ship wasn't a coincidence. They want to know more about us, but I don't think we're in any danger. I don't see any reason why we should cut the mission short."

"I agree, but I don't want to provoke them. I don't think we should do any more weapons testing," Mike said.

"All right, unless there's another incident we'll continue the mission as planned."

An hour later Jeffery's com unit rang. It was Ron. "Hi Ron, do you have anything to report?"

"Yes, I found something missing. We had five spare power modules, now there are only four. I know there were five because I took a major spare parts inventory before the ship launched. Additionally, when Toby went to get some parts to repair the oven two days ago, he remembered seeing all five power modules."

"That's interesting. There was a power module in the Ganymede probe too. I wonder if that's what they want. Please continue your search."

"Yes sir."

Jeffery sent a message to Earth: "I don't believe we're in any danger. However, it's now apparent during the missing three hours the aliens were onboard the Star Rover. One of our spare power modules was taken. We'll continue the mission as planned unless another incident occurs or you ask us to return immediately."

Since it would take over five hours for a message to reach Earth, they still had not received his first message, so Jeffery was not expecting a response anytime soon. He was hoping they wouldn't order him to return immediately.

Another hour went by before Ron reported that nothing else appeared to be missing.

Eleven hours after the first message was sent, Jeffery received a message from Earth:

178

"We received your message and video. Please continue the mission and keep us informed."

A few hours later another message was received. "We don't understand how you could have lost three hours. Are you sure it wasn't an error with the diagnostics?"

Then Jeffery received a response to his last message. "We confirm you had five spare power modules when the Star Rover was launched, so if one is missing, we agree with your conclusion the aliens took it. No one at NASA has any idea how to stop time, but several have expressed a desire to find out how it was done. Keep us informed of any new developments and check all onboard cameras to see if they caught anything digitally."

For the remainder of the mission there were no more incidents, so they headed back to Earth on schedule. While they were waiting for a shuttle to bring them to the station, Jeffery told the crew not to discuss the encounter with the alien ship with anybody, not even with each other. He also told them failure to follow his order would result in dismissal from the ship's crew.

When Jeffery stepped aboard the station, he was not surprised to see Max waiting for him. Max didn't say anything, but motioned to both Jeffery and Debbie to come with him.

They followed him to a small conference room. Max closed and locked the door so they would not be disturbed.

"Okay, tell me what happened," Max said.

Jeffery responded, "To begin with, all we noticed was a brief power fluctuation and an external radiation sensor sounded an alarm. It was determined the radiation was very powerful and like an x-ray. I didn't think any radiation could penetrate the ship's shielding, but apparently I was wrong. Since high power x-rays are not a natural occurrence, I asked Debbie to use our long-range scanner to look for anything that might have generated a radiation burst. The system found the alien ship and we sent you the video. Sometime later, Lieutenant Rice reported that the chronometer diagnostic indicated the ship's time was off by three hours. He ran the diagnostic a second time with the same results. We decided it was possible the ship was boarded during the missing time. I asked Lieutenant Rice and his people to search the entire ship for anything that indicated the ship had been boarded. They found one of the power modules was missing. There were no additional incidents and the alien ship was never detected again. It is my opinion that these are the same beings who took the Ganymede probe and they took it to learn more about how the power module functions."

"That's quite a story," Max said, stroking his chin thoughtfully. "Do you agree, Debbie?"

"Yes, I should add that I never felt we were in any danger. If the aliens wanted to harm us, they certainly had the opportunity. However, if there's any way to increase the range of the long-range scanners that should be done before the next launch. Neither Jeffery nor I believe this meeting with the alien ship was a coincidence. They knew we would be there."

"I agree. I'll ask about the possibility of increasing the scanner range. Is there anything you want to add, Jeffery?"

"No. I assume this meeting with the alien ship is being kept confidential?"

"It absolutely is secret. Did you warn your crew not to talk about it?"

"I did, and I told them if they do, they'll be dismissed from the Star Rover crew. I know none of them want that, so I'm certain they'll keep the information to themselves."

"Good. I'm sending a crew to the ship to go over every square inch to look for anything out of the ordinary. I don't think they'll find anything, but it doesn't hurt to look. Both of you take a few days off, but stay on the station. Thank you both for doing a great job."

A thorough inspection of the Star Rover and its contents revealed nothing new. The only evidence of the aliens' presence was the missing power module. On the positive side, however, they were able to extend the range on the scanner to seventy-five hundred miles by making software changes. For the mission to Gliese 876, that would have to be good enough. For the following mission both hardware and software changes would be required, but the engineers thought they could increase the scanner range to twenty thousand miles.

GLIESE 876

The Gliese 876 mission was scheduled for March 9, 2120. The Star Rover was loaded with enough additional supplies so the crew could survive for a year, although the mission was scheduled to last four months.

For this mission, the hydroponic garden would be used to supply fresh vegetables, so the gardener, Ensign Carol Hobbes, began planting and setting up the garden in late January. This garden was in a separate part of the ship and was designed to rotate slowly so it always had 50% of normal Earth gravity, which was sufficient for the plants to grow normally. Carol thought the garden would be a fairly popular place on the ship because of the constant gravity.

A week before the Star Rover was scheduled to launch, Max called Jeffery and Debbie into his office for a meeting. They arrived together.

Max said, "Please sit down. We have a number of things to discuss. First, I know you're aware we'll have ten paying guests on this mission. They each paid $2,500,000 for their cabins. They'll all be here by February 7, so I want you both to meet with them that evening and let them know what they can expect. They have all been evaluated and the NASA doctors said they were fit for space travel and they've all been through two weeks of training, but I don't know how well they'll be prepared for the length of time they'll have to spend in a gravity-free environment. They need to understand this isn't a pleasure cruise, but I'm sure you'll make that clear to them.

"The next subject is the possibility of meeting with the alien ship again. I think it's likely that will happen, but I'm hoping this time we'll be able to make contact with them. By the way, our guests don't know about the alien ship, so you should explain that to them during your meeting."

"Debbie and I have been talking about that and we agree we'll probably encounter the aliens again," Jeffrey said. "Perhaps with the longer scanner range we can detect them and try to contact them before they surprise us again. I have a few thousand questions for them. I'm not sure how our guests will feel about the possibility of contacting aliens. They may find it exciting, or possibly terrifying."

Max nodded in hopeful agreement and continued, "Next, some of the engineers have expressed concern about using the wormhole generator for forty consecutive days. The system on the ship has never been used for more than fifteen seconds at a time. So, they think you should consider using a series of short hops instead of one long one."

"I thought about that too, and I was thinking perhaps we should use it for twenty hours at a time and then use the sub-light engine for four hours. That way we would have gravity for four hours a day. It would extend the travel time to Gliese by five days. There's no rush to get there."

Max looked pleased. "That's a great idea, and it will make our paying guests happy too. Actually, the crew will probably be pleased as well. The last thing I wanted to talk to you about is NASA's liability if anything goes terribly wrong. Even though the ship has redundant systems, and enough spare parts to rebuild the wormhole system twice, a failure is a possibility.

"If the wormhole system fails and you're stranded near Gliese 876, there's no way you'll ever be able to return to Earth. Even if we had a second ship, we wouldn't realize there was a problem until it would be too late to help. So, every person on the ship has to sign a waiver that absolves NASA and all crew members of any potential liability."

"As far as the crew is concerned, we all know this mission is a risk. Every space flight is a risk. I don't see any problem with them signing the waivers, but what about our paying guests?" Debbie inquired.

"They've already signed waivers and nobody put up a fuss about it."

Jeffery asked, "Who are these paying guests? I hope they're not just rich guys looking for some excitement."

"No, they aren't. They're all college professors, scientists, or engineers. I'll send their resumes to you. None of them paid for their trip. It was paid for by the universities or the companies they work for. I believe they want to participate, as much as possible, in the exploration of the planets in the Gliese 876 system. Additionally, there's a certain amount of pride in being on the first interstellar trip."

"I'm sure it'll be okay. Anything else?" Jeffery asked.

"No, not at this time."

Both Jeffery and Debbie nodded and said, "Okay," as they left Max's office.

Each of the paying guests arrived on the space station the day before the mission was scheduled to depart. They were given a box containing their communicator for use on the Star Rover, information about the ship's layout, their cabin assignment, a list of the crew members, and a notice to be at a meeting in conference room B at 7:30 that evening.

By 7:15 all of the guests were assembled in the conference room and at 7:30 Jeffery and Debbie walked in. Debbie sat down at the head of the table and Jeffery stood and spoke to the group. "Good evening, I'm Captain Jeffery Whitestone and this is Commander Debbie Murphy, my executive officer. She is second in command. All of you have signed a non-disclosure agreement given to you by NASA. The information I'm about to give you is not to be divulged to anybody. If, after receiving this information, you wish to change your mind about going on this mission with us, you're free to do so and your payment will be refunded. Please understand that changing your mind about the mission will not release you from the agreement you signed regarding what I'm about to tell you."

Every person in the room stared at Jeffery and nobody said anything, so Jeffery told them about the encounter with the alien ship and the missing three hours that had occurred during their test mission.

There were several audible gasps from the group, but everyone continued looking at Jeffery, so he started speaking again. "We don't believe this was a chance meeting with the alien ship. They knew we would be there. We're fairly certain that the Ganymede probe was taken by these beings. There is no indication that they wish to harm us in any way. If that was their intention, they certainly could have done that when they boarded our ship during the three missing hours. We believe that they are simply curious about us as we are about them.

"As a result of that encounter, we feel it's likely we'll encounter them again on this mission. The sensor range on the ship has been extended by ten thousand miles, so we hope to detect them before they get too close and we'll try to communicate with them. We obviously don't know what will happen, but we feel you should be aware of the situation."

Jeffery paused for a few seconds and then asked, "Does anybody want to back out?"

Almost in unison, every person in the group said, "No."

Jeffery continued, "Good. I'm glad everybody is still interested in continuing with the mission. It's a 'once in a lifetime' opportunity. Now I want to tell you some other things about our mission that you should know. Please understand this is not a cruise ship. There are no menus, and meals are served four times per day. Basically, every six hours. At 6:00 AM and 12:00 midnight breakfast is served, at 12:00 noon lunch is served, and at 6:00 PM dinner is served. If you want to eat at a different time, snacks are available in a break room near your quarters.

"I'll tell you that eating in 0 g is an interesting experience. So is using a shower and a toilet. I don't think any of you have ever spent a long time in a gravity free environment, so we've devised a plan to make things a little easier. The wormhole system will be used for twenty hours per day. Then we'll switch over to our other engine and set the acceleration at .75 g's. That way you'll have four hours per day at near normal gravity. If you find yourself needing gravity, you can always go to the hydroponic garden area. That area has a constant gravity of .5 g's. There's a bathroom and shower in there that you're welcome to use. There are a few chairs in there as well. Also, all of you have been given uniforms. The shoes and the back pockets of the pants have magnets in them. That enables you to walk and sit almost normally.

186

"Each of you has been given a com unit along with instructions on how to use it. It's very simple. We have a doctor and a nurse onboard, so if you have a medical problem please let them know. They also have pills that can help with nausea in case you have a problem with the lack of gravity. Although you're guests onboard the Star Rover, if a problem occurs and we need your assistance, you'll be expected to help. I don't think that will happen, but you should be aware that it could.

"The last thing I want to talk to you about is excursions to the planets we'll be studying. If you're interested in going on one of the planet excursions, please let me know and we'll do our best to accommodate you. It will require some space suit training, but we can do that during the journey to Gliese 876. Also, be aware that we don't really know what the conditions are on the planets we'll be visiting, so we may not be able to go down to the surface safely. Do you have any questions for me now?"

Nobody asked anything, so Jeffery ended the meeting by saying, "The shuttle will start taking us to the Star Rover at 7:00 AM, and we'll be on our way at 9:00. Please don't be late. Goodnight, I'll see all of you tomorrow."

The following morning the passengers and crew were all in the shuttle boarding area before 7:00. The shuttle could only hold twenty people, including the pilot, so it took two trips to get everybody to the Star Rover. The passengers were going to be in zero gravity until the ship launched, so this was their first extended experience with no gravity.

Jeffery went to the bridge as soon as he got aboard. He had been on the first shuttle, but the rest of the bridge crew were on the second one. They arrived thirty minutes later, and without being told, Mike and Debbie began the pre-launch system checks. At 8:55 Jeffery made an announcement. "Our pre-launch checks have been completed and all systems are fully functional. In five minutes, we'll use our low speed engine to move us away from the space station and position the Star Rover for the first wormhole hop. This means we'll have 50% of normal gravity for thirty minutes. Please be seated until you hear an announcement that it's safe to move around the ship. The first hop will be twenty hours long and we'll travel 1.8 trillion miles, or about 1/3 of a light year. Thank you."

At exactly 9:00, the ship's sub-light engine was turned on at an acceleration of .5 g's and the ship began to move away from the space station. Jeffery announced it was safe to move around the ship. Twenty-five minutes later, Jeffery made the next announcement. "In five minutes we'll begin our first wormhole hop, so enjoy the gravity for five more minutes. During the wormhole hop all of the external monitors will be useless. All you'll see is a light gray screen. There will be an announcement just before we switch over to the sub-light engine so you can prepare for gravity again. The passengers are free to move around the ship. There's nothing that is 'off limits,' but please don't bother any crew members as they all have assigned tasks. If you have any questions, please feel free to come to the bridge and ask. Also, if you feel sick or queasy, please go to the doctor's office and you'll be given some medication to help. Don't forget the hydroponic garden area has gravity, so if you're feeling uncomfortable you can always go there. However, the more time you spend in zero gravity the more quickly you'll get used to it. Let's have a safe trip. Captain out."

The first day went well. There were no problems with the ship and only two of the passengers became ill. Dr. Weber was actually happy to see them because it gave him something to do. A few of the passengers spent most of the day in the hydroponic garden area, but although it had gravity it was very warm and humid, so it was still not a very comfortable environment.

None of the passengers showed up for lunch, but a few hours later they were hungry, so they all showed up for dinner. Zero gravity meals are similar to baby food. Everything is made into a smooth paste so it sticks to the spoon and you suck it off the spoon and swallow it. Most of the passengers did relatively well and by the end of the meal they were all getting the hang of it.

At the end of the meal, Jeffery made another announcement. "I hope you enjoyed dinner. I'm sure all of you read the material you were given before you boarded the ship, but I wanted to remind you that spending time in zero gravity isn't good for your muscles, so it's important you exercise for at least thirty minutes every day. I suggest walking in the hydroponic garden area. Have a good evening."

The trip to Gliese 876 went as planned. Although everybody was expecting to have an encounter with the alien ship, they were all somewhat relieved it didn't happen. However, there was one big surprise they discovered almost immediately after the hop ended. Gliese 876 was supposed to have four planets, but a new planet about three-quarters the size of Earth was discovered between Gliese 876d and Gliese 876c. To retain the same naming convention the new planet was called Gliese 876f.

Due to the mass of the Gliese planets, it would be impossible to land the shuttle on any of them except the one they had just found. They would, however, study them from an orbit as close as possible. The innermost planet in the Gliese 876 system was Gliese 876d. Its mass was six times that of Earth, and even though it was close to the star it was still cold. The surface temperature was about -30° centigrade during the day and about -60° at night. The planet did have an atmosphere that was composed primarily of methane and ammonia. There appeared to be hundreds of active volcanoes on the surface. The Star Rover spent five days studying the planet and taking thousands of pictures.

The hop to Gliese 876f only took a few seconds. Although it was similar in size to Earth, it was nothing like it. It had a very thin atmosphere that was 90% nitrogen. The balance was oxygen and carbon dioxide in almost equal parts. The surface was dotted with volcanoes, although not to the same extent as Gliese 876d. Even though it was farther from its sun, its surface temperature was only slightly cooler than Gliese 876d. It was -40 degrees centigrade during the day and -65 degrees at night. Jeffery was considering making a shuttle trip to the surface when the long-range sensor alarm sounded. He knew what it was without looking.

Debbie said simply, "Captain, we have company."

Jeffery was excited, but did his best to appear calm. "Okay, before they scan us and put us to sleep again, let's try to communicate with them. I have no idea what radio frequency they're using, or even if they have a radio, so let's send out a message on all available frequencies."

Debbie said, "Ready."

"Space ship near Gliese 876d, this is the Star Rover from the planet Earth. Please respond," Jeffery said with what he hoped was an authoritative voice.

Everybody on the bridge was shocked when a few seconds later a voice said, "Hello, Captain Whitestone, we were hoping you would try to contact us. We have been following your progress since you left Earth. Please do not be afraid, we are peaceful and have no intention of harming you. We would like to invite you and Commander Murphy to come to our ship. We have much to discuss."

Everyone on the bridge was surprised by the response. After a few seconds Jeffery asked, "How did you learn to speak perfect English?"

"We have been following events on Earth for over a thousand of your years, and can communicate in any of the major languages spoken there, but since your message was in English, we responded in the same language. If you agree, I will move our ship within shuttle range of the Star Rover. You can come here, or if you prefer, I will go over to your ship. But there are some things I want to show you on my ship."

Jeffery thought about it for a few seconds and said, "Okay, move your ship. Commander Murphy and I will go there."

It only took a few minutes for the alien ship to move close to the Star Rover.

Jeffery thought he should ask something before they went over to the alien ship so he turned on the transmitter and asked, "I assume the environmental conditions on your ship are satisfactory for us?"

190

The voice replied, "Yes, the atmosphere on our home world is almost identical to that of your Earth. We have 2% less nitrogen and 2% more oxygen. We keep the temperature on our ship at about twenty degrees centigrade which, I am sure, will be comfortable for you. I am looking forward to meeting you."

Jeffery said, "We'll be there in ten minutes." Then he asked Debbie, "Are you okay with this?"

"Absolutely! I've been waiting a long time for this moment. Let's go!"

The voice said, "Please approach our ship from the port side. When we see you, we will open a large door and you can fly your shuttle inside. As soon as your shuttle has landed, we will close the door and pressurize the docking bay."

Jeffery said, "Okay," and turned to Mike. "You're in command while we're gone. I'll leave my com unit on so you can listen to what's happening. If you feel we're in any danger, I want you to leave here and go back to Earth immediately. Is that clear?"

"Yes sir," Mike responded, although he looked like he would rather not obey this particular command.

Jeffery and Debbie left the bridge and headed for the shuttle bay. When they arrived they got into the shuttle and Debbie said, "I'll be recording this whole thing."

"Good idea."

They left the shuttle bay and headed to the alien ship. It was probably three or four times the size of the Star Rover. When they were two hundred yards away a large opening appeared on the side. Jeffery flew the shuttle slowly into the bay and landed gently. As soon as the shuttle settled, the opening closed, and he could hear the area outside pressurizing.

Jeffery noticed something and he said to Debbie, "There's gravity here. They must've figured out how to create artificial gravity without using centripetal force. I have to ask how they did it."

191

Almost as soon as the subtle sound of the pressurization stopped, there was a knock on the shuttle door. Jeffery opened the door and saw his first alien.

It was a female, about 5' 8" tall, slender build, black hair, bright green eyes, and her skin was a light tan. She looked human except for her hands. They were somewhat larger than normal and her fingers were probably an inch longer than would have been normal for a human. She was wearing a light green uniform. She smiled and said in a soft voice, "Hello, my name is Brealak. I will be taking you to see Garlut. He is our captain. Please follow me."

Jeffery and Debbie followed Brealak out of the bay and into a long hallway. They walked about a hundred feet down the hallway. Brealak put the palm of her hand on a sensor and an opening appeared in the wall. They went inside and saw a large table with at least a dozen chairs around it. There was a man seated, but when they walked in, he stood up. He was very tall, at least six-foot-five, and had a slender build. He was obviously much older than Brealak. His hair was gray, and his face was somewhat wrinkled. He was neatly dressed in a light blue uniform, and had a perfect smile. He said, "My name is Garlut. I am very pleased to meet you both. Please sit down. Would you like some water?"

"No thank you. Commander Murphy and I are pleased to meet you too. We have a lot of questions," Jeffery said.

"Before you start asking questions, which I will be happy to answer, I would like to explain some things to you. Is that acceptable?"

"Yes . . . If we seem a little nervous, it's because we've never met an alien before. I hope you don't find the word 'alien' offensive."

"The word is fine. We are from a planet we call Coplent. It is twenty light years from here. There are more than five hundred inhabited worlds in this section of the galaxy. My job is to keep watch on twenty-one of those planets with developing civilizations. Earth is one of those planets. This job is inherited. My family has been doing it for over fifteen hundred years, but we only started watching Earth a thousand years ago. I have been doing this for seventy-five years, and I will soon retire. When I do so my daughter, Brealak, whom you have already met, will take over.

"When we first started watching Earth, we were not very careful about hiding our shuttles. The people of Earth frequently saw them. That is probably the reason there are paintings and descriptions of them in your ancient literature. However, we never had any interactions with anybody on Earth. In fact, our ships rarely landed, and when they did it was in remote areas that were devoid of people. You are the first people from Earth we have ever spoken to.

"We realized it was necessary for us to be more careful about being seen as the people of Earth began to increase their scientific knowledge. I do not think one of our ships has been seen for more than two hundred years. Also, I want you to know we are not responsible for the stories about 'flying saucers,' because none of our ships are saucer shaped.

"Part of my job is to make first contact with civilizations when they become capable of interstellar space travel. We have been watching Earth more carefully since you started the regular flights to Ganymede. We were very surprised it took you only twenty years to learn how to travel faster than the speed of light. For most civilizations that process usually takes a few hundred years. Now that you have that capability, we would like to establish a relationship with you. Every culture has unique things to trade, and so we have built relationships all over the galaxy based on trade."

"Did you take the probe we put on Ganymede?" Jeffery asked.

"Yes, we did take the probe, although we intended to have it back before you realized it was gone. Unfortunately, we were unable to return it in time. Your probe had a unique source of electrical power we have never seen before and we took it so we could study it. If you want the probe back, I would be happy to return it to you. Before you ask, we also took one of the power units from your ship during your last mission. However, we did not board your ship. We have a device similar to something I have seen in your television stories. It is a type of transporter, and it can be used over short distances to move objects from one place to another. Unlike your stories, it cannot be used for moving living things and its range is limited to five miles."

"After your ship was placed into a time stasis field, we moved our ship to within two miles of yours. Then we used our device to move the power unit to our ship. We have tried to duplicate the technology, but so far, we have failed. The devices we make do not work. We would like to trade some of our technology for information on how to build these power units."

Jeffery replied excitedly, "I'm sure we can do that. We haven't been on your ship very long, but as soon as we landed I was impressed that you have artificial gravity on your ship. I know that's something we would like to have. The transporter would be very valuable as well. I believe you said there are more than five hundred planets with advanced civilizations in this part of the galaxy. Are they all humanoid? That is, do they look like us?"

"We have found all of the more advanced cultures have humanoid forms. In order to develop a civilization, a species must have the ability to make and use complex tools. That requires hands and fingers. There are a few planets with civilizations that have speech, but they are similar to dogs on Earth. They have a fairly complex language, but are incapable of using tools. So they cannot build the things they need to continue developing. We were surprised when we learned they have a basic understanding of farming and can grow some vegetables for food, but that is not a very difficult task."

"Do all the humanoid people look the same?" Debbie asked.

"For the most part, yes. Some are taller, some are shorter, some have excessive amounts of hair, and others are almost completely devoid of hair. Of course, all of them are mammals, but there are genetic differences too. Although you have only seen two of us, you may have noticed we are somewhat taller and more slender than most people from Earth. I am certain you also noticed our hands are bigger and our fingers are longer than yours. But what is more important is that we have discovered as civilizations mature, they almost universally become more peaceful. Out of all the planets that have advanced cultures, only two are somewhat aggressive, and they are both more than one hundred light years from Earth."

"You said your people never had any face to face contact with the people on Earth, but did you ever consider intervening when we were about to do something stupid?" Jeffery asked.

Garlut smiled and said, "The only time we came close was at the end of what you called World War II. We typically only observe each planet for any extended length of time every ten years or so. Understand, when I talk about years, or any period of time, I am using Earth terms. On Coplent, our year is five hundred forty-one days, and each day is about thirty-one of your hours long. In 1935, we saw the development of the Nazi government in Germany and we were concerned it might lead to a global war that could have set scientific advancements back substantially. We returned almost ten years later and discovered the war had occurred and was nearing a conclusion. We were astounded that scientific advancement had reached a point we didn't think was possible to achieve in that time span. When we discovered the United States had developed atomic weapons we considered intervening, but decided against it since we felt if the weapons were used at all, it would only be to end the carnage. I do not know if you were aware of this, but if Germany had not been defeated in early 1945, they probably would have had atomic weapons by the fall, and we did not think they would hesitate to obliterate most of the major cities in Europe. I do not think we would have allowed that to happen."

Jeffry said, "I'm curious. You mentioned you were surprised at how quickly we developed interstellar space travel. Did we do it right?"

"Yes, your approach to the problem was correct. The only way to travel interstellar distances is by what you call wormholes. However, I suspect you will discover there are ways to increase the speed through the wormholes. We can now travel more than five hundred times faster than light, and I'm certain you will achieve that too in the coming years. But there are other things besides speed that are important for interstellar travel. One of them you have already noted was artificial gravity, and the other technology is the ability to create food from almost anything organic. We have a device that can create edible, and I might add tasty, food by breaking down molecules of any organic material into its component parts and recombining them into food. Basically, everything on our ships is recycled, so we only have to carry minimal supplies."

Garlut paused while Debbie and Jeffery took this in. Then he continued, "One thing we have not been able to create is a communication system that allows radio signals to travel faster than light. So, like you, we are unable to communicate with our home planet in any useful way. We have been working on possible solutions for probably more than a thousand years and we have made very little progress. If the people on Earth could resolve that problem, the entire galaxy would be in your debt.

"I believe it is time for us to meet the people of Earth. I would like to go back to Earth with you because we do not want to alarm anybody. Would that be acceptable to you?"

"Yes, I think that would be fine, but first I'd like to continue our survey of the Gliese 876 system."

"I can tell you there is nothing remarkable about this system. There are no lifeforms on any of the five planets, but if you want to continue your research, please do so. If you decide to do that, we will stay here until you are ready to return to Earth. Would you like to take a tour of our ship?"

Jeffery answered, "I think we'd both like that very much. Also, I'd like to invite you and any of your crew members who'd be interested to come to our ship. I know the people on our ship would like to meet and talk with you."

"I would be pleased to come over to your ship and meet with your crew and passengers."

"Perfect. I want to call my ship and fill them in on the details of our meeting." Jeffery took his com unit off his belt, pressed a button, and said, "Parker." A few seconds later he heard Mike say, "I've been listening. It sounds like everything's okay."

"Yes, everything's fine. I'm sure you heard that we are going to take a tour of their ship. Then we'll come back. I'll contact you again after our tour."

"Okay, I'll be waiting for your call."

"I'm curious, how many crew members do you have on your ship?" Jeffery asked Garlut.

"We have sixty-five crew members. We do not have any guests because our missions are typically several years long."

"The presence of guests onboard the Star Rover was supposed to be a secret. How did you know we have guests?"

"I told you we monitor almost all of NASA's communications. I think we knew about your guests before you did."

"That wouldn't surprise me," Jeffery admitted with a chuckle. "We're ready for our tour anytime."

I will ask Brealak to give you the tour. When would you like me to visit your ship?"

Jeffery looked at his watch and said, "How about eight hours from now? Do you want me to send our shuttle to pick you up?"

"That is the only way it would work. Our shuttle is about twice the size of yours and would certainly not fit into your shuttle bay."

"Perfect. I'll call you when we're ready to leave. Our shuttle will hold twelve people, so if you want to bring anybody else, please feel free."

"I will ask my crew. I am certain Brealak will accompany me, and I will ask our chief engineer to come as well."

At that moment Brealak walked into the conference room. Jeffery was confused because he never saw Garlut call her. Garlut noticed his confusion and said, "We have developed some simple forms of what you call telepathy. We can communicate commands like 'come,' 'stop,' 'help,' and a few others. It is very useful."

"I'm sure it is," Debbie said.

"Brealak, please take our guests on a tour of the ship and answer any questions they have. If you do not know the answer, ask Quat to help you. Make the bridge the last stop on your tour."

"Yes, sir."

As they left the conference room, Jeffery asked, "Who is Quat?"

"Quat is our chief engineer. He knows more about this ship than anyone else. I doubt you could ask a question he could not answer."

"Your English is perfect. I have no idea how you could do that without practice speaking to other people. I speak two other languages, but it took years to learn them," Jeffery said.

"I think our species has a natural talent for learning languages. Our native language is very difficult. It has ninety-two letters and twenty-one vowel sounds. If you can learn to speak that, other languages are easy. Our children are typically fluent by the time they are two years old, and they can read by the time they are four. Je parle aussi le français."

"Moi aussi, mais je préfère parler en anglais."

Understood. I will speak English. Is there anything in particular you would like to see?"

"No, I'm enjoying just looking around at your obviously advanced technology," Jeffery said.

For the next hour, Brealak took Jeffery and Debbie to every part of the ship. They looked at the engine room, the medical facility, typical crewman's' quarters, the dining room, the recreation room, and finally the bridge.

When they arrived on the bridge there were four people on duty, including Garlut. Each crewman was seated at a desk that had at least four screens on it. The data on the screen was obviously in their native language, so it was impossible for Jeffery or Debbie to have any idea what they were looking at, but it was impressive.

Garlut said, "Each operator position in this room is capable of controlling everything on the ship."

Jeffery said, "You said you used your transporter to remove the power module from our ship. Does that mean you can see inside it?"

"Yes, we have a device that generates a signal that can penetrate the hull of your ship and allow us to see inside. It is not a perfect view, but there is enough resolution to easily make out shapes and even read large printing."

"Is it harmful to living things?" Debbie asked, a frown of concern on her face.

"No, it is not harmful unless the exposure lasts for several hours. It also has a very narrow beam, three feet in diameter. That is why it took us so long to locate the area where power units were stored. If we knew where to look, we could have found it very quickly and you may never have known about the time stasis field. Did you like our ship?"

"It was very impressive. The Star Rover hardly compares to this ship. But it's our first interstellar ship, and based on the technology available to us it's perfect."

"I completely agree with you. It is excellent for a first interstellar ship. We would like to give you some of our technology to use on the next ship, and we would like Earth to join our trading association. I think it would be beneficial for everybody."

"Given everything you know about us, I'm sure you're aware I'm in no position to accept or reject your offer. We have a World Council, and that would be their decision. But I don't see any reason why they'd reject your offer to join the trading association. Does that mean there would be aliens on Earth?"

"Yes, some of the planets in the group will want to establish offices on Earth, or perhaps even embassies with a permanent staff. If you are ready to go back to your ship, Brealak will take you back to the shuttle landing area now."

"Thank you. You've been a most gracious host," Jeffery said. Then he looked at his watch and added, "The

199

shuttle will be here to pick you up in six hours. I'll call you first to let you know we're coming."

"Thank you, I am looking forward to meeting the people on your ship."

Brealak took Jeffery and Debbie back to their shuttle. After they were seated inside, the shuttle hatch was closed. Then the exterior door opened and they left the alien ship. They didn't talk for a minute or two and then Debbie said, "I never thought the first contact with an alien civilization would be so easy. At first, I was a little suspicious and I thought Garlut had some evil scheme in mind, but I don't think that any more. I truly believe he wants to be friendly and helpful. I know he wants to build power modules, but I think trading the power module technology for some of the things he has on his ship would be a great deal for us."

"I absolutely agree. Just having artificial gravity is worth the trade."

When the shuttle was fifty yards from the Star Rover, the shuttle bay door opened and Jeffery flew the shuttle inside. As they exited the shuttle bay, almost everybody on the ship was waiting for them in the hallway. Jeffery said, "Mike, get everybody together in the dining room in ten minutes and I'll tell them about our meeting."

"Okay," Mike said, and he went back toward the bridge. Two minutes later he made the announcement about the meeting. By the time Jeffery and Debbie got to the dining room, almost everybody was already waiting for them.

Once the room quieted down, Jeffery began by giving them a synopsis of the meeting with the aliens. Then he told them, "They want Earth to join a trading association. That would make Earth part of an interstellar group of planets. They took Debbie and me on a tour of their ship. It was very impressive. The Star Rover is hardly even in the same class. Anyway, Garlut and his daughter will be here this evening after dinner and they'll answer your questions. They also want to follow us back to Earth and have asked us to cut this mission short. However, since many of you paid to be here, I'll leave that decision to your group. Please get together and let me know your decision at dinner this evening."

Jeffery left the dining room and went back to his quarters. Debbie went to the bridge and while she was there, she loaded the video she had taken on the alien ship to their computer network where everybody onboard could view it. She talked to Mike about the aliens and then went to Jeffery's cabin.

She knocked on the door and went inside. Jeffery rose from where he was sitting at his table and walked over to her. They hugged for a few seconds, kissed for more than a few seconds, and then sat down. Jeffery mused, "We have to stop meeting like this."

Debbie smiled and responded, "I suppose so. You know this is a day I'll never forget. If I had a vote, I'd prefer to go back to Earth immediately."

"I'm a little disappointed in our exploration of Gliese 876. There really is nothing to see here and we can't land the shuttle on any of the planets except 876F, where apparently there's nothing to see on the ground that can't be seen more comfortably from the ship. I'm sure I wouldn't want to cut the mission short if we hadn't met the aliens, but that seems to me to be more important than exploring some dead worlds."

Debbie replied, "I agree. On another subject, we really haven't had an opportunity to be alone since this mission started and I think we need some alone time."

"Okay, the next time Mike has the bridge we can meet on deck D. Nobody will be there because all of the rooms on that deck are empty. Mike knows we're more than friends, so I'll tell him we want some time alone. Is that okay with you?"

You know, Mike's on duty now, and his next shift starts at 8:00 tomorrow morning. So how about if we meet at 8:15 in room D4?"

"It's a date . . . well, probably more than just a date," Jeffery said with a grin.

"You know, sometimes you're really crude."

"I thought that was one of my most endearing qualities."

201

Debbie smiled and said, "I'm going back to my room. I have a report to write. See you at dinner." They kissed goodbye and she left.

Jeffery arrived at the dining room a few minutes before 5:00. He sat at his regular table waiting for Debbie when the guests walked in. They went over to Jeffery and one of them said, "We discussed it and we'll agree to forgo the rest of the mission if you can arrange a tour of the alien ship for us."

"I'll speak to Captain Garlut about that when he gets here, but I'm sure that's not a problem. Mike's going over to pick him up at 6:00. When we get back, I'll also talk to NASA about giving you a partial refund or a discount on a subsequent mission."

"That would be great if you can arrange it. Please let us know."

Mike called Jeffery at 5:50 to tell him he was about to leave to go to the alien ship. Jeffery asked him to call Garlut and let him know he was leaving and Mike said he had already done that.

Fifteen minutes later, Mike called to inform Jeffery he was on his way back, and there were three passengers: Garlut, Brealak, and Quat. Jeffery told him he would meet them at the shuttle bay.

To keep everybody comfortable they kept the ship's sub-light engine engaged at .5 g's.

They didn't go anywhere. The ship simply went in a five-hundred mile circle.

When the three aliens exited the shuttle bay, Jeffery was there to greet them. "Welcome aboard. Our crew and guests are excited to meet you."

Garlut said, "Captain Whitestone, this is Chief Engineer Quat." Jeffery and Quat nodded at each other. Jeffery guessed shaking hands when meeting someone was not an alien custom. Quat was very tall, perhaps six-foot-eight, and he was not as slender as Garlut or Brealak, but he wasn't fat. He looked enormously strong.

"We're meeting in the dining room. Please follow me. Garlut, I asked the guests onboard if it would be okay if we returned to Earth immediately. It's their decision because they paid a lot of money to be on this mission. They agreed in exchange for a guided tour of your ship. I told them I'd ask you about it."

"That is not a problem. In fact, if any of them are interested they can return to Earth on our ship. I am sure they would appreciate the constant gravity. The foods we eat are similar, and if your chef gives us samples of food, we can easily duplicate them and add them to our menu. Please tell them that when you speak to them."

"Of course, I'll be happy to do that."

When the group entered the dining room, everybody stood and applauded. Garlut said, "Thank you, but that is not necessary." He walked to the front of the room and said, "My name is Garlut. I am here with my daughter, Brealak, and my chief engineer, Quat. I am sure Captain Whitestone has told you about our meeting earlier today, so I will not go over any of those details again. However, I did want to discuss the possibility of ending your mission early and returning to Earth immediately. There is really nothing very exciting to see here, and we are anxious to meet with the people on Earth and negotiate a trade agreement. Captain Whitestone mentioned that some of you would like a tour of our ship. That can certainly be arranged. Additionally, if any of you would be interested in making the return trip to Earth on our ship, that can be arranged as well. I think we would both benefit from spending some time together. If any of you have any questions, I would be happy to answer them."

Thomas Mason, the zoologist, asked, "I'm sure you're familiar with the animals we have on Earth. Are they similar to animals on other planets?"

"Yes, they are similar in terms of species. Most planets have felines and canines, although you would probably not consider them cats and dogs. They also have reptiles, birds, fish, and some have amphibians. The inhabitants of most planets do not have pets, which you may find surprising, since pets are a very important part of Earth's culture. The variety of animals is amazing."

"Do you eat the same type of foods we eat?" asked April Barr, one of the two cooks onboard.

"We have much in common with the people of Earth. We are omnivores and we have animals similar to cattle that we raise for food. We also grow plants which are almost identical to wheat and sugar cane that we use to make a variety of things like breads, pasta, and various sweet foods. In case any of you choose to return to Earth on our ship you can try our foods, or if you prefer, we can get samples of the foods you like and prepare them for you."

Dr. Weber asked, "Is your physiology similar to ours?"

"Our DNA is different. We have more chromosomes than humans, but we have similar internal organs. We have two livers and only one large kidney. However, our kidneys are similar to your livers in that they can regenerate. We can also regenerate fingers and toes, but it takes a long time. Our life spans are somewhat longer too, about one hundred of our years, but our years are 50% longer than yours, and our days are 25% longer. If you would like to know more about us, I would be happy to have our doctor speak to you."

"Thank you. I'd like that very much," Dr. Weber replied.

"Garlut, my name is Ron Rice. I'm the chief engineer onboard the Star Rover. I also was part of the team that designed our wormhole drive system. It's my understanding you have the capability of moving your ship up to a velocity of five hundred times the speed of light. How was that accomplished?"

Before Garlut could answer the question, Quat spoke. "What we discovered was that if a ship enters the wormhole at a higher velocity, it will transverse it faster. If we must travel somewhere very quickly, we found that entering the wormhole at 50% of light speed will give us the greatest speed through the wormhole. For some reason, which we do not understand, going faster does not appear to have any additional speed advantage. Also, the speed increase does not become significant until the ship has a velocity of 25% of light speed. Coplent and Earth have similar mass, so the gravitational forces are almost identical. Like you, our bodies cannot withstand more than about 2 g's for any length of time, so we had to find a way of eliminating the effects of inertia. You have already experienced the way we did that. We discovered the laws of physics are not valid in a time stasis field, so during the acceleration phase the entire ship, with the exception of the propulsion systems, is placed into a time stasis field until our desired velocity is reached. Then, when the acceleration stops, the time stasis field is turned off and we can enter the wormhole. Our ships are capable of accelerating at 60 g's, but it still takes six of your days to reach 50% of light speed."

After a few seconds Ron responded, "Thank you for that information. I think, for now, we'll be content with our limited speed. One hundred and thirty-four times the speed of light is fast enough to get almost anywhere we want to go."

Mike asked, "You said there's a planetary trading association you wanted Earth to join. Is this a form of multi-planet government? Are the other members aware you've asked Earth to join the group?"

"It is not a multi-planet form of government. But we have all agreed to a general set of rules regarding trade between planets. The rules are simple. For example, we cannot misrepresent a product's capabilities. If we sell a product to perform a specific function, then it must perform that function. If it does not, the product can be returned for a full refund. If a seller cannot or will not give a refund, they are removed from the association. In the past fifteen hundred years that has never happened. It is also a violation of the rules to sell the same product for different amounts of money. We can set any price we like for a product, but we must always sell the product for the same price. We have a meeting every two years. At the last meeting I told the other members that Earth would probably have interstellar travel within ten years. I was given permission to offer you the opportunity to join the association when that happened. Are there any additional questions?"

"Yes, one more question. How do you pay for the goods you buy? Do you have an interstellar currency?" Mike asked.

"Every trading planet has an account at the Trade Association Bank. When goods are bought or sold, the information is sent to the bank and the appropriate accounts are debited or credited. If a planet does not have sufficient credit to cover a debit, they are asked to cover the shortfall with some type of asset. On Earth you used to use gold, but now you use silver. We use a very rare mineral called hirodim. It is similar to diamonds. Any planet that cannot cover a debit within a specified amount of time has their membership in the trading group suspended until the debit is covered. That has only happened once."

"If Earth doesn't have any hirodim, how can we join your trading group?"

"Typically, this is not necessary. New members usually only sell for a while before they start buying. That way they build up a credit balance. However, if Earth needs hirodim, I am sure Coplent can find something of value to trade for it. Please understand we trade many things other than technology. Most planets have unique spices, plants, or even animals that can be traded. We will explain all this to your World Council during our meeting. Please understand that our trading group has rules, but they are easy to follow and are meant to be beneficial to all the member planets. Are there any more questions?"

Nobody asked anything so Garlut said, "I wanted to let you know I will contact Captain Whitestone in the morning with a schedule so anyone who is interested can take a tour of our ship. While onboard, if you decide that you want to return to Earth on our ship, please let me know. Dr. Weber, please come over to our ship tomorrow with the tour group and I will make sure you have an opportunity to meet with our ship's doctor. Captain Whitestone, you promised us a tour of your ship. Can we do that now?"

"Of course, please follow me." He turned to Ron and said, "Ron, please come with us in case they have a question I can't answer."

They spent four hours looking at every part of the ship, then Jeffery took them back to their ship. When Jeffery got back to the Star Rover he went to the bridge because his shift there was about to start and Debbie's was ending. He walked up to her and said under his breath, "Don't forget about our date tomorrow morning."

She smiled at him and said, "I've been thinking about it all evening."

Jeffery's shift was boring. Nothing happened and he almost dozed off a few times. At 7:55 Mike came in to relieve him. Jeffery looked at him and said, "The ship is yours. Have fun," and then he left to go on his date with Debbie.

When he arrived at the room, the door was slightly ajar so he walked in. Debbie was lying on the bed, naked. He closed the door and turned to look at her. She got up and walked toward him. They embraced and kissed passionately. Then Jeffery quickly removed his clothes and they moved to the bed. Their lust took over, and it took an hour until both of them were finally satisfied. Debbie looked at Jeffery and said softly, "That was wonderful. I love you and I'm sure you love me. We have to be together. We shouldn't have to sneak around to spend time with each other."

"Deb, you're right. I love you and want to be with you. When we get back to Earth, I'll tell Max we're going to get married. What do you think he'll say?"

"I think he'll say two things: 'congratulations,' followed by, 'you're fired.' You know that violates NASA rules."

"Yes, but we're big celebrities now. I don't think Max would want the negative publicity associated with firing us, or changing our jobs. I'm willing to take the risk."

"Me too."

They stayed in bed and talked about the future for a while. Then Jeffery received a call from Garlut telling him they were ready to receive visitors. Jeffery said they would be there in a half hour. He announced that anybody who wanted to take a tour of the alien ship should proceed to the shuttle bay. Debbie told him she would take them over to the alien ship, so Jeffery could get some much-needed rest.

207

All ten of the guests, Dr. Weber, Ron Rice, and Beatrice Woods, the mission photographer, were waiting for Debbie at the shuttle bay. She took them over to the alien ship. After the passengers all got out of the shuttle, Brealak asked Debbie if she was going to stay. Debbie said she had to get back to the Star Rover and asked Brealak to call her when they were ready to return.

When Debbie got back to the Star Rover, she went to the dining room and sat down with a cup of coffee. She hoped she and Jeffery made the right decision. At that moment Linda Gonzalez, the ship's nurse, walked into the dining room. She got a cup of coffee, walked over to Debbie and said, "You look deep in thought. Would you like some company?"

Debbie looked up at Linda, smiled, and said, "Sure, I could use some company right now."

"What's wrong?"

"My life, well more specifically, my love life. It's almost nonexistent."

"You do know your relationship with our captain is one of the worst kept secrets onboard. Is that what's bothering you?"

"Jeffery and I decided that when we get back to Earth we're going to tell our boss we're getting married. But both of us love our jobs and we don't want to lose them."

"I know it's against NASA regulations, but I don't think they'll do anything. You two are returning as heroes. They won't take any action that would reflect badly on NASA."

"That's what Jeffery said, so I guess I should stop worrying. Does everybody onboard know about us?"

"I think so. In any case I wouldn't worry about it. If you two want to spend time together, just do it."

"Thank you, Linda. I appreciate your advice."

"Don't just appreciate it. Take it!" Linda exclaimed with a laugh.

"Okay, I will. If NASA decides Jeffery and I are unfit, then the hell with them," Debbie said resolutely.

The trip to the alien ship went very well. All of the guests decided to return to Earth on the alien ship. Dr. Weber spent the entire time with the doctor from the ship and came back impressed with the aliens' medical equipment and technology. Ron Rice was overwhelmed with what he had seen on the ship and was hoping that they would be willing to give Earth most of what he saw.

That evening at dinner, Jeffery spoke to the crew and guests. "Tomorrow morning we'll take all of our guests over to the alien ship. As soon as the shuttle is back aboard, we'll start our return to Earth. Since it will be only the crew onboard the Star Rover, we'll be traveling by wormhole for the entire trip except for one hour per day. That will give us an opportunity to contact the alien ship and make sure their guests are okay. Although the alien ship can travel much faster than we can, they're going to match our speed and course. We should arrive back at Earth in forty days."

The following morning everything went as planned, and by 10:30 the shuttle was back onboard.

Fifteen minutes later, the Star Rover started the return trip to Earth. After the ship's journey started, Debbie moved her things into Jeffery's quarters, so now the relationship was obvious to all onboard.

The trip back to Earth went exactly as planned. Every day the two ships stopped within one hundred miles of each other. Jeffery checked to be sure his guests were okay, and during the entire trip there was only one minor problem: one of the guests had a severe migraine headache and had left his medication on the Star Rover. Apparently, that was something the alien doctor had never encountered before. To resolve the problem the alien ship moved to a distance of only three miles from the Star Rover and used the transporter to move the medication from the Star Rover to the alien ship.

At the stop on the day before they were scheduled to arrive near Earth, Jeffery called Garlut and asked him to time his arrival near Earth eight hours after he arrived so he could make sure the appearance of the alien ship would not cause any panic. Garlut agreed.

On the following day, May 6, 2120, the Star Rover exited the wormhole fifty thousand miles from Earth. Jeffery immediately called Max. The timing was good because it was 1:30 in the afternoon in Florida where Max's office was located. Max wasn't in his office, but Jeffery spoke to his assistant, who was surprised to hear from Jeffery, but immediately promised to find Max when Jeffery told him it was urgent. A minute later Jeffery heard Max say, "Why are you back so soon? Is there a problem?"

"No, there isn't a problem, but there is a situation I need to make you aware of immediately."

"It must be important for you to cut short a mission that cost slightly more than a trillion dollars," Max said rather dryly.

"It's that important." Jeffery spent the next several minutes telling Max about the meeting with the aliens, and that Garlut wanted to meet with the World Council.

Jeffery stopped speaking and it was several seconds later that Max finally began to speak. "I don't know what to say. We were hoping you would meet with the aliens, but we didn't expect you to bring them home for dinner. I think this is really good news. I'll call President Winters and let him know about this immediately. Where are you now?"

"About fifty thousand miles from Earth."

"Did the ship function correctly? Is there anything else I should be aware of?"

"The answer to both questions is, 'Yes.' The ship functioned perfectly. The other thing you should be aware of is that Debbie and I are going to be married as soon as we get back on Earth."

"I knew there was something going on between you two. But you obviously work together very well, so you have my blessing. I'm not sure how some of the other people at NASA will feel about it, but don't be concerned. I'll handle any problem that comes up. I hope you'll invite me to the wedding."

"Max, you'll be the first person we invite."

210

"You and Debbie did a terrific job. I'm sure the president will want to congratulate you too. I have to call him now and will talk to you again after I've spoken to him."

Debbie was on the bridge next to Jeffery and she heard his half of the conversation. As soon as Jeffery ended the call to Max, she looked at him with a worried look on her face. Jeffery smiled at her and said, "Max wants to be invited to the wedding and said we did a terrific job. He promised that if there are any objections to our marriage, he'll handle them."

She threw her arms around him and they kissed. The crew on the bridge applauded.

Fifteen minutes later, Max called Jeffery. "I just spoke to President Winters," Max told him. "He's going to call an emergency meeting of the World Council on Thursday, three days from today. The meeting will be at the Council Headquarters in New York. We would like Garlut, and any of his crew that he would like to bring with him to the meeting, to stay on the space station until Thursday morning. Then we'd like you, Debbie, and a few security people to escort him to the meeting. We also want you and Debbie to stay close to him while he's on the space station in case there are any problems. Is this okay with you?"

"Yes sir, I realize how important this is and I appreciate the trust you're placing in us."

"Make sure Garlut gets anything he needs while he's on the space station. My assistant has already contacted the station and they'll have two suites ready for him."

"Okay, I'm expecting him to be here in a few minutes. I'll let him know the schedule and if there are any problems, I'll let you know."

"Jeffery, please call me after you speak with him. Even if there are no problems, I want to be aware of what's happening."

"Yes sir, I'll do that."

Max said, "Thank you," and ended the call.

Several hours later, the alien ship materialized three miles from the Star Rover. Garlut contacted Jeffery and said,

"It is nice to be back by Earth and not have to hide. Did you arrange for a meeting with your World Council?"

"Yes, the meeting will be in three days. It will be at the World Council Headquarters in New York City. While you're waiting, they'd like you and any of your crew you'd like to accompany you to the meeting to be our guests at the hotel in the space station. It will give all of you an opportunity to experience Earth culture firsthand. You won't have to observe us from a distance anymore. Debbie and I will also be staying on the station to help you with anything you may need. We'll also escort you to the meeting."

"Thank you. Only Brealak and I will be attending the meeting. The rest of my crew will remain on our ship. However, I would like for them to have an opportunity to spend some time on the space station, if only for a few hours."

"That would be okay. I'll make all the arrangements with the manager of the station. Just let me know when you would like to schedule the visits. I'm sure you realize they'll have to speak English." Jeffery said.

"I will make sure there is an English-speaking person in every group."

"That will be perfect. Please move your ship two miles from the space station. I'm moving the Star Rover as well. Once we're both ready we'll use our shuttle to transport you and Brealak to the space station."

"Understood. I will move our ship after you move the Star Rover."

"Please contact me when you and Brealak are ready to be picked up."

"I will do that."

A few minutes later, Jeffery moved the Star Rover near the space station and the alien ship appeared a mile off their port side. Garlut contacted the Star Rover to let them know they were ready. Jeffery, Debbie, and Mike went to the shuttle. Mike was going to take them to the space station and then return to the Star Rover.

As the shuttle approached the alien ship, the docking bay door appeared and Mike flew the shuttle inside and landed. Just a few seconds after the area was pressurized, there was a knock on the shuttle door. Mike opened it and Garlut and Brealak stepped inside, each carrying a small case. Mike closed the door and when the opening appeared again, he flew out and took them to the space station.

Garlut said to Jeffery, "I am pleased you and Debbie will be with us. It is always easier to get adjusted to new civilizations when we have somebody with us that we know and trust."

"Thank you. Debbie and I are very familiar with the station, and we'll make every effort to keep you comfortable there. I've been meaning to ask you a question for a while now. It's not important, but I was wondering if your ship has a name?"

"It does, but it is not pronounceable in English. I know you have been calling it the 'alien ship' and that is fine with me. Since I expect we will be making frequent trips here in the future, I will give the ship a name that humans can pronounce."

"You could keep it simple and call it Garlut's ship."

"I could, but I will try to think up something a little better."

When they were three hundred feet from the station, Mike stopped the shuttle, waiting for a docking bay to open. A few seconds later a bay opened and Mike flew inside and landed the shuttle. When the bay was pressurized, Mike opened the shuttle door and the four passengers got out and walked to the door to enter the station. They could see through the glass in the door that a small crowd had gathered, including Bruce Mann, who was in charge of station operations.

Jeffery turned to Garlut and asked, "As you can see there are a bunch of people waiting to see you. Is that okay or do you want me to have them dispersed?"

"Jeffery, I expect crowds everywhere I go. It is not a problem."

Jeffery said, "Okay then," and he opened the door.

Brealak went through first, followed by Garlut and Debbie. Then Jeffery stepped inside.

213

Bruce Mann was in the front of the group. He stared at Garlut, slowly walked to within two feet of him and stammering said, "M-my name is Bruce. I'm the operations m-manager for this station. If there's anything I . . . I can do to make your stay here more comfortable, please don't hesitate to ask."

"Thank you, Bruce. My name is Garlut. This is my daughter, Brealak. It is my understanding that Captain Whitestone and Commander Murphy will be helping us get accustomed to this space station."

"Of course. I was simply offering my service in addition to theirs should you need anything. Please allow me to show you to your rooms."

"Thank you, Bruce, but Brealak and I will be sharing a room, if that is all right with you."

"That's no problem at all."

"Do you have a room for Jeffery and Debbie as well?"

"They have rooms in the crew area of the station. If you would prefer, I can give them rooms next to yours."

"Thank you. That would be my preference."

"Please follow me."

Someone from NASA was making a video of Garlut's arrival, and he followed them through the station to the hotel area. Everybody, including the NASA videographer, followed Bruce to the suite. Bruce opened the door into a very large living area. There were two sofas and two large reclining chairs. A large window was opposite the door and through it was a fantastic view of Earth. The room also had a fully stocked bar and an eighty-five-inch video screen. Midway down each of the side walls of the room were doors. Bruce walked over to one and opened it. Inside was a lavishly furnished bedroom that was a little smaller than the living area. There was an enormous bed, a dresser, a video screen, and a recliner identical to the ones in the living room. There was a large area to hang clothes and an open door that led to a massive bath room. Bruce said, "I hope you like your accommodations. There's an identical bedroom on the other

214

side of the living room. I'll leave you alone now, but as I said before, if you need anything please don't hesitate to ask."

"Thank you, Bruce. The accommodations are excellent. The only thing we need is a supply of water."

"I'll have that brought over immediately. Also, Jeffery and Debbie will be in the room right next to yours. You're in room 110 and they'll be in room 111."

"Thank you again, Bruce. You are an excellent host." Then Garlut turned to Jeffery and Debbie and asked, "Would you two mind staying here for a few minutes?"

"Of course not," Jeffery replied and then motioned everybody else to leave.

After everybody else had left, Garlut said, "I noticed there was a man following us around with a camera. Is that a usual practice?"

"No, but you are the first aliens they've ever seen, so that makes your arrival important news. I suspect he'll be following you around while the two of you are on the station. When you're on Earth, there'll probably be a lot of people following you around with cameras. Is it a problem for you?" Jeffery asked.

"No, I suppose that is all right. I did not ask you to suppress the information about our visit to Earth, so I really cannot object. Are there dining rooms on the station?"

"I think you mean restaurants and there are several on the station. The best one is part of this hotel."

"Do they not all serve the same food?"

"No, they all serve different kinds of foods. Some are more expensive than others."

"You mean you have to pay to eat?"

"Yes, except in your case NASA is paying all of your expenses."

"Is NASA paying for this room too?"

"Yes. Is it unusual to pay for things on other planets?"

"On most of them, it is not customary to charge guests for rooms or food. However, most of the planets do not have hotels and restaurants. Typically, when I visit other planets, I stay at the home of the person I am visiting and they provide me with food."

"That happens on Earth too. If I travel to visit friends, I often stay with them. If staying in a hotel makes you uncomfortable, I'm sure I can find somebody from NASA who'd be happy to have you as a guest."

"That is not necessary." Garlut seemed to think for a moment. "Do you have a home on Earth?"

"Not really. When I'm on Earth I either stay at NASA facilities or with my parents. They have a home in Boca Raton. That's a city in Florida. However, Debbie and I are going to be married, and I'm sure after the next mission we'll find a home on Earth so we can live together."

"Perhaps on my next visit I can stay with you. Would that be possible?"

"It would be okay with me, but I suspect the World Council would prefer you stayed at a more secure location."

"Yes, I understand that. I noticed Bruce had a problem with Brealak and me sharing a room. Is that a violation of some Earth custom?"

"No, not really. Parents and young children always share rooms. It's less common with parents and adult children."

"Would you two like to have dinner with Brealak and me?"

Jeffery looked at Debbie, who nodded, and said, "We'd like that very much. We'll come back in an hour. Is that okay?"

"Yes, that will be fine."

Jeffery and Debbie smiled at Garlut and Brealak. Then they left and went to their room. It was identical to the room Garlut and Brealak had. Jeffery asked, with a small laugh, "So which bedroom do you want?"

"You do know that sometimes you act like an idiot, but if you really want to sleep in separate rooms, please let me know now." Debbie replied with a note of sarcasm.

"You don't have to take me seriously all the time, you know."

216

"I'm beginning to think that unless we're on the ship I should never take you seriously. Anyway, we should go get our stuff and bring it here. This is much nicer than our rooms in the crew quarters."

They were back in their room a few minutes later. The first thing Jeffery did was call Max and let him know how things were going with Garlut. Max was pleased with Jeffery's report and he asked him to call him back after dinner.

At the appropriate time, Jeffery and Debbie knocked on the door to Garlut's room. He opened the door a few seconds later and said, "You're right on time." Then Garlut asked, "Are Brealak and I dressed correctly for dinner?"

They were both dressed in the same style uniforms they had been wearing before, except they were light brown. Debbie said, "You both look fine."

"Let's go," Jeffery said. The four of them left the room and walked to the hotel restaurant.

Jeffery had called earlier and made a reservation, so they were seated immediately at a table next to a large window. Each of them was given a menu and the hostess asked if they wanted anything to drink. They all ordered water. After the hostess left, they opened their menus. Jeffery immediately noticed there were no prices, and that made him happy. He didn't want to explain why some items cost more than others. Jeffery noticed a confused look on the faces of his guests. He asked, "Is there a problem with the menu?"

"Do we order all of these items? It seems like it would be too much to eat."

Jeffery did his best not to laugh. "No, you pick one item from each group. So, from the group 'Soups and Salads' you pick something you would like. Then you pick one item in the 'Entrée' group, and two items from the 'Sides' group. If you don't know what something is, please ask."

"Jeffery, I have no idea what I want, and I am sure Brealak does not know what she wants either. Please order for us. I am sure anything you select will be good."

Debbie asked, "How about if we start with a Caesar salad, followed by a bowl of lobster bisque. Then for the entrée, veal cordon bleu, French fries, and the broccoli cheese casserole?"

Jeffery said, "That sounds wonderful. I think we should all have that."

Garlut said, "I thought English was the language used on the station, but part of that was in French. Anyway, I have no idea what any of it is, but I am sure it will be good."

"The food here is excellent. It'll be better than good," Debbie said with a smile.

After a few minutes, the waiter came over to the table to take their order. Jeffery ordered for everybody. The waiter complimented them on their food selection and left. He returned to the table a few moments later with a basket full of small cinnamon rolls.

Garlut looked at the rolls and asked, "Did we order these? They smell wonderful."

Debbie replied, "No, we didn't order them. They give them to everybody who comes here to eat. They actually taste better than they smell. Try one."

Garlut and Brealak both picked up a cinnamon roll and began to eat them. Almost instantly they looked at each other and smiled. Brealak said, "These are wonderful. I do not think I have ever tasted anything this good." Then, looking at her father, she asked, "Do you like them too?"

"I think they may be the best thing I have ever tasted!"

There were at least a dozen rolls in the basket. Jeffery and Debbie each ate one and the rest were consumed by Garlut and Brealak.

"What are these things made with?" Garlut asked.

"The primary flavor is called cinnamon. I would guess the other ingredients are wheat flour, sugar, eggs, and butter," Debbie replied.

"Where does cinnamon come from?"

"It comes from the inner bark of some types of what we call evergreen trees."

"The taste is definitely unique. It is a product Earth should consider exporting."

A few minutes later, the waiter brought the bowls of lobster bisque, and when he noticed that the basket of cinnamon rolls was empty, he asked if they wanted more. Brealak said, "Yes, they are wonderful."

Garlut and Brealak also liked the lobster bisque and the salad, but not as much as the cinnamon rolls. When the waiter brought the main course, the two aliens appeared to eat as if they had never eaten before. They both ate every morsel of food on their plates. Then Garlut asked, "Is all the food on Earth this good?"

Jeffery smiled and said, "The economy on Earth improved substantially after the invention of the power module. As a result, this kind of food is available almost everywhere. However, the food at this restaurant is better than most. Why do you ask?"

"Because this food is not typical of what is available on other planets. I believe Earth could create a very profitable tourist area offering food this good."

"You should mention that to the World Council when you speak to them."

"I will certainly do that."

Then Jeffery asked, "Do you know what chocolate is?"

"No, not really. I have seen it mentioned in videos, but we have never tasted it. Is it as good as the cinnamon?"

"It has a completely different taste and texture, but I think it's better. This restaurant offers a dessert called a chocolate fondue. It includes various types of foods you dip into liquid chocolate. I think we should order that."

When the waiter came over to pick the dishes up, Jeffery ordered chocolate fondue for dessert. He nodded in agreement and said that was an excellent choice.

When the waiter brought the fondue, Jeffery could tell his guests were anxious to try it. There was a large pot filled with the liquid chocolate and surrounding it were sliced apples, sliced bananas, small thin crispy crepes, and marshmallows. Jeffery picked up one of the crepes, dipped it into the chocolate, and ate it. Then Garlut and Brealak did the same thing. Once again, they appeared to be very happy with this new experience.

After tasting the crepe, Garlut said, "I may spend the rest of my life here. This is wonderful."

Jeffery showed them how to use the small forks to pick up the other items on the tray. In less than ten minutes everything was gone.

Brealak said, "This was, by far, the best meal I have ever eaten. But I do not think I could eat anything else, no matter how good it is."

"I think we're all quite full. Would you like us to show you around the station?" Debbie asked.

"That would be perfect," Garlut responded.

They walked around the station for forty-five minutes. Garlut and Brealak seemed to like what they saw. They asked a few questions which were quickly answered and then walked back to their rooms. Garlut thanked them for a wonderful evening and Garlut and Brealak went inside their room.

The next morning, Jeffery received a call from Garlut asking him and Debbie to come to his room. Jeffery told him they would be there in ten minutes. Jeffery and Debbie had been having coffee in their room when the call came. They had already showered, but were not dressed yet. They both dressed quickly and went to Garlut's room.

They knocked on the door and Brealak open the door immediately.

"We came over as quickly as we could. Is there a problem?" Jeffery asked.

"Not at all. We would like your help in preparing our presentation to your World Council. Do you know any of the members of the council?"

"No, I've never met any of them, but Debbie and I will be happy to assist you in any way we can."

"I think Garlut and I learned a lot last night about Earth culture. We have been studying Earth for a long time, but we were not looking at how individual people behaved. Earth seems to be somewhat unique in that everybody is different. You all have different desires. You want to achieve different things during your life. We have watched some of your video programs and we thought they were pure fiction, but many of them now seem to be based on real human emotions.

"Most of the cultures we deal with are not like that. On most planets, one's future is determined at the time one is born. Education is designed to provide the knowledge needed to perform the job that will be assigned. Our social life is more open. We are free to choose a partner, but male and female partners are always from the same social class. It obviously is not that way on Earth."

At that moment, Garlut walked into the living room and said, "Good morning. I am glad you are here. I think we really need your help."

"Brealak was just explaining that last evening you discovered you had some misconceptions regarding Earth's culture. But I don't understand how having dinner with us and our tour of the station could have created that feeling."

"Jeffery, it was more than our dinner and tour. Brealak and I watched news videos for several hours last night and that was when we realized we do not know as much about Earth as we would like. You must understand, this meeting with your World Council is very important to us. As you know, we do not make any attempt to contact a planet until its people achieve interstellar travel. Earth is the first planet in the group I am responsible for that has reached this goal in more than five hundred years. I will only have this opportunity once, and I want to make sure we do our presentation correctly. As I have often heard watching Earth videos, 'You only get one chance to make a good first impression.'"

"Now I understand your concern. As I said before, Debbie and I'll do anything we can to help."

"What do you know about the members of the World Council?"

"I don't know anything specific about them. However, my feeling is that the members of the council are motivated by a desire to help the people whom they represent first and all the people of Earth second. Being a member of the council is a lot of responsibility and the job does not pay very much.

Politics on Earth has changed a lot in the last hundred years. A hundred years ago, politics was all about money. If you had enough, you could give it to a person in power to convince them to do something you wanted done. It would be impossible to do that now without being caught, so that doesn't happen anymore. If you can make them believe the trade agreement will be good for Earth, I'm sure they'll agree to join your trading association."

"I hope you are right. What do you think they would find enticing?"

"I think the offer of advanced technology would be important. I also think they'll like the idea of having interactions with people of alien races. Again, you know our history. We fought wars over religion and skin color for more than five thousand years. It was only in the last century that world peace was finally achieved. The acceptance of other people isn't based on how they look, but how they act is important to them. I'm sure they'd like to have an opportunity to test that with aliens."

"I believe Earth has at least three unique things that would be in large demand by our trading group: the power units, cinnamon, and chocolate. I am certain there are more items that I am unaware of, but as we spend more time here, those things will become obvious."

"I think if you tell the World Council what you just said, there won't be any problems. Advanced technology in exchange for the power module design, cinnamon, and chocolate is an excellent trade. I'm certain they'll agree."

Garlut looked at Brealak and they both appeared to accept what Jeffery had told them. Then Garlut said, "It will definitely be different dealing with people who are not motivated by greed. I think that was what we were worried about. We had no idea how we were going to allow them to benefit personally from the trade agreement. I would still like you two to help me write my speech."

"As I said before, Debbie and I will do anything we can to help make your mission here a success. However, I'm expecting to get something I really want out of this agreement.

222

I want to know how to create artificial gravity for the Star Rover before our next mission."

"I can promise you that will happen. It is not as difficult as one might think."

The four of them spent the rest of the day working on Garlut's presentation, stopping only briefly for a lunch break. Then they went out for another excellent dinner at the hotel restaurant. Once again, Garlut and Brealak were very impressed with the food. After dinner, Garlut asked if it would be possible for him and Brealak to return to their ship for the night. They also wanted to make arrangements for groups of their crew to come over to the station. Jeffery called Mike and asked him to bring the shuttle over to the station. When Mike got there, the four of them went into the shuttle for the short trip to Garlut's ship.

Once they were inside, they all went to a small conference room and set up a schedule for the crew members to go over to the station in groups of ten. Each group would have three hours on the station. Jeffery called Bruce to make him aware of the schedule, and asked him to use one of the space station's shuttles to transport the visitors since Galut's shuttle was too big to park inside the station. It was also decided that someone from Bruce's staff would give each group a tour of the station and then take them to the hotel restaurant for a meal.

As they were leaving, Garlut told Jeffery that he and Brealak would return to the station with the first tour group. Mike took Jeffery and Debbie back to the station and he went to the Star Rover.

When Jeffery and Debbie got back to their room, Jeffery called Max to tell him how the day went. Once again, Max was pleased with his report. He asked Jeffery if he thought it would be okay to give the World Council the information they just discussed. Jeffery thought about it for a few moments, then he told Max that although Garlut had not asked him to keep it secret, but he didn't want Garlut to think anything said to him would be immediately reported. Max agreed he wouldn't speak to President Winters about it.

The first group of crew members was scheduled to arrive at 10:00 AM, and at 10:10 Jeffery received a call from Garlut. He asked if it would be okay if he and Brealak relaxed in the room for the day. Jeffery said that was okay and he asked him if they wanted to have dinner together. Garlut quickly agreed. It was decided that they would meet in the hotel's restaurant at 6:00 PM.

In the early afternoon, Jeffery received a call from Max, who told him a chartered shuttle would pick up the four of them at 9:30 on Thursday morning. The shuttle would take them to the New York City Shuttle Port and would arrive there at 11:00. Then a car would be waiting to take them on the five-minute trip to the World Council Headquarters building. The meeting was scheduled for 11:30 and would be followed by a formal lunch. Jeffery said he would let Garlut know the schedule, and if there was a problem, he would inform Max immediately.

The dinner went well that evening. The restaurant was offering Italian food so they ordered a small pepperoni pizza as an appetizer. That was followed by a bowl of Italian chicken soup, and for the entrée they ordered lasagna. For dessert this time, they ordered crème brûlée. Once again, the meal was an enormous hit.

On the way back to their rooms, Jeffery said, "I should have mentioned this to you earlier. The shuttle will pick us up at 9:30 tomorrow morning for the trip to New York. The trip will take ninety minutes."

"Understood. Will you and Debbie be there too?" Garlut asked.

"Yes, we'll be there. Don't worry. I'm sure everything will be okay. Did your crew like the space station?"

"Yes, they took a vote and decided Earth was going to be their favorite port of call. A few of them asked if they could be assigned here."

"I'm glad they had a good time. We'll knock on your door at 9:15. Have a good evening."

Garlut said, "Goodnight," as he and Brealak went into their room.

Jeffery and Debbie talked a while about what was going to happen tomorrow. Jeffery was glad they were going to be in a secured official car, so no reporters would bother them or their alien friends. Debbie said she was nervous about meeting the members of the World Council, and Jeffery was a little nervous about it too. They talked until midnight when they finally decided to go to sleep.

THE WORLD COUNCIL MEETING

Jeffery and Debbie woke up early, showered, and dressed in their NASA uniforms. Then they went to the restaurant for breakfast, but neither of them were hungry and all they ordered was coffee. They knocked on Garlut's door exactly at 9:15. Garlut opened the door immediately and said, "Good morning, we are ready to go."

The four of them walked in silence to the shuttle bay. When they arrived, they discovered the shuttle had been waiting for them for almost an hour. They boarded the shuttle, which had a capacity of thirty, but they were the only passengers onboard. After the shuttle departed the station, Garlut asked, "Are these flights usually this empty?"

"No, this shuttle was chartered just for us. Normally there are about twenty people onboard. I'm sure they chartered the shuttle for security reasons," Jeffery replied.

The flight to New York was perfect. When they arrived at the terminal there were ten armed security guards waiting for them. There was also a woman from the World Council with the guards. She was gazing intently at Garlut and haltingly said, "Good morning. Please forgive me for staring, but I've never seen an alien before. My name's Heather Swift and I'm an assistant to President Winters. I'm here with a security team to escort you to the meeting."

"Good morning, Heather. I'm Captain Jeffery Whitestone. I'd like to introduce our guests." He pointed to Garlut and said, "This is Garlut from the planet Coplent, and next to him is his daughter, Brealak." Turning toward Debbie, he said, "This is my executive officer, Commander Debbie Murphy."

"It's a pleasure to meet all of you. Please follow me."

Five guards led the procession. They were followed by Heather, the aliens, Jeffery, and Debbie. Behind Debbie were the remaining guards. They proceeded out of the terminal into the parking lot where there were three vehicles with tinted windows waiting for them. Three guards got into the first vehicle. Two guards, Heather, and the rest of the group went into the second vehicle, and the remaining guards got into the last vehicle. The drive over to the World Council building only took a few minutes. In the courtyard in front of the building, more than a thousand people awaited them. Heather said, "They're here hoping to see an alien for the first time, but we'll go into the underground parking area."

They drove around the side of the building, where another contingent of guards was blocking the entrance to the parking area. The guards separated to allow the vehicles to drive in, and then they immediately closed ranks again. Once inside the building, the vehicle containing Heather and her group stopped next to an elevator. The five of them plus the two security guards rode the elevator up to the 60th floor where the conference room was located.

As the elevator door opened, a large crowd of people began to applaud. There were also ten photographers and a few more security guards. Heather, Garlut, Brealak, Jeffery, and Debbie were moved through the crowd into the conference room. Seated at a large table were the members of the World Council. There was a smaller table directly in front of the table where the council members sat and Heather indicated they should sit there. When the group was seated, each of the council members introduced themselves. When they were finished, Heather told Garlut it was his turn to speak.

Garlut stood up and said, "Good morning. My name is Garlut. I am here with my daughter, Brealak, and two new friends, Captain Jeffery Whitestone and Commander Debbie Murphy. I am sure you have all read the reports, so you know we have been studying Earth for a long time. I will not go into much detail here, but part of my mission is to make contact with planets when they develop interstellar travel. You should be very proud of the fact that your scientists and engineers developed interstellar travel only twenty years after you perfected travel within your solar system. That often takes hundreds of years.

"We began to keep a closer watch on Earth after you landed a probe on Ganymede. What really caught our interest was the power source for the probe. We were monitoring your

228

video and radio transmissions so we were aware of the power source, but we had never seen one. That was why we took your probe. We wanted to study the power source to determine if we could duplicate it. We thought we could get it back to Ganymede before you noticed it was missing. I must apologize for taking it. But by our laws we could not legally contact you until you had achieved interstellar travel. We were unable to duplicate it. We also took a power unit from the storage area on the Star Rover. It is not our way to steal things and we intend to make it up to you. Even though our technology is thousands of years more advanced than yours, we still could not figure out how to make them.

"When the Star Rover made its first interstellar trip, we decided it was time for us to finally meet. That is why I am here today. I represent a trading group made up of four hundred seven planets. My goal today is to make Earth the newest member. Every planet has unique resources or products that are wanted by the population on other planets. During the brief time I spent on your space station, I found two items I can guarantee will be in high demand, cinnamon and chocolate. There will also be substantial demand for the power units you manufacture. These three items alone could create a substantial benefit for the people of Earth. I am certain as I spend more time here, I will be able to identify many more items that can be sold through the trading group.

"I must tell you I have travelled to more than half of the four hundred and seven member planets and not one of them can match the food that was available on the space station. Earth could easily start a very profitable tourist business."

At this point Garlut paused and looked at his audience. They were all staring at him, so he continued, "However, I am also sure that Earth would be interested in buying products from other planets as well. Our planet has developed artificial gravity that can be used on your ships. We have a molecular transportation device that allows us to move any non-living object from one place to another within a five-mile radius. We used it on the journey here from Gliese 876 to move some

229

medication that was needed by one of our passengers from the Star Rover to my ship. We have a device that allows us to see through solid objects, and we have a device that can create a time stasis field we use to allow our ships and crew to accelerate to half the speed of light in six days. That requires a force equivalent to more than 60 g's on Earth. Without the time stasis field, no known living organism could survive that amount of gravitational force.

"One of our member planets specializes in medicine. They have found cures for almost every known disease on my home planet. As a result, our life expectancy has increased by more than 50% since we joined the group.

"I have told you about only a small fraction of the goods and services available. If you join our group, many of the closer planets will send trade delegations to Earth. They will explain to you in detail what they can offer to Earth and at the same time you can tell them what products Earth can offer. In the end, everybody will benefit. Also, one of the planets has developed a language translation system. The device has already been loaded with the Earth languages of English and French. This device will completely eliminate communication problems. Before I leave Earth, I will give you five of them as compensation for your probe and power unit I took.

"You should be aware that the funds for the trades are handled by a bank where all member planets have accounts. If you join our group, a branch of that bank will be opened on Earth. When something is purchased or sold, no matter how large or small, your account will be credited or debited as required. New members usually only sell for a while until they build up sufficient credits to begin purchasing items. We do have something we use as an interstellar currency. It is a very rare mineral called hirodim. It is similar to the diamonds you have on Earth, but it is slightly harder and dark blue in color. All small items are priced in fractions of one cubic centimeter of hirodim, referred to as a *hirodim block*. I am not very knowledgeable about money on Earth, but I would guess one hirodim block is worth about $100,000,000. For example, the translators I am going to give you each cost .0019 of a hirodim block. My entire ship would cost two thousand hirodim blocks. Should you decide to join us, the trading group will set up an office on Earth and the people who work there will help make sure your products are priced correctly. They can also assist you in locating products you need or finding additional products to sell. I will also be available to help you should the need arise.

"I realize that joining our association will mean a constant flow of aliens to and from Earth. All of the lifeforms in our group are humanoid. As a matter of fact, with rare exceptions, all of the intelligent lifeforms we have found in the galaxy are humanoid. They may look a little different, but for all enlightened civilizations, that is not a problem. They have two things in common: none of them are hostile and all of them are looking for a bargain.

"Finally, I want to let you know that you have nothing to lose by joining our association and much to gain. However, if you want to think about it, please feel free to do so. I will stay here for ten more days. If you have any questions, please contact me through Captain Whitestone. Thank you for your time."

Garlut sat down at the table and the members of the council began quietly discussing his proposal. Then President Winters asked, "Mr. Garlut, if Earth decides to join your association, can we withdraw from it if we desire?"

"Please call me Garlut. The title is unnecessary. There is actually nothing to withdraw from. We would ask that you notify the bank you will no longer be trading. No planet has ever withdrawn from it, but there is certainly no obligation to be a member."

"How soon would the flow of aliens begin?"

"The first group to come would be from the bank and one or two people who are employed by the trade association. They would probably be here in sixty days. The employees of the trade association will put together a report regarding the products Earth has to trade, and that report will be sent to all the member planets. The members who are interested will first send a delegation of three or four people to evaluate the trading potential. If they like what they see, and I am sure they will, they will want to establish a permanent embassy here. That will probably take more than a year. I would suggest that should you make the decision to join us, you should immediately employ several people who can act as a liaison between the trade association or the member planet representatives and your council. I am sure you do not want to be involved in every decision. However, to answer your question, it will probably be two years before large numbers of aliens would be coming here."

President Winters said, "You've given us a lot to think about, but I feel certain we'll have a decision no later than Saturday."

Garlut finished by saying, "Thank you, sir. I am looking forward to your response." Then he sat down.

President Winters said, "Garlut, I hope you will join us for lunch today."

"It will be my pleasure."

The lunch went well. There were three tables set up and President Winters, Garlut, Brealak, Jeffery, Debbie, and Heather were all seated together at one of them. Conversation was minimal. Jeffery and Debbie were very uncomfortable being seated at the same table as the most powerful people on Earth, but as the meal continued, they became more at ease. Most of the conversation was between President Winters and Garlut. As the lunch was breaking up, President Winters told Garlut the council would be meeting in the afternoon to discuss his proposal and they would contact Jeffery as soon as their decision was made. Garlut thanked him for his time. Then the President excused himself and left the table. A few moments later, Heather got up and asked, "Garlut, do you want to stay in New York or would you rather go back to the space station?"

"I think I would like to go back to the space station. Brealak and I like being there. I suspect if we stayed here, we would be surrounded by security guards all the time. I know that is to protect us, but I find it uncomfortable to be followed everywhere we go. I hope if Earth joins our group, it will not be necessary to have constant protection from the people on Earth while we are here."

"I understand completely. I'm sure as the people here become more accustomed to the presence of aliens, the security guards will no longer be necessary. Many of our citizens have profound religious beliefs that don't allow them to accept the fact there are other intelligent lifeforms. We're concerned they might become violent and we want to make sure that doesn't happen. Please follow me and I'll take you back to the shuttle."

Two hours later, the four of them were back on the space station. Garlut had hardly spoken during the trip to the station. As they exited the shuttle bay he asked, "Jeffery, do think the council will agree to join the association?"

"Yes, I think you made an excellent presentation. I would expect to hear from them in the next few hours. Obviously, I'll let you know immediately when I do."

They went back to their rooms. Garlut thanked Jeffery and Debbie for their assistance. When Jeffery and Debbie were finally alone, Debbie said, "I'm glad that's over. I don't think I've ever been so nervous in my whole life. It would be okay with me if I never met another world leader personally."

"I agree completely, but I suspect because of our friendship with Garlut and Brealak, there will be more of those meetings in the future. You'd better get used to it. You do realize when we go back to Earth unescorted, we'll be set upon by reporters and photographers. We'll probably be remembered as the first people to make contact with an alien civilization and the first people to bring aliens to Earth."

"I suppose you're right, but that doesn't mean I have to like it." Then Debbie smiled and said, "Let's talk about something completely different. When do you want to get married?"

"Not until this situation is resolved. Do you want a big wedding or a small one?"

Debbie replied, frowning, "Do you think Max would allow us to have a small wedding? I would think he'd want to capitalize on the good publicity it would generate for NASA. Perhaps we should do it before Garlut leaves. We could be the first couple to have aliens in attendance at their wedding!"

"I thought you didn't want any unnecessary publicity. Let's call Max later and discuss it with him. I want to ask Garlut if people get married on Coplent."

They decided to relax in their room for a while. They sat down and turned on the news. They were not really surprised to discover the meeting was the main topic for discussion, and although Garlut and Brealak were discussed more than any of the other attendees, Jeffery and Debbie were also mentioned frequently. After watching the news for fifteen minutes and seeing themselves several times Debbie said, "We may never have another moment of privacy unless we stay here or go back to space."

"I think things will die down after a while." Jeffery started to say something else when his phone rang.

"Hello Captain Whitestone, it's Heather. President Winters asked me to contact you. The council has decided to accept Garlut's proposal. He would like the four of you to come back to Earth tomorrow for the announcement which will be shown all over the world. It will be scheduled for 8:00 PM. The shuttle will be there to pick you up at 5:00."

Jeffery, with a big grin, replied, "Thank you. That's great news! I'm sure Garlut will be very pleased. I'm not sure I like being seen all over the world, but I guess that has already happened because of the news coverage of the meeting today. Is there anything we should do to prepare for the announcement?"

"No, I don't think so. President Winters will be doing all the talking. He wants to introduce each of you to the world, but there's no plan for any of you to speak. If that changes, I'll let you know immediately. By the way, you and Debbie should be very proud of the part you played in this affair. You two have profoundly affected Earth's history. I'll be on the shuttle when it comes to pick you up."

Jeffery looked at Debbie and asked, "Did you hear what Heather said?"

"Yes, I heard every word! Let's go to Garlut's room and tell him personally."

They walked to Garlut's room and knocked on the door. A few seconds later, Brealak opened the door. When she saw Jeffery and Debbie smiling, she already knew the answer to the question she was about to ask and instead said, "The council approved the deal, didn't they?"

"Yes, they did!" Jeffery said happily.

"I must tell Garlut immediately! He will be so pleased." She left the living room and walked into the bedroom. Two minutes went by and the two of them emerged from the bedroom together.

"I cannot begin to tell you how grateful I am for your help in this situation," Garlut said. "It never would have happened without you two."

"I'm not sure about that, but Debbie and I are very happy with the results as well. They want us to go back to Earth tomorrow at 5:00 PM so we can take part in a worldwide broadcast that will announce the agreement. I'm sure that's not a problem for you."

"No, that is fine. As a way of showing you how much I appreciate everything you have done, I am going to ask Quat and his engineers to install an artificial gravity system on the Star Rover. There may be some compatibility issues between our systems, but it should only take four or five days."

"Thank you. I'll have to ask my boss if that's okay, but I'm sure he'll approve it."

"I want to leave as soon as Quat is finished with his work on your ship. I must go back to Coplent to let them know about Earth joining the trade association. It is a real problem that it takes longer for communication to reach Coplent than it does to actually go there."

"I'll contact my boss right now and speak to him about this. Is it okay if I use your phone?"

"The only one who ever calls me is you, so I do not see a problem."

Jeffery called Max and announced, "The world Council approved the deal with Garlut."

"I know, Heather contacted me right after she spoke to you."

"Because of the help Debbie and I gave to Garlut, he wants to install an artificial gravity system on the Star Rover. It'll take no more than five days. Since I don't own the ship, I thought I should ask your permission before I tell him it's okay."

"I have no problem with that at all. However, I would like one of our engineers to work with the people who install the system so they can learn something about it."

"Hold on for a moment." Then turning toward Garlut, Jeffery asked, "Is it okay if one of the NASA engineers works with your people during the installation of the artificial gravity system?"

"Yes, of course."

Jeffery continued speaking to Max. "Garlut said it was okay. They want to get started as soon as possible because he wants to return to Coplent."

"I'll send somebody up on the next shuttle. They can get started in the morning."

"Thanks, Max. I want to talk to you about something else, but I'll call you later to discuss it."

"Let me guess. You want to talk about you and Debbie getting married?"

"Are you spying on us? How did you know?"

"Just a lucky guess. Call me in a few hours and we can talk about it."

Turning back toward Garlut, Jeffery said, "Max is sending up an engineer on the next shuttle, so Quat can get started tomorrow morning. Can I ask you a question about Coplent customs?"

"Of course."

"Do people on Coplent get married?"

"No, marriage seems to be an Earth custom. I met Brealak's mother while I was in school. We were both students. We liked each other so we started going places together. Then one day we made the decision to live together. There was no ceremony, no legal contracts, we simply decided to live together. I only see her a few times a year now, but I miss her all the time. That is one reason I am glad Earth decided to join us. It gives me an excuse to go home."

"Why doesn't she go with you on your missions?"

"She has other responsibilities. Her mother lives at our home. She is very old and her health has reached the point where nothing more can be done for her. When her mother passes, my mate, Koltep, will probably join me on my missions. It will mean the three of us can be a family again."

Jeffery didn't know what to say, so he didn't say anything for a while. Then he asked, "Is Brealak your only child?"

"Yes, she is. Shortly after Brealak was born I began working on my father's ship as his aide. I was not home very often and it would have been difficult for Koltep to raise a child by herself. I had worked for my father for ten years when he retired. Then I became captain of his ship. He was ninety years old when he retired. That was sixty-five years ago. The ship was his property until he died. At that time the ship became mine. I will probably retire in ten years. Then Brealak will be the captain."

"Marriages may not be performed on Coplent, but they're a big deal on Earth. Debbie and I will be married soon, and if you're still here, I'd like you and Brealak to attend."

"We would be honored to be guests at your wedding. But please make it soon so I do not have to delay my return home."

"I think we can probably do it before you have to leave. I'll let you know tomorrow. I think Debbie and I'll skip dinner this evening, but please don't let that stop you and Brealak from enjoying a good meal. I'm certain you don't need us to help you order dinner anymore."

"You are correct. I am sure we can handle it. If I have a question, I will ask the waiter."

"Okay, we'll see you tomorrow," Jeffery said as he and Debbie left Garlut's room.

When Jeffery and Debbie were in their room, they sat in the living room next to each other and Jeffery asked, "Who do you want to invite to the wedding?"

"My parents and my sister. I'll have to ask my mother who she wants to invite, but it probably won't be more than ten people. Who do you want to invite?"

"Just my parents. I called them before the meeting yesterday and told my mother you and I were going to get married soon, and if she wanted to see what you look like, she should watch the news coverage of the meeting. I'm sure they watched, but I haven't called since the meeting. I suppose I should do that."

"I should've called my parents, but I didn't. I'm sure they saw the news yesterday. I suspect they're probably upset with me. I'll go call them now."

Debbie went into the bedroom to make the call. When she came back, she sat next to Jeffery and said, "My mom was upset, but everything's okay now. She knew I was on the mission but she didn't know I was going to be at the big meeting. She was surprised to see me. By the way, she thinks you're very handsome."

Jeffery chuckled. "She obviously has remarkably good taste."

"You may be surprised to learn that I agree with her. You are handsome. Anyway, she wants to invite her sister's family. There are three of them, so there will only be five from my family."

"We should invite the crew of Star Rover and Max. Do you want to invite any of the other NASA pilots?"

"No, I suspect they're all on missions anyway. So, we have eighteen people from the crew, Max, five from my family, two from yours, Garlut, and Brealak. That makes twenty-eight guests."

"Okay, I'm sure Max can find us a big room at NASA and I'll bet the hotel manager can find someone to cater it. Then all we need is someone to perform the ceremony. Let's order dinner from room service and when we're finished, I'll call Max."

238

When Max answered the phone later, Jeffery asked, "Can we talk about the wedding now?"

"Why not? Tell me what you two have in mind."

"We have a guest list of twenty-eight people. We'd like to have the ceremony at NASA since we're inviting the crew from the Star Rover. I'll find someone to cater it. But I would like you to find the room and someone to perform the ceremony."

Max laughed for a moment and said, "I think you need to think bigger, actually much bigger. I spoke to Heather a few hours ago and told her that you and Debbie were getting married. She asked me when and I told her it would be soon, but there was no date set yet. Then she asked me to hold for a minute or two. When she came back on the line she told me that all the members of the World Council would be attending with their families. That means at least fifty more people. There will be a lot of people from the NASA high command there as well. That will probably add another thirty-five people. There will also be security guards, photographers, and reporters. You must understand that you and Debbie are celebrities now and you have all the baggage that goes with that status. This is great publicity for NASA and if your alien friends attend, it will be a big help in getting public approval for the trade agreement."

"All we wanted was a small wedding with just a few friends and relatives. You aren't going to let that happen, are you?"

"Do you really want to upset President Winters?"

"No, I suppose not," Jeffery admitted with a little groan.

"What day would you like?" Max asked.

"You know, Max, I never realized you were a wedding planner. I want to have it before Garlut leaves. How about next Friday?"

"Just so you know, my talents are unending. Actually, I'm going to give the date to Heather and she'll do the rest. All you and Debbie have to do is show up."

"I think we can handle that. Thanks Max . . . I think."

"You're welcome. I'm going to call Heather now. I'm sure she'll be contacting you."

After Jeffery disconnected the call, he looked at Debbie. She had a worried look on her face. Then he asked, "Is there a problem?"

"I heard what Max said. Do you really want all those people at our wedding?"

"No, but I don't think we have a choice. If we do this for NASA, they'll probably do almost anything we ask in the future. I've been thinking about the next mission. I'm going to ask Garlut where the closest uninhabited Earthlike planet is. Then I'm going to insist it be our next mission, and I'm sure they'll agree. Don't you think it would be exciting to study a planet like Earth minus the people?"

"Of course I do, but I just can't imagine my family or the Star Rover crew at a party with the World Council."

"I don't know your family, but the crew is probably a little crude for the World Council. But that's not our problem. As Max pointed out, all we have to do is show up."

They were both deep in thought when they were somewhat startled by the phone. Jeffery answered it.

It was Heather. After saying hello, she continued, "I'm really excited. I love big weddings and this one is going to be bigger than most."

"Great, that's exactly what we didn't want. But I know we have to do this."

"Hey, you should be happy. It's a big honor to have every world leader at your wedding."

"I suppose so. But it was a real shock. We only wanted twenty-eight people, and most of those are the crew from the Star Rover."

"There will be a few more than twenty-eight. The wedding will be in the grand ballroom at the World Council Headquarters. It'll be scheduled for Friday at 8:00 PM. I'll take care of all the invitations, but I need names and addresses. Please send that to Max tomorrow. We're working on this together. Since you want to invite the Star Rover crew, you don't need to send that information. I also know where Garlut

240

and Brealak are. It's the information on other friends and relatives we need. Once the guest list is complete, I'll send it to you so you'll know who will be there."

"Okay. I have to admit, I'm a little overwhelmed by all this."

"Don't worry about it. It'll all be taken care of. Okay?"

"Yes, it's okay. Thank you, Heather."

"You're welcome. I'll see you tomorrow at 5:00."

Jeffery and Debbie spent fifteen minutes compiling the list of people they wanted to invite to their wedding and sent it to Max. Despite everyone telling them to be calm, it simply was not working. Both he and Debbie were nervous. They both had trouble sleeping. At 8:30 the following morning, they received a call from Garlut asking them to go to breakfast with him. They said they would be at his room by 9:00. When they arrived, they found the door open so they walked in. Garlut and Brealak were sitting in their living room waiting for them.

Garlut looked at them and said, "You do not look happy. Is something wrong?"

Jeffery tried to smile and said, "Yes and no. The World Council has hijacked our wedding."

Garlut looked confused and said, "I am sorry, I did not know how the word 'hijacked' could be applied to a wedding."

"Okay, that was a bad choice of words. The World Council has taken over our plans for our wedding. It was going to be small, with only the crew of the Star Rover, our families, our boss, and you two. Now the wedding is big. Every member of the World Council and their families will be there as well as the top managers at NASA. There will be security guards, photographers, and more. We've been told it's in the best interest of NASA and the World Council, so we should just try to make the best of it."

"Now I understand. Perhaps if you do what they want, they will reciprocate in some way."

"Yeah, that's what we're hoping for. We'd like to set the parameters for our next mission. Actually, we want your help with that. We'd like to know where the closest uninhabited Earthlike planet is located."

241

"I can help you with that, but I need the charts that are on my ship. I am sure we can do that tomorrow."

"Okay, tomorrow will be fine."

As they were about to leave for breakfast, Jeffery received a message from the Star Rover: "NASA engineer and Quat are onboard to start installation of the artificial gravity system."

Jeffery said, "They're starting the artificial gravity installation."

Garlut said, "Good," and they left the room.

At breakfast they talked about the broadcast that evening. Since none of them were scheduled to say anything, there was nothing to be concerned about. Jeffery did mention they should either have an early dinner, or a late one after the broadcast. They decided on an early dinner and they would meet again in the restaurant at 3:30.

Garlut said he wanted to go to the Star Rover so he could keep watch on the installation. Jeffery called Mike and told him to send the shuttle to the station to pick up Garlut. Jeffery and Debbie went to their room after taking Garlut and Brealak to the shuttle bay.

At 3:30 Jeffery and Debbie, dressed appropriately in their uniforms, arrived at the Hotel Restaurant, and Garlut and Brealak arrived several minutes later dressed in what appeared to be a more formal uniform. After eating dinner and small talk, they left the restaurant and walked to the shuttle bay. Just as before, the shuttle was waiting for them when they arrived. All four were greeted by Heather, who seemed very happy. She asked if everyone was okay, and they all responded with a "yes."

After the shuttle departed, Heather walked over to Jeffery and Debbie and said, "The wedding plans are going well. All the invitations will be delivered tomorrow. Music will be provided by twenty members of the New York Symphony Orchestra, the catering is all set, and a New York Supreme Court judge will perform the ceremony. Included with the invitations to your family members are first class air

242

tickets and airport transfers. Rooms have been reserved at the Hilton hotel next to the World Council building."

Debbie said, "Thank you very much. We really do appreciate what you're doing for us."

"You're welcome. It's going to be a wonderful experience."

The trip to the World Council building was identical to the last one. The security guards were even the same. Once inside the building they went to a room that was set up as a studio. There was a podium where President Winters would speak. On the left of the podium was a table with chairs for the seven members of the World Council. On the right was a table with four chairs for Jeffery, Debbie, Garlut, and Brealak. Apparently, Heather would not be seated with them.

Jeffery and his group were the first to arrive. When President Winters walked into the room, he immediately walked over to Jeffery's table and said, "This is a very important day for us, and all the members of the council appreciate your being here this evening. I want to extend my personal congratulations to you and Debbie on your upcoming wedding. I realize it wasn't what you wanted, but sometimes we have to give up some things for the greater good. I can promise you it will be a memorable event and there will be some personal benefits too. Garlut, we're looking forward to developing a great relationship with the people of your planet and our other new trading partners. I hope we'll see you often. Thank you all again."

President Winters walked to the podium and the rest of the World Council took their seats. At exactly 8:00 PM, he began his speech.

"Good evening. As all of you are probably aware, two days ago the World Council listened to a presentation by Garlut. He's from the planet Coplent. Their ship is currently in orbit two miles from our space station. Coplent is twenty-five light years from Earth. Not close by in normal terms, but in interstellar terms it's one of our closest neighbors. Scientifically, their civilization is far more advanced than ours. In fact, they've been studying Earth for over a thousand years.

243

Coplent is a member of an interstellar trading association. That association currently has four hundred and seven member planets. Garlut gave us a compelling presentation about why we should become the next member. After an extensive discussion, the World Council has agreed to join.

"We believe the benefits Earth will receive will be good for all of us. In fact, we don't see any reason not to join. Being a member of their association means we'll be trading our goods and services with other planets. In the short time Garlut has been our guest, he has found three things we have on Earth that aren't available anywhere else. Two of them are very common food items: cinnamon and chocolate. His people are also interested in our power modules. Sometime in the next few months, the first permanent delegation of aliens will arrive on Earth. They will be setting up a bank to handle our interplanetary trades. They will also be looking at other goods or services we could offer to our new trading partners. In exchange for these items, we will receive marvels of engineering that would probably take us hundreds of years to develop on our own. For example, our first star ship, the Star Rover, is currently being fitted with an artificial gravity system that will make space travel far more comfortable. But there are other advances that will be available to us as well. One of our new trading partners specializes in medicine. On Coplent, these medical advances have led to a 50% increase in life expectancy. There's reason to believe the same can be done for the people of Earth.

"This means aliens will be living among us. You should know all of the inhabitants of these planets are humanoid. There will be some differences, of course, just as there are among humans. We've finally learned those differences are unimportant. So too are the differences between humanoid species.

"Some of the member planets will have embassies on Earth just as we will have embassies on other planets. As we continue to build more star ships and interstellar travel becomes more common, there will likely come a time when some people may decide to leave Earth and live on alien

244

worlds. We think that's a good thing because the intermingling of species will benefit everyone.

"I want to take a moment to thank two people who played a very substantial role in making this great leap forward for Earth. They are the captain of the Star Rover, Jeffery Whitestone, and his executive officer, Commander Debbie Murphy. They are seated on my left with our alien visitors, Garlut and his daughter Brealak. I hope I'm not telling any secrets, but Captain Whitestone and Commander Murphy are going to be married next Friday.

President Winters paused for a few moments as the people in attendance at the meeting applauded. Then he continued, "From this day forward, Earth will never be the same. We're sure it will be better. Thank you for your time this evening. Goodnight."

After the speech, Jeffery looked at Debbie and said, "I told you we're famous now. I'm not sure it's a good thing, but I suppose we'll know in a few months."

At that moment, President Winters walked over to their table again and said to Jeffery and Debbie, "As a way of saying thank you for a job well done, you're both being promoted. Although you'll remain in your positions as captain and executive officer, Jeffery, you now have the rank of admiral, and Debbie, you have the rank of captain. Thank you again. I'm looking forward to seeing you at your wedding."

Jeffery and Debbie were more than a little surprised. They both smiled broadly and said, "Thank you sir," at the same time.

"I hope you don't mind, but I'm not going to call you Admiral," Debbie said to Jeffery with a smile.

"Congratulations on your promotions," Garlut said.

"Thank you. Now let's get out of here and go back to the space station," Jeffery said.

The four of them got up to leave, but Heather stopped them. "Before you make your escape, we'd like you to pose for a few pictures with the council members. Please follow me."

245

They spent the next fifteen minutes posing for pictures. They followed Heather out of the room back to the car. A few minutes later they were on their way back to the station. While walking back to their rooms, Jeffery said, "Garlut, tomorrow morning are we still going to your ship so you can show me where that uninhabited earthlike planet is located?"

"Yes, of course."

"I'll have Mike pick us up at 9:30. Okay?"

"Yes, that will be fine. Since Mike is your navigator, he should probably be there as well."

They were now at the door to Garlut's room. Jeffery said, smiling, "I agree. I wanted Mike there also. That way if he takes us a few light years off course, I'll have somebody to blame. Have a good evening."

"We will see you at the shuttle bay. Goodnight."

When Jeffery and Debbie got to their room, Jeffery called Mike. Mike answered, "Good evening, Admiral. How may I be of service to you?"

"First, stop calling me Admiral. Second, I want you to be at the shuttle bay to pick us up at 9:30 tomorrow morning. We're going to Garlut's ship to look at his star charts. How did you know I was promoted? I didn't think that had been made public yet."

"An hour ago, everybody on the ship received an invitation to the wedding of Admiral Jeffery Whitestone and Captain Debbie Murphy. Thank you for inviting us. There's a rumor that President Winters will be there. Is that true?"

"Not only President Winters, but the rest of the World Council as well. Anyway, I'm sure the food will be great, and the drinks will be free flowing. What more could you ask for?"

"Everybody is looking forward to it. Why are we going to look at star charts?"

"Because I'm planning our next mission. I want to go to an uninhabited Earthlike planet. Garlut knows of one in a system that isn't too far away. I want you to be there since you're our navigator and it's your job to make sure we don't get lost."

246

"Do you think NASA will let you plan your own mission?"

"Why not?" Jeffery replied with a chuckle. "I'm an admiral now."

"I'll be there at 9:30."

The following morning, the four of them were at the bay a few minutes early. At 9:30 they all went into the shuttle for the quick trip to Garlut's ship.

As soon as they were onboard, they went to the bridge and Garlut gave some verbal commands to the computer in his native language. Instantly, a star map appeared on the screen. There was writing on the image, but nothing the humans could understand. Garlut pointed out the system and said, "This is a system we refer to as Procolt. The planet you want is Procolt 2. It is 10% larger than Earth, has an oxygen and nitrogen atmosphere, and the surface temperature near its equator is about twenty-four degrees Celsius, which should be very comfortable for you. It is much colder at the poles, about negative sixty degrees Celsius. I have been there twice and I never saw any animal larger than a small dog. There are very few reptiles on the planet. It has mostly small mammals.

"There is an insect population and we found some of them are mildly annoying, but overall, it is a very nice place to visit. This system is twenty-seven light years from Earth and it is not visible from Earth because Procolt is a small star. There are much larger and brighter stars behind it as seen from Earth. I have some images I took on my last visit which was probably fifteen years ago. I will convert them to a format you can use and send them to you. I can also give you the coordinates for the system, but we will probably need to make some changes in your navigation system to allow input in our format. I will send one of my engineers to the Star Rover to make those changes."

"Thank you," Jeffery said. Then he asked, "How is communication handled between the members of the trading group? I contacted you using an old Earth emergency radio signal. But if we find ourselves in a position where it's necessary to communicate with somebody else, I think we really need to know how to do it."

Garlut blinked his eyes for a few moments, realizing he had forgotten something important, and said, "I should have thought of that before. While my engineers are on your ship working on the artificial gravity system, I will also have them add one of our communication systems. These systems already have the translator built in, so you will not need one of the portable units for that. However, you should have one or two of them onboard for personal communication."

"Thank you again. Can we really get all this done before you want to leave?"

"Yes, I think we can, but if I have to delay my departure by a day or two, that is fine. Brealak and I would like to stay on the ship until tomorrow morning. Can you send a shuttle over tomorrow morning at ten?"

"Consider it done."

"Tomorrow I would like to go over to your ship to make sure everything is going well with the gravity system. I will bring one of our communication units and an engineer to make the changes in your navigation system. I will also bring the images of Procolt 2."

"That would be great. Thank you again. We'll see you tomorrow morning."

Jeffery went to the Star Rover to see how things were going with the artificial gravity system installation. As soon as they exited the shuttle bay, he noticed changes. There was now a plastic coating on the floor. He said, "Mike, can I assume this stuff on the floor is part of the gravity system?"

"Yeah, they're spraying that stuff on every floor. I guess it's a good thing we don't have carpeting. You can't see it, but there's wiring and transducers in that coating. The transducers create gravity waves. They're putting this stuff everywhere except the hydroponic garden area. Carol said she likes the system she has and the plants have adapted to it. So, I told her we wouldn't put it in her area. This isn't the final coating. After everything is working, they'll spray an opaque sealer over this stuff."

248

"Thanks for the update. Who's on the bridge now?"

"Sean and probably Ron."

"Good, I need to speak with Ron." Jeffery picked up the communicator to call his linguistics officer, Ensign Cathy Carter. He pressed the button on the communicator and said, "Carter."

A moment later a voice responded, "This is Cathy."

"Hi Cathy. It's Jeffery. Please meet me on the bridge."

"Yes sir, I'll be there in a few minutes."

When Jeffery stepped onto the bridge, he saw his chief engineer and said, "Hi Ron, how are things going?"

"Oh, good morning Admiral." Ron smiled, saluted, and said, "I wasn't expecting you. Aren't you two supposed to be planning for your wedding or something?"

Jeffery said, "Please, no more admiral stuff. I know it violates military protocol, but you know I want to keep things informal. As far as I'm concerned, nothing has really changed. I'm still Jeffery."

"Yes, sir." Ron replied smiling.

Then Debbie said, "To answer your question regarding the wedding, Jeffery and I have nothing to do. It's all being done by an aide to President Winters. So, we came here to harass you."

"Well, I guess that's okay. They expect the gravity system to be completed within forty-eight hours. So far the tests we've run have all been successful."

"That's great. Please make sure you learn as much as you can about it because if it fails, I think you know who will have to repair it."

"Yeah, I've been learning everything I can. That plastic material they're spraying everywhere is really amazing. I understand how it works, but I can't figure out how it's made. I'll spend some time with Quat before he leaves and try to pry some additional information out of him."

"Good. Tomorrow more people will be coming over from Garlut's ship. They'll be installing a trade association communication system. They're also going to make some modifications to our navigation system so we can utilize their star charts. That will be needed for our next mission."

Just as Jeffery finished, Cathy walked onto the bridge and said, "Good morning sir."

"It's not necessary to call me 'sir,' Cathy. Anyway, tomorrow some people from Garlut's ship will be installing a new communication system that will allow us to communicate with other ships from the trading association. I want you to learn how to use it. The system has a built-in translator so it will eliminate a major problem. In addition to your other jobs, you're now our communications officer. We'll set up a spot for you on the bridge. If we encounter another ship, it will be your job to initiate contact with them."

"Do I get a raise?"

"Do you need it?"

"No, there's nothing for us to spend money on anyway, but I had to ask. Thank you for inviting all of us to your wedding. I think everyone is looking forward to it."

"I'm looking forward to being married, but I'm less sure about the wedding. Debbie and I are going to stay onboard for a while. We'll be in my quarters if you need us."

Debbie and Jeffery left the bridge and walked to his room. His furniture had been moved so the floor could be sprayed, but nobody had moved it back. They spent a few minutes repositioning the furniture and Jeffery sat down at his desk and called Max.

"Good morning," Max said, "are you getting excited about your wedding?"

"I don't think 'excited' is the right word. The reason for my call is that I want to talk to you about our next mission." He told Max about the new communication system, and added, "They're also making modifications to our navigation system so we can use their star charts."

"Why do we need their star charts, don't we have our own?"

"Yes, but ours only reference the stars that can be seen from Earth. For our next mission, I want to go to the Procolt system. There's an Earthlike planet there that has no humanoid population, but does have small animals. I want to explore it. That's why I need their charts."

"How far is it?"

"Twenty-seven light years. Garlut has been there twice. Tomorrow he's bringing some images. I'll send them to you."

"I'd like to see them. I think a visit to Procolt would be okay, but we want you to visit Coplent too. Please discuss that with Garlut. I'd like to know his reaction."

"I think that's a great idea. I'm sure he'll be happy with that decision. Is this a prelude to sending a permanent delegation there?"

"Yes, of course it is. I wish I could go with you, but I'd never pass the physical."

"What's the date for our departure?"

"There's no exact date, but I'd guess it will be about thirty days. I assume you're going to take a few days off for a honeymoon. When you get back, we'll set up a meeting to discuss the mission."

"Okay. By the way, according to Ron the gravity system will be finished in forty-eight hours."

"That's good news. Call me again tomorrow."

"I'll do that." Jeffery turned to Debbie and asked, "Did you hear what he said?"

"Yeah, I'd love to go to Coplent."

"Not that! We haven't made any plans for a honeymoon. Where do you want to go?"

"Well, your quarters are bigger, so we should probably go there."

"That doesn't sound very romantic. How about someplace in Europe like London, Paris, or Rome?"

"You know we spend our lives traveling, so why would we want to travel someplace?"

"I see your point. How about if we just stay in our room on the station?"

Debbie smiled enticingly. "That works for me."

"Okay, but let's tell everybody we are going to Bali or something. I don't want them to know we're still here."

251

"Bali, it is."

When Debbie and Jeffery arrived on Garlut's ship the following morning, they found him with two of his engineers. There were also several large boxes of equipment. When the passengers and equipment were loaded into the shuttle, they left for the return trip to the Star Rover.

Debbie was piloting the ship. Jeffery turned toward Garlut and said, "I received permission to go to Procolt on our next mission. They want us to make another stop too. They want me to go to Coplent."

Garlut smiled and said, "I think that is a wonderful idea. I do not know if you realize that the Procolt system and Coplent are in almost opposite directions. The distance between the two systems is forty-eight light years. For the Star Rover, that is a one hundred-thirty-day trip. Do you know which will be your first stop?"

"No, not yet. Will you be on Coplent when we get there?"

"When I know your schedule, I will try to arrange it. I will also give you some information about who to contact in case I am not there. We have a space station, so that should be your first stop. We do not have a fancy hotel or restaurants on our space station, but I think you will be impressed."

"I'll talk to Max about the schedule later today. Perhaps I can let you know by this afternoon."

When they arrived at the Star Rover, Mike was there to greet them with a big smile on his face. Jeffery and Debbie noticed something immediately. There was gravity. Debbie jumped up a few inches and came back down, then she smiled. "This is wonderful!" she exclaimed.

Mike said, "The gravity system was finished while you were gone. It's working all over the ship now. There are still a few areas where the floor needs to be sprayed and that should be finished in a few hours."

"That's good news. You must have known that before we left, but you didn't say anything."

"I wanted it to be a surprise."

Jeffery smiled and said, "It was, and a very pleasant surprise too. Please get somebody from maintenance to take these boxes where they need to go."

Garlut said, "Everything needs to be on the bridge."

"Okay, I'll take care of it," Mike replied.

Everybody went to the bridge except Jeffery, who went to his quarters. When he got there he called Max, but Max was in a meeting so he left a message telling Max that Garlut thought stopping at Coplent was a great idea, and asking Max to let him know what planet he preferred the Star Rover to visit first.

The day went by quickly. The new communication system was installed and Cathy received several hours of training on using the equipment and the protocol used for communication between trade association members. Jeffery received a message from Max indicating he should make the decision regarding the mission sequence, but he was glad Garlut was happy about the upcoming visit. The modifications were also completed on the navigation system and Mike was fully trained on its operation.

As Jeffery watched Garlut's engineers training Cathy and Mike, he decided he was going to request training for some additional crew members before the next mission. He wanted another navigator and a backup communications officer. He sent a message to Max with his request. Much to his surprise, Max responded by leaving a message an hour later: "Your new staff will be there in a few days. Your additional navigator is Lieutenant Dean Crawford and Ensign Anne Perkins will be your backup communications officer. Both of them have an engineering background. I believe they'll make excellent additions to your crew. They're both very happy with the assignment."

Jeffery told Mike and Cathy about the new crew members. He was concerned they might feel slighted in some way, but actually they were both pleased to have the help.

Later in the day, Jeffery asked Garlut to join him in his quarters. Jeffery left the door open so when Garlut arrived he could just walk in. He said, "I wanted to discuss the schedule for the next mission with you. If we go to Procolt first, it will probably be seven months before we get to Coplent. Does that work with your schedule?"

"It will probably work. There is something I have been meaning to discuss with you. It will make things easier when you are dealing with other members of the association. We have adopted standards for days and years. We do not use months. You must start using the standards if you want to be understood. Our standard day in Earth time is twenty-eight hours, thirty-one minutes, and seventeen seconds. Within the trade association there are twenty hours in a day, and four hundred fifty days in a year. I know it will take some time to get used to it, and it is only necessary to use on your ships. We do not use minutes or seconds. We use thousandths of an hour. It will not be difficult to program your computer systems to handle this change. Can you get this done before your mission starts?"

"Yes. It'll definitely be confusing, but I certainly understand the need to do it. We use months all the time, but now we'll have to express everything in days."

Garlut continued, "A date is expressed as the year and the day within the year. What you would call a Julian Date. Time is expressed as the hour and thousandths of an hour. The current time is 11.563."

"Okay, I'll get our chief engineer working on that. I'll need you to give him the exact time so our time will match yours." Then Jeffery turned to his computer and after a minute or so said, "If my calculations are correct, we'll arrive at Coplent one hundred and seventy-seven standard days after our departure from Earth."

"That sounds right to me. I will do my best to be there before you arrive. But I already sent the information to you about who to contact if I am not there."

"Yes, I have it here. Thanks, I'll call Ron to let him know about the new time standards."

"Good, I will see you later," Garlut said. He left Jeffery's quarters and walked back to the bridge.

254

Jeffery called Ron and explained the problem. Ron replied that he would have the new trading association standard time as well as Earth time displayed on all of the bridge monitors tomorrow and the new time would also be available on all onboard computers.

In what seemed like no time at all it was Friday morning: wedding day. Jeffery and Debbie met Garlut and Brealak at the hotel restaurant for breakfast, but neither Jeffery nor Debbie were hungry. The wedding was scheduled for 7:00 PM with a reception and dinner afterwards. There was a shuttle that would take the twenty-two crew members of the Star Rover, Garlut, and Brealak to Earth at 4:30. Jeffery was somewhat concerned about leaving the Star Rover empty, so two people from the station would be onboard until the crew returned.

That afternoon, both Jeffery and Debbie called their parents. They were all at the hotel across from the World Council Headquarters building. Everybody was very excited about the wedding and they were anxious to see Jeffery and Debbie. Debbie's mother asked her where they were going for their honeymoon. She thought about telling her mother the truth, but told her instead that they were going to Bali.

RUSSELL FINE

THE WEDDING

By 4:15, everybody who was going to the wedding was waiting for the shuttle. The entire Star Rover crew, including Jeffery and Debbie, were dressed in their NASA uniforms. Garlut and Brealak were attired in the same uniforms they wore to the World Council meeting. The shuttle arrived at 4:20, and by 4:25 everyone was onboard. A few minutes later it departed the station for the trip to Earth.

When they arrived in New York, Heather was there waiting for them. She directed Jeffery, Debbie, Garlut, and Brealak to a limo, and the crew of the Star Rover to a shuttlebus. When they arrived at the World Council, the building's courtyard was filled with people. However, just as they had done before, they drove to the side entrance of the parking garage and went inside. Heather led all of them to the ballroom floor. As Jeffery and Debbie stepped off the elevator, they spotted their parents waiting for them.

Jeffery and Debbie walked over to them. Debbie said, "Mom and Dad, this is Jeffery."

Debbie's father reached out and shook Jeffery's hand. Jeffery said, "I'm very pleased to meet you, Mr. Murphy." Then Debbie's mother gave Jeffery a brief kiss on the cheek and smiled at him. "It's nice to meet you as well, Mrs. Murphy."

Then Jeffery introduced Debbie to his parents. After the introductions, they walked inside the ballroom. The room was enormous. Jeffery estimated one hundred and fifty feet long and one hundred feet wide. It was lit with at least one hundred crystal chandeliers. At the far end of the room, an orchestra was playing softly. There were dozens of tables already set up for dinner. On each of the two outside walls, there was a bar and tables with hors d'oeuvres. Jeffery guessed there were already more than one hundred people there, but he didn't see any of the World Council members.

He felt a tap on his shoulder and turned around to find Garlut and Brealak standing there. "I'm sorry. I didn't mean to abandon you," Jeffery said. Then he said, "Mom, Dad, Mr.

and Mrs. Murphy, this is our friend Garlut and his daughter Brealak."

Garlut and Brealak bowed slightly and Garlut said, "We are very pleased to meet you."

Mr. Murphy glared at Garlut and Brealak for a few seconds, and said, "Please forgive me for staring. I've never met someone from another planet before. Garlut, do you like Earth?"

Garlut smiled and replied, "There is nothing to forgive, and yes, I like it very much. I have been studying Earth for a long time. It is nice to finally have an opportunity to meet some of its people."

Then Mr. Murphy asked, "Is Earth similar to your home planet?"

"Our civilization is much older than yours and we have developed more advanced building techniques, so our buildings look different. Also, we do not use wheeled vehicles for transportation. But overall, they are somewhat similar. Jeffery and Debbie will be visiting Coplent soon. You should probably ask them that question when they get back."

"I'm not sure our visit to Coplent was supposed to be public knowledge yet," Jeffery said under his breath.

"I promise I won't tell anybody," Mr. Murphy said.

"Okay, how about if we get some drinks? I'm sure everything will be terrific," Jeffery suggested.

They went to the bar and got drinks. Garlut and Brealak asked for water. They picked up small plates and filled them with hors d'oeuvres. Just as they did this, Heather walked over to them and directed them to the table reserved for them. They took their seats and talked among themselves for a while, mostly the parents asking Garlut and Brealak questions. Suddenly the room became quiet and they turned to look at the entry to the ballroom. They saw the World Council members and their families walk in. All except President Winters walked to the tables that were reserved for them. President Winters walked over to Jeffery's table.

President Winters said, "Hello." Then, looking at Garlut and Brealak he said, "It's nice to see you again. Has your stay here been pleasant?"

"Our stay has been excellent. I am sorry we have to leave shortly, but Brealak and I will be back soon."

"Good, I'm looking forward to that." Looking at Jeffery, he said, "Aren't you going to introduce me to these fine folks?"

"Of course," Jeffery said. "These are my parents, David and Gwen Whitestone."

"I'm pleased to meet you Mr. and Mrs. Whitestone. You should be very proud of your son."

David Whitestone said, "Thank you, we are very proud of him." Then they shook hands.

Debbie said, "These are my parents, Peter and Joyce Murphy."

"It's very nice to meet you. You may not know this, but your daughter is the highest-ranking women in the NASA Space Corps."

"We didn't know that. Thank you for telling us," Peter Murphy said, beaming proudly.

At that moment, the orchestra stopped playing and Heather walked to the center of the room in front of the orchestra.

"It looks like things are about to start. Please excuse me. We'll talk again later," President Winters said as he walked back to his table.

Heather walked to the front of the room. The orchestra stopped playing and she said, "We'll be starting in a few minutes with a brief speech by President Winters. There are two tables close to the front of the room with blue tablecloths. These tables are reserved for the crew of the Star Rover who are with us tonight for this celebration. All of the tables with white tablecloths are open seating. Please take your seats as soon as possible. Thank you."

Five minutes later she said, "I'm pleased to present President Winters." Everyone in the room applauded as

President Winters walked to the front of the room. Heather went to a table and sat down.

As soon as the applause began to dissipate, he began speaking. "As Heather said, I will keep this brief. I just want to introduce you to our guests of honor: Admiral Jeffery Whitestone and Captain Debbie Murphy." He looked toward their table. "Please stand up so everybody can see you."

Jeffery and Debbie both stood up and the applause started again, much louder than before. They looked around smiling at the crowd. Jeffery asked, "Will the members of the Star Rover crew please stand?" The Star Rover crew all stood up and everyone applauded loudly. When the applause finally began to die down, Jeffery and Debbie sat down again.

President Winters continued, "I don't think they realize it yet, but they are true heroes in every sense of the word. They have played a key role in the evolution of Earth's future, and they will continue to do so as they take the Star Rover to meet other members of the trade association we just became members of. On their next mission, they will be going to Coplent, the home planet of our first alien friends: Garlut and his daughter Brealak. Would you please stand up?"

Garlut and Brealak stood up and again the applause started. They looked around and smiled. Once again as the applause died down, they sat down.

President Winters began speaking again. "I want the entire crew of the Star Rover to know we are all very proud of the job they've done and we are looking forward to the things they will accomplish in the future. Now I'm going to stop speaking so Justice William Goldberg of the North American Supreme Court can perform the marriage ceremony."

Justice Goldberg walked up to the front of the room and President Winters went back to his seat. After another brief round of applause, Justice Goldberg began to speak. "I must say I have not performed a wedding in more than twenty years, but I'm looking forward to this one. Will the bride and groom please come up here and join me?"

Jeffery and Debbie walked to the front of the room. Justice Goldberg turned the microphone off and he asked Jeffery, "Do you have the rings?"

Suddenly Debbie had a horrified look on her face and she said softly, "Oh shit! I forgot about the rings!"

Jeffery reached out, grabbed her hand, and said softly, "I didn't." Then he reached into his pocket and handed the rings to Justice Goldberg.

Debbie looked at Jeffery with an expression that conveyed extreme affection and said, "I love you. When did you get the rings?"

"We can discuss that later."

They both turned and faced Justice Goldberg. He turned on the microphone again and began the ceremony. At the end he said, "By the power vested in me by the State of New York, I now pronounce you husband and wife. Please kiss her already."

Jeffery and Debbie had a long sensual kiss while the guests applauded. When the kiss was over Jeffery and Debbie went back to their seats, Justice Goldberg said, "And now the moment we have all been waiting for, it's time for dinner!"

As Justice Goldberg returned to his seat there was a mixture of applause and laughter.

Jeffery and Debbie were congratulated by everyone at their table. After a few kisses and handshakes, they sat down. Debbie looked at Jeffery and asked sternly, "Why didn't you tell me about the rings? You let me look like an idiot in front of a Supreme Court judge."

"How did I know you were going to say 'oh shit' to the judge? Actually, I wasn't sure we'd even need the rings, but I thought I should have them just in case. The concierge at the hotel ordered them for me a few days ago. I got them the next day."

"I know it worked out, but I still think you should've told me."

An excellent dinner was served a short time later. Garlut even commented that he was sorry to be leaving so soon because he was going to miss the food. After dinner was over,

Heather came over to their table and asked Jeffery and Debbie to go to the World Council table. The people at the table had changed places. Prior to the wedding, the World Council members had been seated at two tables with their families. Now the family members were at one table and the members of the council were seated at the other one.

Jeffery and Debbie sat down at the table, and after a few more congratulations, President Winters said, "The decision to join the trading association was an easy one. But we want to make sure we aren't being deceived in any way. When you go to Coplent, try to get out among the people and get to know them. I would like to know how they feel about the trade group. Also, we would like you to initiate contact with the planet that does the medical research. I think that's where our people will find the most direct benefit."

"I'm sure we can do that. You're aware we're going to the Procolt system first, aren't you?"

"Yes, we know you want to time your arrival at Coplent to coincide with Garlut's schedule."

"It will probably be seven or eight months before we arrive at Coplent. I think it would be great if we could communicate our progress during the mission. Unfortunately, you won't know anything about the mission until we get back. In my discussions with Garlut, he said one thing that every member of the trading association wants is some type of faster than light communication system. I'd like to be able to tell him we're working on that. Could we make that a priority for one of our engineering groups?"

"I think that's an excellent idea. I realize we're not as advanced scientifically as some of the other members of the group, but perhaps all it needs is a fresh approach. I would also like to start construction on the next interstellar ship, but I suspect we'll need more technology before we do that. If we don't wait, we may be building something that's obsolete before it's ready for its first mission," President Winters replied.

"I agree. I'm sure Garlut will help us when he comes back to Earth."

262

"Since we already know what products we'll be trading, I want you to take some cinnamon and various forms of chocolate with you and give them to the Coplent government. We'll also give you twenty power modules to be given as gifts to them. Can you find room on the Star Rover for five hundred kilos of cinnamon and a thousand kilos of chocolate?"

"Yes, there's plenty of storage space on the ship, but I'll verify that with the ship's chief engineer."

"Good. I probably don't have to remind you that when you're on Coplent, you are representatives of the entire planet."

"We promise not to do anything that would embarrass Earth. I have a small favor to ask, though. Garlut gave you five portable translators. Could I have two of them to use on the Star Rover?"

"Yes, I should have thought about that myself. They'll be there tomorrow. I won't ask where you're going on your honeymoon, but wherever it is, have a good time. Heather will make any travel arrangements you need."

"Thank you. I'll do that," Jeffery said.

He and Debbie got up and walked over to the other World Council table where Heather was seated. When Heather saw Jeffery and Debbie, she stood up and walked toward them. "Is there something I can help you with?"

"Yes, can you get us a shuttle back to the station?"

"The shuttle that brought you here is still there. Are you ready to go? Perhaps you should say a few words to the guests before you leave."

Jeffery groaned. "Do you really think that's necessary?"

"Yes, I do. Follow me."

They walked back to the front of the room. The orchestra stopped playing and everyone stopped talking and looked at him.

"Debbie and I will be leaving shortly. I want to thank all of you for being here to help us celebrate our wedding. I would also like to thank NASA and the World Council for making this magnificent affair possible. Good night, everyone."

There was a brief round of applause and then the talking and the music started up again. Heather led them back to the limo. As they were getting into the limo Jeffery said, "Heather, please make sure Garlut and Brealak get back to the space station when they are ready to leave."

"Of course."

Fifteen minutes later, they were on their way back to the space station.

When they arrived at the hotel, Jeffery stopped at the front desk and said, "Please don't let anyone know we're still here. If anybody asks where we are, tell them you don't know. Can you do that for me?"

The man at the desk replied, "Yes, of course I can do that. I'll also inform the other clerks. Have a good evening, Admiral Whitestone."

THE PROCOLT MISSION

Jeffery and Debbie walked to their room, went inside, and didn't come out for three days. During that time, Jeffery did speak to Garlut for several minutes. They discussed his upcoming mission and were looking forward to seeing each other again in about two hundred and ten standard days.

A week after the wedding, Jeffery and Debbie were ready to get back to work. He called the Star Rover and discovered Mike had taken the day off and Dean Crawford was on duty. He asked Dean to send the shuttle over to the station to pick them up. Dean said he would do it himself and he would be there in fifteen minutes.

Jeffery and Debbie checked out of their room and walked to the shuttle bay and waited for the shuttle to arrive. They were both happy to be going back to the Star Rover. When the shuttle bay door opened, they walked to the shuttle and got in. Dean said, "I'll bet you're both glad to be back at work."

"You're right," Jeffery replied. "We're both glad all the fuss is over. How are things going on the ship?"

"The gravity system is working perfectly and everybody is happy about that. I've been working with Mike on the navigation system modifications and feel pretty confident I can handle it. Anne and Cathy have been working together on the new communication system and a protocol manual that Garlut gave them before he left. Also, they're upgrading the long-range sensors. They'll be able to operate up to one hundred thousand miles and can now detect lifeforms more accurately. They increased the ability of the systems to detect movement and radiation bursts."

"That should come in handy. Anything else?"

"I don't think so. Did you have a nice honeymoon?"

"Yes, it was wonderful," Debbie answered.

When they arrived at the ship, they went to the bridge. Jeffery called Ron Rice and asked him to join them. After pleasantries had been exchanged, Jeffery asked him when the long-range sensors would be ready.

"It should only be another day or two. They also increased the resolution of our visual scanners. I can now read the screen on someone's phone from a thousand miles away."

"That's pretty impressive. Do you feel confident you can maintain the gravity system?"

"Yes, I went over it with Quat. I really don't see any way it could fail. But in the unlikely event there's a problem, I'm sure we can fix it."

"Before we leave, they'll be bringing the cinnamon and chocolate we discussed earlier onboard. They're gifts for Coplent. Please make sure they're stored properly. We'll also be bringing some power modules for them."

"Okay, I'll take care of it. Anything else?"

"No, not now."

Ron left the bridge and a minute later Jeffery and Debbie left as well. They walked to Jeffery's quarters, which was now their quarters, and found a surprise on the door. The little name plate that said, "Captain Jeffery Whitestone" had been replaced with a ten-inch-square engraved brass plate that said, "Admiral Jeffery Whitestone and Captain Debbie Whitestone." Jeffery and Debbie were both surprised and pleased. The plate was very impressive.

Two days later, the modifications to the long-range and visual scanners were completed. All of the tests the crew performed went perfectly. Jeffery and Debbie were very impressed with the changes, and they were now more confident the Star Rover would be the perfect ship for interstellar travel. However, there was one more surprise. The NASA engineers had completed a modification to the design of the particle beam weapon on the Star Rover that increased the power substantially and the range to thirty thousand miles. Jeffery was not sure if the ship needed a weapon that powerful, but felt it was always better to be prepared for any situation. The weapons modifications would take two weeks. That meant it would be completed only a few days before they were scheduled to start their mission.

Time flew by. The weapons modifications were completed on schedule. Debbie and Jeffery decided they

266

would stop just past the orbit of Pluto again to test the weapons systems before continuing on the mission. Jeffery was told to return to Earth immediately if the tests failed.

For this mission, all but three of the rooms would be occupied. The crew utilized twenty-one rooms since Jeffery and Debbie now shared one. Mike, as third in command, moved into the executive officer quarters and there were twenty-six paying guests. Each guest paid five million dollars for the privilege of being on the eighteen-month mission.

The day before the mission was scheduled to start, all the guests arrived onboard. About half of them were college professors or other members of the academic community. The others were simply very wealthy people who were looking for an adventure. Jeffery was sincerely hoping that "adventure" would be lacking in the mission.

Late in the afternoon, Jeffery received a call from Max who said he was on the station and wanted somebody to pick him up and bring him to the Star Rover. Debbie volunteered to go. She returned to the ship with Max thirty minutes later.

When Max and Debbie walked onto the bridge Max said, "Good day Admiral Whitestone. Are you prepared for your mission?"

"Yes sir. All the passengers are onboard. The new systems have been thoroughly tested, with the exception of the weapons systems. Everything is working normally. The material for Coplent arrived yesterday and is properly stored. We have food and air for two years. I believe we're as ready as we'll ever be."

"Good! I'm glad to hear that. I'd like to speak to you and Dr. Weber. Is he in his office?"

"I'm sure he is. What's this about?"

"I'll explain it to both of you together."

Jeffery and Max walked over to the medical office. When they walked in, they found Dr. Weber reading something on his computer. He looked up and said, "Hello Max, I haven't seen you for some time. Is there something I can do for you?"

"Hi Frank. Yes, there's something I need your help with. Are you aware of an epidemic of a flu-like illness in central Africa?"

"Yes, I've read something about it. The article made it seem like it was under control."

"We've found a way to relieve the symptoms, but we haven't found a cure. We're working on it, but the virus is unlike anything we have seen before. The reason I'm here today is that I want to give you some blood samples containing the virus. We'd like you to take them to Coplent and see if they might be able to find a cure. If they can't, Garlut mentioned a planet that specializes in medical problems. Perhaps you could arrange to have the samples given to them."

"I'll do what I can. Please send all the information you have about the disease to me."

"We're collecting the data now and you'll have it in a few hours."

"Do you realize we won't be back for eighteen months? That would appear to be a long time to wait."

"They've been working on this for over a year. The disease doesn't spread very quickly. To date we have three hundred cases and we have no idea how it's transmitted. So far, forty of the patients have died from respiratory failure. The symptomatic relief does prevent that, but the patients who are receiving treatment are now showing signs of kidney failure. A cure in eighteen months may be the best we can hope for."

"I understand what needs to be done and I'll do my best to help."

"I know you will. Let me know when you receive the information. Please review it as quickly as possible and if there's anything else you need, call me immediately."

"You can count on it, Max."

Max and Jeffery left the medical office and returned to the shuttle bay. Jeffery took Max to the station, where another shuttle was waiting to take him back to Florida.

When he returned to the bridge, Dr. Weber was waiting for him. He said, "I received the information regarding the disease. I think the situation may be more serious than Max realizes. The number of cases has increased by 30% in the last thirty days. If that continues, by the time we get back the number of cases could be astronomical. I'm thankful that at least we can hold the symptoms at bay, so we do have some time. The other positive thing is the resulting kidney failure is mild, but it's certainly a cause for concern. If a patient becomes very ill, we can resort to dialysis. That's not a great option, but it's better than death."

"Do you need anything else from Max? After we leave there's no way to contact him."

"I know, but I believe what I have is sufficient. I'll call Max and let him know."

"Good, but you still have twelve hours before we leave in case you find you need something else."

"I'll go over the material again."

That evening they had a big dinner for the crew and guests. Jeffery gave a speech similar to the one he had given before they left on the first mission, but this time there were no warnings about the lack of gravity.

At exactly noon the following day, June 14, 2120, the Star Rover left Earth's orbit. They accelerated slowly until they were in the correct position. Jeffery made the announcement they would be entering the wormhole in twenty seconds. Then thirty-five seconds later, he announced they had exited the wormhole and were now three million miles beyond the orbit of Pluto.

They spent several hours testing the new weapons systems. Sean Richards, the chief security officer, reported the weapons were working perfectly.

The Star Rover was now ready to begin its journey to the Procolt system. Jeffery announced they would be entering the wormhole again in a few seconds, but this time they were going almost twenty-eight light years, so it would take seventy-six days to travel that distance. He also reminded them that the external monitors would be useless during that time.

The trip to the Procolt system was largely uneventful. A few people got sick, but nothing serious. There were a few falls, the worst resulting in a sprained ankle. The chefs did their best to prepare some interesting meals and the recreational areas on the ship were kept busy. It was boring, but it wasn't unexpected. Since the guests knew what to expect, they didn't complain.

When the ship exited the wormhole, they were just outside the orbit of Procolt 6. Everyone onboard was watching an external monitor when suddenly the Procolt system came into sharp focus.

Jeffery, Debbie, and Mike were on the bridge. Jeffery asked, "Should we go directly to Procolt 2 or should we go into a low orbit around each of the planets in the system before going there?"

Mike said, "Since our paying guests have chosen Dr. Haslet as their spokesman, why don't we ask him?"

"That's a good idea." Jeffery picked up his com unit and said, "Haslet."

A moment later he heard, "Haslet here."

Jeffery responded, "Dr. Haslet, this is Admiral Whitestone. Please come to the bridge."

"I'll be there in a few minutes sir."

When Dr. Haslet walked onto the bridge, Jeffery asked him the same question he had posed earlier. Dr. Haslet thought about it for a few seconds and said, "I think we should go directly to Procolt 2, then if we have time, we can explore the other planets in the system. All of us are anxious to get off the ship for a while and none of the other planets are suitable for exploration."

"Okay Dr. Haslet, we'll do that. Lieutenant Parker, please set a course for Procolt 2."

Mike turned to face his console, typed in several commands, and said, "Procolt 2 isn't in a direct line of sight from here. We'll have to go near Procolt 4 first and then we can go directly to Procolt 2."

"That's fine. Please carry on."

After a brief jump through the wormhole, Procolt 4 was visible in the external monitors. Before Mike could execute the next command, the ship's radiation alarm sounded and there was a brief power fluctuation. Debbie said, "Admiral, it appears we've been scanned again."

Jeffery said, "Locate the ship that scanned us."

A few seconds went by and Debbie said, "Sir, the ship is seventy thousand miles off our starboard side. It isn't the same configuration as Garlut's."

"Lieutenant, try to contact them."

"Yes, Admiral," She sent a standard greeting. Ten seconds later she received a response. "I just received the following message: 'Your ship is intruding on the sovereign territory of the planet of Torblit. You have one standard hour to leave this system or your ship will be destroyed.'"

"That doesn't seem very friendly. Send this message: 'We are the newest member of the trade association. We're from the planet Earth. We were told by Garlut of Coplent we could explore Procolt 2 and it was not inhabited. We have no desire to interfere with anything you're doing or trespass on your territory.'"

The response was: "You now have .992 standard hours to leave this system or your ship will be destroyed. Coplent has no authority to grant access to our territory."

Jeffery was determined to make the mission a success. He thought for a few seconds and said, "Lieutenant, send this: 'We're on a trading mission to Coplent and we're carrying valuable cargo they want. They know we're here and are waiting for us to arrive. All we want is some time to explore Procolt 2 and we will leave.'"

"We are not concerned with what you want or where you are going. We have established a mining colony on Procolt 4 and have claimed the entire system. You now have .983 standard hours to leave this system."

Now Jeffery, desperate to think of a way out of the situation and save the mission said, "These people are traders, perhaps they'll respond to a bribe. Let's try this: 'We would be willing to trade some of our cargo in exchange for granting us permission to explore Procolt 2.'"

This time there was a delay before they responded, "What cargo are you carrying?"

"Well, perhaps that got their attention. Send this: 'We're carrying a food product that is unique to Earth, a valuable spice we use, and electrical power supplies that never run out of power.'"

"We are not fools! There is no such thing as an electrical power supply that does not run out of power."

Jeffery said, "I think we're getting somewhere. Now try this: 'Allow me to bring a sample of each of these products to your ship. I'll come alone in an unarmed shuttle. If you're not happy with these samples, we'll leave this system immediately.'"

After another delay, they received this: "Move your ship to within one thousand units of our ship, then you may use your shuttle to bring the samples to us. If we detect any hostile move, we will destroy your ship without warning."

Jeffery asked, "Does anybody know how big a unit is?"

Cathy said, "That's in the book Garlut gave us. A unit is 1.23 miles."

"Send this: 'We accept your terms. We'll move our ship immediately.' Lieutenant Parker, move the ship."

Jeffery picked up his com unit and said, "Rice." When Ron answered, he said, "Put one case of chocolate candy bars, a ten-kilo bag of cinnamon, and two power modules on the shuttle immediately."

"Yes sir. May I ask why?"

"We'll discuss it later."

"Yes sir."

Mike moved the Star Rover and then they received a message. "You may come to our ship now. Approach from our port side."

Jeffery said, "Captain Whitestone, you have the ship. I'll keep my com unit on so you'll hear everything."

Debbie said, "Yes sir. And, as a personal favor, please don't get us killed. I'll be really mad at you if that happens."

Jeffery gave her a grim smile. "I'll do my best to keep us all alive."

Jeffery picked up one of the pocket translators they had received from Garlut as he left the bridge. When he arrived at

272

the shuttle bay, Ron was waiting for him and asked, "What's going on, Admiral?"

"The other ship has threatened to destroy us unless we leave this system. I'm hoping to bribe them with the stuff you put on the shuttle."

"Good luck," Ron said as Jeffery walked into the shuttle.

The alien ship was much larger than the Star Rover and there were obvious weapons attached in several places around it. It was cigar-shaped, approximately five hundred feet long and a hundred feet in diameter. There were markings on the side of the ship, but Jeffery had no idea what they were.

Jeffery moved the shuttle to a position two hundred feet from the port side of the alien ship. He watched as a large mechanical door opened and flew the shuttle inside the ship.

When the bay was pressurized again, Jeffery opened the shuttle door. Waiting outside were three people. They were all short, none of them taller than five feet. Their skin was a very pale blue, their eyes were dark green, and they wore tight fitting uniforms that were the same color as their skin. They appeared to be devoid of hair anywhere obvious and they had slightly bulging abdomens. The thought that came to Jeffery's mind was munchkins, but they didn't look friendly or happy. Two of them had hand-held weapons that were aimed at him. The one in the middle said something, but Jeffery had forgotten to turn on the translator. He reached into his pocket slowly and took out the translator. The aliens knew what it was and after Jeffery turned it on and put the earphone in his ear, the one in middle repeated what he had said before. "My name is Glencet. I am the captain of this ship. Show me what you brought."

Jeffery went back into the shuttle and returned with the two power modules. He said, "These are the electrical power supplies I told you about. They may not be of any use to you because they're designed to supply twelve volts and that may not meet your needs. But we can make them to produce any voltage and current you require."

"How does it work?"

Jeffery thought about it for a few seconds and said, "I'm not an engineer so I can't explain how it works, but I can verify it does work as I described to you. We use hundreds of them on our ship to provide electrical power."

"What else did you bring us?"

Jeffery returned to the shuttle and this time came back with the chocolate and the cinnamon. He opened the box of candy bars and handed one to Glencet, saying, "This is what we call candy on Earth."

Glencet looked at it, smelled it, and then handed it back to Jeffery and said, "You eat half of it."

Jeffery opened the candy bar, broke it in half, and ate half of it. He handed the other half back to Glencet.

He smelled it again and then took a small bite of the candy bar. Suddenly a big smile appeared on his face and he said, "This is very good. I want more."

"This box is for you. I can bring you one more box, but I have to bring the rest of it to Coplent. If you want more, I'm sure I can arrange for that to happen."

"What is in the bag?"

"This is a spice we call cinnamon. It's usually mixed with sugar to give food a unique flavor."

"Open the bag."

Jeffery opened the bag and put his finger inside it. When he removed his finger from the bag, he showed his finger to Glencet and then licked the cinnamon off his finger. Then Glencet did the same thing, but before tasting the cinnamon he put his finger by his nose and smelled it. He apparently liked the smell and licked the cinnamon off his finger. He said, "This is very good too."

Glencet told his companions they could put away their weapons and he said to Jeffery, "You have twenty standard days to explore Procolt 2. Then you must come back here. When you come back you will bring another box of candy and an engineer who can explain how these electrical power supplies work. I assume you have someone on your ship who can do that. Do not attempt to go to any other planet in this system. Are these terms acceptable to you?"

274

"Yes, they are. I'll be back in twenty days."

Glencet and his companions left the shuttle bay and Jeffery went back to his shuttle. As soon as he closed the hatch, the exterior door opened and Jeffery left the alien ship.

FUTURE WORLD HISTORY

BOOK 2

2120 - 2136

PROCOLT 2
SEPTEMBER 2120

After leaving Glencet's ship, Jeffery flew the shuttle to the Star Rover and docked inside the shuttle bay. He closed the outside door. When the pressure was equalized, he left the shuttle and walked inside.

Debbie was patiently waiting for him. She hugged him while saying, "You're a great negotiator. An hour ago, they wanted to kill us and now they've invited us to stay and explore."

"I'll accept the credit, but I think it's the only logical decision they could make. I knew they would want what we had to sell."

The couple walked to the bridge. When they arrived, Jeffery told Mike to plot a course to Procolt 2 and put the Star Rover in orbit above the equator. Two hours later, the Star Rover was exactly where it was supposed to be. Then he asked Debbie to look for a landing site.

On the second orbital pass, she said, "I think I found the perfect site. It looks like a large meadow near a lake. Scans indicate there are forested low mountains nearby containing a network of caves. It should be a great place to explore."

"Okay, that sounds good to me. Mike, put us in a geosynchronous orbit above the landing site," Jeffery ordered.

Mike responded, "Okay, I'll put us in a fixed position fifteen hundred miles above it."

Mike programmed the navigation computer, and twenty minutes later they were in orbit above the landing site Debbie had identified.

"Debbie, take Dr. Weber, Sheila, Thomas, and two security officers down to the surface. Have Dr. Weber verify conditions are acceptable for us without using spacesuits. I know Garlut told me there were no dangerous animals or plants, but I want Sheila to check out the plants in the area for anything that might be dangerous, and Thomas to look for any animals that might be a problem. I don't want to report that one of our guests was eaten by the local fauna or flora."

"Okay, we should be ready to depart in fifteen minutes."

"Debbie, don't leave the shuttle. I want you to stay onboard in case there's an emergency."

She nodded. "Understood."

Twenty minutes later, the shuttle departed the Star Rover. The trip to the surface of Procolt 2 took less than thirty minutes. Dean watched their descent on the scanner as the shuttle entered the atmosphere. Then he switched to the long-range scanner which clearly showed the shuttle and its position relative to the landing site. As Dean watched, the shuttle approached, circled the area twice, and landed.

The ship's com unit was monitoring Debbie. They heard her say, "We landed. The temperature is twenty-three degrees Centigrade and there's a westerly wind blowing at four miles per hour. Our instruments show the atmosphere is almost identical to Earth's. Dr. Weber is running some tests that will take ten minutes, and if everything checks out, my passengers will begin their assigned tasks. I've instructed that, for the moment, they must stay in visual range of the shuttle. One of the security people will remain on the ship with me and the other one will go with Dr. Weber."

"Good. Keep me informed," Jeffery responded.

Fifteen minutes later, Jeffery received a report from Dr. Weber. "Jeffery, all the tests I've run for potential pathogens are negative. The only problem I found was excessive amounts of pollen. Since I'm not familiar with the plants here, I don't know if that will be a problem. I suggest anybody with allergies stop by the medical office for a non-drowsy antihistamine injection before going to the planet's surface. I've tested the water in the lake for dissolved minerals and for the presence of heavy metals known to be troublesome for us. The results were similar to lakes on Earth, but I would not suggest swimming in it or drinking the water until I can check for any microorganisms that might be present."

"That's good news. You and Debbie should return to the ship so you can continue your testing, and Debbie can bring the temporary housing unit and the maintenance crew down to the surface for set up."

"We can leave in a few minutes."

Jeffery called Ron Rice, his chief engineer, and said, "Ron, have two of your staff bring the portable habitat to the shuttle bay. Debbie will take them to the landing site where they can assemble it."

"My guys will be there within half an hour. Is that okay?"

"Yes, they can take an hour because she's still on the planet. She'll be leaving shortly."

"Great, an hour it is."

The habitat was made up of very light, but strong, plastic panels. When fully assembled it had four bedrooms, two bathrooms, a small kitchen, a dining area, and a central-living area. It would take four or five hours to assemble. It was waterproof and could withstand winds up to one hundred twenty miles per hour. Automatic climate control would maintain a constant temperature of twenty-one degrees Celsius as long as the outside temperature was between negative thirty-two and positive fifty-seven. All the furniture and the plumbing fixtures were part of the structure, but the cushions and mattresses had to be inflated.

The building had a five hundred gallon water supply, but for this mission they would use water from the lake. If tests determined the water to be unusable, a filtration system would be installed to resolve the problem.

Debbie left to go back to the surface a few minutes after she arrived. She took the maintenance crew and the habitat to the surface and immediately returned to the ship.

By the time she returned, Dr. Weber had already given his approval of the water for swimming, but cautioned against swallowing any. During their initial study of the animals and plants, Thomas and Sheila reported they had found nothing they would consider dangerous.

Jeffery announced that in thirty minutes the shuttle would depart for the planet's surface again. They would take fifteen of the guests aboard to the surface on this trip. They

3

should decide among themselves who would go on the first trip. The remainder would go four hours later. There was eight hours of daylight left and he didn't want any of the guests on the surface of the planet the first night. Only crew members were to stay on the planet's surface.

Four people stayed in the habitat the first night on Procolt 2. There was one person from the security staff, Sheila, Thomas, and Daryl. There were no problems except a few howling animals. The next morning just after dawn it started to rain very hard at a rate of three inches per hour, but after a half hour the rain abruptly stopped, the clouds dissipated, and the day became sunny and warm once more.

After the rain stopped, the Star Rover sent the shuttle down to the surface on the first of two trips. The first trip had fifteen of the guests, Dr. Weber, and Jeffery. The second trip would have the remaining guests and Beatrice Woods, the mission videographer.

Each scientific crewmember had been given assignments while on the surface. Thomas Mason, the zoologist, and Beatrice were assigned to find the indigenous animals and take imagery of them. Sheila Nelson was assigned to continue her inspection of the plants in the area and take samples to bring back to the ship for analysis. Daryl Cohen, a geologist, volunteered to take a few of the guests with him as he explored some of the caves in the area.

Jeffery relaxed by the lake where he was joined by Dr. Weber. The water was crystal clear and there was an obvious abundance of fish swimming under the glassy surface. "You know what, Frank?" he said. "I think this would be a great spot for a vacation home. Debbie and I could live in the habitat, build a small boat, and go fishing every day."

"This seems like the perfect spot for that, Jeffery. It makes me wonder why this planet is uninhabited. Perhaps people from other planets don't like to relax the way we do?"

"I suppose that's possible. But I'd be happy to trade several cases of chocolate for the rights to this place."

"You're talking like you're ready to retire."

4

"No, I don't want to retire. I just want a place to go where nobody can disturb me."

Before Dr. Weber could respond, Jeffery got a call on his com unit. After he answered, Daryl said, "I need you and Dr. Weber here immediately! We found something you have to see."

"What is it?" Jeffery asked.

"A body . . . well, more of a skeleton. I think it's human."

"Dr. Weber is with me. We'll be there as soon as possible. Leave your com unit open so we can find you."

"Yes sir."

Jeffery turned toward Frank and asked, "Did you hear that?"

"Yes, I did. But I don't think it's human. I'm certain we're the first humans to visit this planet."

"I guess we'll know shortly."

Jeffery and Dr. Weber followed the signal from Daryl's com unit to the entrance of a cave. A woman Jeffery recognized as one of the ship's guests was waiting for them. As they approached, she said, "We have to go two hundred feet into the cave."

She was holding a bright, lantern-shaped light. Jeffery and Dr. Weber followed her into the cave. A minute later they reached the spot where Daryl and the others were standing. They moved away from the skeleton so the doctor and Jeffery could inspect the remains.

They saw a skeleton that had shreds of clothing around it. Around its neck was a metal tag on a chain. Jeffery took one look at the metal tag and gasped. "It's definitely human. Frank, he's wearing an old military dog tag!"

Frank bent down closer to the remains and looked at the dog tag. The information on the tag was written in English. The name on the tag was Gordon Brown, he had O negative blood, and he was Catholic. It also had a social security number, so he was from the United States.

"How could Mr. Brown possibly have gotten here?" Dr. Weber asked excitedly.

5

Jeffery had a perplexed look on his face. He thought about the situation for a few seconds and replied, "I have no idea, but I do know who to ask. The next time I see Garlut it will be my first question. How long has he been here, any clue, Doctor?"

Dr. Weber knelt down and began a cursory examination of the remains. A few minutes later when he was finished, he stood up and said, "That's a very difficult question to answer. We really don't know very much about the environment here. It does appear small animals were eating the body because there are obvious gnaw marks on the bones. But the lack of decay in the bones would seem to indicate he hasn't been dead very long. Perhaps less than a year or two, but I'm not sure. Do you think we could find out more about him since we have his name and identification numbers?"

"We could if we were back on Earth. However, after the North American Union was formed, the Social Security system was replaced with the Resident Identification System, and the RIS numbers are not in the same format. Mr. Brown had to have arrived on this planet at least 100 years ago. The military stopped using Social Security Numbers back in the late twenty-first century and went to a different numbering system approved by the old Department of Defense. Can you get any information by analyzing the remains?"

"I'm not sure. I don't have the equipment to do carbon dating, but I can do a genetic analysis. It may show any diseases he'd been exposed to during his lifetime which could give us an approximate age."

Then Daryl said, "There's something else over here you need to see."

Jeffery and the doctor walked to where he was. There was evidence of a fire. They found a knife with a blade six inches long, a metal water canteen, and small bones were scattered around the area.

Jeffery thought the knife was the type members of the military were given a long time ago, and the metal canteen was something he had only seen in museums. Jeffery began to think perhaps Mr. Brown was much older than they thought.

6

Jeffery made arrangements for the skeleton to be taken back to the ship. Dr. Weber would accompany it and begin his analysis immediately. Jeffery also began to wonder if there were any other humans on the planet, so he contacted Debbie and asked her to scan for any animal larger than fifty pounds. Garlut had told him the largest animals on the planet were the size of small dogs. However, Garlut had also told him there was a substantial insect population on the planet and he had seen only a few. Now he had more questions for Garlut.

Daryl asked, "May we continue to explore the cave?"

"Yes, but inform me immediately if you find anything unusual."

"Yes, sir."

During that first full day on Procolt 2, there were a few other surprises. During the search for indigenous animals, Thomas and Beatrice discovered most of the animals they saw would be considered rodents on Earth. Perhaps the most unusual was an animal that looked like a giant squirrel. They had the same basic body shape and a long furry tail, but when they sat on their hind legs, they were thirty inches tall, and looked like they weighed at least twenty-five pounds. Additionally, instead of claws they had small hands with four fingers and opposable thumbs.

The team was also surprised by the fact there were very few birds. Most of the things that flew were medium-sized insects similar to grasshoppers and some smaller ones that looked like flies. They didn't see any primates, but they were only looking in a small area. However, they still managed to gain images and video of over forty different animal species.

Sheila's search for plants yielded better results. She found eighty-one different plant species in the first few hours of her search. None of them were unusual and they looked similar to Earth's plants. She planned to widen her search area the following day.

Daryl continued the search through the cave and found no other indications of human habitation. All of the rocks in the cave walls were common on Earth.

Dr. Weber spent hours running tests on the skeletal remains of Gordon Brown, but found nothing that could help him determine age.

After spending several more hours relaxing by the lake, Jeffery decided he had to return to the ship. The next shuttle was scheduled to go back to the Star Rover in twenty minutes. He walked to the shuttle and took a seat inside. A few minutes later, Thomas and Beatrice came aboard.

Beatrice sat next to Jeffery and offered to show him the videos she had taken of the animals.

They spent the next twenty minutes looking at them. When the video of the giant squirrel played, Jeffery stared at it and then asked Beatrice to play it again. As he watched the video the second time he said to Thomas, "This animal appears to me to be very intelligent. Perhaps I'm wrong, but it almost looks like it's posing for the camera."

"I'm glad you said that because I thought the same thing. Tomorrow I'm going to follow one around for a while to see how it spends the day. If it really is intelligent, we should know by the end of the day."

"That's a good idea. Let me know what you find out."

"I'll do that."

After the shuttle landed on the Star Rover, Jeffery immediately went to the bridge. Anne Perkins, communications officer, was seated at the communications console and Jeffery said, "I believe the trade group communication system Garlut installed is going to be more useful than I thought. Anne, please contact Glencet."

Anne called Glencet's ship and a few moments later they heard him say, "Admiral Whitestone, how can I help you?"

Jeffery took Anne's place at the console, pressed a button and said, "I have a question. While exploring a cave this morning my crew members found some humanoid remains, a skeleton and a few shreds of clothing. However, around the neck of the skeleton was a metal tag that identified him as a member of the military of the United States. That country hasn't existed on Earth for almost eighty standard years. Do you have any idea how somebody from Earth could have gotten to Procolt 2?"

"We have not spent much time on Procolt 2. We only go there to replenish our water supply. Also, we have only been here on a permanent basis for less than two standard years. Ships from Coplent have traveled there far more often than we have, although we have not seen any ships other than cargo ships from Torblit and your ship since we have been here. I do remember hearing a rumor that some humanoids were seen on Procolt 2 many years ago, but I always thought it was just that, a rumor. Perhaps your friend Garlut can help you when you see him."

"I'll certainly ask him. Are you making progress with the samples I left you?"

"The box of chocolate is gone. Every member of my crew enjoyed it. I was hoping you could bring more before you leave. I gave the spice to my cook who will use it in a cake. The power modules do seem to work as you described, but their electrical output is not suitable for our needs. When you come back with your engineer, we will explain to him what our requirements are. We would like you to tell us how much they would cost."

"I'm certain the power modules can be designed to provide any type of electrical power that's required. The trade group was going to send some people to Earth to help us price the products we're going to sell. I'm sure that will be done before I return to Earth. I'll let them know what you need and we'll give Torblit a price. However, I won't be back on Earth for almost two years."

"That is not a problem. We all understand trading with new trade group planets is slow at the beginning. Since Coplent is helping you, please inform them of our desire to purchase the power modules and the chocolate. I wish I could have been more helpful regarding the human you found."

"Don't worry about the skeleton. I have a feeling Garlut knows something about it. When we meet again, I'll bring you another case of chocolate."

Glencet said, "Thank you," and the connection was terminated.

Since there were no problems the first night, Jeffery agreed to let some of the guests stay in the habitat on Procolt 2 for the second night. The following morning it rained again, and Jeffery began to wonder if it was going to happen every day.

Once the rain stopped, Thomas and Beatrice went to search for another giant squirrel. Thomas thought perhaps he could make friends with the squirrel, so he took two carrots from the kitchen storage bin before they left the habitat.

Daryl and her group of guests went to explore a different cave and Sheila went looking for more plants. This time one of the ship's guests went with her.

It took Thomas and Beatrice nearly fifteen minutes to find a squirrel. It was standing in a clearing in front of a forested area, its light brown fur shimmering in the sunlight. They were approximately one hundred and fifty feet away and decided to stay out of sight by hiding behind a large tree. The squirrel was sitting on its hind legs looking around. Beatrice began making a video recording, and as they watched, the squirrel was joined by two more. One of them was much smaller and probably a juvenile. They were shocked when they saw what happened next. The squirrels began making sounds that almost sounded like speech. As they continued to watch, it became obvious it was a rudimentary form of communication. They were speaking to one another! Then, much to their surprise, the first squirrel pointed at where Thomas and Beatrice were hiding and said something to the other two squirrels. Then all three squirrels scampered back into the forest and disappeared.

Thomas could hardly believe what he had just witnessed. He stammered when he asked, "Did we really just watch three squirrels have a family meeting and talk about us?"

Beatrice replied softly, "It's hard to believe, but that's what it looked like to me too."

"Did you record what they said?"

"I'll play it back and check the audio."

Beatrice played the video. The squirrel speech was loud and clear. They couldn't understand any of it, but Beatrice suggested they ask Cathy to analyze the patterns.

"I think we should keep looking for more squirrels," Thomas said.

"Absolutely."

They decided to go into the forest to continue their search. A half hour later, they spotted two of the animals sitting on a log. Beatrice started recording the two squirrels and Thomas began walking slowly toward them. The squirrels saw him coming and began talking to each other, but they made no move to run away. Thomas took the two carrots out of his pocket, and as he walked closer, he offered them to the squirrels. The squirrels looked at Thomas, exchanged a few words, and waited for him to come closer. When he was only a few feet away, he crouched down and offered each of the squirrels the food. The squirrels both reached out toward Thomas and they each took a carrot. They smelled them and took a small bite. They obviously liked the carrots because they were both eaten within a few seconds.

When the squirrels were finished, they both looked at Thomas and said something. Although he couldn't understand the words, he was sure they were asking for more. He said, "I'm sorry but I don't have any more now. I'll bring you more tomorrow."

He turned around and started walking toward Beatrice and he heard the squirrels say something to each other, then they jumped off the log and began following him. When he was a few feet from Beatrice he said, "I wonder if they're going to follow us back to the habitat."

"Well, you did want a chance to study them to see if they're intelligent. But I'm sure we already know the answer to that question."

"I'm going to call Cathy and ask her to come down here." He picked up his com unit and after exchanging greetings, he said, "I think we need your language skills down here. Can you come down on the next shuttle?"

11

"Sure, but I thought there was no intelligent life on the planet. Why would you need language skills?"

"You probably won't believe this until you see it for yourself. We discovered some animals that resemble large squirrels with small hands instead of front paws. Beatrice made several videos of them speaking to each other! I'm hoping, perhaps with your assistance, we could learn a few words of their language."

Cathy giggled into her com unit. "Is this a joke?"

"No, right now two of them are following us as we walk back to the habitat. I gave them each a carrot and I think they want more. If you want, I'll ask Beatrice to send a video to you."

"Please do that. I'll get back to you after I see it."

"Okay. I'll be waiting."

Although Beatrice only heard half of the conversation, she realized Thomas wanted her to send one of the videos to Cathy, so she sent it immediately. A few minutes later, Thomas received a call from Cathy.

"This is very hard to believe," she admitted, "but I'm sure you're right. I heard several sounds repeated. They could be common words, names, or even phrases. I obviously don't know what they were saying, but there were definitely words being spoken. I have to talk to Jeffery about this. I'll be down there as soon as I can."

"Okay, we'll be waiting at the habitat."

Jeffery and Cathy came down to the planet on the shuttle. When they walked over to the habitat, they saw several of the crew members, including Thomas and Beatrice and a few of the guests, standing in a circle. As they drew closer, they could see two squirrels inside the circle.

As they approached they were greeted by everyone, and then two of the crew members moved out of the way so Jeffery and Cathy could get a close look at these remarkable squirrels.

Thomas gave a carrot to Jeffery and Cathy. Cathy took the carrot, offered it to one the squirrels, and asked, "Would you like a carrot?"

The squirrel looked at her and said something. Then Cathy asked Beatrice, "Have you been recording them?"

"Yes, by now I have nearly two hours of video."

"I want to study the recordings." Turning to Jeffery she asked, "Can you get a supply of vegetables for me that I may give to them? I'd like to be alone with them and see if I can get some basic understanding of their language."

"Yes, I'm sure I can get you all the vegetables you need. I think we have plenty of nuts onboard too. Are you sure they're actually talking?"

"It certainly appears that way. One of the classes I took in college was about how some of the early explorers in Africa and South America learned native languages. I'm sure the same principals apply here."

"Okay, I'll get you some treats for our new friends. After you learn to speak their language, ask them if they know how Mr. Brown came to be on this planet."

"I know you're joking, but I suspect their language may not have words to ask the question you want. Most simple languages only have words for things that are common in their environment. They may have no real concept of time and probably would not have the ability to understand a question like, 'where did something come from?' However, they may be much smarter than we think they are. I should know in a few days."

"Okay, I want you to stay down here and work with them."

"That's exactly what I want to do. Thank you."

Cathy spent the rest of the day working with the squirrels. She showed them common objects and said the English word and noted the response. After working with them for six hours, Cathy thought that she may have discovered the words for tree, rock, water, sun, and food. In an attempt to teach them her name, she was now convinced that in the mind of the squirrels all humans were "Cathy." It only took them five minutes to learn her name and that was impressive. Cathy also learned their word for squirrel. It was "clorspo."

As evening approached, it was apparent the squirrels were getting uncomfortable. They turned to each other and exchanged a few words. Then one of them turned toward Cathy and said something that included the word "clorspo" and they left. In a few moments they had disappeared inside the forest. Cathy didn't know what they said, but she thought it was probably something like, "We have to go now, but we'll be back tomorrow." At least she was hoping that was what they said.

Cathy went inside the habitat and went to the kitchen to find something to eat. She sat at a table and sent a report on the day's progress to Jeffery. She was very happy with the results so far. The squirrels were sentient, but she was worried they wouldn't return.

After she had finished eating, Beatrice walked into the kitchen, got something to drink, and walked over to join Cathy.

"I was watching you work with the squirrels for a while," Beatrice said. "I was impressed with your ability and the intelligence of the squirrels."

"I think they call themselves 'clorspo.'"

"Okay, I was impressed with the intelligence of the clorspo."

Cathy laughed. "I was too. I just hope they'll come back tomorrow morning. They left in a hurry."

"I'm sure they'll be back. They like our food. There's an extra bed in my room. Do you want to use it?"

"Yes, thank you. Please show me."

Cathy put her dishes in the dishwasher and threw away the garbage. Then she followed Beatrice to the room.

Cathy fell asleep quickly, but woke up well before dawn. She tried to go back to sleep, but after fifteen minutes she gave up. She showered, dressed, and went to the kitchen to get something for breakfast. By the time she was finished, the sun was starting to rise.

She walked outside and realized it was about to rain again. She went back inside and a few minutes later the rain started. As she watched the rain, she wondered what the

14

squirrel word for rain was. After the rain was over, she went outside looking for the squirrels, but saw none. Somebody had brought a few plastic chairs down from the ship and she decided to sit down and wait for them outside.

She didn't have long to wait. About ten minutes later, six squirrels walked out of the forest and came over to her. She set up a camera to record everything.

She watched as the squirrels came closer and then one of them said a few words to her. She understood two of the words: "clorspo" and "spol." She believed "spol" was the word for food. She realized she had forgotten to bring out some of the vegetables and nuts Jeffery sent. As she started to get them, she saw Sheila walking out of the habitat with the food.

Sheila gave Cathy the box and said, "I thought you might want this. Is it okay if I watch for a while? I promise I won't interfere."

"Sure, if you want to. Just get another chair."

"Okay."

Cathy opened the box and found a bag of raw almonds inside. She opened the bag and took out a handful. She gave an almond to each of the squirrels who took and ate it, but two of the squirrels said "plor" to her as they took the nut.

Sheila asked, "Did they just say, 'thank you?'"

Cathy nodded. "I think so."

After three hours, many carrots, and half a bag of almonds had been consumed, one of the squirrels walked up to Cathy and said something that included the words "spol," "plor," and "clorspo." The squirrels then went back into the forest.

Cathy and Sheila walked back inside the habitat. Cathy sat down at a desk in the living room and said, "I think I may have enough information now to understand at least fifty words, perhaps more. This is the most exciting thing I've ever done!"

"Can you load their language information into one of the portable translators Garlut gave us?" Sheila asked.

"Yes, the man Garlut sent to install the communications system showed me how to do it. The problem is I know a lot of nouns, but no verbs so far. I'm hoping to add a few verbs to my vocabulary by the end of the day."

Cathy and Sheila spent the next two weeks working with the squirrels. By the end of that time, Cathy was fluent in their language. Perhaps more surprising was that the squirrels had learned some English. Cathy asked the squirrels about Gordon Brown, but all they could tell her was that the squirrels had been seeing humans for a long time. They really didn't have any meaningful way of measuring time, or any words to describe time, because it wasn't important to them.

There were no more unusual discoveries made during their stay on Procolt 2. Two days before they were scheduled to leave, Cathy called Jeffery to ask if she could meet with him for a few minutes. Jeffery asked her to come to his cabin at 7:00 that evening.

At exactly 7:00, Cathy pressed the entry button on Jeffery's cabin door. The door opened and she went inside. Jeffery was seated at the table. He looked at her and said, "Please, have a seat, Cathy. How can I help you?"

"I know we're scheduled to leave in two days. I've made great progress in communications with the squirrels, and I would like to know if I can stay here for a while so I can continue working with them. They're amazing creatures and are probably more fluent in English than I am in Squirrel. They have a society which has values similar to our own. I really think they warrant further study."

"I agree we should study them, but do you realize it will be years before we'll be able to come back? Are you ready to spend the next three years without human company?"

"Sheila wants to stay here too, so I won't be alone. There's fresh native fruits and vegetables to eat. The water from the lake is drinkable, and the habitat will provide shelter. I'm sure we'll be fine. The only thing I will miss is coffee."

"I'll have to think about it. Is Anne capable of taking your place?"

"Yes, I'm sure she is."

16

"I also have to ask Glencet if you can stay here, since he claims his planet owns this entire solar system. I'll give you my answer tomorrow."

"Thank you."

After Cathy left his cabin, Jeffery walked over to the bridge. When he arrived, Mike and Anne were on duty. He said to Anne, "Cathy wants to stay here and work with the squirrels. Before I can make a decision on her request, I need to know if you believe you're capable of taking over her position. Are you okay with that?"

Anne thought for a minute and said, "Yes, Cathy and I loaded the information on the squirrels' language into the translator together. I've read the manuals and both of us studied the information Garlut left for us on the trade group protocols."

"Okay, now I have to ask Glencet if I can leave two of my people on the planet for three years. Please contact him for me."

"Yes sir."

A minute later, Anne handed Jeffery the headset and he said, "Captain Glencet, may I ask you a question?"

"Yes, of course. Admiral Whitestone."

"While exploring Procolt 2, we discovered something else besides the skeleton of a human. We discovered a race of very intelligent animals. They're similar to an animal on Earth we call a squirrel. Except these animals are not only intelligent, they are much larger, and have hands instead of paws. They have their own language, which one of my officers has learned. This officer and our ship's exobiologist have asked permission to stay on Procolt 2 for three years to study these animals. However, you only allowed us twenty days to explore the planet. Before I give them my answer, I have to know if you would have any objections if they stayed here."

"I am not sure. Are they capable of living on their own for that long?"

"Yes, I'm sure they are. We constructed a small building on the planet which will provide them with shelter, a

17

lake to supply them with water, and there are native fruits and vegetables to eat."

"Do you want me to agree or would it be easier for you if I refused your request?"

"This isn't an easy decision. I'm concerned for their safety, but I understand their desire to stay here. Obviously if you refuse my request, the decision is no longer mine, but I'm not looking for an easy way out."

"I have a suggestion. In exchange for three boxes of chocolate, we will allow your people to stay on the planet. Additionally, we will make monthly trips to Procolt 2 and make sure they are okay. Do they have the equipment to contact us in the event of an emergency?"

"No, we only have one trade group communication system and it's installed on my ship."

"We have some handheld devices. I could give them one to use, but it does not have a translator-built in."

"Do you have a handheld communications system that can send and receive signals from Procolt 2 to Procolt 4? Our handheld devices have a maximum range of only five thousand miles. Anyway, one of the officers who wants to stay on the planet is our language expert. I could bring her to your ship and I'm sure she would be able to learn enough of your language for basic communication in a few days."

"Okay, we can do that. Have you made the decision to let her stay?"

"No, but I will soon. I will contact you again shortly."

"Okay."

Debbie was on the planet, so Jeffery called her and asked her to take the next shuttle back to the ship. When she was onboard, she went to her cabin where Jeffery was waiting for her. "Is there a problem?" she asked.

"No, not exactly. I have a decision to make and I want your input."

"Does this concern Cathy's request to stay on the planet?"

"Yes, it's not an easy decision. Three years is a long time to be on your own."

18

"They aren't alone. Don't forget the squirrels are there. I've been watching them. I'm certain they wouldn't allow any harm to come to either of them."

"I've made an arrangement with Glencet to check on them once a month. Glencet is also going to give them a handheld communicator so they could contact his ship in case of an emergency. So, do you think I should approve their request to stay here?"

"Yes, I think you should."

"Okay, but I want to make sure they understand what they're getting into." Jeffery picked up his com unit and called Cathy. "Hi Cathy. I'd like to see you and Sheila in my cabin at 9:00 tomorrow morning."

"Does this mean you're approving our request?"

"No, it means I want to talk to both of you about your request."

"Yes sir, we'll both be there."

The following morning at 8:57, the entry button was pushed on the door to Jeffery and Debbie's cabin. Jeffery said, "Come in."

Cathy and Sheila walked into the cabin.

Jeffery and Debbie were seated at the small table in their room. They motioned for Cathy and Sheila to sit.

Jeffery said, "Good morning. As I explained yesterday, I want to be sure you understand what you're asking. My decision will depend on what you say. Is that clear?"

Both women said, "Yes."

"When we leave here, we'll probably be unable to return for three years. Remember, this is the only interstellar ship we have. Should something happen to the ship, you would be stranded here for who knows how long."

"I hadn't thought about that, but I believe the odds are fairly remote anything would happen. In any case, I'm willing to accept the risk," Cathy said.

"I'm also willing to accept the risk," Sheila answered.

"In the event I approve this, you should know I have made arrangements with Glencet to send a ship to check on you once every month. Also, Glencet is going to supply you with a com unit you can use to contact his ship in case of an emergency. However, the com unit doesn't have a translator built in. Both of you will be required to go to Glencet's ship and spend enough time there to learn their language. You don't have to be fluent, but you will need to know enough to call for help and understand the response."

"That seems like a very good idea. Is Glencet's ship going to stay here for the next three years?" Cathy asked.

"I don't know, but I already thought about asking him."

"Sheila, how are you with learning languages?"

"I'm not as good as Cathy, but I took several years of French in college and didn't find it very difficult."

"Good, so you're comfortable with this?"

"Yes."

"Very good. I'll contact Glencet today and we'll take you to his ship tomorrow. Please make sure your furry friends know you won't be there for a few days."

"I already told them we might be leaving and would be gone for many days. They have no concept of numbers, but if I'm given the opportunity, I'm going to try to teach them about numbers and time."

"Okay, I'll contact you after I speak to Glencet."

The two women left the cabin and after the door closed Debbie said, "I think Sheila is worried about learning Torblit, or whatever they call their language."

"I got the same feeling. We'll see how she does. She only has to be able to call for help."

"Yes, I know."

Later that morning, Jeffery contacted Glencet and asked him if he could bring his two crew members over there at 10:00 the next morning. Glencet agreed and reminded Jeffery about the chocolate. Laughing, Jeffery replied he would bring the three cases.

At 9:00 the following morning, the Star Rover left the orbit of Procolt 2 and was within ten miles of Glencet's ship by 9:30. Anne contacted Glencet's ship informing them their shuttle would depart shortly. As the shuttle approached the alien craft, the door opened to the hangar bay where the shuttle flew inside and landed. When the bay was pressurized there was a knock at the hatch of the shuttle. As soon as it opened Jeffery saw Glencet and next to him was a man probably six inches taller than Glencet, and significantly stronger looking.

Jeffery put on his translator and heard Glencet tell the man to take the cases of chocolate to his cabin. He said, "Good morning, Captain Glencet. It's nice to see you again. Permission to come aboard?"

Glencet replied, "Please, welcome aboard, Admiral." He watched as the three exited the shuttle and asked, "Are these the crew members who want to stay on Procolt 2?"

"Yes, they are." Pointing at Cathy, he said, "This is Lieutenant Cathy Carter, she's a language expert and our chief communications officer." Then he pointed to Sheila and said, "This is Lieutenant Sheila Roth, she's one of our ship's exobiologists, specializing in botany."

"It is very nice to meet both of you. Please accompany me to the bridge and I will introduce you to your instructor. Her name is Moltas."

They followed Glencet to the bridge and Glencet introduced Moltas. The three women left the bridge. After they left Jeffery said, "I'm sure Lieutenant Carter won't have any problems, but I'm not so sure about Lieutenant Roth. If she's unable to learn what she needs to know to make a distress call, I'll have to withdraw my permission for them to stay on Procolt 2."

"I will contact you tomorrow and let you know how they are doing. Do they both have translators?" Glencet asked.

"No, we only have two. I gave one to Lieutenant Carter."

"Okay, we have a lot of them onboard, but they are not programmed for your language. We will borrow the one Lieutenant Carter has and program our units. Then we can lend one to Lieutenant Roth. Do you have any videos of the animals you found?"

"Yes, I believe Lieutenant Carter brought them aboard. After your translators are loaded, you'll be able to understand my crew as well as the animals. Lieutenant Carter added the animal's language protocols earlier."

"Very good. I will take you back to your shuttle."

"Thank you. I'm looking forward to getting a progress report tomorrow morning."

The following morning, Jeffery had a brief conversation with Glencet who told him both officers were doing well learning the new language. He felt they wouldn't need more than two more days and they could be picked up in the evening the day after tomorrow.

After the conversation with Glencet, Jeffery and Debbie went down to the habitat. When they arrived, they were greeted by a group of squirrels. One of the larger ones came up to him and asked in a squeaky but understandable voice, "Are you Cathy's master?"

Cathy had told Jeffery the squirrels were learning English, but he was stunned by the question. He stared at the squirrel for a few moments and said, "Cathy works for me, so I am her superior, but not her master."

"Are you going to let Cathy stay here with us?"

"Yes, Cathy is going to stay with you. Sheila will stay with you too."

"Good. We like them. We will take care of them."

"Thank you, I want Cathy and Sheila to be happy while they stay here."

"Will they be here when the sun comes up again?"

"No, they'll be here after the sun comes up two times."

Jeffery saw his response to the question resulted with a blank stare from the squirrel. He had forgotten the squirrels had no concept of numbers. After thinking about it, he said, "They will not be here when the sun comes up again. They will be here the next time the sun comes up after the sun comes up tomorrow."

The squirrel seemed to be satisfied with his answer. It went back to the group and spoke to them for a few seconds before leaving the area around the habitat to venture back to the forest.

After the squirrels left, Debbie asked, "Do you think they understood what you said?"

"I think so. I never realized how hard it was to talk and not use numbers." He chuckled. "To tell you the truth, I'd like to stay here too. It's perfect. The temperature is ideal, it rains on schedule, and you can actually talk to the wildlife. What more could you ask for?"

"It does seem nice, but I think after a while I'd get tired of eating vegetables. I like meat, but I know I could never kill anything wild on this planet for food."

"I understand, but if we set up a resort, we could bring in a supply of meat on a regular schedule. I think people from Earth would pay a lot to vacation here."

"Are you planning on building your own starship? I don't think NASA wants to be in the tourist transport business."

"Actually, you would probably need several ships, because with only one ship you would only be able to make two trips per year, and most people can't just disappear for the length of time needed to come here on vacation."

"I think they can if they're very wealthy."

"Well, it was just a thought. But I think we should spend the whole day here since we won't be back for a while."

"You convinced me."

Jeffery and Debbie spent the day relaxing. They took the last shuttle of the day back to the Star Rover. The following day would be spent preparing the ship for the one hundred and thirty day trip to Coplent, which neither Jeffery nor Debbie were looking forward to.

The following morning Jeffery and Ron Rice, the chief engineer on the Star Rover, took the shuttle over to Glencet's ship. Glencet met them as they stepped off the shuttle. Jeffery said, "This is Lieutenant Rice. He can explain how the power modules work. You need to give him the specifications for the power modules you would like to buy."

"The engineer that Lieutenant Rice will be working with has that information," Glencet replied. Then he handed a translator with English capability to Ron and said, "Lieutenant

Rice, please wait here. One of my engineers will be here shortly to speak with you about the power modules."

"Okay, I'll wait here."

Then Glencet said, "Admiral Whitestone, please follow me to the bridge. Your people are there waiting for you."

Jeffery followed Glencet to the bridge. When they arrived, Cathy and Sheila were speaking with some of the members of Glencet's bridge crew.

"Are you two comfortable with your ability to ask for help if there's a problem?" Jeffery asked.

Both women answered "yes" at the same time.

"Then I have no problem granting your request to stay on Procolt 2 until we return."

They walked back to the shuttle bay and found Ron speaking with one of Glencet's engineers.

Glencet, looking at his engineer, asked, "Do you understand how the power modules work?"

"Yes, sir. They are actually very simple."

"Do you believe they will be reliable?"

"Yes, sir. I do."

"Good, please return to your station."

"Glencet, thank you for your assistance. I am no longer concerned about the safety of my people staying on Procolt 2."

"You are welcome. I want you to know that I am scheduled to return home in about a half year, but another ship will take over and they will continue to monitor your crew members. I will return here again in about a year and a half."

"Good, I was going to ask you how long you would be here. I will see you again when I return to Procolt 2."

Then Jeffery, Ron, Cathy, and Sheila boarded the shuttle, and they returned to the Star Rover. A few minutes later the ship was in orbit above the habitat on Procolt 2. Jeffery took the shuttle and went down to the habitat with Cathy and Sheila. The squirrels were waiting for them and appeared to be very pleased to see the two women again.

Jeffery asked, "Are you sure you want to stay here? This is your last chance to change your mind."

Cathy said, "We're sure we want to stay. I'm sure everything will be okay. I don't think Glencet would risk losing his supply of candy."

"I'm sure you're right. When we come back, I'll bring him a few dozen cases, and some usable power modules. I promise we'll come back as soon as possible."

After the "goodbyes" were said, Jeffery returned to the shuttle. He turned back and waved to his two brave officers, then he got aboard, closed the hatch, and returned to the Star Rover. He kept thinking he may have made a serious mistake allowing the women to stay.

THE JOURNEY TO COPLENT
OCTOBER 2120

The first forty-seven days of the trip went perfectly. Even though there were a lot of ways to keep busy on the ship, the guests complained of boredom. However, on day forty-eight, the boredom changed to fear. Just after 8:00 in the morning the wormhole system failed. Jeffery was informed immediately by chief engineering officer, Ron Rice. He wasn't sure what caused the failure, but the entire engineering department was working on the problem. He promised Jeffery he would give him a status report in an hour.

Jeffery made an announcement to the whole ship. "This is Admiral Whitestone. As you probably noticed, we exited the wormhole a few minutes after 8:00 a.m. This was the result of a system failure. Please do not be concerned. We have replacement parts aboard the Star Rover to repair the entire drive. Engineering is working on the situation and as progress develops, I will keep our crew and passengers informed."

An hour later, Jeffery still had not heard from Ron so he called him. Ron apologized and said he had lost track of the time. Additionally, he thought they found the issue, but it would take at least another two hours to verify.

Jeffery made another announcement. "I apologize but I have no new information regarding our situation at this time. Engineering thinks they've found the problem, but the analysis will take some more time. I'll keep you informed."

So far nobody on the ship was too concerned, but as the day wore on the news didn't get any better. The failure wasn't where the engineers first thought, and now they were looking at more than a dozen potential problem areas.

At 9:00 that evening, Jeffery called Ron and asked him to come to his cabin. When Ron arrived, he had a dismayed look on his face. Jeffery asked him for a progress update.

"I wish I knew. Every test we run indicates normal operation. Right now, we think the problem is in the wormhole projector. Unfortunately, that's the most complex part of the system. To make matters worse, we can't access it from inside the ship. I'm sending two men out with replacement parts and we're going to replace every part in it. That will take thirty-six hours. I wish I could guarantee it would fix the problem, but I can't. Jeffery, I can assure you we'll fix it. I just don't know how long it will take."

"I understand. I want you to know I don't think there's anyone more qualified than you to find it. I suspect some guests won't be pleased when I make the next announcement, but I'm sure they understand we're doing everything we can to resolve it. Please call me as soon as you have any additional information."

Jeffery made another announcement and gave everybody the status of the wormhole system.

After the announcement Debbie asked, "What do we do if we can't get the system online again?"

"I don't even want to think about that. We're out in the middle of nowhere, and without the wormhole system, this is where we'll stay. I could bring the ship up to 60% of light speed in three months, but there would still be nowhere to go. I suspect the closest system with an earthlike planet is Procolt, and we're more than fifteen light years from there. If Ron can't repair the system, the best we can hope for is that Garlut will realize there's a problem when we don't show up at Coplent and come looking for us."

The next thirty-two hours seemed to last forever. The mood on the Star Rover was bleak and grew worse as time went on. There seemed to be a general feeling of doom. But everyone knew the risks, so they were generally ready to accept their fate.

Jeffery and Debbie were both on the bridge as hour thirty-three of the repair approached. Ron walked onto the bridge wearing a big smile mixed with eyes that showed exhaustion and said, "We found the problem and everything appears to be working normally! We should be able to get moving again as soon as my men are back onboard."

Jeffery immediately made the following announcement to the entire ship. "This is Admiral Whitestone.

It gives me great pleasure in reporting that Engineering has completed repairs. For those contemplating the thought of dying here in outer space, please put those thoughts to rest. We'll be underway shortly."

Fifteen minutes later, the Star Rover began moving again. The rest of the trip to Coplent was uneventful, and nobody complained about boredom as they all had much to talk to one another about with their surprising impending slow death aboard the starship. They entered the Coplent system one hundred and thirty-four days after they left Procolt 2. The last leg of their journey took them within seventy-five thousand miles of Coplent. Anne contacted the planet and learned they were expected. They were told to bring the Star Rover to a distance of fifteen units from the space station.

RUSSELL FINE

COPLENT
FEBRUARY 2121

Mike plotted the course to the space station and used the sub-light engine to move the Star Rover to the correct location. Fifteen minutes later, the ship received a call from Garlut.

Jeffery put on a headset and said, "Hello Garlut, it's good to hear your voice. We've had a very interesting mission so far and I have many things I'd like to talk to you about."

"I am happy to hear your voice as well. I will be on the space station shortly and will contact you again when I arrive. If it is acceptable, I will take a small shuttle to the Star Rover. I too have many things to discuss with you."

"You're welcome to come aboard anytime. I'm looking forward to seeing you."

"I should be there within three hours."

Three hours later, Jeffery and Debbie walked to the shuttle bay to wait for Garlut.

The shuttle arrived a few minutes later. Garlut and Brealak were both aboard, and after they entered the ship Garlut asked, "Can we go the dining room to get some food? We really miss the cuisine from your chefs on Earth."

"Yes, of course. We don't have the same selection, but I'm sure the cook can prepare something you'll like."

When they arrived in the dining room, Jeffery went into the kitchen and asked the cook to prepare something extravagant for the guests. He also asked her to make some cinnamon rolls because Jeffery knew how much Garlut and Brealak liked them.

When Jeffery returned to the table Garlut asked, "How was your journey? Did you like Procolt 2?"

"It has been rather interesting," Jeffery responded. Then he said, "Procolt 2 was nice, very nice, but we have a mystery I hope you can help us resolve."

"What is the mystery?"

"First, when we arrived at the Procolt System we were threatened with destruction by a ship from Torblit. The ship's

31

captain, Glencet, claimed that Torblit owned the Procolt System and threatened to destroy our ship if we didn't leave immediately. I managed to diffuse the situation by giving Glencet some of the products we were bringing to Coplent. He particularly liked the chocolate. Anyway, he agreed to let us explore Procolt 2 for twenty days. Apparently, they have a mining operation on Procolt 4 and thought we were there to steal whatever it is they're mining.

"During our first full day there, some of our people discovered a humanoid skeleton while they were exploring a cave. Upon examination, we found a metal tag around the neck of the remains that identified the body as a soldier from the United States. We were unable to determine how long the person had been dead, but it didn't appear to be for very long. As you probably know, the United States hasn't existed for eighty-five years. So, I have two questions: How did somebody from Earth get to Procolt 2 and how long ago did he die?"

Garlut said nothing for a few seconds, then he said, "Do you remember I told you we weren't responsible for the reports of flying saucers?"

"Yes, I remember."

"What I did not tell you was I know who is responsible. There were people from Metoba studying Earth. They fly saucer-shaped shuttles. Although they were, and still are, members of the trading group, they didn't feel compelled to follow the rules regarding contact with backward civilizations. They had no problem with flying over major cities and being seen. Although I am not aware of any specific instances where they actually made contact with the people on Earth, but I am certain it happened. I suspect they probably kidnapped people from Earth from time to time, in an effort to study them. I know they are aware of Procolt 2 and it is probable they took their captives there when they were finished with their research. I must also tell you they have not visited Earth for more than one hundred years."

"What do the people from Metoba look like?"

"I suspect you already know the answer to that question. They are thin, hairless, and have bluish-gray skin. They are short. The tallest ones are probably five feet tall. They have large black eyes and their noses do not protrude from their face. They do not wear clothes and the males have no external genitalia. Because the females have no breasts unless they are near the end of or right after a pregnancy, it is impossible to tell the males from the females by looking at them."

"You're right. I would have guessed that, except for the part about the genitalia. I just figured the drawings I saw left off the genitalia for reasons of modesty. We brought the remains with us. Can your people determine how long ago the man died and possibly his age?"

"I am not a medical expert, but I think we may be able to help you. You should also be aware that Torblit has no legal claim to the Procolt System. If they want to file a claim, they must do so by petitioning the trade group members at the yearly meeting. Despite their warning, they would have never damaged or destroyed your ship. That would have caused them to be ejected as members of the trade group and would result in financial ruin for Torblit," he said and then paused awaiting a reaction. "You mentioned you brought some things from Earth for us. Can you tell me what they are?"

"Yes, there are cases of chocolate bars, sacks of cinnamon, and I have eighteen power modules that produce the power Quat requested. I left Earth with twenty, but I gave two to Glencet. He expressed a lot of interest in the power modules and wanted information regarding the pricing and delivery. I have no idea how to communicate that information to him. Even if they wanted to buy something, we have no way to deliver it to them since Earth has only one starship."

"I am sure we can resolve those issues during your visit. Torblit has a permanent trade representative on Coplent and I will set up a meeting with him. I would not be concerned about delivering their purchases. Torblit has a fleet of five hundred starships, and I am positive they will pick up anything they decide to purchase from Earth."

"Good. Can I assume you have an idea about product pricing?"

"Actually, we have trade delegates on Earth now. The first group arrived shortly after you left. They met with representatives of the World Council and created a pricing schedule for the three items Earth will begin trading. Some of the people from the first group have already returned to Coplent and have gone back to Earth again. The bank has opened a branch on Earth as well. Everything is progressing as we anticipated."

"Very good! I would also like to tell you about the other important thing we discovered on Procolt 2. We found a race of highly intelligent animals. They're similar to small rodents called squirrels on Earth, except they're much larger. They have hands with opposable thumbs and have developed a language. I left two of my crew members there to continue studying them. I hope we haven't violated any trade group rules, but we didn't know they were intelligent when we first landed on Procolt 2. Because they aren't humanoid, I didn't think there would be a problem. We aren't going to give them any new technology or make any attempt to change their society. However, I must tell you that in the twenty days we were on Procolt 2, the squirrels managed to learn to speak English and they taught our language expert to speak their language."

Garlut appeared to be deep in thought for a moment before he said, "I wasn't aware there were any intelligent species on Procolt 2, and the planet has been extensively explored. Perhaps this is a small group of animals that only live in the area where you landed. Since they are not humanoid and will likely never develop interstellar travel, I am certain you did not violate any of the trade group rules. I am concerned that you left two of your crew members there. Are you sure they are safe?"

"Before we left, I made arrangements with Glencet to check on them regularly. Also, Glencet gave them communications devices which will allow them to contact his ship in case of an emergency."

"It sounds like you did what was needed to insure their safety. I would also like to send a ship to Procolt 2 to study these animals. Would that be okay with you?"

"Of course. I'm sure Cathy and Sheila would appreciate the company. Your ship should probably contact Glencet so he can let my crew members know they are going to have visitors.

"We left a habitat that can house sixteen people on the planet, so your people can stay there. I have two more things I want to discuss with you. The first is that Dr. Weber has some blood samples from people who have contracted a disease we've been unable to find a cure for. I was hoping we could give the samples to some of your medical experts and ask them to help us find a cure. The other item was, on the way here from Procolt 2, our ship's wormhole system failed. It took us almost four days to repair it. During the outage, many of my crew and probably all of our guests were convinced we were going to be stranded and die out in the middle of nowhere. Is there any system in place we could have used that would have let other trade group members know about our problem?"

"I have contacts at the University Medical Center," Garlut replied. "I think they may be able to help you. Please give me the samples and any other information you have concerning the disease. I will send it to them. Regarding the problem with your propulsion system, you are correct. There is no system in place that would have allowed us to know about your problem. That is one reason why we need to develop a communication system that would allow us to transmit messages at least at the same speed we can travel through space. However, in your case, if you had not arrived here within thirty days of the time you were expected, I would have searched for you. Since you are using our navigation system, I am sure we would have found you."

"That's good to know, although it all worked out so there was no crisis. I want to convince the World Council that we should build more starships. If all the ships follow a specific mission plan and if a ship is late returning to Earth, we'll know where to look for them. I know that's by no means foolproof, but it's better than nothing."

"We have a similar plan here on Coplent. Our ships follow regular trade routes, and because our ships are much faster than yours, our missions are shorter. Typically, half a year, so in the event of a system failure we would be able to locate them fairly quickly. We have never lost a ship. We have had a few close calls with problems similar to the one you experienced, but the problems were always resolved by the ship's crew."

"Perhaps by the time I get back to Earth they'll have made some progress on the new communications system," Jeffery mused.

"Based on your accomplishments, I believe Earth has excellent engineers. I think they will find a solution to the problem, and if they do, it will make Earth very wealthy. I wanted to talk to you before you go down to Coplent. It is not anything like Earth. Almost all of the land surface is densely populated. There are very few single-family homes. More than 95% of the forty-five billion inhabitants of Coplent live in apartments. Many of those apartment buildings are over one hundred stories tall. The only green spaces are in parks, and there are a lot of those. There are also some very nice areas that are unsuitable for building due to environmental or land surface conditions. You will probably find it surprising, but most of our people have no desire to even visit a place like Procolt 2. The open space, the trees and plants, and even the animals make them feel uncomfortable. This is a problem for us since we are running out of space and fresh water. We import almost all of our food because there is so little land available for farming. You should consider this a warning. As the population on Earth increases because of improvements in medical technology, you could be facing the same problem in as little as two hundred years."

"The population on Earth has increased by 50% over the last one hundred years, but we like open spaces, forests, trees, and wild animals. I just don't see it happening on Earth. I suspect, given the opportunity, a large percentage of the population would gladly move to a place like Procolt 2 in a heartbeat. We have areas that sound a lot like Coplent. In our larger cities like New York, Hong Kong, Mexico City, and Los Angeles, people are already living as you describe on Coplent, but they go to the sparsely populated areas for vacation."

Until now, Debbie and Brealak had been listening, but hadn't joined in the conversation. At the lull in the conversation, Brealak said, "Garlut and I would like you and Debbie to be our guests at our home. We have a very large apartment and I am sure you will be more comfortable there than at a hotel."

Without waiting for Jeffery to answer, Debbie said, "Thank you. We gladly accept your invitation."

Jeffery said, "Yes, I agree. We know little about Coplent. Staying with friends will make it much more pleasant for us."

Garlut said, "I am glad that is settled. Please get the samples from Dr. Weber and gather what you need. We will go down to the surface. Is there anything else you need from us now?"

"Yes, I need someone to take the products we brought to you off the ship, and we need to have someone remove the remains we found on Procolt 2."

"I will take care of that as soon as we get to my home."

At that moment, the cook brought out a big platter of cinnamon rolls and placed them on the table. Debbie got up and brought glasses of water for everybody and coffee for Jeffery and herself.

Brealak and Garlut immediately began to eat the cinnamon rolls. Garlut said, "These are different from the ones we ate on the space station, but I think they are just as good. Do different cooks make the same foods differently?"

Jeffery thought that was an odd question. He answered, "There are basic instructions for preparing foods, but many people make changes they think will improve the taste. I could probably find hundreds of different recipes for cinnamon rolls."

"That probably explains why our food is so different from the food on Earth," Brealak said. "On Coplent, every cook prepares the food in an identical fashion. So, if you eat something at home or at a restaurant, it will taste exactly the same. Food preparation is mechanical and it is always done the same way."

"I have to admit that sounds boring. On Earth, food preparation is considered an art. The person preparing the food can cook it any way that seems appropriate. We have hundreds of different seasonings," Debbie said. "These seasonings can make the same food taste completely different depending on how they're used."

A few minutes later, the cook brought the main course. Each was given a small filet mignon covered in a Béarnaise sauce, buttered green beans with sliced almonds, and a dish of macaroni and cheese.

"This is excellent," Garlut said. "Do you always eat like this on the ship?"

"The meat is used for special occasions, but the rest of the meal is normal," Jeffery responded.

After dinner, Jeffery contacted Dr. Weber regarding the blood samples and asked him to bring them to his cabin. They all went to the cabin so Jeffery and Debbie could pack the things they needed for the stay on Coplent. Dr. Weber was already there with the samples when they arrived. He gave them to Garlut and told him what he knew about the disease. While Dr. Weber and Garlut were speaking, they headed to the lab. When Jeffery and Debbie finished packing, Jeffery said, "We're ready to go, but before we leave, I want to know if you can make arrangements for my crew and our guests to tour Coplent."

Brealak answered, "That has already been taken care of. Starting tomorrow morning we will bring down groups of fifteen people and take them on an all-day tour of our planet. We have trained twenty professional tour guides who speak English so your people will not need translators with them. I believe your communications person is already aware of this."

Jeffery opened his com unit and said, "Anne."

38

A few seconds later she answered with, "Yes sir."

"Are you aware of the plans to transport fifteen people from the ship to the planet's surface every day for a tour?"

"Yes, I'm aware of it. Mike and I are preparing the lists right now."

"Thank you. Debbie and I will be going down to the surface shortly. Please contact me if you need our assistance with anything. Also, some people will be coming tomorrow morning to the ship to offload the cargo. Please make sure Ron is made aware. Somebody will also be coming to remove the remains of Mr. Brown."

"Yes sir."

"I think we're ready to go," Jeffery said.

They left the cabin and walked back to the shuttle bay where they boarded Garlut's compact shuttle and left the Star Rover. Jeffery thought they were going to go to the space station before going to the surface of Coplent, but he was wrong. Shortly after leaving the Star Rover, they began their descent to the surface. Jeffery and Debbie both stared out the window waiting for a clear view of Coplent, but they were twenty-five hundred miles above the planet and the descent would take almost two standard hours.

NASA HEADQUARTERS
FEBRUARY 2121

Max Hiller was sitting at his desk drinking his first cup of coffee of the day, thinking about the mission to Procolt and Coplent. Since he had no way to communicate with his crew, all he could do was hope for the best. The problem had existed since the first European explorers began exploring the Americas, but that didn't make it any easier. He was hoping the person he was waiting for would be able to give him some good news about the Interstellar Communications Project or ICP as the developers were calling it.

His meeting was to be with the head of the ICP, Dr. Brandon Simpson, one of the smartest people to ever work for NASA. He had graduated high school at fourteen and obtained his PHD in theoretical physics from MIT at twenty-one. He started working at NASA shortly after his graduation from MIT. Later, he helped develop the wormhole system used by the Star Rover and was working on a new and less complicated system that would be used for the next group of starships when he was promoted to lead the ICP six months ago. Brandon actually looked like the nerd he was. He was almost six feet tall, but slightly overweight. He was unconcerned about his personal appearance and usually looked somewhat disheveled, often wearing clothes with colors that clashed. His dark brown hair was combed back over his head and was so long the ends curled up. However, nobody cared what he looked like or how he dressed.

Brandon was the son of Terry Simpson, who had been the ship's captain during the first manned flights to Ganymede and made the first sub-light space flights. His father was also the first captain of the Ganymede Express. His grandfather was Albert Simpson, the inventor of the power modules still in use today which brought about many profound changes on Earth during the previous century.

Brandon was on time for his meeting with Max. He walked into Max's office and sat down.

41

After exchanging greetings, Max said, "I'm concerned about the Star Rover. I know we aren't expecting them to return for a few more months, but I keep wondering what's happening with them. I was hoping you'd made some progress with the ICP."

"That's what I wanted to talk to you about this morning. The obvious solution to the problem is to find a way to transmit radio signals through a wormhole, because there's no other way to exceed the speed of light. We know how to move solid objects through a wormhole, and those objects are capable of extending the wormhole to their final destination. A radio signal can't do that. However, I think we can build a series of signal relay stations one light year apart. We can then establish a wormhole between the relay stations and insert signal carriers at one-hour intervals. The carriers will be able to travel between relay stations in eighteen hours. The carriers would travel constantly on an elliptical path between the relay stations. When you want to send a message, you send it to the closest relay station. The relay station would send it to the next approaching carrier and the carrier would deliver it to the opposing relay station. That process would continue until the message reached its final destination."

"That's an interesting concept. It would still take several weeks to get a message and a response from Coplent, but it's far better than what we have now. Do we have the capability to do this?"

"No. The basic technology exists, but the carrier design and the relay station design will probably take two years. Then we would have to build a test system and we'll need a starship to do the testing. I would guess the earliest we could even begin to test the system would be in three to four years."

"Have you done any simulations which would indicate this idea is feasible?"

"Yes, the computer simulations indicate it'll work. We've done some of the preliminary design work on the relay stations and we think we know how to make the wormhole curve around the relay stations. The carrier design is fairly simple."

"Good! Put together a formal proposal and I'll submit it to the World Council. I'm not sure they realize we'll never be able to achieve real time communications capability. This may be a real shock to some of them."

"I know. But I really believe this is the best approach to resolving the problem. I'll have your proposal in two weeks."

"Thanks, Brandon."

"I'll call you when it's ready," Brandon said as he got up to leave.

Max watched him leave and thought about the proposal. It would take years to place the relay stations around the galaxy and build a small fleet of starships to maintain them. It would be very expensive, but for now it was their only option. He also realized that if he had it now, he would have been getting regular reports from the Star Rover and would have some idea about what was going on. He decided it was worth whatever the cost would be. He also thought the other members of the trade group would be willing to pay a lot to use the system.

RUSSELL FINE

COPLENT
FEBRUARY 2121

Garlut's shuttle continued the long descent to the surface of Coplent. Jeffery and Debbie were both looking out the window, but there wasn't much to see. Most of the planet was hidden by a thick blanket of clouds. When the shuttle finally dropped below the cloud layer, Jeffery and Debbie were amazed. Everywhere they looked there were tall buildings with very little space between them. There didn't appear to be any streets and they were still too high to make out any small objects, or people, on the ground.

Jeffery asked, "Are there any roads on Coplent?"

Brealak answered, "No, we travel by what you would call a moving sidewalk for short distances. For longer trips, we use shuttles like this one. Most people do not own a shuttle, so if they have to go far from home, they use a shuttle service. That is not much different than the way people travel in the big cities on Earth, except you use ground vehicles instead of shuttles."

Debbie asked, "Where are we going now?"

"We are going to our home. We should be there in one-quarter hour."

"You live with your mother and grandmother. Is that correct?"

"Yes, but my grandmother is unable to communicate now. We talk to her all the time, but she is unable to respond. She is becoming something of a burden for my mother, but in our society the children are responsible for their parents when they are no longer able to take care of themselves. Is it different on Earth?"

Debbie thought for a moment before answering. "It depends on the level of help required to care for an aging parent. Sometimes the child may get somebody to help with parental care which enables the parent to continue to live with their child. In more severe cases where the child is physically unable to take care of them, the parent may be placed in a care facility where they will receive all the assistance they need.

There was a disease on Earth called Alzheimer's that had a devastating effect on brain function and was a serious problem for our older people, but that disease has been eliminated and the need for these facilities has greatly reduced."

"That is interesting. On Coplent, our older people do not normally lose their cognitive abilities. They do lose some of the ability to control their muscles, which occasionally affects their ability to speak. Unfortunately, my grandmother has lost both her ability to speak and walk."

They continued their trip in silence until Garlut said, "The building directly below us is where our home is located. We will land shortly."

The building was enormous by Earth standards. It appeared to be about fifteen hundred feet on a side, and perhaps two thousand feet tall. The roof had parking areas for small shuttles, like the one they were in. Only about half of the shuttle spaces were occupied. Garlut brought the shuttle to a point a few feet above the roof surface and then gently lowered it to its landing spot.

Jeffery looked around as they exited the shuttle. Some buildings were taller than the one they were on, but most were shorter. Everywhere he looked, all he could see were large buildings. The cloud cover had cleared and Coplent's sun was bright in the sky. It appeared to be somewhat brighter than Earth's sun, but it had been so long since Jeffery was on Earth, he wasn't sure. He asked, "How big is this building?"

Garlut answered, "It is approximately one-quarter unit square and one-half unit high. It is one of the larger buildings on Coplent. There are three thousand apartments in the building. The bottom three floors are a shopping area. There are about twelve thousand people living here."

"That's big!" Jeffery exclaimed.

"Too big for me," Debbie said, shaking her head.

They walked over to an area that had a bank of elevators. Brealak said, "We are on the 245th floor. Our apartment is on floor 162." A moment later the door to the elevator opened and they walked in. Brealak said something in her native language and the door closed. The elevator descended quickly and the door opened. They stepped out into an enormous hallway, walked about one hundred feet, and stopped at a door that slid into the wall as they approached. The group stepped inside.

Jeffery looked around the space. They were standing in what must be the living room. On one wall was a large window. He guessed the window was twenty-five feet long and nine feet high, with the wall extending a foot on each side. The material in the window was somewhat darkened so only a small amount of the intense sunlight was able to enter the room. The window was so clear that if it wasn't tinted, Jeffery was sure he would have thought there was nothing there at all. The ceiling gave off a soft, warm glow that illuminated the entire room. The light was evenly distributed across the ceiling, so no shadows were created.

Lounging near the center of the room, watching a large video monitor, was a woman Jeffery assumed was Brealak's mother. The woman smiled at them and said something he didn't understand. Next to her was a woman who appeared to be much older. She had a blank look on her face and appeared to be staring at the view through the window. She did not react at all to them. Both women appeared to be suspended three feet off the floor with no visible means of support. As Jeffery watched, the younger woman moved to a sitting position, stood up, and walked over to Jeffery and Debbie. As she approached, Garlut said, "This is my life companion and Brealak's mother, Koltep, and seated there is my grandmother, Vortin." Then he said something to Koltep in his native language. Koltep smiled and bowed slightly to Jeffery and Debbie.

Garlut walked to a spot on the wall, touched it, and an opening appeared. He reached inside and removed three items. Jeffery immediately recognized them as translators. Garlut pressed a button on the side of two of the translators and said, "English." Then he handed one to Debbie and the other to Jeffery. He pressed the button again and said, "Coplent," and gave the translator to Koltep.

As soon as Jeffery and Debbie put on their translators, they could understand the audio from the monitor. Garlut turned off the monitor and asked, "Would you like a quick tour of my home?"

"Yes," Jeffery responded. "That would be nice, but first please tell me what Koltep was resting on when we came in."

"The same device we installed on your ship to create artificial gravity can also be used to reduce or eliminate gravity. In the floor under where Koltep was lying is a specially designed antigravity system. It turns on automatically as you approach it and projects an image that looks like a large chair with a foot rest. You either sit or lay on it, get into a comfortable position, give the system a verbal command, and it will support you in that position by controlling the gravity around you. It is very comfortable, but it takes a while to learn how to use it correctly.

"The chairs have a similar system. As you sit on the chair, it recognizes the contours of your body and supports you completely. When you are sitting on the chair 95% of your weight is eliminated by the system. That way sitting does not affect your circulation and you do not become uncomfortable after sitting for a long time like you would in a conventional chair. Would you like to try it?"

"Yes, I think that would be interesting."

Jeffery walked to one of two large chairs that looked like recliners. He sat down and he felt the chair lightly on his bottom and back. Then he felt himself being raised slightly off the surface of the chair. He felt like he was sitting on air and was in awe of how comfortable it truly was. After sitting for a few moments, he said, "Debbie, you have to try this. I don't think I've ever sat in anything this comfortable before."

Debbie walked over to the other chair, sat down carefully, and a big smile appeared on her face. "This is terrific. Can we buy two of these for the Star Rover?" she asked their host.

48

"I am sure I can arrange that, but the power you have on the ship does not match the requirements for the chairs," Garlut cautioned.

"Technically, that's correct," Jeffery said, "but we have eighteen power modules aboard that were designed to meet Coplent's power requirements. I'm sure I could have Ron modify one of our backup modules to create the same power output."

"That being true, would you want them installed in your cabin?"

"No, I think we should put them in the recreation room so everybody can have an opportunity to enjoy them."

"I agree," Debbie said.

"I can have them installed within the next few days. You can pay me in chocolate for them when I get back to Earth," Garlut said with a glint in his eyes.

Jeffery smiled, "That's not a problem. I'll get you whatever you want."

They spent the next twenty minutes looking at the apartment. It was very big, probably four thousand square feet. Jeffery and Debbie had a bedroom with a private bath that was equivalent to a room they would have had at one of the better hotels on Earth. Their room had the same glass wall and lighted ceiling that was in the living room. Garlut showed them how to control both fixtures. The room also had a very large bed that had the same antigravity system as the chairs they had tried.

After spending a few hours at the apartment, Garlut and Brealak decided to show Jeffery and Debbie the highlights of Coplent.

They went down to the first floor and spent an hour looking at the various stores and they were amazed at the shopping available in the building. There were lots of clothing stores, furniture stores, stores that sold entertainment systems, stores that sold food and medicines, and there was even a store that sold shuttles like the one Garlut had used to bring them to the planet. The one thing they didn't see were restaurants.

49

After their tour of the building, they returned to the roof and boarded Garlut's shuttle. They flew for a while and landed near a large park. It was a beautiful, warm afternoon with a mild wind that Jeffery and Debbie thought made it very comfortable. Despite the perfect weather, the park was almost empty.

Garlut said, "The government constructed hundreds of these parks, but very few people use them. Many of our people have a fear of large open spaces, as I told you before. Brealak and I like this park and we come here often when we want to get away from the crowds. I think we appreciate it because we spend so much time in space."

They spent two hours relaxing and exploring the park, which had a small zoo with animals unlike anything Jeffery or Debbie had ever seen. There were some small animals that looked similar to a horse, but were only eighteen inches high. They were also a bright shade of blue. There were other animals that looked like bears, deer, and big mice. They were all shades of blue or green.

Garlut said, "These are just a few of the animals that are native to Coplent. Due to the expansion of the humanoid population, these animals no longer live on Coplent except in zoos. Several hundred years ago we transported herds of animals to a nearby planet with an environment almost identical to Coplent. With the exception of birds and fish, there are now almost no wild animals living here."

"Do you have farms where they raise animals or plants for food?" Debbie asked.

"Only a few are left. They are mostly dairy farms. We import more than 90% of the food we consume. We do harvest large quantities of seafood every year, which makes up the other 10%," Brealak answered.

Jeffery was still looking at the colorful animals in the zoo. He asked, "Why are the animals here blue and green? So many of the animals on Earth are mostly black, brown, or gray."

"I noticed that as well when I started studying Earth. After my first extended visit to Earth I asked some of our zoologists here and they had no idea. Their best guess was that the color was due to differences in the light emitted by our sun when compared to Earth's sun," Garlut replied.

After they left the park, Garlut took them on a tour of some of the mountainous areas of Coplent. They were exquisite with no indication of the presence of people.

Jeffery said, "If I had to live on Coplent, this is where I would want to live."

"It may look inviting, but on winter nights the temperature can drop to negative sixty degrees Centigrade. Shall we go back to the apartment? I will treat you to a typical meal on Coplent. Then you will know why we like the food on Earth so much." He chuckled softly.

"Maybe we'll like it more than you do," Debbie suggested.

"Maybe, but I doubt it," was Garlut's reply.

It took an hour to get back to the apartment. When they went inside the smell of cooking was apparent, and not very appetizing. Jeffery and Debbie looked at each other, silently agreeing that the smell was not appealing.

Koltep was busy in the kitchen. She smiled at them and asked through her translator, "Did you enjoy your tour of Coplent?"

"It was interesting," Debbie replied. "Our cultures are very different. Jeffery and I don't like crowds. We like large open spaces. Many of our parks require reservations. Here the parks are almost empty. I think the shopping you have in the building is excellent. I can't imagine any reason to shop anywhere else if you live here."

"I agree. I really do not leave the building very often. Dinner will be ready in about .1 hours. I am sure it will not be up to Earth standards. Garlut and Brealak told me the food on Earth was the best they had ever tasted." Koltep smiled.

"I'm sure it will be very good. It smells wonderful," Debbie lied with a smile on her face.

They sat down to eat and both Jeffery and Debbie were surprised because the food tasted much better than it smelled. The dinner consisted of some kind of meat that tasted similar to pork and a vegetable that resembled a potato, but was blue. There were also some rolls that both of them thought were the best part of the meal. They both ate their dinners and thanked Koltep for an excellent meal.

After dinner, they sat down in the living room. The view from the large window was fantastic. The lights from the city below and from the shuttles above were mesmerizing. As they settled down in their wonderfully comfortable chairs, Garlut said, "I just received a message that the remains of the body you found on Procolt 2 were picked up and are on the way to the university medical lab. I suspect they will have some answers for you tomorrow."

"Wonderful, thank you. I just hope it answers more questions than it creates," Jeffery said.

"I understand how you feel, but I would not worry about it tonight. Our food may not be the best, but the beds are the most comfortable you will find anywhere," Garlut assured his guests.

They talked for another hour or so, but Debbie and Jeffery were both tired and found themselves yawning despite their best efforts to prevent it. Finally, Jeffery thanked Garlut for his hospitality and said that he and Debbie were going to lie down for some rest.

Once they were in their room, they spent some time looking out the window at the view before getting ready for bed. Jeffery darkened the window so they would be able to sleep.

When they got onto the bed, they smiled at each other. "This bed has got to be the most comfortable thing I've ever had the pleasure of lying on!" Debbie said.

"Do you want to play around or just go to sleep?"

"Let's play!" Debbie said and then she added, "Quietly."

The following morning Debbie and Jeffery felt wonderful after their rest. They showered and dressed. They left their room and found Garlut sitting in the living room watching a news program.

He turned off the monitor as they walked into the room and asked, "Did you sleep well?"

"Extremely well. You were right, that bed was by far the most comfortable thing we ever slept on."

"Good. I received the results of the analysis of the remains from Procolt 2. Yesterday, you said you hoped it answered more questions than it creates. I am sorry to say that is not the case. The analysis indicated that the man died not more than fifteen Earth years ago. However, he was approximately one hundred and eighty years old at the time of his death."

Neither Jeffery nor Debbie said anything for a while. Then Jeffery asked, "How is that possible? People from Earth never live that long."

"I have no idea. I have scheduled a meeting with Dr. Kavits for later this morning. He is in charge of the laboratory where the analysis was performed. Perhaps he can answer your questions. While we are there, I will give him the samples I received from Dr. Weber."

"Thank you for arranging the meeting."

"I also set up an appointment for us this afternoon with the trade representative from Torblit."

"It sounds like we'll have a busy day," Jeffery replied.

Later that morning, Garlut took them to the university medical laboratory for the meeting with Dr. Kavits. They didn't use the shuttle. Debbie and Jeffery had the opportunity to experience the moving walkways. They left Garlut's building and walked a few hundred feet to a stairway that went down twenty-five feet and then entered a large room. Around the room were five large doorways with writing over them. Each doorway went in a different direction. Debbie and Jeffery followed their host through one of the doorways onto a slow-moving walkway.

Jeffery looked around. The room was crowded, but the people seemed to ignore him and Debbie. He asked, "Garlut, we are obviously different from the native people, but they don't seem to notice us at all. Are aliens that common?"

"Yes, about 25% of the population on Coplent is alien, and your appearance is not that different."

As they stood on the walkway it began moving faster. It appeared to be solid, but it obviously was not. Jeffery didn't understand how it worked, but he wanted to find out. The longer they stood on it the faster it moved.

Garlut said, "The walkway will match the speed of another one which will appear on our right shortly. We will simply step over to the other walkway that will take us to our next transfer spot."

Jeffery was still confused about how it worked. He said, "Okay, we'll follow you. Can you tell me how this system works?"

"The walkways are made of a material that appears solid, but becomes somewhat fluid when exposed to a strong magnetic field. That allows the speed of the system to vary depending on how the magnetic field is applied. It took a long time to build, but they are very reliable. The one you are standing on has been running for one hundred and fifty years without a failure. Please follow me."

Just as Garlut stopped talking, the other walkway appeared on their right. They stepped over to it without any problems and continued on their journey as they moved along their walkway, others were moving along their own paths. Many other species were around them and then, and as they drew closer to their destination, there were less. A few minutes later, they moved to the right again onto the walkway that went to the university. This one slowed down as they approached their destination. They stepped off and a few moments later they were in a room that looked identical to the one near Garlut's apartment building.

They walked out of the room and up to ground level. Garlut pointed to a large building a half mile away and said, "The laboratory is in that building."

A few minutes later they were in the building. Garlut said something to a receptionist and they walked up one flight of stairs, going through a door at the top of the stairway. Jeffery and Debbie put on their translators as they stepped through the doorway. They followed Garlut to a large office with the door open. Inside was a man who appeared slightly older than Garlut. He was also taller. Jeffery guessed he was at least seven feet tall. The man saw them and walked over. When he was a few feet away he said to Garlut, "Good morning, my friend. Are these the people from Earth you told me about?"

"Yes." Pointing to Jeffery he said, "This is Admiral Jeffery Whitestone. He is the commanding officer of Earth's first starship."

Then pointing to Debbie, he said, "This is his life companion and second in command. Her name is Captain Debbie Whitestone."

"I am pleased to meet you, Admiral. I am Dr. Kavits. Please sit down. I am sure you have some questions."

"Thank you," Jeffery said as they all sat down at a large table. "Please, call us by our first names, Jeffery and Debbie. I have several questions."

After Dr. Kavits was seated he said, "Please ask anything you like."

"Do you know a lot about the anatomy of Earth people?"

"We have been studying them for a long time, almost one thousand years. However, all the information we have is from reports and scans. You are the first people from Earth I have ever met. Regardless of those facts, I am certain our analysis is correct."

"The average life span for us is about ninety of our years. You said the remains we found belong to a man who lived to be more than twice that. I don't doubt your results, but can you explain how he lived that long, and can you determine a cause of death?" Jeffery inquired.

"Our analysis has not been completed. His age and time of death were easy to find, but the cause of his death may be impossible to determine. The examination of his remains showed no signs of trauma. He could have died from starvation, dehydration, or simply old age. We are trying to find out if we can detect anything unusual in his bone material.

You can help with our analysis by providing us with blood samples and full body scans. Are you willing to do that?"

"Yes, we'll be happy to if it will help you. I also have a favor to ask. Garlut has some blood samples from some of our people who have been stricken with an unknown disease. Our doctors have been unable to find a cure. We were hoping you may be able to offer us some assistance."

"It would be my pleasure to assist, but that will take some time. How long are you going to be here?"

"I'm not sure. Since Coplent is sending ships to Earth on a regular basis and your ships are much faster than ours, if you find anything that would be helpful, please send it to Earth on the next outbound ship."

"I think that is a good idea. It will save a lot of time. I will be back in a moment with my assistant, Marcet. She will perform the scans and take your blood samples."

Dr. Kavits left his office and came back a minute later with a young woman wearing a white lab coat. She was tall and thin, like most of the people on Coplent. However, she had red hair and up to this point, everybody Jeffery and Debbie had met from Coplent had black hair. She walked up and said, "My name is Marcet. It is a pleasure to meet you. Please follow me. This will not take long."

They followed Marcet out of the office to an examination room. She said, "Please sit and I will take your samples." They were expecting to see a syringe, but instead Marcet picked up a device that looked like a round plastic tube six inches long and perhaps a half inch in diameter. Both ends of the tube were flat and on the side were several small buttons. She pressed a few of the buttons, then pressed a few keys on a computer terminal on the desk. She walked up to Jeffery and pressed the device lightly against his neck. Jeffery felt a small vibration and she removed the device from his neck saying, "Please remove all of your clothing so I can do the body scan."

Jeffery hesitated for a moment. Marcet noticed his hesitation and asked, "Is that a concern as I do not want to make you uncomfortable?"

"No, it isn't a problem. I was just surprised," Jeffery said as he stood up and began undressing.

While Jeffery was removing his clothes, Marcet took a blood sample from Debbie. When Marcet finished, Debbie stood and removed her clothes.

At the back of the room was a plastic disk three feet in diameter mounted in the floor. Marcet directed Jeffery to stand on the disk with his feet slightly spread apart and his arms pointing forward. Marcet watched as Jeffery got into the correct position and said, "Please stand still for a moment." She had a small device in her hand and she pressed a button. There was a brief, high-pitched sound. "Thank you, we are all done. Debbie, please stand on the scanner."

Debbie went over to the plastic disk on the floor and assumed the same pose Jeffery had done. A moment later, she heard the high-pitched sound again. Marcet said they could both get dressed.

A few minutes passed and they were back in Dr. Kavits' office. "Thank you. I hope you did not find anything uncomfortable, Dr. Kavits said. "Up to this time all of our tissue samples from Earth have been taken from deceased subjects and they are old. The most recent ones are from almost two hundred years ago. Your samples will allow us to compare your DNA to that of the remains. I should be able to complete my analysis before the end of the day."

"Thank you for your help with this. I will be waiting for your report," Garlut said. He turned toward Jeffery and Debbie and said, "We should go so Dr. Kavits can begin his analysis."

They all got up to leave and Jeffery said, "Thank you, Dr. Kavits. We really appreciate what you are doing for us."

"You are most welcome. I will contact Garlut when I have the results."

They left the office and returned to the moving sidewalk. As they stepped on it, Garlut said, "We have to go back and get my shuttle. Our next appointment with the trade representative from Torblit is too far to use the moving walkways."

"How far is it?" Jeffery asked.

"It is a two-hour trip. It will take a half hour to reach the high-speed travel zone, an hour in that zone, and another half hour to land. It will give you an opportunity to see other parts of Coplent."

When they arrived at Garlut's apartment building, they took an elevator directly to the roof. They went to Garlut's shuttle and got in. Garlut turned on the shuttle and pressed a switch on the dashboard. A small keyboard appeared. Garlut typed for a few moments, and then said, "I have to tell the control system where we are going and then we have to wait for clearance. That usually takes .1 hours."

Just as he finished speaking, something appeared on the screen in the middle of the dashboard. "That is our clearance. Once we reach an altitude above ten thousand feet, the automatic system will take over and we can just watch the scenery until we drop down to ten thousand feet again."

"That's amazing. We have nothing like this on Earth. Did you use this system when we flew down to the surface from my ship?" Jeffery asked.

"I did tell the system where we were going, but because we did not use the high-speed travel zone, it was not necessary to use the automatic control. We dropped straight through the zone instead of traveling in it."

Jeffery nodded and said, "A system like this isn't needed on Earth. At least not yet. If we have to travel long distances, we use commercial transportation."

A few moments later, they heard a warble sound and Garlut said, "We're on automatic control now."

Jeffery and Debbie watched out the window as the shuttle gained altitude. As they watched above them, they could see the travel zone. It looked like a busy highway on Earth, but all of the vehicles in it were traveling at the same speed. The forward speed of the shuttle began to increase and then it was merged flawlessly into the flow of traffic. They traveled with the rest of the traffic for a half hour and then veered off to the left and entered another travel zone. This one had fewer vehicles on it. After several minutes, the shuttle dropped out of the travel zone and slowed down. There was another warble sound that indicated Garlut now had control of the shuttle.

"How high were we?" Debbie asked.

"In Earth terms, we were thirty-five miles above the surface. We were traveling at three thousand miles per hour, although I am sure you did not think we were moving that fast."

"I didn't hear a sonic boom when we exceeded the speed of sound. And there were zero G-forces on us. Why not?" Debbie asked.

"Our shuttles are designed to minimize the effects of exceeding that speed. These shuttles also eliminate almost all outside noise. If you were outside, all you would have heard was a soft 'pop.' The G-forces are eliminated by the same gravity emitter used in the beds and chairs in the apartment, just modified for travel."

As they descended, Jeffery noticed this part of Coplent didn't look very different from the other parts. It was filled with big buildings. Jeffery decided he really didn't like Coplent. The people were very nice, but the excessive number of tall buildings and the lack of green space was a turnoff for him.

As he looked out the window, the shuttle approached a building that appeared to be the same size as the apartment building Garlut lived in. They landed on the roof, and after Garlut parked the shuttle, he said, "Here we are, one-quarter hour early."

As they got out of the shuttle, Garlut added, "I have never been here before, but the design of all these big buildings are similar, so I am sure I can find our destination. We have to go to room 90-173."

They followed Garlut to a bank of elevators and took the elevator to the 90th floor. They exited and walked a few hundred feet to their destination. They went inside and found themselves in a room about thirty-five feet square. There were several tables with chairs around them. At the far end of the room a woman was seated at a desk. As they approached, she said, "Good afternoon. How can I help you?"

"We have an appointment with Representative Drabord. My name is Garlut, and this is the commanding officer of the Earth ship Star Rover, Admiral Jeffery Whitestone."

"Representative Drabord is expecting you. Please be seated for a moment while I get him."

"Thank you," Garlut replied.

They sat down but only had to wait a short time before a short, heavy-set man with pale blue skin walked up to them. He looked like Glencet, but older. He said, "I am Drabord. It is a pleasure to meet you. Please, follow me to my office."

Drabord's office was small and there was a large window that took up almost the entire wall. In front of the window was a large but short desk. It appeared to be the perfect size for somebody who was only five feet tall. The chairs opposite the desk were for taller people and they were very comfortable. When everyone was seated, Drabord asked, "How can I help you, Admiral?"

"I met Captain Glencet in the Procolt System," Jeffery said. "We were there to explore Procolt 2. Captain Glencet agreed to allow us to explore the planet in exchange for some of the cargo we had aboard. He liked two of the items so much that he wanted me to contact you when I got to Coplent to arrange to purchase some of them."

"What are these items he liked so much?" Drabord asked.

"The first item was a portable power source that will supply electricity for an infinite length of time. We have units on Earth that still function properly after more than one hundred years."

From the look on Drabord's face, it was apparent he didn't believe such an item existed.

Jeffery continued, "I can see you don't believe such a power source exists, but I can assure you it does. Captain Glencet didn't believe me either, so I gave him one to examine.

60

After he assured himself it was as I described he said he wanted to buy some, but I didn't have a price at that time."

"Do you have a price now?"

This time Garlut answered, "The units will cost .15 hirodim each. They will be manufactured to meet the electrical requirements that Captain Glencet specified and will be available to be picked up in one year. At the present time, Earth has only one starship, so they are unable to make deliveries."

"Are they guaranteed?"

"Of course, all products from Earth have the standard trade group guarantee."

"Can you provide me with a sample unit?"

"Yes, it will be delivered here in two days."

"After I examine it, I will let you know if we want to purchase any. They are very expensive, but if they work as described, I believe the price is reasonable. What is the other item Glencet wished to purchase?"

"It's a food product we call chocolate. I have a sample with me," Jeffery said as he reached into his pocket and took out a chocolate candy bar which he handed to the representative.

Drabord looked at the candy bar for a few moments. Then he smelled it, but there was almost no smell through the wrapper. Jeffery said, "You have to remove the wrapper first."

Drabord didn't say anything. He unwrapped the candy bar, smelled it, and then he smiled broadly. "This smells wonderful." They watched as he broke off a small piece and tasted it. A moment later he said, "This tastes even better than it smells. I can understand why Glencet would want to buy this. How much is it?"

"A case with one hundred fifty bars is only .0005 hirodim," Garlut replied.

"That seems reasonable. Is the time frame the same?"

"No, I'll have ten thousand cases on Coplent in one hundred twenty days. There will be regular shipments arriving from Earth after that time."

"I will contact you after I have evaluated the power supply," Drabord said. "Thank you for coming."

"Thank you for meeting with us," Jeffery replied.

When they were in the hallway outside Drabord's office, Jeffery turned to Debbie and said, "Do you realize we just sold cases of chocolate bars for $50,000 each?"

Garlut smiled and said, "I told you Earth would find being a member of the trading group very profitable. But you should know some of that profit goes to Coplent. We pay Earth .0003 hirodim per case and we sell it for .0005. That gives us some profit and covers the cost of transporting the chocolate to Coplent and other distribution points."

They went back to the shuttle and began the trip back to Garlut's apartment building. Midway, there was a loud beep and an image appeared on the screen in the dashboard of the shuttle. Garlut spent a few seconds reading the image and said, "This is the report from Dr. Kavits. As a result of the information you provided, he was able to determine that his original estimates were fairly accurate. He now states the man you found was one hundred and eighty-four years old at the time of his death and the death occurred seventeen years ago. He also said the DNA found in the remains show signs of mutation. He discovered the DNA samples from the bones that formed the hands and feet were not identical to the DNA found in the hip bone. Dr. Kavits believes some type of radiation exposure must be occurring on Procolt 2 that slowly modifies the DNA of living organisms. In the case of our skeleton it substantially increased his life span, but the effects of radiation may not always be beneficial. He still is unable to determine how Mr. Brown died."

Jeffery thought about what Garlut had just told him for a while and then he said, "I think we should return to Procolt 2 as soon as possible and let our two crew members know there's a potential for danger if they stay. Dr. Kavits said the rate of mutation is slow. Does he know how slow? We've been gone four months. Could Cathy and Sheila already be showing the effects of the radiation?"

"I do not know the answers to your questions, but I will ask Dr. Kavits. I think it is a good idea for you to go back to Procolt 2 and check on your crew members."

"Do you have a problem with Debbie and me leaving in the morning?"

"I think you should wait a few more days. Your guests and crew are still touring Coplent, and I think you should allow them to complete their tours. I do not believe a few more days will make any difference."

"I guess you're right. We'll stay for two more days." Then he asked, "Debbie, do you agree?"

"I'm concerned, but I agree delaying our return to Procolt 2 by two days shouldn't be an issue, although it would be helpful if we had a way to contact them."

"Yes, it'll take four months to get back just to find out if everything is okay."

A few moments later Garlut said, "I have an idea. I own a small ship that can make the trip to Procolt 2 in thirty-five days." Looking at Jeffery, he continued, "It will only hold six people, but you, Dr. Weber, and Brealak could make the trip there and return in less time than it would take for you to get there in the Star Rover. There would still be room for your two crew members if you decided to bring them back here."

Jeffery asked Debbie what she thought.

"I don't like the idea of being without you for almost three months, but it does make sense. I wonder how our guests would feel about being stranded here for that long."

"You know, there may be a real benefit to you, Garlut. While I'm gone our chef, April, could teach some of your people how to cook Earth food."

"That makes me think it is an even better idea. Brealak, is this plan okay with you?"

"Yes, of course it is. I like the idea of being out on my own."

"You will not be on your own. Jeffery will still outrank you."

Jeffery said, "No, that's not right. Brealak, if we do this, I have no intention of ordering you around. As far as I'm concerned, you're in charge. Dr. Weber and I will be there to support you."

Garlut said, "One thing I should mention. There is almost no privacy aboard the ship. Is that going to be a problem?"

"No, that's not a problem for me. On the missions I made to Mars and Ganymede there was no privacy either. I'm used to it."

Brealak said, "Since the ship has not been used for a while, I will bring it to the space station tomorrow to run a complete diagnostic routine before we leave. I will stay onboard tomorrow night."

"I have a question," Jeffery said. "I have no idea how to operate this ship. What if something happens to you?"

"I am sure I can teach you how to operate the ship in a few hours. Most of the systems are automatic. Basically, you tell the ship where you want to go and when you want to leave. The ship does the rest."

"Does the ship understand English?" Jeffery asked.

"The ship control system has a translator feature built in, but I will have to add English to its database. I will do that tomorrow as well," Brealak replied.

When they returned to Garlut's apartment, the first thing they noticed was the smell of something cooking. Much to their surprise, it smelled good. A moment after they stepped inside, they realized why. Inside the kitchen they discovered one of the chefs from the Star Rover, William Peterson, was making dinner.

"Good evening, Ambassador Garlut, Admiral, Captain. You're probably wondering why I'm here. This morning Koltep contacted the ship and asked if we could send somebody down to prepare a typical Earth-type meal. I volunteered. For dinner we're having beef brisket with barbeque sauce, baked beans, and yeast rolls."

"That sounds delicious," Jeffery exclaimed.

Brealak added, "It smells very good too."

"It will be ready in about an hour," the chef announced, smiling.

"Thank you," Jeffery said.

"My pleasure, sir."

The dinner was excellent. Koltep, who had never tasted Earth food, said, "This meal is wonderful. Can you teach me to cook like this?"

William replied, "I don't think I'll be here long enough to teach you very much, but I'll be happy to spend some time with you while we're here."

Jeffery said, "William, you're going to be here a little longer than we originally planned. I have to go back to Procolt 2. In order to make the trip as fast as possible, we'll be using one of Garlut's ships which can reduce the travel time by nearly 70%. So, the Star Rover will be here for another ninety days."

"Well, in that case I'll have plenty of time to teach you how we prepare and cook traditional meals," William said, smiling at Koltep.

"I am looking forward to it."

After the meal they talked for a while. They discussed the situation on Procolt 2, so William now understood why Jeffery had to return.

After Brealak offered to take William back to the Star Rover, he asked, "Is anybody on the ship aware of this plan?"

"Not yet, but I'm going to contact Mike and let him know," Jeffery responded. "I'll need to contact Dr. Weber so he'll be ready to leave the day after tomorrow. By the time you get back to the ship, everybody aboard will know."

A few minutes later, Brealak and William left.

Jeffery picked up his com unit and contacted Mike to give him the details of the report from Dr. Kavits and his plan to return to Procolt 2. He finished with, "Please inform Dr. Weber about our plan and tell him he'll be accompanying us. He should pack whatever he thinks he'll need."

"Okay, I'll let him know immediately, sir. Is Captain Whitestone going with you?"

"No, we're using a small ship that only accommodates six people. I expect we'll be back in seventy-five days. Be sure to let the guests know what's going on as well."

"I understand. I'll take care of it."

"Garlut will be staying on Coplent, so if you need anything, I'm sure he'll be happy to assist you. Brealak will be going with us to Procolt 2."

"Understood. I don't know how the crew and guests will react when they find out we'll be here for another three months, but I'm sure they'll understand."

"Good. Thanks, Mike."

"Godspeed Jeffery."

Ten minutes later, Jeffery received a call from Dr. Weber. He explained everything again. Dr. Weber agreed they should leave as soon as possible.

The following morning when Jeffery and Debbie left their room, they found Garlut in the living room watching the news. When he saw them, he said, "Good morning. Brealak left several hours ago to prepare the ship for the trip to Procolt 2. Is there anything you would like to do today?"

Jeffery replied, "Good morning. We'd like to go back to the Star Rover. I want to meet with the crew and guests before I leave tomorrow. Can you arrange that?"

"Yes, I will take you there myself whenever you are ready. Tomorrow morning a shuttle from the space station will go over to the Star Rover to pick up you and Dr. Weber to take you to Brealak's ship."

"Thank you, Garlut. I also want to thank you for your hospitality. I'm really going to miss that bed. I don't suppose the beds on the ship will be that comfortable."

"No, unfortunately they will not. But I am sure they are no worse than what you have on the Star Rover. Remember, for twelve of the days you are traveling, you will not be aware of anything because of the time stasis field."

"I realize that. But we're still going to be spending more than twenty days in a small ship without much to do. Do you think Brealak could spend some time teaching me your native language?"

"I think she would be happy to do that. However, with the translators that really is not necessary."

"I'd like to be able to read as well as speak your language. Besides, it'll give me something to do."

"I will talk to her about it," Garlut agreed.

Less than an hour later, Debbie and Jeffery were packed and on their way back to the Star Rover with Garlut.

When they exited the shuttle bay, Mike was waiting for them.

Jeffery said, "Hi Mike. Is everybody aboard aware of the plan?"

"Yes, they are and they all agree that rescuing our crew members takes top priority."

"Okay, good. I need to talk with Dr. Weber now. Garlut, please come with me. I'll see you later, Mike."

They walked to the medical office and found Dr. Weber inside looking at a video monitor. He looked up from the screen when they walked in and said, "I'm glad you're back. I've been doing some research and couldn't find any instances of radiation causing mutations in DNA on living creatures. Obviously, our records only cover Earth." Then turning toward Garlut, he asked, "Can you set up a meeting, or at least a conversation with Dr. Kavits?"

"Yes, I will try right now."

Dr. Weber continued, "I'm bringing some standard first aid items and a DNA analyzer.

"Since we have DNA profiles for everybody aboard, it will be simple to determine if there are any changes. However, if there are changes, there's absolutely nothing I can do about it."

"I understand that, but we still have to know if being on Procolt 2 creates genetic anomalies. I'm wondering if the squirrels we found were the result of a genetic mutation," Jeffery replied.

"Without DNA samples from previous generations, there's no way to tell," Dr. Weber stated emphatically.

At that moment Garlut said, "Dr. Kavits will contact me in an hour on my com unit and you can discuss this situation."

"Does Dr. Kavits speak English?"

"No, but my com unit has a translator built in, so you will be able to understand one another."

"Thank you. I really appreciate what you're doing for us," Dr. Weber said with a note of sincerity in his voice.

"Garlut, I have to go to the bridge," Jeffery said. "Do you want to stay here with Dr. Weber?"

"I would like to go to the dining room and have a snack. Will you join me, Dr. Weber?"

"It would be my pleasure, sir. However, please call me Frank."

Garlut and Frank walked to the dining room. They found a large tray filled with a variety of donuts in the food service area. Garlut looked at the donuts and asked, "Frank, what are these things?"

"They're called doughnuts. They're usually made with sweet dough that's fried in oil. Try one. I'm sure you'll enjoy it."

Garlut tasted one that was covered with chocolate frosting. With a big smile on his face, he said, "These are great! I think they are even better than cinnamon rolls. I have heard the word 'doughnut' before, but never realized what it was."

"We have them here every morning," Frank assured him.

Garlut and Frank talked for a while until Garlut's com unit beeped, it was Dr. Kavits getting back to him. He spoke to Dr. Kavits for several minutes in his native language, pressed a button on the side of the com unit, and said 'English.' Then he handed the com unit to Frank.

"Hello, this is Dr. Frank Weber."

"Good morning, Dr. Weber. I understand you have some questions regarding our report on the remains found on Procolt 2."

"Please understand, I'm not questioning your conclusions. However, your report mentions the possibility of some type of radiation present on Procolt 2 that caused ongoing genetic mutations. I did some research and couldn't find any indication of radiation with those properties has ever been found on Earth. Is it common in other solar systems?"

"I would not say it was common, but I have seen evidence of this type of radiation before. However, I never encountered it personally. All I have are medical reports. I was hoping you could search for the source of the radiation while you are on Procolt 2."

"I have no idea how to detect this radiation. Before we went down to the surface of Procolt 2, we did a thorough scan of the planet and didn't find any indication of abnormal radiation. However, our equipment may not be as sophisticated as yours. We aren't using the Star Rover to go back to Procolt 2. We'll be using one of Garlut's ships." He stopped and looked at Garlut, "Does the ship have radiation detection equipment onboard?"

Garlut thought for a moment about what Frank asked. "The ship you will be using does have the ability to detect most types of radiation. But the equipment is five hundred years old. Perhaps Dr. Kavits has something more modern you could use."

Frank repeated Garlut's comment and Dr. Kavits replied, "Yes, I do. Do you know where the ship is now?"

"It's at the space station being prepared for our trip tomorrow."

"Good. I will send the equipment along with somebody to install it in two hours. Please let me speak to Garlut again."

Frank handed the com unit to Garlut. He had a brief conversation with Dr. Kavits, then closed the com unit and said, "The updated equipment will be installed before you leave. He also asked if he could send his assistant, Marcet, on the mission. Will that be all right?"

"Yes, I think we should take advantage of any technical expertise available. Do you think Brealak will object?"

"No, but I will let her know. We should also confirm it with Jeffery."

They talked for a few more minutes before Jeffery came into the dining room to get some coffee. He sat down with Frank and Garlut.

Frank said, "I spoke to Dr. Kavits. He wants us to try and find the source of the radiation, so he's sending over a new radiation detector that will be installed on the ship we'll be using. He also wants to send his assistant, Marcet, on the mission with us. Would you have any problem with that, Jeffery?"

"No problem at all," Jeffery assured him. "Debbie and I met Marcet at the university. She seemed to be very competent and I'm sure she'll be an asset on the mission."

"I am going to leave now and go to the space station so I can meet with Brealak and tell her what is going on. Somebody will be here tomorrow morning to bring you two over there. I do not know if I will see you again before you leave, so I wish you a safe journey," Garlut said.

"I want to thank you for all the help you've given us," Jeffery said.

As Garlut stood up to leave he said, "You are welcome. I will see you when you return."

Jeffery went to his cabin and found Debbie waiting for him. She smiled mischievously and said, "I have plans for us this evening."

"I was hoping for a passionate goodbye. Is that what you had in mind?" he said with a smirk.

"Exactly."

The day passed quickly. Jeffery, Debbie, Frank, and Mike had dinner together. A little later, Jeffery and Debbie went back to their cabin and didn't come out until morning.

They had breakfast in the dining room and every member of the crew came by their table to wish Jeffery good luck on the mission. When breakfast was finished, he went back to his cabin, picked up his bag, and brought it to the shuttle bay. Frank was already there with the equipment he was bringing on the mission. The timing couldn't have been better. At that moment, the exterior door to the shuttle bay opened and a small shuttle flew in.

They watched through the glass and saw Brealak emerge from the shuttle. She saw them watching and smiled. Jeffery opened the interior door to the shuttle bay and as she walked in, he said, "Good morning. Is everything ready for our trip?"

"Yes, the only thing missing are you two."

Jeffery said, "I want to go to the bridge and say goodbye to Debbie. I'll be back in a few minutes." As he turned to go, he saw Debbie walking toward him.

They hugged and kissed goodbye. Debbie said, "Brealak, please take good care of him."

"I promise. This should be a very easy mission, so do not worry."

"I'm sure I'll worry anyway."

Jeffery kissed Debbie one more time, picked up his bag, and walked to the shuttle.

Frank had already loaded his equipment and was seated inside. Brealak stepped into the shuttle right behind Jeffery.

Fifteen minutes later, they were at the space station. After they landed, Brealak said, "Leave all of your things here. Somebody will bring them to our ship."

They followed Brealak through the space station. It was obviously designed to be functional. There were no shops or restaurants, just hallways with lots of doors. Each door had writing on it that Jeffery couldn't read. They walked for only a minute or so when Brealak said, "This is our ship."

They followed her into the small ship. They walked through the hatch and directly into the control room. Brealak gave Jeffery and Frank translators and said, "Marcet does not speak English, so you need to wear these."

Jeffery looked around. The first thing he noticed was, despite the fact the ship was hundreds of years old, everything looked new. There were two consoles which seemed to have identical controls. There were also four more large chairs that looked like recliners mounted on the deck. Three doorways led out of the control room. They walked through the first one.

They were now in the sleeping quarters. It had six sleeping areas, each had a bed, a small chest, and a place to hang clothes. At the opposite end of the room was a door.

Brealak said, "The toilet is through the door at the back of the room. It is the only private area on the ship. To the left of the door are two smaller doors. That is our laundry system. You place a soiled piece of clothing into the upper door. The system scans the garment, disassembles it, and rebuilds it with clean new fabric. When the new garment is finished, it is placed on a shelf behind the lower door. If there are any metal or plastic pieces in the original garment, they will be reused in the reconstructed new one. The process is fast. It takes .03 hours per garment. Please place only one item into the system at a time," she laughed ever so slightly and continued, "If you try it with multiple garments, the results will be both unusual and unwearable."

They followed her out of the sleeping quarters and into the second doorway. "This is our dining room. The ship is equipped with a food generator. You did not know this, but I had samples of food brought over from the Star Rover and loaded them into the system, so you have some Earth foods available. There is a list printed in English next to the controls so you will know what they are."

Jeffery said, "Thank you. Frank and I really appreciate this."

Brealak smiled and said, "You are welcome, but it was not just for you. I prefer your food to ours."

The last doorway was the bathroom. It was small and contained two sinks, a glass enclosed shower stall, and two benches. Brealak said, "I told you there was no privacy on the ship."

Jeffery said, "It's not a problem. The ships we use for trips within our solar system are set up in much the same way. Both of us are used to living like this."

"Good. As soon as Marcet and your personal things are aboard, we will be ready to leave."

Marcet arrived at the ship .1 hours later. When she saw Jeffery, she said brightly, "Hello Admiral, it is nice to see you again. Did you like Coplent?"

"On this journey, it's just Jeffery. It's nice to see you again too. Yes, I like Coplent, but it's so different from Earth it's hard to compare them. This is our ship's doctor, Frank Weber."

"Hello Frank Weber. It is nice to meet you."

"Please call me Frank. It's a pleasure to meet you as well."

A few moments later, a man began bringing in the items that Jeffery and Frank brought for the mission. Jeffery and Frank put their stuff away in the sleeping quarters and rejoined Brealak and Marcet in the control room.

Brealak said, "Please sit down and we will get underway." Then she sat down at the left console, closed the hatch, and separated the ship from the space station after informing the station of their plan.

Jeffery was sitting right behind Brealak so he could see everything she was doing. She maneuvered the ship away from the space station. The video monitor in front of her showed the area in front of the ship. The video monitor on the right console showed the area behind the ship. Jeffery watched as the space station disappeared from view.

Brealak spent several minutes entering commands into the ship's control system. Then she said, "Please get comfortable. In one minute, this part of the ship will be in time stasis. While we are in stasis the ship will accelerate to 50% of the speed of light. Once we reach that speed the stasis field will turn off and we will be on our way to the Procolt System. We will be in stasis for almost six days."

Jeffery was watching the monitor when he heard a beep. The next moment the display on the video screen had changed completely.

Brealak said, "That was the easy part of the trip. Now we will enter the wormhole. We will be at the Procolt System in twenty-four days." She entered a few commands into the system.

The monitor displays turned gray as Jeffery expected. The images suddenly cleared up and Jeffery could see stars. He said, "Our monitors are gray while we're traveling through a wormhole. This is much better. Do you know how they cleared up the display?"

"No, I'm not an engineer. Now I want to spend some time teaching you how to operate the ship. The first thing you have to learn is one word in Coplent's native language. The word is 'dorplan.' This word wakes up the system and then it listens for one or more commands. In order to give the commands in English, you must tell it that first. So, to start the system you would say, 'Dorplan. English.'"

"That seems simple enough." Jeffery said.

"It is very simple. Next you would give the system the command. For example, if you wanted to stop our current journey and return to Coplent the command would be, 'dorplan. English. Stop new destination Coplent execute in point fifteen hours.' That command would bring the ship to a position fifty thousand units above Coplent. Unless a more specific command is given, the ship will always bring you to a position fifty thousand units above the planet's surface. I could be more specific. For example, 'dorplan. English. Destination Earth twenty-five-hundred-unit orbit execute now.' If the ship is already traveling in a wormhole, it will continue on the current course while it calculates the best point to initiate the course change. It will do that with no loss in speed."

"That's amazing. Why didn't it react to your commands?"

"Because I turned the verbal input off. After the calculations are completed it will display the course information on the screen, but not in English so it will not be very useful."

"That reminds me. Did Garlut tell you I wanted to learn your native language?"

"Yes, he did. We will start that soon."

For the next several hours, Brealak taught Jeffery how to use the ship's other systems. By the time the lesson was completed, Jeffery felt sure he would be able to operate the ship in an emergency. Of course, he was not able to actually try out any of his new-found knowledge, but he would have the opportunity when they arrived at Procolt 2.

When the lessons were over, Frank said, "I'm getting hungry. Can we try your food generator?"

"Okay, we will have lunch," Brealak said. All four of them went into the dining room, where Brealak showed Jeffery and Frank the list of Earth food items that were available. Then she said, "The food generator is programmed for English. You just push the red button and tell it what you want."

Brealak pushed the button and said, "Meatloaf with gravy and mashed potatoes." The machine made a soft mechanical sound that lasted for mere seconds. Then the unit made a beeping sound and a panel opened. Inside was a plastic plate that contained hot meatloaf with brown gravy on it and a scoop of mashed potatoes. Brealak reached inside the machine and removed the plate. It looked and smelled like meatloaf.

Marcet said, "That smells wonderful. I would like to try that as well." Looking at Brealak, she said, "I do not speak English. How do I order that?"

"All the Earth foods have to be ordered in English. I did not have time to program the foods in Coplent. I will order for you." Brealak ordered the same thing for Marcet and the two women sat down at the table.

Jeffery looked at the menu, pushed the red button, and said, "Roast beef sandwich." When his sandwich was ready, he took it and sat down. He tried the sandwich and was pleasantly surprised. It actually had the taste and texture of roast beef. Even the bread was good. He said, "This is really very good. I'm impressed."

Brealak said, "The food generator is capable of matching the taste, color, temperature, and texture of almost any food. Yesterday I tried the macaroni and cheese. It was really very good. By the way, it has also been programmed to make coffee."

Frank ordered a ham and Swiss cheese sandwich with potato chips. When it was ready, he joined the others at the table. After he tasted his food he said, "I agree, this is pretty good. But it'll never replace a real cook. We have about twenty-five food items to eat. I think after a couple of months we'll get tired of eating the same things."

"You can always try some of our foods," Marcet said.

"I'll have to give that some thought."

After lunch was finished, Brealak told Jeffery to stay in the dining room so she could start teaching him her native language. She brought some very basic children's books onboard. The books had pictures of common items with the word for the item printed underneath. However, there were ninety-two letters in the alphabet and twenty-one vowel sounds, so this was not like learning French or Spanish. Brealak and Jeffery spent four hours during his first lesson and she was pleased with the progress he made.

While Jeffery and Brealak were working on his language learning project, Marcet and Frank spent the afternoon discussing various medical topics. During the course of the afternoon they both learned a lot about the others' cultures and medicine.

Dinner went smoothly and afterward Brealak said, "I am tired so I'm going to go to sleep. But I wanted to make you aware of a Coplent custom first. On Earth, most people wear some type of clothing when they sleep. On Coplent, we sleep nude. Is that going to be a problem for either of you?"

"No, I have no problem with that. I usually sleep in my underwear, unless it's very warm. Then I sleep nude as well. Nudity is common on our space ships," Jeffery responded.

Frank said, "Please feel free to sleep in the way that's most comfortable for you."

"Thank you," Brealak replied. Then she left the dining room and went into the sleeping quarters.

The others talked for another hour. Then they all decided to go to bed as well.

The journey to the Procolt System went smoothly. The four of them got along very well and they learned a lot about each other's culture. Despite the complexity of the Coplent language, by the time they were ready to begin the deceleration phase of the mission, Jeffery was able to read the books Brealak had brought. He was also able to have simple conversations with Brealak and Marcet in their native language.

The four of them took their seats for the six-day deceleration phase of the mission, but because of the time stasis field it appeared to happen instantaneously. After it was over, they were fifty thousand units beyond the outermost planet of the Procolt System.

Jeffery said, "I think we should go to Procolt 4 first and let Glencet know what we're doing. I left on good terms with him and I don't want to do anything that would upset him."

"I agree," Brealak said, "That would be the correct protocol. I will set up the navigation system to take us there. If we have a clear path, it will take less than .05 hours to get there." She keyed some information into the navigation system and then she said, "There is not a clear path to Procolt 4, so it will take .1 hours to get there."

When they arrived at Procolt 4, they were fifty thousand units above the planet's surface. Brealak tried to contact Glencet, but there was no response. She tried several more times, but the results were the same. She asked, "Jeffery, are you sure Glencet said he would still be here?"

"Yes, he said he would be here for at least another half year and then another ship will arrive to take his place. Can you scan the area to see if his ship is still here?"

"Yes, I will do that now."

After spending some time at the scanner Brealak said, "There is a problem! There is no ship in orbit around Procolt 4. But there are some large metal and plastic fragments that may have been part of Glencet's ship. I am going to move us closer to the fragments so we can get a better look at them."

Suddenly, Jeffery was worried about his people on Procolt 2. His heart was racing when he said, "Yes, please do that."

Brealak moved the ship close to the debris field and began scanning. She said, "The debris shows signs of an explosion, but I cannot tell if it was internal or external. We are twenty thousand units above the surface. I would like to drop down to two thousand units and scan the surface. Is that okay with you?"

"You're in charge of this mission. I'm concerned about my people on Procolt 2, but I agree scanning the surface is a good idea. Glencet told me they had a mining operation. Perhaps we can find that. We should also get to Procolt 2 as soon as we can."

"I think we can complete our scan in an hour. If we locate the mining operation, I will try to contact them. We have to find out if they need help."

"I agree."

Brealak put the ship into an orbit two thousand units above the planet's equator. She then initiated an automatic scan of the planet's surface. The system was looking for humanoid lifeforms, heat sources, and electromagnetic radiation. It only took a half an hour to locate the mining operation. A high-resolution video scan showed it. There were obvious signs the operation had been attacked. Several buildings had been demolished and more than a few bodies could be seen. None showed any life signs.

Brealak tried contacting the mining operation. She didn't expect a response so she was not surprised when she didn't receive one. She said, "I think we should land and search for survivors. We have two doctors onboard who can help."

Frank and Marcet had been silently observing. Frank said, "I'm ready. How about you, Marcet."

Marcet looked at Frank and said, "I will get a med-kit assembled, in case we find any survivors."

Frank asked with some concern in his voice, "Are we prepared to fight in case any of the bad guys are still there?"

"We have several handheld weapons aboard. We will take them with us as a precaution, but my scans did not indicate anything alive down there," Brealak replied.

"Remember, this is a mining operation. Can your scanner detect lifeforms under the surface?" Jeffery asked.

"It is able to detect life forms up to a depth of fifty feet. You are right, we should be prepared for a fight, but I do not think it will happen."

"There's one more thing to consider before we land. If there are any survivors, they might think we're part of the group that attacked them. How do we let them know we're there to help them?" Jeffery asked.

"I spent over a year on Torblit and I speak their language. I can tell them we are not the enemy," Marcet answered.

Jeffery said, "Good! That makes me feel better. We should bring a translator with us anyway."

The ship landed near the mine opening. The air on Procolt 4 was breathable, but it was only 14% oxygenated, not the 20% they were accustomed to. It was also cold, negative fifteen degrees Centigrade. There were some coats that were part of the ship's standard equipment and each of them put one on. They also each took a small canister of compressed oxygen in case it was needed, and a flashlight. Brealak and Jeffery also carried weapons.

They left the ship and walked into the mine. As they walked Marcet called out in Torblit, "We are from Coplent. We are here to help you," every few seconds. The inside of the mine was dark and Jeffery led the way. He was holding his light in his left hand and his weapon in his right. After walking a few hundred feet into the mine they heard a cry for help. They hurried forward and found themselves in a round, rock-walled room thirty feet in diameter. There were three men in the room. All appeared to be badly injured.

One of the men said to Marcet, "We are very glad to see you. We need food. None of us have eaten for a week. I am okay except for the hunger."

"I am a doctor and so is he," Marcet said, pointing at Frank. "Can all of you walk to our ship?"

"Two of us can, but Bendal has a broken leg. My name is Sportec. What made you come to Procolt 4?"

Marcet did a quick examination of Bendal and gave him an injection to ease his pain. While she was doing that,

Brealak handed a translator to Sportec. After he put it on Jeffery said, "Frank and I are from Earth. We recently joined the trade group. We were here before and we met with Glencet. I left two of my crew members on Procolt 2 to study some animals we discovered there and we went to Coplent. While we were there, we found out my crew members may be in danger due to some type of radiation exposure, so we came back to check on them. We decided to stop at Procolt 4 to let Glencet know what we were doing. When we got here, we found that his ship had been destroyed. He told me there was a mining operation on the planet, so we decided to look for it before we went to Procolt 2."

"I am very happy you did! Grober and I will carry Bendal to your ship."

"That won't be necessary. I'm sure Frank and I can do it."

Jeffery and Frank walked over to Bendal. Bendal tried to stand, but was only able to do so with Frank's help. Once he was standing, he put an arm each around Frank and Jeffery and they began a slow walk back to the ship.

When they got back, Sportec and Grober went to the dining room to get something to eat. Frank and Jeffery put Bendal on one of the beds and Marcet began a more thorough examination. She gave him more medication for pain. Once the pain medication took effect, she reset his leg, put a splint on it, and secured it with a polymer wrap. Then she put a device over the break and turned it on. Marcet said, "This device will heal the break in your leg. Please try not to move your leg for .1 hours."

"Thank you for your help. If you hadn't arrived when you did, I am certain all of us would have died."

"Would you like me to bring you some food?"

"No, I am hungry but I can wait until my leg heals."

"Can you tell me what happened?"

"I do not really know much. The three of us were just ending our shift when we felt the ground shake. We thought it was a quake. We walked to the mine entrance just in time to see our main building blow up. The blast knocked us all

80

backward off our feet. I fell and heard my leg snap. Sportec and Grober helped me back to the area where you found us. A few hours later, Sportec went back to see what happened. We had three buildings. All of them were completely demolished. There were twenty-two men working here. The others are all dead. That was eight days ago.

"We had water, but no food. We had been working here for over a year so we adapted to the low oxygen levels. We tried using our handheld com units to contact Glencet, but there was no response. We assumed his ship had been attacked as well, but we were not sure until you told us. Do you have any idea who could have done this?"

"No, I have no idea. We have to go to Procolt 2 and check on Jeffery's crew members. Then we will go back to Coplent. What were you mining?"

"They never told us, but we had our suspicions. There were rumors that Torblit needed money, so we all thought it was hirodim, but we were never told. Each time we opened a new section of the mine, the supervisor would walk through the mine and tell us where to remove the ore. A few of the men asked what kind of ore we were extracting, but they were told that if they wanted to keep their jobs they should stop asking. Since the jobs paid very well, everybody kept quiet."

"If you're correct, that would explain why Glencet was so hostile when Jeffery showed up. He threatened to blow up his ship if they didn't leave immediately. Jeffery gave him some of the goods they were carrying in exchange for some time to explore Procolt 2."

"I heard about that. Apparently, Jeffery had things Glencet wanted, but I do not know what they were."

A few moments later the device over the break in Bendal's leg beeped. Marcet removed the splint and said, "Your leg should be okay now, but take it easy. No running or jumping for a while."

Marcet removed the device, polymer, and splint. Bendal sat up in the bed. He slowly stood up and smiled, while saying, "This is great! No pain! Thank you, doctor."

"You are most welcome. Now we can get you something to eat."

Marcet and Bendal joined the others in the dining room. After the three miners had eaten, Marcet told them to go to the sleeping quarters and try to get some rest. After they left, Jeffery asked, "Brealak, do you have any idea who could have done this? Garlut told me all the members of the trade group were peaceful."

"I believe this was done by Crosus. They are the richest planet in the trade group and have been for more than a thousand years. Being the richest planet gives them a financial advantage. They have the ability to set the terms for virtually all of their trade agreements. They do not negotiate. If you want to buy something, they tell you how much it will cost. If they want to sell something, they set the purchase price. We all believed there was no more hirodim in our part of the galaxy. If Torblit did find hirodim, that could make them wealthier than Crosus, which would weaken Crosus' position in the trade group. I do not think Crosus would find that situation acceptable.

"In the terms of the trade agreements, armed conflict between members of the trade group is prohibited. This would be considered an act of war. If Crosus did this, they would be expelled from the trade group. I am sure that is why they attacked from space. That way no one could prove it was them. We must get back to Coplent as soon as possible so I can report this."

"We have to go to Procolt 2 first. If we have to take my two crew members back with us, this ship is going to be awfully crowded. It was obviously designed for six and we already have seven. Is the ship capable of carrying nine passengers?" Jeffery asked.

"The ship's air, water, and food systems can handle up to twenty. We have two choices: We could use the time stasis field so we will not be awake during the trip, or we could sleep and eat in shifts. We can make that decision after we see the situation on Procolt 2. I am concerned that whoever attacked the ship and the mine may have also attacked your facility on

82

Procolt 2. We will leave immediately," Brealak stated with a grim expression on her face.

Marcet went to the sleeping quarters and told the miners the ship was leaving to go to Procolt 2, suggesting they stay in their beds until the ship landed again. They agreed. Marcet went back to the control room and sat down. As soon as she did, the ship took off. When they were twenty-five thousand units above Procolt 4, Brealak programmed the navigation system to go to Procolt 2. About .15 hours later, they were in an equatorial orbit above Procolt 2. Jeffery used his com unit to try to contact his crew members, but there was no response.

Using the ship's scanners, they were able to locate the habitat. They watched the video monitor as the scanner showed what was left of the habitat. It looked like the entire building had been destroyed.

Brealak landed the ship close to the remains of the habitat. Jeffery and Frank left the ship immediately to search through the wreckage. A half hour later they were sure that nobody had been inside when the attack occurred. That was a big relief, but they had no idea where Cathy and Sheila were.

Jeffery suggested, "They must have taken refuge in one of the caves, but there are dozens of caves in this area. Let's go back to the ship and ask Brealak to use the scanners to search underground for them."

As Jeffery and Frank turned to walk back, they saw one of the squirrels standing ten feet in front of them. As they approached the squirrel asked in a soft, squeaky voice, "Are you Jeffery, the one who is Cathy's boss?"

"Yes, I am."

"Follow me and I will take you to Cathy and Sheila."

"We will, but I must contact my ship first and let them know what's happening."

Jeffery contacted Brealak and told her that apparently Cathy and Sheila were okay and one of the squirrels was taking him and Frank to them. He promised to contact her again after he had a chance to evaluate the situation.

Jeffery and Frank followed the squirrel through the woods and into a cave. After they had walked twenty feet into the cave it was so dark, they could barely see the shape of the squirrel in front of them. Then they saw a shimmer of light ahead. As they approached, the light got brighter. The cave opened into a large room and seated in the center of the room surrounded by squirrels were Cathy and Sheila.

Jeffery smiled broadly and said, "I'm very happy to see you two again. We were very worried. You are okay, aren't you?"

"Yes, but we're better than just okay. Something strange, but good, is happening to both of us," Cathy said.

"That's why we came back so soon. We discovered the remains we found were from a man who died seventeen years ago at the ripe old age of one hundred eighty-four. There's some type of radiation on this planet that causes genetic mutations in living organisms. For Mr. Brown, his life span was substantially increased. What effect is it having on you?"

"Well, I don't know if we're going to live longer than normal, but our strength has increased. Glencet called to tell us he was under attack and he suggested we get out of the habitat because it could be a target for whoever was attacking him. Before we could take his advice, there was an explosion near the habitat that caused the structure to vibrate and then it began to come apart. Sheila and I were both inside. So were seven of our squirrel friends. We were able to hold up the habitat long enough for the squirrels to get out. Then Sheila and I left as well. As soon as we let go, the wall we were holding up fell down. As we were running away from the habitat, there was another explosion and the habitat was completely demolished. We never saw a ship, so we assumed the attack came from space. We tried to contact Glencet after we got a few hundred feet from the remains. There was no response from him, but apparently somebody tracked the signal from our com unit because a few seconds later there was an explosion fifty feet away. We followed the squirrels into this cave and we've stayed here in the dark for a while. We went back to the habitat and found a working power module and a lamp, so we brought them back here along with some pillows and blankets. Is Glencet okay?"

"No, his ship was completely destroyed and unfortunately, it doesn't look as if there were any survivors. The mining operation on Procolt 4 was also attacked. Three men survived the attack and they're on Brealak's ship."

"Why didn't you come on the Star Rover?"

"Because we were worried about you two and Brealak's ship is much faster than the Star Rover. Why didn't you answer me when I called your com unit?"

"We were concerned that whoever destroyed the habitat and tried to kill us would be able to track the signals from the com units we had. One of the squirrels took them far away from the cave and buried them."

Jeffery nodded. "That was a very good idea."

Frank said, "I'd like both of you to come back to the ship for a complete physical. I know you think what's happening to you is beneficial, but I'd like to make sure you're both well."

Sheila, who had been quiet up till now pleaded, "Jeffery, please don't make us leave here."

"We'll discuss that after I get the results of your examinations."

As Jeffery turned to leave, he felt a tug on one of his pant legs. He looked down and saw one of the squirrels. The squirrel said in their typical high-pitched voice, "We have never been inside a space ship. Can we come with you?"

Jeffery looked around and counted at least thirty squirrels. He said, "The ship is too small to take all of you. We can take five of you now. When the first five come back, another group of five can go into the ship." As soon as Jeffery said it, he realized he had forgotten the squirrels had no concept of numbers.

He was about to explain it a different way when the squirrel standing next to him said, "I will split us up into groups of adults. There will be five groups of five and one group of four. Is that okay?"

It took Jeffery a few seconds to realize what happened. In the short time he had been away from Procolt 2, Cathy and Sheila had taught the squirrels the concept of numbers and the ability to do simple calculations. The ability of the squirrels to learn was apparently far greater than the ability of humans. He replied nervously, "Yes, that would be perfect."

The squirrel walked over to their group and selected four others to join him. Then he turned around and said to Jeffery, "We are ready."

"Very well, let's go."

As they walked back, Jeffery asked quietly, "Frank, have you ever seen another living creature that learns as fast as these squirrels?"

"No, their ability to learn is truly amazing. We've been gone for only a few months and now they speak fluent English and do simple math. I wonder how long it will take them to learn to read and write."

Cathy, who was listening to the conversation, said, "They can already read numbers. We were going to start on letters when the habitat was destroyed. However, based on how quickly they learn, I would think we can have them reading simple children's books in six weeks."

Jeffery asked, "Frank, do you have the ability to test their intelligence?"

"No, I don't think it's possible to test their actual intelligence with any degree of accuracy until they're able to read. But a brain scan might give us some clue regarding their ability to learn. Unfortunately, I don't have the equipment on the ship, but I'm sure it's available on Coplent. Do you want to invite them to go back to Coplent with us?"

"No, I don't think that would be a good idea. However, we could bring the appropriate equipment back here on our next trip."

When they got back to the ship, Jeffery said, "Let me go in first and tell Brealak about our guests. I'll be back shortly." He found Brealak in the dining room. He sat down across from her and said, "We have some guests that would like a tour of your ship."

Brealak looked puzzled. "What are you talking about? What guests?"

"The squirrels want to see your ship. In the time we were gone, they became fluent in English. When we left, they had no concept of numbers. Now they not only understand numbers, but they can solve simple math problems too."

"That's impossible. Nothing learns that fast."

"That's the same thing I said to Frank. Is it okay if I bring them aboard? You can see for yourself how intelligent they are."

"I do not see any harm so bring them aboard. I'll be in the control room."

Jeffery left and returned with the squirrels following him. He walked into the control room with his new furry friends. When Brealak saw them, she smiled and spoke to them in English, "Hello, I am Brealak. I am the captain of this ship."

The first squirrel behind Jeffery looked up at her and said, "It's nice to meet you, Brealak. We don't have names yet, but I'm sure Cathy will give us names soon."

Brealak had been expecting a few mispronounced words in broken English at best. She smiled and said, "This is a very small ship, but I will be happy to give you a tour. Please follow me." The five squirrels followed her into the sleeping quarters.

While Brealak was showing the squirrels the ship, Frank asked Cathy to follow him into the bathroom. Frank said, "There's really no private area on the ship, so this is the best I can do. Please wait here and I'll get the equipment I need for your examination."

"Would it be okay if I took a quick shower before you start the exam? I haven't had one in a long time."

"Sure, I'll come back in ten minutes. I'll find something clean for you to wear."

"Thanks."

Frank left the bathroom and walked over to a storage area where there were extra uniforms. He picked up two of them he thought would be the right size. Then he walked over to his sleeping quarters where his medical equipment was stored. When he got back to the bathroom, it was crowded. Cathy was still in the shower and Brealak and the squirrels were looking around. As Frank walked in, Brealak and the squirrels walked out.

Frank said, "I brought a uniform for you to wear and I'll show you how to use the laundry system when we're done. Please step out so we can get started."

Cathy stepped out of the shower and covered herself with a towel. Then she walked over to the closest bench and sat down. She said, "It feels nice to be clean again."

After Cathy was dressed, Frank took a blood sample and put it into the analyzer. A few moments later a report showed up on the screen. He looked at it and said, "The analysis indicates there have been minor changes in your DNA since your last test. However, there's no indication of any medical problem."

Using a medical scanner, Frank checked her heart and lungs. Then he proceeded to check her reflexes the old-fashioned way, with a small rubber mallet from his days in medical school. He found no problems. Then he attached two small electrodes to her forehead and said, "I'm going to do a quick brain activity scan. Please sit very still."

The test took about twenty seconds. When it was over, Frank removed the electrodes and looked at the report. He said, "Your brain is showing increased activity. I'm not sure what that means yet. I'll have to study the report and compare it with your last one. I suspect it may be due to radiation exposure. That being said, I still don't see any immediate problems. But I don't think you should stay here until we've had an opportunity to investigate the changes in your DNA."

"Does that mean you're going to tell Jeffery not to let me stay here?"

"No, that's simply my opinion. I'll tell Jeffery what I found. If he asks me for my opinion, I'll tell him what I think, but the final decision should be yours, and I'll tell him that too. Please remember there are other dangers here. Whoever destroyed the habitat may come back and you are defenseless."

"You're right, of course. I'll discuss this with Jeffery. I'm worried about leaving the squirrels here alone. They have no concept of war and didn't understand what happened to the habitat."

"Think about it for a moment. The squirrels are not a threat to whoever destroyed the habitat. They may be safer if you and Sheila are not here."

"I see your point. I don't want to do anything that would put them in danger, but I really don't want to leave either." She was silent, feeling some remorse and disappointment over the impending decisions she and Sheila would likely face, then she said, "I'd like to get something to eat now, if that's okay."

"Your doctor orders are for you to get a good, hot meal and some sleep. Please ask Sheila to come in here," Frank said with a smile on his face.

Cathy walked over to the dining room and sat down at the table. Jeffery and Sheila were both sitting there. She told Sheila Frank was ready for her. Then she turned to Jeffery and said, "I was going to ask you if Sheila and I could stay here, but after talking to Frank I've changed my mind. I was thinking about us and not the safety of the squirrels. Frank said that if the people who destroyed the habitat come back, they won't be looking for animals. They would be looking for humanoids and our being here, unarmed, could put the squirrels in danger."

"Frank's right. We have to leave here soon, probably in four hours. I think you should use that time to explain to the squirrels why you have to leave and let them know you'll be back as soon as possible. I suspect it will be at least one hundred and twenty days. When we come back, we'll be prepared to defend our position here and you'll be able to spend time with the squirrels without putting them or yourself in danger."

"Okay, I want to tell Sheila the plan and then I'll go talk to my little friends. Frank said I should eat something and then get some sleep, but that will have to wait." She got up from the table and left the room.

A few moments later, Brealak walked into the dining room and sat down. Jeffery said, "I'm glad you're here. I told Cathy we were leaving in four hours and suggested she explain the situation to the squirrels."

"She just left with the first group. I can't believe how intelligent they are. They are the first intelligent non-humanoid species we have found. They speak almost perfect English. Sheila told me how quickly they learned the concept of numbers. It is truly amazing!"

"I told Cathy we'd be back as soon as possible, and we'd be ready to protect ourselves. But the weapons on the Star Rover aren't capable of doing that. Does Coplent have some kind of war ship that could protect the planet?"

"Yes, it has not been needed for a long time, but it can be reactivated very quickly. I want to find out who committed these acts of war. If they are members of the trade group, they will be expelled. But regardless of who they are, we will not allow this to happen again. I still think it was Crosus, but we have no proof."

"How many people does your warship hold?" Jeffery asked.

"I think it requires a staff of ten to run the ship, but it can transport another two hundred."

"Will there be a problem if I bring some of my crew on it?"

"No, I am sure that would be okay," Brealak said.

"Good. I want to have the Star Rover here too, but that will take ninety days and I don't want to wait that long to get back."

The results of Sheila's exam were the same as Cathy's. She showed signs of genetic mutation, but appeared to be in overall perfect health. After her exam, Sheila walked into the dining room and sat down across from Jeffery. She said, "I suspect Cathy and I had the exact same conversation with Frank. I know he's right and we shouldn't stay. I want to go say goodbye to the squirrels as well. Is that okay, sir?"

"Yes, of course. We'll be leaving in less than four hours. Cathy is explaining the situation to your furry friends now. I think you should join her."

"I will. Thank you."

The next few hours went by quickly. Cathy and Sheila spent the time showing the squirrels the ship and explaining that they had to leave, but would return as quickly as possible. They also informed the squirrels that if they see other people, they should hide in the cave and not to use the light in the cave at all because the bad people may be able to detect the electrical energy.

The ship left Procolt 2 on time. When they were fifty thousand units above the planet, Brealak told the new passengers to lie down and the four original crew members each took a seat in the control room. After everybody was comfortable, Brealak instructed the navigation system to start the return to Coplent.

Six days later, the navigation system turned off the time stasis field. The ship was traveling at half the speed of light and everybody aboard was awake. A short time later, the ship entered the wormhole where it would stay until it was time to begin the deceleration phase of their journey.

It was decided that Brealak and Jeffery, being the senior officers aboard, would have permanent positions in the sleeping quarters and everybody else would rotate in using the remaining four beds.

Jeffery continued his language lessons and Cathy decided she wanted to learn the Coplent language as well. By the time the ship was ready for the deceleration phase, both Cathy and Jeffery were able to have simple conversations in Coplent.

When the deceleration phase was over, they were only thirty thousand units from Coplent. Brealak contacted Garlut immediately.

Garlut responded, "I am glad you are back. How was your trip?"

Brealak told Garlut what happened. When she was done, he said, "This is outrageous! It is an act of war! I must inform the Trade Council immediately."

"I will be at the station inside the hour. Please have a shuttle waiting for us," Brealak said.

Garlut, unable to control his anger, commanded loudly, "It will be there. Bring everybody to the Trade Council office."

"We should be there in three hours. I think we should activate one of our warships and return to the Procolt System as soon as possible," Brealak suggested.

"I agree. I will contact the Trade Council and let them know what is going on. Then I will contact Commander Streb and inform him of the situation. I am sure he will activate one of our warships immediately. I will see you in a few hours."

When it was obvious the conversation with Garlut had ended, Jeffery asked, "What happens now?"

"We are going to the Trade Council office and report what happened."

As Garlut promised, when they arrived at the space station there was a shuttle waiting for them. They boarded immediately. As soon as everybody was aboard, the shuttle left the space station for the two-hour trip to the Trade Council office.

When they arrived at the Trade Council office, Garlut was already there. He and Brealak hugged when they saw each other. Garlut said, "I am glad you are back. I wish the circumstances were better. Commander Streb has ordered our newest warship activated. It has not been used for ninety years, but it can be operational in a day or two. I assumed you would want to go back, so I told Commander Streb that you and I will be on the mission to Procolt."

"Yes, I do want to be on it," Brealak replied. "I am sure Jeffery and some of his crew will want to go as well."

"That will not be a problem. Although I do not see the need for a large contingent of soldiers. We should go to the meeting room. The Trade Council representative is waiting for us."

They walked into the room and sat down around a large table. One by one, each of the witnesses gave their account of what happened. After everybody spoke, the Trade Council representative asked a few questions. Finally, he said, "This action is a very serious breach of our agreement. It is an act of war and must be dealt with immediately. Is Coplent in a position to send a warship to the Procolt System?"

Garlut replied, "Yes sir. Our ship will be ready in two days."

"Good. I will send ambassadors to the other trade group planets to inform them of this situation, but we cannot wait for the next meeting. We must take action as soon as possible. Is Drabord aware of these events?"

"No sir, we were going to see him when we leave here," Garlut responded.

"Please keep me informed and assure Drabord that the council will take whatever action is required to resolve this situation and bring the perpetrators to justice."

"Yes sir. I will do that."

As soon as they left the office, Garlut contacted Drabord. Garlut told him there was an urgent situation he had to discuss with him immediately. Drabord said he would stay in his office and wait for Garlut to arrive.

Garlut and the others boarded Brealak's shuttle, leaving his there. Garlut told the pilot their destination and they left immediately.

During the trip Garlut said, "I do have good news for you. Dr. Kavits and his team were able to find a cure for the disease on Earth. The information was put on a ship that left here ten days ago."

Jeffery's eyes lit up and a smile showed as he replied, "That's good news. I'm sure Max will be pleased. Actually, I suspect a few million people will be overjoyed."

Everyone was quiet for a while. Then Jeffery said, "I want to bring the Star Rover back to Procolt 2 so we can continue our research there. However, the ship isn't equipped to fight a battle with another ship. Will the warship be able to protect the Star Rover as well?"

93

"The warship we are sending will place monitors throughout the Procolt System. They will know if another vessel enters the system and will take immediate action. Additionally, we can install ground defenses on Procolt 2 that can protect the Star Rover as long as it stays in a low orbit," Garlut replied.

"That makes me feel better."

When they arrived, Drabord was waiting for them. He was surprised to see three people from Torblit exit the ship. He recognized Garlut and Jeffery from their previous meeting, but didn't say anything. When everyone was out of the shuttle, they went inside to a conference room. As soon as everybody was seated Brealak stood up and said, "Sir, we have just returned from the Procolt System. I am sorry to inform you that both Captain Glencet's ship and the mining operation on Procolt 4 have been attacked. The entire crew of the ship was killed and all but three of the miners were killed as well." Pointing at the three survivors she said, "These three men are the only survivors."

Drabord said nothing for a few seconds. Then, with a scowl in his voice, he asked, "What is being done about this?"

"We are activating one of our warships," Garlut responded. "It will leave for Procolt in two days. When we get there, we will examine the wreckage and try to determine who is responsible. We will stay in the system until we are relieved by a ship from Torblit. If the perpetrators come back, we will deal with them. If they are a member of the trade group, they will be expelled. If Torblit wishes to take additional actions, they are free to do so. There will be no reprisals from the Trade Council," Garlut responded.

"I would like my assistant to be on the ship going to Procolt," Drabord growled.

"I am certain that will not be a problem. I will inform you of the departure time as soon as possible. You should know the Earth research habitat on Procolt 2 was also destroyed. Luckily, nobody was injured as a result of that attack."

"I am pleased the people from Earth were unharmed. I want to thank you for coming to tell me this personally."

"You are welcome. Are you going to go back to Torblit?"

"Yes. It will take me a few days to finish up some things, but I will leave as soon as possible."

Sportec asked, "Sir, can we return to Torblit with you?"

"Of course, and you are welcome to stay here until we are ready to leave."

"Thank you, sir." Then turning to Jeffery and Brealak, he said, "I do not know how we could ever thank you enough for thinking about the mining operation. Had you not come to our rescue I am sure the three of us would have died. If there is ever anything we can do for you, please let us know."

"Brealak and I are glad we could help. Have a pleasant and safe journey home," Jeffery said.

After they left Drabord's office, Jeffery looked at Cathy and said, "I assume you and Sheila want to get back to Procolt 2 as soon as possible. Am I correct?"

Both Cathy and Sheila said in unison, "Yes, sir."

Then Jeffery asked, "Garlut, can you get us back to the Star Rover?"

"Yes, of course. Pilot, please take us back to the space station."

The trip back to the space station took two hours. As soon as they arrived at the station, Jeffery contacted Debbie and asked her to pick them up. Debbie said she would be there in ten minutes.

She arrived on time. As soon as the door opened to the shuttle bay, Jeffery ran inside and over to the open shuttle door. He went inside and first hugged and then kissed his wife.

She said, "I missed you a lot. Please don't leave me again."

"I missed you too. I'm going back to Procolt 2 in two days, but this time you're coming with me. We'll have twenty-six days to get know each other again."

"Why are you going back so soon?" she said with some concern. "What happened?"

Jeffery told her what happened, adding, "Coplent is sending a warship to the Procolt System and we'll be on it."

When they got back to the Star Rover, Jeffery and Debbie went to the bridge.

Mike was there and when he saw Jeffery, he smiled and said, "It's nice to have you back aboard. How was your trip to Procolt 2?"

"The travel was okay, but what we found was not. Please have the entire crew go to the dining room and I'll brief everybody at the same time."

Mike made the announcement.

Within ten minutes, the entire crew was assembled in the dining room. Jeffery stood at the front, smiled, and said hello to each of the crew members as they walked in. When everybody was seated, he said, "I'm very happy to be back onboard the Star Rover, but I'll only be here a short time. We went to Procolt 2 to check on Cathy and Sheila, but the mission parameters changed when we arrived at Procolt 4."

Then he told the crew what happened and about the Coplent mission to the Procolt System.

"Mike, you will command the Star Rover and I want you to leave as soon as possible for the Procolt system after we leave," he gestured to Debbie and himself. "When you get there, stop at Procolt 4 first. If we're there, we'll board the Star Rover and go to Procolt 2 with you. If we aren't there, go on to Procolt 2.

"I also want to give you a brief update regarding the squirrels on Procolt 2. They're extremely intelligent. I believe their ability to learn may exceed any other living being, including humans. They all speak almost perfect English now. Cathy and Sheila have started to teach them about numbers. Now they can read written numbers and do simple math. This is a remarkable achievement considering they learned it all in less than half a year. One of our goals on Procolt 2 is to continue their education.

96

"The last thing I wanted to tell you is that during the brief time Cathy and Sheila were on Procolt 2, they were exposed to some unknown type of radiation. It has caused changes to their DNA. So far, these changes appear to be beneficial. Both have experienced increased muscle strength and brain activity. It's still too early to determine if there are any negative effects of the radiation exposure. For this reason, when we get to Procolt 2 no one will be ordered to go down to the surface of the planet. It will be strictly voluntary. Does anyone have any questions?"

Carol Hobbes, who was in charge of the hydroponic garden on the ship, asked, "Does this mean you're taking the ship into a potential war zone?"

"I don't believe the ship will be in any danger. The Coplent warship will be monitoring the entire system and a ground-based defense unit will be installed on Procolt 2 that will protect the Star Rover. But, yes, strictly speaking it will be a war zone."

Ron Rice asked, "Since we don't have another habitat aboard, do you want us to fabricate one during the trip to Procolt 2?"

"If you have the raw material you need you should do so. It will certainly be more comfortable than living in a cave."

Since there were no further questions, Jeffery sat down at the table where Mike and Debbie were. "Mike, are you comfortable with taking the ship to Procolt 4?"

"Yes, and I don't think there'll be any problems we can't handle."

"Good. The Star Rover will take two months longer to get to the Procolt System than the Coplent warship, and I know that Cathy and Sheila want to get back there as soon as possible."

"Jeffery, it's not going to be a problem. But I'll bet you're going to miss the food."

"You're right. We all will. But I think we'll be able to live through it."

Then Debbie asked, "Are Garlut and Brealak going too?"

"Yes, I'm sure they are."

"Good, it'll be nice to have somebody we know onboard."

Jeffery took Debbie's hand and said, "Please excuse us. If you need me, I'll be in our cabin."

Jeffery and Debbie spent several hours in their cabin. They were on the bed resting when Jeffery's com unit beeped. He picked it up and said, "I hope this is important."

"I guess it is. Garlut called the ship. He wants to talk with you. I'll transfer the call to your com unit."

A moment later, Jeffery heard a click and said, "Hello Garlut. How can I help you?"

"I wanted to let you know the warship has been certified and will be leaving tomorrow morning. You should be at the station by 7:00 a.m."

"That's not a problem. We'll be there."

"Marcet is also going. She wants to study the squirrels and look for the source of the radiation."

"That's a good idea. I'm glad there will be people we know on the ship."

"I'm sure you will find everybody on the ship very friendly. You will also be pleased to know the food generators have been programmed with a variety of Earth foods. While you were gone, William and Koltep worked on at least fifty recipes and they will all be available. I also wanted to let you know you should not bring any personal items with you. Anything you need will be provided."

"You're right. I'm pleased. We'll be at the station by 7:00. So, we shouldn't pack any clothes. What about things like a razor, toothbrush, or comb?"

"You will not need any of those items. Everything will be provided."

"Good, thank you for calling," Jeffery said, and they terminated the call.

The following morning, Mike took Jeffery and the others to the space station. When they stepped inside the station Garlut, Brealak, and Marcet were waiting for them.

Garlut said, "Good morning. Are all of you ready for another long space journey?"

"Yes, we are," Jeffery responded.

"Good, please follow me. Our shuttle is waiting."

They walked to another shuttle bay. Inside was a large shuttle. There were already twenty people aboard. As soon as they were seated the door closed. A few moments later they were on their way.

It took little time to reach the ship. It was enormous, much larger than the size of a cruise ship on Earth. There appeared to be at least twelve levels on the ship based on the number of openings on the side. As they got closer, Jeffery noticed what he guessed were weapons mounted all over the outside.

The shuttle landed inside and Garlut stepped off before anyone else in their group. There, a member of the ship's crew was handing out room assignments cards. He spoke to her, and after a brief conversation got the room assignment cards for everyone in the group.

As they walked out of the shuttle bay, Garlut said, "I arranged for all of our rooms to be together. Brealak and I will share a room. Jeffery, Debbie, your room is next to ours. Cathy, Sheila, and Marcet are sharing the room right across the hall. Please follow me."

Jeffery asked, "Have you been on this ship before? You seem to know your way around."

"I was not on this ship, but I was on an identical ship when I was Brealak's age. It was a one hundred fifty day training mission. Everybody who wants to be licensed to command a ship must go through the training. The training ships do not have real weapons, but they have simulators for weapons training. That is the only difference."

The shuttle had landed on level five and their rooms were on level eight. They walked up three flights of stairs to their rooms. When they got there, Garlut said, "Inside your rooms are watches that use our time system." Remember there are twenty hours in a day and we use hundredths of an hour, not minutes. It is currently 6.20. Please meet me in the hallway at 6.45."

Jeffery and Debbie walked into their room and were pleasantly surprised. The room was square, and each side was about twenty-five feet long. There were two large beds, two desks, and some very comfortable chairs. There were also two small chests. On each chest was a watch as Garlut promised. The watches had a digital display and the time was displayed using Arabic numbers. There were three buttons on the side of the watch.

Jeffery took off his watch and put on the new one. He said, "These things must have been programmed for us. Coplent does not use Arabic numbers. I'll bet these are com units too."

Debbie put on hers and said, "They seem to be a little heavy to just be a watch. We'll have to ask Garlut about it."

Opposite the bed there was a door. Debbie opened it and said, "We have our own bathroom! I wasn't expecting that on a warship. I wonder what we do for clothes."

Jeffery walked into the bathroom. Inside were the same two small doors that were on Brealak's ship for the laundry system. There was also a shower, a toilet, and sink. Hairbrushes, combs, razors, toothbrushes, and a tube of toothpaste were on a shelf above the sink. Jeffery asked Debbie to come into the bathroom and he explained how the laundry system worked.

They relaxed in their room until it was time to meet Garlut again. When they walked out of their room into the hallway, Garlut was already there.

"Jeffery, do you feel comfortable enough with your Coplent language skills to skip using a translator?" Garlut asked.

"No, I don't think my vocabulary is proficient enough for this situation."

"I brought translators for everybody anyway." He handed a translator to each of them. When Cathy and Sheila emerged from their room a few moments later, he gave each of them a translator as well. Then Garlut spent the next half hour showing them around the ship. Although the ship was enormous, only one quarter of the space was devoted to living quarters. During the tour, Garlut also explained how to use the combination watch/com unit each of them was wearing.

When the tour was over, Garlut looked at his watch and said, "We have a meeting scheduled with Commander Streb in .1 hours. We should hurry." He led them to a conference room with a large oval table and at least twenty chairs around it. Seated in one of them was Commander Streb, who said, "You are right on time. Garlut, it is good to see you again."

"It is nice to see you again too." Pointing at Jeffery, he continued, "This is Admiral Whitestone and his assistant and life partner, Captain Whitestone. He is the commander of the Earth ship Star Rover, and she is his first officer. Next to her is Lieutenant Carter and Lieutenant Roth. They were present on Procolt 2 when the attack occurred."

"I read the reports, but there was not much information in them. Was there any evidence that might indicate who was responsible for these attacks?"

Brealak answered, "No sir. We were in an unarmed vessel. After we rescued the three survivors from the mining operation on Procolt 4, we left as soon as we could. We were understandably concerned about the fate of the Star Rover crew members who were on Procolt 2. It appeared the attacks were launched from a great distance. None of the three survivors witnessed the attack on the mining operation because they were inside the mine. I am sure that is the only reason they survived."

"Do we know what they were mining?"

"We cannot be sure, but the miners thought it was probably hirodim."

Commander Streb was in deep thought for a few moments. Finally, he said, "I was concerned about that. If they were mining hirodim, that could jeopardize the positions of some of the planets in the trade group. I suspect Crosus would be the most concerned. They are always arrogant anyway, and if one of the other trade group planets discovered a substantial amount of hirodim they would consider that a threat.

"When we get to Procolt 4, we will examine the remains of the Torblit ship and the mining operation. Perhaps we will find a clue there. On a different subject, can someone tell me about these intelligent animals that were found on Procolt 2? I was there many years ago and I never saw any evidence of intelligent animals."

Cathy gave him a brief description of how the squirrels were discovered. When she finished, Commander Streb said, "I assume Lieutenant, you and Lieutenant Roth, want to return to Procolt 2 to continue your work with them. Is that correct?"

"Yes sir. Neither of us wanted to leave, but we were afraid if we stayed, we might put them in danger."

"I agree. When we get to Procolt 4, I will have one of the smaller ships take you to Procolt 2."

"Thank you, sir. I would also like to suggest that if you have the opportunity you should come to Procolt 2 and meet them yourself."

"That sounds like a good idea. If I have the opportunity, I will do that. Admiral Whitestone, I would like to have you on the bridge when we arrive at Procolt 4."

"Yes sir, I'll be happy to assist you in any way I can."

"Thank you all for coming. Please return to your cabins because we will be leaving shortly. We will meet again after we enter the wormhole."

Jeffery and Debbie were comfortably seated on the chairs in their cabin and they felt the slight movement of the ship as its journey began. Then they heard an announcement: "In .1 hours, the time stasis field will be activated. To prevent injury, all personnel must be seated."

That was the last announcement Jeffery and Debbie would hear for six days. There was no sensation at all when the time stasis field was activated. Then they heard: "Our current velocity is 51.3% of light speed. We will be entering the wormhole in .02 hours."

"That's the third time I've experienced the time stasis field. I think it's amazing. It's hard to believe six days have passed," Jeffery said.

"Actually, it's your fourth time."

102

"Yeah, you're right. I forgot about the time it happened to the Star Rover. Let's go get some food. After all, I haven't eaten for six days." Jeffery chuckled at his own little joke.

During the trip to the Procolt system, Jeffery and Debbie had two more meetings with Commander Streb. The meetings were not to gather information, but to get a chance to become better acquainted. Jeffery also spent time with Brealak, improving his language skills. For the last three days of the journey, Jeffery stopped using his translator. He had a few problems, but he was able to speak and understand the Coplent language in almost every situation. The only time he had any difficulty was when he got involved in technical conversations.

The ship stopped briefly just outside the orbit of the outermost planet in the Procolt system. Then it began its short trip to Procolt 4. The ship was parked in an orbit one thousand units above the planet's surface. As soon as the orbit was established, they began scanning the surface of the planet. It didn't take them long before they were looking at the site of the Torblit mining operation. There was now a small ship on the ground. It was slightly larger than a shuttle and was armed with both particle beam and plasma weapons. Scans of the planet and the surrounding space did not indicate the presence of any other ships.

Commander Streb asked, "Can we identify what type of ship that is?"

The ship's security officer, Groset, responded, "We are working on it, sir. The ship design is somewhat unusual. Ships that small usually do not have much firepower. Also, it does not appear to have a wormhole drive system, so there must be a larger ship nearby."

Jeffery, who was on the bridge, said, "I suspect the mother ship went to Procolt 2. I think we should go there as soon as possible."

"I agree, but I want to send a ship down there first. Groset, please take fifteen of your people down to the surface and secure the area. Place anybody you find under arrest. Try to use minimal force, but do not hesitate to defend yourselves. Keep me informed."

"Yes sir, I was anticipating this so I have fifteen people standing by waiting for orders. We will be off the ship in .15 hours. I will have someone here to take my place on the bridge immediately, sir."

"Good. We will leave for Procolt 2 as soon as you are off the ship. Navigator, plot a course to Procolt 2. Put us in a ten-thousand-unit orbit."

A few moments later, a woman came to the bridge and sat down at the station where Groset had been sitting. Commander Streb looked at her and said, "Lieutenant, we will be leaving for Procolt 2 shortly. As soon as we are out of the wormhole, enable all the shields and begin scanning the entire area for ships either in orbit or on the surface. Make sure all weapons systems are charged and ready."

"Yes sir."

Jeffery asked, "You have shields? I thought that was just science fiction."

"Yes, we do. They draw a tremendous amount of power, at least five times the amount of power required by the wormhole generator. Because of their power requirements, we only use them when it is absolutely necessary. This is why we need your power modules."

"I'm sure we can get you all you need."

"Sir, Groset has left the ship and the shuttle bay door is closed."

"Thank you, lieutenant. Navigator, take us to Procolt 2 now."

"Yes sir, we will have to make two jumps to get there. It will take .9 hours."

Upon arrival at Procolt 2, they immediately detected the presence of another ship. Before Commander Streb could take any action, the other ship opened fire on them. The ship shook a little, but there was no apparent damage.

"Weapons officer, set the power on the particle beam cannon to 50% and fire three times. Then hit them with a full-strength electromagnetic pulse. That should stop them."

"Yes sir."

There was a loud, high-pitched beep followed by a somewhat softer pop each time the particle beam cannon was fired. The electromagnetic pulse made no sound, but it did rock the ship slightly. The other ship appeared dead.

"Scan the ship for life forms."

"Sir, the ship shows thirty-eight lifeforms, but no signs of any electrical activity."

"Lieutenant, send an armed shuttle with four armed men to the other ship. I want to know who they are. If they resist, tell our men to use the stun setting on their weapons if possible."

"Yes sir."

The other ship was fifteen thousand units away from the warship. They watched the monitor as the shuttle approached. When the shuttle was five units away, the other ship exploded. The debris from the ship was traveling at a very high velocity. The shuttle could not get out of the way in time and was struck by several large pieces of the exploded ship. The shuttle didn't explode, but the hull was breached in so many places the four men aboard most certainly died before they had time to react.

Commander Streb yelled something Jeffery didn't understand, but from the sound of his voice, Jeffery was sure he understood anyway.

"I wasn't expecting that. I cannot believe they would kill themselves rather than be captured."

"Sir, did we get enough information about that ship to know where it came from?" Jeffery asked.

"Well, did we, lieutenant?" the commander snapped.

"I believe so, sir. The system said there was a 90% probability the ship is a Crosus design."

"That is what I suspected. I hope my people on Procolt 4 have better luck. Is there any sign of a ship on the surface?"

"Not so far, but I will keep checking, sir."

"Dispatch another shuttle to pick up the bodies on our ship."

"Yes sir."

The warship was in an equatorial orbit above the planet. As they approached the other side, the officer manning the long-range scanners said, "Commander, I have detected a small ship on the ground with five humanoid life forms around it. It appears to be identical to the ship on Procolt 4. I will put the image on your screen, sir."

Jeffery and Commander Streb looked at the monitor. The five people on the surface appeared to be removing the debris left when the habitat was destroyed. Jeffery said, "I would like to go down there with my lieutenants. We could land a few units away and walk to their location. I'm sure we could make a video of them removing the debris and their ship. That would enable us to positively identify who they are."

"You can do that, but you must take some of my security people with you. You will also need a pilot."

Brealak, who was also on the bridge, said, "Sir, I am fully qualified to fly the shuttle and would like to volunteer."

"Okay, the four of you go to the shuttle bay. I will have four of my security people meet you there. Lieutenant, put us in a fixed position above the landing site."

"Yes, sir."

Jeffery went to his cabin. When he went inside, he discovered Debbie was taking a shower. He went into the bathroom and after explaining the situation, he asked, "We're going to the surface. There's a ship down there loading up the remains of the habitat. Do you want to go with us?"

"I do, but it'll take me at least twenty minutes to get ready. I don't think you should wait."

"You're right, I'll get back as soon as possible."

Jeffery went to the cabin shared by Cathy and Sheila and announced his presence. Cathy answered. "What's going on?"

"We're in orbit above the habitat. There's a ship and five people cleaning up the remains of the habitat. We're going down to the surface so we can spy on them. I assumed you and Sheila would want to go with us."

"Of course we do."

106

"Okay, let's go. Brealak will be piloting the ship and there will also be four security guards with us. The plan is to make a video of them and the ship if we can get close enough."

"I have an idea. I'm sure I could show the squirrels how to use the video camera. They could easily get close enough without being noticed."

"Do you think they're still in the cave?"

"I'm sure they'll still be there."

When they arrived at the shuttle bay, Brealak and the four security guards were waiting for them. After everybody was onboard the shuttle left the warship. Brealak landed the shuttle 2 units from the cave where they had last seen the squirrels.

It took them a half hour to walk to the cave entrance. They were still at least one unit from the remains of the habitat, so they were not worried about being noticed. They were not using any communications equipment because they wanted to minimize the chances of being detected. When they were thirty feet into the cave Cathy called out to the squirrels, but there was no response. They walked a little farther into the cave and Cathy called out again. This time a squirrel responded from just ahead of them. It was so dark it was hard to see.

"Cathy, I'm happy to see you again. We all missed you and Sheila. Did you know there are people by the remains of the habitat?"

"Yes, we know about them. We think they're the same people who blew it up. Have you been watching them?"

"Yes, but we don't get too close. They smell bad."

"That's interesting. Anyway, we would like you to help us."

"How can we help?"

"Do you remember the videos I showed you and the camera that made them?"

"Yes, I remember them."

"We have a very small video camera. I'd like to show you how to use it and I want you to make a video of the people who are by the habitat. You have to hide so they don't see what you're doing."

107

"Would they hurt us if they saw what we were doing?"

"It's possible. We'll be nearby and protect you if we think you're in danger. Since you're from this planet and they've probably already seen you, they won't feel you're a danger to them. I'm sure they have no idea you are sentient beings."

The squirrel thought for a moment and said, "We'll do this for you."

"Thank you."

Three of the squirrels, Cathy, and Sheila left the cave. Once they were outside, Cathy showed them how to use the tiny camera.

After the squirrels had practiced taking videos of each other, one of them said, "I think we're ready. We'll try to stay where they can't see us."

"Good. Please remember to take videos of the ship too. I want to go back in the cave and get Jeffery and the security guards. Wait until I'm back before you go."

Cathy went back into the cave and came out a short time later with Jeffery, Brealak, and their security team. When she was close to the squirrels, she said, "Okay, you can go now. We'll be right behind you. Please try to make as little noise as possible, and don't talk to each other. If they hear you talking, they'll be on their guard."

"We'll be quiet."

The squirrels left and began walking through the dense wooded area to where the habitat was. The others followed a short time later. The woods would make it easier to remain unseen, but more difficult to follow the squirrels. Soon they reached an area where they could hear the people from the ship talking to each other. Jeffery quietly asked Brealak, "They aren't speaking Coplent, are they?"

"No, I don't know what they're speaking."

Suddenly there was a loud noise. It took Jeffery a moment to realize what it was. The noise he heard was the door to the unknown shuttle closing. Then they heard the unmistakable sound of the engines starting. The ship was leaving. The timing could not have been worse. It would now be up to Commander Streb to capture the ship.

Jeffery waited a few moments after the ship took off. Then using his communicator, he contacted Commander Streb. "Commander, the ship on the surface just left. I'm not sure yet how much we were able to capture on video. I think you should try to capture the ship."

"We were watching the area and saw the ship take off. They apparently took most of the remains of the habitat with them. I suspect they will return to Procolt 4 and look for their mother ship. They will find us instead. We are leaving Procolt 2 now and will be back when this is over."

"Good! We're going to look around for a while and then go back to the cave. We'll have one of the guards stay outside the cave so you'll be able to contact us. Good luck."

"Thank you, Admiral."

Brealak said, "I think we should look through the remains of the habitat in case there's any evidence that would help us determine what type of explosive was used to destroy it."

They spent an hour looking through the remains, but if there was any evidence it had already been removed. They walked through the woods back to the cave.

Brealak asked the squirrel for the camera so they could look at the video. The squirrel-had done a very good job. The people from the ship could be easily seen and their conversation was recorded. There was also extensive video of the ship.

Jeffery asked Brealak, "Does the video give you what you need to determine who these people are?"

"I am not sure. I need to study this footage further. However, if Commander Streb is able to capture some of these people, that will certainly tell us who is involved."

Three hours later the guard waiting outside the cave came in. He said, "I just spoke to Commander Streb. He wants you to come back to the ship."

Cathy asked Jeffery, "Is it okay if Sheila and I stay here? I don't think we or the squirrels will be in any danger now."

"Okay, you can stay for now. I'm not sure what the plans are. I don't want to go back to Coplent now since the Star Rover is on its way here. Since I won't be able to contact you while you're in the cave, go outside and call me in two hours."

"Yes sir. Thank you."

Jeffery, Brealak, and the four guards left the cave and walked back to their shuttle. An hour later, they were back onboard the warship. Jeffery went to his cabin to tell Debbie what happened and Brealak went to the bridge. He and Debbie followed her a few minutes later.

As soon as they were on the bridge, Commander Streb said, "Jeffery, I think we have a problem. We captured the people from the ships that were on Procolt 4 and Procolt 2. They are not from Crosus, they are from Dorest. They were hired by a Torblit contractor to clean up the areas that were destroyed on both planets and were told to make it look like there was never anything there. Also, they have no idea why their mother ship would blow itself up to avoid being captured. The ships they were using were a Crosus design, but they have owned them for more than ten years. Without their mothership, they are out of business."

"Why did they fire on us as soon as we dropped out of the wormhole?"

"I asked them that too. They think the captain of their ship might have thought we were pirates, but pirates do not have warships. The captain should have known that. I believe them. They did not resist in any way when they were captured."

"So, what do we do now?"

"I have to go back to Coplent. I am sure you want to stay here, so before we leave, I will have my people construct a shelter for you and your crew to use until your ship gets here."

"Thank you, sir. I really appreciate it. How long will it take to build the shelter?"

"It will be done tomorrow. I assume you want it in the same area where your habitat was."

"Yes, that would be perfect."

Jeffery and Debbie went back to their cabin. Once they were inside, Jeffery said, "I'm worried about this situation. Somebody is trying really hard to cover this up. If Brealak and I hadn't come back to Procolt 4 when we did, nobody would know about the attacks. Our coming back really messed up their plans for the cover-up. Our involvement is going to be known and we might be in serious danger."

Debbie shook her head. "I don't think so. From their perspective we were simply in the wrong place at the wrong time. We aren't a threat to them."

"They don't know that. Anyway, I'm still worried. I'm going to ask Commander Streb for some weapons just as a precaution."

By the end of the next day, the warship crew had assembled a sixteen hundred square foot shelter. It had four small bedrooms, two bathrooms, a kitchen, a large common area, and a storage area that included a cabinet that contained a variety of hand held weapons. All of the rooms were appropriately furnished, and the required electrical power was supplied by large solar panels on the roof connected to rechargeable batteries.

The shelter also had a water purification system so they could use the water from the nearby lake for drinking. In the kitchen there was a food generator and two laundry systems like the ones on the ship. To make the food generators work, they had to be supplied with carbon-based materials such as wood, leaves, or grass.

When Jeffery and the other crew members of the Star Rover saw the shelter, they were very pleased. The officer in charge of building the habitat warned Jeffery the batteries would only be able to supply power to the shelter if it remained sunny. If there were more than three consecutive days without sunshine, the system would fail.

111

Since they had never seen a completely cloudy day, Jeffery was not concerned. Besides, he was sure they could live without electricity for a while.

Later that day, Commander Streb contacted Jeffery to let him know they were leaving. Garlut also contacted him and told Jeffery he would be returning to Earth shortly after he returned to Coplent. Jeffery asked him to contact Max Hiller and let him know what was going on, and that the Star Rover would be returning to Earth within ninety days. Garlut said he would be happy to do that.

The following morning, twenty of the squirrels were outside the shelter waiting for Cathy and Sheila. When Cathy and Sheila went outside, the squirrels surrounded them and told the women they were very happy they were there and they wanted to continue their education.

Jeffery and Debbie went outside to greet the squirrels as well. Once the squirrels calmed down and Jeffery could be heard, he said, "One of the items installed in our shelter is a long-range scanner. It has a two-hundred-thousand-unit range. I believe we're safe for the time being, but I want the scanner manned all day. We'll be using standard time here, so we'll all take five-hour shifts manning the scanner. There will be no exceptions. If you're on duty and you have to leave for any reason, get somebody to take your place. I'll take the first shift, followed by Debbie, Cathy, and Sheila. Does anyone have any questions?"

One of the squirrels pulled on Jeffery's pant leg and asked, "Could we help? I'm sure you could show us how to use the scanner. We want to help you."

Jeffery thought about it for a moment and said, "Okay, that's a good idea. We'll train any of you who are interested. Before we do that, I think we need to give all of you names so we can identify each of you. I'm not even sure how many of you there are. Cathy, please take care of that for me."

"Yes sir. We'll do that this morning."

Jeffery and Debbie went back inside the shelter. Jeffery sat down in front of the scanner and turned it on. He was wondering if the morning rain would interfere with its

112

abilities. He looked outside and noticed the clouds were already building up and it would begin raining soon.

When the rain started, Jeffery looked out of the window and noticed the squirrels and the women were gone. He turned his attention back to the scanner. He was pleased to see the scanner continued to function normally and was unaffected by the rain.

Toward the end of the shift, Cathy came back. She sat down on a chair next to him and said, "There are seventy-three squirrels. Seven of the females are pregnant. Since the squirrels understand numbers but can't read yet, I decided to number them instead of giving them regular names. The alpha male is S1 and the rest start at S2 and go through S73. Is that okay?"

"Sure, that makes things easy. If I want them to do something, I only have to ask S1. To me they all look very similar, so I doubt I'll ever be able to recognize them all by sight."

"They're beginning to ask some unusual questions. Like why do we wear clothes, why do we bathe every day, and why do we use toilets? I tried to answer them in terms they would understand, but I'm not sure I was successful."

"Well, I suppose those types of questions are natural. I think they want to emulate us as much as possible. They're becoming more civilized. I thought their comment that the people from Dorest smelled bad was interesting. Animals typically don't think of smells as good or bad."

"I guess they really aren't animals. Tomorrow, we're going to start teaching them to read. I think they'll do very well. Before we left Earth I downloaded some children's books because I thought they might be useful to help people we meet to understand English. I'm going to print twenty copies of one of the books to use as a teaching aid."

"Are you going to try to teach twenty of them at a time? I think that would be very difficult."

"I thought about that and decided the class size should be about eight to ten, but I wanted each student to have a copy of the book. That way I can give them personal help if they need it."

"That sounds good. Please keep me informed."

"I'll do that, sir."

NASA HEADQUARTERS
MARCH 2122

Brandon Simpson sat across the desk from Max Hiller. Thirteen months ago, Brandon was seated in the same position when he told Max about his idea for an interstellar communication system. NASA had spent over two billion dollars on the project so far, and that was only a small portion of the total outlay.

"Yesterday we inserted the last of the carriers," Brandon informed Max. "They were inserted into the system at eighteen hour intervals and they are moving at five hundred times light speed. So far everything seems stable. There's a ship at the distant end of the system, one light year away. We'll be ready to send a test transmission tomorrow morning. The message should reach the ship in slightly less than the carrier time spacing."

"How long would it take to extend the system to Coplent?" Max asked.

"I think it would take three years, unless Coplent wants to help. Since their ships are three times faster than ours, we could probably do it in half the time with their help."

"How much is it going to cost?"

"I think the cost is irrelevant. Once the system is operational it will pay for itself in less than five years. I'm certain if we complete the system between Earth and Coplent, the other members of the trade group will be asking us to install systems for them. Did you speak to Garlut about it when he was here?"

"Yes, of course I did. He was sure that Coplent would be interested. I didn't ask him if they would be willing to help us, but I suspect they will. What time do you want to start the test?"

"I think we should start it at 7:15 tomorrow morning. There will be a carrier passing the Earth end of the system at 7:32."

"Okay, I'll meet you in the communications room at 7:00 in the morning. This had better work or we may both be looking for new jobs," Max said earnestly.

"It'll work. I've tested it over shorter distances and there was no problem. Don't worry about it."

"Fine, I'll see you tomorrow."

Brandon got up and left Max's office. Max watched him leave. He had really stuck his neck out on this one. If it failed, he was sure he would be in trouble, but Brandon had never failed before, so he told himself there was really no reason for concern.

The following morning, Max walked into the NASA communications room at 6:55 a.m. to find Brandon was already there. Max walked over to where Brandon was standing and said, "Good morning. Are we ready for the test?"

"Yes, the system is stable. All the carriers are in their proper positions. Do you want to have the honor of sending the first message at five hundred times the speed of light?"

"You know I do! What do I do?"

"It isn't complex. At 7:15, you press the transmit button."

They waited around, making small talk for almost fifteen minutes. At precisely 7:15, Max pressed the transmit button. A signal was sent to the relay at the Earth end of the system. At 7:31:50 the message was transferred to the approaching carrier. At about 1:00 a.m., the signal on the carrier would be transferred to the relay at the far end of the system, one light year away. That signal would then be broadcast to the waiting ship.

At 1:01:06, the signal was received by the ship waiting for it. The ship then sent a signal saying, "Message Received" and began its return trip to Earth. The message the ship sent would arrive at the NASA communications room 17.52 hours later. The ship would return to Earth about four days later.

The test was a success.

PROCOLT
MARCH 2122

Jeffery woke up early. It was still dark outside but his watch, which used galactic standard time, displayed 9:00. He decided the watch was useless unless you were aboard a ship where night and day were artificial. He didn't remember ever checking the length of a day on Procolt 2, but he decided it didn't matter.

Debbie was still sound asleep. He left their room and walked into the kitchen. He really wanted a cup of coffee, but the food generator wasn't programmed for it, so he settled for water. He was wondering what he and Debbie were going to do for two months until the Star Rover arrived. Cathy and Sheila would be busy with the squirrels, but the two of them really had nothing to do.

Debbie joined him a short time later. She sat down, kissed him lightly on the cheek, and said, "Good morning."

"Good morning. Would you like some breakfast? The food generator can make us scrambled eggs or pancakes."

"Pancakes, I guess. The eggs aren't very good."

Jeffery got up, walked over to the food generator, and set it to make two orders of pancakes. When they were ready, he brought them to the table. When they were done, Jeffery said, "What do you want to do today?"

"I think we should go exploring. We never had the time before. Perhaps we'll make another unusual discovery."

"Perhaps we will. You do realize we'll be affected by the radiation here. I'd like to devise some method to test our strength every day. I know we can't do it with any degree of accuracy, but something is better than nothing. Any idea how to do that?"

Debbie thought for a few moments. "What if we make a spear and check to see how far we can throw it every day?"

"That's a good idea. Let's go look for a long, straight branch we could use to make a spear."

They cleaned their dishes and left the shelter. When they walked outside, they saw several squirrels that appeared to be playing some kind of game. As Jeffery and Debbie walked closer, the squirrels stopped playing. One of them looked up at Jeffery and Debbie and said, "Good morning. My name is S34."

"Good morning, S34. Are you ready to start learning how to read?" Debbie asked.

"Yes, we all are. We're waiting for Cathy and Sheila. Do you know what they're doing?"

"I think they may still be sleeping. Would you like me to wake them and let them know you're waiting for them?"

"No. If they're tired, we'll let them sleep. What are you and Jeffery going to do?"

"We're going for a walk, but it will have to be short because it'll probably start to rain soon."

"We like the rain. Do you like the rain too?"

"Yes, I like the rain, but I don't like getting all wet."

"Don't you get all wet when you bathe?" S34 asked logically.

"Yes, but I don't like getting my clothes wet. It's uncomfortable."

"Then why do you wear clothes?"

"We don't have fur all over our bodies like you do, so we wear clothes for protection."

"Okay, I understand now. I hope you enjoy your walk."

"I'm sure we will."

Jeffery and Debbie walked around the end of the lake toward the hills. The sky was starting to darken, threatening rain. They decided to walk toward the hills and look for a place that would shield them. They didn't find a cave, but they found a space under a ledge that would work. On the way, Jeffery picked up a tree branch that was about five feet long and two inches in diameter. He had a pocket knife with him, so while it was raining, he whittled a spear.

It rained for a half hour. After the rain stopped, they went looking for someplace where they could test the new spear. They decided to walk back toward the shelter. After covering half the distance, they found a large, open field. The grass was only a few inches high, so it would be a perfect place for their test.

Looking around, Jeffery mused, "I wonder why the grass is so short."

"It probably only grows to a height of a few inches and then it stops. It's a little unusual for grass, though. On Earth, most grasses would naturally grow much taller before they stop."

"We need to find some rocks to mark the place where we'll stand to throw and to mark the farthest point we throw it."

Debbie went looking and came back a few minutes later with three fist-sized rocks. She put the first rock down. Jeffery put his right foot next to it and threw the spear. Debbie marked the spot with another rock and said, "I think you should throw it three times." She picked up the spear and brought it back to him. He threw it again, but the second throw was shorter than the first. His third throw was about six inches farther. Debbie marked the spot and they switched positions. Debbie's longest throw was a foot shorter.

They left the spear and the rocks in place and would come back tomorrow to try again.

They did that every day. For the first eight days there was no significant change, but on the ninth day both were able to throw the spear two feet farther. The distance remained unchanged for the next several days. However, two weeks later the distance jumped again by almost ten feet. It became obvious they were increasing in strength.

During the same time, the squirrels had learned to read simple words. Cathy was certain by the time the Star Rover arrived they would be able to read all of the books she brought.

RUSSELL FINE

COPLENT WARSHIP
MARCH 2122

Commander Streb was sitting at the desk in his cabin. They had been traveling in the wormhole for two days and was anxious to get back to Coplent. He was wondering what he would do when he got home when his com unit beeped. He touched a button and said, "Yes."

"Commander Streb, I have something to show you, sir. Can I ask your location?"

"I am in my cabin."

"I will be there shortly, sir."

When Lieutenant Plart walked into the commander's cabin, he was holding a small cube that held several wires coming out of it. The lieutenant walked over and placed the device on the desk in front of his Commander. "Sir, this is the reason the mother ship exploded. This device is designed to explode a half hour after it is exposed to an electromagnetic pulse. I have seen these things before. We found them on both of the ships we brought back."

"Do we know how they got there? I feel certain the crew from Dorest did not put them there."

"Not yet sir. We do know that the person who arranged their contract, Melban Walst, offered to overhaul their ships prior to the start of their mission. I suspect the devices were placed on the ships during this overhaul."

"Do we know where this Melban Walst is now?"

"The crew said he lives on Torblit, but they do not know where he comes from. They have done work for him before, so they trusted him."

"The assistant to the Torblit trade representative is on the ship. Please let him know what we discovered. Do you think we should charge the men from Dorest with a crime?"

"No sir, I do not. I think they were simply doing the job they were hired to do."

"You said you had seen these devices before. Do you know where they are made?"

"Yes, they are made on Crosus. I think you suspected that."

"Yes, I was sure Crosus was involved. But now we need to know if it was a government sanctioned operation. I think that may be difficult to find out. Perhaps Melban Walst will be able to tell us."

"If he is still on Torblit. If he finds out the mission failed, he will probably leave Torblit in a hurry."

"I do not believe there is any way for him to find out. I think it will come as a complete surprise. Did you ask the crewmen from Dorest why their shuttles were so heavily armed?"

"Yes commander, they said the armament was added during the overhaul. They were told there was a possibility they would have to defend themselves. But they were not told who the enemy was."

"I wonder if the weapons even worked. Did they test them, lieutenant?"

"I do not know, sir. But I will ask."

"Good. Please keep me informed. I think you can let the prisoners out of the brig."

"Yes, sir. They do not appear to be dangerous."

Lieutenant Plart left Commander Streb's cabin. Now that he was alone again, Commander Streb began to think there was a possibility of war. Crosus would not accept being rejected from the trade group lightly. If they found out their plans had been thwarted by people from Earth, Earth could be in danger. Earth was the most vulnerable planet in the trade group and it would be up to Coplent to protect them. He made the decision that after their return to Coplent, he would take his ship to Earth. He had heard Earth was a very nice place to visit and the food was exceptional.

Twenty-nine days later, the warship arrived at the space station above Coplent. Commander Streb contacted the Trade Council representative and made him aware of the situation. He also said he was taking his ship to Earth in order to offer them protection from a possible attack by Crosus. The Trade Council representative agreed with his plan. He also said he wanted to speak personally with the crew from Dorest. Commander Streb said they would be at his office before the end of the day.

Now that his plan had been approved by the Trade Council, he made an announcement to his crew. "As you all know, we have arrived back at Coplent. However, I believe there is a substantial possibility we will be at war with Crosus shortly. I know Coplent can defend itself if that happens, but the newest member of the trade group, Earth, cannot. Therefore, our stay here will be brief. We will be leaving for Earth in five days. I expect all of you back aboard one day before we depart."

After the announcement, he called Lieutenant Plart and told him to bring the men from Dorest to the Trade Council office as soon as possible, and then make arrangements for the crew from Dorest and their shuttles to be taken to whatever planet they wanted.

Moments later, Commander Streb's com unit beeped.

"Commander, this is Garlut. Brealak and I were going to leave for Earth on a trade mission in two or three days. We will probably be there a few days before you arrive. Do you want me to make them aware of the situation with Crosus or would you prefer to do that yourself?"

"Am I correct in assuming you already know the leaders on Earth?"

"Yes, I have met them all."

"Then I think you should let them know we are coming and why. That way, they will not be concerned when they see my warship. Do you think this could make them withdraw from the trade group?"

"I suppose that is possible, but the fact we are sending a ship to defend their planet should make them feel better about the situation."

"I will contact you as soon as we are within communication range."

"When you get there, I will buy you dinner. I guarantee it will be the best meal you have ever eaten."

"I am looking forward to it. Have a safe trip."

"Thank you. I will see you in thirty days."

PROCOLT 2
MAY 2122

Jeffery was sitting at the table in the kitchen of the shelter with Debbie. They had been on Procolt 2 for more than two months. He said, "The Star Rover should be here soon. I've been waiting for months to get a cup of coffee."

Debbie grinned. "Is that the only reason why you're anxious for the Star Rover to get here?"

"You know it isn't. I'd like to get back to Earth too. We've been away for more than two years and I miss it."

"I do too, but I really like it here on Procolt 2. I think we should move here."

"I'll only do that if we can bring a few years' worth of coffee with us. Are you ready to retire already?"

"No, but I think it would be a nice place to do that."

"You do realize we don't yet know the effects of long-term exposure to the radiation here? I was also wondering what happens to us when we leave here. Do you remember the story of Shangri-La?"

"I remember it. If you went there you stopped aging, but the years came back as soon as you left. Do you think that could happen here? It didn't seem to have any negative effect on Cathy or Sheila."

"I know, but they weren't here for very long. Anyway, it's something to think about."

"What I was thinking was opening some kind of resort here, serving Earth food and telling everyone about the beneficial effects of the radiation."

"Don't you think it's a little premature to tell people about the benefits? I agree it seems to be good for squirrels and humans, but we have no idea how it will affect other species, let alone us in the long-term."

"I know. It was just wishful thinking."

"Well, if you're up for it . . . it's time for our daily test. The spear awaits."

"Okay."

They walked to the area where they tested their spear throwing ability. In the two months that elapsed since they came to Procolt 2, both were able to double their distance.

Jeffery picked up the spear, cocked his arm, and threw it at least ten feet farther than he had yesterday. He threw the spear two more times, but the distance did not change substantially.

Now it was Debbie's turn. She got into position and threw the spear. It went about twelve feet past her best effort the day before. Her other two throws were the same.

"Obviously the effect of the radiation is increasing. I think we should both have complete physicals when the Star Rover gets here," Debbie said.

"I agree. I also think we should test Cathy and Sheila on their spear-throwing ability."

Neither had mentioned to Cathy or Sheila that they were testing their strength by throwing a spear every day, so at dinner they brought up the subject.

Jeffery started. "I thought you two should know that Debbie and I have been testing our strength improvement by throwing a spear. We do it every day. On the first day, I was able to throw it about thirty feet. Yesterday, I was able to throw it about sixty feet. Today, I was able to throw it at least ten feet farther. So, the effect is obviously increasing. Debbie's results were similar. Tomorrow I'd like to test the two of you."

"Yes, I think that would be interesting. Did you notice any obvious changes in your physical appearance since you got here?"

"No, my muscles appear the same. So do Debbie's. Have you seen any changes in yourselves?"

"Not really. I think I may have lost a little weight, but that's all," Cathy said.

"I haven't noticed anything either. I'd think since we're getting stronger, our muscle mass would increase."

"I want Frank to check us out thoroughly when he gets here. That should be in a day or two."

The following morning after the rain, all of them, and several of the squirrels, walked over to the spear-throwing

126

area. Jeffery and Debbie went first. Their results were about the same as the day before. Cathy threw the spear at least twenty-five feet farther than Jeffery.

Chuckling, Jeffery said, "Debbie, I think you and I should be nice to Cathy, and probably Sheila too, since they can probably beat the crap out of us."

"Colorfully said, but very likely true," Debbie responded.

Sheila threw the spear a few feet farther than Cathy and said with a grin, "I guess I'm the spear-throwing champion."

The squirrels watched the contest. After it was over, S1 asked, "Since Sheila is now the strongest, is she the boss?"

"No," Jeffery responded, "it doesn't work that way. I'm in charge because of my experience and education. Strength has nothing to do with our rank on the ship."

S1 appeared to be thinking about what Jeffery said. "Okay, I think we still have a lot to learn about human society."

Next morning, the shuttle from the Star Rover landed close to the shelter. Most of the squirrels, and all of the humans, watched it land. A few moments later, Mike and Frank got off the shuttle and walked over to where everyone was standing.

Jeffery said, "Hi guys. Did you have a nice trip from Coplent?"

"It was completely uneventful, I'm happy to report," Mike replied. "How are you guys doing?"

"Other than a desperate need for coffee, we're all fine."

"Before we left, some people from Coplent came aboard and replaced the bed in your cabin. I hope you don't mind, but I had to try it. It's fantastic. Frank tried it too, but not at the same time."

"I hope not," Jeffery said with a laugh. "No, I don't mind at all. Let's go inside before it starts to rain and I'll fill you in on what's happened here."

Frank was looking at the squirrels and said, "Hi, how are you guys today?"

S1 responded, "We're doing very well, Dr. Weber. Thank you for asking. My name is S1."

Frank could not believe how much the squirrel's ability to speak had improved. He said, "Your English is excellent. Have you been working with Cathy and Sheila?"

"Yes, we have. Not only has our ability to speak improved, but we can also read simple books. We like to learn new things."

"That's incredible. What would you like to learn?"

"I think we need to learn more about human civilization. Sometimes humans do things we don't understand."

"Don't feel bad about that. Some humans do things I don't understand either."

Once they got inside, the humans sat down at the table in the kitchen. Jeffery filled them in on everything that had happened. After he had brought them up to date, he told Frank about the effects from exposure to the radiation.

Frank said he would give them all examinations tomorrow aboard the Star Rover.

By the time they were finished getting updated, it was around lunchtime and Mike suggested they have lunch on the ship. The habitat dwellers quickly agreed. Then S1 asked, "May I go with you? I would like to see the Star Rover."

Jeffery replied, "I think that would be okay. We could probably take four or five of you. You can join us for lunch. We have lots of fresh vegetables on the ship."

S1 said, "I remember the day we met. You offered us carrots. Do you have any of those on the ship?"

"I think it's amazing you remember that. Mike, do we have any carrots aboard?"

"Yes, we have lots of carrots."

"Good, we really like carrots. They don't grow here. Perhaps somebody from your ship could show us how to grow carrots. Then we could have them all the time," S1 said.

"We have a gardener named Carol aboard. I'll ask her to help you set up a garden where you can grow carrots."

"Thank you. That would be wonderful."

S1 picked four other squirrels to go with him to the Star Rover. The six humans and the five squirrels boarded the shuttle for the trip to the Star Rover.

Everyone was aboard the shuttle when Jeffery realized there was a problem. Once the shuttle was in space, there would be no gravity except the gravity occasionally caused by using the thrusters to align the shuttle with the bay on the Star Rover. It wasn't a problem for the humans because they were in seats with seatbelts. But the seats were obviously not designed for big squirrels.

Jeffery said, "S1, I'm not sure you'll understand what I'm about to tell you. When the shuttle leaves the planet, we'll be in an area where there's no gravity. There won't be up or down and you'll be weightless. The seats on the shuttle are designed for humans. We have to find a way to prevent you from getting hurt during the flight. Does anybody have any ideas?"

Frank said, "We could attach them to the seats with some non-adhesive stretch tape I have in the medical supply kit. It would be a little uncomfortable, but it would only be for a short time."

"Would that be okay with you?" Jeffery asked.

"I'm not sure. Attach me to the seat and I'll let you know," S1 replied.

Frank pointed to one of the seats and said, "Hop up here."

S1 jumped onto the seat and sat with his back against the seatback. Frank got a roll of the tape and wrapped it around S1 three times. Then Frank asked, "Can you get off the seat?"

S1 squirmed and tried, unsuccessfully, to get off the seat.

Frank asked, "Would you be okay like that for twenty minutes?"

"I don't know. How long is twenty minutes?"

Frank thought for a moment and asked, "Can you count to sixty?"

"Yes, I can count to sixty."

"After the engine starts, count slowly to sixty like this." Frank looked at the second hand on his watch and counted slowly to ten. "If you count to sixty at the same speed I counted, it will take one minute."

"I have to count to sixty twenty times and that will be twenty minutes."

"Right, very good. So, do you think you can stay like that for twenty minutes?"

"Yes, I can and the others will be able to also."

Frank spent the next few minutes attaching the squirrels to the seats. When they were all attached, everyone sat down and buckled themselves in. The ship took off and the squirrels were transfixed by the view out the windows. When the shuttle reached the correct altitude, Mike aimed the shuttle at the Star Rover fifty units away and shut off the engine. As soon as the engine stopped, gravity disappeared.

"That feels very strange. I don't like it," S1 said.

Jeffery said, "It will only be for three or four minutes."

"But I still don't like it."

"I understand. I didn't like it either the first time, but now I'm used to it and it doesn't bother me."

When the shuttle had drifted to within a unit of the Star Rover, Mike used the thrusters to orient it correctly. As soon as the thrusters were turned on, S1 said, "That feels much better."

Mike decided to use the thrusters all the way back to the ship. In less than two minutes, they were safely inside the shuttle bay. As soon as Jeffery got off the shuttle, he walked over to a com unit mounted on the wall and said, "Hobbes." A moment later Carol answered and Jeffery said, "Hi Carol. This is Jeffery. We're back onboard and have some guests with us. Please come to the shuttle bay. I want you to show them around the ship and then take them to hydroponics and show them how we grow carrots. When we go back down, you'll accompany us to help set up a garden."

"Yes, Admiral. I didn't think there were any people on Procolt 2. If I may ask, who are they?"

"You'll see when you get here."

"I'll be there in two minutes, sir."

S1 said, "This ship is much bigger than Brealak's ship."

"Yes, this ship can hold over one hundred people, but there are only fifty aboard," Jeffery said.

"Eight of our guests decided to remain on Coplent. Twelve more decided to go back to Earth on a Coplent trading ship. We only have thirty aboard," Mike said.

A few moments later, Carol walked into the shuttle bay. She looked around, then she spotted the squirrels and said, "Sir, are these the guests you want me to teach how to create a garden?"

Jeffery smiled and said, "S1, I'd like you to meet Carol Hobbes. She's our hydroponics, e-r-r-r, gardener," Jeffery said catching himself.

S1 said, "It's very nice to meet you, Carol. We like carrots and Jeffery said you could teach us how to grow them."

Carol's jaw dropped in awe as S1 spoke to her. "I...I would be h...happy to do that for you," she stammered then turned to Jeffery. "I didn't expect them to speak perfect English."

"They not only speak perfect English, but they can do simple calculations, and read."

Carol just stared at the squirrels for a few moments longer before gathering herself and saying, "Please follow me." She left the shuttle bay with all five squirrels following.

Debbie laughed and said, "I think you should have warned her, but that was funny."

"Perhaps we should take them to Earth?"

Frank shook his head. "I don't think that would be a good idea. The people on Earth are already somewhat distressed by the presence of aliens. Talking, sentient squirrels might be too much for some of them to comprehend."

Jeffery laughed. "Let's go to the galley. I need coffee."

The group walked into the dining room. There were several tables occupied by crew members and guests. After the group sat down, the people from the other tables walked over and they talked for a few minutes. While they were speaking,

Debbie got up from the table and walked into the kitchen to speak to the chef.

"Hi April, would you please bring coffee and some snacks to our table? There are six of us."

"Yes, Captain. I'll have a fresh batch of doughnuts ready in five minutes and I'll make a fresh pot of coffee. Welcome back, by the way," April said with a smile as she hurried around the kitchen.

"Thank you. I like Procolt 2, but it's nice to be on the Star Rover again. It's like coming home after a vacation."

Debbie returned to her table and sat down saying, "April is making a fresh pot of coffee and she'll bring us some doughnuts as soon as they're ready."

Jeffery said, "Wonderful! We were just talking about giving everyone aboard an opportunity to go down to the surface for a few days. Do you see any problem with that?"

"No, but I think we should wait until after Frank completes his exams. I don't want to expose any of the crew, or our guests, to potential danger until we're certain the radiation isn't permanently harmful."

"I agree with Debbie. I'll start the examinations tomorrow morning. Cathy, please be at my office at 9:00. Sheila, I'll see you at 10:00. Jeffery, you and Debbie can come together at 11:00. I should have the results by 3:00."

"Okay, that's reasonable. Mike, did you have any issues with the Star Rover on the trip from Coplent?"

"No, there were no problems at all."

"We'll be leaving for Earth in thirty days. If there's any maintenance that needs to be accomplished, please make sure it's completed before we depart."

"Yes, I'll make sure to discuss it with Ron."

Jeffery was about to say something else when April walked up to the table and said, "Hello sir, it's nice to have you back aboard." Then she put a large pot of coffee on the table along with packets of sugar and creamer. "I'll be back in a minute with cups, spoons, and fresh doughnuts."

Debbie and Jeffery inhaled the coffee until April returned with a tray that had glazed doughnuts, spoons, and six coffee cups. She gave each of them a cup and put the tray in the middle of the table.

Jeffery said, "Thank you April. This looks great." After the young chef left, he went on, "I think there's going to be a war. The trade group is going to expel the planet that was responsible for the Procolt 4 attacks. That will have a severe negative effect on the population and I suspect they won't accept expulsion lightly. I'm concerned Earth may be involved."

Frank asked, "Why would Earth be involved in this situation?"

"Because Brealak and I discovered their actions, rescued the miners, and reported it to the Trade Council representative. They'll probably blame Earth and Coplent for their problems."

"That isn't a reasonable thing to do, but I suppose people who start wars aren't reasonable in the first place," Mike said.

After they finished their coffee and doughnuts, Jeffery and Debbie went to their cabin. They went inside and decided to try out their new bed. Within moments they were both sound asleep.

They woke up an hour before dinner when Jeffery's com unit beeped. He answered and Carol said, "Sir, the squirrels are absolutely amazing. I'm certain they learn faster than humans. I'd like to go down to the surface with them so we can start working on their garden. Can you get somebody to take us down?"

"Yes, but are you aware you're exposing yourself to a type of radiation that we haven't completely confirmed is benign?"

"I'm willing to accept the risk, sir. All the people who have spent time on the surface appear to be fine."

"I'll call Mike now. Wait five minutes, then call him and let him know what you want." Jeffery contacted Mike to give him an update. "Carol will be contacting you in a few minutes to go down to the surface with the squirrels. Please do that for her."

"Okay, but I'm in a meeting with Ron now in regards to maintenance. Is it okay if I ask Dean to do it? He's thoroughly trained on shuttle operations."

"Certainly, but make sure Dean knows the squirrels have to be taped to the seats."

"No problem, I'll take care of it."

Jeffery and Debbie showered, put on clean clothes, and walked to the galley. When they arrived, they found the dining room was packed. There was one empty table at the front of the room so they made their way to it. Everyone in the room stood up and applauded.

Debbie sat down, but Jeffery remained standing. He said, "Thank you all for that warm welcome. It's good to be back aboard the Star Rover. We'll be here for thirty days before we return to Earth. All of you know there's some kind of unknown radiation on the surface of Procolt 2. Tomorrow the four of us who were on the planet for the past two months will have complete physicals. If none of us show any signs of problems linked to radiation exposure, each of you will have the opportunity to spend a few days on the planet. The announcement will be made tomorrow at dinner."

After dinner, Jeffery met with each of his officers briefly. When the meetings were completed, he and Debbie went back to their cabin for the night.

By 1:00 p.m. the next day, all of the physicals had been completed. The results were not surprising. Each of them exhibited some modification in their DNA, but there were no negative effects. The only thing obvious was a substantial increase in strength. One of the requirements to be a member of the crew was to be able to lift ninety pounds without difficulty. Each of them was now able to lift one hundred and sixty pounds without a problem.

At 2:30 Frank came to see Jeffery. Jeffery and Debbie were both seated at the table in their cabin when Frank arrived. He came in and sat down with them.

"As near as I can tell," Frank started, "the four of you are in perfect health. In fact, some of the minor problems that were noted during the previous physicals have disappeared.

For example, Cathy had a slightly irregular heartbeat. Because the irregularity disappeared under stress it was not considered to be a problem. However, there's no evidence of that irregularity anymore. The blood work for all of you was almost identical, and all of the values were excellent. Nobody had any vitamin deficiencies, liver and kidney functions were perfect. In fact, everything was perfect. I can now understand why Mr. Brown lived to be one hundred and eighty-four.

"I didn't think about it at the time, but they were telling us his age in galactic standard years, not Earth years. So, he was probably over two hundred and fifty years old when he died. In any case, I don't see any reason not to let the people on the Star Rover visit the planet for a few days."

"I'm glad to hear that. I'll make the announcement at dinner."

Jeffery made the announcement as planned.

All of the crew members and guests spent three or four days on the surface of Procolt 2 during the thirty days the Star Rover remained there.

As Jeffery expected, the day before they were scheduled to begin the return trip to Earth, Cathy and Sheila told him they wanted to resign their positions on the crew of the Star Rover and stay on Procolt 2. Jeffery told them he understood, but reminded them that this time there would not be any help nearby. They were completely on their own. However, the women had made up their minds. Regardless of the danger and the lack of human company, they were determined to stay. In the end, the two women got their way. The following day when the Star Rover left orbit, it was permanently missing two crew members.

The trip back to Earth would take seventy-four days. During that time, Jeffery and Debbie decided they wanted to build a first-class resort on Procolt 2. The resort would have two towers with guest rooms. There would be multiple restaurants, a swimming pool, and a golf course. There would be boating on the lake and cave tours. Jeffery thought that it would probably cost substantially more than five hundred billion dollars to build and between them they had

135

substantially less than a million dollars, but it was fun to dream about it.

The Star Rover exited the wormhole seventy-five thousand miles from Earth. Moments later Mike said, "The long-range scanner indicates two alien starships at the space station. They're both from Coplent. One is Commander Streb's warship. The other ship is Garlut's."

Jeffery had no idea what was going on. He could understand why Garlut was here, but he didn't see any reason for the warship to be here. He said, "Anne, try to get in touch with Commander Streb."

"Yes, sir."

Two minutes later, Anne handed the private communicator to Jeffery and said, "Commander Streb, sir."

Jeffery slipped the headset on and said, "Commander Streb, this is Admiral Whitestone. How are you?"

"I am in good health. I suppose you are wondering why I am here, Admiral."

"Yes sir, I am."

"In a few days there will be an emergency meeting of the Trade Council. The purpose of the meeting is to consider expelling Crosus from the trade group. There is a substantial amount of evidence indicating the attacks on the Procolt System were conducted by Crosus. If they are expelled, they may blame Earth and Coplent for their expulsion. We can take care of ourselves, but Earth is not capable of doing that. So, we are here to defend Earth in case there is an attack."

Jeffery remembered expressing his concerns regarding retaliation from Crosus to Debbie when they first arrived on Procolt 2, but he was surprised when he realized that Commander Streb had the same concerns. He replied, "I thought that an attack from Crosus was a possibility, and I'm really pleased that you're here to help Earth."

"The people of Crosus are very arrogant. I have met many of their officials, and in my opinion, they believe they are perfect and all other species are flawed. That arrogance has resulted in some minor issues before, but they never admit they are wrong. Any problem they face is someone else's fault.

136

Since you and Brealak discovered the attacks on Procolt 4, their punishment is now your fault."

"That doesn't make any sense, but I've notice that arrogant people are often illogical. Where is Crosus?"

"Crosus is about one hundred and ten light years from here."

"It seems to me it will take a long time before they know about the expulsion. If they decide to take action against the Earth, it would be another one hundred days until they get here. It would appear you're going to be here for a long time."

"There is a rumor Crosus has developed an ability to travel much faster than we can. If that is the case, they could be here within thirty days. Crosus does not discuss their technical capabilities with the other members of the trade group. They never sell their technology either. So, we really do not know how proficient they are."

"If you don't know anything about their capabilities, how can you be sure you'll be able to protect Earth?"

"I can't be 100% certain we will be able to protect Earth. But I am 100% certain Earth is not capable of protecting itself, so I do not see any downside to being here. Also, to the best of our knowledge, Crosus does not have any warships. There is no financial advantage to building a fleet of warships and Crosus seldom does anything that does not produce a profit."

"Is there any profit in attacking Earth?"

"No, but as I said, they are very arrogant. That may override their concern for profit. I cannot be sure Crosus will attack Earth, but if they do, we will be prepared. We will stay here for another one hundred and fifty days. Then I will make a decision regarding our return to Coplent."

"That sounds reasonable. Since you're here, you and your crew will have an opportunity to try Earth food."

"I already did that. Garlut was here several days before me. He took me to dinner at the space station. It was probably the best food I have ever eaten!"

"I'm glad you liked it. Do you know where Ambassador Garlut is now?"

"I think he was going to a World Council meeting. I expect he will be back on his ship in a few hours. If I hear from him, I will ask him to contact you."

"Thank you, Commander."

"You are most welcome, Admiral."

Now Jeffery knew why the warship was here and he was concerned about an attack from Crosus. He was also fairly sure just the presence of the Coplent warship would be a deterrent. He was deep in thought when he heard Anne say, "I just received a message that said the space station set up a new mooring system. They sent us a mooring status grid. We're supposed to go to location B37."

Jeffery said, "Anne, give the map to Mike. I want to go back to my cabin for a few minutes."

"Yes sir."

When Jeffery went into his cabin, he found Debbie sitting at the table drinking coffee. He sat down across from her and said, "I think we may be safer if we go back to Procolt 2. Commander Streb is here with his warship. He thinks there's a good possibility Earth will be attacked by Crosus, so he came here to protect Earth."

"Why would Crosus attack Earth?"

"Well, I asked Commander Streb that exact question. He thinks they'll blame us for the failure of their plan to cover up the destruction of the mining operation. If Brealak and I hadn't gone back to the Procolt System when we did, nobody would know about it except for Torblit. They were not in a position to report anything, because they had no legal right to set up the mining operation in the first place."

"I agree with you. I think we should drop off our guests and return to Procolt 2."

"You do realize we don't own this ship. Since NASA does, I think we have to go where they tell us to."

"We could steal the ship. They'd never be able to catch us," Debbie said with a smile on her face.

"I don't think that's a good idea. However, we could resign and ask Garlut to take us back to Procolt 2. We could bribe him with doughnuts and cinnamon rolls."

138

"I just made captain and you're now an admiral. I don't think I'm ready to resign. Are you?"

"No, I'm not. I think you and I should meet with Max tomorrow and find out what they want us to do next."

Two hours later, the Star Rover was moored near the space station. Jeffery contacted Max and set up an appointment for the following morning. He called Mike and told him he wanted the shuttle ready to begin taking the guests and crew members to the space station within thirty minutes. He also made an announcement to the crew and passengers regarding the shuttle departure. He was about to call Max when his com unit beeped.

He opened his com unit, thought for a second, and said, "This is Admiral Whitestone."

Max Hiller said, "I'll bet that's the first time you used your rank when answering your com unit."

"You're actually almost right Max, it's close. I was just about to call you. I want to meet with you tomorrow morning. Is that convenient?"

"How about 10:30?"

"Perfect. What were you calling about?"

"I wanted to ask you about your mission. You've been gone for over two years. I met with Garlut when he arrived and he filled me in on the situation with Crosus. But he wasn't with you on Procolt 2. I'm sure you'll be filing reports, but I'd rather hear the details from you personally."

"Debbie and I will see you tomorrow morning, Max." Jeffery closed his com unit and said, "We're meeting with Max tomorrow morning at 10:30. He wants a report on what happened on Procolt 2."

"That seems reasonable since NASA paid for the mission," Debbie replied.

"Yes, I guess you're right. Do you want to spend the night on the ship, or would you prefer to have a room at the hotel?"

"The bed here is much more comfortable. I think we should stay on the ship."

"I agree."

139

The following morning, Jeffery and Debbie were at the shuttle bay a few minutes early.

At exactly 6:00, Dean Crawford arrived. He said, "Good morning, it looks as though you two are my only passengers this morning."

Fifteen minutes later they were onboard the space station. They ate breakfast at the hotel and then walked over to the shuttle bay where the Earth shuttle would be departing. They boarded and were surprised to see Garlut and Brealak.

"Good morning. I wasn't expecting to see you here," Jeffery said.

"We have a meeting this morning with the Trade Council representative. How did things go on Procolt 2?"

"I think everything went extremely well. The radiation we were exposed to caused both Debbie and I to develop an increase in strength, as we expected. The squirrels can read and their math skills have improved. Cathy and Sheila decided to remain there. I spoke to Commander Streb yesterday and gave him an update on the situation."

"I bet you were surprised to see his ship here."

"Yes, I was surprised. That's why I called him. Do you think we should be worried about an attack from Crosus?"

"I think it is very likely, but they will not be expecting a Coplent warship to be here. Only the crew of the warship and perhaps ten others knew about the plan to send it here. Even if Crosus has spies on Coplent, they would not have known about it."

"Do you think Commander Streb will be able to protect us?"

"Yes, I do not think you have any idea how powerful the weapons are on that ship."

"That's good, but I hope he doesn't have to use them. On another subject, Debbie and I were thinking about opening a resort on Procolt 2. Do you think that would be a good idea?"

"I think it is a great idea. But before you do, you must find out more about the effects of long-term exposure to the radiation there. You will also need permission from the Trade

Council, but that will not be a problem since no single group owns the planet currently."

"We do have another problem. I don't think we have enough money to build it."

"That really is not a problem. When you ask the Trade Council for permission, make sure you tell them that you will need investors to help with the financing. There will be a lot of people eager to help you, including myself."

Jeffery looked at Debbie and said, "Do you really want to do it?"

"We need to think about it for a few days. I think we need to know what NASA's plans are for the Star Rover before we make that decision."

Garlut said, "I already know what your next mission will be. Do you want me to tell you?"

"Yes, the more we know the better prepared we'll be for our meeting with Max."

"Max told me they have made some progress on building a communications system. The first implementation of the system will be between Earth and Coplent. When completed, it will allow us to send messages in either direction in fifteen days. That is half the time it takes for a ship to get here. The Star Rover will be assigned to place relay stations in space between here and Coplent at one light year intervals. After you place the relays, you will have to insert carriers into the system. The carriers will be traveling between the relays at five hundred times the speed of light. I am certain Max will give you a more detailed description of your task at your meeting."

"That sounds like a pretty boring task."

"It will not take that long. You only have to go half way. Coplent ships will be completing the other half. I think you can probably complete the job in one hundred and fifty days."

Jeffery and Debbie arrived at Max's office a few minutes early. The door was open, so they walked in. Jeffery said, "Hi Max, it's good to see you again. It's hard to believe it has been more than two years since our last meeting."

"Good morning. It's nice seeing you as well. Garlut told me a lot of the details of your mission, but he wasn't always with you, so I suspect there are things he doesn't know. I'd like you to fill me in."

Jeffery handed Max a written report of the mission and said, "It's all in here. I think the only thing Garlut isn't completely aware of is the effect of the radiation exposure on Procolt 2 has had on us and the race of intelligent squirrels we discovered."

"Garlut told me about your discovery of the remains of a human on Procolt 2 and a little bit about the squirrels. I appreciate the written report, but as I said, I really want to hear it directly from you."

Jeffery spent the next several minutes giving Max a synopsis of the mission. When he finished Max thought for a while about what was just said and then asked, "Do you think the radiation that increased Mr. Brown's life span is also responsible for the intelligence of the squirrels?"

"I'm certain of it. We haven't found the source of the radiation, but we think it's local to the area where we set up the habitat on our first visit. There's no evidence of obvious genetic mutations in any of the other indigenous animals on the planet. Debbie and I spent three months on Procolt 2. I have no idea if it has increased our life span, but both of us are significantly stronger after exposure to the radiation. Cathy and Sheila, who have been on the planet longer, are stronger than we are."

"I think we need to get a team of geneticists to Procolt 2 to study the radiation, but right now we have a more pressing need for the Star Rover. We've developed a communication system that will allow us to transmit messages at five hundred times the speed of light. That's still nowhere near as fast as we would like, but it's better than anything else available currently. I want to use the Star Rover to help implement the system."

"I already discussed the system with Garlut and he explained what you want us to do, but I think you should speak to Commander Streb about it. He told me yesterday there's a rumor Crosus has developed the ability to travel much faster. If that's true, your system could be obsolete before the first message is sent."

"I agree, I'll contact him immediately. We've already spent over two billion dollars on the prototype. If there's even a small chance this thing will be obsolete before we're finished, we should stop right now. Did Commander Streb have any details?"

"No, he said Crosus doesn't share its technology with other members of the trade group. But he got to Earth as quickly as possible because he wanted to be here in case the rumor was correct and a fleet of Crosus ships suddenly shows up."

"This situation with Crosus has the World Council worried. We all realize you did nothing wrong. In fact, President Winters said he would have done exactly the same thing. You should be aware the public doesn't know about the Coplent warship. They know a ship is here, but they don't know any of the details. Apparently, the World Council is concerned that if the people knew Earth might be in danger, they would want to terminate our membership in the trade group."

"So, let me ask you something, Max. I assume our next mission was going to be placing the relays for the communication system. If that's not going to happen in the short term, can we go back to Procolt 2?"

"I can't answer that yet. I'll have to discuss this with Brandon Simpson. He's the engineer who designed the system. I'll let you know as soon as I can. By the way, I thought you should know that in two weeks, construction will start on the Star Explorer. It will be our second interstellar vehicle. They expect it will take eighteen months to build and a few months for testing before it's ready for its first mission. The plan after the Star Explorer is completed is to start building interstellar transport ships. That way we'll be able to deliver the products we sell. Right now, ships from Coplent deliver most of our products. All of our new ships will have the time stasis field generator, so they'll be able to travel at five hundred times light speed."

"So, my ship will be obsolete in a couple of years?"

"I don't think so. I'm sure we could retrofit it. You and Debbie should take a few weeks off. Go someplace nice and just relax for a while. I'll call you as soon as I know what we're going to do about the communication system."

"Okay Max, I'll be waiting for your call. Can I give the rest of my crew some time off as well?"

"I don't see why not. Give everybody two weeks."

"I'll do that. None of them have been paid since we left. Can you make sure they're paid before their leave starts?"

"I'll make sure that their funds are available by tomorrow morning."

"Thanks, Max."

Jeffery and Debbie left Max's office. As they were walking to the shuttle landing area, Jeffery asked, "What do you want to do now?"

"I'd like to visit my family. Don't you want to see your parents too?"

"Yes, I'd like to do that. So, let's spend a week with your parents and then a week with mine. Then we can come back here and press Max for an answer about our next mission."

"That sounds good. I'll make some calls."

After all of the arrangements were made, they went back to the space station. They had dinner at the hotel restaurant and called Mike, asking him to send the shuttle over to pick them up.

The following morning, Jeffery made an announcement to the entire crew that they had two weeks of leave starting the following morning. He also told them they had been paid overnight so they would have plenty of money to spend while away from duty.

Over the next half hour, crew members except Ron stopped by to thank Jeffery. As they did, he reminded each crewmember they had to be back aboard right after their leave was over as he was not sure when they would be leaving on the next mission.

Jeffery was about to call Ron to ask why he had not come by yet for an update or to check in with the duty roster, when he walked into the dining room not looking particularly amused. Jeffery handed him back the duty roster, signed, and asked what was wrong. Ron said he didn't want to talk about it now. He also asked if it was okay if he stayed aboard the ship. Jeffery said he had no objections and Ron turned and left without saying anything.

Jeffery asked, "Debbie, do you have any idea what's wrong with Ron? I know his wife was killed in an accident about a year before we left, but I thought he had a daughter he'd want to see."

"I have no idea. Perhaps Frank knows what's going on. I'll ask him."

Debbie left the dining room. She returned fifteen minutes later, walked slowly over to the table and sat down next to Jeffery, and said sadly, "I am sorry to have to tell you this, but Frank told me that Ron's daughter died while scuba diving in Hawaii. Frank didn't know the details, but apparently she was Ron's only relative."

"I'm sorry to hear that," Jeffery said as he caressed her hand. "I wish I'd known earlier. Knowing him as I do, he will likely bury himself in work now as a way to handle the grief." Jeffery stopped to think about how it would be to be alone in the universe. "He is a terrific officer, but I feel he may need to talk to someone soon."

"I agree, I wish there was something more we could do to help him," Debbie pondered.

"I'll speak with NASA's psychology department. They may need to speak with him about some grief counseling under the circumstances. He may not be able to return to space until they sign off on him."

The following morning, Jeffery and Debbie left on the first shuttle to the space station. They took a shuttle to New York and from there went to visit Debbie's parents. As planned, they spent a week there and then a week with

Jeffery's parents. Neither gave any thought to the fact that they were now celebrities. Nobody recognized them until they were on their way back to the space station. Apparently, somebody from the company that ran the shuttle service had notified one of the television networks. When they arrived at the shuttle terminal, they were surrounded by reporters and video camera operators. They arrived an hour before the shuttle was scheduled to depart, so they spent most of that time answering questions. They didn't mention anything about Gordon Brown, the squirrels, or Crosus. It all went rather well, and the interviews were seen worldwide for the next few days.

When they arrived back at the space station Jeffery received a call from Max.

"I wanted to tell you that you both did a wonderful job with the interviews," Max said. "I also found some information regarding Gordon Brown. He was part of the D-Day invasion in France that occurred on June 6, 1944. He disappeared five days later and was never seen again. He was twenty-three years old when he disappeared. So, the age estimates you received from the doctors on Coplent were off by about fifty years."

"Garlut told me he's fairly certain how Mr. Brown managed to get to Procolt 2. He said the race of aliens responsible for all the reports of flying saucers that occurred during that time frame took him there. Also, I don't know if you're aware of this, but Ron Rice's daughter died while scuba diving. She was his only living relative. Ron appears to be depressed. He's an excellent officer. I think Ron needs a psych eval before we return to space, it might help with his grief process. I also thought about offering him some extended leave. I'm just not sure how to handle it though."

"It's a tough situation, I think you should speak with him and then let me know what his thoughts are. You should know if he's going in for an evaluation, he'll have to miss the next Star Rover mission. All of the psychological evaluations take at least a few months. We can't have our people out there and feeling this way about their home life. The jobs they do are far too important. Additionally, we got your earlier

146

recommendation for him to be promoted to Command a new ship. I have taken this into consideration in lieu of the psych eval. If he clears that, he will be on my short list. Also, I'd like to have more information about the aliens who kidnapped Mr. Brown. I'll ask Garlut the next time I see him."

"Sounds good Max. Thank you. I'll discuss it with him but only when I get back to the Star Rover."

"Okay. Please let me know his feelings as soon as possible. By the way, there's still no decision on your next mission."

"I'm not surprised. I'll call you as soon as I've spoken to Ron."

The first thing Jeffery did after he and Debbie were in their cabin was to call Ron and asked him to come to his cabin.

The door to the cabin was open, so when Ron arrived, he walked in and asked, "Hi, did you guys have a good vacation?"

Debbie said, "Yes, it was very nice. We spent a week with my parents and then we spent a week with Jeffery's parents."

"I saw the interview you did. I noticed you were very careful with the information you gave out."

"I admit it was difficult not to say anything about the situation with Crosus, but we were told that information was not to be made public. Ron, we heard about your daughter. I know you didn't want to discuss it, but you have our deepest sympathies. If there's anything we can do to help you, please let us know."

"Thank you, but I'm all right now. I just have to try not to think about it too much."

"If you would like to take some time off, I'd be happy to approve it."

"I would prefer to work. It helps keep my mind busy."

Jeffery replied, "I understand. I wanted you to know that construction will be starting this week on the Star Explorer. When it's finished, NASA will begin building a fleet of interstellar cargo ships. You're being considered for the

147

position of command on one of the new ships. Would you like that?"

A small smile appeared on Ron's face, then he said, "Yes, I would. Did you have a hand in that, by any chance?"

"I did mention to Max that I thought you were qualified for the position."

"Thank you, I appreciate it. Is there anything else?"

"Before you can start the training for that position, you know NASA will want to conduct a psych eval on you. And since you just lost your daughter, it will be extensive. But, if you pass that with flying colors, and I know you will, then you will be selected for command training. You won't be able to go on our next mission. All of the candidates will be going through an eighteen-month training program."

"I'll keep that in mind. Do you know what our next mission is?"

"Not yet, but I expect to find out in the next few days."

Ron thought for a few seconds and said, "Please tell Max I'd like to be considered for a position as commanding officer on one of the new ships. I do understand the psych evaluation needs to be performed first. But realistically, I really have no reason to stay on Earth anymore. So, I may as well explore the stars. Right?"

"I completely understand that, Ron. I'll pass the news along."

Ron left the cabin. As soon as he was gone, Jeffery called Max and let him know Ron was interested in becoming a captain of one of the new ships and that he would undergo the psych evaluation first.

COPLENT WARSHIP
AUGUST 4, 2122

Commander Streb was sound asleep in his cabin when the battle station alarm rang. He was up in an instant and was about to call the bridge when his communicator beeped. He answered the call by saying, "Why is the alarm sounding?"

"Commander, four Crosus ships appeared two hundred thousand units away. They are about to disappear behind the moon," the duty officer replied.

"Send out two armed shuttles to follow them. Make sure the shuttles have their shields at maximum. I realize using the shields on the shuttles will make it obvious somebody is watching, but unless they know we are here, they will probably think the ships are from Earth."

"Sir, with all due respect, if the shuttles are using their shields, they will not have sufficient power to fire their weapons."

"Noted. Of course, I am aware, but if the shuttles report suspicious activity, we will take care of it. Before we leave Earth, we are scheduled to procure some of their power modules so the shields and weapons will be able to function at the same time."

"I will order the shuttles to leave immediately, sir."

"Good, I will be on the bridge shortly."

The shuttles left the warship and went behind the moon as ordered. Only moments after they moved to the dark side of the moon, they were fired upon. The shields did their job and the ships were undamaged. Since the moon blocked communication, the shuttles decided to split up. One of them went back so they could update Commander Streb. The other ship continued forward.

When Commander Streb was told the shuttles had been attacked, he ordered the warship to leave orbit and go to the far side of the moon. As they approached their destination, he contacted the shuttle that was watching the Crosus ships. The officer in charge of the shuttle told him three of the four Crosus ships had landed. They appeared to be unloading a large piece of equipment.

Commander Streb had a good idea what the equipment was capable of doing. He was certain the Crosus plan was to destabilize the moon's orbit. That could cause the moon to crash into the Earth and destroy it. However, it was more likely the moon would go flying off into space and would cause devastating problems with earthquakes, flooding of low-lying areas, and other catastrophic consequences. He told his communications officer to try to reach the commander of the Crosus ships.

The only result from their attempt to communicate was the Crosus ship began firing their weapons at the warship. The warships shields prevented any damage, but with them activated he was unable to return fire. He contacted the shuttles and told them to fire their weapons at the Crosus ship. The weapons on the shuttles had relatively low power, but they could still inflict damage.

They were watching the Crosus ship on the monitor when it was hit by a particle beam from one of the shuttles. The Crosus ship stopped firing at the warship and Commander Streb ordered his weapons officer to immediately open fire on the Crosus ship. They dropped their shields and fired at the ship. The result was the targeted ship appeared to lose all power, even the life support systems.

Commander Streb ordered the weapons officer to fire a full-strength electromagnetic pulse at the ships on the surface. He didn't want to destroy the ships unless he had no choice. However, the electromagnetic pulse had no effect. They fired it again, but the results were unchanged. He ordered the ships on the surface to be destroyed. There were three loud bursts of noise when the weapons were fired. They were watching the monitors when suddenly the whole ship shuddered. The Crosus ship in orbit above the moon had fired on the warship. It did sustain some damage, but the shields were brought up before the Crosus ship could fire again.

The ships on the surface were badly damaged, but their crews were still working around them, assembling a large

150

piece of equipment. Commander Streb ordered the weapons officer to target the equipment they were building. A moment later it was destroyed. Most of the crew on the bridge were watching the monitors to see what was happening on the surface, but one officer was watching the ship that had just fired on them. He said, "The Crosus ship that just fired on us is powering up its engines."

Commander Streb said, "Do not let them get away. Their ship is faster and more maneuverable than ours. I do not want to destroy the ship, but if they power up their wormhole generator I will. Weapons officer, if they make any move to escape, try to target their propulsion system."

"Yes sir."

They watched as the Crosus ship began moving away from the moon. As the Earth came into view, the ship suddenly started moving very fast toward the Earth.

"Navigator, follow that ship, but stay ten thousand units back."

"Yes sir."

They followed the Crosus ship until it stopped about five thousand units above the Earth.

"Sir," the weapons officer said, "there was just a large energy surge on the Crosus ship. I think they may be powering up a weapon."

"Destroy them," Commander Streb ordered.

"Yes sir."

The weapons officer fired a full energy particle beam at them. There was a small explosion on the Crosus ship and it began to fall toward Earth.

"Sir, it appears they are still powering up a weapon. But the ship is out of control, so there is no way to fire it accurately," the weapons officer said.

"Where is it going to fall?"

"It appears it will fall into the ocean about one hundred and fifty units east of New York City. It will hit the Earth in .12 hours."

"Communications officer, contact NASA and tell them where that ship will impact the Earth. There may be a large explosion which could result in a tidal wave."

"Yes sir."

There was nothing more they could do except watch. The energy from their weapons would be dissipated by the Earth's atmosphere, making them useless. They watched as the ship hit the ocean and exploded. The energy from the explosion was far greater than what they had expected. Their view was blocked by a thick layer of steam created by the explosion. As the view cleared, it became obvious New York City was in trouble. The explosion had generated a wave .05 units high (more than three hundred feet) and one unit wide. That wave would hit New York City in less than .5 hours. There was no way to evacuate the city quickly enough.

The communications officer contacted NASA again and told them what was going to happen, but they already knew. The falling ship was being observed by both planes and space ships that were flying over the area. New York City's hurricane warning system was activated. There was simply not enough time to do much about it. By the time the wave reached the New York City area a lot of the initial energy had dissipated, but the wave was still .02 units high (almost one hundred and thirty feet) and just less than one unit wide.

The wave caught the western most tip of Long Island before slamming into Brooklyn. It destroyed every building in its path. The wave crossed into Manhattan headed for Hoboken, but it lost all of its energy before that could happen. By the time the carnage was over, more than ten thousand people were dead. Far more than that were homeless since the wave destroyed more than one hundred thousand homes and buildings.

In an emergency meeting of the World Council, they were ready to blame it on Commander Streb. When he told them the intention of Crosus was to destabilize the moon's orbit and what that would mean to Earth, they realized if not for Commander Streb and his ship, Earth might well have been destroyed. They debated what to tell the public because they didn't want them to know how close they had come to total destruction. Additionally, they didn't want to jeopardize Earth's membership in the trade group. In the end it was decided it would be blamed on a large meteor that was undetected until it was too late to warn anyone.

Most of the people of Earth accepted the explanation of the incident. The few people who knew the truth never said anything to contradict the official explanation. It took over three years, and more than twenty trillion dollars, to rebuild the area destroyed by the wave. The truth about the incident was finally revealed in 2504, almost four hundred years later.

During the year that followed the incident on Earth, Crosus was expelled from the trade group. They never attempted to retaliate against Coplent. Torblit received permission to reopen the mine on Procolt 4, and as a result of that mining operation, Torblit replaced Crosus as the richest planet in the trade group.

There was one other casualty from the attack on Earth. Crosus had proved it was now possible to travel at speeds far greater than five hundred times the speed of light. That made the communication system obsolete before it really got started. If ships could travel faster, messages could too. As a result, the communication system designed by Brandon Simpson was cancelled. Crosus had figured out how to travel faster than anyone else, but they refused to reveal how they did it. Brandon Simpson would not give up. He made up his mind to figure out how they did it no matter how long it took.

As a result of the cancellation of the communication system, Jeffery received permission to return to Procolt 2 on the Star Rover. With Garlut's help, he requested permission from the Trade Council to build a vacation resort there. That process would take at least two standard years for approval because the process required the request be made at one meeting, but no decision would be forthcoming until the following meeting one year later. The procedure gave the members of the Trade Council time to evaluate the request.

After his psych evaluation was cleared, Ron Rice was accepted into the training program. The crew members of the

Star Rover gave him a big party at the space station the night before he was scheduled to begin training. Toby Grayson was promoted and replaced Ron Rice as Chief Engineer. NASA assigned Peter White to take Toby's place as Assistant Chief Engineer. Peter had worked with NASA for more than ten years in various engineering positions and he was thrilled with his new assignment. Jeffery, Debbie, and Toby all thought he would be an excellent addition to the crew.

Anne Perkins was promoted to chief communications officer to replace Cathy Carter. Diane Thomas, who spoke several languages and had a master's degree in electrical engineering, was selected to fill Anne's previous position, and Mark Jackson would replace Sheila as the ship's botanist and one of the exobiologists.

THE RETURN TO PROCOLT 2
SEPTEMBER 2122

Jeffery and Debbie were sitting in the dining room on the Star Rover. Frank walked in and sat down across from the couple. As he sat he said, "We left Procolt 2 four months ago. I was wondering if either of you noticed any changes in your muscles since you're no longer exposed to the radiation."

"No, we haven't, but do you have any explanation as to why we have increased strength without any increase in muscle mass?" Jeffery asked.

"My guess is the genetic changes allow you to use your muscles more efficiently. Think about the squirrels for a moment. There's no doubt their enhanced intelligence is due to exposure to the radiation, but the size of their brains didn't increase. They're using their intellectual capacity more efficiently."

"I guess that makes sense. I wonder why the other animals living in the area don't seem to be affected," Debbie said.

"Perhaps they have been affected, but in ways we can't recognize. Think about the squirrels again. Remember they have hands, but we don't know if they always had hands. Perhaps the hands are also the result of radiation exposure. If the other animals in the area have developed physical changes, we would never know it," Frank said.

"Right! You can't tell from looking at us that we have increased strength. So, I suppose if the changes were physical or only moderate changes in intelligence, we wouldn't be able to detect it," Debbie stated.

"Do you know our schedule for this mission yet?" Frank asked.

"Yes, we're going to Procolt 2 first. We'll probably stay there for thirty days. Then we'll go to Coplent. We're delivering some custom-made power modules for Commander Streb. We'll probably be there for ten days. Then we're going to Torblit to discuss trade issues. I have no idea how long we'll be there, but when we finish at Torblit we'll be going back to Earth. I think we'll probably be gone for at least a year."

"Did you find replacements for Cathy and Sheila?" Frank asked.

"Yes, their replacements will be arriving tomorrow. They're both well qualified and I'm sure they'll be excellent additions to the crew. They don't know anything about the squirrels yet and will be surprised. Debbie and I are thinking about moving to Procolt 2. I haven't told anyone else about this, but we're considering opening a resort there. Garlut will be submitting a request to the Trade Council at their next meeting requesting permission on our behalf."

"I think that's a wonderful idea. If you decide you want a doctor as part of your staff, let me know."

"Actually, I was planning on asking you as soon as we receive approval from the Trade Council."

"Good, I think I'd like that."

Debbie had been sitting mostly quiet during the conversation. "Frank, do you think our life spans will be increased too?"

"I have no idea. Just because Mr. Brown experienced an increased life span doesn't mean we will. Let's see how we feel after we're on the planet for fifty years. When are we leaving for Procolt 2?"

"We have to wait until the power modules are delivered to the ship. That's scheduled for the day after tomorrow. I would guess we'll be on our way in three days. If you need any medical supplies, you'd better order them immediately."

"Okay, I'll do that. I'll see you later," Frank said as he got up from the table.

After Frank left the dining room, Debbie said, "I'm not sure it was a good idea to tell him about the resort. We don't know if it will happen."

"Garlut said there's no reason for the Trade Council to deny our request. He also told me we shouldn't be concerned about financing."

"Does he have that much money?"

156

"I don't know, but I think he has some. He also indicated that he knows other people who would be interested in investing in the resort."

The trip to Procolt 2 was, for the most part, very relaxing. The ship functioned perfectly, the crew was comfortable, the food was good, and for the first time on a long trip nobody complained about being bored.

Jeffery and Debbie spent time discussing how they wanted their resort built. Frank also got involved in the planning. By the time they arrived at Procolt 2, the three of them were sure what they wanted to do. They all were in agreement about how the resort would be built, but there were some differences between them on where. Frank thought they should look for a site where the effects of the radiation would be minimal. But both Jeffery and Debbie didn't think the radiation would be a problem. However, they all agreed that when they were on Procolt 2, they would try to find the source of the radiation and determine if the effects were localized. If the radiation was limited to a specific area, they would build the resort in another section that wasn't affected.

When the Star Rover was in a stable orbit above the planet, Jeffery said to Mike, "Debbie, and I are going down to the surface. Contact Cathy or Sheila and let them know we're coming. You have the bridge. I'm not expecting any trouble, but if the scanners detect anything let me know immediately."

"Yes sir. Have a good time."

"Thanks, Debbie and I will be back aboard in less than eight hours."

Jeffery left the bridge and went to his cabin to get Debbie.

As they walked to the shuttle bay he said, "Tomorrow Frank will come with us and we'll look for the source of the radiation. Somebody from NASA gave him a directional radiation detector that should help us find it."

Debbie sat at the pilot's station and Jeffery sat in a passenger's seat. The shuttle left the Star Rover and Debbie landed the shuttle a half hour later. It was early afternoon, the sun was shining, and the temperature was a very comfortable

157

twenty degrees. When the shuttle door opened, they found Cathy and three squirrels waiting for them.

Cathy said, "Admiral, Captain. It's nice to see you again. We've been waiting for your return. Something amazing has happened. Please follow me."

While they were walking to the shelter, Cathy said, "While you were gone two squirrels were born. Both births occurred about one hundred and fifty days ago. By the time the newborn squirrels were one hundred days old, they were speaking English. But even more surprising is that all the knowledge of their parents was passed down to their offspring. They could not only speak, but they could read, write, and do basic arithmetic. They recognized their elders and called them by name. To the best of my knowledge, there has never been an instance where children inherited learned knowledge from their parents."

Jeffery and Debbie were silent while they thought about what had occurred. Jeffery said, "I knew they were very smart, but if they have the ability to pass down learned knowledge from the parents, they'll surpass the intelligence of every other species in the galaxy. Think about this for a moment in human terms. If a couple both had advanced degrees in physics when their children were born, they wouldn't need any education because they would know everything their parents knew. They'd actually be more knowledgeable than either of their parents because they would have the knowledge from both of them. We have to inform Frank."

"Having knowledge is important, but are they smart enough to know how to utilize their knowledge to solve problems?" Debbie asked.

"That's a good question. Over the next few days, Sheila and I will give them problems that will require both logic and knowledge to solve. Then we'll have the answer to your question."

"I'm not sure I'd like the idea of my kids being more knowledgeable than I am."

"You aren't a squirrel, so I wouldn't worry about it," Jeffery said with a smile.

"I'm not a squirrel. But the squirrels might feel threatened by their offspring."

"Debbie, I think you should go back to the ship, get Frank, and bring him here," Jeffery suggested.

"Okay, I can do that. I'm very interested in his reaction."

Debbie went back to the shuttle. Before she took off, she contacted Frank and told him to meet her at the shuttle bay. He wanted to know if there was anything wrong. She told him there was nothing wrong and she would explain everything when she saw him. All the way back to the ship, she kept thinking about the squirrels. She thought it was obvious the squirrels were continuing to mutate, and she wondered what other abilities they might develop over the next few years.

As soon as she landed and the shuttle bay was pressurized, Frank knocked on the door to the shuttle.

He boarded and asked excitedly, "What's going on?"

"While we were gone, two squirrels were born. They appear to be a little higher on the evolutionary scale than their predecessors."

"You're going to have to explain that," Frank said.

"Frank, it appears they inherited learned abilities from their parents. By the time they were one hundred days old, they were able to speak English. I haven't seen them yet, but I was told they appear to have all the knowledge of both their parents."

Frank reflected on that statement. "I know of documented cases where some animals transfer some learned tasks to their offspring. However, these are simple tasks, like using a rock to break the shell of a nut. That isn't even remotely similar to transferring the ability to speak a language to your children."

"It's much more than that. The new generation can also read and do simple math problems."

"This has to be the result of continued mutation due to radiation exposure. I wonder where it will end."

"I was thinking about that on the way here," Debbie admitted. "If their mental ability continues to develop, will they have telekinetic capabilities or even the ability to read minds?"

"I really don't think either of those things are possible, but I could be wrong."

Debbie started the engine and a few moments later they were on their way back to the surface of Procolt 2. They were silent for a while. Then Frank asked, "Are there any pregnant females now?"

"I have no idea. You'll have to ask when we get there. Why?"

"Because I'd like to see if there's a difference in the brain scans between the parents and the fetuses."

"I didn't know you could do a fetal brain scan."

"I'm not sure I can either. It has never been done on a squirrel, but I'd like to try. I also want to do a DNA analysis. It might tell me if there's a difference between the parents and the children. I suppose it might tell me which gene is responsible for this new ability."

There was another brief lull in the conversation. During that time Debbie noticed that Frank was holding a plastic case that looked like a small tool box. She asked, "Is that your new radiation detector?"

"Yes, I got it from NASA just before we left Earth."

When the shuttle landed, S1 was waiting for them. As Frank stepped off the shuttle, S1 said, "Dr. Weber, it's very nice to see you again. Would you like to see our new children?"

"Yes, I would like that very much."

"Please follow me."

They walked to the shelter and in the living room were two squirrel children, they looked like the adult squirrels, but they were only about twenty-inches tall. They were taking turns reading a children's book aloud to Cathy and Sheila.

They listened as S74 and S75 took turns reading the story, each of them reading for about a minute. Their voices were high-pitched and soft, but the enunciation was almost perfect. Frank wondered if they really comprehended what they were reading. Apparently so did Cathy, because when S74 and S75 finished reading the story she asked them questions about the story they would not have been able to answer without understanding what they read. They answered each question correctly and it soon became obvious they were able to both read the story and grasp what they read.

Jeffery, Frank, and Debbie were amazed at the intelligence the young squirrels displayed. But that was only the beginning. When the reading lesson was finished Sheila took over, and on a large monitor she displayed some simple addition and subtraction problems. S74 and S75 solved each problem almost instantly when it was displayed.

Frank said, "Do you realize these squirrels are less than five months old, but they have the abilities of seven or eight year old human children? They're still immature physically, but their minds appear to be fully developed."

Cathy stood next to Frank and asked, "Dr. Weber, is it possible to actually transfer learned knowledge to your offspring?"

"I didn't think so, but obviously that happened." He was silent for a few moments before adding, "I'd like you to teach them how to multiply and divide. Then start some simple algebra. I want to know if they can apply logic to solve math problems."

"Okay, I can do that. What will that tell you?"

"Reading and simple math can be learned, but the ability to use logic to solve a problem requires a much greater level of intelligence. I also think it would be interesting to include a few of the adults in your class. I suspect the adults won't display the same level of intelligence."

Cathy smiled broadly and said, "We'll start on that tomorrow."

Frank decided to stay on the planet overnight. The following morning, after the rain, he planned to begin his search for the radiation source. Jeffery and Debbie returned to the Star Rover.

That evening Frank, Cathy, and Sheila had dinner together in the shelter. While they were eating, Cathy said, "I don't know if this is the right time to bring this up, but I noticed something the squirrels were doing they never did before. They started using the toilets in the shelter. I asked why and S1 told me it was more convenient than going outside. There was no indication of modesty, it was just a matter of convenience."

"I think that proves they're no longer animals. I wonder if they'll start wearing clothes." Frank replied, smiling.

Cathy continued, "I also asked S1 about the garden. He said they're now growing more food than they can eat. They're growing carrots, green beans, and lettuce. I'd like someone to bring some peanuts down from the Star Rover. I'm sure they'll love them. To answer your question Dr. Weber, I don't think they'll ever feel a need to wear clothing. I'm certain they believe their fur would take the place of wearing clothes."

The following day Frank got up early. While he was drinking a cup of coffee, S1 walked into the dining room. Frank said, "Good morning. I have a question for you, if you don't mind. Are any of the females in your group pregnant?"

"I think so. Why are you asking?"

"I'm curious about the increase in intelligence of the children in your group. I'd like to measure the difference in brain activity between a pregnant female and her fetus."

"Can you do that without hurting them?"

"Yes, it's absolutely painless. All I have to do is attach some wires to the female's head and abdomen."

"Then I'll ask if any of the females are pregnant."

"I'd also like to do a DNA test on one of the children and their mother. I only have to swab the inside of their mouths with soft cotton swabs."

"That wouldn't be a problem. We can do that anytime," S1 replied.

"I'm going out to search for the source of the radiation here. I'd like to do the tests when I get back."

162

"Would it be okay if I bring them here just before dinner?"

"Yes, that would be perfect."

Frank began his search as soon as the morning rain stopped. When he was outside the shelter, he turned on his detection equipment. It was a handheld device that was shaped like a pistol. It had a bright metal barrel about six inches long and about two inches in diameter. There was a trigger to turn the device on. On the top of the barrel was a small dual-purpose video display. It was used specify the scan parameters and to display the results of the scan. It detected an unknown form of radiation, but it didn't indicate any particular direction in which the field appeared to be stronger. He decided to walk south of the shelter and stop every few hundred feet to check the radiation levels. As he walked, he found no change in the level of radiation or any indication of a potential source. After he had walked for an hour, he realized he needed a faster mode of transportation. There was a small electric car aboard the Star Rover. He called Jeffery and asked him to have it brought down on the next shuttle.

When he returned to the shelter, he found Sheila holding a class for four squirrels. In addition to S74 and S75, there were two adult squirrels in the class. He watched as Sheila showed her students how to solve some simple algebra problems. They all appeared to be learning very quickly. He didn't want to be a distraction, so he returned to his room.

At dinner time, S1 appeared with another adult squirrel and one of the children. Frank took two sterile cotton swabs out of a package in his pocket. He swabbed both the mother and her child and thanked them for helping him with his tests.

The following morning the shuttle arrived. Jeffery drove the little electric car to the door of the shelter. He went inside looking for Frank and found him sitting in the dining room drinking a cup of coffee.

"I brought the car for you. I didn't think you'd need the protective shell so I didn't bring it."

"Thanks. I agree the shell is unnecessary here since I won't go out until after the rain stops. The car will make my search a lot easier." Then he handed Jeffery two plastic bags containing the cotton swabs from the mother and child. "Please give these to Linda and tell her to run a complete DNA comparison."

"Certainly. I'll give them to her as soon as I get back onboard. Do you think it's possible the source of the radiation is the planet itself?"

"I thought about that. It's a possibility of course, but I think it's more likely to be some object from space that fell on the planet."

"I have nothing to do right now, so if you like, I'll help you with your search."

"Great! Let me finish my coffee and we can go."

A few minutes later they were sitting in the car. The body was small, four feet wide and seven feet long with two seats in front and a large storage area. The axles were placed as far apart as possible to increase stability. The tires were very large, twenty-four inches in diameter and nine inches wide. Each wheel had its own independent drive mechanism meaning the vehicle could be propelled with whatever number of drive wheels best suited the conditions. The seats were well-padded to make the ride more comfortable and minimize the risk of injury to the people riding in the car.

Frank sat in the driver's seat and both men fastened their seat belts. Frank decided to go a different direction this time. The car smoothed out most of the bumps in the rough terrain and they were both fairly comfortable. It had a top speed of thirty miles per hour, but Frank was driving only ten. Every mile they stopped and took radiation readings. The area they were exploring was mostly large meadows. There were a few dense forest areas they had to drive around, but they continued travelling in one direction. After two hours of driving, they decided to end their search for the day. Every reading was exactly the same. The detector said the radiation type was unknown, and the strength measured ten on the display that went from zero to one hundred.

For the next week, Frank continued his search for the true source of the radiation. The terrain west of the shelter appeared to be all meadow land, so he was able to drive much farther. He drove at top speed for three hours and then stopped to test the radiation. He was hoping for a different reading, but it was still the same. After two more disappointing days, he gave up. He decided the search must be done from the air.

By this time, Cathy and Sheila had managed to teach the squirrels basic algebra. They also discovered S74 and S75 were able to learn faster than the adults in the class, although ultimately, they all learned the material. So far, they had only given the students numerical problems to solve. Now they decided to start giving them more complex problems dealing with logic, so Cathy gave each student a set of word problems.

By the time she passed out the problem to the four students, S74, who received the problem first, said, "The answer is 5.08."

Then S75 said, "If you want to be more precise, 5.07690."

The two adults in the class also reached the correct answer, but it took them a little over a minute and they used the paper the problem was written on to find the answer.

Obviously, the problem was too simple, so Cathy and Sheila spent a few hours that evening writing more complex problems.

There were four problems this time. Before Cathy passed out the problems she said, "This test is made up of four problems. Please write the equation you used to solve the problem and your answer."

This time it took S74 and S75 ten minutes to solve the problems. The last of the two adults finished in fifteen minutes. All of the answers were correct.

Cathy told her students class was over for the day. Then she used her communicator to contact Jeffery and asked to see him as soon as possible.

"Is there a problem?"

"Yes. It isn't serious now, but it will be soon. It concerns the education plan for the squirrels."

"Debbie and I'll come down on the next shuttle. We should be there in two hours."

165

"Thank you. We'll be waiting for you."

When the shuttle arrived, Cathy and Sheila were waiting for them as promised. As soon as Jeffery and Debbie stepped off the shuttle Cathy said, "Thank you for coming, Jeffery."

"Actually, Debbie and I were already planning to meet with Frank today. How can I help you?"

"We gave the squirrels a more complex algebra test. All four of our students got every answer correct. S74 and S75 completed the test in ten minutes. The adults took an additional five minutes."

"Wow! That's very impressive," Jeffery responded.

"Yes, I agree. Obviously, the squirrels are very intelligent. I'm sorry to tell you we really don't have the right material to continue their education for much longer. We need more advanced books. And, Sheila and I aren't qualified to continue their education for much longer because they may already be more knowledgeable than we are."

"I doubt that. What subjects would you like books for?"

"We need books for advanced math, physics, and chemistry at a minimum."

"When I get back to the ship, I'll ask our engineers if they have any books you can use. Will the squirrels be able to read the books?"

"I don't know, but the books are for us, not the squirrels. We wanted to use the books to develop lesson plans."

"If anyone aboard still has copies of their textbooks, I'll ask them to send the files to you."

"Thanks, that will help. When you leave here, you're going to Coplent, right?"

"Yes, and then we'll continue to Torblit before returning to Earth."

"When you get to Coplent please let Garlut know about this situation. Perhaps they can send somebody to help."

"Okay, but very few of the people on Coplent speak English. I think it would be better to ask Garlut to discuss this with Max when he goes back to Earth. I'm sure he'll return before us."

"You're probably right. I'm sure the squirrels could learn a new language, but that would probably slow down their education."

Jeffery and Debbie walked into the shelter and found Frank in the dining room. They sat down across from him. Jeffery said, "The radiation detector has been attached to the shuttle. Toby looked at the design and thinks as long as we keep our altitude less than three thousand feet it should work correctly. The output has been routed to the display at the co-pilot's position.

"Did Toby give you any indication regarding speed?"

"Yes, he said during scanning we shouldn't exceed six hundred miles per hour."

"So, if we fly a grid pattern at three thousand feet, how much of the surface will we be able to cover before we leave for Coplent?"

"I would guess maybe 25%, but I don't think we should attempt to cover the planet's entire surface. I think we should go in two hundred-mile increments. So, we fly at top speed for two hundred miles, slow down, take our measurements, and repeat the process until we reach a pole. Then we come back here and do it again, but in the opposite direction. If we do that we should know within a few days if the radiation is equal over the entire surface. If it appears to be stronger in one area, we can cover that area more thoroughly."

"That sounds reasonable. Let's get started."

Debbie stood up and said, "I'll do the flying this afternoon."

Debbie and Frank left the dining room while Jeffery got a cup of coffee. While he was sitting there, one of the squirrels wandered in. He walked over to Jeffery and said, "Hello sir. How are you today?"

"Very well thank you, but I was just thinking we have to leave here in ten days. I really don't want to go."

"Do you have to go?"

"Yes, my job has a lot of responsibilities, and I have an obligation to complete each of my assigned tasks to the best of my ability. Do you understand?"

"Yes, I do understand, but do you have to keep doing your job?"

"Yes, I have to keep doing my job until I return to Earth. Then I could resign, I suppose, but if I resign, I would have no way of returning here."

"I think Garlut would bring you back."

"Yes, I'm sure he would, but I have plans for my return here. Do you know what a resort is?"

"It's like a hotel, but it's bigger and offers food and recreation."

"That's right! Debbie and I want to build a resort here, and when it's finished, we'll come here to live. Dr. Weber wants to do that too."

"Would that bring a lot of other humanoids here?"

"Yes, I'm sure it would. Is that a problem?"

"No, we like humans."

"Good, we don't want to do anything that would upset you. We like you also, and it's important to us that all of the squirrels are happy. I don't know if you realize it, but you're the only non-humanoid intelligent species that has ever been found."

"Yes, I do realize we're unique."

Jeffery intended to continue the conversation, but the squirrel left the dining room and he was alone again. The conversation with the squirrel had increased his desire to live on Procolt 2, and he decided he was going to do everything he could to make sure that happened.

For the next several hours, he wandered around the area near the shelter. He watched Cathy and Sheila teaching the squirrels algebra for a while. He went to the lake and walked along the shore. When he heard the shuttle returning, he walked back to the shelter. By the time he got there the shuttle had landed, so he went inside the shelter and found Debbie and Frank in the dining room.

168

When Frank saw Jeffery he said, "We went north for four thousand miles and south for about the same distance. We never detected any change in the radiation levels or any indication of a source. I'm beginning to think the planet itself is the source, and that means it would be the same everywhere. Tomorrow we're going to go two thousand miles east and then go north and south again."

"I suspect your results will be identical to the results of today's trip."

"You're probably right. But if we have identical results for the next few days, we'll have to do additional tests to determine if long term exposure to the radiation is dangerous."

"Is there any way to do that in a relatively short period of time?"

"I think that depends on your definition of 'a short period of time.' If we bring animals here that have very short life spans, we can watch several generations over a period of a year or so. If we don't detect any serious abnormalities, we can be somewhat certain it's safe."

"I'll ask Garlut about that when we get to Coplent. I'd like to go back to the Star Rover. Are you ready to leave?"

"I'd like to stay here again. Is that okay with you?" Frank said.

"Sure, we'll be back in the morning. See you then."

Jeffery and Debbie left the shelter and went back to the Star Rover. As soon as Jeffery was back onboard, he called Toby and asked him if any of his engineers still had copies of their textbooks. Toby told him he was fairly certain Peter White did because he was teaching classes at a local college before he received his assignment to the Star Rover. Jeffery told him to have Peter send the copies he had to Cathy.

The following morning, Jeffery and Debbie decided they would go with Frank today. They went down to the surface and walked into the shelter. Frank and Sheila were both in the dining room having breakfast. Sheila smiled when she saw Jeffery and said, "Thanks. Peter sent us more than a dozen textbooks. That will provide us with what we need to continue the education of the squirrels for at least two years."

"I'm glad to hear that. It's one less thing to worry about. Maybe we could get them some books on architecture and they could design some buildings for us."

Debbie said, "I'm sure they could, but I would guess their designs wouldn't be suitable for resort use. The designs would probably be based on a squirrel's needs, not the needs of humans."

"You do realize I wasn't being serious."

"Sure, you were," Debbie said with a smile.

"Frank, are you ready to go?" Jeffery suddenly felt the need to get moving.

"Yep," he answered as he picked up his breakfast dishes and put them into the recycler. "Let's go."

For the next seven hours they studied the radiation levels at more than sixty different spots. At every spot, the radiation level was identical. When they returned to the shelter, Frank said, "Let's do this one more time. Tomorrow let's go four thousand miles west and try this again. If the results are the same, we'll have to assume the radiation level is identical everywhere on the surface of the planet."

"Okay, Debbie and I will see you tomorrow morning."

The following morning Jeffery and Debbie were having breakfast when Mike sat down at their table. He said, "I'd like to spend some time on the surface. I haven't had an opportunity to do that very much since we got here."

Jeffery asked, "Would you like to take Dr. Weber on his radiation search today? You can do that. If you want, you can stay in the shelter overnight."

"That sounds great, Jeffery. What time is Dr. Weber expecting to be picked up?"

"Anytime you get there will be okay."

"I'll leave shortly. Thank you."

After Mike left, Debbie said with a smile, "I guess we're stuck with each other all day."

"Yeah, maybe we could spend some time in our cabin doing some interesting experiments."

"That sounds like it could be fun."

Frank gave up on his search for the source of the radiation by the end of the day. Nine days later, they were ready to leave for the ninety-day trip to Coplent. By that time, the squirrels had advanced to solving simultaneous equations with multiple unknowns.

COPLENT
DECEMBER 2122

The trip to Coplent was routine as the crew was now accustomed to long trips through space. Jeffery decided the time spent would be used to cross-train his crew, so every member would be capable of handling multiple tasks. The crew members enjoyed making good use of the time instead of spending it playing games.

By the time the Star Rover arrived at Coplent, the engineering crew was capable of handling security issues and the security members received training in advanced first-aid, communications, and hydroponics. There was now a backup for every staff member except Dr. Weber. Jeffery decided that during their stay on Coplent, every crew member would learn how to pilot the shuttle.

When they were within range, they contacted the space station at Coplent. Jeffery discovered their timing was perfect. Garlut was scheduled to return to Earth in three days and he was on the space station to prepare for his mission. An hour after the Star Rover was moored near the space station, Debbie took the shuttle to the station to retrieve him.

Jeffery went to the dining room. He found April in the kitchen and asked her to prepare a special meal for dinner that evening because Garlut would be joining them. She replied that she knew what he preferred and would have it ready in time. Jeffery was sitting in the dining room when Garlut and Debbie walked in. They were both smiling when they sat down. He asked, "So why are you two so happy?"

Garlut answered, "Because the Trade Council already approved your request to build the resort on Procolt 2. They approved it the day after I presented it to them. They were actually very excited about this possibility and approved a loan from the trade group bank to finance the construction, and additional funds will be available for working capital. The only requirement was that you submit the plans for their approval, at which time, they will be reviewed at their next meeting. If they approve them, and I am certain they will, the money for the construction will be available immediately after the meeting."

"That's great news! We need to meet with an architect as soon as possible. Is there somebody on Coplent who could handle the design?"

"Yes, I know somebody who will do an excellent job for you. I will arrange a meeting before I leave for Earth."

"Thanks. Did Debbie tell you about the squirrels?"

"Yes, she did. I think they are amazing. She asked me to speak to Max about finding somebody to take over their education and I will do that. Marcet wants to go back to Procolt 2 because she still wants to study the radiation. She has spent several months learning English and she may be able to assist Cathy and Sheila with their teaching."

Debbie said, "I think that's a good idea." Then turning toward Jeffery, she asked, "Are you ready to retire from NASA when we get back to Earth?"

"Yes, I think I am. It will be at least eight months before we get there. The next problem is, once we retire, we'll have to find a way to get back to Procolt 2. I don't think NASA will just give us a ship to use."

"I am sure they will not, since they do not have any extra ships, but I do," Garlut said. "I have two ships like the one you and Brealak took to Procolt before. I really do not need both of them, so I can give one to you. I will arrange to have it refurbished before I leave. When it is ready, I will have it shipped to Earth on one of our cargo transport ships. It will be there, ready for you, when you need it."

Debbie and Jeffery looked at each other and smiled. Then Jeffery replied, "That's very generous. I don't know how we could repay you, but I'll think of something."

"You are welcome. No repayment is necessary, but I will expect a free room and meals at your resort when it is done."

"Whenever you or any member of your family wants to visit the resort, everything will be free. Do you think we should use the trade group bank for financing? I thought you were suggesting we use private investors when we discussed this before."

"I was, but if the Trade Council wants you to use the trade group bank, you should do it. You will get better terms, and in the unlikely event the resort fails, they will not pressure you for repayment. They already know the risks and have accepted them."

There was a brief lull in the conversation. Before anyone started to speak, April came to the table with a big dish of cinnamon rolls.

Garlut said with a smile, "You know what I like."

After dinner, Garlut used his communicator to set up a meeting with the architect for the following afternoon. He told Jeffery and Debbie to be at the space station by 9:00 the following morning. He would have a shuttle there to take them to the meeting. He thanked them for an excellent dinner and asked to be taken back to the space station. Jeffery and Debbie both escorted him back.

When they returned to the ship and were in their cabin, Jeffery called Frank and asked him to join them. When Frank arrived, Jeffery said, "The Trade Council not only approved the resort, but they also agreed to finance the construction. We're meeting with an architect tomorrow afternoon and with any luck, we will be able to start construction in a year."

"Wow! That was fast. That means you two will have to resign when you get back to Earth."

"We know. What about you? Are you ready to resign or are you going to continue working for a while?" Jeffery asked.

"I'll have to think about it. We won't return to Earth for at least eight months, so I have some time."

"Yes, you do. By the way, Garlut is giving us a ship so we can get back to Procolt 2 after we leave NASA. I think we should spend the next few hours putting together a basic design for the resort so we have something to show the architect tomorrow."

In five hours, they had a basic design completed. There would be two buildings for guest rooms. Each building would have two hundred and fifty rooms. There would also be a building between the guest room buildings that would have several restaurants, offices, a check-in area, and an indoor/outdoor swimming pool. Around the outdoor part of the pool, there would be a place to get snacks and drinks as well as a shuttle port and a marina.

There was some concern about how to design the rooms because they were not sure if special rooms would be needed for people from different planets. They all agreed that would be something they would have to discuss with the architect since they were sure he would know far more about the other humanoid species than they did.

Debbie, who liked drawing, agreed to make some preliminary designs for the meeting the following day. After Frank left, she started to work and didn't finish until the middle of the night.

After breakfast, Mike took Jeffery and Debbie to the space station. Since Mike was going to spend the day training other crew members to pilot the shuttle, he went back to the Star Rover immediately after dropping them off.

When Jeffery and Debbie walked out of the shuttle bay, they were surprised to see Brealak waiting for them.

Brealak greeted them with a smile and asked them to follow her. They boarded another shuttle and began the trip to the architect's office. During the flight, they discussed the plans for the resort. Brealak was impressed and remarked that she expected the resort would be a fantastic success. During the conversation, Jeffery and Debbie learned the architect they were going to see was named Nandor and had designed many of the parks and the park buildings on Coplent.

When they arrived at Nandor's office, they found Garlut was already there. He had briefed Nandor on the project and he and Garlut were discussing it when the others arrived. After introductions were made, Debbie gave Nandor the plans she had drawn. He studied them for a while. Then he said, "This is a reasonable start. I think I have a good idea of what you want to do." Looking at Jeffery, he asked, "Are there any budget restrictions?"

Jeffery said, "I don't know. Garlut made the presentation to the Trade Council and they arranged the financing."

Garlut replied, "The council felt seven hundred hirodim would be more than sufficient for the construction. They also arranged another one hundred hirodim for working capital."

Nandor replied, "That basically means there are no budget restrictions."

Jeffery said, "I'm very happy the allocated funds are more than adequate. When we were discussing this last night, we wondered if special requirements will be needed to accommodate guests from some of the planets. We've had very little contact with other civilizations, so we really don't know if that will be a necessity."

Garlut responded, "As I told you, all of the advanced civilizations are humanoid, and our needs and desires are similar with regard to room requirements. There will be definite differences in food preferences, so you will have to learn how to prepare some native foods. To minimize potential problems, you should probably limit the resort to people from only a few planets when you open. When you become more experienced, you can open the resort to people from other planets whose food requirements may be somewhat unusual."

"What makes the food unusual?"

Garlut explained, "Well, for example, the people from Morplad only eat live food, usually small animals like the mice on Earth. On the positive side, the people are small, about four Earth feet tall, and they only eat two or three times per week. I think the bigger problem will be drinks. All of them drink water, as we do on Coplent, but on many of the planets there are unique alcoholic drinks. You will have to have the ingredients to make the drinks and you will have to know how to make them. I am sure I can find somebody to help you with that."

"I do not think room design will be of any concern," Nandor said. "I will send the plans to Garlut when they are completed. I am sure the plans will be waiting for you when you get back to Earth."

"Thank you, Nandor."

"You are most welcome. If I have any questions, I will relay them to Garlut."

After they left the office, Garlut said, "We should go back to my home. Koltep has been experimenting with some recipes William gave her and I think they are good. However, I would like to get your opinions."

"Sounds great," Jeffery said, "We're happy to help."

"I have to go to the university to discuss something with Marcet," Brealak said. "I will be home in three hours."

"That is fine, we will wait for you before we have dinner," Garlut responded.

When the three of them were on their way to Garlut's apartment, Debbie said, "I think we have a problem we should resolve before we build the resort."

"And that is?" Jeffery asked.

"Have you considered how our customers would make reservations? They can't just pick up a phone and call us or send us a message," Debbie said with a note of concern in her voice.

Garlut laughed and said, "That is not the way we make reservations unless the resort is local. We do send messages, but typically reservations for off-world locations are made at least a year in advance, and often two years. Unless you own a starship, and most people do not, you have to depend on traders to take you where you want to go and pick you up to get back home. The resorts usually make those arrangements. Remember, if you are going to vacation at an off-world resort, you will probably spend thirty to sixty days traveling in each direction. You will want to spend at least thirty days at the resort. So, you will need to arrange to be gone for at least half a year. For most people, that has to be planned. Part of that plan is communicating with the resort. You send them a message telling them how long you want to stay, and you give them a time frame of at least one hundred and fifty days for your arrival. The resort will make the arrangements and send

178

a message back. Depending on the location of the resort, it could take up to ninety days for them to receive your request. If the resort is popular, there will be trade ships at the resort frequently, so the plans could be completed in a few days, otherwise it could take up to ninety days to make the travel arrangements. After the travel arrangements are completed, the resort sends a confirmation to you."

"Wow, that's a lot more complex than calling to make a reservation. I knew we needed an interstellar communication system and this process is just another reason why," Jeffery said.

"I told you before, we are counting on Earth to invent it. Remember, to begin with, you are going to limit your customers to only a few planets. I suspect most of your customers will come from Earth or Coplent for the first year or two. That will make things simpler. We already have a regular flight schedule between Earth and Coplent. Once the construction starts, there will be regular flights between Coplent and Procolt 2 as well. After the construction is completed, those flights will continue. That will make travel arrangements easier. We will set up offices on each planet and people will be able to go there to make reservations on the spot."

"That sounds okay. I hadn't really thought about the time it takes to travel to vacation spots on other planets. That will certainly be something new to the people who live on Earth. Probably less than five thousand of the people on Earth have traveled off the planet. Giving people the opportunity to travel to another solar system will generate a lot of interest, especially if we can keep the price reasonable."

Debbie asked, "So what would you consider reasonable?"

"That's a good question. I suppose about $250,000 per person for transportation and a thirty-day stay at the resort is reasonable. People pay that for a six-month cruise, and what we're offering is far more adventurous," Jeffery offered.

"And far more dangerous as well. Garlut, what do you think would be reasonable?" Debbie responded.

"Coplent is richer than Earth, so the people can afford to spend more. The typical cost for a thirty-day, off-world vacation for two people is about .015 hirodim, or about $1,500,000. I think the price for travel for a couple from Earth should probably be around half that amount. However, we do not know what the construction costs will be yet. The bank will probably expect to be paid 20% of the gross profits to repay the loan. When we know what the loan repayment will cost, we will probably be able to estimate how much to charge the guests. I already know what the costs for transportation are, but we will probably have to estimate the cost per day to service each guest."

Jeffery and Debbie did not say anything, but they were both wondering how many people on Earth would be able to afford a vacation on Procolt 2.

When they arrived at Garlut's apartment, Jeffery was not expecting the odors that greeted him. Koltep was preparing something that smelled really good and he was pleasantly surprised.

Debbie looked at him and smiled. "That smells wonderful! I wonder what it is."

Garlut explained, "Koltep said she was going to try a few of the things William taught her how to make. I hope you like them. But even if you do not, please tell her how good everything is because she has been working on this all day."

"Of course, but I'm sure everything will be good," Jeffery said.

They were going to wait for Brealak, but she called Garlut to tell him she would be late and not to wait for her. So, they started as soon as dinner was ready. Both Jeffery and Debbie thought everything was very good. They were not sure what they were eating, but they decided not to ask. It was, without a doubt, the best meal they had eaten on Coplent. About midway through the meal, Brealak came home. Almost immediately after she sat down, she said, "Marcet and I want to go back to Procolt 2 for a while. Is that okay?"

Garlut thought for a few moments and said, "It is okay with me, but you will miss the next trip to Earth. I spoke to

180

Marcet about going back to Procolt 2 yesterday, but I did not think she was going to ask you to go with her."

"She told me you spoke to her, but Marcet and I are both anxious to get back there again. She wants to study the radiation there in greater detail and she never had much opportunity to interact with the squirrels. She has no way to get there, so I told her I would ask if it was okay to use the small ship again."

"Yes, it is okay. When do you want to leave?"

"The day after tomorrow. We will probably be gone for eighty or ninety days. I think Marcet is planning on staying for at least a year, so I will be returning by myself."

"You are going to be lonely, but I am sure you can handle it."

Two days before they were scheduled to leave for Torblit, Garlut contacted Jeffery to tell him Nandor had completed some preliminary plans for the resort. They had a meeting scheduled with him the following afternoon.

Jeffery and Debbie met Garlut at the space station late in the morning and went to Nandor's office where they spent nearly two hours going over the plans, which Jeffery and Debbie found very impressive. At the end of the meeting, Nandor said, "I will have the final plans ready in ten days. Jeffery, will you still be on Coplent at that time?"

"No, I have to go to Torblit. You should send them to Garlut. I trust him completely."

"That will not work either because I have to leave to go to Earth in a few days and I will be away for at least seventy-five days. When the plans are ready, please submit them to the bank. I will review them when I get back."

"Okay. I will send the plans to the bank. I think there is an excellent chance the plans will be approved by the time Garlut returns to Coplent. But if changes are needed that will not be a problem."

After the meeting ended, Garlut brought Jeffery and Debbie to the space station. As soon as Jeffery and Debbie left the shuttle bay, Jeffery called Mike and told him to send the shuttle to pick them up. When the shuttle from the Star Rover arrived, they were surprised to see Daryl Cohen, the ship's geologist, piloting. The chief of security, Sean Richards, was in the co-pilot's position.

Jeffery said, "Hi, I was expecting Mike. Daryl, is this your first solo flight?"

"Yes, Admiral. But the shuttle handles exactly like the simulator. It's actually easy to fly. Besides, I'm not alone. If I get in trouble," he pointed over to his co-pilot, "Sean is here to help."

"Does he have any more experience than you do?"

Sean responded, "Yes, sir. I flew it around for two hours yesterday. As Daryl said, it's very easy to fly."

"Good. Take Debbie and me back to the ship."

The landing on the ship was a little bumpy, but otherwise the flight was okay. Jeffery and Debbie walked to Frank's office to tell him about the meeting with Nandor. By then it was dinner time, so they went to the dining room and spent the next hour eating and discussing plans for the resort.

TORBLIT
JANUARY 2123

The following morning, the Star Rover left for Torblit. The trip took sixty-five days, so Jeffery ordered the cross-training to continue. Diane Thomas, the new communications officer, came to see him shortly after the announcement.

"Sir, if it's okay with you I'd like to forgo the training so I can spend my time learning to speak the Torblitian language. I picked up some Torblitian language tools during our stay on Coplent."

"I think that's an excellent idea. When we get to Torblit, you can attend my meetings. I'll wear a translator, but it only translates the words, not how the words are spoken. If you learn their language, you'll probably be able to give me some useful information regarding the conversations the translator misses."

"Thank you, sir. I really appreciate this opportunity."

"Diane, we're very informal on the ship. It's not necessary to call me 'sir,' or 'admiral' all the time. Only when we're on the bridge, or in front of other dignitaries, and of course, NASA officials. Please feel free to call me Jeffery."

"Okay . . . Jeffery, I'll try to remember that."

Three days before the Star Rover was scheduled to arrive at Torblit, Jeffery and Debbie decided they should let Mike know about their plans.

Jeffery called Mike and asked him to come to his cabin. When Mike walked in, he had a worried look on his face.

"Is something wrong?" Mike asked as he entered.

Jeffery said, "No, there's nothing wrong. But as third in command on the Star Rover I felt there was a situation you need to be aware of."

Mike's expression did not change when he asked, "What situation?"

"When we get back to Earth, Debbie and I are resigning from NASA. I'm going to recommend they promote

183

you to captain. I don't know if they'll accept my recommendation, but I wanted you to know about it."

"I knew something was going on, but I didn't know what it was. What are you going to do after you guys retire?"

"We're moving to Procolt 2. We plan to build a resort there."

"I thought you might be planning something like that, but I didn't think it would happen so soon. Is Dr. Weber going with you?"

"Yes, but I'm not sure when he'll be joining us. Debbie and I want to be there during the construction, but there's no reason for him to be there then."

"How are you going to get to Procolt 2? I don't think NASA will let you use the Star Rover."

"Garlut is giving us a small starship. He promised it would be waiting for us when we get back to Earth. Please don't tell anyone else about this. I'll make an announcement shortly before our arrival on Earth."

"My lips are sealed. You know though, Jeffrey . . . I'm going to miss you both. A lot."

"We'll miss you too Mike, but we'll be together for another one hundred and twenty days or so."

Three days later, the Star Rover exited the wormhole seventy thousand units from Torblit.

Jeffery said, "Anne, please contact the space station and ask for Commander Grisom Blort. He should be expecting us."

"Okay."

Three minutes later, Anne said, "Commander Blort is waiting for you."

"Thank you, Anne." Jeffery put on his headset and said, "Commander Blort, I'm Admiral Jeffery Whitestone, commanding officer of the Star Rover. I was told to contact you when we arrived at Torblit."

"Admiral Whitestone, it is an honor to speak with you. I do not know if you realize it, but you are considered a hero on Torblit as a result of your rescuing our three survivors from the Crosus attack on Procolt 4."

184

"No, I was not made aware of that. I don't believe I did anything heroic. I just did what I thought was logical. However, I do appreciate it."

"When will you arrive at our station?"

"It will be within the next two hours."

"When you are fifty units away, please contact the station and they will tell you where to take your ship."

"Thank you, Commander. We'll contact the station when we are in position."

"Once your ship has been securely placed, I will go there. I would like to discuss your meeting schedule."

"Commander, our shuttle bay is small and can only accommodate one shuttle. If it's okay with you, I'll bring our shuttle to the space station. We can either meet there, or I can bring you back to the Star Rover. Whichever you prefer."

"I would prefer to meet on your ship. Perhaps that will give me the opportunity to try some of the wonderful food you have onboard?"

"Okay, I'll bring our shuttle to the station and pick you up. I'll ask our chef to prepare something special in honor of your visit."

"Thank you, Admiral. You are most gracious. I am looking forward to our meeting."

When the Star Rover was fifty units away from the station, Anne contacted them for instructions on where to moor the ship. Anne gave the instructions to Mike. Mike read them and went over to the navigation console, keyed in a few commands, and said, "Jeffery, we should be secured within ten minutes."

"Thank you, Mike," Jeffery turned toward Debbie and said, "Let's go over to the shuttle bay." Then he turned toward Diane and said, "You too."

"Yes, sir."

The three of them boarded the shuttle. Debbie sat in the pilot's seat while Jeffery and Diane sat in the passenger seats. Jeffery asked, "Diane, are you ready for this meeting?"

"Yes, I don't think I'll have any problems."

"Good, then I'll let you handle the formal introductions."

When they arrived at the station, Diane was the first person off the shuttle, followed by Jeffery and Debbie. There was a man waiting for them. Diane walked up to him and in perfect Torblit said, "Commander Blort, I'm Lieutenant Diane Thomas, the assistant communications officer on the Star Rover. I would like to present Admiral Jeffery Whitestone, the commanding officer of the Star Rover, and his wife, Captain Debbie Whitestone, second in command of the Star Rover."

"Thank you, Lieutenant, I must say I am pleasantly surprised you speak Torblit. I am somewhat confused, Admiral Whitestone. You did not inform me of someone aboard who would be able to speak perfect Torblit.

"The lieutenant spent time on the trip here to study your language and become conversationally fluent."

"Okay, I understand. Shall we go to your ship now?"

"Yes, please come aboard, Commander Blort."

The trip back to the Star Rover only took a few minutes. Jeffery asked Commander Blort if he would like a tour of the ship. He said he would, so Jeffery asked Diane to take him on a tour and then bring him to the dining room.

Jeffery and Debbie went to the dining room. April saw them sit, so she walked over and asked what happened to his guest. He told her Diane was taking him on a tour of the ship and they would be in the dining room soon.

April prepared a basket of fresh yeast rolls and chocolate filled croissants and put them on the table. She also put four cups on the table and a thermos full of hot chocolate. Diane and Commander Blort arrived ten minutes later. They sat across from Jeffery and Debbie. Jeffery asked, "Well, Commander . . . what do you think of our ship?"

"It's very nice. It is much smaller than most of our starships, but it does seem to be very comfortable."

"The Star Rover is Earth's first starship. In fact, it's currently our only starship. By the time I get back to Earth, our second ship will be nearing completion. The new ship is bigger and faster than this ship. We're also starting to build our first

186

interstellar cargo ships." Indicating the plate of rolls, he added, "These things on the table are called croissants and yeast rolls, they're a very popular on Earth."

Blort chose a croissant drizzled with chocolate and took a small bite. Suddenly there was a big smile on his face and he said, "These are wonderful. Can your cook show us how to make them?"

"Yes, but I'm not sure you have the necessary ingredients. For these, you will need something we call chocolate. Chocolate can be used in a variety of ways. The beverage you have in front of you is called hot chocolate. Please try some."

Commander Blort picked up his cup and took a small sip of the hot chocolate and said, "This is excellent too. I am sure we have nothing like this on Torblit. Can we purchase some chocolate from you?"

"Yes, it's one of the products we sell."

"Is it very expensive?"

"A large box, which weighs one hundred pounds, would cost .00015 hirodim. That would be enough to make about fifteen thousand chocolate filled croissants."

"Does it come with directions?"

"I don't believe so, but while we're here our chef would be happy to train some of your people on how to make foods with chocolate."

"That would be wonderful. I will have three people here tomorrow morning for training. Do you have any chocolate aboard your ship we can purchase?"

"No, but I'll be happy to give you a box. I'll have it ready for you tomorrow. That way you'll have a few days to try it before you commit to buying any."

"Thank you, Admiral."

"My pleasure, Commander."

They spent a half hour discussing the schedule for the upcoming meetings. Jeffery gave Commander Blort the rest of the yeast rolls and croissants to take with him and he took him back to the station.

They had two meetings scheduled for the following day. There was a meeting with the Torblit representative to the Trade Council in the morning. Torblit was similar to Earth in that the major method of transportation was private vehicles powered by engines which utilized alcohol as a fuel. In the afternoon, there was a meeting scheduled with the largest vehicle manufacturer on the planet to discuss converting to electric motors powered by power modules.

The following morning, Mike took Jeffery, Debbie, and Diane over to the station. Before they left the shuttle, Jeffery told Mike there would be three passengers going back to the Star Rover with him and he should escort them to the kitchen to work with April. When the three of them left the shuttle bay, Commander Blort was already waiting for them. There were three other people with him.

"Good morning, Admiral, Captain, Lieutenant," Commander Blort said. "The three people behind me are here to train with your chef."

"Good morning, Commander," Jeffery responded. Then he gave him a box of chocolate candy bars and said, "This is the box of chocolate I promised you."

"Thank you, Admiral."

"You're welcome."

The three trainees boarded the shuttle and Mike took them to the Star Rover.

After the shuttle left, Commander Blort said, "Please follow me to the shuttle that will take us to the Trade Council office."

They walked to the next shuttle bay. Inside the bay was a very large shuttle. It looked like it could comfortably hold at least one hundred people. However, when they went inside Jeffery was surprised to see there were only seats for fifteen. There were a few sofas and five large, padded chairs that looked like recliners. At the front of the passenger compartment was a counter with six bar stools in front of it. Behind the counter was a woman who watched them as they boarded.

188

Commander Blort said, "This is my private shuttle. The lady behind the counter is Gleestol. She is my life partner and my assistant. She will make sure we are comfortable during our trip to the Trade Council office."

After all of them were seated, Gleestol asked if anyone wanted something to drink or eat. Everyone politely declined, so Gleestol sat down next to Commander Blort. Blort picked up a device sitting on a table. He pressed a button on it and the shuttle door closed. Apparently, that was a signal to the pilot that they were ready to depart. Moments later, the exterior door to the shuttle bay opened, the shuttle engines started, and it began to move slowly out of the station.

The shuttle descended quickly into the atmosphere of the planet. The surface was obscured by a thin cloud layer the shuttle passed through a half hour later. Now Jeffery, Debbie, and Diane had an excellent view of the surface. From their altitude, at about ten units, Torblit looked very similar to Earth. They could see small cities connected by roads. There were lakes and rivers as well.

Commander Blort said, "We will stay at this altitude for an hour while we travel east to our destination. If you have any questions about what you see, please feel free to ask."

"It looks a lot like Earth. How big is Torblit?"

"At the equator, Torblit has a diameter of seventy-five hundred units, so it is somewhat larger than Earth. The gravity is 10% higher, so it will take you a few hours to get accustomed to it. The atmosphere is similar to Earth's, about 20% oxygen, 77% nitrogen, and 3% other gasses, primarily carbon dioxide. Our population is six billion people. 70% of the people live in cities and 30% live in rural areas. Torblit is much colder than Earth, so most of the population lives within twelve hundred units of the equator," Commander Blort replied.

As they looked through the windows, a large city came into view. The shuttle started to descend to its destination. As it approached the surface, they could see both large buildings and small ones that looked like private homes. There were roads everywhere and vehicles that looked a lot like cars on

189

Earth. The shuttle landed on the roof of one of the large buildings. After they landed, Commander Blort opened the shuttle door and all five of them walked out. The air outside was refreshing and a bit cool. Jeffery guessed it was about sixteen degrees with a light breeze.

They walked to a lobby area and went inside. It was obvious they were expected because as soon as they walked in, a girl came from behind the counter and said, "We have been awaiting your arrival. Please follow me."

They stepped into an elevator, the girl pressed a symbol on a large display panel, and the elevator door closed. There was absolutely no sense of motion and Jeffery began to think the elevator was broken, but a few moments later the door opened and they found themselves in the lobby of a large office. The girl said, "Please be seated and I will let Malden Pinder know you are here."

A few minutes later, a man walked over to them and said, "I am the Torblit representative to the Trade Council. My name is Malden Pinder. I am very pleased to meet you, Admiral Whitestone. Please call me Malden. I have a conference room set up for our meeting. Please follow me."

They followed him to the conference room and after they were seated Diane stood and said in perfect Torblit, "Malden, my name is Lieutenant Diane Thomas. I'm a communications officer on the Star Rover. Seated next to me is Captain Debbie Whitestone, she's second in command. Next to her is her husband, Admiral Jeffery Whitestone. He's the commander of the Star Rover."

Malden had a confused look on his face for a few moments and then he asked, "On Earth when a female takes on a male life partner, does she change her name?

"Yes, that's a common practice on Earth," Diane responded.

"We do not do that on Torblit, or on any of the other planets I am familiar with. Anyway, we are not here to discuss social customs, we are here to discuss a trade agreement. We would like to purchase a minimum of one million power modules per year for at least the next ten years. Admiral

Whitestone, are you in a position to negotiate a unit price based on that quantity?"

Jeffery closed his eyes and thought for a few moments. "Yes, if Torblit will agree to a ten-year commitment to purchase one million power modules annually, the unit price for a standard power module would be .0007 hirodim."

"How reliable are they?"

"They're very reliable. There are no moving parts, so nothing can wear out. We've been using them in our vehicles for over one hundred years and I'm not aware of any failures unless the units were physically damaged."

"Do you use them on your starship?"

"Yes, the Star Rover has more than two hundred standard power modules installed to provide electrical power to all areas of the ship. There are also twenty-four high power units that are used in the propulsion system."

"Does your price include delivery?"

"No, at the present time the Earth has only one starship. We're building more, but it will be at least two years before the first ship is ready. If Torblit isn't able to pick them up, we can make arrangements with Coplent to deliver them to you. You would have to negotiate the delivery charges with the Coplent trade representative."

"I am certain that will not be necessary. Torblit has more than five hundred cargo ships. How soon would they be available?"

"If you're in a hurry to get them, I would suggest you draw up the specifications for the product you want and have them taken to Earth on one of your ships. It will take the Star Rover ninety days to return to Earth. I'm sure one of your ships could make the trip faster. Unless the specifications are very complex, they would probably begin manufacturing them in less than twenty days after receiving and reviewing the specifications. Once the manufacturing process begins, they can produce at least five thousand units per day. So, if your ship stayed at Earth for another thirty days it would be able to return with one hundred fifty thousand units."

"Those terms are acceptable. I will have a contract ready for you to sign tomorrow."

"I would also suggest you prepare the specifications for the power modules you need to purchase and allow my chief engineer to review them. He's very familiar with power module designs and would be able to detect any potential problems."

"Can he read our language?"

Before Jeffery could answer, Diane said, "Not currently, but I can. I'll go over the specifications with him."

Malden said, "I believe we now have a plan for Torblit to obtain power modules. Thank you, Admiral Whitestone, for making this transaction very easy."

"You're welcome. Earth has other products to sell besides power modules. Commander Blort has already expressed some interest in purchasing chocolate. In fact, there are three people from Torblit on the Star Rover now who are learning to prepare foods with chocolate. Are there any other Earth products Torblit is interested in?"

"No, nothing that I am aware of. My primary concern is the purchase of power modules. The vehicles we use for transportation use alcohol for fuel. Alcohol is easy to produce, but as our transportation needs grow, the amount of farmland required to grow the plants we use to make alcohol is cutting into our ability to grow food crops. As a result, food prices are rising rapidly. Since there is no way to reduce transportation requirements, the best solution is to find a new source of energy, and the power modules will be that source."

"I understand. As I mentioned, we've been using them for more than one hundred years, which includes powering our transportation needs. If you're interested, I'm sure we can provide technical assistance to help you with the necessary design modifications. Please let me know."

"That might be very helpful. We have no experience using electric motors for vehicles, and some assistance would probably reduce the amount of time needed to start production. Do you think it would be possible for some of your engineers to return on the ship we will be sending to Earth to pick up the power modules?"

"Yes, I'm certain that can be arranged. I'll give you a letter to give to the Trade Council representative regarding your request."

"Thank you. I suspect that this topic will come up again at your meeting tomorrow. If it is possible, you should bring one of your engineers to the meeting in case there are any technical questions. Commander Blort will have the contract with him when he meets you tomorrow. It has been a pleasure meeting you, Admiral."

"Thank you for meeting with us. We'll be here for a few more days before we return to Earth. If I can assist you in any way, please don't hesitate to ask."

Everyone stood up. Jeffery and Malden smiled at each other. Commander Blort also thanked Malden for his time. The five guests left the conference room and walked back to the elevator. As they approached, the elevator door opened. They stepped inside and Commander Blort gave the elevator a verbal command that Jeffery didn't understand. The door closed and the elevator took them quickly to the roof lobby. Once again, there was no sense of motion during the brief ride.

They went back to the shuttle. When they were seated, Commander Blort said, "I thought the meeting went very well. Do you agree, Admiral Whitestone?"

"Yes, I do. Malden's request was very reasonable and I gave him an excellent price. I think the meeting was beneficial for everyone."

A few moments later the shuttle door closed and they began the journey back to the space station. When they arrived, Commander Blort said, "Thank you, Admiral. Please meet me at the same time tomorrow morning."

"You're welcome. Tomorrow I'll have my chief engineer with me."

The following morning, Dean took Jeffery, Debbie, Diane, and Toby to the station. Commander Blort was waiting for them again.

When Jeffery saw him, he said, "Good morning Commander. I'd like you to meet Lieutenant Toby Grayson. He's the chief engineer on the Star Rover."

Smiling, Commander Blort said, "It is a pleasure to meet you, Lieutenant Grayson." Then he turned toward Jeffery and said, "Your chef is an excellent teacher. This morning I had a delicious chocolate cake for breakfast. Actually, the cook called it a coffee cake. I do not really know what that is, but it was excellent."

"I'm glad you liked it. Are you going to order some chocolate?"

"Yes, but I am not sure how much to order. I think I might order a few hundred boxes and then resell them here. I am sure it will be very profitable."

"The sample box I gave you was baking chocolate. It's designed for cooking. You can also buy ready-to-eat bars of chocolate. I'll have some brought over to the station when my shuttle comes to pick me up later."

"Thank you, Admiral. I am looking forward to that." Commander Blort handed Jeffery a large envelope. "This contains the contract for the power modules and the specifications we discussed."

Jeffery took the envelope and said, "Thank you." He opened his com unit, contacted Mike, and asked him to have a box of chocolate candy bars on the shuttle when it returns to the station.

The meeting lasted most of the day. A lot of it was technical and Jeffery was glad he brought Toby with him. They also went on a tour of the manufacturing facility. Vehicle manufacturing on Torblit was not even remotely similar to Earth. There was only one company that manufactured vehicles for Torblit. The vehicles had not changed in twenty years. The people usually drove a vehicle until it was no longer cost effective to repair it and then they bought a new one that was almost identical to the vehicle they had before. There were only four types of vehicles available, and the factory they were visiting made all of them.

One of the vehicles was very small and had three wheels. The engine was mounted in the back and supplied power to the two rear wheels. The single wheel in front was only for steering. There were seats for two people and a small area behind the front seats for packages. This was their bestselling vehicle.

They also made a larger vehicle that could seat four people, with a large trunk in the back. In that vehicle the engine was mounted in the front and supplied power to the front wheels.

The other two vehicles were commercial trucks that were designed for carrying cargo. All of the vehicles were going to be redesigned to use electric motors.

To keep costs down, they decided to use the same power module design for all of the vehicles. Toby and Diane spent an hour looking at the specifications and Toby said the design would not present any manufacturing problems.

When the meeting ended, everyone who attended was satisfied with the results. Commander Blort contacted Malden to tell him the results of the meeting and that he should send a ship to Earth as soon as possible. Malden said the ship would leave as soon as he had the signed contract from Jeffery and the letter concerning the requested engineering assistance.

When the four members of the Star Rover crew were onboard the station, Jeffery called the Star Rover and told them to send the shuttle to retrieve them. He also reminded them there should be a box of candy bars on the shuttle.

After the shuttle landed in the shuttle bay, Mike walked out with the box of candy bars, handed the box to Commander Blort, and walked back to the shuttle.

Jeffery told Commander Blort he would have the signed contract and the letter the following morning. Jeffery, Debbie, and Toby spent the evening going over the contract and writing the letter requesting engineering assistance.

The following morning, Jeffery went to the station with Debbie. Commander Blort was not there but was expected within the hour, so Jeffery left the materials with the station master and returned to the Star Rover.

195

Commander Blort contacted Jeffery two hours later to let him know he had the contract and the letter. He was going to deliver them to Malden later in the day and the ship for Earth would leave in the morning. Jeffery said that since his business on Torblit had concluded, he would like to leave for Earth as soon as possible. Commander Blort didn't see any reason for Jeffery to delay his departure, and Jeffery thanked him for his assistance.

The next morning as the Star Rover was preparing to leave Torblit, Mike noticed something he didn't expect. He was setting up the plot through space at the navigation station of the bridge when he noticed they would be within a half-light year from the Procolt System. Mike debated about mentioning it to Jeffery, but only for a moment.

"Jeffery, I thought you should know, during our return to Earth we'll be very close to the Procolt System."

"How close?"

"About a half light year. It would probably add sixty hours to the trip, plus the time we spend there."

"Debbie, what do you think about stopping at Procolt 2 on the way home?"

"I think it's a good idea. By now Brealak and Marcet have been there for a while. I'd like to know if they have any new information regarding the radiation. It would also be nice to see how the squirrels are doing."

"I agree. Mike, set a course for Procolt 2."

"Yes sir," Mike said with a big smile on his face.

"Why are you smiling, Mike?" Jeffery asked.

"Because I like Procolt 2, and I really want to get off the ship for a while in a place where I can breathe fresh air and walk in a big field with grass and trees."

"Okay, that's reasonable. When we get there, we'll stay for ten days and everyone will have at least two days on the surface for some much-needed R and R."

"Thank you, I'm sure all the crew members will appreciate some time off."

"How long will it take to get there?"

"Thirty-four days."

"Anne, notify the station we're leaving. Mike, as soon as we receive clearance let's get going."

A few minutes later, they were on their way to Procolt 2. During the trip they continued the cross-training. Jeffery decided that Frank and his nurse, Linda, should give every crew member advanced first aid training, and for those who needed a refresher course, he taught them how to use the automatic defibrillators that were scattered around the ship. Jeffery hoped it would never be needed, but he thought it was a good idea to be prepared.

RUSSELL FINE

198

PROCOLT 2
MARCH 2123

They arrived at Procolt 2 on schedule and Anne contacted Cathy to let her know they were making a surprise visit. Cathy was very happy the ship had returned so soon because a lot had happened since they left.

Jeffery, Debbie, and Frank went down on the shuttle as soon as the Star Rover was in a stable orbit.

When they exited the shuttle, they found Cathy, Sheila, Brealak, and S1 waiting for them.

"I'm very happy to see you guys! In fact, I'm sure we're all happy you're here," Cathy said.

"Glad to be back," Jeffery responded.

"Let's sit in the dining room and I'll tell you what's happened since you left."

They all walked to the dining room. Everyone sat down on a chair, even S1, who started the conversation.

"As you know, Cathy gave us several textbooks. We read through them with some help from Marcet. When we finished those books, we found the maintenance manuals for the Star Rover. The manuals not only discussed how to diagnose problems and maintain the propulsion system, but gave a lot of information on the design of the system. We spent several days studying the design. We're positive we can make improvements that would enable the Star Rover to travel at a velocity of ten thousand times light speed."

Jeffery wanted to ask, 'But you're only a squirrel, how could you possibly know how to do that?' However, he said nothing for several seconds and then he said, "It took our best engineers over twenty years to design the system and make it operational. Now, after studying it for only a few days, you can increase the ship's velocity more than fifty times!"

"It's only theoretical at this point, but we're certain the theory is sound. Actually, it will increase the Star Rover's speed almost seventy-five times. However, it's not really the propulsion system that will be modified. It's the wormhole generator that will be changed. If it's possible, we would like to discuss this with one of the design engineers from Earth."

"Can you write a description of the wormhole generator modifications so we can show it to the engineers at NASA when we get back to Earth?"

"Of course. We'll have that for you tomorrow. There's something else you should know regarding these changes to the wormhole generator. If they work the way we think they will, it would also be possible to create an interstellar communications system that would allow messages to travel at the same speed."

Jeffery was speechless for a moment, he just stared at S1 as his mind raced. He knew the squirrels were intelligent, but hadn't expected them to be knowledgeable about starship propulsion and interstellar communication systems. Finally, he said haltingly, "I have no idea how you became so knowledgeable so fast. However, if your theories are correct, you'll be responsible for improvements in space travel and communications we never thought were possible. Every planet in the trade group will be in your debt."

"I'm not sure how we became so knowledgeable either. It seems the more we learned the more we wanted to learn. When Brealak and Marcet arrived, we set up a class for adults who wanted to continue their education. Seven of us, including me, decided to let Brealak and Marcet teach us mathematics and physics. In about twenty days, we'd completed the basic math and physics lessons, so we began learning more advanced mathematics and physics. One of the students, S12, decided to read ahead of the rest of the class. We'd already learned trigonometry and geometry, so she learned calculus and differential equations. Once she felt she understood the mathematics involved, she began studying the advanced physics textbooks. When she finished the physics books, we decided that S12 would be our instructor since her knowledge was superior to any of the humanoids on Procolt 2."

Jeffery was still trying to comprehend everything that S1 said. He almost stuttered when he replied, "Your ability to

200

learn is truly amazing. In ninety days, you've learned more than I did in my last two years of college. If it's okay with you, I'd like you to speak with Toby. He's our chief engineer. Perhaps you could explain to him how the new propulsion system would work."

"We would be happy to speak with Toby. Please have him come to our class tomorrow morning."

"Thank you. He'll be there."

S1 walked back into the shelter. The others just stood staring at each other. Then Brealak said, "I watched them go through the textbooks in a way we never did in school. They read every word, discussed every idea, and every one of them seemed to absorb the material. I am inclined to believe what he says about increases in speed and communications capability. I watched S12 teach the classes, and although my education was excellent, I was not able to grasp the concepts they were talking about as quickly as they did. What really impressed me was when they asked questions about the material, S12 was able to answer the questions and explain the concepts even though her only information regarding the material was from reading the same book."

"Toby is probably the best person on the Star Rover to discuss these concepts with them. He has doctorates in physics and electrical engineering. It'll be interesting to get his response to S1's proposals."

Frank decided to stay on the planet, but Jeffery and Debbie went back to the Star Rover. They returned in time for dinner. While they were eating, Toby walked into the dining room. Jeffery called him over. After he took a seat with them, Jeffery said, "Toby, I have a task for you to do tomorrow. Please come to my cabin tonight at around 8:00 so we can discuss it."

"Yes sir. I'll be there at 8:00."

"I'll see you then."

Toby arrived on time. Jeffery opened the door and said, "Please sit down, Toby."

Toby looked worried as he was sitting. "Is there a problem, sir?"

"No Toby, there's no problem. I know that on our previous visit to Procolt 2 you didn't spend a lot of time on the surface. However, while you were there did you have any conversations with the squirrels?"

"I did speak to them a few times, but I was uncomfortable doing it. I found it difficult to have a conversation with an animal, even though they speak perfect English."

Debbie responded somewhat harshly, "The squirrels are not animals! The fact they aren't humanoids doesn't make them animals, Lieutenant Grayson."

Toby looked shocked for a moment at her outburst and apologized.

Jeffery added to what Debbie had said. "I believe the squirrels are extremely intelligent. I also think what separates us from animals is the ability to communicate concepts and ideas in a meaningful way. Long before we arrived here, the squirrels had developed their own language and were able to speak to each other. They created a social structure to meet their needs. They learned to live in groups in the caves to protect themselves from the environment. They gathered food and stored it at specific locations within their caves. They were very similar to prehistoric humans on Earth.

"I also believe that our coming here triggered a latent desire to learn. We enabled them to use their intelligence for the first time. Their desire to learn is insatiable. Before we left here, we gave them copies of college level textbooks. In the brief time we were gone they studied every book we gave them, and it appears they actually learned all the information in those books. Absorbed it really, and can now create diverse theories from the information. I really don't think you should consider them animals."

"Yes sir. I was unaware they had the ability to learn that quickly. Based on what you've told me I would have to agree they aren't animals."

"We're having this conversation for a reason. By using the information they learned from the textbooks, they believe they can create a propulsion system for starships that would enable them to travel at ten thousand times light speed. They also believe the same technology could be used to create an interstellar communication system and want us to bring one of the engineers from Earth here to discuss their ideas. I said I would do that, but I wanted them to put their ideas in written form so I'd have something to show the engineers on Earth. S1 told me he would have something for me tomorrow. When that paper is ready, I'd like you to review it and then, if the idea has merit, I want you to discuss it with the squirrels and report back to me. Can you do that?"

"Yes, I'm sure I can. However, it's difficult for me to believe they were able to figure out how to do all that based on the books we gave them."

"I understand how you feel, but you must approach this with an open mind."

"I will, and I'll review the documentation immediately after I receive it."

"In the event you're convinced their proposals are sound, who do you think would be the best person on Earth to make those ideas a reality?"

"Without a doubt, the best person on Earth to do that is Dr. Brandon Simpson."

"That was my thought as well. Thanks, Toby. I'll call you as soon as I get the documentation."

"I'm really looking forward to reviewing the material. Good evening."

The following morning, Jeffery and Debbie went down to the surface along with eight other crew members. They landed a few minutes after the regular morning rain had ended and were surprised when nobody was there to greet the shuttle. Jeffery and Debbie went to the shelter while the others decided to go for a hike.

When Jeffery and Debbie walked into the shelter's dining room, they were surprised to see two of the squirrels, Frank, Cathy, and Brealak seated at a table. They were all drinking coffee, even the two squirrels. Actually, the squirrels were not seated at the table, they were standing on the chairs. But it was interesting to watch them holding cups of coffee with their petite hands. It could not be easy to drink from a cup when your mouth isn't designed for it, but they seemed to be doing it without a problem.

As Jeffery and Debbie sat down, one of the squirrels said, "Good morning, Jeffrey, Debbie. I'm S12. I just finished writing the theory behind our ideas down on paper for you. S1 is reviewing it now."

Jeffery replied, "Thank you S12. I'm looking forward to reading it."

"The theory is mostly expressed as a complex formula. I mean no disrespect sir, but I'm not sure you'll understand it."

"You may be right, but our chief engineer has an extensive knowledge of mathematics and physics, so I think he'll be able to understand it."

"I would like to meet him. Can you arrange that?"

"That has already been done. I asked him to review the paper and then speak with you about it."

"Thank you. I'm looking forward to that meeting."

"Does anyone know where Marcet is? I want to find out if she has any new information about the radiation," Jeffery asked.

"She went out cave exploring with members of your crew," Brealak answered.

"When she gets back, please ask her to contact me."

"I'll do that, but I can tell you she doesn't believe the radiation presents any real danger. She has been checking our DNA every few days since we arrived here, and so far we seem to be unaffected by it. I guess people from Coplent are immune."

"That's good to hear. But I would still like to speak to her when she returns."

"Of course, Jeffery. I'll ask her to contact you when I see her."

"Thanks."

They continued talking until S1 arrived. He walked up to Jeffery and said, "Good morning. As promised, I have the documentation regarding the new propulsion and communication systems." Then he handed Jeffery a folder that contained about fifty sheets of paper.

Jeffery looked at the material. S12 was correct. He didn't really understand what he was looking at. After a while he said, "S12, you were right. I haven't looked at equations like this for more than ten years. I'll take this to Toby now."

Debbie said, "If it's okay with you, I'll stay here."

"Okay, I'll be back in a few hours."

When Jeffery got back aboard the Star Rover, he went to his cabin and called Toby. A few minutes later, Toby came in and sat down at the table across from Jeffery. Jeffery said, "Good morning, Toby. This is the documentation I received from the squirrels."

"Thank you, sir," Toby responded. He picked up the folder and began to study the document inside. He didn't say anything for about ten minutes. Then, with a big smile on his face, he said, "It's so simple. I don't know why nobody thought of it before."

"Would you like to explain it in simple terms so I can understand it?"

"Of course, sir. We've known for some time that tachyons travel faster than light. But they're difficult to detect and as a result, we've never been able to measure how fast they really travel. The squirrel's theory is that they actually travel at about ten thousand times the speed of light. Their proposal is to create a tachyon generator which could generate a field around a ship. When the ship started moving it would instantaneously attain the velocity of the tachyon particles. They believe, with good reason, an object encased in a tachyon field would be unaffected by inertia. That's also what happens when we travel through a wormhole."

"Do we know how to build a tachyon generator?"

"Theoretically, yes. That information is also in this documentation. I'm very impressed. I'll certainly never refer to them as animals again."

"Let's go down to the surface so you can discuss this with them."

"Okay, but I need to go back to my cabin and get a few things. I'll meet you in the shuttle bay, say . . . ten minutes."

Once they landed, Toby and Jeffery went directly to the shelter and into the dining room. S1 and S12 were already there waiting for them. Jeffery said, "This is my chief engineer, Lieutenant Toby Grayson. Toby examined the information you gave me this morning and would like to discuss it with you."

S1 said, "Hi Toby, it's a pleasure to meet you. I'm S1 and S12 is next to me. Do you think our proposed system will work?"

"Yes, if your formulas are correct. I'm sure the system will function as described. But I have a few questions."

Jeffery said, "This is way above my head so I'm going to go for a walk. If you need me, please call." He left the dining room and walked out of the shelter. He decided to go to the lake and find a comfortable place to relax for a while.

After he found a comfortable spot on the shore, he thought about how the squirrel's proposal could change things in the future. The trip from Earth to Procolt 2 would take less than two days. The trip to Coplent would be about the same. The enhanced communication system still would not allow for real time communications between solar systems, but it would mean messages within the trade group would be received in less than three days, and in most cases in less than one day.

While Jeffery was relaxing and letting his mind wander, his com unit beeped. He opened it and said, "This is Jeffery."

"Hello Jeffery, this is Marcet. Brealak asked me to call you, but I was going to do that anyway. I would like to speak with you but not on the surface. Can I go back to the Star Rover with you?"

"Of course. Do you want to give me a hint about what you want to talk about?"

"Not now."

"When we go back to the Star Rover we won't be coming back here until morning. Do you mind spending the night on the ship?"

"No, not at all. When do you plan to leave?"

"Probably in two hours."

"That is perfect. I will meet you at the shuttle."

Jeffery was curious about what Marcet was going to tell him and he was more than a little concerned that she didn't want to discuss it on the surface. He assumed she was concerned about the squirrels hearing what she had to say. His only thought was perhaps the squirrels were in some kind of danger as a result of their exposure to the radiation. Now he was worried and his relaxing afternoon was shot. He walked around for an hour and then headed back to the shelter.

When he got back, he went to the dining room. S1, S12, and Toby were still there, so Jeffery asked, "Did you have a meaningful discussion?"

Toby answered, "Yes, we certainly did. I now believe that their proposed systems will work and the results will change space travel forever. I want to get Brandon Simpson to talk to them. Do you think you can make that happen?"

"The order would have to come from Max, but I feel confident I can bring him back."

"When do you think we're coming back?"

"I haven't told you this, but I don't see any reason to keep it a secret anymore. When we get back to Earth, both Debbie and I are resigning our commissions. Garlut brought a small starship to Earth for us to use. We'll be returning here almost immediately. I don't know when the Star Rover will be returning."

"Who will be taking over the Star Rover?"

"I suspect it will be Mike. I'm going to recommend him for the job. I'm certain he's the most qualified person."

"I agree, Mike will make an excellent captain. On the return flight to Earth, I'll prepare a presentation for Brandon. Please make sure he sees it before you give Max your resignation."

"Okay, it's the first thing I'll discuss with Max."

"Thanks."

"We'll be going back to the ship in a half hour. Unless you want to spend the night here, you should be aboard before that time."

"Yes sir."

"Do you know where Debbie is?"

"No, sorry, I have no idea where she is now. I saw her with Brealak about an hour ago."

Jeffery used his com unit to call Debbie and let her know the shuttle would be leaving in a half hour. She said she would be there.

The four of them talked for a few minutes and then Jeffery and Toby said goodbye to S1 and S12 and walked to the shuttle. When they got there, Marcet was already aboard.

"Hi Marcet, it's nice to see you again. Meet Toby, our chief engineer."

"Hello Toby, it is nice to meet you."

"Hi Marcet, it's nice to meet you too."

"Jeffery, please wait for Dr. Weber. He'll be here shortly."

Before Jeffery could answer, both Debbie and Frank got aboard the shuttle. There was little chatter. All of them were mostly silent on the trip to the Star Rover. As they landed in the shuttle bay, Marcet said, "Jeffery, I think we should meet in your cabin."

"That'll be fine, but it's not only my cabin. I share it with Debbie."

As they left the shuttle bay, Toby walked off by himself and the others went to the cabin for a meeting. After they were seated, Marcet said, "I am sorry to be so secretive, but I did not want this information to get back to the squirrels. Can we all promise not to say anything to them about what I'm going to say?"

Heads nodded in agreement.

"Good, because I do not know how they would react. When I came here one of the goals I set for myself was to find out if the radiation could be harmful. Brealak and I brought ten mated pairs of small animals from Coplent. On the trip here I did a baseline DNA analysis on Brealak and myself, and all

208

the animals as well. When we arrived, I placed the animals in cages at various locations near the shelter. The squirrels were curious, so I told them exactly what I was doing. I took DNA samples every ten days from all of us. After sixty days there was absolutely no evidence of any DNA mutation in any of the animals nor in Brealak, or in myself. Thirty days later there still was no indication of any mutation."

Jeffery asked, "Are you saying all living things from Coplent are immune?"

"Yes, that is exactly what I am saying. All of us have been here for one hundred twenty-three days and are still unaffected. Some of the animals have had offspring and they are unaffected as well. I suspect, although I cannot be positive, that only creatures with Earth-type DNA would be affected. I really did not understand what was happening until Dr. Weber arrived two days ago. I asked him if he had ever done a DNA analysis on the squirrels and he told me he did that on his last visit. His nurse sent the results to me and I looked at them yesterday morning. What I discovered is the squirrel DNA is more than 95% identical to your DNA. The squirrels are not native to Procolt 2, they were brought here from Earth. I am certain that is why you think they look like a larger version of the squirrels you have on Earth. They are, in fact, mutated Earth squirrels."

Frank asked, "Are you sure about this?"

"Absolutely. There is no way the squirrels are native to this planet. The reason I did not want the squirrels to know is they appear to be very proud of their heritage. I am not sure how they would react if they knew the truth about their origin."

Jeffery said, "I understand, but now I'm wondering if there are other animals from Earth that were brought here and also mutated. As we explore the planet, are we going to find talking cows, or super intelligent cats and dogs?"

Marcet continued, "I do not know about that. I am not familiar with the animals on Earth. However, I suspect Gordon Brown was not the only human brought here. I am wondering if there is a colony of humans somewhere on the planet."

"When we first arrived, we scanned for any animals larger than fifty pounds and we didn't find any. So, if there are more humans, they must be very small or living in an area our scanners weren't able to penetrate."

"I think we should begin exploring all the caves we can find," Frank said, thoughtfully. "Perhaps they're here, but living in caves. If that's the case, they wouldn't have been detected by the scanners."

Marcet added to Frank's thought. "I was just thinking perhaps exposure to the radiation makes humans sterile. If that were the case, the humans brought here would probably all be dead by now."

"I think you should test Cathy and Sheila," Jeffrey said as he looked at Frank who nodded. "They've been here the longest. If you want to test me, I have no problem with that. I've been on the planet longer than any other male."

"Thank you, Jeffery, I will do that."

Debbie had a very sad look on her face and said softly, "Does that mean, there's a chance that Jeffery and I will never be able to have children?"

"We should not jump to conclusions. I will run the tests tomorrow morning. I will have an answer for you by tomorrow evening."

"Starting tomorrow, I'll assign the crew the task of searching every cave they can find for any evidence of human habitation. Debbie, you know more about the scanners than I do. Can they be set up to find caves?"

"Yes, I'm positive I can reprogram them to do that by tomorrow morning."

"Great, please do that. I'll call a crew meeting after dinner."

After dinner, Jeffery made an announcement to the crew. He said, "Good evening. I know I promised all of you some time off, but now we have an important task. We just discovered evidence there may be an enclave of humans living on Procolt 2. If they do exist, they would be living in caves. Tomorrow morning, we'll begin scanning the surface for any caves large enough to hold a small group of humans. When caves are discovered, we'll dispatch a crew to explore them. Please remember some of the locations we search may be in colder areas of the planet, so if you don't have thermal protection, they are available in the store room on deck 3. If you discover a human population, you shouldn't try to make contact with them, instead, contact the ship and we'll send either Anne or Diane to make initial contact. Questions?"

The new botanist, Mark Jackson, asked, "What makes you think there may be humans on Procolt 2?"

"Mark, you weren't on our first mission here. Are you aware of the skeleton we found in a cave near the lake during our first trip to Procolt 2?"

"Yeah, it was a guy who was in the US Army during World War II."

"Well, we now have evidence some animals were brought here as well. We think perhaps the aliens who brought Mr. Brown and the animals here were attempting to start up a human settlement. So, if there's a settlement, we should try to find it."

Thomas, the ship's exozoologist, asked, "Didn't we scan for life forms when we arrived here the first time?"

"Yes, we did. We looked for any living creature larger than fifty pounds. We didn't find any. However, our scanners are ineffective inside caves, so if they were in a cave, we wouldn't have been able to detect them. That's why we're looking for caves."

There were no more questions, so Jeffery concluded by saying, "Your assignments will be posted in your duty rosters by 0600 tomorrow morning."

That evening, Debbie finished the modifications to the scanner. It was late when she finished, so she decided to test it in the morning. Early the next morning, she went to the bridge and sat at the main scanner. She loaded the modified software and began scanning the areas near the shelter. The ship was in a stationary orbit above that area, so it would be easy to scan. She knew there were several caves in that area and in less than a minute the scanner located seven large caves. All of those caves had been explored, so she began looking for other caves near the equator. She programmed the scanner to look for caves within a five hundred-mile radius of the shelter and left the bridge to have breakfast. If the scanner located anything, the system would notify her.

Just as she took her first sip of coffee, her com unit alarm sounded. She picked up the com unit and read the displayed message. "Three caves found." She decided to finish her breakfast before going back to the bridge. By the time she finished, her com unit alarm sounded four more times. She went back to the bridge and looked at the results. So far, the system had located eleven caves in five different areas. Debbie gave the information to Mike, who promptly dispatched a team to the first group of caves located. The task would have been easier if they had another shuttle, but since they had only one, the team would check out all eleven caves before returning.

It was necessary for the ship to move so Debbie could scan another area. Mike moved the ship one thousand miles east. Debbie began another five hundred-mile radius scan. The next scan found only six caves, all located in the same general area.

After that scan completed, Debbie and Jeffery went to see Marcet in the medical office. She gave them both a fertility test and told them she would have the results in a few hours.

Later that day, Marcet called Jeffery and said he and Debbie should come to the Medical office. When they arrived Marcet said, "The news is not all bad. Debbie shows no signs of infertility. However, Jeffery's test was not as good. His sperm count is about half of what it should be. I do not know if that is the result of radiation exposure or not. However, if you two want to have children you should not wait."

"I have an implant to prevent pregnancy." Concern filled her voice. "Would you remove it, Marcet?"

"I think Frank would be better suited for that task as he is obviously much more familiar with human anatomy than I am."

"I'll contact him immediately. Thank you for doing this for us. I did want to wait for a few more years before I got pregnant, but I guess we won't wait now."

Jeffery had been silent through the whole conversation, but now all he said was, "I'm sorry."

"You have nothing to be sorry about. It's not your fault. However, you better be prepared to have sex on demand until I get pregnant."

He chuckled. "I think I can deal with that."

They went back to their cabin and Debbie called Frank, telling him the test results and requesting her implant be removed. He told her he would do it in the morning and the procedure would only take fifteen minutes.

As the sun was setting, the team reported no evidence of human habitation had been found in any of the caves. It was too late to send out another team that day.

However, the lack of light didn't affect the scanner, so the scanning process continued all through the night.

By morning, twenty-three more caves had been located. That morning two teams were on the shuttle. In one of the areas they were searching there were four caves within two miles of each other, so the shuttle dropped off the first team there. The shuttle then took the second team to an area with two more caves.

Also, that morning Frank removed Debbie's implant and told her the effects of the implant would dissipate slowly over the next thirty days. After that she would be able to get pregnant. He also suggested since there was a possibility Jeffery's condition was going to continue to deteriorate, they should consider putting some sperm in a sperm bank when they get back to Earth.

Two hours after the first team was dropped off, they contacted the ship. They had found evidence of a human settlement including what looked like a diary, apparently written in French. They also found some clothing and evidence of fires that were built near the cave entrance. They didn't find any humans, living or dead, but they were anxious to continue searching the remaining caves in the area.

No other evidence of human habitation was found that day, but the search would continue for a few more days. When

213

the teams returned to the Star Rover, the first team leader brought Jeffery the diary.

Jeffery, counting on his foreign language classes from college, opened the diary and began reading. After a few pages he offered some insights regarding the owner, "The person who wrote this was a French citizen. He was abducted around the same time as Gordon Brown. In fact, I would guess Gordon Brown was part of the same group. He indicated that when he was taken, he had this book and several pencils in his pocket. He also wrote that there were fourteen people on the ship. Eight of them were French, three of them were American soldiers, and three of them were German soldiers. All of the people were subjected to various medical tests, and after what he guessed was several months, they were put on a smaller ship which landed and they were all escorted off the ship. The ship left them here, stranded. They had no idea where they were. They initially thought they were still on Earth although they saw plants and animals they didn't recognize. Eventually, they realized they weren't on Earth anymore when they discovered the days were not twenty-four hours long."

The search for more caves and additional evidence of human habitation continued until the day before they were scheduled to leave. They had searched seventy-one caves, but none of the other caves showed any further evidence of human habitation. Also, during their search they found no other animals they could absolutely be certain were originally from Earth.

Jeffery and Debbie were disappointed with the results of the search. As Jeffery continued to read the diary, he hoped there were some names included. Unfortunately, the person who was writing the diary did not refer to anyone by name. It was basically just a list of their daily activities.

The diary described their search for food and water. There were a few fruit trees and the fruit seemed edible, albeit not very tasty. They noticed animals eating seed pods from some of the trees, so they tried those. The seeds tasted a little like peanuts and everyone in the group seemed to enjoy them. The American soldiers also made bows and arrows for

214

hunting. Since there were so few birds, they didn't have a source for feathers, so the bows were only accurate for about fifteen feet. They did hunt some animals they described as looking like large rats. The diary said the meat was tough, but it tasted decent enough. Water was no problem. There were fresh water lakes all over the area, but there was no mention of fishing. Jeffery thought they probably lacked the equipment needed to fish. As the diary ended, they were looking for something to make new clothes from, but hadn't found any suitable material. The diary ended abruptly. There were still twenty blank pages in the book, but Jeffery speculated the author no longer had anything to write with.

The night before the Star Rover was scheduled to leave, they had a party at the shelter. A special meal was prepared by the Star Rover cooks with several kinds of meat for the people and an assortment of cooked vegetables for both the squirrels and the people to share. All of the crew members of the Star Rover attended. They had to do it in shifts so the ship was not left unattended. As the party ended, Jeffery met with S1 and the people who were staying on the planet. He promised to return as soon as possible, but he thought it would be at least a few months before he would be back.

The Star Rover left the next morning for the journey back to Earth. As the ship left the Procolt system behind, Jeffery thought about how nice it would be to have the new propulsion system so they could make the trip to Earth in only two days.

During the trip, Jeffery and Debbie rehearsed how they were going to let Max know they were resigning. Jeffery also suggested Max might be expecting them to resign since by now he knew Garlut had left a starship on Earth for them.

EARTH
JUNE 2123

Every member of the crew was elated to be home. As they approached the space station, Jeffery noticed there were several large ships nearby. Two of the ships were from Coplent, but four other ships had a design he didn't recognize. After the Star Rover was securely moored, Jeffery contacted Max.

Max answered almost immediately. "This is Max Hiller. How can I help you?"

"Hi Max. We're back."

"I was expecting your call. Did you have a good trip?"

"Yes, we did. Max, I really need to meet with you as soon as possible. How soon can you fit me in?"

"If you like, I'll meet you at the space station for dinner at 6:00."

"I think that would be perfect. Debbie and I'll be there. We have a lot to talk about."

"I'm looking forward to it. See you later."

Jeffery and Debbie decided they would spend the night at the space station after dinner. All of the crew members were given two weeks leave. By the time Jeffery and Debbie had to leave, only Dean, Toby, and April were still aboard. Dean took Jeffery and Debbie over to the space station. He told them that he agreed to stay on the Star Rover for the next three days. Then, Mike was going to come back, so he could go down to the surface for a few days.

When Jeffery and Debbie arrived at the restaurant, Max was waiting. As they approached the table, he stood to shake Jeffery's hand and give Debbie a friendly hug.

"It's nice to see both of you again," Max said as he sat. "Based on a conversation I had with Garlut several weeks ago and the visit by the Torblit representative, it appears your mission was a success."

Jeffery said, "Actually, you have no idea how successful it was. I know you have a Ph.D. in physics. I want you to look at something." He handed Max the folder that

217

contained the information on the new propulsion and communication systems.

"What's this?" Max asked, an expression of confusion on his face.

"Please, look at it. I think it's self-explanatory, but if there's something you don't understand, please ask."

Max took the folder and began looking at the material inside. He didn't say anything for a few minutes. Then he closed the folder, looked at Jeffery and asked, "Is this for real?"

"Absolutely. Toby spent several hours with the designers and was convinced it will work."

"Who are the designers?"

"You probably won't believe this. These systems were designed by the squirrels on Procolt 2."

"What? You're kidding me, right? I don't believe it! You are joking, aren't you?" Max replied with a big grin on his face.

"No, I'm not. Before you tell me they're just animals, there are some things you should know. We stopped at Procolt 2 twice. When we first arrived, we discovered newborn squirrels inherit all of their parents' knowledge. When we arrived the first time, the children were about five months old. They were already capable of speaking, reading, and writing English. During the time we were there, they learned algebra. They were able to solve word problems without difficulty. Before we left, Cathy asked me for some college level textbooks they could use to continue the squirrels' education. We gave them copies of all of Peter's textbooks. By the time we returned to Procolt 2, eight months later, they'd gone through every book they had. They decided that since they knew more than any of the people there to assist with their education, they would now use adult squirrels as teachers. Believe me when I tell you they're significantly more intelligent than we are," Jeffery's face was dead serious as he spoke.

218

"Okay, they're obviously intelligent. I don't know if I agree that they're more intelligent than us. However, if this information is correct, I may be forced to agree with you."

"I think we should show this to Brandon," Jeffery said.

"I agree, but I don't think we should tell him where it came from." Max was looking over the paperwork again and thumbing through the designs one at a time.

"Does he know about the squirrels?" Debbie asked.

"No, I don't think so. We haven't kept it a secret, but it hasn't been widely discussed either. In any case, talking animals are not in the same category as advanced physicists."

"I think there's one more thing you should know about the squirrels. They're not native to Procolt 2. They're from Earth," Jeffery said just before taking a long swallow of his water.

Max's jaw dropped open. Then he shut it with a snap and asked, "How is that possible?"

"One of the people on Procolt 2 currently is a doctor from Coplent there to study the radiation on the planet's surface. She's also a geneticist. She checked the squirrels' DNA. It's not similar to any DNA found in other animals on Procolt 2. In fact, it's over 95% identical to our DNA. She also believes there's a possibility only Earth-type DNA is affected by the radiation. We think the squirrels were brought there at the same time as Gordon Brown and other people from Earth were taken to Procolt 2," Jeffery continued.

"What other people?" Max nearly choked on the words. "Did you find more human remains?"

"No, but we found evidence of a group of humans living in a cave. There was even a diary." Jeffery handed Max the book. "It's written in French."

"You know French, don't you? Did you read it?"

"Yes, it says fourteen people were abducted from France shortly after the D-Day invasion. There were eight French civilians, three American soldiers, and three Germans. There are no dates. It mostly describes how they managed to survive. It ended rather abruptly. I assumed the author no longer had anything to write with, but that's only a guess."

219

"That's interesting. I'll get this translated immediately. I'll also set up a meeting with Brandon for tomorrow afternoon. Do you want to be there?"

"I wouldn't miss it for anything. I think Toby should be there too."

"That's a good idea. Now I have a very important question for you."

"What's that?"

"Why did Garlut leave a starship at the space station for you?"

"Oh, well . . . I was waiting for you to ask about that. Debbie and I, uh, I'm not sure how to say this."

Then Debbie said, "Jeffery, sometimes you're such a coward. Max, we want to resign from NASA and go live on Procolt 2. We're planning on building a resort there."

"Well," he paused to contemplate his next words for a moment. "I can't say I'm surprised. I am, however, disappointed. I was hoping you'd be around for at least one more mission. The Star Explorer will be ready for testing in less than a month and I'd like to have you two in command during the testing phase. Please consider that."

"Okay, we'll think about it. I assume the testing would be less than a year."

"Actually, it will be only six months. After our meeting with Brandon tomorrow, I'll take you on a tour."

"Thanks, I think we'd both like that." Jeffery looked at Debbie, who nodded in agreement.

After they finished dinner, Max left to catch a shuttle back to NASA headquarters and Jeffery and Debbie checked into their room. When they were inside, Debbie said, "I'm not sure how you feel, but I don't think I want to spend six months testing the new ship. I want to go back to Procolt 2 now."

"I agree, but we owe it to Max to at least look at the new ship."

"Okay, we can look, but I don't think it'll change my mind."

The following morning, Jeffery received a message from Max asking him to be at his office at 2:00 p.m. for the

220

meeting with Brandon. Jeffery called Toby and Toby said he would be able to attend as well.

They arrived at Max's office a few minutes early. Brandon had not arrived yet, but Toby was already there. After greeting Max and Toby, Jeffery and Debbie sat down across from Max. At that moment Brandon Simpson walked in.

Max said, "Good afternoon Brandon. I'm sure you already know Jeffery, but I don't think you've ever met his wife, Debbie."

Brandon said, "Hello Jeffery. It's been a few years since we last met." Then turning toward Debbie, he said, "It's a pleasure to meet you, Debbie."

"It's nice to meet you as well. I've heard a lot about you, and all of it is positive."

"Thank you," Brandon said. Then he turned toward Toby, extended his hand and asked, "You are?"

"Hello. I'm Lieutenant Toby Grayson, chief engineer on the Star Rover. It's an honor to finally meet you, Doctor Simpson."

"Well, I appreciate that thought. But I'd rather be on a starship instead of designing them. And please, call me Brandon. We're all friends here."

Max said, "Which brings us to the reason for this meeting. Jeffery brought this to me yesterday. I would like your thoughts on it." He handed the folder to Brandon.

Brandon studied the material in the folder for about a minute and said, "This is amazing! I don't know why I didn't think of this. Whose idea was this?"

Max said, "It came from an advanced non-human civilization. Do you think we can make those proposals into real systems?"

"Yes, I'm sure of it." Then turning to Toby, he asked, "Did you review this?"

"Yes, and I came to the same conclusion."

"Max, I'd like to get started on this as soon as possible. But I would like to meet whoever came up with the idea first."

"I was hoping you'd say that because they want to meet with you too," Jeffery said.

"Where are they?"

"They're on Procolt 2."

Brandon had a confused look on his face and said, "I read the reports on Procolt 2. There was no mention of an intelligent race living there. There was some mention about some large rodents that displayed some intelligence, but that was all."

Brandon looked at Jeffery, who just smiled and nodded his head.

"Are you telling me this came from a bunch of rodents?"

"Actually, they look like large squirrels. But that's where the resemblance ends. They are extremely intelligent," Debbie offered.

"Okay, I can't argue with their ideas. I'd like to meet them. But the trip there and back would take the better part of a year. I know the Star Explorer could reduce that time significantly, but it will be a month before we can even begin testing."

"I have access to a ship from Coplent that can make the trip in less than a month. I'll take you there . . . that is . . . if Max agrees."

"Max, you have to let me go," Brandon pleaded.

"I'll make you a deal, Jeffery. I'll let you take Brandon to Procolt 2 if you promise to do the testing on the Star Explorer."

Jeffery looked at Debbie, who sighed before saying, "Okay Max, we'll do it. We'll give you another six months. Have you thought about the fact the Star Explorer may already be obsolete?"

"Yes, I've been thinking about that since our meeting yesterday. But this new propulsion system isn't going to be ready for years. I think it will be quite a while until the Star Explorer is obsolete."

Brandon said, "It may happen a lot faster than you think. It may be possible to retrofit the Star Explorer with the new system in less than three years, possibly a lot less. I'll have a better idea after I've had an opportunity to study this material in greater depth."

Jeffery said, "Max, we can leave tomorrow if that's okay with you and Brandon's demanding schedule."

"Yes, I guess that's okay. Can you be ready to leave that fast, Brandon?"

"Absolutely. Just let me know what time and I'll meet you at the space station. What do I need to bring?"

"All you need is a couple of days' worth of clothes and toiletries. Everything else will be available on the ship. Meet us at 8:00. I must warn you there's no privacy aboard the ship."

"I really don't care about that at all."

"Okay, we'll meet you at the shuttle bay tomorrow morning at 8:00. Debbie and I are going to leave now so we can make sure the ship's ready."

Jeffery and Debbie went back to the space station and had to ask where the ship Garlut left for them was. They got the information and a small device that would remotely open the shuttle bay door on the ship. Jeffery called the Star Rover and asked them to send the shuttle to pick them up. They went back to the Star Rover, packed what they needed, and then Dean took them to their ship. Jeffery opened the shuttle bay door and Dean flew the shuttle in. Dean wanted to look at the ship, so after the shuttle bay was pressurized, they all got out of the shuttle and went inside the small ship.

The ship was identical to the one Jeffery, Brealak, and Marcet used to travel to the Procolt System.

Debbie's only comment was, "You weren't kidding when you said there was no privacy. It must have been interesting for you on your trip with Brealak and Marcet."

"Interesting isn't the right word. I think frustrating would be better."

Dean said, "Thanks for the tour, Admiral. I know this ship is faster, but I think I'd rather be on the Star Rover. Have a good trip, sir."

"Thanks for bringing us over. We should be back in three months." Jeffery said.

After Dean left, Jeffery checked out the systems on the ship and everything appeared to be functioning normally and within parameters.

Now that Jeffery was finished with the systems testing, they went into the kitchen and ate dinner with food from the food generator. After dinner, Debbie said, "Since this will be our last night alone for a while, I think we should make the most of it."

"Mrs. Whitestone, you certainly do not have to tell me twice," Jeffery said with a sly smile.

The following morning, Jeffery contacted the station and asked them to send a shuttle to pick him up. Debbie was going to stay aboard. The shuttle arrived twenty minutes later. He arrived at the space station at 7:45 and found Brandon was already there.

Brandon got on the shuttle and a few minutes later, they were aboard the ship. Jeffery gave Brandon a quick tour.

"I never dreamed a starship could be so small," Brandon stated looking around the close quarters. "I'm glad I have stuff to read. Is the food from that thing in the kitchen any good?"

"Yes, the food is actually pretty good, but there aren't very many choices. Still, it's much better than the food they eat on Coplent."

Jeffery contacted the station to tell them they were leaving. He started the engine and moved away from the station. When they were fifty units from the station, Jeffery told Debbie and Brandon to make themselves comfortable because they would be asleep for the next six days. Jeffery set the course and activated the stasis field timer. They all got comfortable and then, in what seemed no time at all, six days passed and the ship was traveling at slightly more than half the speed of light. Moments later, the wormhole system turned on and they entered the wormhole. They had nothing to do now for twenty days.

Brandon had never been on a long space flight and the lack of privacy was a minor issue for the first couple of days. After dinner on the third day of the flight, he said, "If you two

224

would like some privacy I'll stay in the kitchen for the next hour. I don't mind at all."

Before Jeffery could answer, Debbie said, "Thanks Brandon, we really appreciate it." Then she grabbed Jeffery's hand and they went into the sleeping quarters. They came out some time later and Debbie thanked him again.

Six days prior to their arrival at Procolt 2, the deceleration phase of the trip began. Again, the time passed instantly and when they woke up, they were one hundred thousand units from Procolt 2. Jeffery put the ship into a low orbit above the equator. When they were over the shelter, he contacted Cathy to let her know they would be landing shortly. Cathy was surprised they had returned so soon, but was very happy about it. Jeffery also told her to let S1 know Brandon Simpson was with them.

Jeffery landed the ship near the shelter. By the time they disembarked the ship, there was a crowd waiting. Cathy, Marcet, and Brealak were there, and there were several squirrels as well.

"It is nice to see you still know how to fly our ships, Jeffery," Brealak said playfully. "Did you have a pleasant journey?"

"I really enjoyed the fact the trip took one third the time it took in the Star Rover. Pointing at Brandon he continued, "This is Dr. Brandon Simpson. He's the most knowledgeable engineer at NASA."

Brandon had a confused look on his face as he gazed at the squirrels before him. Then S1 said, "It's a pleasure to meet you, Brandon. I'm S1, the leader of the squirrels. Next to me is S12. She wrote the proposal for the new propulsion and communication systems. Did you find her proposal satisfactory?"

Brandon said nothing for a few seconds. He knew the squirrels were intelligent and could speak English, but knowing it and experiencing it were two different things. When he regained his composure, he said, "It's a pleasure to meet you as well. However, I must tell you that S12's proposal is far more than just interesting. It has the potential to simplify space travel in a way we never thought possible. Once it's implemented, it will reduce the time required and the cost for interstellar travel by more than 90%. If I had to pick a word to describe S12's proposal, it would be 'astounding'."

"Thank you," S12 said. "We have heard a lot about you and your opinion is very important to us. We would like to meet with you as soon as possible so we can discuss how we can implement the new systems. We understand the theory, but we don't have any practical knowledge about building anything."

"We can meet right now, if that's convenient for you."

"Right now is excellent. I would like to meet where there will be minimal interruptions. Do you have any suggestions?"

Brandon responded, "How about in the dining room on our ship?"

"That would be perfect," S1 said.

The two squirrels and Brandon walked back to the ship. Jeffery watched them go and once they were aboard he asked, "Marcet, did you learn anything new about exposure to the radiation here?"

"I cannot be certain about this, but it appears that long term exposure to the radiation affects male potency in creatures with Earth-type DNA. The squirrels told me 'a long time ago', whatever that means to a squirrel, there were many more births. In the last year there have been only a few. They also said previously most of the newborn squirrels died shortly after birth. Now there are fewer births, but all the newborns are healthy."

"Maybe they're having sex less."

"Based on my observations, that is certainly not the case."

"You watched them?"

"Jeffery, you do realize that while they have amazing intellect, socially, they are still animals. They cannot be embarrassed and have absolutely no modesty. Regardless of what they are doing, if they feel like having sex, they do it."

"Is there anything else I should be aware of?"

226

"Yes, the lifespan of the squirrels would appear to be increasing. I do not have any accurate records, but it appears as the birthrate has declined, the lifespan for the squirrels has increased. I do not know how long squirrels live on Earth, but similar animals on Coplent live about ten years. S1 has told me he remembers living through at least twenty winter seasons."

"I didn't notice a change in seasons here. The weather seems to be the same all the time."

"The temperature doesn't change much, but many of the trees lose their leaves in the winter and more flowering plants bloom in the spring. That's what S1 remembers. So, the squirrels are experiencing the same things humans from Earth experience in regard to sexual potency and lifespan."

"I guess that makes sense if our DNA is so similar."

Four hours later, the meeting between Brandon and the squirrels broke up. They walked into the dining room in the shelter and sat down at the table with Jeffery and Debbie. Jeffery asked Brandon, "Did you have a productive meeting?"

"Absolutely," Brandon said. "I'm certain this will work and I'm fairly certain how to build it. I suspect we could retrofit either the Star Rover or the Star Explorer in one hundred and fifty days. The only major modification required for the existing hardware would be to the wormhole generator. However, the navigation systems will have to be completely redesigned. You see, the navigation systems perform two functions. They tell the ship where to go, but they also make sure the ship doesn't fly into any solid objects. The systems are based on the speed the ship is traveling, so the systems we have now aren't fast enough to guide a ship safely when it's traveling at ten thousand times the speed of light. We'll need significantly faster computers."

"I thought the computers we have now can't run any faster."

"You're right. So, we need to redesign them to handle the new navigation system requirements. However, S12 and I have a plan to do that too."

227

"That's very impressive. What kind of timeframe are we looking at for everything?"

"I believe the projects can be done simultaneously, but the computer design will take longer, and the software design can't begin until the computer design is finished and working. I'd estimate it will take two years to make the systems fully functional. I think we should return to Earth as soon as possible so this project can be started. Also, I want to take S12 and her mate, S31, with us. I need her help with these projects."

Jeffery looked at S12 and asked, "Are you sure you want to go back to Earth with us? You'll be gone for a long time. You should realize that Earth is not like Procolt 2. It's much warmer, and there are millions of people that live in the area where you would be working with Brandon. Even the food is different."

Brandon said, "I've already discussed this with her. I have a five thousand-square-foot house with two pools, one indoor and one outdoor. The house is in the middle of a walled, five-acre lot filled with fruit trees. I think S12 and S31 will be very comfortable there."

"Okay, it does sound wonderful. I just hope the press doesn't find out about them."

Brandon thought for a few seconds and replied. "I think it would be best if we find a way to get S12 and S31 to my house in total secrecy. I'm sure Max can make that happen. But, at some point in the future the public will have to be told about them. I think it would be healthy for people to learn there are other intelligent species that aren't humanoid. Sometimes humility is a good thing."

Debbie said, "I was thinking the average person on Earth would feel threatened, not humbled."

S12 said, "I do not understand the situation. Do you really think people on Earth will feel threatened by a big squirrel?"

"Yes, I do," Jeffery answered. "I think the best plan is to keep your visit a secret. I would love to have a news briefing with you and S31 there, but this is not the time. Perhaps, after the new systems are functional would be a better time. Anyway, since the squirrels will be traveling with us, we probably need to reprogram the food generator on the ship to produce vegetables. I think Brealak knows how to do that."

Brandon said, "I'd like to wait here for a few days. I'm not that anxious to spend another twenty days on the ship. A few days with some open space and fresh air will be very nice."

Brandon and the squirrels walked away, and Jeffery looked at Debbie and said, "You were fairly quiet. Are you okay with my decision?"

"I don't think you could have done anything else. The squirrels will be fine, as long as nobody knows they're there. If the press finds out, NASA will have to post armed guards around Brandon's house."

"Yes, but I'm confident Max can handle it."

The following morning, Jeffery and Debbie were sound asleep on the ship when Brealak came in to wake them up. She shook Jeffery gently and a few moments later Jeffery opened his eyes. "Good morning Brealak, is something wrong?"

"No, but I wanted you to know Garlut will be here in a half hour. He is here with Nandor to look for areas to build the resort. I did not know he was coming and he did not know you were here, but he would like you and Debbie to go with him while they search for potential building sites."

"Okay, give us a few minutes to shower and get dressed. We'll go over to the shelter as soon as we can."

Jeffery and Debbie arrived at the dining room where Brealak and Marcet were waiting for them. Jeffery and Debbie each got a cup of coffee. Jeffery asked, "Where are the others this morning?"

Brealak responded, "Cathy and Sheila are out walking. They do that almost every morning, but usually after the morning rain. This morning they left early instead. Brandon went to the squirrel cave this morning with S1 and S12. I think Brandon really wants to learn as much as he can about the squirrels while he is here."

229

"I can understand that, they're very interesting. Since he's planning on living with two of them for a couple of years, I think he wants to convince himself there won't be a problem."

"I was listening to Brandon describe his home on Earth. He must be very wealthy."

"Brandon's grandfather was Albert Simpson. He invented the power module. As far as I know, Brandon is his closest living descendent. He still collects a small royalty for every power module sold. Those small royalties' amount to a substantial amount of money. I would guess Brandon is one of the wealthiest people on Earth. I'm sure he can afford anything he wants."

"Why does he work if he doesn't need money?"

"Because he likes what he's doing. I think he considers his job at NASA a hobby. It isn't something he has to do. It's something he wants to do."

The conversation was interrupted by the sound of a shuttle landing. The four of them went outside to meet Garlut. When Garlut and Nandor got off the shuttle, Garlut looked around and said, "It is nice to see all of you." Looking at Jeffery and Debbie, he continued, "I am especially pleased you two are here. It is a very pleasant surprise. Did you resign from NASA?"

"No, we did tell them we wanted to resign, but we agreed to work for another half year so we could test a new starship once it's completed. This trip was unexpected. We're here with one of NASA's chief engineers. I think you'll be fascinated when you find out why. Hello, Nandor."

"Hello, Jeffery. Like Garlut, I am surprised but very pleased that you and Debbie are here."

"We should go inside and you can enlighten me as to why I will be fascinated," Garlut said happily.

They went in and sat down. Jeffery started, "We made a stop here on our way back to Earth from Torblit. When we arrived, we found out the squirrels had a plan to create new propulsion and communication systems that would revolutionize space travel. They believe, and our NASA engineers agree, they can make a propulsion system that would allow a starship to travel at ten thousand times the speed of light. The communication system would use the same technology and enable messages to be sent at the same speed."

"The squirrels came up with this plan?" Garlut asked incredulously.

"Yes, their knowledge has progressed to a point where they're probably the most intelligent beings in the galaxy. I took the plan back to Earth, where it was analyzed by NASA. They agreed the theory behind the plans was sound. The squirrels asked me to bring back a NASA engineer with whom they could discuss the plan and how to implement it. So, I came back with Brandon Simpson. He has spent hours discussing this with the squirrels and is absolutely convinced the plan will work. We're bringing two of the squirrels back to Earth with us. We were planning on leaving in two days, but now that you're here, we may delay that for a while."

"You are right. This is fascinating. Do you realize what this means? When the Trade Council gave you permission to build the resort, they gave you the rights to all of the planet's resources. That would include the squirrels, so you own the plans for these new systems."

"I do not own the squirrels, or their designs, regardless of the Trade Council's decisions. I will have to discuss this situation with S1. Also, I'm not in a position to either develop or market products. If I had the rights to the designs, I'd probably turn them over to NASA and let them do the product development."

"I understand how you feel, but the rights to these developments have the potential to make you and Debbie one of the wealthiest families in the trade group. You would not need to borrow any money to build the resort."

"I really appreciate what you are saying, but I will not take advantage of our relationship with the squirrels. Debbie, do you agree?"

"Yes, we have to discuss this with S1 before we can continue this conversation."

Jeffery said, "Give us some time to find S1."

Garlut replied, "I think that is a good idea. While you are gone, Nandor and I will spend some time searching for a good location for the resort.

Jeffery knew Brandon was with S1 and S12 so he contacted him and asked Brandon to bring S1 and S12 to the shelter's dining room.

Twenty minutes later Brandon walked into the dining room with S1 and S12. He asked, "Is there a problem?"

Jeffery replied, "No, I don't think so. S1, as leader of the squirrels there is something you need to be aware of. Debbie and I have been granted the rights to Procolt 2, and all its resources, by the Trade Council. Garlut feels that means that I own the plans to the new systems, but I disagree. I believe that you own the plans to the new systems."

S1 immediately replied, "Then I will give them to you and you will own them. Is that acceptable?"

"You should know that the plans are very valuable."

"Jeffery, we have no use for money. You and your crew have been supplying us with everything we need, and we are very happy. So, let us make an agreement: We will give you the plans, and you will agree to continue to provide us with whatever we need."

"Then we have an agreement. But you must promise me that if you ever need something you will ask us for it."

"I promise. Do you want to put this agreement in writing? From what I have read that seems to be the way humans do these kinds of things."

"I suppose so," Jeffery replied. "I'll ask Garlut about it when he comes back.

Brandon and S1 left, but Jeffery and Debbie stayed in the dining room. They began discussing the situation and before they realized it almost two hours had passed. They heard the sound of a shuttle landing. Jeffery said, "Garlut and Nandor must be back. I wonder if they found a suitable site for the resort?"

They walked over to the shuttle and when Garlut and Nandor stepped out Jeffery said, "I spoke to S1 about the rights to the designs and we agreed that they would give Debbie and I the rights to the plans in exchange for us taking care of them."

Garlut smiled and said, "That seems fair. The squirrels really don't need money. What they want is primarily food, shelter, and protection."

"S1 suggested that we sign a written agreement. I'm not sure that's necessary. What do you think?"

"I suppose it's reasonable, and it does protect you and Debbie."

"Okay, do you have a contact at an attorney's office we could speak with, or perhaps the bank?"

"When I get back to Coplent, I will set up a meeting with the manager of the bank branch," Garlut said. "He will have an attorney there that will make certain you are fully protected. However, you must make sure that NASA understands you and Debbie own the rights to these new systems."

"I don't know how they'll react to that information, but I guess I'll find out when we get back."

"I do have a personal request. When the system development is completed, I would like to have my ship retrofitted with the new systems. I will pay any expenses that will be incurred by NASA for the work." Garlut looked directly into Jeffery's eyes for this statement.

"Consider it done. I'll make sure NASA understands that in exchange for the right to use the new systems, they'll have to install them in your ship."

"Good, I'm glad that is resolved. Nandor and I looked at several sites from the air, and some of them looked promising. But there are a lot more to look at."

They spent the next several days scouting for possible build sites. They finally selected an area along the equator but five hundred units east of the shelter. It was a level area surrounded by mountains. The valley was fifty-one square units and included a lake that was thirty-four square units. The site was both beautiful and tranquil. Everyone agreed it was ideal.

Now that the site selection process was completed, Jeffery told Brandon they would be leaving the following morning. Brandon said he would inform S12 and S31 about the departure schedule.

Later that evening, Jeffery was just finishing dinner when S1 walked into the dining room saying, "Good evening, Jeffery. I was told you would be departing for Earth in the morning. I'm worried about S12 and S31. Please make sure they feel comfortable in their new surroundings and try to bring them back as soon as possible."

"I promise I'll do that. I also want to ask you a question. As you know, Debbie and I are building a resort five hundred units from here. The area is really beautiful. There will be construction crews on the planet for at least three years. While they're here, I can have them build a much larger shelter for you and the other squirrels, if you'd like. I'm sure it will be more comfortable than the cave. It'll have lights, running water, and a food generator to prepare meals. If you think that's something you would want, please let me know and I'll make sure it's built."

"As our intellect grows, so does our desire to be more comfortable. A year ago, we were very happy living in the caves. We didn't mind that it was dark and damp all the time. Now we take turns spending nights in the shelter. We also have grown accustomed to using toilets. It's much more convenient than going outside the cave to relieve ourselves. So, the answer to your question is 'yes.' A shelter large enough for all of us to be comfortable would be very nice. Although we're just beginning to understand money, I know building a shelter would be very expensive. Do you have the money to pay for it?"

"Yes, I can pay for it. I'll ask Nandor to design something that will be a comfortable home for at least two hundred squirrels. That way there will be room for growth."

"Could it also have rooms to use to teach our children?"

"Yes, of course. Why don't you think about it while I'm gone? When I come back, we can discuss it."

234

"Thank you, Jeffery. We'll do that."

The following morning, Jeffery and Debbie were aboard the ship running pre-flight diagnostics when Brandon and the two squirrels arrived.

"Good morning. Is everyone ready for the trip to Earth?" Jeffery said.

"S31 and I are concerned because we've never spent very much time in such a small space," S12 replied.

"I understand and this is a very small ship. I thought perhaps you and Brandon could work on some of your designs during the trip. I'm not sure what S31 would like to do. We have an unlimited supply of food, if he likes to eat. We also have games he might be interested in playing."

"I think unlimited food will keep him occupied."

"Good. Did Brandon explain how this ship works?"

"He did tell me about the stasis field that's used to minimize the effects of inertia while we're accelerating or decelerating."

"After we're five thousand units from Procolt 2, I'll set the course for Earth. A few moments after I start the engines, a stasis field will envelop the living areas on the ship. We won't be aware of anything while we're in stasis. When the field collapses and we wake up it will be six days later, we'll travel for twenty days, and then we'll be placed in stasis for six days again while the ship slows down. When we wake up the second time we'll be just above Earth," Jeffery continued. "Please find a comfortable place and sit or lay down."

Brandon sat in one of the passenger seats and S12 and S31 laid down on seats. Jeffery was happy this ship was equipped with artificial gravity, so no taping of the squirrels was necessary. After everyone was ready Jeffery, started the engine. A half hour later, the ship was ready to begin the journey to Earth. Jeffery looked at the squirrels. They were both sound asleep, so he set and initiated the course for Earth.

Six days later, they woke up when the stasis field turned off. S31 looked up at Jeffery and asked, "Are we ready to start the trip to Earth now?"

Jeffery smiled and said, "We left Procolt 2 six days ago. We're several light years away now. In a few moments, we'll enter the wormhole and begin the longest part of our journey to Earth."

During the trip, Brandon and S12 spent time working on the new computer hardware that would be required. The processor chip would use tachyons to send information inside the chip instead of wires, which would increase the speed of the processor by several orders of magnitude.

Debbie taught S31 how to play some card games, including an old Earth favorite, solitaire. He seemed to really like it, so he split his time between playing cards and eating. He appeared to be enjoying not only the food, but some of the classic card games.

Neither of the squirrels had ever taken a shower, but after watching the humans take showers for a few days, they decided to try it. The showers were automatic, a few seconds after anything enters the shower the water turns on and it stays on until the shower stall is empty. S12 and S31 went into the shower together and played for almost an hour. They decided it was fun to take showers and did it almost every day during the remainder of the trip.

When they arrived at Earth, both S12 and S31 were a little disappointed the trip was over because the journey was full of new wonderment for them.

Shortly after docking at the space station, Jeffery called Max.

"Hi Max, we're back. And we have two surprise guests with us."

"I'm almost afraid to ask, but who are the surprise guests?"

"S12 and S31 from Procolt 2 are here. S12 wrote the proposal you read, and Brandon thought it would be helpful if she was here during the construction of the prototypes."

"Do you think the world is ready for squirrels that are more intelligent than we are?"

"No, not really. So, they're going to stay at Brandon's house."

"Don't you think somebody will notice them when they walk through the station?"

"Yes, so we aren't going to go through the station. This ship can land on Earth, so I'll land it near Brandon's house and we'll get them to his house unseen."

"I know Brandon's house is out in the middle of nowhere, but somebody will see the ship and it will be seen by air traffic control as well."

"I'm sure you can take care of that."

He sighed. "I suppose so. I'll need some time to arrange everything. I'll call you in the morning. Is that okay?"

"That's fine. Have a good evening, Max."

"Yeah, I'll try."

Early the next morning, Jeffery received a call from Max who told him to land the ship at NASA Headquarters, but not to leave it. Max would bring a bus out to the ship and then take them to Brandon's house. Jeffery said they would leave as soon as possible, probably within fifteen minutes.

It took a little longer than Jeffery had estimated. Twenty minutes later, the ship left the docking area for the space station and began the descent to NASA Headquarters. Less than an hour later, Jeffery landed the ship and moved it to the end of a taxiway so it didn't interfere with any other craft.

A few minutes after they stopped, the ship was approached by a small bus. It stopped by the ship's hatch and Jeffery opened it. Max walked aboard accompanied by an armed guard.

When Jeffery saw them, he said, "Hi Max. Did you think we were going to attack you or something?"

"Not likely. The guard is here to protect you and your passengers, not me. I'm anxious to meet them."

"Max, I'd like you to meet S12 and S31."

"Hello Max," S12 said. "It's very nice to meet you. Brandon has told us a lot about you. I must say you really don't look scary."

"Brandon said I was scary? I'll have to discuss that with him later. Before your ship becomes the center of attention, we should all get on the bus and leave."

"We're all ready. However, I want to come back here tomorrow and moor the ship by the station," Jeffery said.

Max responded, "That's a good idea. I'll pick you up in the afternoon and we can make the trip together."

Everybody walked over to the bus. Jeffery closed the hatch with the remote and boarded the bus last. The guard took the driver's seat and after everyone was aboard, the bus started moving.

Jeffery was watching the squirrels who were staring out the windows. They had never seen anything even remotely similar to things they saw as the bus traveled through central Florida. They had never been in a civilized area before and were obviously fascinated. After driving for a half hour, they turned off the main road onto a narrow country road. All of the signs of civilization disappeared. There were large fields filled with palm trees and palmetto plants. Ten minutes later, they arrived at Brandon's house. There was a nine-foot brick wall around the property and a guard at the only road leading into the walled compound.

Brandon walked to the front of the bus and waved to the guard who opened the gate. They drove up to the house and stopped in front.

S31, who had not said a word since they got off the ship, looked at the house and then, looking at Brandon, asked, "You live here by yourself?"

"No, I have two people who work for me who live here too. There's a woman who cooks most of my meals and keeps the house clean. Her name is Bess. Her husband, Tom, takes care of the outside of the house and the swimming pools."

Everyone except the guard got off the bus. The driver asked Max if he should wait for him. Max told him that he would be here for a while and not to wait. The others walked into the house where Bess was waiting for them.

238

"Hi Brandon," Bess said as they all came into the foyer. "It's nice to have you home and I see we now have some pets."

"Hi Bess, these aren't pets. They're from Procolt 2 and will be our house guests for the next year or two. I'd like you to meet S12 and her mate S31."

Bess had a confused look on her face, which became more pronounced when S12 said, "Hello Bess. It's very nice to meet you."

Stammering she said, "It's n-nice to m-meet you too." Then looking at Brandon, she asked, "Is this some kind of trick?"

"No Bess, S12 and S31 may look like animals, but S12 knows more about theoretical physics than I do. She'll be helping me design new propulsion, communication, and computer systems for NASA."

Looking at the squirrels again, she said, "I'm sorry. You're the first aliens I've ever met and I guess I expected aliens to kind of look like we do. Please forgive me."

"There's nothing to forgive," S31 responded. "We understand you were surprised by our appearance."

Brandon said, "Bess, let Tom know about our guests. They'll be staying in the main guest room next to the indoor pool. So, please make sure it's ready for them."

"I'll take care of that right away."

"Since none of you have been here before," Brandon offered. "Let me show you around."

The house was built around a central atrium that contained a large indoor pool and many small palm trees and other flowering plants. The squirrels were obviously amazed with the pool area.

"This is like a small indoor lake," S12 said. "I think we're really going to like it here."

The guest bedroom, where the squirrels would be staying, was very spacious. The room contained a large bed, several comfortable chairs, a big video monitor, and had its own bathroom.

Behind the house, there was a pool much larger than the one inside. There were also chairs and resort style chaise lounges scattered around. The pool also had a diving board. Surrounding the pool area were much larger palm trees and other native Florida plants. Adjacent to the area was another smaller house where Bess and Tom lived.

After looking around, Jeffery asked, "Brandon, would you like to adopt Debbie and me?"

Brandon laughed. "No, I really don't, but you're welcome to stay here. The house has three more unused guest rooms."

"This is definitely a lot nicer than what we have at NASA," Debbie said with a smile. "Thanks, Brandon, we'll think about it."

"Brandon, can S31 and I play in the pool for a while?" S12 asked.

"Of course, please enjoy yourselves. Tomorrow we'll continue working on the computer design. By the way, there's something you should be aware of. This area isn't like Procolt 2. There are many large predators here. So, for your own safety, please don't leave the compound. Inside the compound, in the grassy areas, you'll probably see some large birds. They won't hurt you, so you don't have to be afraid of them. I know there aren't very many birds on Procolt 2, but this area has a lot of them."

The squirrels ran to the pool and jumped in. They stayed in the shallow end of the pool since they didn't swim very well. The others watched them play for a while and then went back in the house. They walked into the atrium and sat down at a table overlooking the pool.

Jeffery said, "Max, I think you should consider halting construction on the Star Explorer until the new systems that Brandon and S12 are designing are ready. The ship would be obsolete before construction is completed."

Before Max could respond, Brandon said, "We have three large projects to complete. The new propulsion system, the new communication system, and we'll need a new navigation system as well. The current navigation systems

240

aren't fast enough to work effectively with the new propulsion system. I believe that we can have all three projects completed in less than two years."

"I see your point," Max said. "Unfortunately, it's not my decision. I'll have to discuss it with the directors."

"There's something else you should be aware of," Jeffery said as he looked at the pool. "Debbie and I have an agreement with the squirrels. We agreed to provide for all their needs in exchange for the rights to the new systems. As a result, Debbie and I own the rights to the new systems. NASA is free to use them at no cost, but I suspect NASA will soon find itself in the business of outfitting ships from other systems with the new designs. When that happens, Debbie and I will be entitled to a royalty on each new system."

Max thought for a few moments and said, "Since NASA will be paying for a lot of the development, I would think we would actually own the rights to the completed systems."

"Max, NASA will make billions from these systems. I'm only looking for a small piece so I can finance the construction of the resort. I really don't think adding 5% to the cost for Debbie and me is asking too much."

"I guess you're right. If it wasn't for you two, none of this would be happening. I'll contact someone in our legal department to draw up a contract."

"Thank you. One more thing: I promised Garlut that when you start retrofitting ships with the new systems, his will be first."

"I'll bet you told him we would do it for free too."

"Yes, I did. But if I have to, I'll pay for it out of my royalties. You should consider the experience NASA gains from retrofitting Garlut's ship will result in a substantial amount of new opportunities. NASA could become the primary source for building and retrofitting starships in the trade group."

"I suppose that's a possibility, but NASA is primarily a research organization. I suppose we could create a subsidiary that would build and retrofit starships. Now I have two items for discussion at the next directors' meeting."

The rest of the day was spent relaxing. Jeffery and Debbie decided to accept Brandon's offer to stay there for a while. The squirrels spent most of the day playing in the outdoor pool and sleeping. They woke up around dinner time and walked into the house asking Brandon where they could get food. Brandon told them dinner would be ready soon and Bess had prepared a roast beef dinner with roasted potatoes, green beans, and glazed carrots.

When dinner was ready, Bess asked Brandon, "Should I set places at the table for S12 and S31?"

"They're very civilized and know how to use silverware, but they still prefer to use their hands. So, to answer your question, yes, you should set places for them at the table."

Dinner went very well. The squirrels loved all of the vegetables, and the others were grateful for a meal that was not prepared by a food generator.

After dinner, Jeffery and Debbie took Max back to NASA Headquarters using one of Brandon's cars. After they dropped him off, they went to their quarters and picked up what they would need to stay at Brandon's.

Max came back the following afternoon and took Jeffery to where the ship was. Jeffery flew the ship up to the space station and secured it. Four hours later, they were back at Max's car.

Jeffery, Debbie, and S31 spent a few days enjoying all that Brandon's house had to offer. The food was excellent, their room was both comfortable and private, and Bess and Tom made sure they had anything they needed. S12 and Brandon spent the same two days completing the design for the new computer systems.

Brandon and Max had been speaking to each other several times a day. Max scheduled a board meeting and wanted both Brandon and S12 there. Since Max didn't want to bring S12 to NASA Headquarters, the meeting was going to take place at Brandon's estate.

In addition to Max, there were nine other directors at NASA. By 10:00 a.m., they had arrived at Brandon's house and were seated at his conference room table. Edward Nichols, the chairman, called the meeting to order at 10:15. Then he said, "This meeting is very informal. I'm going to ask Brandon Simpson to speak with us about some new projects. Brandon has already started doing preliminary work on one of the projects with his partner, S12."

When the chairman sat down, Brandon stood up and said, "Good morning. In front of you is a report prepared by Admiral Jeffery Whitestone concerning the events and discoveries that have occurred on Procolt 2. Before I continue, I would like each of you to spend a few minutes reading the report."

Brandon sat down and studied the faces of the directors as they read the reports. Several of them showed obvious disbelief, but he knew that would change shortly. When everyone had finished reading the report, he stood up and said, "I'd like you to meet my partner, S12."

The members of the board were aware that S12 was not humanoid, but it was still a shock as they watched her walk into the room.

S12 got up on the chair next to Brandon. She looked around at the directors and said, "Good morning. I wanted to elaborate on the information in the report you just read. When we first encountered Jeffery and Debbie, we'd already developed a simple spoken language. It had only about two hundred words, but it was sufficient for our needs. We were familiar with our environment and we weren't the least bit curious about what existed in other places. We had food, water, and shelter. That was all we really needed.

"However, that all changed very quickly. Jeffery introduced us to new foods and Cathy Carter decided to learn our language so she could speak to us. We surprised her because while she was learning our language, we learned to speak English. We discovered we had an insatiable desire to learn new things. We had no concept of numbers or time. Cathy and Sheila taught us those things. Once we understood those concepts, our education really began. Within a half year, we'd learned what most humans take twelve years to learn. Then, after we received some college level textbooks, we continued our education. Two women from Coplent helped us for a while, but it soon became apparent we were more knowledgeable than they were, so I took over the responsibility of teaching.

"My knowledge of theoretical physics is quite extensive. By utilizing this knowledge, I was able to create the proposals that led to Brandon's trip to Procolt 2, and ultimately, my being here today." S12 sat down.

Brandon stood up and said, "I can attest to S12's knowledge of physics. When it comes to theoretical physics, she's certainly more knowledgeable than I am. However, she's unable to convert the theory into practical applications. That's something I do very well, so together we make an excellent team. I know it's hard for you to believe what you just heard. When I first met S12, I simply couldn't believe something that looks like a big squirrel could be intelligent. I now believe, and I'm not alone in this opinion, the squirrels from Procolt 2 have a greater capacity for learning than any other species we're aware of."

Brandon spent the next several minutes explaining the proposed systems. Then he said, "I estimate it will take two years to bring these proposed systems to the testing phase and possibly another year to test the systems before we can begin installing them into starships. Once we do that, the entire trade group will be here asking us to build new ships for them or retrofit their existing ships. The development will not be cheap. I would guess we're looking at three to five trillion dollars, but we'll make that back very quickly. I suspect you have questions. Please let Max speak and then we'll answer all of your questions."

Brandon sat down and Max stood up, cleared his throat and began. "When Jeffery came back from his previous mission, he brought the proposal S12 wrote to me. I'm enough of a scientist to know the proposal looked promising. I gave the proposal to Brandon and he confirmed everything in the proposal was plausible, so I sent him to Procolt 2 to discuss it in depth with S12. Brandon is now certain the systems will work as indicated. I've also had some discussions with the Trade Council representative on Earth. He assured me that if we build these systems, every member planet will become our customers. Earth will become the wealthiest planet in the trade group. We don't have to do all the actual work. We can use subcontractors on other planets, but we'll get a large slice of each transaction. If the final cost does turn out to be five trillion dollars, we'll be able to recover that in less than three years.

"I realize NASA doesn't have the money to finance this endeavor, but the World Council does. It must be brought to their attention as soon as possible. If they turn this down, another planet will build it. I urge you not to let that happen."

Max sat down.

"I'll call the president about this today. I'm sure the World Council will agree to finance the project," Edward Nichols stated.

There were only a few questions. One of the questions regarded the construction of the Star Explorer. Max purposely hadn't brought it up because he was sure one of the directors would ask about it. Max said construction should be halted until the new systems are available. Every director at the table agreed.

After the meeting was over, Max called Jeffery. "Jeffery, I have some good news for you. I'm releasing you from your commitment to test the Star Explorer. The directors have halted construction until the new systems are available. I'd still like you and Debbie to do the test missions because you two are the most qualified pilots we have, but I would certainly understand if you decline."

"Thank you for the information. We'll probably return to Procolt 2 in a few days. At this point, I obviously don't know what we'll be doing two years from now. However, I'm sure we'll make a few trips to Earth during that time, so I'll keep in touch. Do you know when the Star Rover is scheduled to return to Earth?"

"Right now, it's at Coplent. They're installing a time stasis system and will return to Earth as soon as that's completed. They should have arrived at Coplent five days ago. The time to complete the installation is ten days so, after the system is operational, they'll be able to return to Earth in thirty days. I would guess they should be back here in thirty-five or forty days. Why?"

"I wanted to talk to Frank Weber about something."

"Is Frank going to quit on me too?"

"I don't know for sure, but he did tell me he wanted to work at the resort when it's completed. I do know he loves what he's doing and he's very good at it. I just want to let him know what the schedule is."

"Garlut told me on his last visit it would take three years to build. I think they may have already started construction."

"I think you know more about the resort schedule than I do. Maybe Debbie and I will be surprised when we get back. Please let Frank know the schedule when you see him. This lack of communication is going to drive me insane. As soon as the new communication system is ready, I want Procolt 2 to be a part of it."

"I think that's a reasonable request. Since you're living with Brandon, I'm sure you're aware the communication system will be developed as soon as the new computer systems are finalized."

"Yes, I discussed that with him and S12 yesterday. They may be ready for initial testing of the communication system in about one hundred and twenty days."

"Maybe you should delay your return to Procolt 2 until after the initial testing has been completed."

"I'll discuss it with Debbie, but I don't think we want to wait that long before we return. I'll call you tomorrow to let you know."

Jeffery and Debbie discussed it and decided they didn't want to delay their return to Procolt 2. Jeffery called Max and told him about their decision to return to Procolt 2 almost immediately and Max wished them a safe journey.

They spent their last day before their departure relaxing at Brandon's house, swimming and watching the squirrels play. That evening, Brandon drove them to NASA headquarters and they took a NASA shuttle to the space station. Once they were there, they arranged a ride to their ship on a small shuttle. They checked out the systems on the ship and everything functioned normally, so they left immediately.

Once they were a few thousand units from the space station, Jeffery programmed the navigation system to take them to Procolt 2. A minute later the time stasis field initialized and their trip to Procolt 2 started.

Since they were alone on the ship, they took advantage of the situation and tried their best to start a family. It made Debbie wonder if she would ever get pregnant, but she didn't discuss it with him. Finally, when she was expecting her period to start, it never came. She purposely didn't mention it to Jeffery until she was sure about her condition. She was thrilled about being pregnant, but now she had another concern. Did she actually want to give birth on Procolt 2? She would have to make that decision quickly.

When they landed at Procolt 2, Cathy, Sheila, and S1 were waiting for them to get off the ship. As soon as they did, Cathy said, "We weren't expecting you to return so soon. How did things go on Earth with S12 and S31?"

"Everything is fine," Debbie said. "They're living with Brandon and almost nobody knows they're there. S12 and S31 are having a great time. They spend hours every day playing in and around the pool. S12 and Brandon were working on a new computer system. Once that's completed, they're going to start working on the new communication system."

S1 said, "I'm glad they're happy. Did the people at NASA have any problems with S12's proposals?"

"No, there was a meeting at Brandon's house with the board of directors," Jeffery said. "During the meeting both Brandon and S12 spoke to them. I think that convinced them they had merit."

Sheila said, "You just missed Marcet and Brealak. They went back to Coplent two days ago. Brealak said she had something to discuss with Garlut and Nandor concerning the resort, but she didn't say what. You should also know a ship from Coplent arrived twenty-five days ago and they're doing some of the preliminary work on the resort."

"Tomorrow Debbie and I will go over there and see what they're doing. Did Brealak or Marcet say when they expected to return?"

"Brealak said they were going to spend a few days there and then come back."

Debbie said, "I hope they come back soon. I have a question for Marcet."

Jeffery looked at her. He had a rather puzzled look on his face and asked, "What question do you have for Marcet?"

"I probably should have mentioned this before, but I missed my last period and I wanted her to check to see if I'm pregnant."

Now Jeffery smiled, hugged her, picked her up in the embrace, and then kissed her. As he set her back on her feet he said, "That's great news! I sincerely hope you are, but I'm a bit concerned about the lack of medical facilities."

"I've been thinking about that for several days now. This may be my only opportunity to have a baby, and I want to be sure nothing goes wrong."

Cathy said, "Perhaps you guys should go back to Earth right now. You should absolutely take every precaution to be sure you have a normal pregnancy."

"Cathy's right," Jeffery said, showing some concern in his voice. "Marcet won't be back for at least sixty days."

"I've had some medical training," Sheila offered. It has been a while but before I decided to become a botanist, I was a pre-med student. I also worked for two years as an Emergency Medical Technician. During that time, I participated in three births. If you decide to stay here, I'll help you in any way I can."

"Thanks Sheila, I'll have to think about this for a few days. I'm not absolutely sure I'm pregnant, but if my period doesn't start in the next few days I'll know for sure. As long as we're here, I want to see what progress has been made on the resort."

"Okay, but if it turns out you are, we should probably return to Earth as soon as possible." Jeffery tried to not make it sound like an order.

"I understand how you feel, but I just don't want to go for another trek through space right now. There's another consideration too. I don't know if exposure to the time stasis field would have any negative effects on the baby." Debbie placed a careful hand on her abdomen.

"I hadn't thought about that. I guess we have some thinking to do."

They all went inside and sat in the dining room. Cathy got coffee for everyone. Nobody said anything for a while until S1 said, "I realize we're physically different from humans, but I suspect our reproductive systems are similar since we're both mammals. Some of our females have been trained as what you would call a midwife. Perhaps they could be of some help in this situation."

"Well, that would be interesting. I could be the first human to give birth with the assistance of squirrels. I really do appreciate the offer. If I do decide to stay here, I'll gladly accept any help I can get."

The following day all four humans went to the resort construction site. There were at least thirty people working there. The workers had already prepared the surface for the buildings and all the buildings were staked out. Jeffery landed the ship nearby and as he walked toward the construction site a large man, at least seven feet tall, walked toward them. When he was ten feet away, he said, "I am Kransk, manager of this operation. I will bet you are Admiral Whitestone. Garlut told me to be expecting you."

"You're right, Kransk, I'm Jeffery Whitestone. Please call me Jeffery. This is my wife Debbie, and our friends Cathy and Sheila. How are things going?"

"I am pleased to tell you we are ahead of schedule. The land was much easier to prepare than we thought. We will be able to complete the base for all three buildings within fifteen days. Then my crew and I will go back to Coplent and the exterior construction crew will take over and build the actual structures. They will probably arrive a day or two before we leave. I believe Nandor will be here for the initial part of the construction."

"That's good news. I hope the rest of the project goes as smoothly. Is it okay if we look around?"

"Sure, I thought you should know, every member of my crew really likes this location. All of them would like to come back here for a vacation if they can afford it." He laughed a bit with the remark.

"I'm sure we can arrange for the entire construction crew to come back here when the resort is finished at no cost. That way you can check out all the things you built and correct any problems before we open."

Kransk thought for a few moments and said, "I think that is a wonderful idea. Do you think we could bring our families too?"

"I'm sure that would be okay. How many construction workers do you think will be working on the project?"

"All the crews are about the same size. My crew has thirty-four people. Two more crews will also be working on the project. One will do the exterior construction and the other will finish the inside. I believe there will be about one hundred and twenty people."

"I'm certain we'll be able to handle one hundred and twenty families. I'll ask Nandor for a list of all the workers and when we're ready, we'll send out invitations. Are all the workers from Coplent?"

"We all live on Coplent now, but many of us are from other planets. Is it okay if I tell my workers about this?"

"Of course, but remember it will probably be at least two years before the resort will be ready for guests."

"That is okay. A free vacation in two years is worth waiting for. Thank you. If you need anything or if you want to look at the plans, just stop by my office."

"Okay, I may do that since I've never seen the finished plans."

The four of them walked around the construction site for a while and then went to Kransk's office. Kransk showed them the plans. Jeffery was truly impressed. After reviewing the plans for a while, he asked, "Debbie, did you ever think we'd own something like this?"

"No, of course not. I'm still having trouble believing it. But the plans look wonderful. Since these are only exterior plans, I think it would be nice to see what the inside is going to look like, but I guess that will have to wait."

Jeffery rolled up the plans and gave them back to Kransk. "Thank you. We'll probably stop back in ten days or so to see how things are progressing."

"You are welcome. Please feel free to come back anytime."

Jeffery and the women went to their ship and were soon back at the shelter. As they got off the ship, Debbie looked at Jeffery and said, "I don't want to go back to Earth to have the baby. I want to stay here and watch our resort being built. Besides, we both really like it here and I'm sure Marcet will be here to help."

"I don't want to go back either, but I want it to be your decision. I'm sure the baby will be fine and you'll have all the help you need."

Debbie sighed deeply, feeling comforted by the show of support, "I'm glad that's settled."

Ten days had passed and Debbie was positive she was pregnant. She was still certain she made the right decision about staying on Procolt 2, and Jeffery had his worries but supported her decision to stay.

They went back to the construction site and now, instead of stakes and string markings, there was a plastic-type substrate slab at least three feet thick at the base of each building. As they looked at the slabs, Kransk walked over and asked, "What do you think about our progress, Jeffery?"

"I don't know much about construction. I wonder if plastic would be strong enough to support a building."

"This plastic is probably the strongest building material I have ever worked with. What you do not see is that

251

each base has four supports that go about 2/10 of a unit into the ground for the tower buildings. That is more than twice the height of each of the buildings."

"That sounds pretty impressive. In Earth terms, each base support goes almost thirteen hundred feet into the ground."

"We are now five days ahead of schedule and will be finished by the end of the day tomorrow, but since we have no ship to take us back to Coplent, we will have to wait for the next work group."

"Isn't the ship scheduled to arrive in a few days?"

"Yes, we do not mind waiting. Speaking of waiting, I wanted you to know every one of my workers is excited about returning here. They do not make enough money to pay for off-world vacations and this is a once in a lifetime opportunity for them."

"I'm happy to do it. Please tell them they did an excellent job."

"I will pass that on to them. They will appreciate it."

The group left the construction site and went back to the shelter. A few days later, Jeffery was contacted by Kransk who told him the new crew had arrived and they would be returning to Coplent immediately. Jeffery wished him a good journey and said he would look forward to seeing him again when the resort was completed.

That evening while they were eating dinner, Jeffery said, "We have to come up with a name for the resort. I don't want to keep calling it 'the resort.'"

Debbie said, "How about Procolt Paradise?"

"Oh, I like that. Does anybody else have any suggestions?" Jeffery asked.

"How about Squirrel Haven?" S1 said. Then he did something they had never seen before, he laughed. It was the first time any of the squirrels had made any attempt at humor.

"I like Procolt Paradise better," Jeffery said with a smile. "If you like, we could build Squirrel Haven next to Procolt Paradise."

"I think we would like that very much. We really don't want to live in caves anymore."

"S1, I promise you I'll have Nandor design Squirrel Haven for you and we'll build it. Would you like it here or near Procolt Paradise?"

"I haven't seen the area where Procolt Paradise is being constructed. Can you take me there?"

"Of course, we can go tomorrow. I'm sure you'll like it."

"Are you going to have to tape me to the seat again?"

"No, we won't be going into space so gravity isn't an issue."

"Good, that was very uncomfortable."

The following morning, after the rain ended, Jeffery, Debbie, and S1 flew over the area where Procolt Paradise was being built. S1 liked what he saw and said he would like Squirrel Haven built nearby. Jeffery landed the ship, and just like before, the manager of the construction crew walked over. He was much shorter than Kransk and somewhat heavier. As he approached Jeffery said, "Good morning. I'm Jeffery Whitestone, the owner of this property."

"Good morning. Kransk said you would probably stop by and I should call you Jeffery. Is that okay?"

"Yes, of course. What's your name?"

"You can call me Treb. My name is long and difficult to pronounce."

"Okay Treb, it's nice to meet you. We're living in a shelter five hundred units west of here. I'll probably be coming by every few days just to see how things are going."

"That is okay. You are welcome to come by anytime. Right now, we are just getting started. In two days, a freighter will be here with the building materials we will need for the remainder of our portion of the construction. If you want to see any progress, you should come back in fifteen days." Then looking at S1 he asked, "Is that your pet?"

Before Jeffery could respond, S1 said in perfect Coplent, "No, I'm not his pet. I'm a native of Procolt 2. I don't belong to anyone."

Treb said, "I am sorry. I did not mean to offend you. I always thought all intelligent species were humanoid."

S1 said, "No apology is necessary. Before you ask, I learned to speak your language from two females from Coplent. They're named Brealak and Marcet."

"Is Brealak the daughter of Garlut?"

"Yes, she is."

"I have met her several times. She is very nice. Is she here now?"

S1 said, "No, she went back to Coplent with Marcet, but they'll be back here soon."

"When she gets back, please tell her I am here and ask her to stop by."

"I'll be happy to do that."

They left the construction site and returned to the shelter. Now they really had nothing to do for a while. Jeffery and Debbie spent the days relaxing, hiking, and swimming. The days seemed to go by quickly. They waited for the fifteen days as asked, and returned to the site. They didn't land, but from the air they could clearly see one building was already about thirty feet tall and there was work being done on the other tower building as well. They decided to check on the construction every ten days.

During their fifth visit, Jeffery's com unit beeped. When he answered it, an excited Cathy said, "Marcet and Brealak are back!"

"I'm very happy to hear that. We'll be back within the hour."

When they arrived at the shelter, they could see Brealak's ship and Jeffery landed his nearby. Marcet, Brealak, and Cathy were waiting for them. As Debbie stepped off the ramp, Marcet said, "I understand congratulations are in order."

"Thank you. I'm very glad you're here. I hope you're planning to stay for a while."

"Brealak and I are planning to stay here permanently, if that is okay with you and Jeffery. We really like it here and I think both of us have skills you can use."

254

"You're welcome to stay as long as you want. Brealak, a man named Treb said to tell you he's here and he wanted you to go see him."

"Treb is an old friend of our family. I have not seen him for a while and it would be nice to see him again."

"Debbie," Marcet began, "on the trip here, I set up a complete medical facility on Brealak's ship. If you like, I would be happy to give you a complete examination anytime you are ready."

"I'm ready now. I don't want to wait. I want to know for sure the baby is okay."

Marcet and Debbie walked over to Brealak's ship and went inside. Jeffery and Brealak walked back to the shelter and went to the dining room. Jeffery got a cup of coffee and sat down across from her. After a few seconds she said, "I need to tell you why we went back to Coplent. It was obvious the squirrels were becoming more civilized on an almost daily basis. Both Marcet and I felt they needed a building of their own that would give them a comfortable place to live. It would shelter them from the weather, and give them a place to eat and sleep. Since they now bathe regularly and prefer to use toilets, the shelter would have several bathrooms too. We decided to go see Nandor and ask him to design the building for them. Garlut thought you would not have a problem paying for it, but he also said if you refused to pay for it, he would."

Jeffery smiled and said, "We're going to call it Squirrel Haven. I discussed this with S1 shortly after we got back here. I told him it would be built near Procolt Paradise and I would pay for it. I assume Nandor agreed to do the designs."

"Yes, he did. He said he would send the plans with the next ship that comes here from Coplent. I would like to go see Treb tomorrow. Would you come with me?"

"Sure, I'd be happy to do that."

"Are you excited about the baby?"

"Yes, I'm excited, happy, and concerned all at the same time. I think raising a child in this environment won't be easy. There are no other children around to play with, or at least no human children. I'm sure we can provide a loving

255

home and an excellent education, but social development may be a problem until Procolt Paradise is open. I think when we start looking for staff, we'll look for families with children."

"How many people do you expect to have working here?"

"At least two hundred to start. As the business grows, we'll add more."

"With one hundred families living here, I am sure there will be a lot of children for your child to play with. In fact, you will probably need to set up a small school. That is something I would really like to do."

"Okay, you're now officially in charge of the school."

"Thanks, I think. Marcet wants to be your staff doctor."

"That's okay too. But we'll probably have two doctors. Frank Weber wants to work here as well. Since we'll only be open for people from Coplent and Earth, having a doctor for each group would probably be a good plan."

"Are you going to build staff housing?"

"Not initially. Each tower in the resort will have one thousand four hundred guest rooms and one hundred apartments. The apartments are for the staff. When we add additional staff, we'll probably have to build some additional housing, but that probably won't be needed for three or four years after we're open."

"I did not realize it was going to be that big. I am not sure a staff of two hundred is enough."

"The squirrels are going to help out too. S1 asked me if they could work at the resort and I think that's a great idea. I'm just not sure what they can do yet, but I'll think of something."

A few minutes later, Debbie and Marcet walked into the dining room. Both of them were smiling. Debbie said, "We have a healthy baby girl. She'll probably be born in a little over six months. Marcet assured me she could handle the delivery."

Jeffery said, "You do realize you just took the mystery out of your pregnancy."

"I'm sorry. You can forget what I told you and act surprised when she's born."

"I don't think that will work. Anyway, I'm very happy. While you were gone, I hired Brealak to set up a school here for the children of the staff."

Marcet asked, "What about me?"

"You'll be one of the two doctors we'll have here. The other doctor will be Frank Weber."

"That sounds perfect. I really like Frank and I am sure we can work together."

The days passed quickly. They continued monitoring the construction of Procolt Paradise. The exterior structures were almost finished by the time Debbie was ready to deliver. When the time came, Jeffery and Brealak were there to observe the delivery as were several of the squirrels. Marcet gave Debbie some medication to reduce the pain, and after less than four hours of labor, Jeffery and Debbie's daughter was born. They wanted an unusual name, so after some discussion they decided to name her Mystic.

Mystic didn't have a birth certificate. In fact, none of them even knew the Earth date. Brealak's ship provided the galactic standard date: 5407.162. So, Mystic's birthday was the one hundred and sixty-second day of the year. It was difficult for Jeffery and Debbie to stop thinking about weeks and months, but after Mystic's birth they decided to only think in terms of days and years.

One hundred thirty-seven days after Mystic's birthday, the exterior construction of the buildings for Procolt Paradise were completed. Treb and his crew were waiting for the new crew to arrive with the ship that would take them home. The new crew arrived nine days after the exterior construction was completed. But in addition to the ship that had the crew and the materials needed to finish the construction, Garlut's ship had also come to Procolt 2. Nandor was a passenger on Garlut's ship. When the ship was in a stable orbit, Garlut and Nandor took one of the shuttles down to the shelter area.

As the shuttle approached, the noise drew the people in the dining room outside to watch it land. Brealak knew immediately it was Garlut's shuttle and they walked over to meet it. Moments after the landing, the shuttle hatch opened and Garlut and Nandor stepped out.

Debbie was holding Mystic in her arms. She said, "Hello Garlut, I'd like you to meet my daughter, Mystic."

Garlut walked over and looked at Mystic. Then he smiled and said, "Congratulations, she is beautiful." Then looking at Brealak he said, "Brealak, it is nice to see you again. Your mother and I miss you, but we will be spending a lot of time here on Procolt 2 in the future so we will be able to see each other more often."

"I miss you too, but I really like it here. After spending time here, I realized I like open space and fewer people more than the large, overpopulated cities on Coplent. I am going to stay here and manage the school that will be built for the children of the people who will be working here. Marcet is also staying here and will be one of the resort's doctors."

"That is wonderful news. I am very happy for both of you. I am not sure if all of you have met Nandor. He is the person who is designing the resort."

Nandor looked around and stared at S1 for a few moments before he said, "You must be one of the squirrels I have heard so much about from Brealak and Marcet."

S1 stepped forward and said, "Yes, I am. It's very nice to meet you. I've been told you'll be designing a new home for us and I would like to discuss it with you."

"I will be happy to meet whenever it is convenient for you. I came here to see how the construction is going and to spend some time with Jeffery and Debbie to finalize the plans for the interior spaces."

Jeffery asked, "How long will you be staying?"

"Probably thirty days, but neither Garlut nor I are in a hurry to leave."

Brealak said, "Please come with me and I will show you around the area."

The four people from Coplent left the shelter and walked to the lake. When they arrived, there were several squirrels playing in the sand. One of the squirrels walked up to the group and said, "Hi Brealak, who are these people?"

"This is my father, Garlut, and the man who is designing the resort. His name is Nandor."

"Hello Garlut and Nandor. I'm S42. It's very nice to meet you."

"Hello S42, it is nice to meet you as well," Garlut said. "Nandor does not speak English so he did not understand what you said."

S42 repeated his introductions in perfect Coplent.

Looking pleasantly surprised, Nandor responded, "It is nice to meet you as well. Do all the squirrels speak Coplent?"

"Yes, we learned it from Brealak and Marcet. We all speak English too."

"That is truly amazing. Most of the humanoid species in the trade group cannot speak Coplent."

There were some chairs near the lake shore and the people from Coplent sat down. After a minute or so of relaxing, Nandor said, "I can see why you girls like it here. This is wonderful, no noise, except for the sound of the breeze wafting through the trees and the waves lapping at the shore. No crowds of people rushing to get somewhere. Just peace and relaxation."

After relaxing by the lake for an hour or so, they strolled back to the shelter. Nandor said he wanted to go to the construction site. Jeffery said he would take them, so Garlut, Nandor, and S1 all went to Jeffery's ship for the trip. Upon arrival, everybody seemed to be busy and ignored the landing. They left the ship and started to look around. Each of the tower buildings was six hundred and fifty feet tall. Between the two towers was a smaller building that would have offices, restaurants, medical facilities, and the school. There was also a large apartment where Jeffery, Debbie, and Mystic would live.

Nandor went to look for the construction manager while Garlut, Jeffery, and S1 continued to wander around. Behind the center building, a crew was working to build the two large swimming pools. Inside the center building, several groups of workers were installing interior walls. As Jeffery walked around, he noticed that everywhere he looked the

259

workers were using electric tools powered by modules from Earth. He wondered if they would have been able to do this job so quickly without them.

NASA HEADQUARTERS
SEPTEMBER 2124

Brandon and Max were sitting in Max's office when Max said, "I'm very pleased with the progress on the new systems. The new computer is several hundred times faster than the ones we're currently using, and the new communication system is almost completed."

"It actually is completed. S12 and I finished the lab tests yesterday," Brandon reported. "I'm having a unit installed in one of the cargo ships now. The installation should be completed in two days. I've already programmed the ship to go fifty thousand miles beyond the orbit of Pluto. When it gets there, it will begin sending a series of time-coded messages with the new system. When it receives a response, it will indicate the time the response was received and return to Earth. It will take the ship eight days to arrive at its destination. We should be able to launch it as soon as the system is installed."

"Where do we stand on the propulsion system?" Max asked.

"We have a problem there. The tachyon generator we designed isn't strong enough. We either have to make it bigger or more efficient. S12 is working on that today."

"Good. You know I still can't imagine you working with a squirrel. The whole idea strikes me as . . . well . . . nuts!"

"I know, but when you work with S12 you don't think about her appearance. She is, without a doubt, the most intelligent partner I've ever worked with. I couldn't have done this without her," Brandon said emphatically.

"When all these projects are completed, I'm going to hold a news conference and let everybody on Earth know about her," Max said.

"I think that's a wonderful idea. However, to answer your question regarding the propulsion system, it will probably take thirty days to get a usable tachyon generator. As you know, the principle is the same as the communication system. It's only a matter of scale. Once we have the generator

261

working, we can probably get it installed in a ship in forty-five days." Brandon hesitated, then asked, "Did you find a ship to use?"

"Not yet, Brandon. I'll get one of the Ganymede crew ships we no longer use."

"That will work. You should make sure to test the ship in the next two weeks in case my thirty-day estimate is off. Once the propulsion system is ready, we'll need the new navigation system to make it usable. I think that project will take more time than all the others combined. I believe we'll need a year to make it fully operational. That includes designing new long-range scanners."

"I do understand and I'll arrange to test the ship tomorrow."

"Thanks, Max."

The installation of the new communication system was completed without any problems and the computer-controlled cargo ship left Earth orbit on schedule. It arrived at the test location over two and a half billion miles from Earth, and began transmitting messages every ten seconds. A message sent by radio would have taken 3.9 hours to reach Earth. With the new communication system, the messages reached Earth in less than two seconds.

Brandon sent a message to the ship. If the message was received, the ship would cease transmitting and begin the return trip to Earth. The message was obviously received because the ship stopped transmitting. The system had performed flawlessly.

Brandon went back home to tell S12 about the success of the communication system. Max went to his office to call the representative from the Trade Council and let him know about the success of the test. By the end of the day, the news was known all over Earth.

Within a few days, a meeting was held between the Trade Council representative and the World Council. The Trade Council wanted Earth to install the communication systems on every planet in the trade group. The task was far more complicated than simply installing transmitting and receiving systems on each of the member planets. The signals were directional and traveled in straight lines, so in order for the system to be functional, an unknown number of relay stations would be required. Two decisions were made by the end of the meeting. The first being that Earth would have thirty standard years to have the system operational and the second, Earth would be paid ten thousand hirodim for each member planet. Each of the planets would pay half of the cost within one standard year and the balance when the system was installed and operational on their planet. They agreed to meet again in ninety days to discuss the status of the communications installation program and a schedule to begin installations on starships.

The result of this agreement was that Earth would soon become the wealthiest planet in the trade group and consequentially, Jeffery and Debbie would become wealthy as well.

Brandon's estimate of the time required to build the new tachyon generator for the propulsion systems was underestimated. It actually took one hundred and twenty days to get the new generator operational, but the extra time proved to be a benefit because the generator they created was able to produce a field large enough to encompass ships ten times the size of the Star Explorer.

Now that the tachyon generator was ready, the installation of the new propulsion system was started on a thirty-year-old ship which had been removed from service more than five years ago. The installation took almost six months. Virtually every part of the control system was replaced. The NASA construction crew also installed the new communication system. By the time they were ready to test the modified ship everything was ready, except the new navigation system. At a meeting with the NASA directors which included Brandon and S12, the decision was made to postpone the test until the new system was ready. The directors were anxious to test, but both Brandon and S12 explained that without the navigation system operational, it would be difficult, if not impossible, to control a ship that traveled that fast without accurate computer control.

The installation of the communication system was progressing better than expected. The meeting held ninety days after the first communication system meeting went well. It was agreed Earth would supply the systems for starship installations and the technical assistance required in exchange for a payment of one thousand hirodim. If no technical assistance was requested, the cost would be reduced to five hundred hirodim. They decided to continue to meet every ninety days until the installations became routine.

By the time the following communication system meeting occurred, the systems had been installed on Coplent and on two of Coplent's starships. Before communication between Coplent and Earth could be established, three relays stations needed to be placed. That task was given to the Star Rover and was expected to take one hundred and twenty days. They decided to postpone the next meeting until after the relay stations were in place and the systems were tested between Coplent and Earth.

At the same time, progress was being made on the new navigation system. It was currently being installed on the test ship which was now named the Star Racer. The installation was expected to take sixty days. Max wanted Jeffery to test the Star Racer but that was impossible, so command of the ship was given to Captain Ron Rice, who recently completed a new ship training module with NASA. Brandon would act as the ship's navigator, and S12 was now the chief engineer.

The first test for the Star Racer would be very simple. The ship would energize the tachyon field and travel for ten seconds. If the ship functioned as expected, it would be eighteen and one half trillion miles from Earth. If that test went well, the next trip would be to Procolt 2. The twenty-seven light year trip would take one day. The Star Racer would spend some time on Procolt 2 and then proceed to Coplent. It would stay at Coplent for thirty days before returning to Earth.

The installation of the new propulsion and navigation systems was ahead of schedule. It was completed within fifty-two days. The diagnostic tests of the new systems indicated there were no problems, so the first test was scheduled the following day. Aboard would be Ron, Brandon, and S12. There was a safety concern for the crew, so it was decided they would wear space suits during the test. The suits for Brandon and Ron were not a problem. However, they had never made a suit for a non-human. It took more than a week to produce the suit for S12 conversely, it took less than a day to make the suits for Brandon and Ron.

There was no way to hide S12 any longer. When she boarded the shuttle with Brandon for the trip to the space station, the other passengers on the shuttle could not prevent themselves from gawking which made her feel a little uncomfortable, so she decided to talk to them. She said, "Hello, my name is S12. This is my friend Brandon. He and I designed and developed the systems that we'll test on the Star Racer tomorrow."

Suddenly all of the passengers stopped talking. Brandon took the opportunity to speak. "I'm Dr. Brandon Simpson and I'm Chief Engineer in charge of systems development at NASA. I want you to know the designs for the new systems we've developed over the past few years are the direct result of the theories S12 presented to us. The development of these systems would not have been possible without her assistance."

Somebody asked, "S12, what planet are you from?"

"I'm from Procolt 2."

After some murmuring among the other passengers one of them began to applaud, and the applause grew until every passenger was clapping their hands loudly. Brandon stood up, smiled, and said, "Thank you."

The rest of the trip was without incident. When they arrived at the station, another shuttle was waiting to take them to the Star Racer. Although the ship was capable of recycling air and water, it was stocked with enough for six months to prevent problems if the recycling systems failed. There was also enough food for six months.

They ran diagnostics on all of the systems again, then retired to their quarters for the night. They tried to sleep, but were too excited. The next morning, Ron contacted the space station to tell them they were ready to embark. He moved the ship to a position twenty thousand units from the station and contacted NASA. The flight control crew verified that everything looked normal. Ron, Brandon, and S12, already wearing their suits, sealed their helmets. Each of them took their positions. Ron simply said, "Let's do this."

S12 energized the tachyon generator. Fifteen seconds later, the ship moved into the tachyon field, but in a fraction of a second the field collapsed. The navigation system indicated the Star Racer had moved over a million miles.

Ron said, "What happened?"

S12 answered, "The tachyon field collapsed. I don't know why, but I'll find out."

Once verifying nothing was wrong with atmospheric levels, they unsealed their helmets. Ron contacted NASA to let them know about the problem while Brandon and S12 began working on a resolution. Two hours later, they traced the problem to a faulty control board. They had spare parts, so they replaced the board and ran the diagnostics again. Everything checked out, so they all donned their helmets and once again, took their positions at the controls. S12 energized the tachyon field. Brandon moved the ship into it. Ten seconds later, the field collapsed. Brandon checked their position. They were now more than eighteen trillion miles from Earth. Ron, utilizing the new communication system, contacted Earth. He said, "Star Racer to Earth. The Star Racer functioned normally. We'll be returning to Earth in a few minutes."

Twenty-five seconds later, the Star Racer received a message.

"Congratulations, Star Racer. Be prepared for a big party tomorrow with the World Council."

Brandon programmed the navigation system to return to the space station and ten seconds later they were in the exact same position they were in when they first tried the system.

Two hours later, they were on a shuttle going back to Earth. This time they were the only passengers.

RUSSELL FINE

THE STAR RACER
AUGUST 2126

Several people were added to the Star Racer crew for its first interstellar voyage. In addition to Ron, Brandon, and S12, there were two other engineers who had worked with them on the project. Both Ron and Brandon had fully trained assistants and Frank Weber was assigned as the ship's doctor. S31 was aboard as well.

The ship left orbit and was positioned five hundred miles from the space station. Brandon programmed the navigation system to take them to Procolt 2. A few moments later he said, "Because we'll have to stop and make course adjustments, the trip will take about twenty-seven hours."

Frank added, "The last time I made this trip, it took seventy-three days."

The navigation system did everything automatically. They arrived on schedule at Procolt 2. An hour later, the ship was in a stationary orbit two thousand units above the shelter. They decided to surprise Jeffery and Debbie. The crew of the Star Racer with guests in tow got aboard the shuttle, which now had seats designed for squirrels, and went down to the surface. It was early afternoon when they approached the shelter area. Jeffery, Debbie, and S1 were sitting in the dining room when they heard the unmistakable sound of a shuttle on approach. They walked out and watched as the unfamiliar shuttle landed.

When the hatch opened and the occupants stepped out, Jeffery smiled and said, "It's wonderful to see all of you again. Does this visit mean the new systems are working?"

Brandon said, "Yes, everything S12 proposed is working. We made the trip from Earth in twenty-seven hours."

"That's great news! I want you all to know Debbie and I have an addition to our family. We have a two-year-old daughter named Mystic. We'll introduce you when she wakes up from her nap."

"Congratulations," Frank said. "That's terrific. How's the construction on the resort going?"

"The resort, which is named Procolt Paradisc, will be ready to open in ninety days. The first group of guests will be the construction crews and their families. We're already taking reservations on Coplent. We hired one hundred and six people to help staff it and they'll be here in sixty days. I think now is a good time to start advertising on Earth, and we still need another one hundred or so employees. I'd like them to be people from Earth."

"I can take care of those things when I get back," Frank said enthusiastically. "We're going from here to Coplent and then back to Earth. We should be there in less than thirty days."

"Good, I'll go over our advertising and personnel needs with you before you leave. Would you like to see Procolt Paradise?"

"Yeah, that would be great," Brandon said.

S1 said, "S12 and S31, I'm very happy to see you again. Obviously, your mission was a success, but I suspect you're glad to be home."

"Brandon's home was wonderful. We really liked it there, but we missed you and the other squirrels. It's nice to be here again."

"You'll be happy to know Jeffery had a place built for us, so we don't have to live in caves anymore. It's near Procolt Paradise and was designed to hold two hundred and fifty squirrels. While you were gone, we had two new births, so now there are seventy-seven of us."

They spent an hour or so telling each other about what happened in the previous two years. While they were talking, Mystic woke up from her nap and Debbie introduced her to everyone. Mystic had been talking for six months and she was able to talk to them a little bit.

Frank and Brandon really wanted to see the resort, so everyone boarded Jeffery's ship and they flew to Procolt Paradise. The buildings were almost finished. The center building was complete except for some of the medical equipment that had just been shipped from Coplent. They were

270

installing power modules in each guests' room. All of the staff apartments were completed.

The pool area was finished, all that was needed was water. All of the restaurants and bars were ready for guests. They had installed a moving walkway that led from the pool area to the lake like those on Coplent. At the lake they built a marina with dock space for thirty boats and another restaurant. Twelve boats were already docked, and the others were on a shipment scheduled to arrive in a few days.

Jeffery took them on a tour of several of the guest rooms and one of the staff apartments.

Everyone was impressed. S1 said he wanted to show them Squirrel Haven. It was near the pool area, but hidden by some trees. When they arrived, S1 showed them through the new home for the squirrels. There were seventy-five family units and each unit had two areas. One area contained a large bed for the family to sleep on. The other area was a bathroom that had a toilet and a squirrel-sized bath tub and shower combination. There were also three rooms set up as class rooms, and several large meeting rooms. S1 explained this was more space than he thought they would ever need, but he really liked it.

They spent two hours touring the resort. When they were done, Frank said, "I don't want to go back to Earth. I want to stay here. This place is wonderful."

"I already told Marcet you were going to be half of the medical staff. But now I need you to go back to Earth and find some people to work here and start an advertising campaign."

"I know that, but I have no idea when I can get back here, and I have no way of contacting you either."

"Brandon, how long would it take to install the new systems on my ship?"

"Probably sixty days, but I have no idea when I could get it on the schedule. Right now, all efforts are on completing the Star Explorer."

"Does Max still want Debbie and me to test it?"

"I think he'd jump at the opportunity to have you two at the controls for the maiden voyage."

"Okay, I have an idea. Debbie and I will go back to Earth and offer our services to NASA in exchange for making my ship the next one to be converted. By the time you return to Earth, we'll already be there. We can get the advertising and the search for employees started. You'll be back before we leave on the Star Explorer. We'll make Procolt 2 our first stop with the Star Explorer and you can stay here. By the time Debbie and I get back to Earth, the work on my ship should be nearly completed. When it is, we'll return here with our first group of employees."

Debbie said, "I assume we'll be taking Mystic with us."

"Yes, of course we'll be taking her with us. I'm sure Marcet and Brealak can handle the operations at Procolt Paradise until we get back here again. I think we can get back permanently in one hundred twenty days. Brandon, can you teach us how to use the new systems?"

"Sure, we can start tomorrow. I'm certain you'll be able to learn how to use the new systems in a few hours."

At dinner, Jeffery told Marcet and Brealak about his plans to go back to Earth to get his ship retrofitted with the new systems. They assured Jeffery they could handle the operations at the resort in his absence. Additionally, they expected Garlut to be here when Procolt Paradise opened and he would be able to help too.

The following day, Jeffery and Debbie spent the morning with Brandon and S12 learning the new systems. They were designed to be very simple to use. The only potential problem would be if one of the systems failed. They would have no idea how to fix it since the maintenance documentation had not been completed. Jeffery was concerned because there had been a failure on the maiden voyage of the Star Racer. If it happened on his ship, he would have a bigger problem. When he mentioned this at dinner that evening, S12 said she had the solution.

"S31 and I were thinking about staying here, but we decided to stay on the Star Racer until the mission is completed. We'll stay with you on both the Star Explorer mission and your return trip here. I'm fully capable of handling any problem with the new systems as long as I have spare parts available."

"That's perfect. There's nothing stopping us now. Thank you. We'll leave tomorrow morning."

Debbie said, "I'm really glad Mystic is already toilet-trained. That's going to make this trip a lot easier. Brandon, can we stay at your home again?"

"Of course you can. I'm sure Bess and Tom will be happy to see you. You should call them and let them know you're coming as soon as you land."

"Okay."

The following day Jeffery, Debbie, and Mystic began their trip to Earth. After they secured their ship, Jeffery contacted Max. He told Max why they had come back to Earth and what his plans were.

Max agreed to Jeffery's requests. He was anxious to meet Mystic and suggested they take the next shuttle back to NASA headquarters. He would meet them at the shuttle station.

Their shuttle landed four hours later, and as promised, Max was waiting for them. He shook hands with Jeffery, hugged Debbie, and then said, "Hi" to Mystic.

She smiled at him and said, "Hi" back.

They went to a nearby restaurant for dinner and then Max drove them to Brandon's house. Debbie had called so they were expected. Bess made a big fuss over Mystic and took her into the kitchen to give her some ice cream. It was something she had never eaten before, and as expected, she loved it. Max, Jeffery, and Debbie went outside and sat by the pool.

Max said, "We're expecting the Star Racer to return to Earth in ten days. The Star Explorer will be ready for testing in twenty. As soon as the testing starts, I'll have the team begin modifications on your ship. The first Star Explorer mission is going to go to Procolt 2, as you requested, to Torblit, and to Coplent before returning to Earth. We have communication systems that will be installed at each location. I expect the

273

mission to take forty-five days. Your ship should be ready by the time you return."

"That's perfect. I really appreciate this, Max. I want you to know, anytime you want to come to Procolt Paradise everything will be on us."

"I have every intention of taking you up on that."

"I'd expect you to. One of the things we'd like to accomplish while we're here is starting an advertising campaign and hiring some people to work at Procolt Paradise. Could you ask somebody from the PR department to contact us? I'm just looking for some advice. I'm sure they have other tasks and I don't want to take up much of their time."

"No problem, I'll ask Josh Rawlins to call you tomorrow. He's in charge of that department."

Jeffery and Debbie were feeling the effects of travel and neither of them slept well on the trip to Earth, so they were looking forward to a good night's sleep. Mystic was already asleep with a full belly of ice-cream. After saying their good nights to the others in Brandon's home, all three of them were asleep within minutes.

Josh Rawlins called the following morning. Jeffery told him what they needed. Josh said he would arrange a news conference for the following day. He also gave Jeffery the name of somebody they could use to set up an online job application and reservation system. He was sure they could have it running by the time the news conference was over.

Jeffery asked Debbie to take care of the online tasks while he prepared something for the news conference. Josh called back two hours later to let him know the news conference would be at a hotel near NASA headquarters at 3:00 p.m. the following day.

Shortly after Jeffery finished his call with Josh, Debbie told him both online applications would be ready by tomorrow morning.

Jeffery and Debbie were celebrities, so there were lots of people at the news conference from different media outlets. Jeffery started the conference by telling them about Procolt Paradise. It was the first off-world vacation destination offered to people on Earth. He told them when it would open and how to make a reservation. He also announced that people were needed to work at the resort and if they were interested how to apply for the jobs.

The question he knew would be coming, but he really didn't want to answer yet, was how much it would cost.

He said the cost would be the same if all the guests were staying in the same suite. Each suite was designed for up to six guests. For a thirty-day stay at Procolt Paradise, the cost was $350,000 per suite. This included transportation, meals, drinks, and activities.

He said at the present time the trip to and from Procolt 2 took thirty days, but within two years that time would drop to less than two days.

The news spread quickly and by the next day, they had over four thousand reservation requests. They also had over three thousand people who applied for jobs.

That evening, Jeffery and Debbie realized they now had two new problems. First, the number of reservations far exceeded what he thought they would receive. They had expected only fifty or so. Although Procolt Paradise could handle the people, there was no way to get them there yet. He needed a ship at least the size of the Star Rover and he didn't have one. Second, he had no idea how to review three thousand job applications.

They decided to hire a company to take care of the reservations and another one to screen the job applicants. They spent the next morning interviewing potential companies to handle the jobs and by the end of the day, they were satisfied they found what they needed.

The company handling the reservations would contact everyone who requested a reservation and tell them they would be contacted again within ninety days to confirm the departure date. They were also told the departure date could be up to two years from now.

The company screening the job applications said they would be able to narrow down the number of applicants to one hundred and fifty within twenty days.

Jeffery had to find a ship, and he didn't have much time. He contacted the Trade Council representative on Earth and explained his dilemma. The representative said he could arrange the purchase of a used ship that would accommodate three hundred passengers with a wormhole drive and a time stasis generator for four thousand hirodim. Jeffery asked if there were pictures or drawings of the ship. The representative said he had both and would send them immediately.

An hour later, Jeffery had the images. He reviewed them with Debbie and they were impressed with what they saw. He contacted the Trade Council representative and told him he would purchase the ship. That didn't resolve the problem, but it was a step in the right direction. After he had possession of the ship, he would have to make arrangements for NASA to retrofit it with the new systems.

They decided they needed somebody to manage the Procolt Paradise operation on Earth, but they didn't even have an idea where to start. While they were discussing it, Bess was listening to their conversation and suggested they should try contacting somebody who was already in the resort business and set up a partnership with them. Thinking that was a good idea, Jeffery did some research and found the ten largest vacation resort companies. He started contacting them but was unable to reach any of the company managers until he tried Vacations Everywhere. The person who answered the phone had seen the news conference and knew immediately who Jeffery was. She asked him to hold on for a moment and less than a minute later, Jeffery was speaking to the owner of the company.

"Hello Mr. Whitestone, my name is Martin Dressler. How may I help you?"

"I'm looking for someone who can manage the operation of Procolt Paradise on Earth. I need a company that can handle the reservations, personnel requirements, and supply shipments. Do you think Vacations Everywhere can do that for me?"

"We're doing that now for more than one hundred resorts. I'm sure we're capable of handling your needs for

Procolt Paradise. Obviously, there will be some differences since travel to your resort is substantially more complicated, but all we need is a plan to solve the transportation problem."

"Mr. Dressler, I would like to meet with you to discuss this in person. When would it be convenient to do that?"

"Please call me Martin. Our office is in New York, but I know you're in Florida. I could come there the day after tomorrow with my director of operations. Would that work for you?"

"That would be perfect. If you fly into Orlando, I'll pick you up."

"I have my own transportation. If you can get me permission, I can fly to NASA headquarters."

"I'm certain I can arrange that. I'll call you again in a half hour."

"I'll be waiting for your call."

Jeffery called Max and made the arrangements for Martin to land at NASA headquarters. He set it up for 1:00 p.m. and called Martin to give him the information. Two days later, Jeffery and Debbie met Martin and Valarie, his operations director, as they stepped off their plane. Jeffery took them to Brandon's house. They spent the next several hours discussing what was needed on Earth for Procolt Paradise. The key part of the operation was the retrofit of Jeffery's ship to utilize the new systems. Once that was completed, they would begin regular weekly service between Procolt Paradise and Earth. They agreed to a commission plan to compensate Vacations Everywhere for the work they were going to do. Then Jeffery and Debbie took Martin and Valarie back to their plane.

Once they were back at Brandon's house, they felt a sense of relief. Now all they had to do was wait until the work on the Star Explorer was completed. Three weeks later, the Star Explorer was ready. During that time, Vacations Everywhere had selected one hundred and six people for the available positions on Procolt Paradise. Jeffery had asked that preference be given to families where both the husband and wife could work. Ninety-two of the positions were filled that way. The remaining fourteen positions were filled by single people who would share apartments.

Jeffery wanted to get his employees to Procolt 2 as soon as possible. He knew the Star Explorer would be going to Procolt 2 as part of the test and he wondered if Max would allow him to take his employees on the maiden voyage. If he didn't approve this plan, it would mean they would have to wait until his current ship was ready and then he could only take eight or nine at a time.

The other possibility was to wait for his new ship, take the employees to Procolt 2, and then bring the ship back to Earth for the retrofit. That trip alone would take two months. He called Max and made his request. Max told him he would have to discuss it with the board. If they approved, everyone would have to sign agreements releasing NASA from any liability if there was a problem.

Two days later, Jeffery and Debbie were scheduled for the initial test of the Star Explorer. They went to the space station the night before and a shuttle took them to the new ship early that morning. The design of the Star Explorer was similar to the Star Rover. It was 30% larger, but everything looked familiar. Jeffery and Debbie had spent some time studying the new systems and they were anxious to try out what they learned. That would happen today. NASA assigned a navigator for the test flights. She was already on the bridge when Jeffery and Debbie came in.

"Good morning, Admiral and Captain Whitestone. I'm Lieutenant Harris, your navigation specialist for the test flights."

"Good morning, Lieutenant Harris. I'm no longer an admiral and Debbie is no longer a captain since we resigned from NASA. Please call us Jeffery and Debbie."

"Actually, that's not correct, sir. You were both reinstated at midnight."

Jeffery was speechless for a moment. He hadn't even thought about that. Then he smiled and replied, "Okay, Lieutenant. But you can still call us Jeffery and Debbie. I assume you've been thoroughly trained on the new systems?"

"I received personal training from S12, sir. She's really quite remarkable."

"I know that. I was expecting her to be here for the test flight to Procolt 2. Do you know when they are expected to be back?"

"Yes, sir. They're scheduled to leave Coplent in two days, so they should be back here in four days. To be honest, I'd be more comfortable with her aboard. She knows the systems far better than anyone else."

"I think we can delay the long test until S12 is available. I'll speak to Max about it."

An hour later, they were ready to begin the short test. Jeffery manually moved the Star Explorer away from the space station and pointed it toward empty space. Lieutenant Harris programmed the navigation system for a fifteen-second flight.

"All systems go, sir," Lieutenant Harris said.

"Okay, let's do this."

The external screens blurred for a few seconds and then showed the stars moving rapidly across them. There was no sense of movement at all. When the tachyon field collapsed the Star Explorer stopped, but again there was no sense of movement. The only way to tell if the ship was moving was to look at the external monitors.

Lieutenant Harris checked the location of the ship with the navigation system. The Star Explorer was now twenty-eight billion miles from Earth. In the monitors, the sun was the brightest object that could be seen, but it was little more than a dot.

Jeffery contacted NASA. "NASA Command. This is the Star Explorer. After a fifteen-second trip, we're twenty-eight billion miles from Earth. The propulsion and navigation systems functioned as expected."

A few seconds later, a surprising response was received. "Star Explorer, please run another test. This time allow the propulsion system to run for one hour. Note your position relative to Earth and return to the space station."

"Okay NASA. We'll contact you when we get back to the solar system."

"Good luck and Godspeed, Star Explorer."

"That was unexpected. Lieutenant Harris, please find a nice empty spot in space and punch it."

"Yes, sir."

An hour later, they found themselves more than a light year from Earth. Lieutenant Harris took some readings from the navigation system and programmed it to bring them back to Earth.

After another hour, they were a few thousand miles from the space station.

Jeffery contacted NASA again. "NASA Command. Just wanted to say, hi everyone. We have returned. No problems at all."

"Hi Jeffery, it's Max. After you get back to the station please take the first shuttle back. I want to meet with you and Debbie."

"Okay Max, we'll see you in a few hours."

Three hours later, Jeffery and Debbie were sitting in Max's office.

Jeffery said, "The test went perfectly. I think we're ready for a longer test, but I'd like to wait for a few days. I want S12 aboard before we go."

"That's not a problem. However, I'm sorry to tell you the board turned down your request to use the Star Explorer to transport your employees to Procolt 2."

"I expected that," Jeffery admitted, although he was still disappointed. "I just have to figure out how to get them there so we can open the Earth side of the resort."

"Your ship will be ready by the time you get back from your next mission. Since the trip is short, you could probably take eight or nine people at a time."

"I'm not sure what I'll do. I bought a refurbished starship. That ship will hold three hundred passengers. It should be here shortly after we return from our mission. I think the best plan would be to use that ship to take my employees to Procolt 2 and then bring it back here to be retrofitted."

"If you do decide to do that, I'll try to get your new ship worked on as quickly as possible. Garlut's ship was supposed to be next, but I suspect it'll be okay with him if we do your ship first."

"Garlut should be on Procolt 2 when we get there with the Star Explorer. I'll discuss it with him."

"You should also know the engineers working on the ship upgrades think they can reduce the time required to install the new systems to thirty days. Your little ship is next. If they can complete the installation in that time frame, you'd could begin taking some of your new employees to Procolt 2 then."

"I agree. We'll see where we are when we get back from Coplent. Lieutenant Harris said S12 should be back in a few days. As soon as she's ready I'd like to start the mission."

"That's okay with me. Frank also wants to go, but I think he plans on jumping ship when you get to Procolt 2."

"I'm sure you're right."

Four days later, they were ready. There were only five of them aboard. This ship had food generators instead of a kitchen, so nobody had to prepare any meals. Jeffery and Debbie had the captain's cabin. Lieutenant Harris took the next largest cabin right across the hall. Frank's cabin was next to hers. S12 decided she didn't need a cabin. She was very comfortable in a chair on the bridge.

The ship left Earth and arrived at Procolt 2 twenty-seven hours later. They went down to the shelter and were surprised to discover that, aside from a few squirrels, nobody was there. They went to Procolt Paradise and found everyone there instead. The resort was finished and the workers were preparing to leave. All of the furniture was in place, the pools were filled, and everything was ready except the restaurants. Even the squirrels were in the process of moving into Squirrel Haven.

Jeffery and his small group found the others relaxing by the pool. Brealak and Marcet were nude and had apparently just gotten out of the water. Cathy saw them first and yelled, "Hi, it's nice to see you again. We're really enjoying your resort. You should stay here for a while. The only problem is the food. It isn't very good."

"Great to see all of you too. Sorry about the food situation. I guess for now, you'll have to continue to eat generated meals until the restaurants are operating. Otherwise, I'm glad you like it. I noticed the squirrels are making themselves at home."

"Did you come on the Star Explorer?" Brealak asked.

"Yes, and it was great! We made the trip in twenty-seven hours. I didn't even have enough time to explore the whole ship."

"Who is watching Mystic?" Marcet asked.

"She's staying at Brandon's house with Bess and Tom. They really love her and I'm sure they'll take very good care of her while we're gone. We miss her, but this is a test flight and her safety is much more important than our feelings," Debbie responded.

Jeffery and Debbie went to their apartment and really liked what they saw. The furniture not only looked nice, but was very comfortable as well. They were sure they were going to like living there. They spent a couple of hours in the apartment, then rode the moving sidewalk over to the lake to look at the marina. Like everything else at the resort, it was very well done. They took one of the boats and went exploring on the lake for an hour. All the people met by the pool and Cathy brought an assortment of food from the ship for dinner.

The next day, Jeffery went back to the Star Explorer to pick up Lieutenant Harris and bring her down to the resort. She was very impressed and told Jeffery she could understand why everybody who had been here wanted to stay.

They stayed at Procolt Paradise for a few days. When it was time to go on to Torblit, Frank decided to stay on Procolt 2 and Jeffery mentioned he expected that. The four remaining crew members went back to the Star Explorer for the trip to Torblit.

The purpose of the three-day trip was to show off Earth technology. When they arrived at the space station above Torblit, Jeffery was told where to secure the ship, and as soon as the ship was moored, the Trade Council representative would come over to the Star Explorer.

An hour later, Malden Pinder arrived on the Star Explorer. Everyone aboard was there when Malden stepped out of the shuttle bay. "Hello, Admiral Whitestone. It is nice to see you and your life partner again. When we last saw you, your ship was the slowest starship in the trade group. This ship is now the fastest. That is an amazing leap of technology in just a few years."

"Yes, it is but the new technology onboard this ship is due to a partnership we have with S12 and her peers," Jeffery responded, pointing at S12.

"It is nice to meet you, S12. Where are you from?"

"I'm sorry, we don't have a translator for her, so she can't understand you. She speaks English and Coplent. She's from Procolt 2."

Malden nodded. "I heard something about them. Well, congratulations on your technical achievement. It is my understanding you will be here for ten days. During that time, I will bring people interested in purchasing this technology aboard. It would be helpful if you could demonstrate some of the ship's capabilities. Would that be possible?"

"Yes, of course. Please inform me of the schedule so I can be sure we're ready."

"I will do that. The first group will be here tomorrow morning."

"We'll be ready."

During the next ten days at Torblit, Jeffery and his small crew demonstrated the propulsion and navigation systems to fourteen groups. Every one of them was impressed with the capabilities of the Star Explorer. Jeffery didn't realize it at the time, but the demonstrations resulted in the sale of sixty new ships and retrofits for another one hundred and twenty. It would be enough to keep Earth busy for several years.

The Star Explorer went to Coplent next. Jeffery had hoped to see Garlut when he got to Procolt 2. Now he hoped Garlut would be on Coplent when he arrived. As it turned out,

Garlut was there. When Jeffery had an opportunity to speak to him, he quickly agreed to relinquish his spot in line for conversion to Jeffery. Jeffery spent twenty-eight days on Coplent. Almost every day demonstrating the ship. Before they left for Earth, Garlut told him he would be traveling to Earth soon in an effort to secure the manufacturing rights for the new systems. There was no way Earth would be able to keep up with the demand for them. Jeffery invited Garlut to return to Earth with him, but he declined because he had some other things to take care of first.

When Jeffery arrived back on Earth, he was surprised to see his ship docked near the space station. It was not where he had left it, so he hoped the retrofit had been completed. As soon as the Star Explorer was secured, he contacted Max who confirmed the conversion on his ship was complete and the systems had been fully tested. He also told him they had been able to complete the retrofit in only twenty-two days.

The station sent a shuttle to retrieve the four Star Explorer crewmen and bring them back to the station. They took the first available shuttle to NASA headquarters. Brandon was there to pick them up and he had Mystic with him. She was overjoyed to see her parents again, she squealed and ran to them, her arms outstretched. Jeffery bent down and picked her up, hugging her and kissing her lightly on her forehead. Debbie took her from Jeffery and held her. They smiled at each other and Debbie kissed her too. On the way back to Brandon's house, they told him everything that happened during the mission.

That evening, Jeffery and Debbie decided to use his little ship to begin taking employees to Procolt Paradise. There were six passenger seats and six beds. It would be cramped, but they could take ten at a time. The next morning, Jeffery contacted Vacations Everywhere to tell them he wanted to take ten of his new employees to Procolt 2 in two days. Martin Dressler called him back a few minutes later to tell him he had already told the new employees to be prepared to go on a moment's notice. He would have the first ten at the space station in the morning on the day of departure. Jeffery also told him he would be back for another group in a week, but he also wanted twenty-five hundred pounds of food to take to Procolt Paradise on the next trip.

For the next twelve weeks, Jeffery, Debbie, and Mystic commuted between Earth and Procolt 2. On each trip after the first, they took ten people to Procolt Paradise. While that was happening, Jeffery's new ship was being fitted with the new systems and all of the employees from Coplent arrived. After Jeffery's last weekly trip, the resort was fully operational.

Invitations were sent to the workers who had built Procolt Paradise and their vacations were set to start in thirty days. Jeffery really wanted to use his new passenger ship to bring the workers to Procolt 2. He thought about it for a few days and decided to go back to Earth to see if the work was nearing completion.

The following day Jeffery, Debbie, Brealak, and Mystic went to Earth. On the way, they were trying to decide on a name for the ship. They finally decided to call it the Paradise Express.

When they arrived at Earth, Jeffery contacted Max to get the status of the systems installations for his ship. He was very happy when Max told him that the systems had been installed and were scheduled to be tested the following day. Jeffery said he wanted to be onboard for the testing. Max said he would arrange it and call him back later in the day.

Jeffery and Debbie had never seen the ship, but they recognized it from the pictures they had when they purchased it. As the shuttle approached the ship, they realized how big it was. It was at least twice the size of the Star Explorer. Once they were inside, they were amazed. Everything looked brand new. There was no way to tell that the ship was really more than three hundred years old. They went to the bridge and Jeffery was surprised to see Lieutenant Harris at the navigation console.

"Good morning Lieutenant Harris, it's a pleasure to see you again. What's on the agenda for this morning?"

"Good morning, Admi—Jeffery, it's nice to see you and Debbie again too. This morning we'll test all three new systems. First, we'll travel for thirty seconds and test the communication system. Then we'll travel two light years away. Once we're there, I'll program the navigation system to take us back to a point sixty thousand miles above the Earth. We put a small object in orbit at that altitude and the idea is for the navigation system to locate it and take the ship within one mile of it, all without any human intervention."

"That's impressive. Who's the acting captain of the ship today?"

"As far as I know, you are, sir. After all, it's your ship."

"Okay. Anytime you're ready, we'll get started."

Jeffery sat down at the main console. The control layout was identical to his little ship. Everything appeared to be operating normally. He said, "We can go anytime. I'll contact the station to let them know we're leaving."

Thirty minutes later, the Paradise Express left the station. After the thirty-second flight, Lieutenant Harris contacted NASA. Thirty-five seconds later, NASA responded. They traveled for less than two hours and were now two light years from Earth. Lieutenant Harris programmed the navigation system and initiated the program. They were back to Earth again in less than two hours and the small object placed in orbit for the test was one mile ahead of them. The test was a complete success.

By the end of the day, Jeffery, Debbie, and Mystic were aboard the Paradise Express. Brealak was on her way back to Procolt 2 in Jeffery's small ship with ten new employees.

The next morning, the Paradise Express began its first journey to Procolt 2. When they arrived, Jeffery put the ship in orbit above Procolt Paradise and took one of the three shuttles onboard to the surface. They were now ready for guests.

Procolt Paradise was a phenomenal success. After operating for a half year, they were booked up with guests from both Coplent and Earth for the next two years. By the time the resort had been open for a year, the required communication relays were in place and high-speed communication was available between Earth, Coplent, Torblit, and Procolt 2.

Starships were being retrofitted at facilities on Earth and Coplent. As a result of the profits from the resort and the royalties from the new systems, Jeffery and Debbie were the wealthiest couple among the trade group planets.

CROSUS and COPLeNT

That information reached the controlling government on Crosus, and they were not happy their enemy had done so well while the entire planet of Crosus was on the brink of financial ruin.

They found the situation unacceptable and were determined to do something about it. It was decided the best way to get revenge was to attack Procolt Paradise. They wanted to destroy the resort, but even more than that, they wanted to push the Earth, Coplent, and the Whitestones into bankruptcy.

Their plan was to attack the resort and blackmail Jeffery into giving them the plans for manufacturing the new starship systems and the power modules. They felt that once they knew how to make their own, they would be able to sell them for much less and steal all of the business from Earth and Coplent. After they obtained the plans, they would demolish Procolt Paradise.

To put the plan into motion, they had to enlist help from some people living on either Earth or Coplent. Since there were already people from Crosus living on Coplent, the decision was to use them for the attack. First, they had to get a spy on Coplent. Since Crosus had been expelled from the trade group, their ships were no longer allowed to go there, but no one would refuse help to a ship in distress.

They used one of their oldest ships for the mission. The hold of the ship was filled with cargo they still occasionally traded with other planets, even though that violated Trade Council rules. There was only one person on the ship. His name was Valik and he was the spy they needed for the mission. The ship went to the primary shipping route between Coplent and Torblit. Valik turned off all of the power except what was needed for life support, communications, the artificial gravity system, and the long-range scanner.

When the scanner detected a ship from Coplent, Valik began broadcasting a distress signal. The Coplent ship contacted Valik.

"My power system is almost dead," Valik lied. "I only have enough power to keep the life support systems running for three or four more days. Can you tow me to Coplent so I can get the system repaired?"

"I can take you close enough for you to contact the Coplent authorities and request assistance," came the reply.

"Thank you. That would be very helpful."

The Coplent ship moved to a position very close to the front of Valik's ship and put a tow beam around it. Once Valik's ship was secure, the Coplent ship resumed its journey home. Since they were towing a ship, they had to use the sub-light engines for the remainder of the trip. That would take them more than two days. Valik used some of that time to short a few relays and control boards in the power system, so when Coplent sent someone to evaluate the problem they would verify his report.

They released Valik's ship from the tow beam fifty thousand units above Coplent. Valik thanked them for their assistance and he contacted the Coplent space station. He explained the problem and was told they would have to contact the appropriate authority on the planet before they could offer any assistance.

An hour later, Valik was told a repair ship would be there to evaluate the problem shortly and he should be prepared to pay for evaluation and repair. When the repair ship arrived, Valik opened the shuttle bay to allow it inside. Valik was waiting for the repairman as he exited the shuttle bay. He took the repairman to the area where he had damaged the power system and left him there. A short time later, he went back and the repairman was waiting for him.

"The system will take several days to repair, and it is so old I am not sure we have the parts we need. You will probably have to be here for at least five or six days."

"Can you arrange for my ship to be towed to the station for the repair?"

"Yes, I will take care of that when I get back to the station. There is no place for you to stay on the station, so you will have to go down to the surface and stay there until your ship is ready."

"That is fine. I have some friends on Coplent. I am sure I could stay with them for a few days."

The repairman left Valik's ship. An hour later, a tow ship arrived to take Valik's ship to the repair area near the station. After his ship was docked, a shuttle was sent to pick him up and bring him to the station.

When the shuttle arrived, the station master was there to greet him.

"Please understand we do not welcome people from Crosus on Coplent, but we realize this is not a normal situation. The charge to repair your ship is one hundred and fifty hirodim and it must be paid in advance."

Valik handed him a bank card and said, "The charges can be deducted from this account. I was told I will be here for several days. Is there a way I can contact some friends who live here?"

"Of course, please follow me."

Valik contacted one of the Crosus families living on Coplent.

The remaining Crosus families living on Coplent were infiltration spies. Their help would be activated by using a keyword, and Valik was about to do that.

"Hi, I do not know if you remember me. My name is Valik Marstal. We met several years ago at a trade conference."

"Yes Valik, I remember you. Are you here on Coplent?"

"I am currently on the space station. The power unit on my ship failed and I will have to be here for several days while it is being repaired. I was hoping I could stay with you."

"Of course you can stay with us. I can pick you up on the station in two hours. It will be nice to see you again."

"Thank you. I will be waiting for you."

Valik thanked the station master for his help and walked over to the shuttle bay area to wait.

While he was waiting, the station master gave him back his bank card and said, "You have permission to remain on Coplent for ten days. You must report to a local police station before the end of the day and tell them where you will be staying. You will be subject to arrest if you do not comply with these instructions."

"I understand. I appreciate your helping me and I will not break any of your rules."

"One more thing, I need one of your hands, palm up. I am going to insert a microscopic tracker. It will dissolve in thirty days."

Valik offered him his right hand, palm up.

The station master pressed a small device onto Valik's palm. He said, "This will not hurt." Then he pushed a button on the top of the device.

There was a short, high-pitched sound.

"You were right. It did not hurt."

The station master smiled at him and went back to his office. About a half hour later, a shuttle arrived. Robelt Flemm stepped out of the shuttle bay looked at Valik, smiled, and said, "Valik, it is good to see you again, my friend. Melda is anxious to see you too."

Valik and the man hugged briefly and they went together into the shuttle bay and then into the small shuttle docked there. As soon as the shuttle hatch was shut, Valik took a small pad of paper from his pocket, wrote a note, and handed it to Robelt.

The note read: 'Do not talk about the mission. They put a transmitter in my hand.'

Robelt read the note and said, "Melda is making you a surprise dinner. I am sure you will like it. Most of the native food on Coplent is awful."

"Thank you. I am looking forward to it."

They said very little on the descent to the home. Once they were inside, Valik discovered Melda did indeed prepare a special dinner. They had a friendly conversation during dinner, but there was no discussion of the reason for Valik's visit. After dinner they went into a room that was set up as an office and sat down by a table. Robelt handed Valik a pad of paper and while they talked about old times and mutual friends, Valik wrote down the assignment. Robelt read it, wrote, "I need money" on the note, and handed it back to Valik. Valik handed him a bank card and wrote on the paper, "There is two thousand hirodim in the account," and he said, "I have to report to the police to let them know where I am staying. Can you take me?"

"Sure."

They spent the next three days talking a lot, but saying nothing of consequence. At the end of the third day, Valik received a message indicating his ship would be ready the next morning.

The next day, Valik was taken back to the space station where he waited a short time until a shuttle was available. Once aboard, it took him back to his ship and he immediately left Coplent. His mission had been successful.

The same day Valik left, Robelt made a reservation at Procolt Paradise for him and Melda. The first available reservation was almost two years away, but that was okay because it gave him time to plan the attack.

RUSSELL FINE

PROCOLT PARADISE

Procolt Paradise was hugely successful. The new communication system really simplified the reservation process. When the resort first opened, the squirrels wanted to play a part in the operation, so they were put in charge of reservations and were doing an excellent job.

S43 was going through the reservations for the next ten days and he ran across one that concerned him. The reservation was for Robelt and Melda Flemm. They were residents of Coplent, but the name Flemm was unusual for Coplent. After a little research, he discovered that Flemm was a common name on Crosus. A further check with the records on Coplent indicated that Robelt and Melda had emigrated from Crosus to Coplent ten years ago. S43 still remembered the attack on Procolt 2 and was uncomfortable with somebody from Crosus staying at the resort. He sent a message to Jeffery about the reservation and then forgot about it.

Jeffery received the message, thought about it for a few moments, and decided there was no reason for concern.

Fifteen days later, in the middle of the night, there was an explosion. Everyone at Procolt Paradise was awakened by the sound. Moments later, Jeffery received an anonymous message.

"The marina has been destroyed to prove to you that we are fully capable of destroying Procolt Paradise. So far, no lives have been lost, but that will change if you refuse to meet our demands. Explosive devices have been placed in both guest towers. Do not try looking for them. They are both very powerful and very small. You would never find them. These are our demands: Two hundred and fifty thousand hirodim are to be placed in account 347299064201 in the Trade Group Bank. The complete design specifications for the new propulsion, navigation, communication systems and power modules must be placed in box 3794 at the Trade Group Bank Branch 17 on Coplent. You have five days to comply with these demands. Additionally, no ships are to arrive or depart from Procolt 2. If you fail to comply with these demands, thousands of your guests will die."

Jeffery had never expected an attack on the resort. They had no weapons except for a few handheld units on the ships, and they had not been used for years. He showed the note to Debbie.

After she read it, she asked, "What do you want to do?"

"I don't know. The money isn't a problem, we have at least three times that much in our accounts. I'm sure I could get the plans for the systems as well, but I don't want to give in to terrorists."

At that moment, the door chimed. Jeffery opened the door and S1 was standing there. He walked in and said calmly, "I know what's going on and I think I have a solution to the problem."

FUTURE WORLD HISTORY

BOOK 3

2136 – 2500

PROCOLT PARADISE

Jeffery looked at S1 and asked, "What's your plan to defuse this situation?"

"I was hesitant to tell you this earlier, but now I have no choice. Apparently, we are still being affected by the radiation. About a half year ago we began to notice that when we're near humanoids we were able to read their emotions. Please understand, we can't read minds. I can't tell what they are thinking, but I can tell if they are, for example, happy, sad, excited, worried, or confused. I was concerned because I wasn't sure if you would be comfortable knowing we could do that."

"Wow! That's definitely an interesting development, but I don't see how it helps us."

"In the tower for the guests from Coplent everyone is sad, worried, or excited. Only one couple is happy. They are in room 5217."

Suddenly Jeffery remembered the message he received from S34 regarding Robelt and Melda Flemm. "Are the people staying in that room named Flemm?"

"Yes, how did you know?"

"I received a report from S34 about them that said they were probably from Crosus, but I decided to ignore it. Obviously, that was a serious mistake. They said they've placed explosives in both guest towers. I don't think they're going to just let us in without blowing up the other tower."

S1 smiled and said, "I haven't told you everything yet. We also discovered we can activate something in a humanoid brain that causes them to fall asleep instantly. Would you like me to demonstrate it for you?"

"Uh, no, I don't think so. I assume you have tried this on people."

"Yes, we have, but only when people are relaxing around the pool. They only sleep for a few minutes and there doesn't appear to be any harmful effects that resulted from our experiments."

1

"In this case, I'm not very concerned about harmful effects. Do you have to be close to them to make this work?"

"No, I'm sure I can do it from here. But I can only do one person at a time. If you want me to do this, I'll go and get S4 to help."

"Okay, go get S4. While you're doing that, I'll get one of our doctors to whip up something that will keep them unconscious until we can get help here."

Jeffery left his apartment and walked over to the medical office. He was surprised to find both of the resort's doctors, Frank and Marcet, there. He spent a minute or two filling them in on what happened and then he asked, "Do you guys have something that will keep the Flemms unconscious for a few days?"

Marcet replied, "They are from Crosus, not Coplent, so their physiology is different, but I'm sure I can make something you can use that will keep them out for at least a day."

"That should be okay. I think once they are unconscious, we can bind them with wire ties and take them to a cave a few hundred units from here. When help arrives, we can go pick them up and take them to Earth or Coplent for trial."

Marcet said, "Give me a half hour to make my magic potion. I'll bring it to you when it's ready."

"Thanks, I'll be waiting for you," Jeffery said as he left the office.

When Jeffery arrived at the apartment, he was surprised to see the door was open. Inside S1 and S4 were talking to Debbie. When S1 saw him he said, "We're ready. We've never tried this on anybody from Crosus before, but I see no reason why it won't work."

"I want to wait until Marcet has her sleeping potion ready."

Marcet and Frank arrived at the apartment a half hour later. Marcet gave Jeffery two vials of medication and an air pressure syringe. "This should keep them out for at least a day.

They will probably feel like shit when they wake up, but I don't think you really care about that."

"Personally, I think that's a real plus," Jeffery said. Turning to Debbie he said, "I'll call you after they're sedated. Send a message to Earth and tell them what happened and ask them to send help."

"Okay."

Jeffery walked over to his computer and opened a screen that showed the rooms on the fifty-second floor of the Coplent Guest Tower. There were two vacant rooms on that floor. He called his chief maintenance engineer, Jim Roberts. When Jim answered Jeffery spent a few minutes telling him what happened and then Jeffery said, "I need your two strongest guys in my apartment as soon as possible and tell them to bring some big wire ties that are suitable for binding hands and feet."

"Is this going to be dangerous?"

"I don't think so, but feel free to ask for volunteers."

"Okay, I'll have two guys there in a few minutes."

"Thanks Jim," Jeffery said as he terminated the call.

A few minutes later two men showed up at Jeffery's apartment. The door was still open so they walked in. Jeffery told them what was going on and asked them to go to room 5224 in the Coplent Tower. He also told them to use the service elevator so they wouldn't have to walk by room 5217. Jeffery and the two squirrels left a few minutes later.

As soon as they arrived at the room Jeffery told S1 to put the Flemms to sleep. Jeffery watched as both S1 and S4 closed their eyes and began to concentrate on the task. A few seconds later S1 open his eyes and said, "We are finished. Both of them are sleeping."

Jeffery and the two maintenance men walked over to room 5217 and opened the door with a pass key. Once inside they found both of them sound asleep on the couch. Jeffery gave each of them a dose of Marcet's sleeping potion and asked, "Can you guys carry them out?"

"Yeah, that's not a problem," one of the men answered.

3

"Okay, use the wire ties to bind their hands and feet, take them to the shuttle, and strap them in. I'll be there in a few minutes. The medication I gave them will keep them out for at least a day."

Jeffery called Debbie and told her the Flemms were no longer a threat and asked her to send the message to Earth.

"I don't think we should do that yet. I think we need to make sure they don't have some kind of automatic device that will trigger the explosives if we send a message. I'm going to get Brealak and the two of us will search their room first."

"I didn't think of that. Please contact me and let me know what you find."

"Okay."

Jeffery decided he didn't want his prisoners to die waiting for the ship from Earth, so he stopped at the break room and picked up fifteen bottles of water and twenty protein bars. When Jeffery arrived at the shuttle, the two maintenance men were just finishing strapping their prisoners to their seats. When everyone was ready Jeffery flew a thousand units north of the resort and landed near a cave he had explored two years ago. He turned to his maintenance men and asked, "Did you search them for weapons or electronic devices?"

"Yeah, but we didn't find anything," one of them answered.

"Okay, let's put them at least a hundred feet inside the cave. That way if we missed something, they won't be able to use it anyway."

Since the Flemms were still unconscious, they had to be carried inside the cave. Jeffery brought a lamp and left it with them so when they woke up, they would know they were inside a cave and realize they had been captured. He unbound their hands but not their feet and left the water and protein bars next to the lamp.

When they returned to Procolt Paradise Jeffery called Debbie. "Hi, we're back. I left our guests in a cave a thousand units north of here. I'm sure they will be very uncomfortable when they wake up."

4

"Good, they deserve it. Brealak and I searched their room. We found some communication devices and two other devices that looked like they could be used to trigger their explosives remotely. We took everything and put it inside the hotel safe."

"Okay. When you send a message to Earth about our situation, ask them if they have something we could use to help us locate the explosives. I'm not going to feel safe until they have been located and disarmed."

"I'll send the message out immediately. I'll also send a memo this morning to all our guests explaining what happened."

"That's a good idea, but I'm not sure what to do about our guests. What if the explosives have timers on them that are already armed?"

"I'll mention that possibility in my message to Earth. I'm sure that even if they put timers on the devices, they wouldn't go off for several more days. Obviously, if they went off before you had time to meet their demands, they wouldn't get what they want."

"That's a good point."

Debbie sent the message to Earth a few minutes later. They would get the message in two days. Now all they could do was wait.

Four days later they received a response from Earth. They were going to send out an armed ship immediately. The ship had a six person crew and was equipped with explosive detection equipment. They would take control of the prisoners and help locate the explosives before returning to Earth.

The ship arrived three days later. It was a small ship, but like all the ships currently being built, it had the newest propulsion system that enables it to travel at ten thousand times the speed of light, so it could travel the twenty-seven light years from Earth in three days. The Captain of the ship was Glen Turner. Captain Turner, like everyone else at NASA, knew about Jeffery and Debbie, and he was anxious to meet them.

5

Jeffery was informed the ship was landing and he and Debbie went to the landing pad to meet them. Captain Turner was the first one off the ship. He looked at Jeffery and Debbie, smiled, and said, "Admiral Whitestone, it's a pleasure to meet you and Captain Whitestone. I have heard a lot about both of you. You're both legends back at NASA headquarters. I'm Captain Turner, but please call me Glen. This is Lieutenant Durst, my first officer."

"It's nice to meet you as well. I'm sure you're aware of our situation. After we determine if there are any explosives on the resort grounds and disarm any we find, I'll be happy to treat you and your crew to an all-expense paid vacation."

"Thank you, sir, we'll get right on it. It would be helpful if there was somebody we could work with who is very familiar with the structures here."

"I'll have our chief engineer, Jim Roberts, here in a few minutes to help you. We also have two prisoners stashed in a cave a thousand units from here. You'll have to retrieve them and take them back to Earth for trial. Take your time, they aren't going anywhere."

"I'll contact you as soon as we're finished."

"Thank you," Jeffery responded. Then he called Jim Roberts and told him there was a crew here to scan the resort for explosives and they wanted his help with the building layout. Jim said he would be there in a few minutes.

Jeffery and Debbie went back inside. They went to the staff break area where each had a cup of coffee. Shortly after they sat down S1 walked in. He sat across from Jeffery and asked, "Is that the ship from Earth that just landed?"

"Yeah, they will be scanning for explosives shortly. It's too bad you couldn't read the minds of our prisoners. Then we would know if they planted any bombs."

"Perhaps we will develop that ability in the future."

"What you did was amazing. You may have saved thousands of lives. I have no words to express how much we appreciate it."

6

"We will always help you in any way we can. If you and Debbie had not come to Procolt 2, we would still be living in caves."

"Okay, I guess we've helped each other."

Then S1 asked, "What are the plans for rebuilding the marina?"

"I don't know yet. I sent a message to our architect, Nandor, yesterday telling him what happened. I expect to receive a reply in two or three days. I hope we can start on the replacement very quickly."

"When you do could you also build an area for us? We would like to have four or five rooms like we have in Squirrel Haven."

"That won't be a problem. I'll let Nandor know."

"By the way, we now have three pregnant females."

"That's wonderful! It'll bring your population to one hundred twenty-two."

"Yes, our group is certainly growing. It will be years before we outgrow Squirrel Haven, but several members of our group asked if they could have a place to stay close to the lake."

"When I receive plans on the new marina from Nandor I'll let you review them."

"Thank you."

"You're welcome."

S1 left the break room and for a while Debbie and Jeffery were alone. Then Jeffery's com unit beeped. When he answered Glen Turner said, "Hi Jeffery. So far we have found three explosive devices. There was one in each guest tower in the elevator equipment room. We also found one in the main dining room kitchen. They all look like they have remote triggers, but we will disassemble them and let you know what we find."

"Thank you, Glen. You should also check around the marina, or what's left of it, to see if any devices are there as well."

"No problem, but we want to leave in a half hour to pick up your prisoners. We don't know where the cave is, so we will need your help."

"Okay, just let me know when you're ready to go."

"I'll call you."

A half hour later Glen, Jeffery, and two other members of Glen's crew were on their way to pick up the Flemms. Glen landed the ship near the cave. As they entered Glen and his men took out their weapons. When they arrived at the area where the Flemms were left several days earlier they found them sitting on the floor with their backs against the wall. They managed to free their feet but made no move to get up as the four men approached them.

Robelt Flemm said, "Is there any additional cost for the cave tour? You should know that Melda and I really didn't like it very much. The accommodations are awful."

Glen said, "I'm placing both of you under arrest for destruction of property and acts of terrorism. You will be taken back to Earth for trial."

Robelt started to say something but changed his mind.

Jeffery said, "We found the explosive devices you planted and they have all been disarmed."

"Are you sure you found all of them?" Robelt asked as he smiled.

Jeffery ignored the question.

Each of the crewmen escorted a prisoner to the ship. Once they were inside each prisoner was placed in a seat and belted in. Glen looked at the prisoners and said, "Those belts are locked so don't bother trying to get up."

The trip back to Procolt Paradise was uneventful. However, after Glenn and Jeffery got off the ship Glen said, "I don't want to deal with our prisoners during the return to Earth. Can you give me more of the sedative you used on them?"

"Sure, I'll ask Marcet to give you some. Is there anything else you need?"

"No, I'm going to leave two of my guys here with all the equipment. I'll have them check the buildings again. I want

8

to leave as soon as I get the medicine. I should be back in six or seven days."

"Okay, let's go to the Medical Office and see Marcet."

When Jeffery and Glen got to the office, Marcet was there bandaging one of the guests who had fallen by the pool. She looked up and said, "Hi Jeffery, I'll be done here in a minute."

Marcet finished bandaging her patient and said, "That should be healed by tomorrow morning. Please be more careful around the pool. It does get slippery sometimes."

"Yeah, I noticed that a bit late. Thank you, doctor."

"You're welcome. Please let me know if there's a problem."

"I will," the patient said as she got up and left the office.

"Okay Jeffery, how can I help you?" Marcet asked.

"Glen would like more of the sedative so his prisoners won't be a problem during the trip to Earth."

"I think I still have ten doses." She walked over to a cabinet and took out some vials and a pressure syringe and gave them to Glen. "Each dose should render them unconscious for at least fifteen hours, so this should be enough to get you back to Earth."

"Thank you." Glen said.

"You're welcome."

Jeffery said, "I arranged for rooms for your two crewmen who are staying. Just have them stop at the registration desk. When you come back if you would like to stay for a while just let me know."

"Thank you, that's very generous. Is it okay if I come back with my wife?"

"Sure. I really appreciate your help with this situation."

"It's all part of our job. I'll see you again soon," Glen said as he walked back to his ship.

Thirty days after the Flemms were brought to Earth they were tried for the crimes they committed at Procolt Paradise. The evidence was overwhelming and the trial only

9

lasted for two days. The jury found them guilty on all counts and they were sentenced to twenty years in prison.

CROSUS

Bejort Griss, the current leader of Crosus, was mad. Every attempt to retaliate against Earth and Coplent had failed. He was sure the attack on Procolt Paradise would succeed. The attack was meticulously planned. He was positive every potential problem with the plan had been resolved. Obviously, he was wrong. The next time there would be no mistakes. His plan was to destroy the entire Procolt System, and he was sure he would soon have the ability to do it.

Hasin Tork, the person in charge of weapons development, was already a few minutes late for his appointment. Bejort didn't like waiting. He was not a patient man. He considered tardiness an act of disrespect. He thought about throwing Hasin in jail for a week as a warning not to be late again, but he needed the weapon Hasin was working on.

Hasin arrived .2 hours after the scheduled time. Bejort was almost wild with rage, but he contained himself. When Hasin entered Bejort's office he said meekly, "Sir, I'm sorry I'm late for our appointment. Please forgive me. I was waiting for the latest test results and it took a little longer than I expected."

"If you are ever late for an appointment again, you will be punished. Is that clear?" Bejort said angrily.

"Yes sir. I promise it won't happen again."

"So, what were the results you wanted to have before our meeting?"

"Small scale tests indicate the device will be capable of destroying an entire solar system. However, the process will take much longer than we anticipated. It could take up to a year, far longer than our original estimate of thirty days."

Bejort looked at Hasin. The hate he felt for Hasin was obvious when he screamed, "That is entirely unacceptable! You assured me the weapon would work within thirty days. Now I will give you thirty days to make whatever modifications are necessary to meet your original estimate. Failure to meet that goal will result in a most unpleasant experience for you and your entire family. Now get out of here."

Hasin did not reply to Bejort's outburst. He simply turned around and left the office. As Hasin walked back to his office he made a decision. He was going to leave Crosus. He didn't know where he was going to go yet, but the first step was to leave the planet. By the time he arrived at his lab he knew exactly what he was going to do.

He spent two weeks making some modifications to the design of the weapon. Computer simulations indicated that the changes would speed up the process by more than a hundred days, but that was still far slower than his original estimate. Since he couldn't find a way to speed up the process, he decided his only reasonable course of action was to cheat.

He spent the next few days modifying the simulator that was used to test the weapon. When he was finished, he ran the same test he had run previously. Now the results indicated total destruction of all planets within a two hundred-million-unit orbit around the star in twenty-seven days. He was pleased with the results and hoped Bejort would be as well.

He wrote up a report based on his latest test results and sent it to Bejort along with a request to test the weapon on a nearby system that had only one planet within its effective range. Since the Lundalt System was uninhabited, nobody would know or care if the system was destroyed. The prototype of the weapon would take one hundred fifty days to build.

Bejort was pleased with the report he received from Hasin and ordered him to proceed with the test. Hasin and his team began building the prototype. When it was about half finished Hasin told his wife what was going on and told her to go to Beljang with their two children to visit her sister. Beljang was not part of the trade group so there were no restrictions on traveling there. It was also one of the few trading partners that Crosus still had.

Hasin was worried that Bejort might try to stop his wife and children from leaving the planet, but there was no problem. Hasin and his team finished the prototype several days ahead of schedule. Hasin arranged for a small ship to use that would take him and the weapon to the Lundalt System where it would be tested. The day before he was scheduled to leave he destroyed all the design data for the weapon.

When he left Crosus he programmed the navigation system to take him to the system where the test was supposed to occur. The ship stopped seventy-five million units from the systems sun. He sent a partial message back to Crosus indicating the navigation system had failed and brought him only twenty million units from the systems sun. Then he disabled all the telemetry systems that sent automatic messages back to Crosus. The weapon was already loaded into a small probe that was supposed to be launched at the sun. However, he aimed it at the system's only planet, a large ball of methane and ammonia, and launched it. He thought now Crosus would never be able to recover the weapon or build another one. He was only half right.

He programmed the ship to take him to Beljang. He had originally decided to destroy the ship when he got there, but changed his mind. He decided to sell the ship and use the money to take him and his family to some other planet in the trade group where he felt they would be safe. He knew that since Crosus did not have the new communication system, he would arrive and leave Beljang before Crosus received his message.

BELJANG

Two days after he arrived on Beljang he sold the ship for twelve hirodim blocks. More than enough for him and his family to get to another planet and live there for a while. He discussed it with his wife and they decided to try and emigrate to Torblit. They went to the Torblit embassy and filled out the appropriate paperwork. They were told decisions can take up to one hundred fifty days.

He was surprised to hear from the Torblit embassy fifteen days later. They wanted him to come in for an interview. He made an appointment for the following day. When Hasin and his wife arrived at the embassy they were taken to a small office. The man behind the desk said, "We do not normally allow people to emigrate from Crosus. However, I noticed you were involved in scientific research. What kind of research did you do?"

"I did weapons research and design. I was ordered to design a weapon that would be capable of destroying an entire solar system. I actually completed the design, but the process was too slow to be useful. I was ordered to improve the system or my family and I would suffer as a result of my failure. I decided I didn't want to design a weapon that could potentially kill billions of people or put my family at risk. So, I sabotaged the project by destroying the prototype and all the design data except one copy of the data I saved for myself. I had previously sent my wife and our children here so they would be out of the reach of the Crosus government. Now we would like to go someplace where the government of Crosus can't bother us."

"That's quite a story. Can you provide us with any proof that your story is true?"

"I have my copy of the design data for the weapon with me. I sold the ship I was supposed to use to test the prototype as soon as I arrived here. If you have spies on Crosus, I'm sure they could verify that I was involved in weapons research."

"If what you have told me is true, all of us in the trade group are in your debt. I'm sure I can verify some of what you told me. Because communication with Crosus is slow that

15

verification may take sixty days. If you are discovered here, come back to the embassy and we will give you asylum."

"Thank you, sir. We will be waiting to hear from you."

Hasin and his wife thought the meeting went well, and although they liked Beljang, they both realized they were still in danger. The next forty-two days went by slowly. Each day their concern for their safety grew. Hasin had decided that if he didn't hear from the Torblit embassy within two days, he was going to ask them if they could arrange for his children to go there so at least they would be safe. That turned out to be unnecessary. Later that day he received a call from the Torblit embassy asking him and his wife to come in the following morning.

When they arrived at the embassy, they were taken to a large conference room. There were several people in the room already. After Hasin and his wife sat down, the person at the head of the table stood up and said, "Thank you for coming on such short notice. I'm Portug Freedit, the Torblit Ambassador to Beljang. I want you to know that we were able to verify your background information. We sent that information to Earth. They reviewed the information and they have a proposal for you to consider. Please put on the translators that are on the table in front of you."

The ambassador sat down and the man next to him stood up. "Good morning, my name is Brandon Simpson. I'm in charge of research at NASA. I don't know if you know anything about NASA so I will give you a little background. NASA was founded almost two hundred years ago on Earth in a country called the United States. It originally stood for National Aeronautics and Space Administration. The United States, and several of its neighbors, joined together to become the North American Union. About the same time NASA's mission had changed. It was now only involved in space travel. Now NASA stands for North American Space Administration. NASA developed, with the help of some beings from Procolt 2, the new propulsion and communication systems that are being used everywhere except Crosus. We are in the process of setting up a new research facility on Procolt 2. We would like to offer you a position at that research facility. It will include an excellent salary and free housing for you and your family. I can promise you will be safe there. Procolt 2 is protected by Coplent. Since the last Crosus attack there is a Coplent war ship in orbit around Procolt 2 at all times. Are you interested?"

"Yes, I'm very interested. But do you realize that one of the primary goals of the Crosus government is to destroy Procolt 2?"

"I'm aware of that. We are hoping you can assist us in developing something that will protect Procolt 2 against any weapon Crosus might develop."

"I must tell you I feel I'm responsible for the development of the weapon Crosus planned to use, so I feel compelled to assist you with that type of deterrent. I don't want to develop offensive weapons anymore."

Brandon said, "I'm very glad to hear you say that. The research facility should be completed within a half year, but you are welcome to emigrate to Procolt 2 at any time. Until the facility is completed, you and your family are welcome to stay at Procolt Paradise."

Hasin and his wife looked at each other and smiled. Hasin asked happily, "Can we leave tomorrow?"

"I will be leaving here in two days. You and your family are welcome to travel with me to Procolt 2."

"Thank you, sir. We are happy to accept your kind offer."

"You're welcome. Please call me Brandon. My ship is small, so there isn't much room for you to take personal items. Just bring what you will need for the trip. Anything else can be acquired on Procolt 2. I'll have someone pick you up and bring you to my ship. Do you have any questions?"

"How long will the trip to Procolt 2 take?"

"Not long, about five days. The distance to Procolt 2 is seventy light years. Is that okay?"

"Yes, of course. I was just curious. Thank you again for your kindness."

"You're welcome. Please keep the translators. I'll have two more on the ship for your children. I'll see you the day after tomorrow."

The meeting broke up and Hasin and his wife went back home. They were both very happy. When their kids heard the news about them moving to Procolt 2 they were happy too, but when they heard they would be living at Procolt Paradise they were absolutely thrilled.

The day they were supposed to leave, all of them woke up very early. They had already packed their clothes and a few small personal items in their suitcases. Nobody was hungry so they skipped breakfast. The car arrived to pick them up at 9:00. By 10:30 they were aboard Brandon's ship. When they arrived, Brandon gave them a quick tour of the ship. There were three cabins, each with its own bath. There was also a control room, a kitchen, and a recreation room. It wasn't very big, but Hasin and his family were very pleased with their accommodations.

Once the ship was underway Brandon asked Hasin to come into the recreation room because he wanted to ask him some questions. After they were both seated Brandon said, "Please tell me how this weapon you designed was supposed to work."

"The device is designed to accelerate the sun's aging process and bring it quickly into the 'red giant' stage. Depending on the size of the sun, it could expand enough to engulf any planets within two hundred million units. Our simulations indicated the device will work, but I originally thought the sun would reach its maximum growth within thirty days. It will actually take almost a year. That would give the people on the planet more than enough time to evacuate, and that was unacceptable to the Crosus government."

"Are you absolutely certain Crosus will be unable to develop the weapon now?"

"No, I'm not. I destroyed the prototype and the design data, but it's possible they will start the development process again. The people who assisted me are still there. They probably could start the project over again, and they would

18

have a significant head start because of their existing knowledge."

"How long do you think it would take them to complete the weapon again?"

"I would guess in about two or three years they could be at the point where I destroyed the data and the prototype. But remember, the government insists the weapon must work within thirty days. Neither I nor my assistants have any idea how to do that."

"I don't think we can safely assume they won't figure it out. Do you have any ideas on how we can protect ourselves from the weapon?"

"I've been thinking about that for several days and I have a few ideas."

Brandon and Hasin spent the next two hours discussing possible ways to disable the weapon. Together they came up with a plan, but Brandon said, "We need to discuss this with S12 when we get to Procolt 2. She is a native of Procolt 2. She and I developed the new propulsion and communication systems together. The design was hers. I supplied the knowledge to make the systems a reality. She is, without a doubt, the most intelligent physicist I have ever met. You will be surprised when you see her, but after you talk to her for a few minutes you will be absolutely convinced she is brilliant."

"I don't judge people by their appearance."

"Just remember that when you see her."

They landed at Procolt Paradise three days later. Brandon contacted Jeffery to let him know when they would be arriving and asked Jeffery to bring S12 with him to meet Hasin and his family at the landing pad.

PROCOLT 2

Jeffery, Debbie, their daughter Mystic, and S12 were all there to greet Brandon and the Tork family. Brandon got off the ship first, followed by Hasin, his wife, and the two children.

Hasin stared at S12, but didn't say anything. Brandon said, "Hi, it's really nice to see all of you again. Mystic, you have really grown since the last time I saw you."

Mystic smiled and said, "Hi, Uncle Brandon. I'm almost four years old now."

Brandon bent down and kissed Mystic lightly on her forehead and said softly, "You're getting to be a big girl."

Mystic giggled.

Then Brandon turned toward S12 and said, "I would like you to meet Hasin Tork, his wife Frazen, and their two children, Altin and Symbit."

Hasin was still staring at S12 when she spoke, "It's a pleasure to meet all of you. Hasin, I'm very anxious to speak to you regarding the weapon you developed for Crosus."

Hasin, stammering, replied, "I'm available at your convenience."

Brandon said, "We'll meet you in the main restaurant in two hours."

S12 responded, "That will be fine." Then she turned around and walked back to the resort.

Debbie said, "Please come with me and I'll show you your new home."

"I'll come to your apartment in 1.75 hours," Brandon added.

Debbie and Mystic guided the Tork family to the Earth guest tower. On the way, they pointed out the amenities the resort offered. They explained everything was included with the apartment which NASA was paying for.

They took the elevator to the fifty-eighth floor. Then Mystic led them to their apartment. As soon as they walked in the entire family smiled. They had never lived in a place as nice as this apartment. The family walked from room to room exploring it together. It had three large bedrooms, four full bathrooms, a large kitchen, a dining room, and a big living room. From the window in the living room they had a beautiful view of the lake and the newly rebuilt marina.

While the Torks were busy getting accustomed to their new home, Jeffery and Brandon went to the restaurant for a cup of coffee. After they sat down Brandon said, "I think we have a reason to be concerned. On the way, I spoke to Hasin about the weapon he developed. He believes, as do I, that even though he destroyed the prototype and the design plans for the weapon, Crosus will eventually be able to build it."

"What does the weapon do?"

"It causes the sun to enter into the red giant phase of its life cycle. That would destroy all the planets within a two hundred- million-unit orbit around the sun."

"They must really be pissed off at me to want to destroy the whole Procolt System!"

"It's not just you. They want to destroy Earth and Coplent too."

"Does Hasin think he can build something that will counteract the effects of the weapon?"

"Yes, he does. He explained the process to me, and it sounded reasonable. However, I want him to discuss it with S12. I would like to get her opinion."

"I could tell that you never told him S12 was a big squirrel."

"You're right, but I did tell him that he would be surprised by her appearance."

"And he was. Please let me know the results from your meeting this afternoon."

"Of course."

When Brandon knocked on the door of Hasin's apartment, Hasin opened the door almost immediately. He looked at Brandon and asked, "Why didn't you tell me S12 was a rodent?"

"I don't consider her a rodent. I consider her an equal. She may look like an animal, but that's where the resemblance ends," Brandon responded sternly.

"I'm sorry, I didn't mean to offend you or her. I just find it unsettling to speak to her. Do you know why she's so smart? Are there more like her?"

"I do understand how you feel. I felt the same way until I had an opportunity to speak to her. I'm sure you will feel better about working with her after our meeting. The reason she is so smart is there's some type of radiation on the surface of this planet that affects living organisms with a specific type of DNA. For squirrels, it affected them physically and mentally. They have developed hands with opposable thumbs, their life spans have increased substantially, and they have developed the ability to use more of their brain than any other living creature. They also have one other really unique capability. Their offspring have all the knowledge of their parents. S12 has not had any children, but if she does her children will be born with all her knowledge. I think the squirrel population is about one hundred. Jeffery built a home for them called Squirrel Haven."

"Okay, let's go to our meeting."

Brandon and Hasin went to the restaurant and found S12 was already there waiting for them. After Brandon and Hasin were seated, S12 said, "Hasin, I realize you find it uncomfortable speaking to a squirrel. I've noticed this many times in my interactions with humanoids and I'm not offended. I hope after we have spent some time together you will be more comfortable with the situation."

"Just hearing you say that already makes me more comfortable. Have you had an opportunity to look at the plans for the weapon?" Hasin asked.

"Yes, it took a while because at first I was unable to read your language. I sent a message to Coplent asking them to send some language learning material so I could learn it. It took me two days to learn, so now I have no problem reading the material. The design is most impressive, and I have an idea of how we might be able to terminate the reaction if we find out about it within ten days. After that, it may be unstoppable."

Hasin looked at S12 and removed his translator. S12 removed hers as well. It was obvious Hasin intended to test

23

S12's ability to speak Crosus. Then Hasin asked, "What two elements are used to cause the primary reaction?"

S12 responded, in perfect Crosus, "The two primary elements used to cause the reaction are platinum and carbon. Did I pass your test?"

"Yes, you passed the test. I'll never doubt you again. Please forgive me. It was very rude of me to do that," Hasin said meekly.

"I understand, but there is nothing to forgive. However, you need to use the translator so Brandon can participate in the discussion."

Hasin put his translator back on. They spent the next three hours discussing different methods for terminating the reaction. At the end of the discussion they had a plan. Hasin was going to build a computer simulation of the weapon while Brandon and S12 worked on a series of tests to evaluate several different methods to terminate the weapon's reaction.

S12 went home to Squirrel Haven while Brandon and Hasin went to Hasin's apartment. As they stepped into the elevator Brandon asked, "What is your opinion of S12 now?"

"I believe her participation in this project greatly enhances the likelihood that we will be successful. She is, without question, the most intelligent scientist I have ever met."

"I'm very happy to hear you say that. I feel exactly the same way. The laboratory facility won't be completed for at least one hundred fifty days, so I'm going to ask Jeffery if we can use one of the empty apartments as our lab until the facility is completed. I'll also order all the equipment we will need. I think we should be able to get started in ten days."

"So, I have some time to enjoy the place with my family for a while. That's wonderful! We have never had an opportunity like this before. I don't have the words to tell you how grateful I am."

The elevator stopped, and as Hasin stepped out Brandon said, "I'm glad you're happy, but when the temporary lab is ready your vacation will be over."

Hasin looked back over his shoulder and said, "I know, but I'm looking forward to working with you and S12 too."

It took almost a year for Hasin, S12, and Brandon to find a way to terminate the actions of the Crosus weapon. All the computer simulations indicated it would work, but they had no way to test it. Now Hasin wished he hadn't sent the prototype to the planet in the Lundalt system. It was a gas giant and he could not think of any way to retrieve it, but he decided to ask Brandon and S12 anyway.

"We need to find a way to test our theory with a real weapon. There are two possibilities. We could build one, which would probably take one hundred fifty days, or we could retrieve the prototype weapon that I sent to the planet in the Lundalt System. The weapon sends out a homing signal which would enable us to locate it, but I have no idea how to retrieve it. Do either of you have any ideas?"

"Since the planet is a gas giant, it probably has fairly low gravity at higher altitudes. If the weapon is in the upper atmosphere, we might be able to retrieve it with a ship and the transporter system Coplent uses," Brandon responded.

S12 was silent for a minute then she said, "I think the range of the Coplent transporter is only about five units. I believe the plan would work if we could increase the effective range to five hundred units. Brandon, can you get me the plans for the device?"

"I'm sure I can have them here in two or three days. I'll send a message to Coplent today. Do you think that modifying the transporter design will be faster than building a duplicate of the weapon?"

"Until I have had a chance to study the plans I don't know if it will be faster, but I feel it will be safer. I don't want to build a weapon that powerful."

Hasin said, "I understand how you feel. If we built it and Crosus found out, they could try to steal it. A small band of Crosus soldiers could easily land here undetected by the Coplent warship that is in orbit to protect us."

Brandon said, "I agree. Let's try to retrieve the prototype."

CROSUS

Bejort Griss and Jensor Kiltor were seated at a table in Bejort's office. Jensor said, "Sir, I'm sure you're aware that Hasin Tork should have returned from the Lundalt system by now. He was due back more than thirty days ago. I think we must assume his mission was a failure."

"You are correct, of course, but I don't like the idea of starting over with the weapons design. I find it difficult to believe the plans for the weapon and Hasin are both gone."

"Sir, I think Hasin's team could rebuild the weapon in less than two years. Even though the plans were lost, they are certain they can duplicate the last prototype."

"Okay, get them started on it immediately. I also want a team to try to duplicate the communication system the trade group is using. We've lost a year because our communication is too slow to be useful."

"We have some information regarding the communication system. We were able to obtain a unit on Beljang. It doesn't appear to be that complex. I think we may be able to duplicate it in less than a year."

"I'm counting on it. You know the consequences for failure."

"Yes sir, I do. I won't fail."

RUSSELL FINE

28

PROCOLT 2

After the meeting with Hasin and S12, Brandon wondered if the Coplent Warship had a copy of the plans for the transporter. He contacted the commander of the ship and asked about it. The commander told him he would have the plans sent immediately. Brandon had them a few moments later. He called S12 and she walked over to the Development Lab immediately.

She sat at a low table that was specifically built for her and began studying the plans. About an hour later she said, "Brandon, I believe the range of the unit is limited only by the amount of power supplied to it. It was designed to work with a minimal drain of the ship's power system. However, we don't have any limitations on available power. I believe we can increase the range to two hundred units by simply altering the power supply."

"Do you think that will be enough to allow us to retrieve Hasin's prototype?"

"Since we don't have any idea where the prototype is located, I can't answer the question. If they have a spare transporter on the warship, I think we can modify it in a few days."

"I'll contact them and find out if they have a spare unit."

Brandon walked into his small office and called the warship's commander. The commander was very excited about the possibility of extending the range of the transporter. He told Brandon there were two spare units onboard, and he would have one brought down to the surface immediately.

Brandon went back into the work area and said, "We'll have a transporter here within two hours."

S12 responded excitedly, "Perfect! I'll start working on modifying a power module immediately."

The transporter was modified and ready for testing two days later. Brandon took a small tool box with him and drove one of the resort's all-terrain vehicles to about twenty units north of the resort. He stopped and contacted S12. She turned

29

on the viewer that was part of the transporter system and locked onto the signal from Brandon's communicator. She used the viewer to locate the toolbox and activated the transporter. A few seconds later the toolbox was a few feet from her, in the lab.

When Brandon returned to the lab S12 said, "The test at twenty units was perfect. Let's try it at two hundred."

Brandon picked up the toolbox and said, "I'll take this to my ship and call you in about .2 hours." Then he left the lab and went to his ship that was parked about a half unit away. He flew the ship to a location two hundred seven units west of the resort. After landing in a large meadow, he contacted S12 again to tell her he was ready. A few seconds later the toolbox disappeared. Then Brandon received a call from S12. After Brandon answered she said, "The test was not successful. The toolbox was destroyed. It actually looks like it was melted. I need to look at the plans again."

"Okay, I'll head back to the lab. I'm sure we can resolve this problem fairly quickly."

When Brandon got back to the lab, S12 and Hasin were both studying the transporter plans. Brandon joined them and they spent the next six hours analyzing the plans. Hasin thought he had a solution to the problem. He felt the toolbox image was lost because there was no actual receiving device. He suggested they design a receiver that would be able to detect weaker signals. S12 and Brandon agreed.

It took three days to design the receiver and two weeks to build it because they needed parts from Coplent. When it was completed they tested it with items in the resort. It seemed to work perfectly. Brandon picked up a small plastic box and said, "I'll go to the same spot where it failed before."

When he landed he contacted S12 and she activated the transporter. This time it worked perfectly. On his way out, Brandon had grabbed a container of coffee from the restaurant. It was empty now and sitting in a holder next to his seat. Brandon called S12 again.

"I'm going to go five hundred units above the resort. There is an empty coffee container you can use for the test."

The test at five hundred units was also successful. That meant they were ready to try to retrieve the prototype weapon.

They decided to leave as soon as the transporter was installed in Brandon's ship. Four days later they were ready to go. Brandon contacted Jeffery and told him they were leaving. Jeffery wished them good luck and went to the shuttle port because a group from Earth was scheduled to arrive in .5 hours.

Jeffery or Debbie greeted every group that arrived and it was Jeffery's turn. As the people stepped off the ship he smiled at them and directed them to the check-in desk in the lobby.

RUSSELL FINE

32

LUNDALT SYSTEM

Brandon's ship was in orbit above the only planet in the Lundalt system. Hasin had already programmed the ship's computer to scan for the signal generated by the weapon. The ship was fifty thousand units above the atmosphere of the planet. At that distance they would be able to scan about 11% of the area. Each scan took several hours, so they did not expect to find the weapon anytime soon.

On the third scan the weapon was located. It was deeper in the atmosphere than they hoped. The gravity at that altitude was almost three times the surface gravity on Procolt 2. In order to retrieve the weapon they would have to place Brandon's ship in a parallel orbit a hundred units higher than the weapon. Their velocity would have to be slightly faster than the weapon, and that presented a problem. If they were traveling faster than the weapon, their altitude would increase. In order for the plan to work, the speed and altitude of the ship had to be controlled with extreme precision.

They had two other problems as well. Ships like Brandon's only required the use of their conventional propulsion system for landing, takeoff, and maneuvering the ship in space. The ship only had enough fuel for a single attempt. After transporting the weapon aboard, there would only be enough fuel to increase their orbital speed enough that they would be free of the planet's gravitational pull in about thirty hours. After they got back to Procolt 2 they would have to get help from the Coplent warship above the planet in order to land. The other problem was, once they were inside the planet's atmosphere it was probable the communication system would not function correctly.

They spent the next day running simulations with the ship's computer. The last simulation indicated an 83% chance of success. It also indicated that even if they managed to successfully transport the weapon to the ship, there was a 30% chance they would not have enough fuel to escape the planet's gravity.

33

Brandon sent a message to Jeffery telling him their plan. The message also said that if Jeffery did not receive another message within thirty-six hours, he should send a ship to rescue them.

They had to wait three hours before the weapon would be in the correct position for the plan to work. The piloting of the ship was being done by computer, so they could only wait and see what happens. Once they were close enough to the weapon the transporter would be activated manually. They only had one pass. After the ship passed the position of the weapon it would begin to accelerate and bring them out of orbit.

Two minutes before the maneuver was to start each of them took their seats. S12 was seated at the console that controlled the transporter. Her display also showed the position of the weapon relative to the ship. They would enter an orbit around the planet twenty thousand units behind the weapon and one hundred units above it. The ships speed was five thousand units per hour faster than the orbital speed of the weapon. The ship would be in range to transport the weapon twenty minutes after entering orbit for about one minute.

The ship bounced around as it entered the desired orbit, then a few moments later the ride smoothed out. S12's monitor indicated that the weapon was slightly more than nineteen thousand units ahead and one hundred seven units below their path.

The plan was to launch a small probe containing a transporter receiver at the weapon. The probe contained a very strong magnet which would attach itself to the weapon if it was less than ten feet away. S12 studied the signal from the weapon and said, "We won't need the receiver. I'm sure I can program the transporter to use the signal from the weapon instead." It took her less than ten minutes to modify the transporter's program.

Eight minutes later the weapon was one hundred seventy units in front of them. S12 watched the monitor and when it indicated they had closed the horizontal distance to less than one hundred units she activated the transporter. Thirty seconds later the weapon was on the bridge. The transporter automatically shut off after the transport was complete.

As they passed the position where the weapon had been, the ships engines turned on. Brandon watched as their velocity increased. In thirteen seconds the ship speed would be sufficient to escape the planet's gravitational pull. Unfortunately, the engine ran out of fuel two seconds too soon. They were trapped in an orbit around the planet.

PROCOLT 2

S37 had been trained to operate the communication system. When he received the message from Brandon about the plan to retrieve the weapon, he contacted Jeffery immediately.

Jeffery was sitting in the restaurant with Debbie and Mystic having lunch when he received the message. After S37 read the message Jeffery thanked him and closed his com unit. Then he said, "Debbie, would you be interested in a quick trip to the Lundalt system?"

With more than a little concern in her voice she asked, "What's wrong?"

"Maybe nothing. I won't know for sure for another thirty-six hours. Brandon, Hasin, and S12 found the weapon they were searching for, but it was not in an easily accessible location. They were going to try to retrieve it, but there was a substantial possibility they would end up in orbit around the planet and not have sufficient fuel to escape."

"If that happens, how are we going to rescue them? The transporters don't work with living things."

"I think we will have to dock with them and use our ship to carry them out of orbit."

"That's never been done before. Are you sure it will work?"

"I'm not absolutely certain, but I don't see any reason why it wouldn't. We don't have to accelerate from zero, so the strain on the docking mechanism would be minimal. Anyway, I'll discuss this with S1. I'm sure one of the squirrels will have the answer. But this is all theoretical at the moment. I'm hoping the rescue mission won't be necessary, but I want to be prepared."

"This will be a dangerous mission. If you have to go, take Brealak with you. I don't want Mystic to be an orphan."

"I understand. I asked you if you wanted to go, but I never had any intention of putting us both in harm's way."

Jeffery used his communicator and asked S1 and Brealak to come to the restaurant immediately. Both of them arrived ten minutes later. Jeffery explained the situation. Brealak agreed to accompany Jeffery on the mission. S1 said he would discuss the technical aspects of Jeffery's plan with some of the other squirrels immediately.

An hour later S1 contacted Jeffery and told him that the docking mechanism would have to be modified slightly to handle the strain unless the level of acceleration was kept below two units per minute. Jeffery thought for a few moments and then responded that the limitation would be acceptable.

The next day Jeffery and Brealak spent two hours preparing a ship in case a rescue was required. There was about twelve hours left before the thirty-six hour time limit would elapse and the closer that time came the more Jeffery was concerned about the mission.

An hour before the time limit expired Jeffery was sitting in his apartment with Debbie. Every few minutes Jeffery looked at his watch to see how much time was left. Debbie noticed what he was doing and asked, "Why are you so nervous about this rescue mission?"

"I've been wondering about that myself. I know the mission is dangerous, but I've been on dangerous missions before and I never felt this way. I'm concerned I may not be coming back. If that happens, please tell Mystic as she grows up how much I love her."

"That won't be necessary because I'm sure you're coming back and you can tell her how much you love her yourself. You are usually very self-confident. I think the reason you're so concerned is because you're now responsible for someone besides yourself."

"You're probably right, but that doesn't make me feel any better about the mission."

"Consider this, you and Brealak are probably among the most experienced pilots in the trade group. Other than the docking maneuver, you have done all this before many times. I'm sure the docking maneuver will be done by the ship's computer. All you have to do is watch."

"I know all that, but I'm still worried."

38

They continued to talk for a while. Then Debbie looked at her watch and said softly, "It's time to go."

Jeffery walked over to Debbie, smiled at her, and then kissed her goodbye. Mystic was taking a nap so he walked quietly into her bedroom. He watched her sleep for a minute and thought about how much he loved her. Then he bent down and kissed her goodbye too.

Fifteen minutes later he walked into the ship they would be using for the rescue mission. Brealak was already aboard. When she saw Jeffery she said, "They finished installing the auxiliary fuel tank about an hour ago and both tanks are full. We are all set to go."

Jeffery didn't respond immediately. Brealak noticed the look of concern on his face and she asked, "What's wrong?"

"I have a bad feeling about this mission. Debbie told me not to worry. She assured me the two of us can take care of any problem that arises, but I'm still worried."

"If I had to make a guess why you are so concerned, I'll bet it would be because of Mystic."

"You're right. Debbie and I just discussed it a few minutes ago. If everything is ready, let's go."

"Okay, take your seat and we will be on our way in two minutes."

RUSSELL FINE

LUNDALT SYSTEM

The trip to the Lundalt system was uneventful. Brealak put the ship into an orbit thirty thousand units above the atmosphere of the planet and began scanning for Brandon's ship. Three hours later Brealak said excitedly, "I found it!"

"That's great! How close do you think we will have to be for our com units to work?"

"According to the computer the atmospheric conditions are not conducive to radio frequency transmissions. I would guess we would have to be less than three thousand units from their ship."

"Give me the information you have regarding their orbit and I'll program the computer to get us in com range. I think we'll have to maneuver manually to within .25 units of their ship before we can begin the docking procedure."

Brealak printed out the position report generated by the ship's computer and handed it to Jeffery. He spent the next hour programming the computer and running simulations. When he was satisfied with the results he said, "We have to wait for about four hours before their ship will be in the proper position to start our rendezvous."

The time seemed to go by quickly. Everything would be done automatically, so Jeffery and Brealak watched the external monitor. From this distance above the planet it looked beautiful. There were numerous breaks in the cloud cover and through those openings they could see red, orange, and yellow patterns. They were both watching when the computer announced that the maneuver would begin in .025 hours.

They felt the increase in gravity as the ship began the descent into the planet's atmosphere. The ship began to bounce around as it was buffeted by a combination of the atmosphere and the increased gravity from the planet. They both watched the monitor as it showed the distance to Brandon's ship decrease. When it indicated the ships were less than three thousand units apart Jeffery tried to contact Brandon.

41

Brandon answered, "Hi Jeffery, thank you for coming to rescue us. I guess you got our message."

"Yes, Brealak and I are about three thousand units behind you. I'm going to maneuver my ship to within .25 units of yours and then we will begin the docking procedure."

"What happens after we are docked?"

"We will begin to accelerate slowly until we reach escape velocity. I didn't want to wait for modifications to be made to the docking mechanism, so we have to limit our acceleration to 2 units per hour. At that rate it will take about one hundred two hours to reach the speed we need."

"Okay, we don't have any fuel to move the ship so you will have to do it all on your own."

"I assumed that when I programmed the computer to do the maneuver. I'll contact you again when we are close enough to start the docking procedure."

"Okay, we'll talk again soon."

An hour later Brandon's ship was visible on the short-range monitor. Brealak contacted Brandon and she described what was happening. The computer was displaying how far Jeffery's ship was from the optimum position to begin the procedure. It was a slow, painstaking process. Almost an hour had passed until the computer indicated the ships were properly aligned. Then the computer took over. The docking procedure went smoothly and .25 hours later the ships were locked together.

Jeffery began the acceleration process. The passengers on both ships felt the slight increase in gravity and everyone was relieved. Now all they could do was wait until they were out of reach of the planet's gravity. With each hour, the pull of the planet was noticeably reduced as the increase in speed caused the height of their orbit to increase.

Just as the computer calculated, one hundred two hours after the acceleration started, they were free of the planet's gravitational pull. Enough fuel was transferred to Brandon's ship so he would be able to land when he returned to Procolt 2. The ships undocked and .15 hours later Brandon's ship began the journey to Procolt 2. A few minutes later Brealak programmed the computer to take them home. The mission was a complete success. Brealak looked at Jeffery, smiled, and said, "I told you that you had nothing to worry about."

Both ships arrived at Procolt 2 three days later. Debbie and Mystic were there to meet Jeffery as he stepped off the ship. He hugged and kissed them both. Then the three of them, and Brealak, went to the restaurant to get some real food.

When Brandon's ship landed Brandon called the maintenance department and asked them to bring the weapon to his lab. Then Brandon and Hasin went to the restaurant and S12 went home to Squirrel Haven.

The next morning Brandon, Hasin, and S12 were in their lab. S12 arrived a few hours before the others and spent the time studying the weapon. By the time the others arrived she had completed her analysis. She said, "After examining the weapon I'm certain that in addition to our plan to restore a star to normal after it has been exposed to the weapon, I believe we may be able to prevent the device from activating at all if we bombard it with high energy radio waves. It takes about twenty hours for the process to begin, but the components are not well shielded, so the high energy radio frequency radiation will destroy many of the components rendering the weapon useless."

Hasin said softly, "I should have thought about that possibility myself. I'm sorry. But if we want to test that we'll have to build a duplicate of the control system."

"I'm positive we can do that, if we can get identical components," S12 responded.

"Hasin, please get me a list of components and I'll order them from Coplent," Brandon requested.

"I'll have it for you in two hours. But nothing can be substituted. They must be identical."

"I understand, but that may not be possible since I can't order them from a supplier on Crosus."

Hasin nodded his head to indicate he understood the problem. Then he said, "I think that since we now have the weapon here, we have to start building the device we believe will neutralize it in the event that the plan to destroy the control system is a failure."

S12 said, "I agree. We already know what the device has to do, and I have been thinking about the design for a while. I should have the plans completed in a day or two. I don't think it will take more than three months to build."

The Crosus weapon worked by producing radiation that would exponentially increase the fusion reactions in the star. That would increase the energy released inside the star, and the increased energy would cause an even greater increase in the level of fusion. The only way to halt the self-destructing actions in the star was to first eliminate the radiation being generated by the weapon and then flood the star with heavier elements that would bind with the hydrogen atoms. As these heavier elements dispersed through the star, the level of fusion reactions would slow down because there would be less free hydrogen to fuel them.

One of the biggest problems with the device they had to build was to make it so it would be able to withstand the surface temperatures on the star, but Hasin had already developed that part of the technology.

Ten days later the parts to build a duplicate control system for the Crosus weapon arrived. So did some of the components that were needed to build their star-saving device. Hasin worked on building the control system while Brandon and S12 worked on the other project.

Hasin's task was much easier, and he had the control system completed in eight days. He tested the completed control system to make sure it functioned correctly. When he verified it was functioning, S12 began building the device that would destroy it.

Because there was a possibility that the destruction of the control system would cause an explosion or a fire, they decided to perform the test away from Procolt Paradise. Brandon loaded the equipment needed and they flew a hundred units north of the resort.

Hasin and S12 set up the test while Brandon watched. When all was ready Hasin powered on the control system.

44

Then S12 turned on the high-power radio frequency signal
generator she designed. Almost instantly the control system
failed. A second later it began to crackle and then it burst into
flames. The test was a complete success, and further evidence
of S12's ability to analyze and resolve problems quickly and
correctly the first time.

After the test was finished Brandon said, "I'm glad we
did the test here. I think Jeffery would have been upset if we
set fire to our lab." Then looking at S12 he asked, "Do you
think there is some way to create a defense system with this
technology?"

S12 looked thoughtful, or at least as thoughtful as a
squirrel can look, for several seconds. Then she said, "I think
it's possible, but I'm not sure it's practical. I'll have to think
about it for a while."

Hasin said, "If we could create a defense system, it
would be unnecessary to build a star-saving device."

S12 responded, "I'm not sure about that. Unless the
defense system is 100% foolproof, there is still a possibility
the Crosus weapon could hit a star, and I don't believe any
defense system could be perfect.

Brandon said, "S12 is correct Hasin. We still have to
build the Star Saver."

"I like that name, we should call it the Star Saver
instead of just calling it the device," S12 added.

"I like that too," Hasin said.

For the next several weeks Hasin and Brandon worked
on the Star Saver, while S12 worked on the defense system.
During that time S12 hardly said a word to Brandon or Hasin.
She immediately rebuffed any attempt at conversation. She
was constantly deep in thought.

Then one morning everything changed. When Brandon
arrived at the lab S12 was already there. She said cheerfully,
"Good morning Brandon, it's going to be a wonderful day!"

"It's nice to see you talking again. Hasin and I were
both very worried about you."

"I know and I'm sorry, but sometimes when I'm
thinking about a complex subject I have to block out

45

everything else. However, I figured out how to build the defense system."

"That's great! Would you like to explain it to me?"

"The basic problem was how to flood the area around a star with high energy radio waves. I was trying to figure out a way to transmit a signal that would cover the surface of the star we were trying to protect. Once I realized it would be impossible to do that, I started thinking about other options. What I thought about was the original idea you had to utilize drones traveling between relay stations that were one light year apart for a high-speed communication system. All we have to do is build a drone capable of traveling around a star in a series of circles. The circles would be about a thousand units apart. Each orbital pass would be completed in a fraction of a second, and we would be able to cover the entire surface of the star like Procolt in less than two seconds. The drone would constantly blast the area around it with the appropriate radio waves. I am certain I can make a transmitter that will have an effective range of a thousand units, so each pass would overlap with the previous pass."

"Yes, that's a great idea! Since the weapon has to travel slow enough that it won't be destroyed on impact, I'm positive your plan will work."

"I can have a prototype ready to test in sixty days. Then we can deploy it around Procolt and test it with dummy weapons."

"I think we should concentrate on this and put the Star Saver on hold for a while."

"I suppose we can do that, but you know the risk."

"I do, and I think the risk is minimal for now. Once this defense system is deployed around Procolt, we can go back to working on the Star Saver."

"Once we validate that it works on Procolt, we will have to install it in the Coplent system and around Earth's sun as well."

Just at that moment Hasin walked into the lab. He saw Brandon and S12 and immediately realized that S12 was out of her depression. He said, "S12, it's nice to see you happy again. What's going on?"

S12 explained the defense system to Hasin. Like Brandon, he thought it was a great idea. They started work on it that day. They decided to call the device they were building the Star Defender.

Brandon thought S12's estimate of sixty days was probably a little optimistic, but with all three of them working on the project, it was actually ready two days ahead of schedule.

Hasin built three more control systems and mounted them in disposable probes. They loaded the drones and the Star Defender on Brandon's ship and moved into an orbit halfway between Procolt 1 and the Procolt sun. The computer on the Star Defender had been programmed with the orbital requirements and they launched it. The Star Defender had a small tachyon propulsion system and was traveling at about thirty times light speed in just a few seconds. They waited for an hour watching the Star Defender to be sure it was in the correct orbit. Since the system was passive, all they had to do was launch a probe at Procolt and see what happens.

Hasin adjusted the probe to travel at one hundred thousand units per hour and launched it. At that speed, it would take about three hours before the probe would pass the orbit of the Star Defender.

They were all watching the monitor as the probe approached the critical orbit. As it passed through the orbit it exploded. Then they tried the two remaining probes launching them only a few minutes apart. They were destroyed as well.

Brandon believed the mission to eliminate the threat posed by Crosus had been successfully completed.

Within three hundred days the Star Defender had been installed in the solar systems of every major member of the trade group. During that time Brandon, Hasin, and S12 completed the design of the Star Saver and built a prototype. They planned to test it in the Lundalt system within thirty days.

THE SQUIRRELS

The test of the Star Saver was successful. Three days after Brandon, Hasin, and S12 returned something happened that had a profound effect on the squirrel population.

Jeffery, Debbie, and Mystic were having breakfast in the restaurant when S12 walked up to their table. She looked sad, but before Jeffery had a chance to ask her what was wrong she said sadly, "I'm sorry to inform you that S1 died last night."

No one said anything for a few seconds. Then Jeffery said, "I'm sorry to hear that. I always considered him a friend." Jeffery paused for another moment and continued, "Actually, he was much more than a friend, he was part of our family. He will be missed by all of us."

Mystic began to cry and Debbie did her best to comfort her. It was the first time Mystic had to deal with the death of someone she knew.

S12 said, "We would like your help. His death is the first that has occurred since you arrived here. Our old method of dealing with a death is no longer appropriate for us. I've read about how humans hold funeral services when one of you dies, but we have never had any experience doing that. Could you arrange something for us?"

Debbie responded, "Yes, of course. I'll be happy to do that for you. Do you know what you want to do with his body?"

"When we lived in the caves and one of us died, we took the body out of the cave and placed it in a shallow grave that we dug in one of the meadows. But now that just doesn't seem right. We have no religion, and we don't believe in God, or in life after death as many humans do. However, we would like his body to be placed in a location where we can erect some kind of monument to commemorate his life."

"I understand, and I'm sure we can do that for you," Debbie responded.

"Thank you. We are holding a meeting of all the adult squirrels tonight. We need to find a new leader."

49

"Please express our condolences to all the squirrels at the meeting. If any of them are scheduled to work, please let them know they are free to attend the meeting instead of working."

"I'll do that. Thank you for your help," S12 said. Then she turned around and walked in the direction of Squirrel Haven.

Debbie spent the afternoon arranging the goodbye ceremony for S1. She also ordered a small coffin from Earth and arranged for a grave to be dug near Squirrel Haven. She wanted to have some kind of grave marker made as well, but she hesitated because she felt he should have a name, not a number.

The next morning S12 called Jeffery to set up a meeting with him. He said he was in his office with Debbie and now would be the perfect time for a meeting. S12 said she would be there in a few minutes.

When S12 arrived at Jeffery's office she walked in, said "Good Morning," and climbed up on a chair.

Debbie said, "Good Morning S12. How did the meeting go last night?"

"The meeting went very well. A lot of decisions were made. That's what I wanted to talk to you about. Probably the most important decision we made was for each of us to have names instead of numbers. We want our civilization to mimic the social structure humans use. At the meeting it was decided that each squirrel would have a last name that corresponded to the job they do. In family groups the job of the lead male in the group would be used for all the family members. Each squirrel could choose their own first name."

"Did the group pick a name for S1? I wanted to have a name on his grave marker, not a number."

"Yes, they did. They selected the name George Leader for him. My name is Jessica Teacher. Name tag necklaces are going to be made for every squirrel, except the infants. The group also decided that the most intelligent adult should be the leader of the squirrels. Since they considered me to be the most intelligent, I was selected. We also decided that the Leader

50

would retain the position until they either died, resigned, or were no longer capable of leading the group."

Jeffery asked, "Are you going to continue assisting us with the product development?"

"Yes, for now. However, the squirrel population is growing. There are now two hundred thirty-six of us. As that number grows, I may have to spend most of my time handling the responsibilities as Leader. On a personal note, my friend S31, whose name is now Glen Baker, and I are going to become a family group. I want to have a child. Once that child becomes an adult, he or she will take my place in product development."

"Will your name change to Jessica Baker?" Debbie asked.

"Yes, when my child is born. I have to go now and help prepare the Star Saver test, but I wanted to let you know about the results of the meeting."

"Thank you, Jessica," Jeffery said.

Jessica said, "You're welcome," and left the office.

Debbie ordered the grave marker. George Leader's body was taken to Earth to be embalmed. It would be back in ten days and would be shipped with the grave marker. The service for George was scheduled two days after the delivery.

When the new marina was built a banquet hall was included in the design. The hall had been used frequently for parties and weddings, but this would be the first time there would be a memorial service held there.

A burial site was selected near the main entrance to Squirrel Haven. The resort maintenance people dug the grave and mounted the eight-foot tall grave marker the day before the service.

Jeffery was scheduled to speak first at the service. He arrived with Debbie and Mystic about ten minutes early. The hall was already filled with mourners. All the squirrels were given the day off, and every one of them was there in a show of respect for George. Most of the resort staff were in attendance as well.

51

At exactly ten o'clock the lights in the hall dimmed and everyone became silent. Jeffery walked up to the podium. There was some brief applause and then Jeffery began to speak.

"When we first arrived here, almost eight standard years ago, we never expected to find any intelligent beings. The very first time we observed the squirrels we knew we were wrong. We realized immediately that the squirrels had a language and had developed a society. It was another half year before we realized how intelligent they are. As our interactions with the squirrels increased, it became obvious we needed a primary contact. George Leader, then known as S1, assumed that position."

"Over the years we worked together, became friends, and then, despite the obvious physical differences, we became more. Now all of the full-time residents of Procolt 2 are one big family. That means we love and care about each other and help others whenever it is needed. Although most of us are from either Earth or Coplent, our family has people from twenty-seven of the trade group planets. Today we all mourn George Leader."

"George's finest moment was when we were faced with a potential disaster caused by two terrorists from Crosus. After they destroyed the marina, they sent me a list of demands and threatened to kill thousands if I failed to comply. George, using an ability he had kept secret until that time, located the terrorists and put them into a sleep state which enabled us to capture them before they could do any further damage. The two terrorists are still in prison on Earth."

"At this point I would like to turn this memorial service over to Jessica Teacher, formerly known as S12."

Jeffery left the stage and Jessica went to the podium. A stool had been placed behind it, so she climbed up and stood on the stool. She was now high enough to make eye contact with the people in attendance. There was some applause and when it stopped, she began to speak. She talked about things Jeffery knew nothing about. What George did to organize them and how he helped them overcome some of the problems they faced as their society grew. She said he was their first teacher, and he was the first squirrel to learn English. Then she spent some time recounting events that George played a critical role in over the years. Finally, she said, "George was an exceptional leader and it will be impossible for me to fully replace him, but as your new Leader I will do my best to make this difficult time a little easier for all of us."

Then they all walked to the grave where George would be buried and watched as his little coffin was lowered into the ground. Many of the humans cried, and although squirrels are unable to cry, their sadness was obvious.

PROCOLT CITY

Ten days after the burial of George Leader, Jeffery received a note from one of his guests, Oscar Goodman, requesting a meeting with him. Jeffery contacted Oscar and asked to meet him at his office at three o'clock.

At exactly three o'clock a man appeared at the door to Jeffery's office. Jeffery looked up at him and the man smiled. Then he said, "Good afternoon Admiral Whitestone. Thank you for seeing me."

"Please come in. I'm no longer an admiral, and please call me Jeffery. We are very informal here. How can I help you?"

Oscar walked in and sat down across from Jeffery. Then he said, "Jeffery, it's a pleasure to meet you. I represent a group of people from a small city in central Kansas. We have all been here on vacation for the past month and we have a proposal we would like you to consider."

"Okay Oscar, I'm listening."

"We have noticed that every other day a supply ship arrives with commodities that are needed to keep Procolt Paradise running. The primary part of every shipment is food. I'm positive shipping food from Earth or Coplent is very expensive. Is that correct?"

Jeffery thought he knew where this conversation was going. He responded, "Yes, shipping food is very expensive."

"Have you ever thought about growing your own food on Procolt, instead of paying to have it shipped?"

"Yes, I've thought about that frequently. But nobody here has the knowledge or the desire to become a farmer."

"I would like to change all that. Our group is made up of farmers, tradesmen, shopkeepers, and others and we all have one common desire. We all want to leave Earth and move someplace less crowded where we can live a simpler life. We all love it here on Procolt 2 and want to make it our home. We can build the farms and within two years supply you with most of the food you will need. That would benefit all of us."

55

"I haven't been to Earth for a long time. Has it changed?"

"It's beginning to look more like Coplent every day. The population is now more than twenty billion. Many of the largest cities have banned private vehicles. There are too many people, even the national parks in the United States are overcrowded. Right now, the earliest I could get a reservation at any park is three years away."

"How many people are in your group?"

"Our group here is fifty-four, but we represent about two thousand people."

"It sounds to me like you want to build a small city."

"Yes, that's exactly what we want to do. We are prepared to sell everything we have on Earth, come here, and start a new city. But we can't do it without your approval, and some initial financial assistance. Any financial assistance would be repaid once we start producing the food supplies you need."

"Oscar, that's a very intriguing proposal. When do you return to Earth?"

"We have fifteen more days here."

"I must tell you it has been bothering me for some time that everything we need we have to buy from Earth or Coplent. I'm sure you were here for the memorial service for George, the leader of the squirrels. I had to send his body back to Earth to have it embalmed and I had to order his coffin from Earth as well. That situation made me realize how dependent we are on others, and I think that should change. Can you provide me with a list of the people who want to relocate here and their professions?"

"I'm sure I can have that for you tomorrow. Would you like to meet at three again?"

"Sure, I'll have Debbie and Jim Roberts here too. Jim is in charge of maintenance and construction here. We can discuss what you will need to get started. If we agree to do this, you must pick a location for your new city before you return to Earth. While you are gone, we can construct some

56

temporary housing for you and your people to use until permanent structures can be built."

"Thank you, Jeffery. This means a lot to us and I promise we won't let you down."

"Okay, I'll see you tomorrow at three, Oscar."

That evening at dinner he discussed the proposal with Debbie. Like Jeffery, she thought it was a great idea. Then Jeffery called Jim Roberts and told him about the proposal and the meeting.

The next afternoon at three Oscar showed up at Jeffery's office. Jeffery smiled and waved him in. Debbie and Jim were already there, seated at a small conference table. Oscar sat down and pushed a memory card over to Jeffery. Jeffery took it and made the appropriate introductions. Then Jeffery asked, "Does this contain the information I requested yesterday?"

"Actually, it has more. There is a brief biography of every adult who wants to relocate here by family group. The list includes children who will be coming as well."

"How many total people are involved?"

"There are two thousand seventy-four people. Four of the women are pregnant, so the number may increase slightly before we relocate."

"Are you aware of the radiation here on Procolt 2 and how it affects humans?"

"I've heard rumors about some unusual radiation, but no specifics. Apparently, it isn't harmful or you wouldn't be here."

"You're correct, of course. In actuality, the radiation is beneficial. I will explain the details after we have an agreement."

"Okay, by the way, one of the people who will be coming is Craig Whitman. Craig is now a farmer, but he did own a funeral home and is an experienced embalmer."

"I hope we won't need his services for a long time, but I suppose it's good to know we have somebody with that capability. Do you have a plan of what you want to do? I don't want more than two thousand people to suddenly show up here with no place to go."

"Yes, the plan is on that memory card as well. To begin with, about one hundred of us will come here. Many of them have experience in construction. They will build the structures required for phase one. When the structures are finished another two hundred will come and phase two will begin. These people will set up the farms and begin construction of single-family homes. They will also build stores, offices, and roads. When phase two is complete the rest of the people will come. We plan on raising cattle and pigs as well as fruits and vegetables."

Jeffery thought about telling him that raising the animals could be a problem because they had the potential to become intelligent, but he decided not to mention it at this time. Instead he said, "I'll go over your plan this evening."

Jim said, "Jeffery, I could build a temporary structure that would be able to house three hundred people in about thirty-five days. That way they could bring three hundred people initially."

"Do you have everything you need to build it?" Jeffery asked.

"Yes, we actually have enough material on hand to build six of those structures."

"Okay. Oscar, tomorrow morning meet me at the shuttle port at eight o'clock and we'll go looking for locations to build your city. The shuttle holds twelve, so if you want to bring a few more people that would be fine. Have you given any thought to what you are going to call your city?"

"We haven't made a final decision yet, but so far everyone likes Procolt City."

"That sounds perfect," Jeffery said.

After everybody left Jeffery's office, except for Debbie, he asked her, "What do think about this?"

"I think it's a great idea, but we don't know anything about Oscar and his people. I think we should do some checking before we make any commitments."

"I agree. I'll compile a list of names and send it to Earth. We should get the information back in less than ten days."

The next morning Jeffery sent a message to one of his contacts on Earth requesting information on Oscar and his group. Then Debbie, Mystic, and Jeffery went to the shuttle port. Oscar was waiting for them with two other people. When Jeffery was a few feet away he said, "Good morning Oscar. This is our daughter Mystic."

"Hello Mystic, my name is Oscar. And these are my friends, Trevor and Carol."

Mystic replied, "Hello, it's nice to meet you. My daddy said you want to move here and build a city."

"That's right. Today we're going to look for a good spot to build our city. You can help us."

Mystic smiled and said, "Okay, I think that will be fun."

Oscar said, "Trevor is an architect, and Carol is in charge of our finances."

Jeffery shook hands with Trevor and Carol. Then he opened the door to the shuttle and said, "Let's go."

After everyone was seated Jeffery announced, "The temperate area of Procolt 2 extends about four hundred units from the equator. Beyond that the winters are very severe, with temperatures below freezing for months at a time, so I think we should concentrate our search near the equator. Since you will need a source of water, we should probably look for a location near a lake. All the lake water here is drinkable, although we filter it anyway."

"Lakes provide recreation too, Oscar said. Then he asked, "Are there fish in the lakes?"

"Yes, but we haven't found any that taste good. All the fish we serve comes from Earth."

"Part of the plan was to build a large fish hatchery," Carol said.

"I'm not sure that's a good idea. You mentioned you wanted to raise cattle and pigs yesterday. I was going to wait before I discussed the radiation here, but I think now is the time to tell you something about the environment of Procolt 2. As you know, the entire surface of the planet is bathed in radiation. It appears to have no effect on anything, except people and animals from Earth. It's beneficial, for the most part. Humans from Earth experience a substantial increase in muscle strength and extended life spans. Other species experience increased intelligence. I'm sure you are aware of the squirrels here. What you don't realize is that they are the result of mutated squirrels from Earth. If you bring animals here, they may experience the same increase in intelligence. I don't think you would want to raise animals for meat that you could have a conversation with."

Oscar and his group were silent for a few moments. Then Oscar said, "That's an interesting development. I was wondering why there were no pets here. Now I know."

"Actually, there is no rule regarding pets. The situation has never come up. However, I don't think I would want the planet overrun with animals that are as intelligent as we are. If you want to raise animals for consumption, you'll just have to import them from any planet other than Earth."

"With increased life spans, is this place the 'Fountain of Youth'? Do you have any information regarding lifespans for humans?"

"When we first arrived here we found the remains of a human who had been brought to this planet at the end of World War II. Tests indicated that he was about one hundred eighty years old when he died."

"Well, that would seem to be another excellent reason to move here."

"We have not made that information available to the public, and I'd like to keep it that way. Of course, none of us have been here long enough to validate the increased life spans for humans. However, on Earth squirrels live for about ten years. Many of the squirrels here are over thirty. By the way, the squirrels believe they are native to Procolt 2 and they are very proud of that. Please don't discuss this information with them."

"Of course not, nor will we discuss the increased life spans with other members of our group. If that information became public knowledge, there would be billions of people here in a relatively short time."

"Exactly," Jeffery agreed.

The shuttle took off and Jeffery took them to a location a few hundred units east of Procolt Paradise. The area was surrounded by low mountains on three sides and there was a large lake in the valley. Jeffery guessed it was about twenty square units. Around the lake the land was mostly flat and filled with grass and trees. It looked like a perfect place to build a city.

"This was one of the locations we thought about for Procolt Paradise, but our lake is much larger. This lake is called Lake Meadows," Jeffery said.

"This looks perfect," Trevor said.

"I agree, I couldn't imagine a more idyllic place to build a city," Carol stated.

"Do you want to keep looking?" Jeffery asked.

"Can we land here and look around before I answer that question?" Oscar asked.

"Sure."

Jeffery landed the shuttle about two hundred feet from the lake. They all got out and began to look around. Everyone in Oscar's group was thrilled with the location. Mystic and Debbie went for a walk along the lake shore. The sky, which was clear, began to cloud up. It was almost time for the morning rain. As the first few drops fell, they all went back to the shuttle.

Once they were inside Oscar asked, "What other places did you have in mind?"

"There is a location with a similar landscape three hundred units north of here. The biggest difference is the mountains are taller, and they are snowcapped. The temperature in the valley is cooler than it is here, and it does occasionally drop below freezing in the winter."

"Can you take us there?"

"Of course. I'll go slow so you can look at other areas. If you see something that looks interesting, let me know."

"Thanks Jeffery."

Each member of Oscar's group was seated by a window. Jeffery kept the speed at about one hundred fifty units per hour so the trip would take two hours.

During the trip to the next location nobody found anything of particular interest. When they were almost there Jeffery said, "Look out the windows on the right side."

Almost in unison the three people in Oscar's group said, "Wow!"

Jeffery circled over the area for a while and then he landed the shuttle. The temperature outside was a brisk forty-two degrees. Jeffery handed each of them a jacket before they got off the shuttle.

Oscar said, "This place is really beautiful, but it's a little too cold to be comfortable. Is it always this cold?"

Debbie responded, "It's early winter here. In thirty days, the high temperatures will hover around twenty-five degrees."

"How tall are those mountains?" Trevor asked.

"The air is very clear and it's difficult to judge distances by looking. The base of the mountains is twenty-five units north of our location. These are the tallest mountains on Procolt 2. They are all over one unit high, or in terms you are more familiar with, about six thousand five hundred feet," Jeffery said.

"Can you ski on the mountains?"

Jeffery shrugged his shoulders and said, "I don't know. I'm not into winter sports."

Oscar, with a note of authority in his voice, looked at Trevor and Carol and exclaimed, "As far as I'm concerned, the first location you showed us is perfect."

"I agree," Carol and Trevor said together.

"Good, let's go back to Procolt Paradise," Jeffery stated.

When they were back at the resort Jeffery suggested they meet at 10:00 the next morning in the main restaurant. Everyone agreed.

Jeffery arrived at the restaurant a half hour early. An area at the back of the restaurant was set up where they would have some privacy during their meeting. He thought about holding the meeting in a conference room, but wanted it to be informal.

Everyone arrived on time. Jeffery said, "Please sit down, relax, have some coffee and donuts. Jim, Oscar's group has chosen the valley around Lake Meadows for their city. How soon can you get started on their habitat?"

Jim thought for a few moments and said, "I can get started in two days. It will take three days to get the equipment and materials there to build it. When the outside of the building is finished, I'll order the furniture, plumbing, kitchen fixtures, and other items needed to complete the job. The building will be ready for occupancy in thirty-five days."

Oscar smiled and said, "That's amazing. On Earth that project would probably take two years. There is a minor shortage of power modules on Earth now, so it would probably take a half year to get them. Where do you get yours?"

"Normally from Coplent. But we probably have at least five hundred in stock. If I order them, my order always arrives in less than ten days. It's possible I'm getting special treatment, but I certainly never asked for it."

Oscar was obviously thinking about the timetable for the construction of the habitat. Then he asked, "I know we paid for more time here, but would it be possible for us to leave early and arrange to come back as soon as the habitat is ready?"

"If there's space available, I don't see any reason that couldn't be done. But the passenger ships are usually booked hundreds of days in advance. I believe you told me there are fifty-four people in your group. It may be difficult to accommodate that many people on short notice."

"Could you arrange for a charter ship to bring us to Earth and wait for us there until the habitat is ready and bring us back?"

"I'm sure I could do that, but it would be expensive."

"Please look into it. We plan on selling our property on Earth and that will give us the money we need to pay for the charter. If the ship is large enough, I am sure we could have three hundred people from our group on the return flight."

"I will need five or six days to check for available ships. I'll send out a request today."

"Thank you. I don't think you realize how much this means to us."

"You're welcome."

Then Trevor asked, "Do you have any maps or images of the Lake Meadows area so we can plan our development?"

Jim responded, "Yes, we do. I would also like you to tell me where you would like the habitat to be constructed. Can you come to my office this afternoon at two o'clock?"

"We'll be there."

Jeffery sent out requests for a charter ship to Earth, Coplent, and Torblit. Every time he sent out messages, he thought back to how easily things were accomplished on Earth and wished it was possible to have instant communication again. But the distances involved made that unlikely to ever happen.

The following afternoon Jim met with Oscar and his group. Within an hour they had a preliminary plan for Procolt City and selected the construction site for the habitat. After the meeting ended, Jim called his construction foreman and asked him to come to his office. When the foreman arrived Jim went over the plans with him and told him to start construction on the habitat as soon as possible.

Two days later the delivery of materials to the building site began. Although it wasn't required, a cement foundation was used as a base for the habitat. The building was less than a hundred feet from the Lake Meadows shoreline, and if the lake overflowed its banks, he didn't want the habitat damaged. Most of the time the habitats are not intended to be used as permanent structures, but in this case it would probably be actively used for ten years or more.

The morning after the foundation was poured, Jeffery and Oscar were scheduled to go to the site to see how things were going. Before Jeffery went to meet Oscar, he stopped at his office to see if he had received a reply concerning his request for information about Oscar and his group. The reply was there. Jeffery read it quickly and was relieved to see there was nothing derogatory in it.

Oscar was waiting for him when he arrived at the shuttle port. After they arrived at the construction site, Oscar looked around and was very impressed. He said, "It would probably take a year on Earth to get this far, and your people have only been working on it for six days!"

"There's nothing to delay a building project here. No permits, environmental impact reports, or building inspections to contend with. If we want it, and have the material, we build it. By the way, I expect to get some response to my request for a charter ship today. We should stop by my office when we get back and check."

Oscar nodded his head in agreement. They spent another half hour wandering around the construction site and then returned to Procolt Paradise. They went directly to Jeffery's office, and as he expected, there were several responses to Oscars' request for a charter ship.

The most interesting response came from Greg Dorland. He was a space pilot who worked for NASA for twenty-five years. Greg found some financial backers, purchased a used ship, and spent a substantial amount of money refurbishing it. They took possession of the ship thirty days ago and were looking for their first charter. They were offering to do the charter for half of what the others were asking.

After looking over the bids Oscar asked, "Since you know people at NASA, could you check out Greg Dorland for me? The other bidders have all done charters before, but it's hard to ignore his price."

65

I agree. Actually, Brandon Simpson is on Procolt now, and he still works for NASA. Perhaps he can give us some information regarding Greg. I'll call him now."

When Brandon answered Jeffery said, "Hi Brandon, I have a question for you?"

"Okay, ask."

"Are you familiar with Greg Dorland?"

"Yes, I know him quite well. We have been on several missions together. He is an excellent pilot and engineer. Why?"

"He apparently has resigned from NASA and is now operating a charter business. I requested some bids on a charter from Procolt 2 to Earth and back again thirty days later for one of our guests. Greg's bid was the lowest, by about 50%. But my guest is skeptical since he will be Greg's first customer."

"I wouldn't hesitate to book the charter with Greg. I would trust him with my life."

"That's exactly what you do if you book a charter. Your life is dependent on the ability of the captain of the ship."

"Yeah, tell your guest to go with Greg. I would."

"Okay, thanks Brandon. By the way, when are you leaving to conduct the Star Saver test?"

"At least another ten days."

"Okay, thanks Brandon."

Jeffery looked at Oscar and said, "Brandon knows Greg. He said Greg is an excellent pilot and engineer and he would trust Greg with his life."

"Okay, I guess we have selected our charter ship."

"I'll send him a message now telling him you agreed to his terms. When do you want him here?"

"As quickly as possible."

"Okay, I'll take care of it." Jeffery sent the message to Greg as soon as Oscar left the office.

Six days later Jeffery received a response from Greg that said he would be at Procolt the following day. Jeffery immediately informed Oscar. Oscar, and the other members of his group, spent the rest of the afternoon packing and planning for the return to Earth.

The next morning while Jeffery, Debbie, and Mystic were having breakfast in the main restaurant, a squirrel that Jeffery recognized walked up to their table. "Good morning Nathan, is there a problem?"

"No sir, everything is fine. But I was asked to find you and let you know that Greg Dorland would be landing on the next shuttle and he would like to meet with you."

Jeffery looked at his watch and realized the shuttle would be landing in less than ten minutes. "Contact the Captain of the shuttle and ask him to inform Mr. Dorland that I will be waiting for him here."

"Yes sir," and Nathan walked out of the restaurant.

"Who is Greg Dorland?" Debbie inquired.

"He's an ex NASA pilot who resigned and opened a charter company. He has a contract with Oscar's group to take them back to Earth and then return here when their habitat is ready."

"I'll bet when he sees you he calls you Admiral."

"You're probably right."

Fifteen minutes later a man walked up to their table. He looked to be in his mid-forties. He was tall, and very muscular. He looked like a soldier. When he was just a few feet from the table the man said, "Good morning Admiral Whitestone, good morning Captain Whitestone. I'm Greg Dorland. It's an honor to meet both of you."

"Thank you. It's a pleasure to meet you as well Greg. Please call me Jeffery and my wife Debbie. This is our daughter, Mystic. Please sit down and join us."

"Thank you, sir, uh, Jeffery."

"I was told you wanted to talk to me, but I have a question for you as well. Why did you resign from NASA? Brandon Simpson told me you were a top-notch pilot and engineer. I'm sure you would have had an excellent future at NASA."

"I resigned from NASA because of you."

"What! You're going to have to explain that."

"You are responsible for the changes that have occurred at NASA over the past six or seven years. NASA is

67

no longer a research organization. They are now a business entity, and one of the biggest on Earth. Their primary function is to build new ships and retrofit old ones. They also manufacture drive and communication systems for the entire trade group and are now the largest employer in the North American Union. And, as I stated before, these changes are your fault. You started them on the path."

"Okay, I see your point. The excitement is gone."

"Exactly. When was the last time you were on Earth?"

Jeffery looked at Debbie, hesitated for a few moments, and said, "It's probably close to nine years since we've been there."

"More than just NASA has changed. The native population on Earth has increased by 30% in the last four or five years, and there are now about a billion aliens living there too. Most of the major cities have outlawed private forms of motorized transportation. Inside the cities the number of single-family homes has plummeted. The homes that were there have been torn down and replaced with high rise apartment buildings. New York, Los Angeles, London, Tokyo, and Mexico City all have more than fifty million residents."

"Now I know why Oscar and his group want to move here."

"Oscar and his group are just the tip of the iceberg. There are groups like his all over the North American and European Unions. I'm sure you'll be hearing from them soon."

Everyone was silent for a while and then Greg continued speaking, "It's more than just the increases in population that are driving people away from Earth. The attitude of people has changed. Many of them have become lazy. The governments now provide 'cradle to grave' support for people who have no desire to work, and that number is growing every day. If you're happy with your life, why mess it up with work?"

"It seems to me that other civilizations in Earth's history have been in a similar position, and those civilizations withered and died. Is that what you think is going to happen on Earth?"

"Yeah, without innovation and exciting new products, Earth's finances will definitely take a turn for the worse. Someday somebody will invent a way to improve interstellar communications or develop a faster drive system and Earth will be left in the dust."

"They must realize that."

"You would think so, but I see no signs that anything will change in the future."

"They'll still have their food product exports, won't they?"

"Sure, but those exports only represent about 18% of the total export revenues. About 9% of our export revenues come from power module sales. However, our ability to manufacture products for our own use has fallen so far that there is now a six month wait for power modules. We manufacture them by the millions for export, but there is only one factory left that makes them for domestic use."

"So now the cities are overcrowded with people who are too lazy to work, and Earth no longer has the ability to meet its own energy requirements."

"Yup, that's pretty accurate. I think, or at least I hope, that eventually the people in charge will realize what's going on and take some action to reverse the situation."

"We are talking about politicians, aren't we? Until it affects them directly, they are unlikely to change things."

Greg sighed deeply and said, "I guess you're right. Anyway, how's the food here?"

"It's great, and it's free."

"That's a good combination. Do you know when Oscar and his group want to leave?"

"I suspect they will want to leave this afternoon. I told Oscar you would be here today."

"After breakfast I'll go find him."

Greg and Oscar's group left that afternoon. They were scheduled to return in twenty-seven days. The habitat was finished a few days ahead of schedule, so when Oscar

69

returned, this time with two hundred thirty-three people, everything was ready for them. Jeffery sent two shuttles to the space station to bring the new settlers directly to Procolt City.

The city grew rapidly. With the help of some of the construction people from Procolt Paradise, a half year later there were three more habitats built. One hundred nineteen farms, complete with homes, were ready to begin operation. There was a small shopping area too. Unlike Procolt Paradise, in Procolt City money was needed to buy things, so Jeffery had to begin producing currency. Something he knew nothing about, so he hired an experienced banker from Coplent to handle all the money issues.

By the time Procolt City celebrated its first anniversary, the population was twenty-seven hundred. Construction of farms was continuing and construction of some small factories were started. The first factory was going to make power modules. The second factory was going to make small electric vehicles for use in the city.

Procolt City continued to grow. As the fifth anniversary approached, the population was almost two hundred thousand. The city now had everything cities on Earth had. There were two hospitals and four shopping centers. The factories and farms were selling much of their output to Jeffery, but they were beginning to export things to other trade group members as well.

There was a big celebration for their fifth anniversary, and Jeffery was there with his family. Mystic, who was now almost fifteen, was there too, but she was not alone. She came with a boy named Stan. It was her first date.

During the ceremony Jeffery announced that he had been contacted by a group from the European Union that wanted to build a settlement as well. Construction on the new city would begin in about thirty days and was going to be named New Paris. Jeffery was worried the people from Procolt City might be concerned with competition from another city, but that wasn't the case. Oscar actually offered to help with construction.

70

During the five years since the first group of settlers came to Procolt 2, Greg Dorland's business grew as well. He now had five ships and the only charters they ran were between Earth and Procolt 2.

CROSUS

About the same time the construction of New Paris began, Bejort Griss was finally about to receive the final version of the weapon he had been waiting for. It took almost three years longer than the engineers originally estimated, but he decided that by now his enemies would probably have forgotten about Crosus. But he was about to jar their memories. He summoned the commander of his armed forces.

When General Jastmore appeared at his office, Bejort found himself in an unexpectedly good mood. "General, please sit down."

"Thank you, sir."

"I'm sure you are aware that our new weapon is ready to be used to destroy our enemies. We will have three devices available in thirty days. I want you to arrange simultaneous attacks on Earth, Coplent, and Procolt."

The general smiled at Bejort and said simply, "No."

Bejort's mood changed instantly. He screamed, "What do you mean? Are you disobeying a direct order?"

"No sir, you are simply no longer in a position to give orders anymore. The planet is now under military control, and will remain that way until elections can be held."

"Are you out of your mind? I'm in charge here!" Bejort screamed.

Calmly the general said, "Screaming won't change anything. We have decided that we no longer have any desire to take revenge against those who were only protecting themselves from you and your inability to accept defeat. The other planets in the trade group where we were once a member are all flourishing, while our standard of living has fallen so far that in some parts of Crosus our people have almost no food."

Bejort looked at the general with hate in his eyes and said, "General, you are under arrest. You will not live to see tomorrow."

"Go ahead, call your guards."

73

Instead Bejort decided to take matters into his own hands. He opened a desk drawer, removed a weapon, pointed it at the general and said, "You're dead." Then he tried to fire the weapon. Nothing happened.

The general laughed and said, "Your weapon was disabled early this morning."

At that moment two guards walked in. The general said, "Please escort our former leader to the prisoner holding area in the Crosus Court Building."

One of the guards responded, "It will be our pleasure sir."

Once Bejort realized he was beaten, he surrendered completely.

Bejort's trial began two days later. He was charged with, among other things, more than five thousand counts of murder. He made no attempt to defend his actions and the trial ended quickly. Bejort was sentenced to death.

The day after his trial was finished, Bejort was taken to an old shuttle and was strapped into a seat. Next to him on the shuttle floor was the only completed weapon that had occupied almost his entire existence for the last eight years. Before the door to the shuttle was closed the general walked into the shuttle.

The general was smiling when he said, "You and your weapon, which has been disabled, will be able to spend your final moments together. After I close the hatch, this shuttle will be sent on a course directly to the sun. You have about two hours to live. I hope that perhaps you will spend your final moments thinking about all the misery you caused to the people of this planet, but I suspect you really have no remorse for the things you did."

General Jastmore left, closed the hatch, and moments later the shuttle departed. The general watched as the shuttle disappeared from view. Then he walked to his office, which was formerly Bejort's office, and sat down behind the big ornate desk. Prior to the coup he had arranged a meeting with the civilian leaders of Crosus for the next morning.

There were seventeen other people in the big conference room. General Jastmore stood up and said, "Today is a great day for Crosus. We are no longer controlled by a deranged leader whose only thought was revenge. However, I believe we have two tasks that must be completed as soon as possible in order to begin restoring our previous standard of living. The first is that we take whatever action is required to become members of the trade group again. I'm certain we will never regain our previous status with the group, but that doesn't matter. We need to be able to trade with other worlds to restore our finances. The second is that we must hold free elections. As soon as those elections are held, I will step down and turn control of the government over to the elected civilian leaders. My assistant and I will be leaving for Earth later today. They are the most powerful member of the trade group now and we owe them an apology for our previous actions. We will be gone for about seventy days. I expect that while I'm gone the elections will be held. Is there anybody who disagrees with this plan?"

The other people in the room looked at each other, but nobody spoke. General Jastmore watched them and when he was sure there were no objections he said, "One more thing. While I'm gone I want all weapons research terminated. When I return we will consider filing criminal charges against some individuals involved in the development of the new weapon. In my absence, General Yowlend will be in charge."

That afternoon General Jastmore and his assistant, Torpi Grwes, left for their mission to Earth. They were using a small unarmed ship they thought would not be considered a threat. It was equipped with the newest Crosus drive system, so it would take less than thirty days to travel the one hundred light years to earth. During the trip, the General and Torpi spent most of their time rehearsing the upcoming discussions.

When their ship passed the orbit of Mars, they contacted Earth's space station.

The General pressed the transmit key and said, "Earth station, I am General Jastmore from Crosus. I realize you don't allow ships from Crosus to dock at your location, but I'm hoping you will make an exception in this case. I would like to meet with a representative from the trade group to express our regrets for previous actions Crosus has been involved in, but the government on Crosus has changed and we want to rejoin the group."

A few moments later General Jastmore received a reply to his request. "General Jastmore, I don't have the authority to allow you to dock your ship here. Please hold your current position until I can discuss this with my superiors."

"Thank you, we will wait here. Please be advised that there are only two passengers onboard, myself and my assistant, Torpi Grwes. We, and the ship, are unarmed. You are welcome to inspect the ship if you desire."

"Please wait. I will contact the appropriate people immediately."

The general's ship was scanned several times. There were no weapons onboard so none were found. However, the name Crosus is synonymous with death and deception. Several hours later the general received a call.

"General Jastmore, my name is Harlis Croter. I'm in charge of the trade group delegation on Earth. Your appearance here was something of a shock. We never expected any peace overtures from Crosus. I cannot permit your ship to dock at the space station at this time, but I can meet with you at our base on Mars."

"Thank you, Mr. Croter, I appreciate this opportunity very much."

"I'll send you the coordinates of the Mars base. Meet me there in three standard hours. They will be expecting you. Please don't be offended when they search you for weapons."

"I understand the situation. We will not be offended by the search."

"Good, I'll meet you in three hours."

The Mars base consisted of six large interconnected transparent domes. There was one central dome and five domes around the perimeter. Each dome was connected to the central dome and each of the perimeter domes was connected to both of its neighbors. The domes were one unit in diameter and a half unit high. The base also extended about a half unit into the ground under the central dome.

The general contacted the base and was given instructions on where to land. He landed the ship in the center of a large landing pad. As soon as he shut off the engines the pad began to sink into the ground. It continued to drop for a while and then it suddenly stopped. The general received a message telling him to move the ship forward, off the landing pad, and stop.

The general followed the instructions. As soon as the ship was off the pad it began its return to the surface. It appeared to rise much faster than it went down. Then the ship began to move forward. Ahead the general could see a pressure door. As the ship approached the door opened. Once the ship moved inside, the door closed and the general could hear the sound of the area pressurizing. Then a vehicle appeared and stopped next to the hatch of the general's ship. He opened the hatch and four soldiers stepped inside. Two soldiers began inspecting the ship. A third man began checking the general and Torpi for weapons. When they were satisfied the fourth soldier said, "Please follow me, Harlis Croter is waiting for you."

The general and Torpi followed the soldier into the vehicle. A short time later the soldier led the general and Torpi into a conference room. Inside three people were seated at the table. The man in the center stood up and said, "General Jastmore, I'm Harlis Croter. On my left is Krans Yondic. He's the local representative for the trade group bank. On my right is Colonel Halstead. He's in charge of the military contingent on Mars. Please tell us why you are here."

"I'm not sure where to start. About fifteen years ago it became apparent that Crosus was losing its position within the trade group. We needed money and discovered that Torblit had set up a hirodim mining operation on Procolt 4. The plan was to attack the mining operation and take the hirodim for ourselves. The Crosus leader hired some mercenaries to attack and kill the miners. The plan was that we would set up our own mining operation. It was thwarted by two people, one from

Earth and one from Coplent. As a result of our murderous behavior, Crosus was expelled from the trade group. We have been suffering since that time."

The general paused for a moment and then continued, "The leader demanded we take revenge against both Earth and Coplent. He launched an attack to destroy Earth which failed, but killed more than ten thousand of Earth's people. He was not concerned about the deaths. He was only concerned that Earth survived and he lost again. He was overcome with rage and demanded our people build a weapon that would destroy Earth's sun. It took eight years to perfect the weapon. When I learned of his plan to use the weapon in simultaneous attacks on Earth, Coplent, and Procolt I arranged to take over the government and remove him from power. He is now residing on our sun for eternity."

"His lust for revenge almost bankrupted the planet. Many of our people are suffering from food shortages. Unemployment reached more than 50%. Without a change, we are doomed. I'm hoping you will consider allowing us to join the trade group again. We understand we owe reparations to both Earth and Torblit, and when we have money again, we will honor our obligations."

"We have idle factories and highly talented people who are anxious to return to work. Please allow us an opportunity to prove we can be a valuable part of the trade group again."

The three men looked at each other, all of them apparently surprised by the general's request. Then Krans Yondic said, "Prior to the expulsion of Crosus from the trade group, Crosus was our largest depositor. The funds in that account were frozen at that time. Since then we used the funds to pay reparations to Earth for the deaths and destruction of property caused by the attack. The families of the miners on Procolt 4 also received substantial payments from the account. Additionally, Coplent was reimbursed for the costs it incurred defending Earth. However, there is still more than two hundred thousand hirodim in the account. If Crosus becomes a member of the trade group again, those funds would be released."

The general smiled and said, "Thank you, I had assumed the money in our account was used to pay for our crimes, but I had no idea the remaining balance was so high. That money would allow us to buy things which are desperately needed."

Harlis Grwes said, "General, are you familiar with the name Hasin Tork?"

"Yes, he was in charge of weapons research. He disappeared several years ago."

"He didn't disappear. He defected and has been living on Procolt 2 with his family for several years. He assisted us in developing a system that would protect trade group planets from the device Crosus developed. That system has been deployed to protect most of the trade group planets. The attack your leader was planning would have failed again."

"I'm very happy to hear that, but even if I knew that our weapons would fail prior to the coup, it would not have changed anything."

Harlis Croter continued, "Will you agree to disband your military and allow the trade group to place military outposts on Crosus?"

"Certainly, that's a very reasonable request under the circumstances. I have directed the civilian leaders of the planet to hold elections in my absence. When I return I will step down and turn control over to the newly elected government."

"Does Crosus have substantial silver deposits?"

"I don't know, but I'm sure Torpi has the answer to that question."

Torpi said, "Yes, I do. Crosus has substantial silver deposits. Our manufacturing operation used more than one million golas of silver ever year. We don't use the same systems for weights, but one gola is slightly more than a eight ounces. Since manufacturing has declined by 80% after we were expelled from the trade group, silver mining has halted, but it would not be difficult to start it again."

"We have a problem here on Earth that Crosus may be able to assist us with. I'm sure you are familiar with the power modules we developed on Earth. We export them by the millions every year, and exports take priority over manufacturing them for our own use. As a result, we are experiencing shortages that are holding up major construction projects. Would you be interested in manufacturing them for us?"

"Yes, of course," the General replied.

"I'll have to discuss this with other trade group leaders. I'll need ten days to do that. I would like you to stay here while those discussions take place. Is that acceptable?"

"Yes."

"Good. We'll find a place for you to stay. You'll need visitors' badges to obtain the things you will need during your visit. We'll also give you communicators. Please feel free to explore the base here. A hundred thousand people consider this home. We have parks, restaurants, theaters, and a large sports complex. We don't use money on the base. That's why you'll need the badges. I'll make all the arrangements. Please wait here. I'll have somebody here to help you shortly."

The three men got up and left the room. After they were gone the general said, "That went much better than I expected. I was concerned we would be arrested and charged with war crimes."

"Bejort convinced us that the people from Earth were all evil and didn't deserve any of the benefits of being in the trade group. Obviously, it was all propaganda."

A short time later a young woman walked into the conference room. She said, "My name is Yolanda Grace. During your stay on Mars I'll be available to help you with anything you need." Then she handed the general and Torpi badges and small communication devices.

"If you need me press the green button on the communicator and say my name. The badges will be needed to obtain food or other items you need. Please follow me and I will show you to your apartments."

Yolanda, Torpi, and the general spent the rest of the day together. After she showed them their apartments she took them on a tour of the base. They ate lunch at one of the restaurants and it was the first time either General Jastmore or

Torpi had experienced Earth food. They were both very happy with their lunch.

After lunch she took them to one of the many parks on the base. This one had a small zoo and the General and Torpi were fascinated with the animals, which were completely different from the animals on Crosus. Then they went to the sports complex. Inside were areas for snow skiing, water skiing, swimming, golf, and tennis. Neither of the men from Crosus had even seen snow and they both decided to come back and try snow skiing before they went home.

By the time they returned to their respective apartments the General and Torpi were exhausted, and both went to bed early. For the next six days they explored the base and thoroughly enjoyed themselves. There was no place even remotely similar on Crosus. The general made a promise to himself that he would change that.

On the morning of their seventh day on the base General Jastmore's communicator beeped. He answered the call and Yolanda said, "Good morning General Jastmore. Harlis Croter asked me to bring you to the conference room at 11:00 this morning. I will be at your apartment at 10:30 to bring you there."

"Thank you. Do you know what will be discussed at the meeting?"

"No, I was just asked to bring you there. I have no details at all."

"Okay, I'll expect you at 10:30."

Yolanda showed up right on time and found the general and Torpi waiting for her.

"Good morning gentlemen. Are you enjoying your stay here?"

"Yes," the general answered. "There is no place like this on Crosus. I can understand why so many people like living here. I've spoken with some of the people here and they all say it's much better than living on Earth."

"The big cities on Earth are overcrowded. There are lines everywhere. If you want to go to a restaurant for dinner, you can usually expect to wait at least an hour for a table. If

81

you want to go to one of the national parks, you have to make reservations at least a year in advance, and if you want to stay at the park the usual wait is three years. Besides, many of the cities are located in areas where it's too hot in the summer and too cold in the winter. Here everyone has plenty of room, there are no lines for anything, and the temperature is always perfect."

"Can anyone just come here to live, or is there some process you have to follow?"

"In order to come here to live you have to have a job here. Every time we have any position available, we get at least a hundred people applying for the job."

"What kind of jobs are there here?"

"This part of the base is all residential, but about ten units north of us are two more domes. There are factories inside those domes and we manufacturer a lot of things, primarily small electronic devices and pharmaceuticals."

"How do the people get to their jobs?"

"There is a tram under the central dome. The tram runs between this area and the manufacturing area constantly. It's capable of moving fifteen thousand people per hour. The factories work on staggered shifts so the trams never become overcrowded." Then Yolanda glanced at her watch and said, "We have to go. We don't want to be late."

When they arrived at the conference room the same three men were waiting for them there. Harlis Croter said, "Good morning General Jastmore. I have discussed the Crosus situation with several of my colleagues and we are willing to give Crosus a chance to prove they can be a responsible member of the trade group again."

"Thank you. You really have no idea how much I appreciate this opportunity."

This time Krans Yondic, the military commander on Mars spoke. "General, the day after tomorrow a Coplent warship will be in orbit around Mars. Your ship will be placed in its hold and then you and your assistant will leave for Crosus. The trip will take four days. When you get there, you will turn control of your armed forces over to the commander of the Coplent ship. By the time you arrive the bank will have released ten thousand hirodim from your account. We want you to use that money to restart silver mining operations."

"That is all acceptable. Do you know what kind of facility will be needed to manufacture the power modules?"

Harlis responded, "No, but there will be two industrial engineers from Earth onboard the ship. They can give you the details of what is needed. I want you to assign somebody who is familiar with your manufacturing facilities to work with them. We are hoping that power module manufacturing can begin within one hundred days, with the first deliveries twenty days later. We will need at least five million units a year."

"Can we produce some for our own use?"

"Yes, as long as you meet your quota first."

"Will you guarantee us a specific profit margin? Obviously, we have to earn a profit on the devices we sell."

"We want you to keep accurate records of your costs for both labor and materials. We will pay you five times your cost on the first five million units. If additional units are needed, we will discuss terms at that time."

"My only concern with any of this is that I will arrive at Crosus at least twenty-five days ahead of schedule. It's possible that the elections will not have occurred prior to my arrival."

"I'm sure you will be able to handle any domestic problems. I think you should arrange to speak to your people as quickly as possible."

"I agree, our previous leader had some supporters and I suspect they will not be happy with our arrangement, but I believe I can convince them that this arrangement is good for everyone."

Krans Yondic said, "I hope that it won't be necessary, but if military action is needed, your own military and the Coplent ship will be more than capable of handling the problem."

"I'm positive that won't be necessary, but it's always good to have options."

Harlis Croter said, "You and Torpi have another full day here. You should go enjoy yourselves."

"I think we will do exactly that."

Two days later they were on their way to Crosus. Shortly after the trip started, the general and Torpi were both in the general's cabin. They were discussing what they would do after they returned to Crosus. The door chime sounded and Torpi answered the door. There was a young female officer who asked, "I'm Lieutenant Kindler, are you General Jastmore?"

"No, I'm Torpi Grwes, his assistant. May I help you?"

"Yes, Captain Grotok asked me to bring you and the general to the bridge. Would it be convenient for you to come now?"

The general walked up to the door and said, "Of course lieutenant, we would be honored to meet Captain Grotok."

The Coplent Warship was at least three times the size of the biggest ship in the Crosus fleet. It took almost a quarter of an hour to walk to the bridge. When they arrived Lieutenant Kindler led them to a door and knocked lightly.

A voice from inside said, "Enter."

The lieutenant opened the door and walked in followed by the general and Torpi. Once they were inside she said, "Captain, this is General Jastmore and his assistant Torpi Grwes."

The Captain stood up, walked over, shook their hands, and said, "It's a pleasure to meet both of you. Please sit down."

The general and Torpi sat down. When they were seated it became obvious there were two more people in the room. The Captain said, "Gentlemen, I would like you to meet Luther Vandor and William Burtell, they are manufacturing engineers who will be assisting you with the manufacturing facility needed to build the power modules."

The general said, "Gentlemen, it's nice to meet you. Please be assured that you will have our full cooperation in this endeavor."

William said, "Perhaps we can get together after dinner to discuss the requirements for the building."

"William, my assistant Torpi, is very familiar with the status of available manufacturing facilities on Crosus. I'm certain he can help you."

"Good, that's exactly what we need. Thank you general. We'll come to your cabin at 8:00 if that's okay with you."

"That will be fine. Captain Grotok, I wanted to make you aware that Crosus has a substantial planetary defense system. It has a sensor range of more than three hundred thousand units. Please stop the ship at a distance of four hundred thousand units and I will contact them to let them know your ship is coming and not to take any hostile action."

"Thank you for the warning General Jastmore. I was going to ask you about that before we arrived anyway. I'll send somebody to bring you to the bridge at the appropriate time."

The two engineers arrived at the general's cabin right on time. Inside the cabin was a small round table and the four of them sat down. William Burtell began the conversation. "General, we want this endeavor to be a success as much as you do. The lack of power modules is beginning to have a negative effect on Earth's ability to provide housing for the constant flow of new immigrants. We need to build ten thousand homes every month to keep up with demand, but without an adequate source of power modules, we are unable to meet demand."

"Why can't you use some of the units you are producing for export?" the general asked.

"Because the units used for export don't meet the power requirements we need for domestic use. I believe you know we have only one factory producing the units we need."

"Yes, Harlis Croter told me that during our first meeting."

"Anyway, what we need is a supply of pure silver, iron, and nickel. Those are the primary elements of the silver alloy rod that is the main component of the power modules."

"We have an abundance of those elements," Torpi said.

"The facility must have a high temperature furnace to melt the materials used to create the alloy and combine them

85

with extreme precision. There is virtually no tolerance for error in mixing the components. After the alloy has been made, it must be machined into rods. The size of the rod also must be exact. No dimension can be more than .0025 inches off. Do you know what an inch is?"

"Yes. After Earth joined the trade group their system of weights and measures was distributed to all the member planets. Since Crosus was still a member at that time, we have the information," Torpi responded.

"I wasn't aware of that. Are you familiar with the basic concept of the design?"

"Yes. We managed to get some units and we took them apart trying to reverse engineer them, but we were never successful."

"The reason you were unsuccessful was because you didn't have the exact ratio of silver, iron, and nickel in the rod. If it's off by more than .02 grams, the rod will be useless."

"That would make it almost impossible to analyze correctly."

"Exactly, that's the reason nobody has been able to duplicate the device. So, the power module is basically a transformer and the silver alloy rod acts as a magnetic amplifier. An unbelievably strong magnetic field is created when a small electric current runs through the coil around the silver alloy rod. The positioning of the silver and iron rods is also critical. In power modules for use on Earth there is additional circuitry to convert the output of the transformer to a sine wave."

"Will you be supplying the circuit boards for the sine wave conversion?"

"No, you will have to build everything. We will supply you with the designs. Also, Luther and I will stay on Crosus until the factory is running. We will be able to provide any technical assistance you may need."

"I can think of several closed factories that have the facilities that will be needed. The best one is probably a factory that was used to produce various types of steel wire used in construction projects. It has the furnace we will need and it has assembly lines where the wire was wound on spools and packaged. I believe it could be converted in less than sixty days. We may not have everything we need, so we'll probably have to purchase some items from other trade group planets. That may be a problem."

Luther Vandor replied, "If there is something you need that is unavailable on Crosus, let me know and I will get it for you. We will not allow the fact that you are not a full member of the trade group to stand in the way of this project."

"Thank you."

Then Luther, William, and Torpi spent two hours going over the power module design and the manufacturing process. It was way over the general's head, but he listened anyway.

When the meeting broke up and William and Luther left, Torpi said, "The situation on Earth must be critical. I'm grateful for that, because it works to our advantage. However, I can't help wondering why they just don't build another factory on Earth. There is something they're not telling us."

"I agree, but we must take advantage of the situation. I suspect we will eventually find out why they need us so badly."

The rest of the trip to Crosus went smoothly. They had a second meeting with Luther and William, but it was even more technical than the first one.

On the morning of the day they were scheduled to arrive, the General and Torpi were having a leisurely breakfast when Lieutenant Kindler appeared at their table. She said, "The ship will be stopping in .25 hours so you can contact Crosus security. Please come to the bridge with me."

When the General walked onto the bridge, Captain Gortek said, "Good morning General Jastmore. We will be stopping four hundred thousand units from Crosus in a few moments. There has been no evidence the ship has been scanned, so they are probably not aware we are here."

When the ship stopped, Captain Gortek took the general to one of the communication consoles. The general set the transmission frequency and said, "Crosus planetary defense command, this is General Jastmore. Please respond."

A few moments later a voice responded, "What is the pass phrase?"

"Bejort has passed."

"Thank you general. You are not due back yet. However, I can see from this transmission that you're nearby."

"Yes, I'm a passenger on a Coplent warship. We will be parking at the space station shortly. My trip to Earth has been very successful and I would like to speak to the whole planet. Please arrange a press conference for us as soon as possible after our arrival and let General Yowlend know I have returned."

"Yes sir. I will take care of it. I'm very pleased your mission was a success."

"As am I."

An hour later the ship was parked. Captain Gortek, General Jastmore, and Torpi took one of the shuttles over to the space station. As soon as they stepped inside a group of at least thirty people applauded. The general held up his hand and the applause stopped. One man, in military uniform, stepped through the crowd and walked over to General Jastmore. The man said, "General Jastmore, it is both an honor and a pleasure to meet you. I'm Commander Grimles. I've notified General Yowlend that you have returned and a representative from the government press office is waiting for you in my office."

"Thank you, commander. Have the elections been held yet?"

"No, the election is scheduled for ten days from today."

"Please lead the way to your office."

When they arrived at Commander Grimles' office they found that the waiting area had been converted into a studio of sorts. There was a desk at one end of the room, and a camera was mounted on a tripod a few feet in front of the desk. A man walked up to the general and said, "Sir, do you want me to ask you questions or do you just want to speak."

"I'll just speak."

88

The general sat down behind the desk. The lights in the room brightened and the man from the press office said, "Please speak now general."

"People of Crosus, I'm General Jastmore. I have just returned from a mission to Earth aboard a Coplent warship that is now parked at our space station. The purpose of the mission was to ask that Crosus be admitted to the trade group again. As you all know, we were expelled from the trade group for actions taken by our previous leader. To make the situation even worse, after our expulsion Bejort Griss almost bankrupted the planet in his attempt to take revenge against those he felt were responsible for our defeat."

"I have assured the trade group that we are no longer a threat to any other planet and want to rejoin the group so we can begin our recovery from the disastrous leadership of Bejort Griss."

"They have agreed to give us an opportunity to prove ourselves. We will immediately begin preparations to manufacturer a product for export to Earth. To manufacture this product, we will first have to reopen our shuttered silver mining operations and start retrofitting a factory to build the product. We expect the factory alone will employ at least five thousand people, and reopening the silver mines will get thousands of miners back to work. Our goal is to begin production within one hundred days."

"This is only the beginning. If we can attain full membership status in the trade group again, everyone will benefit."

"I have been asked to turn over control of our military to Captain Gortek, the Captain of the Coplent Warship, and I have agreed. After the elections I will turn control of the government over to the new leader."

"I hope all of you are as excited as I am about this change in our relationship with other planets. It will take time to rebuild and get our economy strong again, but I know we can do it. Thank you."

The reaction to the general's speech was overwhelmingly positive, although Bejort Griss still had supporters, they were quickly silenced. The day after the speech a movement began to ask General Jastmore to run for leader. Five days before the election, the two civilian candidates who were running for the job contacted General Jastmore and asked him to run. They both said that if he agreed to run they would drop out. The general had no family so he discussed the situation with Torpi, who also thought he should run. Two days later the general reluctantly agreed.

When the election was held the general received 90% of the vote. After the election he resigned from the military, so now he was Leader Nalick Jastmore.

Two days after the election the first of the silver mines began operation again, after being closed for almost four years. Torpi, Luther, and William began touring potential sites for the factory that would build the power modules, and ultimately decided on the wire factory Torpi had originally suggested.

Work on refurbishing the factory began immediately. The old assembly lines were removed and the furnace was tested to make sure it was still functional. Luther and William worked for several days on the plans for the new assembly lines and gave Torpi a list of the things that would be needed. As it turned out, everything that was needed was either already available on Crosus or could be made within the required time. Nothing had to be imported.

They began hiring workers for the factory immediately. All would initially work on rebuilding the factory and then move into their permanent positions after the factory was operational.

While work was going on at the factory, three more silver mines were reopened and two facilities that produced pure silver bars from the extracted silver ore were reopened as well.

Luther and William were both impressed with the way things were going. It appeared they would have enough silver to build three hundred thousand power modules the day the factory began production. The required iron and nickel were brought to the factory site.

The circuit boards for the power modules were being built by a factory that was currently making electronic devices for domestic use, but they added another five hundred workers to build and test the power module boards.

Another factory was given the task of building the cases for the devices, and they too had to hire more workers to handle the task.

The effect on the Crosus economy was small, but for the first time in more than eight years it was moving in the right direction. Leader Jastmore received credit for the changes and in a poll taken a few days before the power module factory was scheduled to open more than 90% of the population was happy with the job he was doing.

The factory opened on schedule. During the first three days the factory was opened they produced fifty thousand silver alloy rods. That was enough to begin production of the power modules. To meet their quota, they had to build almost seventeen thousand units per day. It took almost ten days to reach that daily requirement, but once it was reached, it never faltered.

Every ten days a cargo ship from Earth would arrive to pick up the finished products. Within one hundred days the power module shortage on Earth began to disappear.

Crosus had proved itself and their membership in the trade group was restored. Almost immediately orders for products that Crosus had previously sold began to come in.

Additionally, now that Crosus was a full member of the trade group again, the new communication and propulsion systems were available to them. They sent ten of their cargo ships to Coplent to be refurbished.

Now that everything was running smoothly, Luther and William went to see Leader Jastmore to tell him they were returning to Earth. At the meeting Leader Jastmore asked the question that had been bothering him since their initial meeting on the Coplent warship, "Why didn't Earth simply build a new factory to make the power modules?"

Luther replied, "The people on Earth no longer want to work. Since the government has so much money, they have

91

become reliant on it for their needs. We could have built the factory, but it would have been almost impossible to find people to work there. Additionally, there is a silver shortage on Earth again."

Leader Jastmore said, "That situation, if it's allowed to continue, will have a substantial negative impact on Earth's economy."

"We know that. In fact, most of Earth's population realizes it. However, the people in a position to do something about the problem either don't know there is a problem or refuse to take any action they think might jeopardize their positions. Until the economy starts to falter and forces the people in authority to do something to correct the situation, there isn't much that can be done. Over the next year Crosus will probably be asked to manufacture more products for Earth. Can I assume you will be interested?"

"Yes, our economy is recovering, but it will take years before all the people who want to work will be able to find jobs again. I'm open to anything that will speed up the process."

"Thank you for your hospitality. It has been a real pleasure working with you and your people," Luther said.

"Thank you for your help. Without it I doubt we would have been able to accomplish the task that needed to be done."

For the next several years the economy on Crosus continued to improve. By the time Leader Jastmore had finished his five-year term as Leader of Crosus, it had become one of the main planets in the trade group again.

PROCOLT 2

While Crosus was rebuilding their economy, Procolt 2 was just beginning to develop theirs. There were now two large cities on Procolt 2. The larger one, Procolt City, had a population of almost a million residents. New Paris had a population of more than five hundred thousand people. The cities were booming and new residents arrived almost constantly.

Procolt 2 no longer relied on imports. Almost everything they needed, with the exception of some foods, was available from domestic sources. While the cities had grown so did the resort. It now had six guest towers, and tourists from almost every trade group planet had spent time there.

However, neither Jeffery nor Debbie were really happy with the situation. There was no real central government. By default, Jeffery was in charge, but he wanted that situation to end. Both Procolt City and New Paris had formed local governments, and each had a mayor. Jeffery contacted them and asked them to come to a meeting.

There were only five people at the meeting. The two mayors, Jeffery, Debbie, and Mystic. Mystic was now almost eighteen and for the past several years she had been taking over more of the responsibility for running the resort. When everyone was seated Jeffery stood up and said, "Thank you for coming. As we all know the population of Procolt 2 will soon be two million people and we have no central government. Debbie and I have been doing the job, but it's not something that either of us wants to continue to do. I would like you two to work with us to form a planetary government, and when we are ready, we will have an election."

"In the near future we'll probably begin exporting some of our manufactured products. Thanks to the ingenuity of the squirrels, we have products that are not available anywhere else in the trade group, and I'm certain there's a market for those items. We need to have our own currency and stop utilizing money from Earth. We need our own fleet of cargo and passenger ships. Additionally, at some point, we

93

may want to curtail immigration. All these things, and more, are within the scope of a planetary government."

Mayor Haskell from Procolt City said, "I agree, Jeffery. We probably should have started on this a few years ago, but we were more concerned with local issues. I'm sure Mayor Cook feels the same way."

"I do. So far neither city has a crime problem, although we both have small police departments. Both cities have almost no unemployment, and I'm sure that the availability of jobs is what is keeping crime to a minimum. However, as the population of our cities grow, we may soon find ourselves with some of the same problems they have in cities on Earth. The one I'm most concerned with is drug use. We must maintain zero tolerance for drugs. Unfortunately, what few drug problems we have had have been the result of tourists bringing drugs here. You have to end that."

"I know, and we are taking steps to do that now. About a hundred days ago we started scanning all luggage and people for drugs as they leave their passenger ships, but if we find anything, we have no laws to prosecute them. All we can do is refuse entry to the planet. We have been giving them partial refunds, but that's going to stop."

Mayor Cook said, "That's a step in the right direction, but you're right, we need a planetary government. I suggest we take ten people from Procolt City, five from New Paris, and two from Procolt Paradise and give them the responsibility to draw up a constitution and some basic laws. Once that is finished we will have an election. I believe that anyone who lives here permanently has the right to vote, and I think that should include the squirrels."

"That sounds good to me," Jeffery said. "I think we should get started as soon as possible. As mayors of your cities you should be able to pick the people you need, but if you want to elect them, that's okay too."

"I'm sure I can find ten people for the committee," Mayor Haskell said.

"And I already have five people in mind. Jeffery, do you have any thoughts about your two members?"

"Yes, I was thinking about Mystic and Jessica Teacher."

"Those are interesting choices. I have no problem with either of them, but I'm curious about why you picked them."

Then Mystic said, "I'm curious as well Dad. Why do you want me on the committee?"

"Because I think Mayor Haskell and Mayor Cook are going to need leaders in their communities to represent their cities, which is perfectly logical. But I thought there should be some representation of our younger residents and the squirrels."

"Okay Dad, I guess that makes sense. But I don't think Jessica has the time to be a member of the committee."

"If that's the case, I'll let her decide who should replace her. I would like the members of the committee to be finalized within ten days, and the first meeting scheduled as soon as possible after the committee members have been selected."

"I believe the North American Union has a constitution we can use as a start to build ours," Mayor Cook said.

"I'll get a copy of it and send it to both of you," Mystic responded.

"One thing I think you should consider. Instead of directly electing a president, you may want to allow the government representatives we elect to pick somebody from their own ranks for the job."

"That would eliminate a lot of the problems I have seen with the governments on Earth. Sometimes it's impossible to accomplish anything when the president and the congress have opposing points of view," Mayor Cook said.

Jeffery stood up and said, "At this point I'm removing myself from this situation. However, if you need my help with anything, please don't hesitate to ask. This meeting is adjourned."

After the meeting broke up Jeffery called Jessica and told her about the committee and that he had suggested she should be a member of it. She said she was honored that he thought about her, but she was way too busy to take on the additional responsibility. She also said she was pregnant and that would occupy some of her time as well. Jeffery offered his congratulations on her pregnancy and asked her to select another squirrel to take her place. She said she would get back to him in a day or two at the latest.

After the conversation was over, Jeffery began to think about the implications of Jessica's pregnancy. Since her child would inherit all of Jessica's knowledge and would learn more as it matured it would, in all likelihood, be the most intelligent being in the galaxy. He wondered what that would mean for Procolt 2.

Jessica did contact him and said she felt that her assistant, Timothy Baker, would be an excellent choice. Jeffery agreed and contacted the two mayors to let them know his selections had been finalized.

Two days later all the members of the committee had been selected and the first meeting was scheduled to begin at the Procolt City community center five days later and would last for ten days.

After six long meetings, the job was done. Copies of the Procolt 2 Constitution were distributed to all permanent residents and a vote was scheduled to ratify the constitution in thirty days.

The constitution was approved by 93% of the voters. Part of the constitution stated that there would be one representative in the Procolt 2 Congress for every hundred thousand people, except people who lived at Procolt Paradise would have two representatives. So, the first congress would have seventeen members. The same as the number of people who were on the committee to create the constitution.

The election was held thirty days after the constitution was approved. Most of the same people who were on the committee were also chosen for the congress, with one notable exception. Oscar Goodman was chosen as one of the representatives from Procolt City. At the first meeting of the congress, he was chosen as president.

As his first official act, President Goodman chose Mystic Whitestone to be his vice-president. It was an interesting choice. President Goodman was the oldest person in the congress and Mystic was the youngest.

The congress began work immediately. They created the Procolt Dollar as their currency, and set the value to be .0001 hirodim. This decision had to be approved by the trade group bank, and it was, but the bank required Jeffery to place one hundred thousand hirodim into an escrow account as a backup for the currency. That was not a problem. They also passed a 1% tax on all sales on Procolt 2 which was needed to fund the government. There were a few complaints about the tax, but in the end, it was accepted.

The decision was made to only pass laws that were needed to maintain the quality of life the people on Procolt 2 already enjoyed. They passed a law forbidding the distribution, use, or possession of drugs for recreational purposes. They also passed a law forbidding the development of new cities without the approval of the congress. The last thing they did before they adjourned was to create a police force and allocate the funds necessary to build two police stations, one in each city, and a small jail.

Until that time, personnel from Procolt Paradise manned the space station. Now that job was turned over to the police.

Jeffery and Debbie were sitting in Jeffery's office, each telling the other how happy they were with the way things were going. Jeffery said, "Now I'm able to devote all of my time to running the resort." But he admitted to himself that it was also a job he no longer desired.

"It's nice not to have to worry about a whole planet. I'm very proud of the job Mystic is doing as vice-president."

"I am too," Jeffery responded. He was about to say something else when Jessica walked into the office.

"Hello Jessica, how is your son Lance doing?" Debbie asked.

"He's doing great. I expect him to begin speaking in another ten days or so. Anyway, I have something exciting I want to discuss with you."

"Okay, what is it?" Jeffery asked.

97

"Currently small electronic devices like communicators and hand-held computers use batteries. Battery technology has not exactly kept pace with other scientific advances, although most devices only require a battery change annually. My team and I have developed a new battery, based on cold fusion technology, which will last forever."

"That is exciting!" Jeffery exclaimed. "What would be involved in producing them?"

"First, we have to finish our testing, but so far we have not encountered any problems. The batteries are fairly simple to make, but they will be expensive to manufacture in small quantities. However, I estimate that once we are making a few million of them per year, the cost will drop to about three Procolt Dollars each."

"How long before the testing is complete?"

"Probably less than a hundred days."

"Can you build some samples for me?"

"Of course. I need to know the size, voltage requirement, and how many you need."

"I would like the type that fit into communicators. I think I'll need at least fifty of them."

"I can do that. I'll have them for you in five or six days. What are you going to do with them?"

"I want to take them to Earth and sell them. Since Earth manufactures almost all the communicators used in the trade group, it would seem like the best place to start. In the meantime, I'll contact one of the industrial engineers in Procolt City and have him come here. I would like you to meet with him and discuss the manufacturing requirements."

"Okay, I must tell you that this is the most exciting thing I've done since I worked on the communication and propulsion systems."

"Thank you for doing this. These batteries are going to do wonders for the Procolt 2 economy, which was doing well already."

"You're welcome."

After Jessica left Debbie said, "You know I'm going to Earth with you."

"I wouldn't dream of going without you. It's been years since we've gone back to Earth. I know it's changed a lot since our last visit, and not for the better, but I want to see it for myself."

The next day Jeffery sent a message to Terrance Brennan, the Director of Operations at NASA, telling him that he and Debbie were coming to Earth for a visit and they would be there in fifteen days. They were planning on staying on Earth for two weeks and he wanted to meet with him during that time.

He also sent a message to Kimberly Thompson, the Director of Research and Development at Apex Electronics. Apex Electronics supplied more than 70% of the hand-held communicators used on the trade group planets. He had met Kimberly before at a conference that was held several years previously on Coplent. He told her he had something that he was positive she would be interested in and asked her to set up a meeting while he was on Earth.

Six days later he received responses from both of the people he contacted. Both of them gave him several choices for dates and times. He selected a date and time for both meetings and sent that information back to confirm them.

The next day a squirrel delivered fifty sample communicator batteries to his office. He called Jessica, thanked her, and then told her he was leaving for Earth the following day.

RUSSELL FINE

EARTH

Jeffery arrived at the space station three days later. He contacted them, identified himself, and asked for a parking location.

The man Jeffery was speaking to on the space station was so surprised he was almost unable to speak. He stuttered when he said, "Admiral Whitestone...It is an honor to speak with you sir...I was told you were coming. Please bring your ship to shuttle bay seven. You can park your ship inside the station."

Jeffery said, "Thank you." As he approached the exterior door opened and he flew his ship inside and landed. The exterior door closed and he could hear the shuttle bay pressurizing. An alarm sounded when the pressurization was completed. When he heard the alarm, Jeffery opened his ship's hatch. He grabbed the suitcase they had brought and followed Debbie off the ship.

Seconds later the door to the interior of the space station opened and a man wearing a uniform Jeffery did not recognize walked up to him and Debbie. He extended his hand toward Jeffery and said, "Hello sir, it is a pleasure to meet you and Captain Whitestone. I'm Captain Kingsley, the manager of the station. Please follow me. There is a shuttle waiting to take you to NASA headquarters."

Jeffery shook his hand and said, "Thank you, Captain. I was not expecting this kind of greeting. Neither of us are in NASA anymore."

"We know that sir, but both of you are still celebrities on Earth."

Captain Kingsley led them to a shuttle bay a few hundred feet away and opened the door for them. Inside was a small shuttle. Jeffery and Debbie walked inside, and Captain Kingsley followed them. He smiled and said, "I'm also your pilot for today. Please make yourselves comfortable. The trip will take about an hour and a half."

Debbie said, "Thank you, Captain Kingsley."

"Things have changed since your last visit. The area around NASA headquarters is now filled with tall buildings. All of them are a combination of apartments, offices, and stores. For many NASA employees, there is no reason to ever leave their building."

"Is that a good thing?" Debbie asked.

"Well, to be honest, it's not the lifestyle I would choose, but for some it's perfect."

The shuttle landed and Captain Kingsley said, "We didn't announce your arrival at headquarters so you won't be mobbed. I was told to take you directly to Director Brennan's office."

"We have a meeting scheduled with him in five days. Why would he want to meet with us today?" Jeffery asked.

"He didn't tell me anything other than to bring you to his office as soon as you arrive. You'll have to discuss the other meeting with him."

As they stepped off the shuttle there was an open tram waiting to take them to the headquarters building. The tram ride was short, less than a mile.

They entered the building and stopped at the security desk. There were badges already waiting for Jeffery and Debbie. The man at the security desk said, "Good morning Admiral Whitestone," as he handed Jeffery his badge. Then he said, "Good morning Captain Whitestone," and gave Debbie her badge.

Noting the rank of the man at the security desk Jeffery said, "Thank you, Corporal."

Captain Kingsley said, "I won't be attending the meeting. However, I will be waiting for you here. I'll have a car here in a few minutes and I can take you wherever you want to go."

"Thank you. We'll be staying at Brandon Simpson's home while we are here. Is that okay?"

"Of course, I was there once for a party. It's a beautiful place."

"Yes, it is. Although it's been a long time since we've been there, I'm sure it hasn't changed very much."

102

Jeffery and Debbie got into the elevator and took it to the top floor. When they stepped off the elevator a young woman was waiting for them. She said, "Director Brennan is waiting for you. Please follow me."

They followed the woman to a large, and rather ornate, wood door. She opened it, and then moved to the side so Jeffery and Debbie could enter the office. Jeffery scanned the office. It was enormous, at least fifty feet long and thirty feet wide. The walls were covered with a beautiful dark wood paneling, and on the walls were pictures commemorating the greatest moments in NASA history. Included were several pictures of Jeffery taken during his years as a pilot. There were also pictures of Debbie, and three pictures taken during their wedding.

A tall, broad shouldered man got up from behind the desk at the far end of the room. He walked over to them and as he approached he said, "It's a pleasure and an honor to meet both of you. As you can see from the pictures, you two were a very important part of our history. Please allow me to introduce myself. I'm Terry Brennan. But call me Terry. If it is okay with you, I'll use your first names as well."

"Actually, we prefer it, Terry. Debbie and I never liked titles."

"Please sit down. Would you like something to drink?"

"Yes, a real cup of coffee would be very nice," Debbie said.

Terry picked up his phone and a moment later said, "Please bring in coffee for us." Then he looked at Jeffery and said, "I know we have a meeting scheduled for five days from now. That's an official meeting, this one isn't. May I ask what brings you to Earth again? I believe it's been eight years since your last visit."

"The length of time since our last visit is one of the reasons for this one. I'm sure you are aware that more than one and a half million people have immigrated to Procolt 2 in the last five years. The stories they have told me about life on Earth doesn't match my memories. I want to see it for myself. Debbie feels the same way."

"There is no doubt that Earth has changed, and many of those changes can be traced back to you two. Because of you, Earth has experienced a level of economic prosperity we had never experienced before. That's the good part. However, the governments were unable to contain themselves. They spent the money they had, and a substantial amount they didn't have. They were positive the good times would last forever. Wages and benefits increased all over the planet. Then the governments decided to raise the standard of living for everybody. They began paying people who didn't work almost as much as the people that did. As a result, it became difficult to find workers for factories, so a lot of those jobs were replaced with machines. That meant many of the people who were working became unemployed, but it didn't really matter because they were getting paid anyway. However, it did matter to the governments. With fewer people working, tax revenues plummeted. None of them are bankrupt yet, but it could happen."

"So, because of a lack of workers Earth had to outsource a lot of their manufacturing to Crosus?"

"Yes, exactly. As you probably know NASA is now the largest employer in the trade group. We have more than eight hundred thousand employees. We build new ships on Earth, Coplent, and Torblit, and we have large maintenance facilities where we maintain and retrofit ships on Earth and Coplent. Almost all of this work has to be done by people. It can't be done by a machine. We pay well, more than twice what you would get from the government for not working, and that's a starting salary. It goes up from there."

"It sounds like you should have people banging on your doors looking for jobs."

"You would think so, but we don't. We currently have more than two thousand job openings at this facility. During a good week we might find twenty people who actually want to work."

"So, Earth is a victim of its own success," Debbie said.

"Yes, we are. We have been forced to import workers from other planets, which is adding to an overcrowding

104

problem in the major cities all over the world. While you are here you should go spend some time in New York or Mexico City. You will probably think you're on Coplent, not Earth. By the way, the European Union is now considering a ban on extraterrestrial workers."

"That will probably make a bad situation worse."

"Yeah, I'm sure it will. Anyway, you said there were two reasons why you are here. What's the other one?"

Jeffery reached into his pocket and retrieved one of the sample batteries. He handed it to Terry and said, "This is the other reason."

"It's a battery. Is there something special about it?"

"Yes, it's a cold fusion battery that will last forever. It was developed by my research and development group."

"You mean the squirrels, don't you?"

"Yes, they surprised me with this about twenty days ago. I had no idea they were even working on it."

"Do you expect it to replace the power modules?"

"No, it's a low power device. It's designed specifically to be used in low voltage and low current applications, like communicators and hand-held computers."

"You'll be able to sell these by the millions. Where are you going to manufacturer them?"

"We're going to build a factory on Procolt 2. Tomorrow we have a meeting with Kimberley Thompson of Apex Electronics. I'm sure she will be interested."

"Yes, I agree. Tell me, do you have a willing work force on Procolt 2?"

"Yes, our unemployment rate is about 1%. There are no welfare benefits on Procolt 2. However, we've formed a government now so that may happen in the future. The people who came to Procolt 2 to live want to work and be productive. They weren't looking for handouts. These people built their own cities. They built homes, stores, farms, and factories. I provided some of the money, but they did the work."

"Would you be interested in having a NASA facility on Procolt 2?"

"I'll certainly think about it. How big would it be?"

"There would be a space station used for large ship assembly and a factory complex where small ships and parts are manufactured. I would guess it would require about ten thousand employees."

"That's an interesting proposition. We don't have ten thousand unemployed people, but I'm sure we could get people from Earth to move there. I'll discuss it with you at our next meeting."

"Be prepared to be mobbed by reporters at the next meeting."

"Okay, I'm not worried about it. I've handled reporters before."

"Jeffery and Debbie, once again, I want you to know it was very nice finally meeting you both. I'll contact you the morning of the meeting and arrange to have somebody pick you up."

"Thank you, Terry. Debbie and I have a lot of thinking to do before our next meeting."

As promised, Captain Kingsley was waiting for them in the security lobby. Jeffery and Debbie returned their badges and followed the Captain to the car. It was a big car, probably twice the size of any car they had on Procolt 2. Once they were comfortably seated Jeffery asked, "Captain, why is somebody with your rank driving us around?"

"I volunteered for the job, but I have an ulterior motive. I want to discuss something with you in private."

"Okay, I can't imagine anything more private than a car. What did you want to talk about?"

"I have advanced degrees in electrical engineering and physics, but on Earth we don't do much research and development anymore, and that's what I want to do. I would like to work on Procolt 2 in your research labs."

"Do you realize that the research and development on Procolt 2 is done primarily by squirrels?"

"Yes, I know that. But that doesn't bother me. I know how intelligent they are and that demands respect. Their physical appearance means nothing. I have seen some videos of S12 speaking and she was very impressive."

106

"I have something I want to show you when we stop."

"Because of traffic it will probably take at least an hour to get there. Would you like to stop somewhere for lunch?"

"I'll leave that to you. The rest of our day is free."

"Okay, I know the perfect place."

They drove for a while before the Captain stopped the car in front of a restaurant called, Mark's Old Fashioned Diner. He said, "This place has terrific food. I'm sure you will like it. All the meat here is real, not made from vegetable protein like most of the meat that's served on Earth now. That stuff may be healthier, but it tastes like crap as far as I'm concerned."

"On Procolt 2 we import beef, pork, and chicken from Earth and Coplent. It's all very good," Jeffery responded.

"I thought there were farms on Procolt 2. Doesn't anybody raise animals for consumption?"

"No, there are no animals raised for food on the planet."

"That's strange. Why not?'

"It's something I'm not prepared to discuss at this time."

The Captain looked like he was going ask something else but finally said, "Okay."

The restaurant was crowded and they had to wait for a table. That was something Jeffery and Debbie had not experienced for a long time. After they were seated and ordered their lunch, Jeffery reached into his pocket and took out a sample battery. He handed it to Captain Kingsley and said, "This is our latest development. It's a cold fusion battery that will last forever."

The Captain took the battery, looked at it for a while, and said, "This is exactly the kind of project I would love to work on."

"If you're sure you want to move to Procolt 2, send a message to Jessica Teacher, she was S12 when she was visiting Earth, and tell her you want to join her group and why. Include all your qualifications and what you think you could add to the group. If she says she wants you, it's a done deal."

"I'll do that this evening. Thank you."

107

"If you join her group, you will be the second human in it. Brandon Simpson is also in the group. Have you met him?"

"A few times when he passes through the space station, but we've never really talked other than the normal pleasantries. Because he usually uses his own ship, he doesn't come to the station very often."

When they arrived at Brandon's house Bess and Tom were waiting for them. Jeffery introduced Captain Kingsley. There were a few hugs and Bess said, "Your room is ready, and if you tell me what you want for dinner, I'll make it."

Debbie responded, "We're not that particular. Make whatever you want. I'm sure it will be fine."

"Okay, I hope you like peanut butter and jelly."

Debbie laughed and said, "If that's what you want to make, that's okay with us. I don't think I've had a peanut butter and jelly sandwich for twenty-five years."

"I'll surprise you with something for dinner, and it probably won't have peanut butter in it."

"I have to get back, but if you need me to drive you someplace just let me know," the Captain said.

"Thanks for the offer, but Brandon has several cars here we can use if needed, although neither of us has a valid driver's license anymore."

"That's not an issue. They stopped requiring driver's licenses several years ago. The only requirement now is you must be over sixteen. Since all the cars have collision prevention devices, there are very few accidents. Most cars can also be driven by the onboard computer, so everything is automatic. I prefer to drive myself, but most people like the automatic driving capability."

"Perhaps we'll see you again when we go back for our next meeting with Terry."

"Probably not, I'll be on the space station. Please let me know as soon as you hear from Jessica."

"I promise."

When Jeffery and Debbie were alone Jeffery asked, "Do you like the idea of having a NASA facility on Procolt 2?"

"I've been thinking about it since Terry mentioned the possibility. I think it's probably a good idea. It helps make us more independent."

"Ten thousand new jobs probably means another fifty thousand people on the planet. I know that's not a problem now, but I think now is the time to start thinking about controlling immigration."

"That's not your problem anymore. You gave up control, and now you have to live with that decision."

"I know, and I think it was the right decision to make. But I still can have opinions, can't I?"

"I suppose."

The meeting with Kimberley Thompson was set up for the following morning at Brandon's house. Kimberly arrived a few minutes early and Bess brought her to a table by the indoor pool where Jeffery and Debbie were waiting.

Jeffery stood up as Kimberly approached and said, "Good morning Kimberly, it's nice to see you again. This is my wife, Debbie."

Kimberly reached forward, shook hands with Debbie and said, "It's a pleasure to meet you, Debbie. Jeffery said a lot of very nice things about you when we were together at a conference on Coplent a few years ago."

"I was planning on going to that conference with him, but our daughter was sick and I didn't want to leave her. Anyway, it's nice to meet you as well. Please sit down."

Jeffery and Kimberly both sat and Kimberly said, "You promised me something that I would be interested in, so what is it?"

Jeffery picked up a small open box that was on the floor and put it on the table in front of Kimberly. She removed an item from it, looked at it, and said, "It's a communicator battery, I have a hundred thousand just like it in stock."

"No, you don't. I guarantee you don't have any like these batteries."

"Really? What's so special about these batteries?"

"They'll last forever. They use cold fusion technology. Unless they are physically damaged, they will continue to produce power indefinitely."

Kimberly smiled and said, "That is interesting, but what do they cost?"

"That depends on how many you buy, but it'll be a small fraction of what you'll be able to charge for them. I promise you, I won't sell them directly to your communicator customers."

"I assume these are for me to use for evaluation purposes?"

"Yes, those are for you."

"Where are they going to be manufactured?"

"I recently decided that since Procolt 2 has a permanent population approaching two million people, any new products we develop will be manufactured on Procolt 2."

"That's a wise position to take. I heard Procolt 2 now has a government. Is that true?"

"Yes, and my daughter, Mystic, was selected to be vice-president."

"Congratulations, how old is she?"

"Almost eighteen."

"That seems very young to have that much responsibility. Will she be able to handle it?"

"Yes, she's been running Procolt Paradise for over a year, and we have over ten thousand employees. Debbie and I are not involved on a daily basis. About the only thing we do is greet visitors as they arrive."

"I'm sure if she can run your resort successfully, she is qualified to be vice-president. Usually vice-presidents don't do very much, but it's good experience if she wants to make a career in politics."

"I think she wants to continue running the resort. I would guess she's not really interested in politics. Anyway, let's get back to our discussion of the batteries. Assuming you find the samples acceptable, how many do you think you would need going forward?"

110

"We sell about a hundred thousand units per month, and I would guess 90% of those sales would include your battery. I would also expect to sell an equal number of batteries to existing users. So, for the first few years, about two and a half million units per year."

Jeffery said, "Okay, I'll get back to you with a cost estimate in ten days or so. That will give you time to evaluate the samples. I would suspect that battery sales to existing users would drop after a few years as units in the field are fitted with the new ones."

"You're probably right, but if Apex is the only company selling communicators with these batteries, our market share will probably grow and new unit sales would increase. How soon can you begin manufacturing?"

"About one hundred fifty days after we receive a signed contract."

"I have one more question. Is there any danger of a radiation leak if the batteries are physically damaged?"

"No, the reaction generates almost no radiation, and the battery components are minimally radioactive. Industrial antistatic devices are more radioactive than the battery components are. I also have a question for you. How does Apex find workers to build the products you manufacture?"

"We don't look for workers, we build them. We even have robots to maintain the robots on the production line. It's almost impossible to find workers on Earth now. The factory that builds the communicators only has nine employees. Their primary job is to program the robots that build the communicators."

Kimberly left a little while later and Jeffery immediately sent a message to Jessica with production requirements. He also told her that she would be receiving a resume from Captain Kingsley. Jeffery realized he didn't know Captain Kingsley's first name and made a mental note to ask him the next time they meet, which would probably be before their next meeting with Terry.

At dinner that evening Debbie asked, "We said we were going to stay on Earth for ten days. I want to spend two

111

days with my parents and sister. We haven't seen them since they came to the resort last year. What do you want to do with the rest of our time here?"

"I want to spend a day or two with my parents too. After our meeting with Terry, I think we should go to New York, San Francisco, and Paris. We're isolated here. I want to see if things in the big cities are as bad as we've been told. We may have to extend our stay by a day or two."

"I like your idea. Two days in each location should be sufficient for us to see what's going on."

"I'll make all the arrangements this afternoon. We'll go see your mother first."

"Let me call her before you make any reservations. I want to find out what her plans are."

"Okay, when we know their schedule, I'll call my father."

Debbie went to Brandon's office to call her mother. She sent her a message before they left Procolt 2, so her mother was expecting the call. It was a long conversation. Her mother started the conversation by complaining about living in a big city. After listening to her diatribe for a while Debbie asked, "Would you like to live on Procolt 2? There are no crowds, no lines, you can use your own car to get around, and we'll get to see each other all the time."

"I was hoping you would ask me that question, so I wouldn't have to ask you. We're ready to go tomorrow. Your sister wants to move there too. Would it be okay if we came down to Florida to see you instead of you coming here?"

"Sure, we're staying at Brandon Simpson's house. It's really beautiful. I'll make the arrangements and call you back."

"That isn't necessary. Your father and I can pay for our own tickets. We can even afford to buy Connie a ticket too."

"I'm sure you can, but Jeffery and I are probably the wealthiest people in the trade group. We have more money than we can ever spend, so please let me take care of the tickets. When do you want to move?"

"I wasn't kidding when I said we're ready to go tomorrow. If there is room on your ship, we would be happy to go with you when you go home."

"Will Connie be ready to leave immediately too?"

"I'm sure she will be, but I'll ask her."

"Should I just buy one-way tickets?"

"I'll call you back in a half hour."

"Okay, I won't do anything until I hear from you."

Debbie went back by the pool area to tell Jeffery about the conversation. She sat down at the table and said, "There's been a change in our plans. My parents and Connie are coming here tomorrow."

"That's not a problem. There's plenty of room here. We just have to let Bess know so she can get two more guest rooms set up."

"There's more. They don't want to go back home again. They want to move to Procolt 2 and want to go back with us."

"I think that would be okay. Do they want to live at Procolt Paradise or one of the cities?"

"I don't know. We can discuss that with them tomorrow. They would have to stay at the resort until we can get a house built for them anyway."

"Are they going to let us have a house built for them? Your father is a very proud man."

"I'm not sure. I just had to convince my mother to let me pay for the tickets to Orlando."

"Perhaps tomorrow we can discuss the financial part of this move. They own property here. Are they going to sell it?"

"Good question. I have no idea. Anyway, you should call your Mom and Dad. Do you think they want to move too?"

"I actually offered to build them a house in Procolt City if they want to move. My Dad said he would think about it, and we haven't discussed it since then."

"You should tell them my parents are moving. Perhaps that would help them reach a decision."

"I'll mention it to him."

Jeffery left the pool area, and like Debbie, went to the office to call his parents. They knew he was on Earth because he sent them a message the previous evening. When he called his father answered the phone.

"Hello Jeffery, we've been waiting for your call."

"I've been tied up in meetings since I got here, and this was really the first opportunity I've had to call you. How are you and Mom doing?"

"We're doing great! When we heard the news that Mystic is now vice-president, we were so proud of her. I wish we could see her more often."

"You can. We discussed this last year. Debbie and I would really like to have you and Mom living on Procolt 2. Debbie's parents are going home with us and they're going to stay there."

"I discussed this with your mother before. She said she has friends and obligations here, but I'll ask her again. Debbie's mother and father live in one of the cities, don't they?"

"Yeah, and they don't like what's happened. That's why they want to move. I realize you live in a rural area and don't have the same problems, but Procolt 2 is a much nicer place to live."

"I agree, I'll talk to her tonight at dinner. Are we going to see you and Debbie while you're here?"

"Of course, I'll call you tomorrow and let you know when we'll be there."

"Can you call me in the morning around 10:00? I'll make sure your mother is here."

"That's no problem. I'll call you tomorrow."

He walked back to the pool area and saw Bess. He told her Debbie's parents and sister were coming tomorrow and would be staying for a while, and asked her to prepare two guest rooms for them.

Bess said she liked having more guests and was happy to make up the rooms.

When Jeffery got back to the pool area he sat across the table from Debbie and said, "I spoke with my Dad. I'm

114

sure he wants to move, but he's not sure how my mother feels about it. He's going to talk to her tonight and I'm going to call him back at 10:00 tomorrow morning."

"While you were talking to your Dad, Connie called me. She said she wants to move immediately too. So, it looks like we'll have three passengers on the return trip.

The next morning Jeffery called his parent's house and his mother answered.

"Hi Mom, how are you?"

"I'm fine. Your father and I had an interesting conversation last night about moving to Procolt 2."

"And did you come to a decision?"

"There's something you don't know. Your father has some health issues. He's developing one of the few diseases that we haven't found a cure for. That is Parkinson's. I'm sure he didn't tell you that."

"No, he neglected to mention it. But you should know we have doctors, hospitals, and all the latest medical equipment on Procolt 2. I doubt there's anything that can be done to help him on Earth that we can't duplicate."

"I think you missed the point I was trying to make. He's sure he doesn't have very long to live, and wants to finish his life on Procolt 2. Despite the fact I will be leaving lifelong friends, he comes first. So, I agreed to move. But we are going to need some help."

"I'll get you all the help you need."

"We have to sell our house and all our household items first, don't we?"

"No, you don't have to sell anything. I'll take care of all your expenses. You can either stay at the resort or I'll have a house built for you. It's your choice. We'll put the house up for sale after you move."

"Are there really good doctors there? I'm worried about him."

"I know Mom. Yes, we have two excellent doctors on staff at the resort, and I have access to the best medical care in the trade group if that becomes necessary."

115

"Okay, I know medical care can be expensive, but I also know that you and Debbie are very wealthy. Will his expenses be a problem?"

"No Mom, I'm sure I can afford whatever medical help Dad needs. Please don't concern yourself with money."

"Thank you. Are you coming here to see us?"

"Debbie's parents and sister are coming here today. We're going to spend two days with them and then we'll come and see you and Dad. We'll be there the day after tomorrow, probably in the afternoon."

"It will be nice to see you again."

"After you move we can see each other as often as you like, especially if you are living at the resort."

"Your father is out walking. I'll let him know about our conversation when I see him. Please don't mention his medical problems unless he brings them up first."

"Okay, I'll see you in a couple of days. Bye."

"Goodbye Jeffery."

Jeffery found Debbie sitting in the living room listening to music. It wasn't something she did frequently, but she was obviously relaxing and enjoying it. She didn't even notice when he walked into the room. But when he tapped her lightly on her shoulder, she looked up at him, smiled, and asked, "What's the verdict?"

"They're moving. My Dad has Parkinson's and is convinced he's going to die soon, and he wants to spend the end of his life on Procolt 2 with us. So, my mother agreed to move."

"I'm glad they're moving."

"Me too. We have to go and pick up your parents and sister. Their flight will be arriving in less than two hours. Tom picked out a car for us to use."

"Is it fully automatic, or will you have to drive?"

"Do you trust me to drive?"

"No, not really."

"I don't trust myself either. The car is totally automatic. All we have to do is tell it where we want to go."

They got into the car. Jeffery was sitting in the driver's seat. He pushed the start button and a voice asked, "Destination please?"

"Orlando airport."

"Arrival or departure?"

"Arrival."

"Airline and flight number?"

"North American Air Express, flight number 1684."

"That flight is currently on schedule to arrive at two o'clock. We will be there fifteen minutes earlier."

The car began its journey. Neither of them had ever ridden in a self-driving car before, and they both found it somewhat disconcerting. After about ten minutes they realized there was no reason for concern, so they started talking about their parents.

When the car stopped the voice said, "We have arrived at our destination. The flight has been delayed by five minutes. Please take a remote from the compartment in front of you and push the button when you are ready to be picked up. When the light turns green it means I will be here in three minutes."

Jeffery opened the compartment and took one of the small remotes. Debbie took one too. They got out of the car and walked inside the terminal. A large monitor hanging from the ceiling had flight information displayed on it. The flight they were waiting for had landed, but would not be at the gate for another fourteen minutes.

They sat down in the gate area and waited for the flight. While they were waiting, a security officer walked up to them. He said, "Are you Jeffery and Debbie Whitestone?"

"Yes, is there some problem officer?"

"Not really. But for security reasons we don't allow famous people to wander around the airport unescorted. So, if you don't object, I will be staying with you until you leave."

"How did you know we were here?"

"Your car informed us."

"That's interesting, the car making sure we're safe," Debbie said with some amusement in her voice.

"Please join us, officer."

117

"Thank you, sir, may I ask why you're here?"

"My parents and sister are arriving on flight 1684," Debbie answered.

"I know a lot of people have left Earth and moved to Procolt 2. It's in the news all the time. Is Procolt 2 that much nicer than Earth?"

Jeffery said, "Why don't you come and see for yourself?"

"On what I get paid? My wife and I would have to go for ten years without eating to be able to afford that kind of vacation."

"I think I can take care of that. Give me your name and address and I'll arrange for a free thirty-day vacation for your family. Do you have any children?"

"No sir, it's just my wife and me."

"The vacation is for six, so if you want to invite anybody else just include them on the reservation form. All I need is your name and communication number."

The security officer stammered when he said, "Thank you sir, nobody has ever done anything like this for me before. I can't tell you how much I appreciate it." Then he handed Jeffery a card and said, "This is my contact information."

Jeffery took the card, glanced at it, and said, "Your welcome, Officer Jensen. Somebody from reservations will call you in about seven days." Then Jeffery handed him one of his cards and said, "If you haven't heard from them in ten days, call me and I will take care of it personally."

At this point the officer was speechless, so he just nodded in agreement.

When the plane reached the gate, Debbie's parents and sister were among the first to disembark. There were hugs and kisses and then Jeffery asked, "How much luggage do you have?"

"We each brought two suitcases. We figured that anything we didn't bring we could buy," Debbie's father responded.

"Okay, let's go get your luggage."

118

By the time they arrived at the baggage claim area their bags were waiting for them. Officer Jensen brought over a luggage cart and put the bags on it. Then he said, "I've already called your car, it should be waiting by the time we get to the curb."

The car was waiting for them. Officer Jensen put the bags in the trunk. Then he turned to Jeffery and said, "Thank you again, sir. May I contact you again when we are at Procolt Paradise?"

"Of course. Thank you for your help with the luggage."

"You're welcome."

After everyone was in the car Debbie looked at Jeffery and said, "You just gave that guy a three hundred-thousand dollar tip!"

Jeffery smiled and said, "It was the least I could do since he was risking his life to protect us."

They spent the time in the car talking about things that had happened in the past year. Nobody discussed the move to Procolt 2.

When they arrived at Brandon's house, Bess and Tom were there to greet their guests. Jeffery introduced everyone and Bess showed them to their rooms. Then she gave them a tour of the property.

While Bess was giving them a tour, Jeffery received a call from Captain Kingsley who told him he would be there at nine o'clock to pick them up for their meeting with Terry. That evening at dinner Jeffery told Debbie's parents and Connie that he and Debbie had a meeting the next morning with the director of operations at NASA. They expected to be gone most of the day.

Connie said, "I could easily spend a month here. I think we can survive for a day without you guys."

"Yes, I'm sure of that. If you need anything, just ask Bess."

Captain Kingsley arrived right on time. After they were seated Jeffery asked, "What's your first name? I don't want to call you 'Captain' all the time."

"It's Vince. This is supposed to be a secret, but there will be somebody else at your meeting with Director Brennan this morning. Gerald Wilson will be there as well."

"That was unexpected. Why would the president of the North American Union want to meet with us?"

"They don't tell me anything. I found out only because I saw his shuttle land this morning at seven o'clock. I checked the security roster for the day and saw that he was scheduled to meet with Director Brennan at eleven. Can I assume you haven't heard from Jessica yet?"

"Yes, the earliest I would expect a response is tomorrow. I'll call you as soon as I get her message."

Vince dropped them off at the NASA Headquarters Building and said, "I'll be back in an hour and the meeting is scheduled for two."

Debbie and Jeffery walked into the building. The same security guard was on duty. He said, "Good morning," and handed them their badges.

When they got off the elevator the same woman greeted them and took them to Terry's office. She knocked, opened the door, and moved aside so Jeffery and Debbie could step into the room.

Seated at a conference table was Terry and President Wilson. They both stood up. Jeffery and Debbie walked over to the table and Jeffery said, "Good morning Mr. President. This is an unexpected pleasure."

President Wilson shook hands with Jeffery and Debbie and said, "Good morning. It's nice to meet the two people who I have read so much about over the years. Are you really surprised to see me here?"

"No, the man who drove us saw your shuttle this morning and saw this meeting on the security logs. But it's still a pleasure to meet you."

They all sat and President Wilson said, "The reason I'm here is because I want to discuss something with you."

Jeffery nodded and President Wilson continued, "I'm sure you are aware we have labor problems on Earth. There is an extreme shortage of factory workers. It's beginning to undermine our ability to remain competitive within the trade group. I know this is a problem we created, but neither I, nor any of my advisors, have any suggestions to resolve the problem. I was hoping that perhaps an outside viewpoint might be helpful."

"I was made aware of how serious this problem is only a few days ago, and I've been thinking about it. I think the only thing you can do is cut the fluff out of payments to those who don't want to work because they are very comfortable. You have to make them uncomfortable enough so they will want to return to work."

"That's a perfect recipe for losing the next election."

"First, I think if you are honest with the people, they will respect your decision. They may not like it, but as long as they realize the need for it, the majority of the people will continue to support you. Even if you lose the next election, you still have the satisfaction of knowing that you did the right thing."

"What do you think, Terry?"

"I agree with Jeffery, I don't see another solution. We can't continue to outsource our manufacturing and retain our standard of living. We either have to reduce our standard of living for everybody, or just for those who don't want to work. You should know that because of a labor shortage, I asked Jeffery if we could build manufacturing and repair facilities on Procolt 2."

"Did you agree?" President Wilson asked.

"I haven't given him my answer yet, but Debbie and I have discussed this and believe it's a good idea. Even though I'm not a part of the Procolt 2 government, I will do everything I can to make us self-sufficient. At the time Procolt City was being built, we imported everything. Now we make about 80% of what we need. Most of the remaining 20% are food items we can't produce on Procolt 2."

Terry asked, "I thought you were importing cars from Earth?"

"We were until sixty days ago. We are still taking delivery of cars purchased prior to that time, but there will be

121

no new orders. Our factory in New Paris is now making about three hundred cars a day, and we could increase that by adding additional workers. If we were running the factory around the clock, we could make over a thousand cars per day."

"Do you use all manual labor?"

"No, some repetitive tasks are done by machines, but 85% of the manufacturing utilizes manual labor."

"Are all the parts made on Procolt 2?"

"Yes, we don't have to import anything."

"That's amazing. I'm sure at some point we could have done the same thing on Earth, but it would be impossible now," President Wilson said.

Nobody said anything for perhaps thirty seconds, then President Wilson said, "Jeffery, the measures you are suggesting are not something I can do on my own. It requires Congress to pass new laws. Would you be willing to speak to a joint session of Congress and tell them what you just told me?"

"Why me? I'm not a great public speaker. I'm positive you could present the same information much more eloquently than I could."

"People think of me as a politician. You, however, are considered a hero by most people of the world. They believe all the good things that have happened on Earth over the last twenty years are because of you and Debbie, and they are right. You made contact with the people from Coplent, you played an important role in our joining the trade group, and finally the technology developed on Procolt 2 is the primary factor in Earth's phenomenal economic growth."

"So, you're saying you think they will take action if I tell them something, but if you said the same thing it will just be political claptrap."

"Yes, that's exactly what I'm saying. Will you do it?"

"Okay, but I need a few days to prepare something. Do you have a speech writer I can work with?"

"Of course, I'll have Brenda Murray contact you tomorrow. She helps me with most of my speeches."

"Debbie and I were planning on going home in ten days or so, but I guess we can stay a little longer."

Debbie, who had not said a word during the conversation, said, "This is very important and delaying our return by a few days isn't a problem. I know you don't like speaking to large groups, but you've done it before and did it very well. I'm sure you'll do just fine."

"Okay, I'll call a joint session of congress in ten days. That will give you plenty of time to prepare."

The meeting broke up a short time later. Vince was waiting for them in the lobby of the building. Jeffery told Vince what happened at the meeting and the three of them spent the entire trip back to Brandon's house discussing what Jeffery should say in his speech.

As they pulled up to the house Jeffery said, "Vince, I should have received a message from Jessica this morning. Do you want to come in?"

"Of course. I'm very anxious to hear from her."

They went directly to Brandon's office. Jeffery checked his messages and there was one from Jessica. He told Vince about the message and then opened it. The message said, "I'm sure you wouldn't have asked Captain Kingsley to contact me if you didn't feel he was qualified to work here. His credentials are excellent. So, as long as you feel he would be an asset to our work, I'm all for it."

"The job is yours. Call me whenever you're ready to go."

"Thank you, sir. I'll have to give NASA a thirty-day notice that I am leaving. I'll send that in tomorrow."

The following day Jeffery and Debbie spent the morning working on Jeffery's speech. In the afternoon Brenda Murray called. Jeffery told her the speech was mostly completed and she asked him to send it to her. He did that as soon as their conversation ended.

The next morning Jeffery received a message from Brenda. Attached to the message was the finished speech. Jeffery read it and thought it was very good. He gave it to Debbie and she liked it too.

Jeffery and Debbie decided to postpone their trips to the big cities. They spent two days with Debbie's family and then they went to visit Jeffery's parents. After greeting each other they sat on sofas in the living room and Jeffery's father said, "We've talked it over and decided we would like to move to Procolt 2. We appreciate your offer to buy us a house, but we would prefer to live at Procolt Paradise. Is that possible?"

"Of course, Dad," Jeffery responded. "You can have one of the high-rise apartments or a house. It's your choice. Regardless of the one you choose, you will get daily maid service, all your meals are free, and you can use any of the resort's facilities."

"We will need thirty days or so to do some things before we leave. Can you arrange for transportation?"

"That won't be necessary. Debbie and I aren't very busy anymore, so whenever you're ready send me a message and we'll come back and pick you up. We'll be here three days later."

"Thank you."

"You're welcome."

Jeffery and Debbie spent two days with his parents before returning to Florida. After they returned Jeffery's mood changed. It was obvious he was concerned about the speech and that concern intensified as the big day approached. He practiced the speech every day, and now he remembered the whole thing.

Vince contacted him the day before the speech to tell him he would be there to pick them up at six-thirty in the morning. The speech was scheduled for one o'clock.

The morning of the speech Jeffery's mood was better. He realized he was not a politician, and if he didn't deliver the speech perfectly it really didn't matter. His life was on Procolt 2, not Earth.

There was a NASA shuttle waiting for them when they arrived at the shuttle port. The flight to Washington was smooth and relaxing. He and Debbie talked about their parents and other things, but neither of them said a word about the speech.

A limo met them at the shuttle port in Washington. When Jeffery and Debbie stepped off the shuttle, Beth Kessler, the vice president, was there to greet them. They shook hands and got into the limo. They went directly to the chamber where the event was to be held. Then Ms. Kessler took them to a room where there was coffee and snacks. Jeffery and Debbie each had a cup of coffee. They sat there until five minutes before one. Ms. Kessler stood up and said, "it's time to go."

She took Jeffery to the staging area, and directed one of her staff to take Debbie to her seat. At precisely one o'clock the Sargent-At-Arms announced Beth Kessler. She walked up to the podium and spent several minutes speaking about Jeffery's past. Finally, she introduced him and Jeffery walked up to the podium. They shook hands again and Jeffery said, "Thank you, Madam Vice-President, for that wonderful introduction. I don't remember doing all the things you mentioned, but my memory probably isn't as good as it used to be."

There was some laughter and applause. When it quieted down Jeffery began speaking. "Thank you all for coming today. I have never spoken to a group like this before, but the message I have for you transcends my discomfort with the situation. Earth is in trouble. Like many of the great civilizations of the past, Earth is about to become a victim of its own success. It happened to the Greeks and the Romans. I can only hope it won't happen again.

"The financial success of the last ten years has brought unprecedented wealth to the governments of Earth. It's natural for governments to distribute some of that wealth to the people they govern. They are elected by the people to their positions and feel compelled to give something back. That's not a problem when it is done in the form of tax breaks, free education, and health care. Responsible governments also provide assistance for those that are unable to take care of themselves. However, it becomes a problem when governments provide direct financial assistance to those people who simply don't want to work.

"The average unemployment rate in Earth's largest metropolitan areas is at an astounding 19%. It's not because jobs are unavailable, it's because the people who receive payments from the government collect only slightly less than what they would be paid if they worked. In their minds, they can easily forgo some material items in exchange for not having to get up and go to work every day.

"Because it's no longer possible to find workers for Earth's factories, many of those products are now being manufactured on other planets. Earth alone is responsible for the financial resurgence on Crosus.

"I would like to tell you about a situation I discovered shortly after I arrived on Earth. I had a meeting with the director of operations at NASA. He told me that at any given time NASA has about two thousand job openings at their location in Florida. Many of these jobs do not require advanced education or special skills, they only require a desire to work. NASA will provide the training required for the job. These positions go unfilled because during a typical week only twenty people apply for jobs.

"On my home planet, Procolt 2, we did not have a government until recently. There was no welfare and everybody worked. Now that we have a government, I hope they will pass whatever laws are needed to provide assistance to those who truly need it. But I'm positive they will never pass a law that provides financial assistance to people who don't want to work and expect the government to take care of them. However, laws like that would never be considered since the people who came to Procolt 2 did so because they saw what was happening on Earth and wanted to escape before the governments here collapsed. These people built their own homes, stores, and offices. They started farms to provide their own food. They built the roads, shuttle ports, and bridges. In short, they built their own cities.

"That attitude still exists among many of the people on Earth, but it is up to you to rekindle the spirit of your citizens. To do that you will need to pass some unpopular legislation. You must reduce the payments to those who are unwilling to work to a point where it makes them uncomfortable. Millions of people will be upset with you if you do this, and you may lose the next election, but you will save the Earth for future generations. Thank you."

Most of the people in the audience applauded. Others sat in their seats and were obviously upset with Jeffery's comments.

The following day the media and some of the more influential members of congress reacted to Jeffery's speech. The conservatives felt the speech was to the point and accurately outlined the problem. The more liberal members of congress and the media were actually offended by his comments. Jeffery really didn't care what anybody thought. He did what President Wilson had asked, and now it was up to President Wilson and others in government to resolve the problem.

The day after the speech Jeffery, Debbie, and her family all left Earth for the trip to Procolt 2. Vince called Jeffery that morning to tell him that he had given his thirty-day notice to NASA, and he would be available to start work on Procolt 2 immediately after that. Jeffery said he was coming back to Earth in thirty days anyway to pick up his parents and bring them to Procolt 2 and Vince could join them.

During their trip back to Procolt 2, legislation was introduced in the congress of all seven of Earth's governments. President Wilson and other conservatives were more than a little disappointed that Jeffery's speech was not as well received as they had hoped. President Wilson's economic advisors told him that without the legislation, the government would have to begin borrowing money again to pay the benefits required under the current laws. He also knew what would happen if the legislation was passed by the North American Union, but not the other governments: The people who were happy being dependent on the government for their existence would move to other parts of the world. That would not be a bad thing for North America, but it could be devastating for the other groups. He decided that was not something he was going to worry about.

127

Jeffery's ship landed at Procolt Paradise. Mystic was there to greet them. She didn't realize her grandparents and aunt were coming, so she was pleasantly surprised to see them. Jeffery said, "Your grandparents and Connie are staying here permanently. Please find them nice two-bedroom apartments."

"Okay, Dad. Several apartments were just vacated on the sixty-third floor overlooking the lake and the marina. I'm sure they'll like them. Come on, I'll show them to you."

Debbie's mother said, "I know it's been a while since we've been here, but you have really grown up. Your Dad said you are running the resort now and you are also Vice President. That seems like a lot of responsibility for somebody your age."

"I guess you're right, but I don't think about it very much. It all just seems to come naturally."

Debbie's parents and Connie went with Mystic to look at the apartments. Jeffery walked over to the lab to speak with Jessica.

When he walked into the lab Jessica looked up from what she was doing and asked, "How was Earth?"

"It's changed a lot, and not for the better. I'll tell you about it later. I want to let you know that Apex expects to buy two and a half million units per year initially, so we need to begin working on both the manufacturing facility and the process to make them in large quantities."

"Would it surprise you if I said I was already working on that?"

"No, it wouldn't surprise me at all."

"I would like to use squirrels to build the batteries. They are better suited to work with the very small components in the batteries."

"That's not a problem. All the squirrels are excellent workers. Where do you want to build the factory?"

"I would like to build it near Procolt Paradise, in the meadow about a unit north of here."

"Okay, the resort won't expand in that direction anyway. When can you have the design complete so Jim can start construction?"

"Probably twenty days from now. Some of the heavy equipment will have to be ordered from Earth, but I'll get that ordered in a few days."

"Do you think we could be in production in a hundred days?"

"Probably, but give us an extra twenty days just in case we find an unexpected problem."

"Okay, I'll send a message to Kimberley at Apex and let her know. She's going to ask about the cost, so I'll need a price in six or seven days."

"Actually, I should have that for you by tomorrow."

"Thanks Jessica, as usual, you are doing a wonderful job. I'm going back to Earth in thirty days to pick up my parents who are moving here. Debbie's parents and sister are here permanently too. They came back from Earth with us. Anyway, when I return Vince Kingsley will be with me, so you might want to think about his first assignment."

"Okay, I'll think about it."

The following day Jeffery received a call from Jessica who told him the manufacturing costs for the batteries, in Earth dollars, would be $2.17 each. Jeffery thanked her for the information and immediately sent a message to Kimberley telling her the cost for the batteries, based on annual purchase of two and a half million units was $12.17 per battery. The profit from the sale of the batteries would easily pay for the manufacturing facility.

Jeffery received a message from Kimberley six days later agreeing to the terms. She said the samples were excellent, and was sure she would be able to sell them for $35. Obviously, everybody was going to make a profit on this product.

Jeffery and Debbie went back to Earth on schedule, picked up his parents and Vince, and returned immediately to Procolt 2. When they landed Mystic was there to greet her grandparents. She had already selected an apartment for them, so after an affectionate greeting, she took them to their apartment.

Jeffery, Debbie, and Vince went to Jessica's lab. Jeffery made the appropriate introductions and then he and Debbie went to the restaurant to get something to eat. Jessica gave Vince a brief orientation, showed him to his apartment, and took him on a tour of Procolt Paradise.

While Jeffery and Debbie were eating, Jim came over to their table and told them that construction had started on the battery factory. He expected it to be operational in less than one hundred twenty days.

When Jeffery returned to his office there was a message from Terry telling him he would be coming to Procolt 2 in thirty days to discuss the NASA facility he wanted to build. Jeffery realized now that Procolt 2 had a government, he had to inform them about his discussions regarding the NASA facility. He called Mystic and asked her to come to his office.

Mystic walked in and said, "Hi Dad. What's up?"

"You need to put on your Vice-President hat for this. When I was on Earth the first time, NASA asked me about the possibility of building a facility here that would build and repair ships. Before I left I agreed, but I neglected to inform you or Oscar. Anyway, Terry Brennan will be here in thirty days to discuss the details and somebody from the government needs to be involved."

"I have a meeting with Oscar tomorrow morning. I'll discuss this with him then. I assume they want to build here because they can't find employees on Earth."

"You're exactly right."

"I can't imagine Oscar objecting, but I'll let you know what he says after our meeting."

"Thanks."

"You're welcome, Dad."

During the next year and a half several things happened. The battery factory was finished and was producing more than ten thousand batteries every day. Construction had begun on the NASA facilities. The new NASA space station was only about half completed, but the ground facility had opened for business ahead of schedule. Business at Procolt

Paradise grew at an almost alarming rate, so two more guest towers were built and ready to open. Both towers were already fully booked for a year.

Everything on Procolt 2 was going well. The new government appeared to be functioning well, and Mystic was doing a great job as vice-president. Unfortunately, Earth was experiencing some serious issues.

EARTH

A year and a half after Jeffery's speech, things on Earth had gotten worse with the exception of North America and Asia. They passed laws to limit the payments of those who simply refused to work. President Wilson's prediction that the people who expected the government to support them would move to other locations where that policy was still in effect proved to be correct.

The influx on new residents in Europe and Africa forced the governments there to raise income taxes and they added other taxes that hit the middle and upper classes the hardest. As a result, the productive people left these areas and moved to either North America or Asia.

Now the European Union and the African Union were facing bankruptcy. Both had debts they would never be able to repay, so they turned to North America and Asia for financial help. Although the money was available to bail them out, both North America and Asia refused unless the laws were changed to eliminate the problem.

After the refusal, the European and African unions decided to cut back services and eliminate government jobs in order to attempt to balance their budgets. It was a dismal failure. Finally, in an act of desperation, the people of Europe elected new government leaders. New laws were passed and the European economy began a slow recovery. The unemployment rate dropped to under 10% for the first time in more than ten years, and as unemployment dropped, tax revenues increased. It appeared Europe was on its way to becoming solvent again.

When the Africans saw the European recovery they also began to implement the same policies. A year later Africa was on the road to recovery as well.

RUSSELL FINE

EARTH 2284

Terrance Mason was elected to the Presidency of the North American Union in November 2284. The economic problems Earth had suffered through ended more than twenty years earlier. Earth was going through another economic boom, unemployment was at 1%, the population stabilized at twenty-two billion people, and life expectancy on Earth had reached a new high at one hundred ten.

President Mason was in the third month of his term, when Dr. Richard Grant, called and asked for a meeting to discuss an urgent situation. The president asked him for details, but Dr. Grant said it was best to explain the situation in person. The meeting was scheduled for 10:30, and Dr. Grant was right on time. The president's secretary opened the door to his office and escorted Dr. Grant to a chair across the desk from President Mason.

After the secretary left the room the President said, "Good morning Richard. What's the urgent problem?"

"The entire western half of the North American Union could be destroyed in a cataclysmic volcanic eruption in two years! I believe that should be considered urgent," Richard responded.

"If you're correct, that is certainly an urgent situation. Please explain what you think is going to happen."

"I'm sure you know we are now able to predict Earthquakes with 90% accuracy within a thirty day period. The accuracy drops to 50% at a year. Four months ago a team from the University of Montana predicted a 2.7 magnitude Earthquake in the Yellowstone Basin within sixty days. There was a quake fifty-eight days later that registered 2.8 on the Richter Scale. After that quake, they predicted another one in forty days that would register 3.1. That quake occurred two days ago. Since the first 2.8 quake, there have been hundreds of smaller quakes occurring every day, but those quakes are slowly increasing in strength. Since then there have been nineteen quakes that were over 2.0, and five of those were over 2.5. Yellowstone National Park is sitting on one of the largest

135

volcanically active areas in the world. I believe a major eruption will occur there within two years. If my calculations are correct, the eruption will occur in conjunction with a 9.8 quake. The strongest Earthquake ever recorded was 9.5. This quake will be significantly larger. I think the area between Juneau and San Diego will be demolished."

"More than a billion people live in that area! What can we do?" the president asked anxiously.

"I believe that the only way to stop the quake is to find a way to release the pressure building up under the Earth's crust, but I have no idea how to do that. I have spoken to a few engineers I know and asked them if there was any way to release the pressure that is being generated by a pool of lava. They all basically said it was impossible."

President Mason was silent for a few seconds and then he said, "I thought earthquakes only occur on fault lines where tectonic plates meet."

"Your right, most earthquakes are along the edges of tectonic plates. However, earthquakes directly beneath a volcano are caused by the movement of magma. The magma exerts pressure on the rocks above it and eventually they crack resulting in a quake."

"Maybe we just need better engineers?"

"Yes, I agree. I want to go to Procolt 2 and discuss this with the squirrels."

"Okay, I'll send a message to Jeffery telling him that we need his help."

"I thought his daughter, Mystic, was running the place now. I know she took a vacation from running the resort while she was president of Procolt 2, but that was almost thirty years ago."

"She has been running the resort since that time with her husband, a man from Procolt City named Virgil Griffith. They have a son named William who is now about fifteen years old. Anyway, Jeffery is still involved in research projects, despite the fact that he is now over eighty years old. He was here for my inauguration and looked like he was in his forties. Take the ship that leaves on Friday. That way Jeffery will have some time to prepare for your arrival. I'll let him know why we need him as well."

"Thank you, sir. One more thing. I think you should consider closing Yellowstone and Grand Teton. If the predictions are correct, the next powerful quake will occur in about sixty days, and that quake will be about 4.2. That's enough to damage roads, bridges, and masonry buildings."

"I don't want to scare people. Let's try to get some answers first."

"Okay, sir. I understand. I'll get you the information as quickly as possible."

RUSSELL FINE

138

PROCOLT 2

Jeffery sat down at his desk and checked his messages. He was surprised to see an urgent message from Terrance Mason. He met Terrance when he came to Procolt Paradise for vacation twenty years ago, and he and Terrance had been friends ever since. The three-day travel time between Earth and Procolt 2 meant they didn't see each other very often, but they sent messages to each other frequently. This was the first time he received one marked "Urgent".

He opened the message and immediately called Jane Teacher. She was Jessica's daughter and had been running the research lab since Jessica's death fifteen years earlier. He asked Jane to bring Vince with her to his office. When they arrived Jeffery said, "Please sit down. I just received a very disturbing message from Earth. They need our help. Vince, I'm sure you've heard of Yellowstone National Park, correct?"

"Of course. I went there on vacation a few times with my parents. It's a fascinating place."

"Yes, it is, and this fascinating place sits on top of the largest and most active volcanic area on Earth. The message I received said that they are predicting a major volcanic eruption coupled with the largest earthquake ever measured sometime in the next two years. Unless it can be prevented, as many as a billion people will be killed in the event. They want us to help them stop it. The president of the North American Union has sent a scientist here to discuss this with us. He should be here in a few days."

Vince said, "I have no idea how to stop an Earthquake. Do either of you?"

Jane said, "Volcanic eruptions are caused by pressure generated by large quantities of magma. If we can find a way to relieve the pressure, it might prevent the eruption and the corresponding quake."

"Something tells me saying it is a lot easier than doing it. I don't think we could just drill a big hole to take care of the problem," Vince said.

"I'm sure you're correct, drilling a big hole won't help. But I'm confident that between the two of you you'll come up with a solution. This is now your top priority project," Jeffery said.

Jane and Vince left Jeffery's office and walked back to the lab together. Jane was, in Vince's opinion, the most intelligent being in the galaxy. Jane's mother, Jessica, was the most intelligent being when she was alive, and all of Jessica's knowledge passed down to Jane. Jane was reading by the time she was about four months old and continued educating herself by reading every text book she could find. Now, at the age of twenty-one, she was a walking encyclopedia. But she wasn't just knowledgeable, she knew how to apply the knowledge she had to solve the most complex problems. He was sure that if anyone could figure out how to stop a volcano from erupting, it was Jane.

As they walked into the lab Jane said, "Since we can't drill a hole to release the pressure without creating an eruption, maybe we could move the magma to another location?"

"You mean with a transporter? That's only capable of moving something that weighs, at the most, five hundred pounds. Additionally, the range is limited to five hundred units, and that's through empty space. I have no idea what the range would be through solid material."

"You're right, there are limitations to the current transporters, but that doesn't mean we couldn't improve their capabilities. Anyway, it was just a thought."

"Could we drill sideways into the magma chamber, giving it a different path?"

"That's also a possibility. If I remember correctly, Yellowstone is about a thousand units east of the Pacific Ocean. We could outfit a submarine with a drill of some kind and drill down and east into the chamber to release the magma into the ocean."

"We would have to invent a drill capable of drilling through more than a thousand units of soil and rock, but that might be an easier task then modifying the transporter."

"Let's think about both ideas tonight and we'll discuss it in the morning."

Vince said, "That sounds reasonable." Then he looked at the time display on his communicator and said, "I have a dinner date with Sybil in an hour, so I'm going to go home and get ready. I'll see you in the morning."

"Okay, have a good time."

The next morning Jane and Vince were both in their lab by eight o'clock. They both thought about the suggestions and Jane said, "I think your idea is better. It's easier to implement and would take far less time to build. What do you think?"

"I thought about both proposals. I agree that modifying the transporter is a very complex task and it might take too long to accomplish. If we had ten years instead of two, I think it would be a better choice. I can think of a lot of applications for an improved transporter. Other than mining, or road building, I don't think there would be a lot of practical applications for the drill."

"Okay, let's work up a preliminary plan for the drill. I'd like to have something to show the representative from Earth when he gets here."

Jane and Vince spent the entire day discussing different ideas for the drill. It had to create a self-sealing shaft to prevent the shaft from collapsing. The only way to do that effectively was to melt the shaft walls. They tested some high-powered lasers to see if they were capable of melting soil and rock into a hard surface, but the lasers were incapable of generating the heat required. Testing indicated that only a fission or fusion reaction would be able to generate the heat required for the task.

They spent the next day thinking about ways to create a controlled nuclear reaction, and by the end of the day they had an idea of how to build their device. The scientist from Earth was due to arrive the following afternoon, so in the morning they created a preliminary design for the device.

Vince and Jane were there to greet Dr. Grant when he arrived. Dr. Grant saw them as soon as he was off the shuttle.

141

He walked over and said, "Good afternoon, I'm Richard Grant. Since you are here to meet me, President Mason must have sent you a message saying I was coming."

Jane said, "It's a pleasure to meet you. I'm Jane Teacher. I manage the research and development area on Procolt 2, and this is my assistant, Vince Kingsley. We did receive a message about your visit. Also, we know the purpose for your visit. Vince and I have been working on possible solutions to the problem. If you would like to accompany us to our lab, we can share the progress we have made so far."

"You've actually made some progress! Our people on Earth said it couldn't be done and wouldn't even consider trying. Obviously, I made the right choice when I asked the President about coming here."

"Richard, we don't believe there's any problem that can't be resolved. We came up with two possible solutions, but eliminated one because we were not sure we would be able to finish it within the two-year time frame. The solution we chose requires no new technology, but using current technology in a different way. Do you want to check in before you come to the lab?"

"No, let's go to the lab. I'm very anxious to see what you've come up with."

Jane led the way to the lab, and once inside they went to a conference room. At the front of the room was a large video monitor that displayed an image of the west central part of North America. Vince walked to the front of the room by the monitor, Richard sat down on one of the chairs, and Jane climbed up on a chair and stood facing the monitor.

Vince said, "The approach we decided to take to resolve this problem is to dig a tunnel from a point a thousand units west of Yellowstone into the magma pool and allow the magma to flow into the ocean. That would eliminate the pressure building up in the pool."

Richard looked skeptical and asked, "How are you going to make a tunnel a thousand units long?"

"With our fusion drill," Vince responded.

"What is a fusion drill?" Richard asked.

"It's something Vince and I are working on. It's a small fusion reactor mounted on a robotically controlled underwater vehicle. The tip of the drill is four feet in diameter and the reactor heats it to about four thousand degrees. This design will allow the drill to melt the material in front of it and harden the surface of the tunnel so the walls won't collapse. It's still pretty early in the design process, but we think we can drill twenty units per day."

"We don't know the exact location of the magma pool. Won't that have to be located first?" Richard asked.

"Yes, but I'm sure your people are capable of finding it. We'll also need a submarine to act as a base of operations during the drilling process."

"You're right. I'm positive our mining engineers can figure out a way to locate the magma pool. How long do you think it will take you to build the drill?"

Jane answered, "About one hundred twenty days."

"I'll send a message to the president as soon as I get into my room asking him to assign someone to get a team together to locate the magma pool."

Jane asked, "We have a preliminary design for the fusion drill. Would you be interested in looking at it?"

"Yes, I would. I'd like to review it this evening and we can discuss it tomorrow. Is that okay?"

Jane handed him a piece of paper and said, "This is the file name and password for the fusion drill design file. Of course, we can discuss the design tomorrow. Have a good evening Richard. Vince and I are usually in the lab by eight o'clock, but you don't have to be here that early. This is a great place to relax and you should take advantage of it."

Richard said, "It's going to be difficult for me to relax when the lives of a billion people are at risk. I'll be here at eight." Then he left the lab to go check in.

Richard arrived at the lab a few minutes after eight. Jane and Vince were already there. Richard said, "Good morning. Jane, you were right, this is a great place to relax. When all this is over, I'm going to come back with my wife and spend a month here. I spent a few hours going over the

143

design and I think it's very clever. I don't see any reason why it won't work. Do you already have the components to build it?"

"I believe we do, but all the components are available to purchase from Coplent. We could have them in six days. I think all three of us should review the design today and I'll check our inventory for parts when we're finished."

Richard said, "Okay, let's get started."

The three of them spent the day going over the design. Richard could not believe how intelligent and knowledgeable Jane was. As they were reviewing the design Jane saw every flaw before Richard or Vince. By the end of the day the design had been modified slightly, but all three of them were convinced it was correct.

Jane cautioned, "I know the design is complete and it looks reasonable, but until we have a working device, we have to assume there will be failures, and we should be prepared for them. If all the parts are in stock, we can start building the electronic parts of the device tomorrow. I'll send the drawing over to our metal working group so they can start on the housing for the device. I don't know how long that will take, but probably not more than four or five days. I would hope to have the device built in two weeks. Richard, are you going to stay or are you going back to Earth?"

"If the president will let me, I'll stay here until we know the device works."

"We're going to have to test it on Earth because it will have to be tested under water and controlled from a submarine. We don't have any submarines on Procolt 2."

"I'll arrange everything."

That evening Richard sent a status report to the president and asked if he could stay until the device was finished. After the message was sent he received a message from the University of Montana. It said, "A new analysis of the situation at Yellowstone has just been completed. It was done because we are now experiencing a swarm of quakes and all of them are over 2.5. The analysis indicates that we'll have only twenty months until the super quake occurs."

144

Richard read the message twice. Then he called Jane and told her about it. She said the shortened time frame means that they will have to increase the power of the device so they can go at least thirty units per day.

They were all in the lab at eight o'clock again the next morning. Jane said, "I spent the night thinking about the design. We were originally going to use one large fusion reactor to heat a four- foot diameter area. Now I think we should use four smaller fusion reactors. Each one heating a two-foot diameter area, overlapping with the adjacent areas so there is continuous coverage. My calculations indicate that this would allow us to increase the drill speed by 50%, allowing us to go thirty units per day. If we only have to go twelve hundred units, and I think that figure is accurate, it would only take forty days to complete the tunnel."

It took the rest of the day to finish the drawings. The next morning Jane sent the new case design over to the metal shop for fabrication and she checked their parts inventory. Everything was in stock except for two small fusion reactors, so she ordered them from her supplier on Coplent.

They started assembling the electronic components immediately. When the finished case arrived four days later, Vince and Jane began mounting the components into the case. The fusion reactors were converted into small rocket engines. The exhaust gases produced by the reactors were very hot, almost four thousand degrees. The reactors were mounted so their exhaust ports were protruding slightly from the front of the device. Each reactor would create a two-foot diameter circle of heated plasma fifteen inches from the front of the device.

It took ten days to complete the construction of the fusion drill. The device was about seven feet long. It was basically a three and a half foot diameter metal tube that was surrounded by rows of casters that would allow it to travel smoothly through a four foot diameter hole. On the front were the four fusion reactor exhaust ports, and on the back there was a large propeller and a directional control mechanism that would allow the fusion drill to be piloted through water.

Richard sent a message to the president regarding the status of the device and reminding him they needed the use of a submarine for testing. The day after the fusion drill was ready to be tested, he received a response that said a submarine had been placed on permanent assignment for Richard's use.

Jeffery and Debbie had been looking for a reason to get away for a while, so they offered to take the team and the fusion drill to Earth on their ship. The following morning the three passengers, the fusion drill, Debbie, and Jeffery were aboard the ship and ready to go. There were also several boxes of spare parts and the equipment necessary to diagnose any problems that might arise.

The trip to Earth would take three days. This time they were not stopping at the space station. Instead, Jeffery was going to land at the Treasure Island Naval Station near San Francisco. The submarine they were going to use was based there and would be ready to depart as soon as the fusion drill and the three passengers were aboard.

EARTH

When Jeffery's ship arrived at Treasure Island, the base commander was there to greet them. As they got off the ship he said, "Good afternoon. I'm Commander Portman. It's a pleasure to meet all of you. Unfortunately, I have to report some troubling news. While you were in transit from Procolt 2 another swarm of quakes struck the Yellowstone basin. This time several of the quakes were over 4.0 and the president ordered Yellowstone and Grand Teton closed to visitors. Many of the roads through Yellowstone were severely damaged, and two bridges were considered unsafe. The only way to travel to Yellowstone now is by helicopter."

Jeffery said, "I don't believe we're needed, so Debbie and I are going to take a short vacation here before we go back to Procolt 2. Good luck, and if you need anything from us let me know."

Richard was sure their timeframe was reduced again. He did some quick calculations in his head and said, "Jane, based on this information, I think we have less than a year. Perhaps, a lot less."

Jane replied, "I agree. We must begin testing as soon as possible. Have they calculated the best place to start drilling?"

Commander Portman looked at Jane as she spoke. He clearly found her appearance somewhat disconcerting. A few moments later he answered, "Yes, I received those coordinates yesterday. The sub can be there in three days. The starting point is estimated to be seventeen hundred miles from the magma pool. That's about fourteen hundred units."

Richard said, "Then we shouldn't waste time. Let's get going as soon as possible!"

The base commander said, "I agree. Jane, I do want to caution you about something. The men aboard have never seen an intelligent squirrel and I don't know how they will react to you. I hope they don't do anything to offend you, but it's possible."

147

"Commander Portman, I do understand and I won't be offended. Although I have never been to Earth before, I have been to Coplent several times. When I walk with humans there, the locals think I'm a pet. If they stare at me, I usually say, 'Hi, my name is Jane. Is there something I can help you with?' They are invariably surprised I can speak fluently. Then they get embarrassed and turn away."

"That's a clever way to handle it. I'll have all the material you brought moved to the sub. It should be ready to go in an hour."

As the three of them boarded the sub several of the men aboard gawked at Jane, but nobody said anything. As they stepped onto the sub the captain greeted them, "Welcome aboard. I'm Captain Marshall."

He handed each of them a small communicator and said, "These communicators are for you to use while you are on the boat. They have been programmed with your first names. To use them just push the green button and say the name of the person you want to speak to. You can also use a title. For example, if you want to speak to me you can say 'Chuck' or 'Captain'."

Jane took the communicator from the captain and looked at it. She was somewhat surprised to see her picture on the back. She said, "Thank you captain, it's a pleasure to be here."

Jane, Vince, and Richard followed the captain to the officer's area of the sub. Each of them had their own cabin. The cabins were small, but fully equipped. There was a bed, a dresser, a small closet, a desk, and a private bath. When the captain showed Jane her room he said, "I hope this is okay. The room was obviously designed for humans, but if you need anything to make yourself more comfortable, don't hesitate to ask. I suspect you're going to be here for a long time, so if it's necessary I can have my men make any alterations you need."

"Thank you, but that won't be necessary. I think the only thing I will need will be a waterproof stool that I can stand on in the shower."

"I'll have one brought over. Anything else?"

148

"Yes, we need a space to set up the control equipment for the fusion drill."

"We've already cleared out a space for you in the officer's mess area. We put some work tables in there and a few chairs. If you have any special power requirements, let me know immediately."

"We brought our own power modules, so electrical power won't be a problem. Please ask your men to move all the equipment we brought to that area and we'll set it up and test it shortly."

"Do you need the fusion drill too, or can I place it in the hold until we get onsite?"

"As long as we have access to it, that will be acceptable."

"I'll make sure it's placed so you'll have the access you'll need. We should be ready to leave in an hour."

A half hour later all the control equipment was in the officer's mess. Richard and Vince began unpacking everything and putting it on the work table the captain provided. Jane was too small to lift anything, but she immediately began connecting all the control units together. Two officers were sitting drinking coffee and watching the three of them working. They appeared to be amused as they watched Jane, but they didn't say anything.

Just as the last piece of equipment was placed on the table there was an announcement that said the boat would be departing in five minutes. Captain Marshall walked up to them and asked, "Are any of you interested in watching our departure from the deck?"

Richard responded, "Thank you for the offer, but we have a few more hours of work to get all this stuff wired together. Then we're going to test the controls and make sure the fusion drill propulsion system is working properly. I suspect we'll be working for the next seven or eight hours."

"Okay, by the way, if you want something to eat or drink just ask the chef. He'll get you whatever you want."

"Thank you, captain. I'm sure we'll all take advantage of that shortly."

149

Then Captain Marshall asked, "Jane, do you need a special diet?"

"I eat fruits and vegetables. I drink water, coffee, and occasionally soft drinks. I don't need anything special. Thank you for your concern."

"You're welcome. I just received a message from President Mason that stated this submarine and its crew are available to provide any assistance you may need to complete your task. So, please don't hesitate or think you are bothering us. If you need anything, just ask."

"Okay, we understand. For now, we're fine. We'll probably need some assistance when we start testing the drill's drive mechanism. If we do, I'll contact you immediately," Richard said.

Six hours later they were ready to test the drive mechanism, but took a break for dinner first. After dinner Richard called the captain and told him they were ready to begin testing and he needed somebody handy with tools. The captain said he would have someone there in a few minutes.

Five minutes later a man carrying a toolbox walked into the officer's mess. He looked around and saw Vince standing in front of the table with all the control equipment. He walked up to Vince and said, "Hi, I'm Machinist Mate Dennis Crawford. The Captain sent me over to help you."

Vince said, "I need you to take me to the hold where the fusion drill is stored. We will have to uncrate it and open it so I can connect the power module. Can you help me with that?"

"Yes sir."

"Okay Dennis, lead the way."

It took Vince and Dennis an hour to unpack the fusion drill and connect the power module. When it was done Vince called Jane and told her they were ready.

Jane said, "I'll run the standard tests first. Is the prop clear?"

"Yes, you can start whenever you're ready."

The propeller began to rotate and the directional control mechanism began to go through a series of gyrations.

The test took two hours. When it was finished Richard and Jane went over the reports. Everything looked good. The following day they were going to test the communication system.

They all met in the officer's mess at 8:00 the next morning. Captain Marshall saw them as they walked in and asked, "How are things going?"

Jane replied, "The propulsion system tests ran perfectly. Today we're going to check the communication system. We're going to keep reducing the power to the transmitter to simulate long distance communication. This will determine if we'll need repeaters in the tunnel. After we finished last night, I was thinking about what happens when we penetrate the wall enclosing the magma pool. The fusion drill is designed to withstand temperatures in excess of three thousand degrees, so it wouldn't be damaged by exposure to the magma alone. However, we have no idea what the pressure is inside the magma pool. If the pressure is very high, the magma may be forced out through the hole at speeds approaching a thousand units per hour. That would probably destroy the control mechanism and the drill would be stuck in the tunnel, effectively trapping the magma."

"Okay, so what do you suggest?"

"I think we need to use an explosive and not the drill to break into the magma pool."

"Can the drill carry it there?"

"With some modifications, yes. I'll get started on that immediately. How big would the explosive device be?"

"We have some small torpedoes. They are four and a half feet long and five inches in diameter, and can be fit with an explosive capable of demolishing a rock wall ten feet thick and four feet in diameter."

"Is the case of the torpedo magnetic?"

"Yes."

"That would be perfect, captain. Thank you."

Jane climbed up on a chair in front of one the computers and began working on the design changes. Vince and Richard began testing the communications system.

Two hours later Jane had finished the design modifications. There was now a five-foot long and six-inch wide slit in the wall of the drill with a remote controlled removeable cover over the slit. Inside were three powerful electromagnets. The magnets would hold the torpedo firmly in place until it was ready to be dropped. She printed out the drawing of the modified case and the formula for the metal alloy used to make the case of the fusion drill. Then she called the captain.

When he answered she said, "Captain, we need to make a new case for the fusion drill. I have the plans ready. However, the case has to be made from a special alloy. I have the formula for that also. We need this done as soon as possible."

"I'll come over and pick up the plans. Then I'll contact the president. I'm positive we'll have someone working on this immediately."

Jane told Vince about the changes that were needed. He told her he would have them finished in four hours after the communications tests were completed. The results of the communications tests were inconclusive. The probability they would be able to communicate with the fusion drill through fourteen hundred units of rock was 62%. They couldn't take the chance. Something would have to place repeaters every two hundred units in the tunnel. Jane would have to discuss that with the captain. They had all lost track of time. It was almost ten o'clock and none of them had eaten dinner. So, Jane decided to wait until the morning to discuss the communication problem. Vince had the wiring and circuit changes finished in the timeframe he promised.

The next morning Vince started working on the modifications to the fusion drill's electronics and made the electromagnets from parts he found on the sub. Jane contacted the captain and asked for a meeting. He told her to come to his cabin.

When she got there the door was open so she walked in. Captain Marshall was seated at a small table and said, "Good morning Jane, would you like something to drink?"

152

"No, thank you. Since we have been aboard things have not gone as smoothly as I had hoped. The results of the communication test indicated that in order to insure the success of this mission we will need to install signal repeaters every two hundred units. That will have to be done by something other than the drill."

"I have several programable submersibles aboard. I'm certain they could be programmed to place the repeaters. I'll discuss this with my chief engineer, but I don't think it's a problem. I thought you should know that the new case will be finished sometime today and they will bring it to us at the drill site tomorrow morning by helicopter. We will be there by 11:00 tomorrow morning. How long do you think it will take to move the components into the new case?"

"Probably two days. I know that puts us a day behind schedule, but there was no way I could predict the density of the rock in this area before we got here. I did my calculation based on the soil on Procolt 2, but the soil on Earth has a much higher iron content and is more resistant to radio signals."

"I don't think losing a day will make a big difference. There have been no reports of unusual seismic activity in the Yellowstone basin in the last few days. At least we know things have not gotten worse."

"Captain, I believe that our timeline is critical. Richard and I both agree we probably have less than a half year before the eruption occurs. Every day we lose is critical."

"I understand, and I would like this completed as soon as possible too. If any of my men can be of assistance to you, please let me know."

"The only thing I will need is for your men to put the drill into the water as soon as it's mounted in its new case."

"Just contact me whenever you're ready."

The sub arrived at the drill site a half hour earlier than scheduled. At 11:00 a helicopter was approaching the sub and landed a few minutes later on the deck. Three crewmen from the sub removed the new drill case from the helicopter and took it to the officer's mess. Vince, Richard, and Dennis unpacked the drill case from the crate and Vince immediately began checking it. After a half hour he said the case was made correctly and the process of moving the drill components into the case began.

After two eighteen-hour days, the redesigned fusion drill was ready for testing. The testing took three hours and was completely successful. Jane called the captain and told him they were ready to put the drill in the water.

The starting point for the tunnel was at a depth of one hundred ten feet. The sub dove to the correct depth and was positioned fifty feet from the starting point. Three divers took the drill out of the sub and moved it into position.

Jane powered on the propulsion system on the drill and it began to move forward slowly. A problem was detected almost immediately. There was a four knot current over the drill site and the directional control system was unable to compensate for it. Jane called the captain and explained the problem.

Captain Marshall replied, "The divers are still in the water. Would it be safe for them to hold the drill until the first few feet of the tunnel were drilled?"

"I'm not sure. I don't want to injure anyone. I think it would be safe as long as they were ten feet from the drill."

"I can have the machine shop make some ten foot metal poles. The divers can use them to hold the drill in place while you start the tunneling process."

"That's a good idea. How long will it take to make the poles?"

"Probably less than two hours. I'll contact them now. Do we need to bring the drill back aboard?"

"No, I can keep it roughly in the same position until the poles are ready."

"Good, I'll call you as soon as they are ready."

The poles were ready in less than an hour. The divers who came back aboard to wait for the poles left the sub again, each of them armed with a ten foot steel pole. The end of each pole was fitted with a small hook that could be hooked around the casters that surrounded the drill case.

Jane moved the drill close to the rock wall and the divers moved it into position so that the front of the drill was touching the wall. Jane powered on the fusion reactors up to 50% power. Instantly the rock wall in front of the drill began to disintegrate. The divers kept the drill steady as it slowly penetrated the rock. A few minutes later the tunnel was five feet deep. Jane turned off the drill. The divers unhooked the poles and returned to the sub.

Jane restarted the drill and this time brought the power level in the reactors up to 75%. The drill began to move forward. The drill's path was already programmed into the control unit and after fifteen minutes the tunnel was two thousand feet long. The drill was working perfectly. Jane notified Captain Marshall, and Richard sent a message to President Mason.

The drill was now beginning to move slightly downward and would continue on the same path until it was at a depth of thirteen units. Then it would go east, directly toward the magma pool.

Jane, Vince, and Richard were all taking eight hour shifts monitoring the drills progress, but there wasn't really much to do. The drill was doing the job, they just had to keep watch in case something went wrong.

After forty-eight hours the tunnel was sixty units long. Jane called the captain. When he answered she said, "Captain Marshall, the drill is still functioning as expected. The tunnel is now sixty units long. I think it's time to prepare the first submersible. I'm sure it's significantly faster than the drill, but I would like to have the repeater in place shortly after the drill passes the two hundred unit point."

"The submersible travels at about fifty miles per hour, so it can go two hundred units in about five hours. Tomorrow we'll prepare it for launch and launch it the next day. The submersible can hold ten repeaters, a few more than we need. We'll drop one on the bottom of the tunnel every two hundred units."

The submersible was launched on schedule and dropped its first repeater just over two hundred units into the tunnel. Things were going very smoothly until thirty-two days after the launch. Vince was watching the images coming from the drill when the image began jumping. Something was shaking the drill violently. Vince turned off the fusion generators and backed up the drill so he could have a better view of the end of the tunnel. The rock at the end of the tunnel appeared to be moving. It had to be an Earthquake. If the tunnel collapsed behind the drill the project would fail. The shaking stopped about twenty seconds after it started. Vince switched the view to the rear camera and the tunnel appeared to be intact, but it only showed the area twenty feet behind the drill.

Vince picked up his communicator and called Jane. When she answered he said, "We just had another quake. The drill started shaking. The area in front of the drill looks okay. I looked behind the drill and the area right behind it looks normal, but I have no way of knowing if the tunnel behind the drill is still open. The quake lasted about twenty seconds."

"The tunnel is only about four hundred units from the magma pool and I'm sure that's close enough to be affected by a quake in the Yellowstone Basin. I'll call Richard and let him know. I think you should turn the drill back on and continue drilling."

"I was going to do that, but I want to make you aware of the situation first."

It was in the middle of the night but Jane called Richard anyway. He answered the phone by asking, "What?"

"I'm sorry to wake you, but I believe there has been another quake. Vince said the drill started shaking. He's worried that the tunnel may have collapsed behind the drill. Anyway, we have to find out more about that quake."

"I'll make some calls immediately."

Twenty minutes later Richard called Jane and said, "We're in trouble. It was indeed a quake that Vince experienced. It was centered in the Yellowstone Basin and preliminary information is that the quake registered 5.9. They are going to analyze the situation and call me as soon as the analysis is complete, but the guy I talked to said we may have less than fifteen days before the big one."

"You have to inform the president. We have to drill for another twelve days to reach the magma pool. Then we have to drop the torpedo and back the drill out of the tunnel. It will go much faster, but it will still take ten days to back out."

"Were still running the drill at 75% power. If we increase the power we may be able to cut two or three days off the drilling time."

"Yes, but that also increases the risk of some kind of failure. I don't want to do that unless we have no choice. Call me as soon as you get the report."

It was only five o'clock in the morning when Richard called President Mason. Richard identified himself to the man who answered the phone and said he had to speak to the president immediately. A minute later the president was on the phone. He said, "I assume this is very important Richard, otherwise you're fired."

"I'll let you make the decision. There was another quake in the Yellowstone Basin about an hour ago. It was the strongest one yet, and preliminary estimates show the quake was 5.9 on the Richter scale. Vince was watching the drill when it started shaking violently, so our operation was affected. The guy I spoke to at the university said he thought the big one might occur in less than fifteen days. We need twelve days to finish drilling and ten days to back the drill out of the tunnel."

"Okay, you're not fired. Is there anything you can do to speed up the process?"

"We are only running the drill at 75% power. We could increase it to full power and that would probably shave two or three days off the drilling time, but Jane is concerned that it would also increase the possibility of a failure. The drill is a very complex device, and if it fails there is no way to finish the task in time."

"Wow! It sounds like we're screwed. Are they certain about the reduced timeframe?"

"No, they're analyzing the data now. They will call me as soon as it's complete."

"And you will call me the moment you hear anything."

"Yes sir, I'll do that."

Two hours later Richard received a call from the university. The man who called said, "Richard, the quake was more powerful than we originally thought. We now think it was a 6.1. More worrisome is that the system predicted there is a 71% probability that in eighteen days Yellowstone will explode for the first time in more than six hundred thousand years. The quake six hundred thousand years ago was probably the most powerful one that ever occurred on Earth. This next one may be hundreds of times more powerful."

Richard was unable to speak for several seconds. The situation was far worse than he ever expected. He finally said, "I wish the news was better, but thank you for the information. I have some calls to make," and he ended the call.

Richard called Jane and gave her the bad news. She thought for a moment and said, "Let's increase the drill to 95%. I also had an idea. I think I may be able to cause the fusion reactors to explode and destroy the drill. That way it wouldn't block the magma flow."

"Yes, but an explosion thirteen units underground could create an Earthquake."

"I realize that's a possibility, but it would be far smaller than the one predicted for Yellowstone."

"We really don't have a choice."

Jane called Vince and said, "I just got word on the quake you noticed. It was a 6.1 quake in the Yellowstone Basin. The computer models indicate the big quake will occur in eighteen days. At the speed the drill is currently going, it will take us twelve days to reach the magma pool. We have to cut that time by as much as possible. Increase the power to the reactors to 95% and push the drill as fast as you can."

"If we only have eighteen days and we use ten of them to get to the magma pool, that only leaves us eight days to back the drill out of the tunnel. There's no way we can do it that fast."

158

"I know, I'm working on that now."

Vince increased the power to the reactors as Jane requested. After two hours the tunnel length was increased by almost two units, a 25% increase in forward speed. Richard took over for Vince a few minutes later. Vince told him about the increase in speed. They both said they hoped it would be enough.

Before Jane took over she completed the programming necessary to cause the fusion reactors in the drill to explode and loaded the program into the control computer. Once the program was executed, the drill would explode in less than two minutes.

Nine days later the drill's job was completed. They were close enough to the magma pool that the surface temperature on the rock in front of the drill was three hundred forty-one degrees. They dropped the torpedo in the tunnel and began backing the drill out.

Jane notified the captain and told him he should be prepared to fire the torpedo at a moment's notice. He said he would keep the launch control switch with him at all times.

The actual length of the tunnel was thirteen hundred eighty-seven units. The drill was traveling backwards through the tunnel at sixteen units per hour. At that rate, it would take eighty-seven hours to back the drill completely out of the tunnel. If the prediction for the quake was correct, the drill would be out of the tunnel a few days before the quake.

Twenty-eight hours later the drill was just past the position it was in when the last quake occurred. Just as Vince had feared, the tunnel had partially collapsed. The camera showed a layer of loose rock a foot-high blocking the tunnel. There was no way for the drill to get past that point. It was designed to travel on smooth surfaces.

Jane called Captain Marshall and asked him to come to the drill control area. When he arrived, she said, "We have a problem," and she showed him the tunnel.

While the Captain was looking at the monitor Jane said, "The pile of rocks appears to be about a foot high and

159

several feet deep. The drill will not be able to move through that, so it's basically stuck at its current position."

"Which is where?" the Captain asked.

"It's four hundred fifty units west of the magma pool, under the Columbia Plateau in eastern Oregon."

"Are there any populated areas there?"

"The closest city is Burns, and that's about fifty units west and twenty units south of the drill's position."

"Is the area geologically stable? If we blow up the drill, will it cause a quake?"

"Probably, but I think it would be a small one, less than 5.0. But, that's a guess. There's no way to accurately predict what will happen. It's also possible that there is sufficient area in front of the drill to relieve the pressure in the magma pool."

"I'm not prepared to make this decision," Captain Marshall said. Then he turned toward Richard and said, "Richard, you have to contact President Mason. This has got to be his decision."

Richard went to the phone and placed a call to the president. They had a brief conversation. Richard came back and said, "The president wants to discuss this with some of his advisors before he makes his decision. He said he would call me back in a few hours.

However, the next call Richard received was not from the president. It was from the Lab at the University of Montana. The man, petrified with fear, told Richard that a new swarm of more powerful quakes had just started. He said the big quake would occur within minutes.

Richard hung up the phone and yelled, "Captain, set off the torpedo now!"

The Captain took the torpedo fire control switch out of his pocket and activated the torpedo. Then the Captain looked at Jane and said, "There's no time to wait for the president to make a decision. Blow the drill."

Jane typed in a command and said, "In two minutes the drill will explode."

Then the Captain asked, "Won't the explosion collapse the tunnel?"

"Yes, but it will also create a huge pocket where the drill is currently located. I believe that the pocket will have sufficient area to hold the magma that comes through the tunnel. Richard, I think you should call the university and find out what's happening."

Before Richard could get to the phone it rang. Richard answered it. It was the same man who had called a few minutes earlier. This time he said, "The swarm of quakes stopped. Did you do something?"

"Yeah, we opened the tunnel to the magma pool. The magma should be flowing out of the chamber and through the tunnel."

"But you didn't have time to get the drill out of the tunnel. What did you do?"

"We blew it up."

"Was the drill under eastern Oregon?"

"Yes."

"That explains the quake that just occurred there."

"How strong was the quake?"

"The preliminary estimate is 4.8."

"Is that strong enough to cause any damage on the surface?"

"Yeah, but in that area there is nothing to damage."

"Good, please keep me posted on this."

"Sure, I'll call you back in fifteen minutes."

Richard walked back to the group, and with a big smile on his face, said, "It appears that our mission was a complete success!"

Captain Marshall looked at Richard, Vince, and Jane and said, "You have just saved the lives of millions of people. I don't know how we can ever thank you."

Jane said, "We were just doing our jobs. No thanks are necessary."

The captain said, "I'm sure President Mason won't feel that way."

That evening, on a worldwide broadcast, President Mason told the world about the problem, and that due to the

161

efforts of two scientists from Procolt 2 and one of his science advisors, the lives of perhaps a billion people were saved.

Two days later, at a formal dinner at President Mason's residence, the president personally thanked them for their efforts and gave each of them a medal. It was the first time a squirrel had ever been so honored.

PROCOLT 2

When Jane and Vince returned to Procolt 2 they went to see Jeffery. He already knew the mission was a complete success, but they wanted to talk to him about the fusion drill. They found him in the restaurant at his favorite table in the back, drinking a cup of coffee.

Jeffery saw them coming, and when they were by the table he said, "Congratulations, you both did an excellent job."

Jane said, "Thank you, but I think there was some luck involved too. Anyway, we wanted to talk to you about the fusion drill."

"I've been thinking about it too. I think it would be a very useful product to build. I'm positive every member of the trade group would buy them to build roads and use for mining operations. We could probably sell thousands of them every year."

Jane said, "That is exactly what we were discussing on the way back from Earth. There's an empty building in New Paris that would be a perfect place to manufacture them."

"Yes, I'm aware of that. Why the sudden interest in manufacturing? I thought you were more concerned with the technical aspects of the things we do here."

"I'll admit I have an ulterior motive. I want money to build a small city for the squirrels. There are now almost ten thousand of us, and we are spread out in small groups all over. I would like to build one location for all of us to live."

"You should know me well enough by now to realize that all you had to do was ask and I would have given you anything you wanted."

"I know, but I didn't want charity. I wanted to earn the money, and I think this will do it."

"I'm sure you're correct. Where do you want to build this city?"

"Not far away. Most of us work here and I want the commute times to be reasonable."

"Do you want me to hire an architect to work with you or do you want to design it yourself?"

163

"Actually, I've already spoken to Justin Younger about it. He should have the plans completed by now."

"Why don't you and Justin find a location and then set up a meeting with me? I'd like to see what you want to build. As far as manufacturing the fusion drills is concerned, I think you should finish the designs and then, if the building is still available in New Paris, we'll turn it into a manufacturing facility. If it has been spoken for, we can always build a new building."

Vince, who had been quiet up till now said, "I think we need three different size devices, based on the diameter of the tunnel. I would suggest we build ten-foot, thirty foot, and fifty-foot models."

"That seems reasonable. Remember, they have to be able to fit in the hold of a ship, unless you want to assemble them on site."

Vince responded, "Since the designs aren't even started, we don't know how big the finished product will be, but we'll make certain not to create a shipping problem."

Jane said, "It will take thirty days or more to finish the designs. I'll let you know when they are ready. Also, I'll contact Justin and find out if the habitat plans are completed. I'll meet with him and make sure I'm happy with them before we set up a meeting."

"Perfect," Jeffery replied.

Ten days later Jeffery received a call from Jane telling him the plans for the new squirrel habitat were finished and she was very happy with the results. A meeting was set up for the following afternoon.

In addition to Jeffery, Debbie, Jane, and Justin, Glen Kelly, the vice-president of Procolt 2, was there representing the government. Also present was the supervisor of Jeffery's construction crew, Derick Tremble. Justin presented the plans and everyone in the room was very impressed. The habitat was more like a city. There were places that dispensed food, medicine, and clothing. The squirrels did not usually wear clothes, but many of them liked to wear shoes, hats, and gloves. Also, some of the jobs they worked in required them to wear protective clothing.

There were three thousand apartments, each capable of housing a family of up to six. There were moving sidewalks everywhere, so the squirrels could get where they needed to go quickly. There was also an automated tram system that would take them to Procolt Paradise.

When the presentation of the plans was finished, Justin showed an aerial view of the construction area. It was located twenty units northeast of Procolt Paradise. The area was currently a large flat meadow, dotted with trees, and there were three small rivers flowing through the intended construction area.

Jeffery asked, "Derick, what do you think about the design?"

"I like it, and I think it will be easy to build. However, it will probably still take a year to finish. After I have a chance to review the plans more thoroughly, I'll be able to give you an accurate estimate of time and construction costs."

"Have you picked a name for the place?" Jeffery asked.

Justin responded, "Yes, we naming it after Jane's mother, Jessica. It's going to be called Jessica's Meadow."

Jeffery nodded and said, "That's a wonderful idea. I really like it."

Jane said, "There is something else I wanted to discuss with you. It appears the designs for the fusion drills will take longer than I anticipated. Apparently, the empty factory in New Paris is now spoken for. Procolt Engineering just received a contract to build the control electronics for the ships NASA is building and refurbishing here, and they signed a twenty-year lease for the factory. I would like to build a new factory near Jessica's Meadow, and I want the factory to use squirrels as employees."

"Give me a couple of days to think about that."

"Jeffery, the unemployment rate among the humanoid population of Procolt 2 is about 1%. Among squirrels, it's 13%. They need to feel useful. They don't like sitting around doing nothing, and this would give them something to do."

165

"How many squirrels would you expect to be employed there?"

"It depends on sales, but I would guess about seven hundred fifty."

"That would take care of the unemployment problem."

"Yes, it would."

"Okay, you make a good point. But I still want a day or two to think about it."

"I'm sure you'll come to the correct conclusion. You always do."

Jeffery said, "Derrick please get whatever you need from Justin and report back to me in ten days."

"Okay, that's fine. Tomorrow I'll go out to the proposed site and make sure there aren't any problems."

Jeffery ended the meeting. After everyone was gone Debbie said, "Jeffery, I want this to be your last major project. I think we're both getting too old to do this kind of stuff."

"I'm sorry, but I don't agree. I know we're both almost a hundred, but I don't feel any older than I did when we first got here. If you're feeling old, it's probably physiological, not physical. Besides, I want to keep active. I don't want to sit around and watch the world go by. However, I won't go looking for new projects, but if one comes along, I can't promise you I won't get involved."

Debbie sighed and said, "I suppose that's the best I can hope for."

Ten days later everybody was together again. Derrick opened the meeting by handing out copies of his report and saying, "I've gone over Justin's designs, examined the proposed construction site, and I'm very pleased to say everything looks good. As you can see, the cost will be approximately one hundred thousand hirodim. There is something about this project that I'm sure you're not aware of. This will be the first major construction project on Procolt 2 that will not require us to import any materials from another planet. We now manufacture everything that will be needed. That means that the entire cost for the project will go back into the economy of Procolt 2."

166

Jeffery smiled and said, "That's good news Derrick. I've always wanted Procolt to be as self-sufficient as possible, and it's obvious we are moving in that direction."

Derrick continued, "I believe the first phase of the project should be the construction of the tram that runs between Procolt Paradise and the construction site. That will enable the construction workers to get to the site easily. It will also help with getting supplies to the site. I can begin construction of the tram in five days, and it will be completed thirty days later. While the tram is being built, I'll get the equipment and materials needed for the first five buildings brought to the site. I don't have enough people on my staff for this project, so we will need to hire at least two hundred additional people."

Jane asked, "Can any of those positions be filled by squirrels?"

"I hadn't thought about that, but I would guess half of the jobs could be done by squirrels. I'm sure they could handle any task that doesn't require a lot of physical strength."

"I can have a hundred squirrels for you whenever you need them."

"I'll let you know ten days before they'll be needed."

Jeffery said, "I need to discuss this with Debbie before we get started. I want to study Derrick's report. Debbie and I will discuss this tonight and I'll give you my answer tomorrow morning. Thank you all for coming."

Derrick said, "If you have any questions regarding the report, please contact me immediately."

"I'll do that. Thank you, Derrick."

After the others left Debbie said, "A hundred thousand hirodim is a lot of money. I know we can afford it, but I thought this project was going to be paid for by sales of the fusion drills."

"I'm sure it will be, but we'll have to put up the money first. Is that your only concern?"

"Probably, but let's talk about it at dinner. I'm hungry."

"Okay."

Jeffery and Debbie both decided to go ahead with the Jessica's Meadow project and the following morning Jeffery contacted Derrick, Justin, and Jane to tell them the project was approved.

Construction of the tram was started five days later. The plan was to build a road from Jessica's Meadow to Procolt Paradise. In the center of the road was an area wide enough for two trams to travel. The trams were basically driverless buses that would travel at fifty units per hour, so the trip would take less than a half hour. The trams would run in a circle continuously and would be spaced one tenth of an hour apart. The road took twenty-five days to build. While the road was being built, a company in Procolt City began building the trams and Derrick's people began constructing the tram stations in Procolt Paradise and Jessica's Meadow.

Six days after the road was completed, the first tram began its test run. Jeffery, Debbie, Jane, Derrick, and Justin were all onboard the tram for its maiden journey. The trip was quick, comfortable, and without problems. The other trams would be put into service as soon as they were completed.

The designs for the fusion drills took longer than Jane and Vince thought. Jane's original estimate of thirty days was off by more than ninety days. The smallest one would be externally controlled, but the two larger ones were designed to be manually operated. Jane insisted they had to be designed so the size of the person operating the unit was irrelevant. This significantly increased the design time and the manufacturing costs.

At first Jeffery thought the requirement to accommodate any size operator was a waste of time and money. Jeffery had assumed Jane insisted on this so the drills could be operated by a squirrel, but he was wrong.

Jeffery had begun taking orders for the drills before the designs were complete and an order for four units was placed, including two fifty foot models, by the government of Fardrin. Jeffery had never met anyone from Fardrin, but he soon discovered they were humanoids, but the tallest of them was less than four feet.

168

It took a year to finish Jessica's Meadow, but the first buildings were ready to be occupied sixty days after construction started, and squirrels by the hundreds moved in. The fusion drill factory was finished forty days after Jessica's Meadow.

When the factory began building fusion drills they started with the fifty foot models, because they represented a majority of the orders. When the first drill was finished it was tested in the factory, and it passed all the tests. Jane wanted a real test so she had the first drill moved to a valley fifty units east of Jessica's Meadow.

The fifty foot model would create a tunnel that was a semicircle, with a fifty foot wide flat base. The drill was an engineering masterpiece. It was forty-eight feet wide and thirty-five feet long. Since this device moved through air, not water, the propulsion system was completely different. It moved on six metal alloy wheels, each wheel powered by its own large electric motor. The movement of each wheel was controlled by a computer that was attached to a joy stick on the operator console. The front of the drill was adorned with twenty-four fusion reactors. Since there was no water to carry away the heat on the sides of the tunnel, the drill drew in large amounts of cooler air from behind it and blew it at the walls of the tunnel to solidify them.

The drill was transported to the test site by a large shuttle. Jane drove it off the shuttle and stopped twenty feet from the mountain. Jeffery, Debbie, Vince, and Derrick were there to watch the test. The observers could hear Jane speak through their com units.

Jane powered up the fusion reactors and said, "Reactors at 50%. Moving forward now."

They watched as the drill moved forward and when it just a few inches from the side of the mountain the rock began to glow and melt. Jane said, "Setting forward speed to one half unit per hour."

Slowly the drill moved into the mountain, creating a perfect semicircle. They watched as the mountain engulfed the drill. It seemed to be working perfectly. A quarter of an hour later the drill was a few hundred feet into the mountain. Suddenly there was a loud cracking sound coming from the tunnel. It grew in intensity until it was almost painful. Jeffery screamed into his com unit for Jane to back out of the tunnel, but it was too late. It sounded like an explosion when the tunnel collapsed, burying Jane and the drill inside the mountain. There was no way to rescue her. She was gone.

No one said anything, they all just stared at the mountainside where the tunnel had been only a few moments earlier. Finally, Jeffery broke the silence and said, "Vince, you're in charge now. All production stops until we figure out what went wrong. Do you think there is any way to rescue her?"

Vince looked at a monitor and said, "The telemetry indicates she is three hundred fourteen feet inside the mountain. It would take at least ten days to reach her. There is no way she could survive that long."

Then Jeffery began to cry, and said softly, "I'm going to miss her."

Debbie said tearfully, "We all will."

Then Jeffery said, "When we are able to recover her body, I want you to give her a proper burial."

Vince said, "Jeffery, I promise you I will do everything I can to recover her body."

Jane never had children, so her knowledge, and Jessica's, was lost forever. Jeffery and Debbie took on the task of finding the most intelligent squirrel on Procolt 2.

After more than thirty days they selected a male named Elliott. He was teaching computer engineering at the school, and seemed to have extensive knowledge about almost everything.

Jeffery met with Elliott to tell him that he had been selected to take over Jane's position and Elliott said he would be proud to follow in her footsteps. Jeffery said his first task was to figure out why the tunnel Jane was drilling collapsed, and what needs to be done to prevent it from happening again.

Elliott nodded and said, "Thank you, sir. I'll get started immediately."

Six days later Jeffery received a call from Elliott. He said, "Sir, I believe that I figured out what happened with the fusion drill. I examined the rock near the cave entrance and found there were large amounts of soft soil mixed in with the rock. I'm certain there is a layer of soft soil under the rock and that soil would not provide adequate support for the rock above. That resulted in the collapse of the tunnel. You should know that there was no way Jane could have known that. Soft soil is very unusual in any mountain on Procolt 2."

"That sounds logical. How do we prevent that from happening again?"

"I think we need to make a small drill that can be used to bore into the rock first and analyze the material we will be drilling through. If we find soft soil, we have to change the drilling location or drill until we reach the pocket of soft soil and remove it by using conventional methods. Then as the soft soil is removed, we will have to build perimeter supports to prevent the tunnel from collapsing. It may also be possible to make modifications to the drill to handle soft soil if it is detected."

"How long will it take to build the small drill?"

"About thirty days."

"Please start on it immediately. I have orders for more than a hundred drills and although I explained to them the drills will not be delivered for a year, I know they will start getting impatient soon."

"Yes, sir. I understand."

"Elliott, I know this is a personal question but I'm concerned about our research and development lab. When Jane died, we lost the knowledge of both Jane and Jessica. I don't want that to happen again. Therefore, I need to ask you something. Have you selected a female partner yet?"

"Yes, I have. We are living together in an apartment in Jessica's Meadow. I believe you interviewed her for the position I was given. Her name is Melody, and she teaches advanced mathematics at the school. I'm not offended by your question. I think it was both reasonable and logical. Also, she told me just a few days ago she is pregnant."

171

"That's wonderful! Congratulations Elliott!"

"Thank you, sir. Melody is far more knowledgeable in mathematics than I am, so our child will be perfectly suited to manage the lab when the time comes."

"Thank you for that information. Please keep me informed on the status of the small drill."

"Of course. One more thing I thought you should know. The construction on the park and recreation area in Jessica's Meadow is almost finished. At a meeting yesterday we decided to name it Jane Teacher Park. Inside the park we're going to build a memorial for her," Elliott said.

"I think that is a very nice gesture. She was the driving force behind Jessica's Meadow, so I'm glad she'll be remembered, and don't concern yourself with the cost. I will take care of it."

"Thank you."

The small fusion drill was ready for testing thirty days later, as Elliott predicted. They took it to the same place where Jane was killed. The drill worked perfectly and confirmed Elliott's thought about soft soil. There was still a problem. Elliott decided that manual drilling in soft soil was still dangerous, so he made the decision to modify the drills to work in a soft soil environment.

It took Elliott and his team another thirty-five days to find a solution to the problem. They developed a plastic resin that could be sprayed onto the cave walls if soft soil was detected. The resin hardened in a few seconds into a smooth surface as strong as a one- inch thick steel plate.

They tested the modified drill on the same mountain. This time the drill was controlled remotely. The drill had been fitted with sensors to detect soft soil, and when it was detected, the forward speed of the drill was slowed to one quarter unit per hour and the power to the fusion reactors was reduced to 25%. The resin was sprayed onto the walls a few seconds after the tunnel was formed. This time the test was a complete success.

Jeffery did not want to take any chances, so he told Elliott to run more tests on other mountains over the next twenty days. If all the tests were successful, they would begin shipping the drills to customers.

At the end of twenty days only a few minor problems were found, and they were quickly resolved. Shipments of the drills began ten days later.

Elliott and Vince decided that it was now safe to locate and remove Jane's remains, so they started on that project immediately. Three days later they reached the fusion drill Jane was driving. It was a tricky maneuver, but they managed to clear the debris around the control cabin of the drill and that allowed them access to her body. The drill sustained very little damage, so after Jane's body was removed, they managed to free up the drill and back it out of the mountain.

Two days after Jane's body was recovered, they held a memorial service for her at Jane Teacher Park. There were more than a thousand squirrels and an equal number of humans at the service.

Jeffery began the memorial service. He said, "It is a sad event that brings us all together here. Today we're going to talk about some of Jane's accomplishments, and there were many. But I think she will be most remembered for the task she and Vince performed on Earth that saved a billion lives. When President Mason was told about her death he was deeply sadden by the news. Two days ago I received a message from him that said the congress of the North American Union voted unanimously to rename Yellowstone National Park. It is now Jane Teacher National Park."

Jeffery paused because of the loud applause caused by his statement. When the applause died down, he continued, "We don't have any national parks on Procolt 2, but we will soon start construction on a memorial for Jane, and it will allow future generations to get to know her. Now I'm going to turn the microphone over to Elliott Teacher, who is following in her footsteps, and that is a very difficult task."

For the next hour, a secession of squirrels and humanoids took turns recounting their experiences with Jane. It was very moving.

The day after the memorial for Jane the squirrels held a meeting to elect a new Leader and Elliott was elected unanimously.

Sixty days after Jane's memorial service, when the Jane Teacher Memorial Pavilion was opened, there was a second memorial service for Jane. The crowd was even bigger than it was for her first one. In addition to the residents of Procolt 2, this one was also attended by all the members of Earth's World Council. President Mason spoke at the service and said the Earth owed a debt to Jane that could never be repaid.

After the drills began to ship, Jeffery and Debbie decided it was time to retire. The management of the lab was turned over to Elliott, and Mystic was in charge of Procolt Paradise.

VANDOR

Fifteen years had passed since the completion of Jessica's meadow, and the squirrel population living there exceeded ten thousand. The humanoid population on Procolt 2 was more than a billion, and the planet now had ten major cities.

Jeffery and Debbie both retired. Their only task was to greet the new visitors as they arrived. It was Jeffery's turn. He watched as the shuttle from the space station landed.

One of the passengers stepped off the shuttle, looked around, saw Jeffery, and walked over to him. He said, "Hello Jeffery. My name is Vandor. It's very important that you and I have a conversation."

"Okay, Mr. Vandor. What would you like to talk about?"

"First, I'm not Mr. Vandor. Vandor is my entire name, although occasionally I used the name Luther Vandor. What I would like to discuss with you is the past history of this galaxy and your part in its future."

"You look human, but something tells me you're not. Would you like to explain?"

"I look human because I am human. However, I was not born on Earth. I'm from the planet Zandrax. I've been living on Earth for most of the last seventy thousand years."

"Is this a joke? I've never heard of Zandrax."

Vandor put his hand on Jeffery's shoulder. Everything around him seemed to evaporate. All he could see was unending white. A few seconds later Jeffery found himself on a large grassy field. There were tall snowcapped mountains in the distance. At the base of the mountains was a large blue lake. It was beautiful, but the vision he was seeing was not on Procolt. It took him a few seconds to realize where he was. He had been there before, many years earlier. He was in northwestern Wyoming inside Grand Teton National Park. Vandor took his hand off of Jeffery's shoulder. Then he smiled at Jeffery and said, "I believe you now realize this isn't a joke."

"Yes, that was very convincing. Are we really on Earth or is this just an image you're projecting into my mind?"

"We're on Earth. I'm sure you recognize this place."

"I do. I was here a long time ago on a vacation with my parents. Do you have the ability to transport yourself to any location in the galaxy?"

"Only if I have been there before. But the ability it not limited by distance. Zandrax is about five thousand light years from here. I can go there too. That's why I came to Procolt 2 on one of your ships. Now that I've been here, it won't be necessary to travel by spaceship again."

"You said you've been on Earth for most of the last seventy thousand years. Are you immortal?"

"No, but we don't age at the same rate you do. During our first twenty years or so we age like you, but then the aging process slows down. A few years after that we reach a point where we age at about one day for every ten years. I am the equivalent of somebody who is in his early forties from Earth, although I'm more than seventy-five thousand years old."

"I have a lot of questions I would like to ask you about Earth's history."

"I'm sure you do, and I will be happy to answer them if I can. But we must discuss something else first."

Vandor put his hand on Jeffery's shoulder again. When Jeffery's vision cleared, they were back on Procolt 2, near the shuttle landing area. "Why don't we go to the restaurant and talk there?"

Jeffery said, "That would be okay."

They walked to the restaurant and Jeffery went to a booth in the back that was devoid of other people. A few moments after they sat down a waitress walked over to the table and said, "Hello sir, is there something I can get for you?"

"Just coffee for me. Vandor, would you like something?"

"Coffee would be fine."

176

A minute later the waitress brought two cups and a carafe filled with coffee. Then she said, "Please let me know if you want anything else."

Jeffery said, "Thank you," then turned towards Vandor. He said, "So, what do you want to talk about?"

"First, I think you need some background information. The civilization on Zandrax is, as far as we know, the oldest in this part of the universe. Humans have existed there for more than two billion years. It was decided we would take it upon ourselves to plant the seeds of civilization on any planet we believed would be capable of supporting human life. In our quest to do that we discovered Earth about three hundred fifty million years ago. At that time dinosaurs were the dominate species. There were only a few small mammals. We introduced a few larger mammals similar to the cats and dogs that currently live on Earth. We wanted to see if they could survive. They did more than survive, they flourished. We studied Earth regularly for a while, coming back every few thousand years to see how things were going. It became obvious the climate was cooling and the dinosaurs would probably not be able to adapt to the changing conditions. We decided to let things on Earth happen without our interference. We left and didn't return for about ten million years. By that time the dinosaurs were gone and the climate was beginning to stabilize. We were sure we could bring primates to Earth and they would be able to survive, which is what we did. About a million years ago we began flooding the surface of the Earth with radiation similar to the radiation that is currently on Procolt 2. That radiation caused mutations in the primates, and within a hundred thousand years the first humanoids were born. It took another three hundred thousand years until your ancestors were born. We removed the radiation sources and left Earth on its own. We returned only sporadically for the next few thousand years. When I first came to Earth, men were just beginning to live in groups, and they discovered how to use simple tools. They made spears for hunting, and with a little help, discovered how useful fire can be."

"Are you saying you were the one who taught early man how to use fire?"

"Yes, I'm sure they would have figured it out on their own, but it might have taken another thousand years. I watched as civilizations developed and died. It became obvious the humans on Earth had one fatal flaw. That flaw was greed. It didn't matter if it was land, water, gold, or anything else. The people in a position of power always wanted more, and they were willing to kill to get it."

Jeffery thought about what Vandor told him for a few seconds and then said, "I don't think that changed until about one hundred fifty years ago. The invention of the power module seemed to have precipitated a change in the attitude of people all over Earth. Once energy became abundant and cheap, we began to focus more on science and medicine and became more satisfied with our lives."

"That was our plan. I made sure Albert Simson discovered the right formula for the silver alloy rod that was the primary component in the power module. I don't know if you realize how many times he said during his interviews with the press how lucky he was to have stumbled across the exact formula for the silver bar."

"Yes, Brandon, Albert's grandson, has mentioned it to me several times. He's retired now and spends half of his time here and the other half on Earth."

"There is something else about the people from Zandrax you should know. We've developed the ability to predict major events in the future based on current or recently passed events. We can't predict the actions of a single person, or even a group of people, but we can predict, with about 90% accuracy, the actions of an entire planet's population. For example, we knew Crosus would not tolerate the loss of their position in the trade group, but because our ability to predict future events is only about 90% correct, we didn't know Crosus would attack the mining operation on Procolt 4, or later attack Earth. We also knew they were going to build some kind of super weapon, but we didn't know what it would be. On the plus side, we were almost positive somebody from Earth

178

would build the resort here with the help of people from Coplent, but we did a little covert manipulation to make sure it happened."

"Why did you want us to build a resort here?"

"It's very simple. We want the people from Earth to continue to slowly mutate until you are our equals. The radiation here on Procolt 2 is similar to the radiation on Zandrax. It may take a thousand generations, but eventually it will happen."

"So, the radiation here is not natural?"

"No, it's not. We put sources of radiation all over the planet about four hundred years ago. Then we made an earlier attempt to populate the planet. We arranged for a ship from Metoba to capture some people from Earth and bring them here about three hundred years ago. They were unable to cope with the changes in their environment. As a result, they all died."

"We know about them. The first day we were here we found the remains of a soldier from Earth in a cave. Later we also found a diary that gave us some information about their ordeal.

"Why did you bring primates to Earth and wait for them to mutate? Why didn't you just populate Earth with people from Zandrax?"

"Because we aren't perfect. We have very strong emotions, and that causes problems. Shortly before I came to Earth there was a war on Zandrax that killed thousands of people. The two sides were fighting over a piece of virtually worthless land. For some unknown reason, we often find ourselves being ruled by our emotions instead of logic. Jeffery, we have a lot more to talk about, but for now, I would like to take advantage of some of the things you offer here. Can we continue this tomorrow afternoon? You can use that time to decide what questions you would like to ask me."

"Of course, would you like to meet here tomorrow afternoon at 2:00?"

"Yes, that will be fine."

Vandor got up and walked over to the check-in area. Jeffery called Debbie and asked her to come down to the main restaurant as soon as possible.

Ten minutes later Debbie walked into the restaurant, saw Jeffery, and walked over to him. "Hi honey, what's up?"

"I just had a very interesting conversation with one of our new guests. His name is Vandor. He's from the planet Zandrax, and has been living on Earth for the past seventy thousand years."

"Is he mentally stable?"

"Yes, he is. To prove his point, he put his hand on my shoulder and a few seconds later we were in Grand Teton National Park."

"He took you back to Earth in a few seconds? That's incredible! Did he explain how he could do that?"

"He said the people on Zandrax have developed the ability to transport themselves to anyplace they have been before. We're going to continue our conversation tomorrow at 2:00. I would like you to be there."

"I wouldn't miss it for anything. It's not often you get to talk to a person who has lived through all of Earth's recorded history."

"It's not just the Earth's history I'm interested in. I want to know something about the future, and he said he wanted to discuss that with me."

That evening Jeffery and Debbie decided on a list of questions they were going to ask Vandor. It took a few hours because they wanted the questions to be about historically significant events.

Jeffery and Debbie arrived at the restaurant fifteen minutes early. They both ordered coffee. While they were drinking their coffee, Jeffery kept scanning the list of questions.

Vandor arrived at exactly 2:00. Jeffery looked up at him as he walked up to their table and said, "Good afternoon Vandor. This is my wife Debbie. I hope it's okay for her to join us?"

180

"Of course, I expected you to bring her." Then he looked at Debbie and said, "It is a pleasure to meet you Debbie. I assume Jeffery told you all about our conversation yesterday."

"Yes, he did, and I am still a little bit skeptical, but Jeffery is convinced you are who and what you claim to be."

"If you need proof, we could continue this conversation on Earth? Just tell me where you want to go and I can take us there in a few seconds."

"I don't think that's necessary."

"Okay, did you prepare some questions for me?"

Jeffery said, "Yes we did. One of the things about our history that has bothered me for a long time is how civilizations that were separated by vast distances and had no interaction with other civilizations all utilized pyramids as a religious symbol. Were you responsible for that?"

"Yes, I suppose I was. Pyramids are easy to build and are very durable, so they make ideal religious symbols."

"Many of the primitive societies utilized human sacrifices as part of their religious ceremonies. Are you responsible for that too?" Debbie asked.

"Those sacrifices were part of their ceremonies long before I got involved with them. I did my best to convince them it was wrong and unnecessary to kill people to appease their Gods, but they didn't believe me. They had, what they thought was evidence, the sacrifices were effective. They told me the sacrifices ended droughts and stopped epidemics on numerous occasions. We know it was coincidental, but it was impossible for me to convince them."

"Our ancestors were often very cruel people, but that began to change prior to what we called the 'dark ages'. Did you push us in the right direction?" Jeffery asked.

"That's an interesting question. I was involved with some of the early attempts at democratic reform. As Christianity spread all over Europe it became the center of human development. By the year 1000, Europe was ruled by kings, whose power was absolute. Absolute power is always corrupting, so I put myself in situations where I hoped I could foster the development of more democratic forms of government. My first real attempt was to convince the Archbishop of Canterbury to write the Magna Carta. It was designed to limit the power of the king with respect to the church and the barons, who were in charge of the local populations. It really didn't accomplish very much, but it was the first attempt.

"I also helped the rebels during the French revolution, believing they would establish a democracy if they were successful in overthrowing the king. However, after the rebels won they proved to be as bad, and in some cases much worse, than the king. Nothing really changed until after the United States was formed and became somewhat successful. They established the first real democracy with a government that was elected by the people. It was the first time a country's leaders were not chosen based on family. However, even though the government was elected by the people, it did not prevent them from mistreating many of the people who lived there. It took almost ninety years for them to abolish slavery, and another forty years before they began to treat the people they referred to as 'Indians', with a modicum of respect and dignity."

Jeffery said, "If I remember my history right, the last remnants of prejudice weren't eliminated until about the year 2040."

"You're right, and there was a brief resurgence of prejudice when the first aliens began arriving on Earth, but it ended quickly." Vandor responded.

"Yesterday, you said that you helped Albert Simpson invent the power module. Why did you do that?"

"It was all part of a long-term strategy to force Earth to develop interstellar space travel. I worked with Albert's father in propulsion development and when he retired, I took over his position. I provided Albert with the original list of elements to be used in the alloys he was testing. I thought it would take him a few years to find the magic combination, but it only took a few weeks. It was a pleasant surprise. I knew enough about him to know he would immediately realize how to utilize the

182

alloy to make the power module. Almost anyone with a knowledge of physics and electronics would have quickly known that the silver alloy could be used to make an unlimited self-contained source of electrical power."

"I suppose you also had a hand in creating the silver shortage that started us on the road to interstellar space travel?" Debbie asked.

"Not directly. I knew that eventually the Earth would run out of silver, but it also happened much sooner than I expected. I knew about the extensive silver deposits on Ganymede, so I made sure a probe was sent there. The rest was just a happy coincidence. I didn't know a ship from Coplent was going to steal the probe, but it all worked out. I couldn't have planned it better."

"Did you have a hand in Debbie and I being selected for the test of the Star Rover?"

"Absolutely. I had decided, after doing some extensive research on NASA employees, you were the most logical choice. I used my position at NASA to lobby for you. Despite my involvement in the design of the Star Rover, it still contained a lot of untested technology. That made the selection of the captain extremely important. I expected there to be problems, and I knew there wasn't anybody more qualified to handle the unexpected than you.

"I also knew about your relationship with Debbie. I know you tried to keep it a secret, but it was actually common knowledge among NASA pilots. I was confident that you would choose her to assist you on the mission, and I thought the two of you could solve any problem that arose."

"That's quite a complement, thank you," Debbie said.

"You're welcome, but the complement was well deserved. I followed your exploits, and although I had never met either of you, I was sure that once you came to Procolt 2 you would fall in love with it and want to stay. When Garlut and Brealak came to Earth for the meeting with the World Council, I sent them a report regarding Procolt 2. I'm sure they he had no idea why they received the report. I knew after your first mission you would want to go someplace with a friendlier environment. I was sure you would ask Garlut about it, because there was no one else to ask. I hoped he would remember the report on Procolt 2 and suggest you go there. Obviously, that worked."

"I suppose you knew we would discover the squirrels."

"Yes, I had them put there so they would be mutated into the species they are today. If you hadn't figured out how intelligent they were, I was prepared to intervene. I'm really glad that wasn't necessary."

"Did you make us want to build a resort, or was that a coincidence?" Debbie asked.

"I needed you and Jeffery to come here to live so you would be exposed to the radiation. I was certain you would like it here, and I was fairly sure you would figure out something that would allow you to live here. I told Jeffery yesterday that our analysis indicated somebody from Earth would build a resort here. I have friends in high places on Coplent and they were prepared to do whatever was required to make sure the resort was built."

Jeffery said, "Why did you need us to come here, as opposed to some other couple?"

"Although you were the best qualified people for the mission, there was another reason I wanted you on the Star Rover. I wasn't going to tell you this for a while, but I really don't see any reason to wait. Both of you have an uncommon active gene. It makes you more susceptible to the effects of the radiation. The first people from Earth who came here lived to be about one hundred eighty. You two will probably exceed that by 200%, and so will all of your offspring."

"So, Jeffery and I are going to live to be more than five hundred years old?" Debbie asked with obvious disbelief in her voice.

"Unless you die as a result of an accident. The combination of the gene and the radiation make you, and your children, virtually immune to disease. I would guess you won't even notice anything you would associate with growing older until you are close to five hundred."

"How common is this gene we both have?" Jeffery asked.

"It occurs once in every twenty-five thousand births. The odds of a couple having the gene is so rare it may have never occurred before. I was prepared to work with any couple where one of them had the gene, but when I found the two of you I knew you would be perfect for the task I am going to ask you to perform."

"What task would that be?" Jeffery asked.

"One I'm not prepared to discuss with you yet, but I will answer any other questions you have."

Jeffery was silent for a few moments and then he asked, "Were you involved in the American Revolution?"

"Not at the beginning. I was in France when the war started, and I met Benjamin Franklin when he assumed his position as ambassador. We had several conversations regarding the American Revolution. I was very impressed with their plans for a democratic government, so I traveled to North America for the first time. I was appalled at the condition of George Washington's army and I wanted to help, but there was very little I could do. I knew how to make weapons that were far more advanced than the muskets they were using, but they didn't have the equipment and raw materials I needed to build them. So, all I could do was watch from the sidelines as they lost most of their battles. I was finally able to help defeat the British at the Battle of the Chesapeake. The French and the British were evenly matched, and the battle was a stalemate. I was aboard one of the French ships and I had a small weapon that could easily sink the British ships without being obvious. I sunk four of them, and that was enough to turn the tide. The French won the battle and the British were unable to bring in reinforcements to assist General Cornwallis in Yorktown. That ultimately resulted in the Americans winning the war."

"Weren't you concerned about getting injured or killed? Medicine at that time was very crude."

"You're right, doctors were, for the most part, useless. But I have an implant in my body that constantly measures my blood pressure, pulse rate, blood chemistry, and brain function. If it detects any anomaly, I am instantly transported back to Zandrax where I would receive immediate medical attention. Unless I was killed in a massive explosion, I would probably be able to recover."

"So, if you fell down and broke your leg you would disappear?"

"Yes, instantly. However, if it was just a broken bone, I'd be back in about an hour."

"Did you get involved in any of the wars in the twentieth century?"

"No. Shortly after the American Revolution I went back home and didn't return to Earth for about two hundred years. It's probably better I wasn't on Earth for the second world war. I'm not sure I would have allowed either side to develop nuclear weapons. Fission bombs based on uranium or plutonium are extremely inefficient and cause more deaths from radiation exposure than the actual explosion. Fusion bombs based on hydrogen are more efficient, but the radiation is still more deadly than the explosion."

"What types of weapons do you have on Zandrax?"

"We primarily use particle beam weapons, like the type you have on your starships. We have very small ones like this." Then Vandor reached into his pocket and took out a small plastic rectangle and put it on the table in front of Jeffery. Then he said, "That's the weapon I used to sink the British ships."

"How powerful is it? It looks like a toy."

"At its maximum setting, it's probably twice as powerful as the weapons you have on your starship. A starship mounted version would be capable of destroying an entire planet, but we've never done that. I believe that the largest thing we ever destroyed was an asteroid that was about sixty units in diameter. It was going to crash into one of our moons and would have caused catastrophic damage."

"If you were on Earth during the second world war, would you have helped the allies win the war?"

"Yes, I've thought about that often. I find it difficult to believe that any sane person could have believed in Hitler's

186

policies. I'm not sure what I would have done, but I would not have allowed Germany and Japan to win the war."

"When did you come back to Earth?"

"I don't remember the exact date, but it was during Bill Clinton's second term as president. When I returned, I decided I wanted to work for NASA, so I hacked into the databases of several of the most prestigious universities in the United States and created multiple advanced degrees for myself. I also built a file on myself in the US government databases. It was never necessary before, but by that time people only trusted what they could see on computer generated reports. In any case, it was sufficient for me to get a job as an engineer at the NASA facility in Houston. I was assigned to propulsion system development, and that was where I met Albert Simpson's father, Charles."

"Were you trained as an engineer?"

"Yes, all the children on Zandrax are extensively educated. Our basic education takes twenty-five years. Then, if you want to work as a professional, you may need up to another ten years of education."

"You said the radiation on Procolt 2 is similar to the radiation on Zandrax. Do you have the same problems with impotence that we have experienced?"

"Yes, we've found that all the races with long life spans have problems producing offspring. However, the effect of the radiation on impotence diminishes quickly when exposure stops. Since the radiation on Zandrax is natural, we can't limit exposure. As a result, our population is stable, at about five billion people. Each year two million die, and the same number are born. Because there are thousands of schools spread all over the planet, it means the schools don't have a lot of students, so each child receives a lot of personal attention during their education. We all receive education in science, math, engineering, and medicine. That doesn't mean we're all doctors, but we all know a lot more about our bodies than we probably need to."

"Does that mean that if Debbie and I leave Procolt 2 we could have more children?"

"Definitely. It would take a year for the effects to completely dissipate. You'll be pleased to know leaving would have no effect on your increased life span."

"That's interesting," Debbie said. Then she looked at Jeffery and asked, "Do you think Mystic would like a little brother or sister?"

"Mystic is seventy-three. I don't really know how she would feel about a new baby in the family. Anyway, I don't really want to leave Procolt 2. Do you?"

"No, I like our life here."

Vandor said, "Tomorrow let's get together again at the same time. We'll discuss the future. Is that okay?"

Jeffery and Debbie both said, "Yes," at the same time.

They all arrived at the restaurant at the same time the next afternoon. After they were seated Vandor said, "Yesterday I told you I have a task for you. I wanted to go back to Earth and get some information before our meeting, and I did that last night. The task I would like you to do is similar to what you did here on Procolt 2. The genetic engineers on Zandrax believe we may have finally found a way to create the ultimate human species. One that does not have the greed that many of the people on Earth possess or the tendency to have fits of rage like the people on Zandrax. The key to that is the gene both of you have. We have been studying people with that gene for more than a hundred years and found that in addition to making them more susceptible to the effects of the radiation, they have more mellow personalities."

Debbie asked, "So, you want Jeffery and I to populate a whole planet? I don't think we're capable of that, although it might be fun to try."

Vandor smiled and said, "That's not exactly what I had in mind. What I want you to do is select five hundred people from Earth who have the gene to go with you to a new planet and start a new species. I have a list with almost names on it. The list, in addition to the name, also contains a brief description of the person's education, job history, and any remarkable achievements."

188

"What do you consider a 'remarkable achievement'?" Jeffery asked.

"One of the people on the list won a Nobel Prize for literature."

"Okay, I agree. That's definitely a remarkable achievement. Tell me about the planet."

"It's at the edge of the galaxy. There are very few solar systems in that region. In fact, the closest neighbor is more than a hundred light years away. The planet is very much like Earth. Unlike Procolt 2, the temperate zone starts eight hundred units north or south of the equator, and extends 1100 units in the direction of the pole. The surface of the planet is covered with several large oceans that cover about 65% of the surface. The planet is 8% smaller than Earth, so the gravity is slightly less. The atmosphere is primarily nitrogen and oxygen, although the oxygen level is about 10% higher than it is on Earth. It has almost no indigenous land animals, and the ones we have seen are all small mammals, nothing much bigger than a rat. Also, all the land animals are herbivores. There are insects and birds, but we have not had an opportunity to study them very much. The oceans are very different. They are filled with life. We've discovered more than a thousand different species of animals in the oceans. By the way, the oceans are fresh water."

"Are there mountains, rivers, and lakes too."

"Yes, the land in the temperate area is covered with dense forests. It's a beautiful and very tranquil place."

"It seems to me we will be very isolated. How will we get the supplies we'll need?"

"We're building a transporter system that will allow people and materials to travel to Zandrax instantly, but we are hoping you will be able to use the resources on the planet for your needs. We'll build homes and other infrastructure for the people who move there initially. There will be a small hospital, but you will have to supply the staff. We'll also supply you with the tools you will need to clear land for farming, and build whatever else you need. I'm hoping the transporter would only

189

be used in case of an emergency. We want you to be self-sufficient."

"Can we bring animals from Earth?" Debbie asked.

"I was going to get to that later, but since you asked, I'll tell you about that now. In order to increase the life spans of the initial people who populate the planet, we are going to install radiation sources. But they will be different from the radiation sources we have used previously. Because the people there will have the gene, the radiation will be much weaker than what we have used previously. It will have no effect on animals from Earth, so you can bring whatever you want. Also, it will probably only be needed for five or six years. As you know, while you are exposed to the radiation there are problems with impotence, so if we are trying to build a new species, making them impotent is counterproductive."

Jeffery asked, "Would it be possible to build the transporter to go to Earth instead of Zandrax?"

"Yes, it's possible, but it's not a good idea. We really want you to break your ties with Earth. If we built a transporter that allowed you to go to Earth, I'm concerned that you would become dependent on it. Also, we don't want additional people from Earth coming to the planet."

"I guess that makes sense. It's just that we're asking the people who come with us to sever all the ties they have with friends and family. That's difficult for a lot of people."

"That's why I'm giving you a list with so many names on it. If there's going to be a problem, select somebody else."

"What if somebody changes their mind after they get there? Can they go back?"

"Only if they can build their own starship. This is a one-way trip. The people are all volunteers and you have to make it clear to them that if they decide to go they will spend their lives on the new planet. That's true for both of you as well."

Jeffery said, "I understand. I think Debbie and I need to discuss this before we make a decision."

Debbie nodded her head in agreement and asked, "I know it's not important, but does this planet have a name?"

190

"No, you can name it whatever you want."

"Janus is the Roman God of beginnings, so how about if we call it Janus?" Debbie suggested.

"I like it," Jeffery agreed.

"Okay, henceforth we will call it Janus."

"Debbie and I will discuss this and we'll try to have an answer for you by tomorrow afternoon."

"There is no rush. Please take as much time as you need. I want you to be positive that your decision is the right one for both of you. I'll be here again tomorrow afternoon." Then Vandor got up and left.

Jeffery looked at Debbie and said, "Our lives here have become boring. We're simply not needed here. Mystic is running the place without our help. The government is doing a good job. I've been thinking about going back into space and doing some exploring, but this sounds better."

"Our lives may be boring, but they are comfortable. Are you ready to go back to eating food from a replicator?"

"Yes, we've been here for almost a hundred years. I want a change. I also think it would be nice to have more children. I think I'm ready to be a father again."

"You know we'll never see Mystic or William again. I'm not sure I'm okay with that."

"I understand, and I'll miss them too. Of course, William is working on Earth now so we only see him once a year. Tomorrow I'll ask Vandor about it. Perhaps he could bring Mystic and William there to visit once in a while."

"Let's not ask, let's make it a condition if we agree to do this. I'll bet all the people on Vandor's list are single. We'll probably be the only people on Janus with a child and a grandchild, so it won't seem as if we are receiving special treatment."

"Are you saying you want to do this?"

"Right now, I'm saying I want to think about it for a while. I know how you feel, and to some degree I feel the same way. I just want to be sure."

Jeffery and Debbie were up most of the night discussing the pros and cons of Vandor's plan. By morning

191

they had made the decision to do it as long as Vandor agreed to bring Mystic and William to Janus occasionally.

Jeffery and Debbie were eating breakfast in the restaurant when Mystic walked up to their table. When she was a few feet away Jeffery said, "Good morning. You look bright and cheerful this morning. What's going on?"

"I'm pregnant. I never thought it would happen again, but it did. I haven't told Virgil yet, but I know he'll be pleased. I'm not sure how William will feel about having a baby brother or sister."

"Congratulations honey, I know how much you wanted another child," Jeffery said happily.

"I'm so happy for you!" Debbie exclaimed.

"I have to go tell Virgil and send a message to William. I'll talk to you later. Bye."

After Mystic walked away Debbie said, "I guess that changes our plans. I'm not going anywhere while Mystic is pregnant."

"I agree, but perhaps Vandor can put everything off for a year. I don't think this was going to happen very quickly anyway."

"Okay, let's discuss this with him this afternoon."

That afternoon Jeffery, Debbie, and Vandor all arrived at the table at the same time again. Vandor said, "I heard Mystic is pregnant. Congratulations. Soon you'll have another grandchild."

"How did you find out?" Debbie asked.

"It's not a secret. I think everybody who works here knows. Pregnancies are not very common on Procolt 2, so they are always news," Vandor responded.

"I was wondering why everyone was smiling at us, now I know. I guess you and I are a little out of touch with the other people here," Jeffery said.

Debbie said, "We were ready to accept your offer, if you agreed to some conditions, and then we found out about the pregnancy. This changes everything."

Vandor smiled and said, "This plan will take at least two years to implement. The baby will be born long before you have to leave to go to Janus."

"If we agree to do this, can you bring Mystic and her family to Janus to visit occasionally?" Jeffery asked.

"I'm sure that could be arranged, but since Mystic has the gene, perhaps she and her family would like to be part of the initial group on Janus. I know her husband doesn't have the gene, but we could make an exception in his case. You must realize that because Mystic has the gene, she will probably outlive her husband by more than three hundred years. She would probably be more comfortable with people who have the same life span she does."

"I hadn't thought about that," Debbie said.

"I think we need to have a talk with our daughter about all this."

After the meeting with Vandor, Debbie called Mystic and said, "Something very important has come up and we need to have a family meeting this evening."

"Mom, we haven't had a family meeting since I was a teenager. What's going on?"

"I'd rather discuss the situation with you in person."

"Should I bring Virgil?"

Debbie hesitated for a few seconds and then said, "I don't think that's a good idea. You'll have to discuss the situation with Virgil, but right now I want to make this just between the three of us."

"Okay, I'll be there at 8:00."

Mystic walked into their apartment a few minutes early. Debbie and Jeffery were sitting in the living room when Mystic arrived. She walked in and asked, "What's the big mystery? Is there something wrong?"

Jeffery said, "Please sit down. Something has happened that you need to be informed about. It concerns the whole family."

Mystic sat down, stared at Jeffery, and said, "Okay Dad, tell me the bad news."

193

"Three days ago a man arrived here. I was there to meet the ship. He came up to me and told me his name was Vandor and he needed to discuss the past and future with me. He said he was human, but not from Earth. I thought he was some kind of nut and then he put his hand on my shoulder. We were instantly transported back to Earth. I suddenly found myself in Grand Teton National Park. Then a minute later he brought us back."

"Dad, are you sure this wasn't a dream or something?"

"Yes, I'm sure it wasn't a dream. We went into the restaurant and he told me some amazing stuff."

For the next ten minutes Jeffery gave Mystic a synopsis of his first conversation with Vandor. When he was finished Mystic said, "So, this person has been controlling the destiny of human life on Earth for all of recorded history. That's hard to believe."

"I understand your skepticism. The next afternoon your mother and I met with him. We asked him questions about Earth's history. We obviously have no way of verifying the things he said, but I believe him. Then he said he wanted to meet with us again to discuss the future, because he was trying to recruit your mother and I for a substantial task."

"Did he want money?"

"No, the subject never even came up. Yesterday he told us that your mother and I both have a gene that makes us more susceptible to the effects of the radiation here. In fact, he made sure I was selected to be the pilot of the Star Rover, and he was positive I would choose your mother to be my assistant. Yesterday he told us that people with the gene, and their offspring, would have a substantially longer life. Our lifespans will exceed five hundred years, which means you will outlive Virgil by more than three hundred years. That was why we wanted to meet with you alone."

Mystic was silent for a while, obviously thinking about what her father had just told her. Then she said, "What about William? Does he have the gene?"

"I don't know, but I'm sure we can find out. Every person on Procolt 2 has a complete DNA analysis on file. I

194

don't know what to look for, but I'm positive Vandor does. If William has the gene, he needs to know about his increased life span."

"How am I going to tell Virgil about this?"

Debbie said, "I'm not sure you should. What purpose would it serve?"

"None, you're probably right. I shouldn't tell him. For some reason, I'm positive you have more to tell me. What's the task Vandor wants you to do?"

"The people of Zandrax are trying to develop the ultimate human being. They have found a planet at the edge of the galaxy that is very similar to Earth. They want your mother and I, along with five hundred people from Earth who also have the gene, to start a new civilization. If we decide to do it, we'll never be back. It's a one-way trip."

Mystic yelled, "You won't be here to watch my new baby, your grandchild, grow up! I don't like that idea at all!"

Debbie said, "Please calm down. First, we haven't told him we would do it yet. Additionally, he promised to bring you and your family there to visit us on a regular basis. He also suggested that you, Virgil, and the new baby could be part of the initial group."

"If I left, what would you do with Procolt Paradise?"

"I'd give it to the government. I don't need the money."

"How soon would all this happen?"

"Not less than two years. The plan is to construct a place for us to live and all the necessary infrastructure before we arrive. They're also going to build a transport system between Zandrax and Janus, that's the name of the planet, that can be used in case there's an emergency."

"I have a bunch of questions. Are they going to install radiation sources on Janus? Will there be medical facilities and schools?"

"Vandor said they are going to build a hospital, but we have to staff it. They are going to install radiation sources, but they will be removed after five or six years. That will be sufficient exposure to start the mutation process. I don't think schools will be necessary for about ten years. You know that exposure to the radiation makes people almost impotent. But after the radiation sources are removed fertility returns, and the ability to conceive normally will be restored. If you move there, your baby will likely be the only child on Janus for a long time."

"I know you haven't said your definitely going, but I think you're leaning in that direction. Why?"

Jeffery said, "I'm bored. My life is too predictable. I want some adventure in my life again. If we don't do this, we're going to take our ship and go exploring for a few years, but this sounds more exciting."

"Can Vandor take us to Janus so we can see it for ourselves?"

"I don't see why not. I'll call him now and ask him."

Jeffery picked up his communicator, called Vandor, and explained what he wanted. Vandor said he would be there shortly.

A few minutes later the doorbell beeped. Mystic got up and opened the door for Vandor. He walked in and said, "You must be Mystic. It's a pleasure to meet you. My name is Vandor, but I'll bet your parents already told you that."

"Yes, they did. It's nice to meet you as well. However, I really don't like the fact that you are trying to break up our family."

"I'm not trying to break up your family. I truly believe that your parents are the ideal candidates to manage the development of Janus. I also think you should go with them. You've been running Procolt for almost fifty years, wouldn't it be nice to do something else?"

"You know, I hadn't really thought about that. We have over ten thousand employees, and keeping the place running is a lot of work. I haven't even taken a vacation in a couple of years."

"Setting up a new community on Janus will be a lot of work too, but the three of you can share the load. Anyway, your father said that you wanted to see Janus for yourself."

"Yes, but I think all three of us want to go. I'm sure you know I'm pregnant. Is this going to be safe for my baby?"

"Yes, it's perfectly safe," Vandor assured her. Then he walked into the center of the living room and said, "We all must hold hands. I'll take us to the location where we plan to build the town. I don't know the time on Janus. It may be the middle of the night. If that's the case we will do this again in about eight hours."

Debbie and Jeffery stood up and they walked over to Mystic, who was already holding Vandor's hand. They formed a circle and Vandor said, "Here we go!"

At first all they saw was bright white then the view began to change and they were standing in a meadow dotted with tall trees. The sun was either setting or rising, they didn't know which.

Mystic looked around. The meadow they were standing in was enormous, and appeared to be surrounded by a dense forest. There were snow-capped mountains off in the distance. Something was bothering Mystic and it took her a few seconds to realize what was wrong. There was no sound. There was a very gentle breeze blowing, but there were no birds or insects. However, the place was beautiful.

"We picked this area because it's near the confluence of three rivers. There are lots of fish in the rivers for food, and the soil is very fertile. It will be easy to grow crops here. And the weather is perfect. In the last three years the lowest temperature was twenty-eight degrees and the highest was seventy-seven."

"That sounds absolutely perfect. What is the annual rainfall?" Debbie inquired.

"It's averaged fifty-seven inches per year for the past three years. It does snow occasionally in the winter. The deepest snowfall so far has been six inches, but the snowfalls are usually less than two inches."

"Was this meadow natural, or did you clear the land?" Jeffery asked.

"It was natural. We're about a unit west of the rivers. Do you want to go see them?"

"Yes, I would like that." Mystic responded.

They walked for about a tenth of an hour and the rivers came into view. There were two rivers, each of them more than fifty feet wide, and they connected into a single large river that was at least a hundred feet wide. They walked to the edge of the large river. The water appeared to be moving rapidly. In the water they could see several different kinds of fish. Some only a few inches long, and others close to three feet in length. The water was crystal clear. It was an idyllic setting.

Jeffery asked, "Why did you decide to build the town a mile from the rivers?"

"Because they occasionally overflow their banks and flood the area nearby. I'm sure we could build something that would prevent the flooding, but we wanted to keep it as natural as possible. The area where we are planning to build is about sixty feet higher, so there's no possibility it would flood."

"What exactly are you planning to build?" Debbie asked.

"Basically, were prepared to build whatever you and Jeffery feel is needed."

"How far are we from Procolt 2?" Mystic asked.

"Five thousand two hundred light years. It will take you about a half a year to get here by ship, and Zandrax will be supplying it. The ship we will be using is much larger than anything you have. Right now, it is designed to move only passengers, but it will be modified so that in addition to carrying up to six hundred passengers, it will be able to move hundreds of animals, and any personal items the passengers want to bring with them. Anything else you are likely to need will already be here when you arrive."

Mystic looked around, sighed deeply, and said, "I really like this place. I'd like to bring Virgil here. Can you do that for me?"

"Of course. I really want you to be a part of this. It's obvious you have excellent organizational skills and would be a real asset to the project."

"Thank you. I appreciate that."

"I know this is personal, but I hope you aren't considering telling Virgil about the differences in your life spans. As a matter of fact, I have no intention of telling any of the colonists about it, and I don't want you to either. Because of the advances in medical technology, many people on Earth are already living to be more than one hundred thirty, and it's common knowledge that on Procolt 2 life spans are usually more than one hundred eighty. I think we should let them know their life spans will be about the same as they are on Procolt 2. That should be enough to get you all the volunteers you will need."

Jeffery said, "The knowledge regarding the longer lifespans on Procolt 2 has created a problem. We now have a waiting list of more than three million people who want to immigrate there. As a result, we are constantly arresting people who try to go there without first obtaining permission. Many people think it's worth the risk, and if they end up in jail for a while, it's okay because even in jail they are exposed to the radiation. However, they are in for a big surprise. We just finished building a facility on Procolt 4 to hold our prisoners, and the people currently incarcerated for violation of immigration laws are being moved there. Any new offenders will be sent there awaiting trial, and if found guilty will be sent to the prison there."

"I was not aware of that, but it may resolve the problem. Unless anybody has an objection, I think we should go back now."

Mystic said, "I'm ready to go back home. Can Virgil and I meet with you tomorrow?"

"Yes, I'll meet you by the shuttle pad at 10:00."

They all joined hands again and a few seconds later they were standing in Jeffery and Debbie's apartment. After Mystic and Vandor left Debbie asked, "Did you like Janus? I was very impressed."

"Yes, I liked it a lot. It reminded me of what Procolt 2 was like when we first came here. If Mystic likes it too, and I think she does, we should agree to Vandor's plan."

"Yeah, you're right. I think we should probably do it even if Mystic decides not to join us, but I really don't think that will happen."

"Are you going to miss this place? I think I will, at least for a while."

"I suppose I will too, but I'm beginning to like the idea of having some adventure in my life again."

The next morning Vandor took Mystic and Virgil to Janus. Virgil liked it as much as Mystic did, so they made the decision to join the initial group of settlers.

That afternoon Vandor met with Jeffery and Debbie again. He gave them the list of candidates and said, "The selection of people for the group is entirely up to you. Please remember that you will need people with all types of experience to make this a success. You'll need doctors, nurses, carpenters, farmers, plumbers, electricians, and more specialists that I probably haven't thought about. But they all must be willing to do the manual labor required to build your new settlement too."

Jeffery said, "You know Debbie and I have already done that once before, although we didn't have a list of names to choose from. We'll get started on this immediately. We're going to leave for Earth in a few days, and we plan on staying there until we have five hundred candidates selected, and at least fifty alternates."

"That sounds like a good plan. You'll probably be swamped by reporters when you arrive. That would probably be the best way to get the publicity you need so people will know why you are there. That way when you contact prospective candidates, they'll have some understanding of your task."

"I'm going to prepare a speech before we leave. When it's finished, I'll read it to you and you can make any comments you feel are appropriate."

"Thanks, I'll be happy to do that."

Jeffery and Debbie spent the next day preparing the speech. When it was finished, he called Vandor and asked him to come over to critique it. Vandor arrived a half hour later.

After he sat down in the living room Jeffery picked up the speech and began to read, "Thank you for this wonderful welcome. Debbie and I are both very happy to be back on Earth again. It has been more than ten years since our last visit. However, we are not here on vacation. We have had a series of meetings with a representative from the planet Zandrax. They are humans, much like us, but their civilization is more than two billion years old. For the last billion years they have been searching the galaxy for planets that would support human life. When they found one they placed radiation sources on the planets and brought primates there, knowing that the radiation would eventually cause the primates to mutate into humanoids. Earth was their most successful test. They are also responsible for the radiation on Procolt 2, although the radiation was put there for a different purpose. Their goal was to create the ultimate human. They knew their own civilization was prone to fits of rage, and they wanted to eliminate that flaw. On Earth they were close, but people from Earth have a major flaw as well. We're greedy, we want what our neighbor has. It doesn't matter if it's power, money, land, water, or anything else. If we want it, some of us will kill to get it."

Jeffery paused for a few moments and then continued to read, "The people from Zandrax look exactly like us, and have been living on Earth, unnoticed, for most of the last seventy thousand years. They recently discovered that some of us, including Debbie and I, have a gene which makes us unique. We have no greed, or fits of rage, and the genetic engineers on Zandrax feel that people from Earth with that gene will eventually mutate into what they believe will be the ultimate human. They have found a planet with an environment almost identical to Earth's at the edge of the galaxy which we have named Janus. They want Debbie and I to select five hundred people from Earth who have the gene to go with us to Janus and start a new species. We have a list of three thousand people and we will begin contacting them shortly and give them more details. Thank you."

201

Jeffery put the paper down the paper with the speech and asked, "Did you think that was okay?"

"Yes, I did. You paused at exactly the right time too. I think it will be effective and probably create some controversy, but that is okay. You want people to think about what you said."

"Good, I'm glad you liked it. Debbie and I are leaving tomorrow morning. How long are you staying here?"

"Probably at least another thirty days. I really like it here. Let me know where you are staying and I will stop by occasionally, since it only takes a few seconds to get there."

"I wish I could do that," Debbie said.

"We decided to stay somewhere that's away from crowds in the big cities, so we're going to stay on the space station until the task is completed."

Vandor stood up and as he walked toward the door said, "Okay, I'll stop by in thirty days or so to see how you're doing. Have a good trip."

Three days later their ship was approaching the space station. The ship was automatically identified by the system at the space station, and when they were about one hundred thousand units away Jeffery received a call. A young woman asked, "Sir, am I speaking with Admiral Whitestone?"

"Yes, this is Admiral Whitestone, or at least I was Admiral Whitestone until I retired eighty years ago. Please call me Jeffery."

"Sir, that would be disrespectful."

"I promise I won't be offended. My wife and I are here, and will be staying on the space station for a long time. Please let me know where I can park my ship."

"Sir, uh, I mean Jeffery, please land at Shuttle Bay 3. Welcome back to Earth. The Station Master will be there to meet you."

"Thank you. I appreciate the excellent service."

A half hour later Jeffery parked his ship in Shuttle Bay 3. As soon as the bay was pressurized there was a knock on the hatch. Jeffery opened it and a man in a NASA captain's uniform walked into the ship and said, "Sir, I'm Captain

Collins. I would like to welcome you to the station. It's an honor to meet both of you. Are you staying on the station or would you like me to book a shuttle for you?"

"Thank you, Captain Collins. We have an open reservation at the Hilton. We will be staying on the station until our task is finished, and that could take ninety days or more."

"Okay, sir."

"Captain Collins, please call me Jeffery, and my wife Debbie. We have been out of NASA for a long time, and even on the ships I commanded everyone called me Jeffery."

"Okay Jeffery, I'm sure you realize you're a legend around here. You probably know that every large city on Earth has a Whitestone High School."

"Yes, I'm aware of that."

"There are two reporters out there waiting to speak to you. I could make them go away if you want me to."

"Instead of making them go away, tell them I will be holding a brief news conference tomorrow morning at 10:00. At that time I will make an announcement and answer questions."

"I'll take care of it, Jeffery."

Captain Collins walked out of the bay and came back almost immediately. He said, "They both ran to call their supervisors. I expect you'll have a lot of people at your news conference tomorrow morning."

"Captain, that's exactly what I want."

"Please follow me to the hotel. Leave your luggage. They will send somebody to pick it up."

Jeffery and Debbie walked with Captain Collins to the hotel. When they arrived at the check-in desk the clerk said, "Admiral and Captain Whitestone, it's an honor to meet you. Welcome back! When I saw your reservation, I thought it was someone's idea of a joke, but then I heard your ship was arriving. May I escort you to your room?"

Debbie replied, "Yes, of course."

As they were walking to their room Debbie said, "I remember the first time we stayed here. Garlut and Brealak

203

were in the room next to ours. It's hard to believe that was probably eighty-five years ago."

Jeffery smiled and said, "Yeah, it only seems like fifty."

Debbie said, "You really haven't grown up much in those eighty-five years. You're still a smart ass."

"I know, I guess some things will never change."

The desk clerk opened the door for them and handed each of them a key. Jeffery reached into his pocket and took out his wallet.

The clerk raised his hand and said, "Sir, I appreciate this but I can't take your money. We're not allowed to accept tips anymore."

"Why?"

"First, no one carries cash anymore. We did away with cash about ten years ago. Also, all the employees were given raises to compensate for the loss of tips."

"It's been ten years since our last visit to Earth. Obviously there have been some changes. Anyway, thank you for the service."

"You're welcome."

After the clerk left Debbie said, "This place really brings back memories. It doesn't seem like it's been that long since the first time we came here. I do miss Garlut and Brealak."

"I do too. I think we should go to the restaurant and order the same meal we did that first night we were here. I think we ordered lobster bisque, veal cordon bleu, French fries, and creamed spinach."

"That sounds good to me. Let's do it."

The next morning Jeffery and Debbie were eating breakfast in the hotel restaurant when a man walked up to their table and said, "I'm sorry to disturb you, but there are at least twenty reporters in the lobby waiting for you to make an announcement. I'm moving them to the large conference room to wait for you. Don't hurry, you said you would speak to them at 10:00, so you have a lot of time to finish your breakfast. I'll let them know you will be there on time."

204

"Thank you. Where is the conference room?"

"Walk past the front desk and turn left at the hallway. The conference room is the third door on the right. The door has a big 'A' on it."

Jeffery and Debbie walked into the conference room a few minutes early. There were probably forty people waiting for him. As he walked in they all stood up and began applauding. Jeffery walked up to the podium, smiled at the audience, and asked them to be seated. He took his prepared speech out of his pocket and read it. When he was finished the room was silent for several seconds. Then the questions started.

"Do you know how the list of names was compiled?"

"No, all I know for sure is that all of the people on the list have the gene."

"Where is Janus?"

"As I said, Janus is at the edge of the galaxy. It's more than five thousand light years from Earth. However, I do not know its exact location."

"Will the people going with you to Janus have extended life spans?"

"Yes, everyone there will be exposed to radiation for five or six years. That exposure will begin the mutation process. The immediate effects of exposure are an increased life span and decreased fertility. Once the radiation sources are removed, fertility will return to normal, the extended lifespan is permanent, and will be passed down to all their children."

"Are you taking anything else with you to start your settlement?"

"Yes, we will be taking farm animals, although I am not sure how many at this point. We will also be taking anything our farmers think they will need to grow our food supplies."

"Won't you be using food replicators?"

"Yes, but not for any longer than absolutely necessary. Food replicators are wonderful, but the food is missing some of the more subtle flavors you get with real foods. Try comparing a steak from a food replicator and the real thing. Believe me, there's an obvious difference."

"Have you been to Janus?"

"Yes, both Debbie and I spent an afternoon exploring the area where the settlement will be built. It's a beautiful area and the weather is perfect. The highest temperature during the year is seventy-seven and the lowest is twenty-eight. The area averages about fifty-seven inches of rain per year, and does have minor amounts of snowfall in the winter."

"How are you going to get there?"

"Zandrax will be sending a ship to Earth to pick up the people and animals that will make up the settlement."

"Are you concerned about being isolated from the rest of the trade group planets?"

"Yes, I am. The nearest system to Janus is more than a hundred light years away. We will be on our own. Also, because Janus is so remote, this will be a one-way trip. The people who agree to go will be leaving Earth forever."

"If Janus is so remote, how did you get there for an afternoon?"

"I was waiting for somebody to ask that question. The people from Zandrax have the ability to transport themselves instantly to any place they have been to before. Additionally, anyone they are in physical contact with is transported as well. They expect humans from Earth will develop that ability as well in the future."

A few seconds went by and nobody asked a question so Jeffery said, "Thank you all for coming today. I appreciate your help in getting the word out about Janus." Then he took Debbie's hand and left the room.

When Jeffery and Debbie got back to their room Jeffery said, "Before we start contacting people on the list, we need to call William. We have to let him know what's going on. I'm sure he saw the news conference."

"I'll call him and explain the situation. If he has the gene he should come. If not, he should probably stay on Earth."

"We should probably check the list to see if William is on it. If he isn't, we'll have to ask Vandor about it."

Debbie turned on her computer and brought up the list. Then she checked to see if William was on it. She yelled, "Great news! William Griffith is on the list! I'm going to call him right now."

William answered the call and Debbie said, "Hi William. It's your Grandmother. How are you?"

"I'm fine. I saw the news conference and I was really surprised. I got a message from Mom telling me she was pregnant again, but she didn't mention anything about you and Grandpa coming to Earth."

"William, we're staying on the space station. We haven't seen you for a year. Can you come up here and spend a few days with us? We want to discuss this in person with you."

"Okay, I'll take a shuttle up there tomorrow."

"Perfect, we'll see you then."

Debbie ended the call and said, "William will be here tomorrow. I hope he agrees to go to Janus with us."

"Well, it's our job to convince him. Anyway, now the real task begins. I think we should split this up. One of us should look for doctors and other medical personnel, and the other should look for farmers. Once we have those selected we can work together on finding the other tradespeople we will need."

"Okay, I'll look for the medical people and you can look for farmers."

"Let's get started."

They spent the rest of the day preparing for the calls they would make tomorrow. The entire news conference was broadcast all over the Earth. Jeffery was certain that anyone they called would know about Janus.

By the following morning they were ready to get started. Debbie had a list of twenty-two doctors and thirty-one nurses. It was midday in the North American Union so she made the first call there. She called the first doctor on her list, Michael Frost.

A woman answered the phone, "Dr. Frost's office. How can I help you?"

"My name is Debbie Whitestone. Would it be possible to speak to Dr. Frost?"

"Oh my God! Are you the famous Debbie Whitestone?"

"I suppose so."

"Wow! Please hold for a moment."

About a minute later a man said, "This is Dr. Frost. How can I help you?"

"Dr. Frost, this is Debbie Whitestone. Did you see my husband's news conference yesterday?"

"It would have been hard to miss it since it was repeated so many times."

"You are the first person we are calling regarding the Janus mission. Would you be interested in joining us?"

"You know, since I saw that news conference yesterday, I have been thinking about what I would say if I was asked that question. I must say I never really expected it to happen, but now that it has, I'm not sure. I like the adventure and the idea of starting a new civilization, but Earth is all I know. I've never even been to the space station."

"Dr. Frost, we will be somewhat isolated, so we need the best medical personnel we can find. Your references are excellent and I'm sure you would be a real asset to the group. Zandrax is building a hospital for us, so we will have the most modern equipment available. Probably even things that aren't available on Earth yet."

"Would I be able to pick my staff?"

"If they're on the list, that wouldn't be a problem. If they aren't on the list, then we would have to verify they have the gene before we could accept them."

"What do you know about the gene?"

"Nothing, other than it's relatively rare. It occurs once in every twenty-five thousand births."

"Everyone on Earth has a complete DNA analysis on file. Can you find out what gene we are looking for?"

"Yes, I'm sure I can do that. I'll call you back as soon as I can."

After she ended the call she said, "I wasn't expecting that. We need more information about the gene."

"I'll send a message to Vandor and ask him to come here."

"That's a good idea."

They were discussing their plans for the day when there was a knock on the door. Jeffery answered it and was surprised and pleased to see William standing there.

William had a big smile on his face and said, "Hi Grandpa." Then William and Jeffery hugged briefly and William walked in. He went over to Debbie, kissed her on the cheek and said, "Hi Grandma. It's really nice to see both of you."

Debbie said, "It's wonderful to see you too. I hope you didn't have a problem getting time off to come here."

"Didn't Mom tell you I bought the company last year? Since I own it, getting time off is not a problem."

"No, she never mentioned that. That must have happened after your last visit to Procolt 2."

"Yeah, right after. Mom gave me the money to buy it while I was there."

Jeffery said, "That may complicate things a bit. Please sit down William, we have something very important to discuss with you."

William sat down on one of the recliners and said, "Okay, let's talk."

Jeffery said, "Your name is on the list of potential Janus settlers. Your Mother, Father, and their new baby will be coming with us. We want you to go there too."

"I like my life here and I really don't want to go live in a primitive settlement."

"There are some things you don't know. You grew up on Procolt 2 and were exposed to the radiation there during that whole period of your life. That means you already have an increased life span. What you don't realize is that because you have the gene you will live to be well over the age of five hundred."

"I have a girlfriend now, and we have talked about getting married. I don't want to leave her."

"I understand, but you should know that you will outlive her by hundreds of years. She will begin to show her age while you will still look and feel like a young man."

William was silent for a while, then he asked, "What if Tina has the gene too?"

"Even if Tina has the gene, she has to be exposed to the radiation for five or six years to be affected by it. If she has the gene, we can arrange for her to go to Janus as well."

"How can we find out?"

Debbie said, "Give me her last name and I'll check the list. But the list only has three thousand names on it, and there are probably millions of people on Earth with the gene."

"Her last name is Gardner."

Debbie checked the list and her name was not on it. She said, "There is no Tina Gardner on the list. We'll send a message to Vandor and ask him about her."

William was obviously upset by the situation. He said softly, "I don't want to watch her grow old and die by herself. I always thought that was something we would do together."

Jeffery said, "I'm sorry William, but this is something you had to know about."

William said, "I guess all I can do is hope she's has the gene. Please excuse me, I'm going to get a room and think about this for a while. I'll come by later." Then he got up and left.

Debbie said, "That went rather badly."

"I think he just needs some time to work things out. In the meantime, I'll send another message to Vandor and find out if Tina has the gene."

They spent the rest of the day contacting people on the list. Jeffery had much better luck with farmers. He managed to get four who would grow crops and two who would raise cattle and pigs. Every one of them liked the idea of being in new place with new equipment in an area that had a "small town" environment.

Debbie only enlisted one doctor. Dr. Thomas Jarvis was a surgical resident at a large hospital near New York City, and like the farmers, he longed to live in a small town. He really wanted to have the freedom to spend whatever time he felt was appropriate with his patients, not the time dictated by the insurance companies. He also offered to help Debbie with her enlistment of other medical personnel, which she gratefully accepted. Dr. Jarvis asked Debbie to send him the list of other potential candidates with medical backgrounds, which she sent out immediately.

That evening Jeffery and Debbie decided they would need, at the most, four doctors, six nurses, and ten farmers. In Jeffery's conversations with the farmers, he told them they would each have two hundred fifty acres. Every one of the crop farmers said they didn't need that much land to grow food for only five hundred people. The two livestock farmers felt that much land would be very helpful. Jeffery also told them that all the farmers would get together and discuss what to grow and how much to plant before they left for Janus. That way they would be able to bring any supplies they would need on the trip.

The following day the recruiting went much better. With Dr. Jarvis's help Debbie was able to recruit three more doctors, including Michael Frost. They also managed to find three nurses. Jeffery also signed up the rest of the farmers they would need.

When they were done for the day Jeffery said, "Every person I spoke to had already been thinking about Janus before we called them. I'm sure the news conference was responsible for that."

"I'm sure you're correct. The cities on Earth are magnificent places, but they are all overcrowded. Moving to Janus allows people to live a more relaxed lifestyle, and I think that was a factor as well."

"Nobody mentioned living longer, but I'll bet they were all thinking about it."

"Yeah, I was actually surprised nobody asked about it."

"So, tomorrow you need to find three more nurses. I'll start on the tradespeople we will need.

The following morning, they went to the restaurant for breakfast. They were discussing their tasks for the day when they realized someone was standing next to their table. Jeffery looked up and was surprised to see Vandor.

Vandor smiled at him and said, "I received your message."

"Thanks for coming, please join us."

Vandor sat down and said, "Thank you. How are things going?"

"Better than I expected. We have four doctors and three nurses. As far as medical personnel are concerned, we only need three more nurses. I also signed up ten farmers. I don't think we will need anymore. However, we have a personal issue that I think you can help us with."

"You know I'll help you if I can. What's the problem?"

"Our Grandson, William, is on your list. We spoke to him yesterday and he told us he has a girlfriend named Tina Gardner and he doesn't want to leave her. We need to know if she has the gene."

"I can find the answer to that in just a few moments." Then Vandor sat down at the table and took a small device out of his pocket. He gave the device a verbal command that included Tina's name. The device beeped. Vandor looked at the device and the expression on his face changed. He said, "I'm sorry to tell you Tina does not have the gene."

Debbie said, "That's not the answer I was hoping for. I'm not sure what he will do now."

"We're making an exception for Virgil and possibly for Mystic's new baby already. I suppose we could make an exception for Tina as well."

"Jeffery and I will discuss that with him this afternoon."

"Okay, please let me know what he decides. If he would like to visit Janus, I'll be happy to take him there.

Regarding your selection of medical personnel, I think that's a good start. I probably should have mentioned this before, but we have androids that can assist with most manual tasks. They look and act almost human, they breathe, their eyes blink, and their skin feels human. You can use them to do the chores most people hate, like cleaning. They can also assist the nurses at the hospital or teach when that becomes a requirement."

"I like the idea of using robots to clean, but I think people would appreciate a human taking care of them if they are confined to a hospital. I'll have to think about using androids as teachers, although we already utilize computers extensively in our schools on Procolt 2. I'm not sure there's much difference between the two."

Debbie said, "I realized this morning there was one medical position we forgot about. We're going to have hundreds of farm animals on Janus and I'm sure there will be pets too. We'll need at least two veterinarians. Vandor, are there any on your list?"

"Yes, although I don't remember how many. However, I'm sure there are more than two. Also, regarding the gene, I'm not divulging any information about it at this time. We have searched the DNA scans of almost every human living on Earth, and we know who has the gene. I'm concerned that if more information about the gene was made public, people would try to fake having it in order to get on the Janus list."

"Why would we need the list again?" Jeffery asked.

"We have to consider the possibility that many of the original settlers could die from accidents or some unknown disease. If that happened, we would need to find replacements."

"We're already picking fifty alternates."

"Yes, but many of them will probably be used to replace any original settlers who change their mind about going. I guarantee you that will happen."

"I think after we select people, we should send them to Procolt 2 and have them live there until we are ready to go to Janus. There would be less temptation to change your mind if your away from Earth," Debbie suggested.

Jeffery agreed, "That's a good idea. I'm sure we can find room for them at Procolt Paradise."

Vandor went back to Procolt Paradise to discuss finding space for the Janus settlers with Mystic. Once that situation was resolved, he went back to Earth so he could help Jeffery and Debbie.

Later that afternoon William came back to Jeffery and Debbie's room. He didn't look happy. He sat down and asked, "Does Tina have the gene?"

Debbie answered, "No, she doesn't. However, Vandor has offered to make an exception so she can go to Janus. Your father is going, and he doesn't have the gene either."

"That's the answer I was expecting. I've decided that in the event Tina didn't have the gene, I'm going to stay on Earth so I can be with her. Tina is very close with the other members of her family and I know she wouldn't want to leave them."

"I'm not sure you are making the right choice, but if that's what you want to do, I'll support you. I'm positive your mother won't like your decision either."

"Tina and I love each other, and I want to spend as much time as I can with her. Nothing anybody says will make me change my mind."

"Okay, but please try to spend some time on Procolt 2 over the next two years, and bring Tina with you so we can meet her."

"I promise I'll do that, and if Vandor can bring us to Janus occasionally, I will visit there when I can."

"Please send your mother a message today."

"Yes, Grandma. I'm going back to Earth on the next shuttle. I'll send her a message as soon as I get home." William walked over to Debbie and kissed her on the cheek again, then he and Jeffery hugged briefly, and he left.

With Vandor's help the entire group of five hundred settlers and fifty alternates were chosen in less than ninety days. During that time, a new facility was completed at Procolt Paradise to house the settlers. Jeffery, Debbie, and Vandor realized that the city Zandrax was building on Janus needed a name, so they decided to call it Janus Prime. The construction of Janus Prime had begun as soon as Jeffery and Debbie agreed to become part of the Janus group, and many of the buildings were completed by the time the last of the settlers were selected.

The Janus settlers were scheduled to arrive at Procolt Paradise in groups of twenty-five every ten days until all five hundred were there. After they were settled into their temporary homes, Vandor brought them over to Janus for a brief visit in groups of three or four. Almost all of the settlers were impressed and anxious to get there, but nine of them decided to leave the group. Jeffery selected nine replacements from the group of alternates, so now the group was complete.

Seven months after Jeffery and Debbie returned to Procolt 2, Mystic gave birth to her second child. It was a boy, and Virgil and Mystic named him Toby. A few days after Toby was born a DNA scan was performed. Toby had the gene.

The schedule was set for them to leave Procolt 2 in one hundred twenty days. The ship from Zandrax would make a brief stop at Procolt 2 to pick up the livestock farmers and then go to Earth to pick up the farm animals destined for the farms on Janus. Then it would return to Procolt 2 to pick up the rest of the settlers. The trip to Janus would take one hundred ninety days.

Several of the settlers asked Jeffery why they needed to take a ship to Janus instead of being brought there by Vandor. Jeffery told them the trip would give them the opportunity to get to know each other better and also give them time to delegate tasks for each settler that they would be required to perform once they were living on Janus.

Jeffery and Debbie turned over the ownership of Procolt Paradise and all of their other businesses, with the exception of the research lab, to the government of Procolt 2. They gave the research lab to the squirrels. In order to be sure the squirrels would be able to continue to develop new products. Jeffery and Debbie set up a fund with five million hirodim in it so the squirrels could draw from it to fund future projects.

The day before the settlers were scheduled to leave, the staff at Procolt Paradise had a big going away party for Jeffery, Debbie, Mystic, Virgil, and Toby. There were more than a thousand people and several hundred squirrels in attendance. It was a tearful goodbye. The next morning all of the settlers were shuttled to the ship that would take them on the one-way journey to Janus. It was both an end, and a new beginning.

EPILOG

The year after the settlers departed from Procolt 2 for Janus, the radiation on Procolt 2 disappeared. It was assumed that people from Zandrax removed the radiation sources, but no one knows for sure. When it became known that the radiation on the planet was gone, the immigration problem disappeared.

For the next two hundred years Earth received only sporadic reports concerning the settlement on Janus. That information was provided by occasional visitors from Zandrax. Despite repeated attempts to find out the location of Janus, our Zandrax visitors refused to divulge the information. They said the civilization on Janus must develop without any outside influence.

There were some brief discussions about attempting to search for the planet, but searching for something more than five thousand light years away is an impossible task. The reports we did receive indicated that everything was going well. Jeffery and Debbie had another child. This time it was a boy, and they named him Zack. Debbie was now the oldest person from Earth to have a child. At the time of Zack's birth, she was one hundred seventy-four years old.

The last report we received from Zandrax concerning Janus was more than a thousand years ago, in 2497. The population on Janus at that time was almost twenty thousand. They were no longer totally dependent on Zandrax for supplies, and as a result no further visits to Janus were planned. However, Zandrax still could be contacted in case of an emergency.

Some other things happened in 2497 too. Zandrax joined the trade group that year and set up transporter stations on Earth and several other trade group planets. The non-human population on Earth exceeded 10% for the first time and English became the primary language on all trade group planets.

RUSSELL FINE

NOTE FROM THE AUTHOR

A few years ago I had an opportunity to speak to a Zandrax trade representative about Janus. Initially he was somewhat hesitant to talk about it, but I convinced him there was no further need for secrecy concerning Janus. I told him about the books I had written about Earth's history, and I said that the information concerning Janus would allow me to complete my work. He finally agreed and we spent most of the following year together gathering information for the final book in this series. The book is now finished and available. Not surprisingly, the title is *Janus*.

Russell Fine

06/04/3509

Made in the USA
Columbia, SC
16 September 2024

41857464R00439